# Morton Thompson

# The Cry
# and the Covenant

**Buccaneer Books**
**Cutchogue, New York**

With the exception of actual historical person-
ages identified as such, the characters are entirely
the product of the author's imagination and have
no relation to any person or event in real life.

Published by arrangement with Doubleday & Co., Inc.

Copyright © 1949 by Morton Thompson

International Standard Book Number: 0-89966-758-9


For ordering information, contact:

Buccaneer Books, Inc.
P. O. Box 168
Cutchogue, New York 11935

For Bella Pindyck

And I will establish my covenant with you;
Neither shall all flesh be cut off any more by the waters of a flood;
Neither shall there any more be that to destroy the earth. And
    God said,
I will remember . . .
And I will remember my covenant,
Which is between me and you
And every living creature of all flesh . . .

*The Book of Genesis.*

# ONE

THE uterus of the woman on the bed contracted according to its cellular intelligence. Without command the vertical muscles squeezed downward. The woman moaned. The sound rose slowly in the thick bed. The downward rippling of the vertical muscles jammed to a halt against the horizontal muscles at the bag's narrow neck. The uterus was wide, its neck was narrow, the horizontal muscles strove outward now to make the circle wider. At this time, in the timelessness of the cell, the contractions of the uterus were occurring at three-minute intervals. The widening neck had stretched to an opening large enough to grudge the admission of three fingers. This labor had been in progress for eight hours without flaw and without volition and beyond command and the intellect of the cell was now the woman, herself.

When the first tentative contractions splayed in her pelvis, the will of the uterus barely fingered the threshold of pain. The woman was breakfasting. She ate, she scrubbed the pewter plates, she reached for a towel. The first pain came. Her hand stopped, upthrust, her eyes widened, the room was gone, the day vanished, and the cosmos became the uterus, solitary, without other meaning, a single stalk in an empty field. The first pain had come. It passed. Now the room had air again. She stood, her mouth a little open, breathing slowly, listening, looking inward, testing, smelling small breaths, waiting, at bay. And when her senses stirred at last, and made a message for her, she trembled, hearking, and suddenly loneliness shook her and fear to be the dwelling of such inexorable things, waiting, enduring and unneeded and alone. Then the thought of other women came shamingly on her and custom, and her tissues became a remembered body again. The hand that rested upon the towel seized the towel and functioned among the dishes.

7

Thereafter she chored her household the more determinedly. But when the pains came even faster she turned to the bedroom and there she made her bed again, smoothing a layer of old sheets over the blankets. And that was done. And she looked brooding over the low, spotless room. She pondered a new chore. But the pains pressed her now, they were closing in, and from her three dresses she took her best and put it on, she put on her best rings and the necklace of seed pearls, and her best shoes, and she lay upon the bed, her head upon the high feather pillow, and when her husband came in he found her thus and tiptoed out and rushed away to say her time had come. The woman smoothed at her dress. Her attire reflected her husband's caste with the middle-class restraint with which she now stifled those cries which the mechanism of the uterus so endlessly ignored.

The name of this woman was Semmelweis and the termination of her labor occurred in the upper floor of a two-story house at Number One Burgauffahrt, in Ofen, Hungary, on the first of July, in the year 1818.

When Joseph, her husband, opened the bedroom door again he was followed by two midwives. They were veiled. They came into the room quickly and behind them Joseph locked the door. Thereafter he put his back against it and listened and watched, and the pains pierced his ears.

The first midwife approached the bed. Thérèse Semmelweis shut her eyes. Deprecatively, the midwife's hands thrust under Thérèse's dress, delicately and modestly pressed her knees apart, slipped into her body to discover the state of her labor. The second midwife, face averted, repeated the examination. From a pocket of the dress one midwife produced scissors, a sharp knife, the vectis, cord, and a kind of corkscrew, and the point waited to twist into the head and the handle waited to be drawn, to crush and draw forth the bones of the skull as a cork from a bottle, if the head would not be born, if the head stuck and would not pass the arch of bone in the pelvis.

Their veils were carefully heavy. It was important to Thérèse that the midwives could not see her flesh for now the agonies of her embarrassment were greater than the birth pains. In a little time there would be no modesty and the woman would be a grunting animal, crazed, straining as though at stool. But later there would be remembering, later when the room was clean and the pains forgot. Then Thérèse would be glad for the veils the midwives wore. The midwives were content, for the veils hid their beards. These were doctors. They were dressed as women because until very lately it had been against the law for a doctor to deliver a child and jail terms and death were the penalties, and because many of this generation still were outraged that a man should look at a woman's private parts. But Joseph Semmelweis and other Josephs in Buda, and Josephs in

Vienna and Josephs throughout the world had begun to prefer doctors. Midwives, for instance, had revived a fashion for bathing the newborn child in dog urine. The last midwife to attend Mrs. Semmelweis had tied the birth cord around Mrs. Semmelweis' leg.

"I do not wish it to creep up inside her again," the midwife explained to Joseph.

The afterbirth had not come forth after many hours. The midwife had fished for it with a sharpened hook. Then she had dragged on the cord until she broke it. Thérèse had somehow lived. No one knew why.

So now there were doctors in her room, decorously veiled men, and despite their veils Thérèse Semmelweis shut her eyes and between pains fretted with embarrassment. Joseph leaned against the door. Another man. Three men in the small room and one woman. She shut her eyes, she blotted out the world, it is not my fault, she said to herself, and she held her eyes closed and waited.

Her forelocks were curled in two sausages of hair on either side of her forehead. The remainder of her head was decently covered with a bonnet of fluted and ruffled white linen tied under her chin. Her heavy Sunday dress covered her to the toes of her well-polished best shoes. Her house was in order. The gambits were complete. Each detail was a prescribed ritual, as anxiously and all-importantly observed as to a Balinese is the faintest movement perilously urgent and meaningful in the traditional gambit of the Temple dancers.

And then in a twinkling, as sudden rain might scatter the gambit of the Temple dancers, or an earthquake or some other element of nature, the moment of beginning birth crashed, and there was no modesty and no game, no dress, no room, no husband, no world but a riven void, empty, rending, ringing with the unbearable.

From the woman's mouth came sound. It was not birth. It was sound, the woodwinds of pain, remote, a noise in a different part of the bed. The sound begged the low rafters. The sound begged the darkness. The uterus, which had nothing to do with these things, laced muscular fingers and squeezed downward again. The uterus was full. The passage of intelligence from cell to cell, from month to month, from hour to hour, now communicated with the divinity of growth, and these cells in turn strove in their intellect, knowing completeness in that place, in that instant, ready for freedom.

The doctors worked without ever lifting the woman's dress. Thus and so her child would be born beneath that dress and drawn forth and the cord cut and the afterbirth delivered and the hem never raised above the woman's ankles. Elsewhere, the intellect of surface tension, the impulse of cytoplasm, the osmotic will to transmit, of inexorable thoughts from cell to cell, knowing how far and no farther, when to begin and when to begin an end, moved with refinement and precise delicacy, entirely living, mighty beyond good and evil and beyond the bitten groans of the woman who was now not even an instrument or a spectator, but other tissues, elsewhere.

This child, her fourth, presented his head and was born. His birth was accomplished without incident. When it was over the doctors wrapped the products of birth in the cloths Thérèse Semmelweis had provided, thrust that which they had wrapped into the porcelain kitchen stove, washed their hands, peered from the window, exited watchfully and silently and criminally into the night.

In the bedroom Joseph Semmelweis sat at his wife's beside and welcomed with his eyes the new child, the fourth boy. He reflected. He named the child Ignaz Philipp Semmelweis.

# TWO

ON the third day Thérèse Semmelweis spoke longingly of home.

"I wonder how it is with them, Joseph?"

"I will go see. Father Müller will be glad to learn of this one." Joseph Semmelweis turned from dressing and smiled at the cradle. The child lay quietly between the twin beds.

"I should like to see Father," said Thérèse. She meditated, her large black eyes staring upward.

"I will bring him, then. I will bring him in a carriage."

There was a knock at the bedroom door.

Joseph beamed broadly. He winked. He waited. Thérèse smiled at him reproachfully. He turned to the door.

"Come in!" boomed Joseph.

Instantly the door flung open and seven-year-old Joseph, five-year-old Karl, and three-year-old Ignaz rushed into the room, halted, bowed, said good morning, ran to the cradle.

"This morning he looks like you, Papa!"

"He looks like Mama!"

"He looks like me!" cried small Ignaz jealously.

Young Joseph snatched the babe from the cradle.

"Put him down!" roared the father.

Joseph raced to the door with the child.

"I want to show him! The children are waiting!"

"Joseph!"

The boy stopped instantly.

"Yes, Father."

Joseph glared.

"He is not a sausage."

"No, Father."

"Do not carry him like a sausage "

11

"No, Father."

"Do you love your brother?"

"Oh yes, Father!"

"Then take him out and show him to the other children."

The door banged behind them. The clatter of their footsteps sped out of doors. The echoes settled. In her bed Thérèse blinked. Her wide mouth opened softly.

"You are a good man, Joseph."

He came to the bed instantly, a stern-faced man of forty whose brows frowned while his eyes twinkled, whose mouth wried always a little to the left and upward.

"You work too hard."

"I? I work too hard?"

"You work too hard, Joseph."

"Tell me—are you thinking of a younger man?"

"My father worked too hard."

"Thérèse——"

"A grocery is not easy. You must take care of yourself. Always."

He considered her, puzzled. Still frowning, he smiled with his mouth.

"I will be specially careful."

Her left hand moved a little. Her fingertips touched his knuckles, then slowly returned to the coverlet. She spoke to the ceiling, brooding.

"The children must always be loved."

"My darling! They are our children. You know I shout. I love to shout! Do I shout too much? Do you think they fear me? Oh no, Thérèse! I am ashamed. I love them when I shout. That is how I love them. But hereafter——"

"If you have to—if another woman—if you marry—it is natural——"

"Thérèse!"

"Only the children—they must love her too."

The room was silent. The air swelled, the silence thickened, his throat dried. His lungs hungered. There was no breath. His heart pumped dry, his thought fled.

"She will be good to you. She must be. Yet—you would not forget me, Joseph? Sometimes?"

He licked the rustling paper of his lips.

"Ha! HA!" he croaked. He tried to chide archly, and his eyes were blind-sick. "Shall I call the priest, then? Ha HA, Thérèse! The priest maybe?"

Her face softened. She looked at him.

"Why not?" She smiled. "It is always good to see a priest. See now, Joseph! There is nothing wrong! How strong I am! How right you are, Joseph! A woman talks and talks, a thought strikes her, a breath, a shadow—and she babbles. And straightway her husband sends for the priest!"

Smiling his crooked smile, he put his hand on her forehead. It was burning hot. He blinked. He kept his hand there.

"You were restless last night, Thérèse," he said diffidently. "You were dreaming of some other man maybe?"

"Do you think it is nothing for a woman to lie here and worry about four troublesome male creatures doing God knows what in her house?"

"Ha HA! The male creatures! Your head is hot, Thérèse."

"My head is hot. The dust is gathering everywhere and he tells me——"

"Do you feel pain, Thérèse?"

"Pain now! Where should I feel pain?"

"Your head is very hot."

"Get the priest, then! Call in the priest, tell him my head is hot, tell him you want another wife——"

"And your lips are dry. Thérèse, your eyes are bright—your eyes are very bright——"

"When I was a girl in my father's house you liked my eyes, you liked how bright they were. Now——!"

"And your head is so hot—it burns. It burns my hand."

"Take it away, then! Take your silly hand away!" And she moved her head irritably, and his hand fell to the pillow. The pillow was wet.

"Thérèse——" And there was horror in his voice.

"Oh, leave me! Leave me, Joseph!"

"Thérèse!" He seized her hands.

She turned then and looked into his eyes, miserably. "I am sick, Joseph," she said, ashamed.

He stared at her.

"I am sick down there," and her shame made her voice a whisper.

"Is it—is it——?"

"It is the sickness of childbed. Must I die, Joseph?"

"You will be fine. It is nothing. I will go quickly. I will bring the doctors. It is nothing. Many have it. It is nothing. It is healthy!" he roared suddenly. "A little fever—a little nothing! Who cares? Who cares for such a thing?"

"I will die, Joseph. As all women die of it."

He was already at the door. He turned and smiled broadly at her, the sweat dribbling down his ribs from his armpits, his knees cracking under him.

"What color eyes have you got, Thérèse?"

"Blue."

"Just once say black. Just once."

"Blue," she said stubbornly, for they were very black.

"When the doctor leaves I will kill you myself!" he roared, and he turned to go.

"Joseph."

He turned.

13

"I love you, Joseph." Her face was pillow-white.

"I love you, Thérèse," he said numbly. His mouth wried up to the left. He blinked at her.

"Ha HA!" he roared. He trembled. And he was gone.

The door closed behind him. He had gone without his hat. Ah, Joseph! She moved her body. She sighed. She lay still. She willed not to think. Life was a wraith, and it tiptoed through her body like a child in the dark, dreading, irresolute, peering the invisible, the frightful, the deadly, the incomparable. Past known pain, known fever, known sweat. Past the boundary. Into the abyss. And her being returned to her a stranger, trembling, for it had seen death. Thérèse Semmelweis was still. When the children returned with the baby she closed her eyes. They put the child in the cradle. They tiptoed out. The door closed. The child slept. Her hand strayed to the cradle. She stared at the ceiling. She swallowed.

Now in the streets, in the windows of houses, humans watched Joseph Semmelweis run and craned their heads, saw he was bareheaded and gasped, remembered it was the third day, and exhaled understanding, fear, and the common defeat. Frau Semmelweis had come to term. Her child was born. Now it was the third day. She was sick. The birth sickness of women had come to her. And so she was living. And so she was dead. Speak gently, neighbor. Death is not deaf.

Death loped easily beside Joseph, diffidently, negligently, as he ate the wind, his teeth grating, sprinting madly to the doctors. Death loped quietly behind the three as they rushed to Thérèse.

And in the bedroom Death listened attentively as the frightened doctors leaned in a corner, head to head, and spoke of the cell they knew not in the protocol of the known. So in the old times the medicine men painted symptoms and life on the walls of caves.

"One reason for this—she is very dark-complected."

The second doctor put his mind to this, recollecting all he had heard about the complexion of women and its relation to the deadly fever of childbirth.

"Naturally," the first doctor said, watching his colleague think, "naturally being dark-complected her labor would be in the first place more difficult."

The second doctor thought of other possibilities and weighing them he selected one.

"I would say—milk fever. Yes . . . But then—she has milk."

"It is undoubtedly puerperal fever."

"You think so? What have we got?" He began to quote the authorities. "Is what she has an illness that is independent as an entity but variable as a phenomenon?" He thrust out his lip. "Has she measles—but no measle spots? Mumps with no swelling? Smallpox without sores? To these and to other diseases each of which has a clearly recognizable sign one must answer—yes. This patient has a disease. It is symptomatic of any disease we know. But it has not the cardinal sign of any. Therefore——"

"As I said. Puerperal fever."

"I am afraid so."

"But I rather incline to the theory that puerperal is zymotic. I think we should treat for fermentation."

"Also—Hunter." He said the name reverently. "Hunter considers puerperal is a colitis—an inflammation of the omentum——"

"But doesn't he also say it is an epidemic influence?"

"Yes, he does. In your opinion, what does he mean?"

"I shall say—the influence of an epidemic."

"That wouldn't hold here." They turned and looked at the woman on the bed. They looked at Joseph, who stared at them hungrily, then conscientiously back at each other.

"How about Mauriceau, or Smellie? Puerperal fever can be due to suppression of the lochia. She certainly hasn't had the discharge a woman normally has after delivery."

"But she *is* discharging. A foul and purulent spirit. Not lochia, of course. Still . . ."

"Of course Cruveilhier still feels puerperal fever is simply a miasma and if that's so the weather certainly hasn't been of the best lately, certainly not of the best, and according to the cosmic-telluric school puerperal comes from the atmosphere——"

"It's true. Let's see. 'As the result of weather changes comes a miasma—a miasma that may hover, invisible, over a room, or over a building, or, if it chooses, over a whole city. And in this miasma is puerperal fever. And a woman who contacts this miasma after she has delivered her child——' "

On the bed lay the woman. Against the wall pressed her husband. In a corner the two doctors consulted with all that a primate can learn, absorbed, honest, indefatigable. In another corner Death lolled indolently, waiting.

"As to this miasma"—they were digging deep, now, into the very bottom of all medical knowledge of puerperal fever—"they say in England that during birth the peculiar anatomical condition of the sexual organs is taken up by a miasma and circulated in the blood. That seems possible."

"Yes, that's true."

"They say that a pregnant woman or a woman who has just had a child is unique in nature. That her blood and her tissues are loaded. And that because of this loading, this unstable equilibrium, she is constantly on the verge of fever." He shook his head despondently. "It's very likely, though Gordon says—he says it is simply erysipelas. Gordon of Aberdeen . . ."

15

"Erysipelas?" The other glanced at Thérèse. "Without rash?"

"Without any rash whatsoever."

"Ah—but without burning?"

"Without burning."

They thought a while in silence. They had come back, full circle. Appendicitis without an appendix, jaundice without yellowing, diarrhea without bowel movement, any disease of known symptoms which did not present the known symptoms was puerperal fever.

"There is another school of thought," the first doctor said conscientiously but without prejudice.

"I know. The *Divinum Aliquid* . . . The unknowable . . . The something divine . . ."

There were no other theories worth discussing. Now they had really come to an end. They stood in silence, considering,

"How does she look?"

"I should say the prognosis is bad."

"Two days?"

"Two. Perhaps three."

"That's how she seems to me. I've noticed there's one sign —she has a sort of erysipelatose tumor, dusky red, on her knees—about the size of a shilling—almost invariably a fatal sign."

"And treatment?"

"Well—a small dose of spermaceti——"

"Certainly can't do any harm. Perhaps some hemlock in a mild saline draught, and, ah, let's put an opium plaster on her side."

"Right. You wouldn't bleed her?"

"I don't think so." He looked at the bed. "I don't think, really——"

"No, you're right."

Well, it had come to an end, then. They had done what they could do. They had spoken of that of which they could speak. It was over. They turned and stared at the woman on the bed. She stared back at them. There was not much hope in her eyes. There was no hope whatever in the eyes of Joseph, his back against the door. For these were doctors. There was greatness and majesty in them. Behind their eyes, implicit in them, was knowledge. And in the ritual of the layman's respecting awe, in the gambits of their thinking, was clear acceptance that through these great and fine and entirely noble men would come, when they chose to speak, the unbearable wisdom of God. Their frock coats, heavy with significance, medaled with gouts of long-dried blood, stiff and crusted, like jewels, with a decade's honored decorations of white and green and yellow pus, ribboned with the sanious fluid of putrescent corpses, these things bore witness to the size of their practice, the number of their cases, the breadth of their knowledge, the

16

depth of their experience, the vast nobility of their wisdom. They were great doctors. God would speak through them. In all Buda there were no better. The fever—the terrible childbed fever—they knew the fever. Beyond their wisdom lay only God.

In the body of the woman cells divided, cells fought, cells devoured, rallied, were defeated, multiplied anew, solitary, without passion, implacably, perfectly, unheeded, and beyond plan.

For a while the doctors meditated remedies. There were emetics, there was the first napkin of a virgin, there were purges of mercury. Death lolled, waiting. Their thoughts roved from school to school, system to system, Mauriceau, Baudelocque, Smellie, Willis, Denman, Charles White of Manchester, even Galen.

In the end they settled upon the Divinum Aliquid.

For this, there being no remedy, they bled her after all, took her urine to taste, and departed. Death shrugged and went with them.

On the fourth day the fever rose. In the night Thérèse was delirious, cried for the new baby, crushed him, and wailed of home, babbled of her girlhood, glared unseeing at the tear-swollen eyes of Joseph. On the morning of the fifth day she wakened toward noon from a deep coma. She saw him on his knees.

"Joseph," she whispered. Then her eyes closed again.

From the morning of the sixth day onward Thérèse began to improve. She was long abed. She rose emaciated, helpless, more than a month later. The grateful family prayed thanksgiving. Friends came to call. So long, they stayed. A measure. No longer. The dust in the house began to vanish. Elsewhere, the unrejoicing cells moved in the continuum of their unremembering perfection. Small Ignaz Philipp had a mother. Joseph had a wife. Seek for a reason. The pattern has reason. The pattern has chain and cause and effect. The pattern is the Divinum Aliquid. The pattern is God and infinite pity and the perfect intellect of the cell and in the end, and in the beginning, and in the brilliant wailing of the unborn, and the future, it is Semmelweis. Ignaz Philipp Semmelweis.

The pattern had begun.

17

# THREE

IT IS 1369 in the wilderness of years and Charles Robert has come frowning from Anjou to king Hungary and died, and Louis, his son, ponders in Buda an empire Hungary will never reckon again. And in Buda a count has built the house Ignaz Philipp Semmelweis will be born in. In this year the Black Death ended winnowing and the ripe harvest lay stacked and rotting throughout the land. The house, raw-new, crouched just below the fortress of Buda.

The count who built the house stayed prudently within its walls, for the smell of the harvest marched the empty streets and rats fought hungry dogs to gorge on the heaped dead on the cobblestones. And the dead were buried and the streets were sweet again and high in the palace Frenchman Louis supped Poland and spread a map and Hungary was Central Europe, from Pomerania to the Danube and from the Adriatic to the Dnieper. In the windows of the count's house petunias bloomed, and in the fields the peasants rose and blew the plague from their noses and some grew wheat and some grew grapes, bright wheat, yellow grapes, loving petunias, flowering statecraft, and the empire bloomed. And in the end a hardier plant burgeoned suddenly and the *Baccillus pestis*, smaller than a petunia, hungry as wheat, flowered in men's bowels, and the Black Death, come again, harvested one man in every four men in Hungary.

This time the stone walls of the two-story house were no sanctuary. The plant sifted in, the count ate of it and died of its hunger.

The empty house gaped at the street and the hours played with silence on the cobblestones and grew to months and silence followed the carted dead and the cobblestones were

18

sweet again and the months, grown to sober years, paced behind the coffin of Louis and Sigismund was king.

At the house where the Black Death had been the doors swung idly and tempted no one.

Now Jesuits took the house, and from Genoa Columbus has sailed for America and from the house the Jesuits moved richly on, in time, and then the house held Paulists, and while the Paulists reaped the Templars came, and now the loot was thinning and through it all the nobles fought the towns, the crazed and plundered peasants rose bloodily, were crushed, raped, burned, disemboweled, and fleeing jumped screaming into the deeper chasms of slavery.

One hundred and fifty years of Turkish rule pass, and in England Elizabeth is dead and Shakespeare, and the Pilgrims have left the *Mayflower* and Cromwell has fallen and the fire of London is at hand. And in the house are cells, for it is a jail now and the home of the commandant of nearby Buda fortress. Thereafter the house slowly decayed, graying and sloughing fragments like the faces behind its bars. The neighborhood, fouled by the jail, became a furtive place of rag-flapped shadows, and the tiles of the house had begun to fall unheeded from the roof before the jail emptied and moved elsewhere.

Buda is the capital of nothing now, and Hungary is part of Austria and Maria Theresa is empress and the house, remodeled, is an inn, days, the playground of Danube sailors, and at night it is a whorehouse. A little while and Napoleon quickens and Francis I is King of Austria-Hungary and the house is a tavern tapstered by Capuchin monks, and Napoleon stirs and on the roads is the rumble of kingdoms and Napoleon mounts and the house blusters with trembling garrison but Napoleon falls and far away in Buda the house is empty again and in the forsaken rooms silence suckles the hours and a tile falls and the months pass and now it is 1812.

To Number One Burgauffahrt, in the year 1812, a stocky, baldish man wanders. And now he stops. And now he smiles his one-sided smile. And Joseph Semmelweis goes to the military and buys the house.

The rumble of kingdoms is birthright, now, inveterate habit, a sound in each man's living. And in Transylvania the unnationed, granite with pride, hearken unceasingly, fevering independence, anguished for anarchy. The wild soul of Hungary is refuged in Transylvania. Voivode of the Vlach, ban of Czoreny, unmending land, Austria kings you, now. Here is 1818. Here is Hungary. Here is kingless Buda. Here in Buda is the house. And of Ignaz Philipp Semmelweis here is the boy.

He is four years old now, and he is fat and happy. He stands at the window in his nightshirt, superintending the dawn, and as usual during the nighttime someone has minted

19

new rooftops, and the day, too, is not even the remote brother of yesterday, and he grins warily into the morning over Buda, a dawn and a city argosied with newness, secret, expectant, impatient, waiting.

His breath comes faster. And as he watches the summons is suddenly unbearable.

"I am coming!" he shouts to the imploring day. He pounds the window sill. "Wait!"

Behind him in one of the five small beds two-year-old August jerks upright. He gazes at his brother, who peers tensely to be sure the day will wait. And even as August watches Ignaz Philipp has whirled and is racing to his clothes.

"G'up," says small August.

"Go back to bed! Ohhhh! Go back to bed! August! I'm ashamed!"

And Ignaz Philipp races to the washstand. August looks doubtfully at the four empty beds in the small room. Joseph, Karl, and Philipp are gone to school. Ignaz Philipp is fumbling at his wet hair. Soon the room will be empty.

"G'up!" cries August.

Snatching his jacket, Ignaz Philipp runs to the bedside.

"Ooohhh! August! Lie down! Quick! You're sleepy!"

"G'up."

"No, no, NO, August!" And he pushes the child's shoulders back to the pillow. August stares up at him. Ignaz Philipp puts his finger to his lips, shakes his head warningly, tiptoes toward the door. August's eyes follow him. Ignaz Philipp turns to look at August again.

"Shhh!" He bends to pull up his stocking. He puts out a hand to steady himself. The small hand rests for a moment on the porcelain stove. He cries out. He jerks it back. His fingers fly to his mouth.

"G'up?" says August hopefully.

"You see? Look what I did! Aren't you ashamed? Now go back to sleep!" He looks at his hand. He looks mindfully at August. Then he puts his burnt fingers behind him and rushes down the hall to Mother's room. He puts on his jacket. He smooths it down. He dabs at his flattened hair, wipes his wet hand on his trouser leg, raises it quickly, and knocks.

"Come," calls Mother.

But the boy is already in the room, and in the next instant his head is pushing beside hers on the pillow.

"Ignaz! Ignaz Philipp! Must you rush so!"

"*Gruss Gott*, Mama!"

"Gruss Gott, child!"

He nuzzles her neck.

"I love you, Mama."

"I love you, child."

He kisses her cheek. He kisses her again.

20

"Kiss, Mama!"

She blinks and pecks at him quickly.

"Let me see you!"

He stands up. He keeps one hand behind him.

"Your hair!"

He dabs at his hair.

"And, oh! Your stockings!"

He pulls quickly at one stocking.

"Did you see the day, Mama? Do you know what happened? It's new, Mama! Everything is new!"

"Of course it is new."

"Somebody has changed everything! Somebody, in the night—somebody came——!"

"No. It is just new. Nobody came, Ignaz Philipp! Why are you keeping that hand behind you?" She rises quickly on one elbow. "Come here!"

He comes slowly to the bed.

She takes his arm. The hand comes from behind his back. She looks at it. She looks at him, her large black eyes worrying and sorrowful.

"It doesn't hurt, Mama." And his eyes fill for her sorrow.

"Oh, Ignaz Philipp! Always rushing! Go quickly! Tell Papa to put a spiderweb on it! Hurry!" And when he has reached the door:

"Ignaz!"

"Yes, Mama?"

"Where is August?"

"I left him—he is in his bed, Mama—I——"

"You did not dress him again! Did you put him on the pottie, even?" The boy swallows. "Run quick! Put him on the pottie!"

"Yes, Mama!"

"And dress him!"

"Yes, Mama!"

"And bring him to me!"

"Yes, Mama!"

"Go, child! What do you want?"

He waited. Her face softened.

"I love you, child!" Now he smiles. "Hurry! And then go to Papa!"

He looks at her a moment longer.

"Will you have my little sister today? Today, Mama?"

"Go, go!"

And he rushes down the hall and back to August.

"G'up?" says August gravely.

"Hurry!" says Ignaz Philipp. He feels his little brother. It is not too late. He staggers up with him and sits him down.

"Hurry! See my hand? Papa will put spiderwebs on it!"

"Milk?"

"You will get your milk." He looks proudly at his hand. "Spiderwebs!" And he lifts August and leads him to the washstand, and waters him liberally, and fumbles him into his tiny clothes and, still streaming, half-buttoned, pulls him down the hall, leaves him with Mother, and rushes downstairs to the grocery.

"Ha!" says Joseph. He surveys him. "HaHA!"

The boy puts out his hand.

"Oooh!" says Joseph. He purses his lips.

"Spiderwebs!"

"HaHA!"

"Mama says put spiderwebs!"

"Come, then!"

"To the cellar?"

"To the cellar!" And smiling and frowning Papa takes the boy's hand and starts toward the wide and magic door.

A bell tinkles. A customer enters. Papa drops the boy's hand and walks toward the sound.

"God help us, Mr. Kastner."

"For health, Mr. Semmelweis."

In the low vaulted room their voices cadenced a worn pattern, then, unworded, became only sound. Mr. Kastner's wife was sick—for recovery, Mr. Kastner!—God willing, Mr. Semmelweis—so the man shops—in a good hour, Mr. Kastner!—yes—well, and so perhaps a little salt, Mr. Semmelweis . . .

The boy sifted crimson coffee berries voluptuously through his fingers. Over the marble counter Papa pushed a kilo salt crystal in a cone of paper and waited expectantly. The boy shut the coffee drawer, languished past the tea, brooded vacantly into the soap vat, and then aware of it dipped his finger and watched the soft, greenish slime thread downward. And the mill, Mr. Kastner? Ah, the mill, Mr. Semmelweis! The cursed mill costs me dearly! He put a pewter mug on the counter. A little raspberry syrup, please. When the government owns the very salt——! Poor Hungary, Mr. Kastner! Our day will come, Mr. Semmelweis! In a good hour, Mr. Kastner! They shook hands. Then they looked about them fearfully. A few lamp wicks, Mr. Semmelweis—a little vinegar . . .

The boy's fingers licked the glossy roundness of the carriage whips. From the whips his hand passed to the women's head shawls, lingered, lolled, then swooped excitedly into a keg of axle grease. He stared at the stiff curling daub. He smelled it. He started at it again. He put it in his mouth. And now, walking on, his fingers picketed the rowed carriage candles, the slimmer house candles, the spokes of a wagon wheel. And now they opened a drawer of yellow paprika, touched the powder, tasted, and now the red paprika, and now slowly he tore a dried peach and dropped the flat strips into the keg of shoe wax, licked the last of the axle grease from his teeth, and

22

began crumpling the edge of a broad tobacco leaf. My regards to Mrs. Kastner, dear sir! As God wills, Mr. Semmelweis! A thousand thanks, Mr. Kastner! My good wishes, Mr. Semmelweis! To see you again, Mr. Kastner! To see you again, Mr. Semmelweis! The bell tinkled. The door opened. A troop of sunbeams raced inquisitively into the dark and spicy shop, stampeded back and out in the nick of time as the door closed behind Mr. Kastner.

"HaHA, boy!"

"HaHA, Papa!"

"Forty kreutzer, boy!"

"Show me, Papa!"

Joseph thumped a ledger.

"It's in the book, boy!"

The boy's fingers pushed into a slab of bacon crusted with paprika.

"You like to examine things, eh, Ignaz?"

The boy tasted his fingers.

"Tastes good? Come! Now we fix the hand."

They walked to the marvel-guarding door. "I put my hand on the stove, Papa."

"HaHA!" Joseph shoved a clanking key into the beam-thick door. The boy jumped impatiently. "I didn't cry, Papa!" He bumped into Joseph trying to get out of the way as the door creaked open.

"No, boy. You don't cry. No one can say you cry."

The cellar yawned beneath them. Down each stone step the boy pressed his feet.

"Don't go too fast, Papa!"

But the steps ended finally. And now, deep in the rock of the mountain, the cellar lay about them.

"First we get cobwebs." Joseph lit a candle. They walked in the shadows of dead and towering tuns. The boy rapped. The tuns boomed emptily.

"What was in there, boy?"

"Wine, Papa! The count's wine!"

He ducked to shout into a spigot hole.

"Ho, Count! Are you in there?" In the lifted candlelight Joseph scrutinized spiderwebs. "I would let him out, Papa."

"There's a good one!"

The boy looked up. Joseph lifted him ceilingward.

"Lick your hand first!"

The boy licked his smarting hand. He looked at Joseph.

"That's right! Now grab it!"

The boy looked at Joseph again.

"With Papa holding you?"

The boy looked at the spiderweb. He reached. He put his hand in the thick web. He clutched. The filaments tore, stringing thickly over his slobbered palm, between his wet fingers.

23

Joseph set him down.

"Things change. When I was a boy we thought spiderwebs were good only for cuts."

"I wasn't afraid. Not when Papa holds me. Never!"

"And now we go upstairs, eh?"

"First the door, Papa! First the secret door!"

"You'll catch cold," protested Joseph, but he led the way to the small and secret door.

It was set in the rock. Stored high on either side were ice blocks, sawed from the Danube last winter, covered with sawdust. And in the midst of the tiered ice was the magic door.

"So there it is."

"Kick it, Papa."

Joseph's heavy boot thudded the thick wood. A little dust fell. The boy's eyes widened. He licked his lips.

"Where does it go to, Ignaz?"

"It goes to the castle. First there is a tunnel. Then there isn't any more tunnel. Then there are steps. Then a long, long way off—there is a door."

"And you open the door——"

"And there is the prince!"

"And here is my little boy"—Joseph caught him up—"and here is his empty stomach"—he turned to the stairway—"and upstairs is breakfast!"

And they left the ancient tunnel by which long-dead Rudolph stole from palace to town, and as the cellar door shut behind them the little bell tinkled again and Joseph pushed the boy in the direction of the kitchen and strode toward the sound.

In the courtyard there were flagstones and grass grew between the chinks, and in the middle of the courtyard was a red marble fountain and a radiant brass faucet, and in the corner was a vinegar tree and from its branches hung a swing.

And the new day had indeed made everything different and the doored archway for delivery carts was easily the prince's door, the door to the tunnel, but small August was frightened and ran back to the silvery vinegar tree, and for a while they played Mr. Kastner and Mr. Semmelweis—as God wills, dear sir—and then the forgotten cobwebs washed off in the fountain which was the Danube and the sun was high and August cried for dinner.

This day, the dinner eaten, Papa called for his hat.

"Take him with you, Joseph."

"And August, too, Thérèse?"

"To the market place, Papa? Do I go to the market place?"

"Leave August with me. Stop jumping, Ignaz!"

And now the shop door was locked behind them and they were on the cobblestones. They were standing in the street. Out in the world. Out in the open street.

Across the river was dusty Pesth and over the cobblestones they rollicked, and the smell of the Danube teased, fled, and beckoned again.

"Someday, maybe, we will all go to Pesth."

They turned a corner, they left the Taban, they were in the Christianstadt.

"What is it like, Papa? Can I go? Can I go too?"

"How should I know what it's like? It costs a kreutzer just to cross the bridge!"

And now they wheeled out of the gardened Christianstadt into many-alleyed Watertown, and Buda sloped riverward, and the smell of the Danube was all the air to breathe.

"Boats, Papa!"

"That's it, boy! That's the bridge!"

"Where, Papa?"

"Look, silly. See the boats? See how they've tied them? There they are, end to end, clear across the Danube! That makes the bridge."

"Yes! Let's go on it, Papa! Come on, Papa!"

"And why?"

"To go to the other side, Papa."

"Hungary's on the other side too. Hungary is Buda—Hungary is Pesth. It's all Hungary. For a kreutzer we'll stay here."

"Poor Hungary, Papa?"

"That's right. Poor Hungary, child."

He quickened his steps. Ahead a small group was forming about a man from the country. He was sitting on the curbing, his embroidered cape over his shoulders, his low-crowned, wide-brimmed hat between his feet. The man sat with his feet in the gutter in complete silence. The group about him was silent, they watched him, their eyes deprecating their presence, angry and sympathetic. Joseph stood a moment, watching. Then he drew one of the crowd aside and they whispered together.

"*Több is veszett Mohácsnál!*" A man cried suddenly.

And the whole group took up the cry, shouting sadly, murmuring, sighing, to the man on the curb. He sat on, motionless, unheeding.

Joseph and Ignaz Philipp moved on down the street.

"What does that mean, Papa? Több is veszett Mohácsnál?"

"Do you see that poor man back there? He's a countryman, Ignaz Philipp. He's just in from the country. This morning he tied his horse in the market place, his best horse, and a tourist, an Englishman, came by and liked the horse and got on it and rode away."

"The man should tell the police, Papa."

"The man hasn't any right, Ignaz Philipp. There's nothing he can do about it. He's a peasant. The Englishman saw the horse, liked it, got on it, and rode away. That's the way it is."

25

The boy gripped his father's hand tighter. His eyes were frightened. He looked up at Joseph, then down again at the sidewalk.

"And that's how a Hungarian is sorry with a Hungarian. He says: 'More was lost at Mohacs.' That's what we all say, Ignaz Philipp. Több ís veszett Mohácsnál. Mohacs was a big battle, boy. A big, big battle. It happened many years ago. And when it was over the Turks had won Hungary. And they kept it for a hundred and fifty years. They sucked it like an orange. The farms became swamps. The people were slaves. And then, after many years, the Hungarians pushed the Turks out of the western part, the part nearest Austria. They were very happy. Now there was a Hungary again. A little piece, anyway. And the nobles met to choose a king. Do you understand, boy?"

"Yes, Papa. They wanted a king."

"Yes. But they were very jealous. Half of them elected a king. The other half went to the strongest King of Europe, Ferdinand of Austria. They asked him to be King of Hungary and he said he would. They thought this strong king would fight the Turks for them and win back the rest of Hungary and we would be a great nation again. And of course this Ferdinand was very glad to get Hungary, and he promised to uphold the Hungarian constitution and live in Hungary and let Hungary be governed by Hungarians."

"Did he beat the Turks, Papa?"

"He never fought them. He was afraid that Hungary might get strong. And from that day on there has been one foreign king after another, worse than the Turks."

"Where are the Turks, Papa?"

"Nowadays they're back in Turkey. A hundred years ago Hungary threw out the Austrians and beat the Turks. And then the Austrians came back and beat Hungary and gave the Turks back what the Hungarians had won. But the Turks moved out, all the same. And where they left, the land was a desert. And to settle the land the Turks ruined, they sent in thousands of Slavs, Serbians, and Germans, mostly from Saxony. They thought these people would always be their friends. But they became more Magyar than the Magyars. That's where we come from, boy. Your great-grandfather was a Saxon. We knew those tyrants from the old country. That's why we love Hungary so much. That's why we will one day be free."

"I will fight, Papa."

"You will fight, son." He looked about him hastily. They were alone in the street. No one had overheard. "You must not speak too loud, boy. You never can tell who is listening."

They walked a while in silence.

"What did Great-grandfather do, Papa?"

"He made the desert bloom. He and the rest of them. That's

26

the Alfold, the middle of Hungary, once a desert, now a wheat field. But now, of our twelve million people, nine million are serfs, men without any rights whatever. Like that poor fellow whose horse was stolen. And the spies, boy, the spies are everywhere. They're afraid of another revolution. They're trying to keep us divided. They're trying to set noble against peasant. Be careful, boy. Be very careful."

"Papa!" Ignaz Philipp had screamed suddenly and thrown himself against his father's leg. He clutched the rough cloth and the skin beneath with tight, pinching fingers.

"What's the matter, boy?"

"What's that!"

"That noise?"

They turned a corner. The market place swarmed before them. The great square hummed, brawled, rumbled, and clamored. The boy halted. As he stared, a scream leaped at him and he whirled, his arms clutching Joseph's leg again.

"Ignaz! See? It's nothing."

Very near a short peasant leaped high to cut the throat of a pig swinging overhead. As he leaped, the pig screamed again, but the knife this time severed an artery and the scream blurred, became a bubbling, and below two gray women with basins jostled on the cobblestones to catch the blood.

"Look here, Ignaz! See the baths!"

The boy peered to the other side, fearfully.

"Come on! Hai! You're walking on Papa's foot! That building—that's the famous Raizan Baths, the Turks built it—someday you and me and Mama and all of us—— Ignaz!"

In front of the building a half-naked man lay on a rug on the cobblestones and on his bared back a black-capped hunchback dropped wriggling leeches.

"Ignaz!"

But the gaping boy would not budge, and Joseph hoisted him to his shoulder and sat him there and so they passed on. Over the cobblestones dogs scampered between the wheels of passing carts, excited peasants streamed in a tide of white kerchiefs, billowing skirts, crimson jerkins, bobbing hats, and from the encamped vendors thundered a babble of bargaining and feigned anguish and beckoning screams. The boy clung tighter. Suddenly from the smell of people, of animals, of unknown things a new odor eddied.

"Papa!"

Joseph stopped. He looked at a cauldron of hot oil, squinted cunningly at the boy goggling at what lay on a plank.

"Hey, Ignaz?" And he strode to the plank, gave the woman a coin, picked a cake, and passed it up to the boy.

"*Krapfen*, Ignaz! Smells good, hah? Careful! It's hot!"

The boy stuffed most of the warm, holeless doughnut in his mouth, then instantly forgot to chew. Next to the krapfen lady a barber was cutting a man's hair, and beside the barber a sitting man howled while a foot doctor trimmed his toenails and cut into a bunion, and as he goggled a waiter scurried by balancing a tray of sausages and beer, almost tripping over a beggarwoman with a harp on his way to a spread blanket surrounded by peasants, gambling.

"Aaahh-CHEW!" the boy sneezed suddenly.

Instantly the racing waiter stopped and turned, the foot doctor paused, the patient stopped howling, and on all sides men and women halted and turned.

"God bless you!" they chorused.

Then the barber resumed cutting, once more the bunion howled, the waiter raced on again, the babble surged as before.

The boy sighed. He relaxed. He looked bravely around. He smiled a little. And the day marched, and the tumult rose and prodigies multiplied. And at last there was sunset.

Now Ignaz lay abed, and his brothers lay asleep about him, and in the dark streets even the dogs were silent, and it was night.

Thérèse Semmelweis stared into the darkness. In the next bed Joseph pondered dreamily. He sighed.

"Joseph."

"Hello, darling."

"Tomorrow I know I'll feel better. Tomorrow I'll help you in the shop."

"Rest, Thérèse. The doctor says rest. The shop is nothing. Thérèse?"

"Yes, Joseph?"

"I wonder—will it be a girl this time?"

"It doesn't move much. I think it may be a girl."

"Make it a girl, Thérèse!"

"Make it a girl!"

He chuckled.

"That Ignaz!"

"What did he do, Joseph? Was he frightened?"

"Frightened! Do you know something, Thérèse? That boy—he's an adventurer!"

"An adventurer! Now may God defend him! What——"

"I showed him the bridge—immediately he wants to go to Pesth!"

"What does he want to go to Pesth for?"

"Who knows why an adventurer wants to go to Pesth? Even I have never been to Pesth. Home is good enough. But he's an adventurer."

"To Pesth, mind you!"

"Yes. And all day long he is sorry for everybody. He is sorry for the poor chickens, he pities the man getting his hair cut, he is sorry for a man killing a cow, then he is sorry for the man getting blood all over him. First he is afraid, then all

28

day he is sorry. Such a boy. And I told him about Hungary."

"Oh, Joseph! Did he understand? Any of it?"

"Maybe."

"What will he be, Joseph?"

"Ignaz? I don't know."

"Not a grocer, Joseph."

"Your father was a grocer! I am a grocer!"

"Still——"

"No. Not a grocer. Young Joseph shall be the grocer. . . . Karl I shall send to Agriculture School. Karl shall be a farmer. . . . Philipp shall study theology and be a preacher. . . . August I think I will make a carpenter. . . ."

"And Ignaz——?"

"My adventurer! HaHA!"

"Sssh, Joseph!"

"Ignaz shall be a military auditor!"

"Joseph! A military auditor! To think of it! Our Ignaz!"

"He likes to examine everything—an auditor! He's an adventurer—the military! He shall go to Officers' School. He shall be a military auditor. It is not only a good career, such a man can help Hungary."

Thérèse smiled happily at the ceiling.

"You're a good, good father, Joseph. It will cost so much . . . I hardly believe it."

"Grusch sends his boy to such a school."

"Grusch! Grusch is a rich man! He must be worth three thousand dollars. Heaven knows what he makes. Grusch works at the palace, after all. He sends his maid to shop——"

"He spends with me as much as thirty dollars a month——"

"To say nothing of the maid who costs him easily thirty-two dollars a year!"

"Still——"

"No! You're a good man, Joseph! A fine, wonderful father. And to me——"

"An old, old man, Thérèse."

"I want no better husband."

In the darkness Joseph reddened. His body warmed.

"Thérèse——"

"Hai! Wonder child! Stop it! Stop it!"

"What is it, Thérèse? What's the matter?"

"It kicks! I think we will have a donkey!"

He sighed deeply. There was a little silence. He closed his eyes.

"I wonder," he said drowsily, "perhaps this one . . . perhaps a girl . . ."

He slept. And when his quiet breathing filled the room Thérèse closed her eyes and the house was silent, and she sighed once and then all the house slept.

Far away, in Vienna, in a small room in the palace, Lucas

29

Johann Boer stood at bay among a company of his fellow doctors and an array of curious courtiers.

There was triumph in the room, and hatred was a long-nursed cancer and Lucas Boer stood alone. For thirty years he had stood alone, and the Lying-in Division of the great General Hospital of Vienna was born under his direction, and for thirty years he fought death in its corridors and envy in the air and hate and jealousy and intrigue throughout the palace.

He stood at bay, now, for the last time. In his hand was a paper, and on the paper was the hospital record for the year past, twenty-six dead out of 3,066 patients, a mortality of .84 per cent. The paper was no shield, no buckler against his fellow doctors. They had found an excuse.

"You will not permit midwifery to be taught on the cadaver instead of the phantom?"

Lucas Boer dropped his eyes wearily. He tried to smile.

"I am sorry, gentlemen."

The room was alive with triumph. Men lowered their lids to hide it.

"That is all, then, Doctor."

He left the room and the palace and walked out into the night.

A little fawning man came forward. He smiled ingratiatingly and his fat body trembled. He licked his lips. His name was Jacob Klein. He would be the next director of the Lying-in Division of the Vienna General Hospital. His entire career would depend upon his fellow doctors and official favor. He had been Boer's assistant.

Now cadavers replaced phantoms. Now rotting flesh replaced a harmless doll.

In the first year of Klein's directorship 237 patients out of 3,036 died from infection, a mortality of 7.8 per·cent. For Klein it was a good year. Perhaps his best.

# FOUR

*"ARMA virumque cano,"* the teacher said. The phrase plucked the violins of his memory. He read on, and his voice became in his ears a conch shell humming the sad, exultant ocean of the past. He put his hands behind him, he closed his eyes, he rode the wind, he prowed the far-bosomed waves.

"Arma virumque cano, Trojae qui primus ab oris . . ."

He opened his eyes. He blinked. He inspected the schoolboys dully.

"Ignaz Philipp!"

The boy rose. He looked at the master. He looked at the book. He licked his lips.

"Yes! Well!"

In the room the dust hung still. Terror kicked him. The boy plunged.

"The arms—the arms, that is, the arms sing of the man . . ."

The master frowned. He narrowed his eyes, incredulous.

"Wait! Wait! I sing of the man . . . of the arms . . ." He paused. He stared fascinated at the teacher. The teacher stared back, unbelieving.

"This is review," the teacher said at last. "This is review, Ignaz Philipp." His voice rose.

"The man sings . . . the arms . . . I sing—— Wait! I am singing——"

"Stop!" shouted the teacher.

His gaze swiveled from boy to boy. He looked incredulously again at Ignaz Philipp. He stepped from the platform, walked down the aisle, and with a sidewise buffet knocked the husky boy into his seat. Ignaz Philipp slumped there, relieved, uncomplaining.

"You fool! You stupid fool!"

"I am singing——" shrilled a voice.

31

"The arms are singing——" pealed another.

"Silence!" shrieked the teacher. The room was instantly silent. He waited for a sound. The boys held their breaths, they stared at their desks. He turned, strode up the aisle, mounted the platform. Mentally he chose the next reciter.

Ignaz Philipp raised his hand.

The teacher swallowed.

"Sir teacher Albers—what kind of arms?"

The class sucked in a breath. Mr. Albers stared.

"Arms?"

"With respect—'the arms,' it says here."

"Weapons, blockhead. Weapons to fight with."

He nodded at another boy. The boy rose.

"Arma virumque cano . . . I sing of arms and the man . . . Trojae qui primus ab oris . . . who first from the coasts of Troy . . ."

The boy droned on, words, a remembered thing, perfectly remembered. The paragraph ended. He looked at Mr. Albers expectantly. Mr. Albers nodded. The boy sat down. Mr. Albers looked at his watch. Two boys done with. The school day was ending. A titter reached him. He looked up. Ignaz Philipp had raised his hand again.

Mr. Albers smiled terribly.

"You want another chance, perhaps? Aha! This time you will distinguish yourself! You know the second paragraph before I give the Latin?"

Ignaz Philipp lowered his head. He touched the book on his desk diffidently.

"Yes! Well!"

"With permission, sir teacher Albers . . ." His voice was high. He swallowed. "The arms——"

"The arms? Again?" He stepped menacingly forward.

"What did they look like," blurted the boy, "that is, the kind—what they looked like——"

His voice crumbled. He stood, waiting. Then his eyes despaired and steadily Mr. Albers looked on at him, his face crimsoned, he looked down, answer me, he prayed, and as he stood Mr. Albers looked away swiftly, gave the next paragraph, called out a name.

"*Musa, mihi causas memora* . . . Muse, tell me the cause . . ."

"The reason!"

"The reason . . . *quo numine laeso* . . . *quo numine laeso* . . . that the divine will . . ."

The boy looked up, helplessly.

Mr. Albers laid down his book. He glanced at the beating cane in the corner, decided time was insufficient, rose, walked to the boy, clouted him, felled him to his seat with a second blow, walked back to the platform.

32

"Hirschler!"

*"Musa, mihi causas* . . . Muse, tell me the reason . . . *quo numine laeso* . . . that the divine will . . . *quidve dolens* . . . why such suffering . . ."

The lesson lagged on. At last it stumbled to an end. The pupils rose, formed a file, shambled to the door, escaped. From out of doors came the customary roar of their freedom. Mr. Albers looked up. It appeared Ignaz Philipp was still in his seat.

"You may go home, Ignaz Philipp."

"Yes, sir." He rose. He looked despairingly at Mr. Albers. "If you please, Mr. Albers—a great favor"—his eyes begged him not to be angry—"all I wanted to know—I thought—if you would tell me——"

"You are a bad pupil, Ignaz Philipp. You do not study. You do not pay attention. You will not apply yourself. What will happen to you, Ignaz Philipp? Do you know what will happen to you?"

The boy hung his head, miserable.

"Answer me, Ignaz Philipp."

"I will study."

"But you do not study."

"I start to study, but it is very hard——"

"Do you think you are clever, with your questions? Let me tell you something. A boy is like a brook. He will wander, he will play, he is here, he is there. But he must be mastered, he must be straightened, he must be led straight to the mill, then the wheels will turn and flour will be made and the world will prosper."

"Yes, sir teacher Albers."

"It is nothing to ask questions. Questions are a brook, wandering. Wandering is worthless. All boys ask questions. You are not unusual, Ignaz Philipp. No, we are not unusual."

"No, sir teacher Albers."

"You have a good enough mind. And yet—I don't know. I really don't know what to do with you. I have tried everything, it seems. And then today——"

"It was about the arms. I was studying, and then I started to think about the arms."

"It was review. That is what is so terrible."

The boy hung his head.

"What is it, Ignaz Philipp? What is it about the arms?"

"Aren't they important, sir teacher Albers?"

"They are not important. We are not studying arms. Don't you see that?"

"Yes, sir."

"We are studying Latin. We are studying a language, a certain tongue . . . *arma virumque cano* . . ." He shaped his voice

33

to descend into the ages. "Don't you feel that? Don't you see what I'm telling you?"

"Yes, sir teacher."

"You see nothing. You feel nothing. Go home and study. Remember it is the language. Go home. Go in peace. Only the language . . ."

He remained at his desk a space after the boy had left. He thought a moment, he looked among his books. Aha! Ancient arms . . . but it seemed they were all old German weapons . . . no, no, Greek . . . it was of no consequence. He closed the book. From out of doors he heard a shriek "What kind of arms?" as the boys greeted Ignaz Philipp, then the shrill noises of flight. He looked down, he saw the book of ancient weapons, abruptly the shouts irritated him.

"If he does so badly with me, what is he doing in the classrooms of the others? This son of a grocer?" He thought about this. Then he put his books away, shut the drawer with a little slam, rose, and left the classroom to find out.

Outside, the interminable soccer game recessed and the boys panted slowly in the direction of a boy who lay on the ground and would not get up. They formed a ring around him and put their hands on their hips and waited, breathing hard.

"Poldi——" a boy shouted to the recumbent one.

The boy on the ground breathed hoarsely, his face white, his eyes closed.

"Hey, look——"

"He's wetting his pants!"

"He's fainted!"

"What? Again?"

"Somebody kicked his kneecap."

"Ignaz Philipp!"

"I was miles away!"

"Nah! All he needs is a touch. You don't need Ignaz Philipp——"

"Just touch his kneecap——"

"One day I was chasing him and he tripped—blam! He fainted."

"It's no fun, all the same."

"Well then, sing to him, Ignaz Philipp."

"Wait a minute. Hey, Poldi! Here he is. He's coming to."

Poldi Hirschler sat up, dazed. He looked wonderingly at the boys ringing him, he remembered, he looked at his kneecap. He began to pale again. They watched, curiously.

"Wait a minute!" Ignaz Philipp kneeled beside him. "Put your head down."

"That's right——"

"Put your head down, Poldi——"

"Come on, he'll be all right."

"Come on, Ignaz Philipp!"

34

"Get back to your goal, our dear singer——"

"I can't." Ignaz Philipp shook his head sadly. He looked at Poldi, sidelong. "I forgot. I promised. I've got to go home."

"Maybe you're going to faint too?" observed a boy.

"Maybe you'd like a hit in the stomach?" asked Ignaz Philipp.

"No," said the boy quickly. "I wouldn't."

"Well, come on," shouted another. "Don't coax him. Get another goalie."

The two teams surged away.

"You've got to give up one man."

"Ohhhh no! It's not our fault you lost your goalie."

"By rights Ignaz Philipp is worth two men! Give up Georgi and Louis!"

"Georgi and Louis! Only listen to them! Georgi and Louis——"

Poldi got to his feet shakily. Suddenly he noticed his pants. Ignaz Philipp looked awkwardly away. Silently they left the playing field. Poldi stopped beside a tree. Ignaz Philipp mastered a wince, kept his face impassive.

"It hurts, eh?"

"Nah. It seems it's tender."

"A pad, perhaps——?"

"I tried. Then I can't run. If you can't run——"

"Yes. That's the truth."

"You don't have to stay. I'm fine now. Go on back and play."

"I'll tell you something. I didn't really leave the game because of you. I could see you were all right. I've got to go home anyway."

"Since when?"

"Yes, that's so. That's really so."

They walked slowly from the school, Poldi stopped again, they continued slowly down the street. A block from his home Poldi stopped determinedly.

"I thank you, Ignaz Philipp."

"You're all right? No pain?"

"As good as new. Maybe better."

"Yes. Well. So long then."

"If you should have trouble with your Latin——"

"It's nothing. Well. So long then."

"Until tomorrow."

Poldi turned and limped down the street. At the block's end he turned. Ignaz Philipp was still standing there.

"It limps a little," Poldi shouted. "Stiff, I think. Until tomorrow." He waved and turned the corner.

Ignaz Philipp looked at the sun drooping westward over the stones of Buda. There was a small autumn haze. He followed it to the Danube. He would be late again.

He stared out at the harbor. A ship sailed slowly out. As he watched it the ship seemed to be quitting not the dock but his heart. It was intolerable. He ached instantly for the parting. He blinked, a passing whore jostled him, he looked down and where he looked the cobblestones became a focused few, myriad with detail, grained and soiled. Now he looked up, and wherever he stared the buildings became stones set one upon another, they lost the shape of buildings and became squares and rectangles and then an infinity of smaller angles, rhomboids, triangles. Suddenly he remembered the ship. He turned quickly. But it had almost disappeared down the Danube. And when he looked around again the narrow dirty street in the Christianstadt was bulk again, the details vanished, a sailor stumbled into the gutter, he sat there a moment blowing a horn, he took the horn from his mouth and began to vomit.

Ignaz Philipp looked away and the sky was leaden. The ship was gone. A new one was starting out. He began to walk homeward. *"Arma virumque cano,"* he said to himself. "Arma virumque cano. I sing of arms and the man. Now I will study. Now I will really study." He frowned, thinking.

At dinner he ate silently. Several times he sighed.

"Are you sick, Ignaz Philipp?" asked Thérèse.

"He is thinking," grinned Joseph, the eldest brother. "He always looks sick when he thinks."

"It hurts him," said Philipp.

"Papa," said Ignaz Philipp, "I would like to know something."

"Aha!"

"Listen, everybody," said Karl.

"What is it, boy?"

"I would like to know, Papa, what kind of arms did they have when there were Greeks?"

"HaHA!"

"Johann! August! Julia! To bed!" called Thérèse. They rose, lingering.

"What kind, Papa?"

"Why do you ask me, boy?"

"To bed!" Thérèse cried sharply. The little ones jostled through the door.

"I want to know, Papa."

"Well, boy—the same kind of arms *I* have."

"Maybe they were longer," said Thérèse. "In the old days—I think I have heard such a thing—people had longer arms."

"He doesn't mean arms," said Karl.

"To fight with," said Joseph.

"HaHA! The Greeks are like the Turks, maybe? Curved swords, perhaps? Scimitars?"

"What do you worry about such things, Ignaz Philipp?" said

36

Thérèse. "Fighting and bloodshed—where do you learn such things?"

"It was in school, Mama. It was something we learned today."

"I think it was swords," said father Joseph.

"When I was a girl I saw a Roman sword," said Thérèse, "short and a little handle, broad, old, iron."

"I don't think so, Mama. I don't think the Greeks——"

"Why don't you ask your teacher?"

"He won't tell me. I asked him three times."

"The teacher wouldn't tell you——?"

"Wait a minute, Papa," said brother Joseph.

"What did you learn today?" asked Karl.

"*Arma—arma something,*" said Ignaz Philipp.

"*Arma virumque cano,*" said brother Joseph. "I sing of arms and of the man——"

"That's review for you, isn't it?" said Karl.

"Yes, but what kind of arms?"

"The bow, silly. A longbow. And a spear. And of course a sword. Sometimes they threw stones——"

"With a slingshot," said Karl.

"A longbow," Ignaz Philipp repeated reverently. "And a spear and a sword. And sometimes a slingshot . . ."

Father Joseph beamed proudly. Thérèse beamed back.

"You see? In this house everyone is smart. Here's a krone apiece."

"Thank you, Papa."

"Study hard, boys."

"Yes, Papa."

"You, Ignaz Philipp. Ask questions. Ask everybody. Even the teacher. With respect."

"Yes, Papa."

"Help Ignaz Philipp, Joseph."

"Yes, Papa."

"You, too, Karl."

"Yes, Papa."

"My boys are very bright," said father Joseph.

"Boys are boys," said Thérèse sharply.

"You will not always be boys. You, Ignaz Philipp, someday you will be a military auditor. Do you know what that can lead to?"

"No, Papa."

"To politics, my boy. Yes, perhaps even to politics. Do you know what that means?"

"Leave the boy alone," said Thérèse.

"He is a Hungarian. This is Hungary. Under this roof it is not Austria. May the day come. Who shall say that he will not make Hungary free—this one?"

"Joseph!"

37

"Make your father proud, boys." He beamed at Joseph. "The old Greeks, eh? Nothing is hidden from you. You, too, Karl. And my wise Ignaz Philipp. Ask about everything." He beamed down the table. "Soon you will know more than your father."

From the floor below came the tinkle of the store bell.

"At this hour?" said Thérèse.

"Go see, Joseph," said the father.

The boy clattered downstairs. He returned wide-eyed.

"It is sir teacher Albers," he said, breathless. "To see you, Papa."

"Your coat, Joseph," cried Thérèse, and the father dashed back into the room, struggled his coat on, dabbed at his hair, rushed downstairs.

Thérèse looked at them.

"It is I, Mama," said Ignaz Philipp.

"What have you done, Ignaz Philipp?"

"It is not his fault, Mama," said Karl.

"Everyone knows the Ofen School is the worst in Hungary," said Joseph.

"What is it, Ignaz Philipp?" Her forehead tightened with sudden horror. "You have been going to school, haven't you? You go straight to school every day?"

"We see him every day, Mama," said Karl.

"Every day," said Joseph.

"Be quiet. I know your 'every day.' You saw him every day the time he spent a whole week down at the docks. Ignaz Philipp?"

"I go to school, Mama. But I don't study."

"Now, now, Ignaz Philipp. Be truthful. Tell Mama."

Thérèse put her arm around his shoulders. Her face softened. "Is it something bad, Ignaz Philipp? Is it something you don't prefer to tell Mama?"

The boy stared at the table.

"Tell me! Tell me quick, Ignaz Philipp! Papa is coming! I can help you!"

The door opened. Behind Papa stood sir teacher Albers. No one looked at teacher Albers. They looked at Papa. There was no expression on Papa's face. He looked briefly at Mama. Then he seated Mr. Albers.

"Go to bed, boys," he said, and Joseph and Karl bowed where they stood when the teacher entered, bowed at the door, and left the room.

"Sit down, Ignaz Philipp. Now let us begin. Do me the honor, sir teacher Albers, will you say again that which you had the kindness to relate to me downstairs?"

"It is not that he is a bad boy," Mr. Albers began deprecatingly.

"A glass of tokay, sir teacher Albers?"

38

"A small glass, perhaps." He glanced respectfully about him. "One can see he comes of a good family."

"He fears God, sir teacher Albers."

"He is a good boy."

"Honored wife, he is a good boy."

"Has he done something wrong?"

Mr. Albers looked carefully at Joseph. He raised his glass to his lips. Thérèse looked fearfully at her husband.

"He does not study," Joseph said wonderingly. "He is failing. He is failing in everything." He said this carefully, word by word, anxious to omit not a syllable, not a clue, to these words which were to him without meaning. He turned to Mr. Albers. "Are you sure this is the one? We have a large family. You mean perhaps Joseph? Or Karl? Or better—Philipp—or Ignaz? This one," he said anxiously, "this one is Ignaz Philipp."

Mr. Albers sighed.

"This is the one," he said sadly.

"But he knows so much," said Thérèse.

"He is forever asking questions—questions from class."

"Sometimes we cannot answer. Not even Joseph, two years ahead of him."

"Questions," said Joseph, "always questions."

"And so bright," said Thérèse.

Mr. Albers nodded.

"I know his questions," he said.

They looked at Ignaz Philipp. The boy kept his shame-filled eyes down. His body, large for a boy of twelve, trembled, he put up a clumsy hand to the disorder of his yellow hair.

"Questions are not study," said Mr. Albers. "Every boy asks questions. Also, it is necessary to study."

"Ignaz Philipp?" said Joseph. "What is it? What has happened?"

"Speak, Ignaz Philipp," said Thérèse.

"I am so sorry, Papa," the boy said in a low voice. "So sorry, Mama. I—I am so sorry."

"Why don't you study?" asked Joseph, as if study were a word newly invented, the meaning of which was not clear to him, a thing that clearly did not apply to his son, something new, just stumbled upon.

"What is it that he doesn't study?" he asked Mr. Albers.

"He studies nothing," said Mr. Albers. "Not arithmetic——"

"But he helps me keep the books—he is always so correct——"

"Nor his Latin——"

"But just tonight he spoke Latin——"

"Nor composition, nor grammar, nor spelling, nor punctuation, nor German——"

"With respect, sir teacher Albers," Joseph interrupted. His

39

face was wary, now, and the confusion was gone. "You are German?"

"His German is atrocious," Mr. Albers said sadly.

"We—ah—we are Hungarians," said Joseph. "Of course we are Hungarians, you understand."

"Yourself?" asked Thérèse.

"I, too, am Hungarian," said Mr. Albers.

"Albers," said Joseph. He savored the word. "A Hungarian name?" He turned to Mr. Albers.

The teacher reddened.

"We are one country, Mr. Semmelweis. Austria and Hungary. And the mother tongue of this united nation is indeed German. It is very necessary that a boy speak German if it is the speech of his fatherland."

"I speak a little German," said Joseph. "My wife speaks very good indeed. I have forgotten much. But I manage. Still—this is Hungary."

"Austria-Hungary, with respect, honored Mr. Semmelweis."

Joseph turned from Mr. Albers and looked steadily at Thérèse.

"But it is not alone German," Mr. Albers cried. "The boy is failing in everything. You must understand, sir. He does not, will not study!"

"Do you beat him, sir teacher Albers?"

"Of course I beat him. It does no good. Naturally I beat him. It is not his teacher who fails, Mr. Semmelweis. I assure you I have failed in nothing. It is he—the boy—who has failed. Not I."

"You beat him and he does not speak good German." Joseph nodded his head slowly. In his mind the riddle was over. The incredible had become a simple situation after all, ludicrous really, completely understandable. And at the end of the table Ignaz Philipp felt his exoneration and it was unbearable, and he raised his eyes humbly.

"He is right, Papa. I do not study. It is not the German, Papa——"

"No," said Joseph politely. "It is not the German and it is not the beatings. You do not study."

"It is true, Papa."

"He is a good boy, Mr. Semmelweis. But if he does not study he will have to leave school."

Thérése caught her breath. Her mouth opened and her eyes widened. Joseph glanced at her from the corner of his eye. He became the merchant and the protector and the diplomat.

"HaHAH!" he said heartily. He clapped Mr. Albers on the shoulder. "Another glass, sir teacher Albers! Come, drink up, drink up! A little matter, you might say, a matter between men, shall we say? HaHAH! Serious, yes, certainly serious!" He glanced severely at Ignaz Philipp. His frown cleared and he smiled engagingly. "Let us have no talk of leaving school. Ha! Here is a little boy—there is a big school—here is a great teacher"—he leaned forward confidentially—"the greatest, one has heard, in all Ofen, in all Buda, in all Ofen, certainly. Perhaps in all Hungary." Mr. Albers looked down modestly.

"I beg of you, Mr. Semmelweis——"

"Do you see, boy?" roared Joseph. "You must study! Then you will become great. A great man like Mr. Albers here!"

"With respect, Mr. Semmelweis——"

"He will show you! He will teach you all he knows. Speak up, boy."

"Yes, Papa."

"That's right. That's the spirit. You see, Mama? A great man like Mr. Albers, so fine a teacher, look at him as he sits there, honoring our humble house, he will never let a little boy leave his school a failure. How could he? How could a learned man like, that do such a thing?"

"I beg of you, honored Mr. Semmelweis——"

"Stand up, boy! Stand up!" Ignaz Philipp rose. "Do you think you are smarter than sir teacher Albers, than this great man?"

"No, Father. Never."

"Do you think so learned a man is to be conquered by a schoolboy? A little boy? A thing like you?"

"Never, Father. It is not Mr. Albers. It is me, Papa. I—don't know why. I just don't study."

"You don't study," echoed Joseph mockingly. He turned to Mr. Albers. "He doesn't study," he repeated, one man to another.

"And do you think," he roared, "that will defeat Mr. Albers? Hah? Oh no, boy. I have lived a long time, I have learned a thing or two about men. You will never defeat such a man as sir teacher Albers, I can tell you that, Ignaz Philipp. Give up trying. He will get the best of you. You will never win. He is too clever for you. You will graduate no matter what you do. He is too much for you, my boy."

"Yes, Papa."

"Sit down, Ignaz Philipp," said Thérèse. "Another glass, sir teacher Albers, if I may presume on your learned good nature?"

"With great respect—a small glass, perhaps."

"It is a fabulous thing to meet you," said Joseph. "I am overcome that you honored us with your visit."

"If all parents were like you, honored Mr. Semmelweis——"

"Perhaps they do not know a man of intellect when they see one," said Joseph.

"Your health, good and honest sir."

"Your health, respected sir teacher Albers."

41

They set their glasses down.

"Go to bed, Ignaz Philipp," Thérèse said levelly.

"Wait!" Joseph held up his hand. "I am glad you are here," he turned to Mr. Albers. "The boy has been plaguing us. I have, you understand, no great education. Hah! What need for Latin to run a grocery store! He asks questions, sir teacher Albers."

"I know."

"I cannot answer him. That is natural. All right, Ignaz Philipp. Here is your teacher. Go ahead, ask."

Mr. Albers turned magnanimously to the boy.

"Go ahead, Ignaz Philipp," he commanded.

"It is nothing," the boy mumbled.

"HaHAH! Nothing! Now you are dumb, are you! Ask about the arms!"

"Still the arms?" Mr. Albers said wearily.

"Joseph told me." Ignaz Philipp hung his head.

"They carried bows, my boy," said Mr. Albers. "Spears, swords, whatever they wanted. Is that enough? Are you satisfied now?"

"You see, boy? That's your teacher! Are you through?"

"What kind of wood?" said Ignaz Philipp in a low voice.

"In the bows? Just wood from the trees."

"From our kind of trees?"

Mr. Albers frowned.

"What does it matter what kind of trees?"

"I thought—if perhaps I wanted to make myself such a bow—if I knew the kind of tree——"

"You study your lessons," said Mr. Albers, "and you won't have time to play with bows. You might hurt someone. Have you thought of that?"

"Last week it was how do birds fly?" said Thérèse intently. She waved her hand as though it did not matter.

"How do birds fly?" Mr. Albers smiled. They all turned and looked at him, waiting. He looked back at them smiling, and then with a little laugh he shrugged. "They fly," he said. "I suppose there is no doubt of that?"

"No, sir teacher Albers."

"You see?" said Thérèse.

"But how?" the boy asked eagerly.

"Because they are so light, my boy. That is why."

"I know," said the boy. "And yet when : found a dead bird I tossed it into the air and it did not float like one of its feathers could float. Oh no. This bird fell back to the earth like a stone. With respect, sir."

"And a few days back it was 'Why does cement hold stones together?' and once before: 'What is the lightning?'——"

"And 'why do we not speak Latin'?" broke in Joseph.

"And what makes holes in cheese——"

42

"And why does a candle burn——"

They stopped for a moment and stared, Ignaz Philipp, Joseph, and Thérèse, at Mr. Albers.

He laughed heartily. They continued to stare at him hopefully. He stopped laughing. He paused a moment to consider these things. He looked back at them, serious.

"He is not sent to school to ask questions, Mr. Semmelweis. He is sent to study. The courses are all laid down by the Imperial Austrian Government. I am there to instruct him. I do my best."

"You need not say more," said Joseph.

"Not a word," said Thérèse.

"Naturally," said Mr. Albers, waving his hand dismissingly, "such questions——"

"I would not dignify them with answers," said Thérèse.

"You should be ashamed, Ignaz Philipp," said Joseph.

"I am ashamed, Papa."

"He must study, Mr. Semmelweis. That is the whole of it."

"I will study, Papa."

"He must try very hard."

"Particularly German," Joseph said earnestly to the boy.

"It is very important," Thérèse said severely.

"And you must respect your teacher, just as if it were I, even though he beats you," said Joseph.

"It is for your good," said Thérèse.

"That is all, then," said Mr. Albers, rising. "I see I am to have your co-operation."

"Honored sir, you have our entire confidence." Joseph rose. "This visit—I am overwhelmed—so distinguished a teacher—Hungary is honored——"

"Austria-Hungary, with respect——"

"Austria-Hungary, sir teacher Albers."

"And the boy——?" Thérèse said anxiously.

The two men looked at Ignaz Philipp, then at each other.

"I think we can take care of that," said Joseph, smiling at Mr. Albers, "we—this greatly distinguished teacher and this humble and unlearned grocer."

"He will be all right," Mr. Albers said graciously. "I will take personal interest."

He turned to Thérèse.

"God's blessing, honored wife——"

"God's blessing, honored sir——"

"God's blessing, child——"

Ignaz Philipp stared at the floor a moment, then came slowly forward, took Mr. Albers' white hand and kissed it clumsily.

"HaHAH!" roared Joseph. "Another glass? No? Come! I will walk down with you! Perhaps you will do me the honor —take a bottle home with you—a new shipment—for the nobility only—but, then, humble grocer that I am I can tell a noble when I see one——"

He laughed a great shouting laugh.

Mr. Albers made a deprecating gesture. He licked his lips. They passed downstairs together. The noise of their footsteps ended.

"Well!" said Thérèse.

And Ignaz Philipp looked at her a moment, then ran and put his head on her shoulder. Her hand went to his hair. Her fingers felt the yellow hair, the texture of the child she had borne.

When Joseph came back to the room he found them thus. Ignaz Philipp stood up.

"You see?" said Joseph. He went to the door and closed it carefully. "You see? A German. Did you ever hear of a Hungarian Albers? He's a German!"

"It's not only that, Papa. It's so hard for me to study——"

"You must study, Ignaz Philipp," Joseph said mechanically. "But he is a German," he said to Thérèse. "And the boy, thank God, is Hungarian. You are Hungarian, boy."

"Oh yes, Papa. And I will study. You will see. This will never happen again."

"Are you ashamed, boy?"

"I am so ashamed, Papa, I could die."

"Don't say that," said Thérèse sharply.

"He has never come here because of Joseph or Karl or Philipp or Ignaz or anybody. Only because of me."

But Joseph and Thérèse barely heard him. It was clear that he should be ashamed. It did a boy no harm. But the fingers of their minds peeled the problem and felt the layered kernel, and their faces cleared. They smiled relief at each other. A fool could see that Ignaz Philipp was at least as bright as any of the others. Why should he fail? He studied with the rest, he helped as well as the others, and he asked more questions than all the others put together.

"He beats the boy," Thérèse said.

"He beats him," Joseph assented heavily.

"He beats him!" Thérèse said helplessly.

"It doesn't hurt, Mama," said Ignaz Philipp.

"And he is German."

"And the boy will not learn German."

"He was not born a German."

"He was not born an Austrian, either, with no language of his own. He was born a Hungarian, a Hungarian child, under a God-fearing, Hungary-loving Hungarian roof."

"I must learn German, though, Papa," the boy said humbly. "The other boys learn it. I can learn it if I study."

"Why don't you study, boy?" Joseph asked curiously.

"I don't know," the boy said miserably. "Sometimes I study,

sometimes I don't study. Sometimes the world is so full of things and I start thinking about them and time flies and all of a sudden I am in class——"

"It is the same for all boys," Thérèse nodded. "And for girls too."

"And the questions," Joseph shouted suddenly. "Did you see? Did you watch his face? A teacher!" He spat the word. "A teacher cannot answer a child's simple questions? Who is the smarter? Tell me that? Who is the smarter, the child or the teacher?"

"Joseph!" Thérèse reproved anxiously.

"Do you think honored sir distinguished Albers ever thought of such questions?"

"Joseph, the boy——"

"That is why he is a teacher. That is why a poor grocer, an unlearned man, can give him a bottle of wine he cannot buy ——"

He turned suddenly to Ignaz Philipp.

"And that is why you must study, boy. Do you see that? Do you want to be a teacher? And take a grocer's charity? That is why you must study and study and study. That is why, when you are a military accountant——"

"If God is willing," said Thérèse.

"That you can rise and rise and rise."

"Yes, Papa."

"And perhaps, in the will of God, be a great politician. And on that day you will remember Hungary and Hungarian children beaten by Germans and Hungarian children forced to learn a language that is not their own. And free Hungary. Free Hungary, my boy. Remember, free Hungary. For one day we who are free in our souls will be free as a nation. And who knows what you will become that day? What will you give Hungary?"

"I will do it, Papa! I swear it! I will study forever!"

"You are pleased with what I have in mind for you, boy? You are pleased to be a military auditor? There is nothing else?"

Ignaz Philipp looked at his father lovingly. His whole simple heart shone from his eyes with adoration.

"Whatever you say, Papa."

"Eh, boy?"

"Whatever you say."

"I love you, boy."

"I love you, Papa."

And advancing, Joseph gave him such a hug as cracked his ribs. Mama stooped, only, and kissed his cheek.

# FIVE

IN the birth wards of Vienna Death was weary, and the rotting cells, foaming daintily in chill and bluing tissue, the cold and waxen uteri, sleek with a new moisture, the fermenting rinds of the fruit he had sucked lay upon wooden tables, and seven hundred and fourteen women were dead in childbirth.

There were years when he was not so weary, when the ceilings were wet with the breaths he had chilled, when every third woman died, every fourth, every fifth. This year, this happy 1834, he yawned and ripped the life from one in fourteen. Go fearfully, woman, go fearfully, virgin, whore, wife, poxed and whole, come with your bellies big, fourteen will enter, one will remain.

And one and one and one and one until there are seven hundred and fourteen. And one and one and day by day, out of the bed, warm still, wet with agony, wet with blood, wet with pus, out of the bed, onto the stretcher, out of the birth room, into the death room. Her hair hangs over the table edge, it is not seemly, put it beside her head, it belongs to her, straighten her legs, pause, and now let us see.

The yellow knees part sullenly, she is Death's now, and would be faithful, but the puzzled fingers of the living slide into the cold vagina, press inelastic muscle, slit the chill skin, dabble the pus, puncture a membrane, squeeze a breast, and the nostrils smell and the eyes peer, the fingers grope, and she is colder now, she has begun to stiffen, she is more than ever Death's, and in the wards another woman howls, another fourteenth, another one in fourteen, and at the door, big-bellied, a woman knocks for admittance, and in a marriage bed a woman sighs, wet with new seed, and in the death room the baffled fingers withdraw, are wiped upon coat lapels, and the body is borne away, the second body today, and tomorrow there will be two more.

In London a paper is published in English concerning a discovery made eighteen years before. "In 1816 I was consulted by a young woman presenting general symptoms of disease of the heart." This is a shy man, a man of delicacy, a man the least impropriety would confuse, a modest, chaste, and bashful man, and the bosom was young and pink and buxom. His ears tingled, they reddened. And yet he must—he must hear with them, he must press ear to that breast, he must listen. The girl hung her head. "Owing to her stoutness, little information could be gathered by application of the hand and percussion. The patient's age and sex did not permit me to resort to direct application of the ear to the chest. I recalled a well-known acoustic phenomenon, namely, if you place your ear against one end of a wooden beam the scratch of a pin at the other extremity is most distinctly audible. It occurred to me that this physical property might serve a useful purpose in the case with which I was then dealing. Taking a sheaf of paper, I rolled it into a very tight roll, one end of which I placed over the praecordial region, while I put my ear to the other. I was both surprised and gratified at being able to hear the beating of the heart with much greater clearness and distinctness than I had ever done before by direct application of my ear . . ."

The discoverer was René Laënnec. The discovery was the stethoscope.

In Vienna, Joseph Skoda waits apprehensively in the office of Jacob Klein. Dr. Klein is visiting a ward.

"And how is our chest this morning?"

"My chest—the pain—that is, I don't know," the patient stutters. The head of the Lying-in Division of the Vienna General Hospital is visiting her, in person.

Dr. Klein lifts the thin arm, drops it on the coverlet, fingers the stringy pulse.

"And Dr. Skoda—is he taking good care of you?"

"Oh yes, sir."

"And tell me something, did he examine you today?"

"Yesterday, sir doctor. Today, not yet. Today, with respect, I haven't seen sir doctor Skoda——"

"Yes. And how does he listen to you? He puts his ear on your chest perhaps?"

"With respect, sir doctor Klein, he uses a—a stick."

"A stick. Yes. Well . . . a stick . . ."

Dr. Klein goes to another bed, a middle-aged woman.

". . . he puts a tube, a stick tube, a listening thing against my chest . . . he pokes here, he pokes there . . ."

"It hurts you?"

"Hurts, no. But I don't understand . . . What's he doing? . . . It makes me uneasy . . ."

And to the bedside of a young woman.

". . . it tickles, the stick sir doctor Skoda puts to my breast is something new?"

And to the bedside of another.

". . . he pokes at me for weeks now. I am very brave. It does not frighten me in the least . . ."

Skoda rises. Dr. Klein seats himself at his desk. For a measured interval he busies himself with papers. And now he looks up.

"Dr. Skoda, a month ago I received complaints about you and I called you here to discuss these complaints. I did not, to be frank, believe the nature of these statements. It was related to me that in your wards you were annoying the patients by poking their chests and abdomens with a—a stick—which you were good enough to explain to me was a device put forth by a Frenchman for listening to noises in the patient's body. A device, I need hardly say, which has not come to my attention, or to the already large selection of instruments now at the disposal of reputable physicians."

"It is a stethoscope, sir director Klein, it is called a stethoscope, invented by Dr. René Laënnec, of Paris, the heart, the lung sounds are greatly magnified by it——"

"At that time I suggested to you that such innovations are out of place in such an institution as the Vienna General Hospital and that grave scandal could arise through the use of untested and unauthorized instruments, rightly reflecting upon myself, as a director of this institution."

"Dr. Laënnec's paper has been translated into English and German. It is a harmless instrument, sir director, of no peril to the patient, possibly of much use to medicine—the sounds are greatly magnified——"

"When you left my office it was my understanding that you were henceforth to discontinue annoying patients with this childish toy and that I, as your director, was to regard myself no longer as your unwitting accomplice in this childishness."

"If the director, with all respect, were to listen through this instrument——"

"I have, however, to my utter amazement, continued to receive intimations that you have disregarded my wishes. This morning I called you to my office and made your rounds. I have personally found out from your patients that you are continuing to annoy, tickle, and otherwise plague them with this unprofessional piece of wood. I discovered one woman in a fever which I have no doubt can easily be ascribed to your continual poking at her. That there were not graver findings in the other patients can only be described as fortunate."

"It is true. I have continued to use the stethoscope."

"You have continued to endanger your patients, to disobey your director. Dr. Skoda, I no longer find your conduct childish. I find it—insane. You are twenty-nine years old. You have

48

been a physician for three years. You spent your first year as cholera doctor in Bohemia. Your first year here at Vienna was exemplary. I find now that your experience has not been sufficiently rounded. You apparently have a gift for innovations, for the inventive. I am going to deal with you leniently. Your new post will afford you full opportunity to labor among the inventive. I am transferring you to the St. Ulrich's Lunatic Asylum. You are relieved, as of this instant, of all duties at Vienna General."

"But, sir doctor, sir director Klein——"

"I could dismiss you altogether."

"I wish only to say——"

"You may consider this interview has ended."

Joseph Skoda had, as it happened, no great political backing. But someone, Dr. Klein could not remember who, had sufficient influence to recommend him.

"I am going to speak to you now, not as a director, but as a fellow physician. I hope for your sake you will remember what I say. The wise physician keeps to the middle ground. He eschews innovations. His path lies neither among those who are far behind the times nor with those who leap among the unproved paths of conjecture. He follows. He lets others try. He learns, when he is old as I am, that there is nothing new, nothing worth trying. There is nothing under the sun worth endangering a career for. And here is a little secret: we have learned all there is to learn. Everything of real consequence. There is nothing new to be discovered. For a whim you have placed me, as your director, in a position of considerable jeopardy. I forgive you. You may go."

Joseph Skoda left the Vienna General Hospital that afternoon. A porter carried his trunk to a waiting carriage. Skoda embraced with his eyes the far-reaching buildings of the hospital, the cathedral of European medicine with which suddenly he was no longer a communicant. Standing thus, outside, dispossessed, the small, thickly built man staring through gold-rimmed glasses trembled in a spasm of insecurity, shame, and loss.

"Where to, honored sir?" the driver called.

Skoda stared a moment longer, then he turned and walked to the carriage.

"St. Ulrich's Lunatic Asylum," he said. Then he smiled at the shock in the driver's face. "It's all right. I'm a doctor. I belong there."

Sitting in the carriage, Skoda resolutely put away confusion and terror, bent himself to review his career. Which device, he demanded of himself, was responsible for the catastrophe? He forced himself to be detached. Was it the stethoscope or the plessimeter? He remembered reading Laënnec on the stethoscope. He remembered his first listening through a

49

wooden tube against the patient's chest. From that moment, hearing the tube's magnification of sound, he knew how senseless was diagnosis based on the fainter sounds detected by the ear alone. On the other hand, if the instrument evoked terror it might retard the patient's recovery. But how deep was the patient's distrust and terror and how prolonged? And when the patient found the wooden tube did not hurt him and he was bound to find this out in less than sixty seconds, then how much harm could be blamed on the wooden tube?

It was the same with the plessimeter, he decided swiftly. The plessimeter was simply a disk of wood or metal or ivory. It was placed on the patient's body. Tapping this disk produced sound. The tap was gentle. The accentuated sound that resulted was not a new discovery. Brewers and vintners had been using it for centuries. They tapped a barrel with their fingers or a mallet. A full cask returned a dull sound. An empty one resounded like a drum. A half-empty one produced a sound midway between the two sounds. An expert vintner or brewer could tell almost to a pint how much a barrel held. It was simply a matter of practice. Practice, and much listening.

And with the human body it was much the same. Auenbrugger had discovered this and applied it with success. A normal abdomen, tapped, returned a certain sound. A distended abdomen sounded like a drum. An abdomen or a chest or any other cavity, full of water, pus, or tumor tissue, returned a dull sound. At first Auenbrugger merely laid three fingers flat on the patient and tapped the three fingers with the middle finger of his other hand.

For a time Skoda had contented himself with this manner of producing sound. Then he had heard about the plessimeter. The plessimeter had these advantages: it magnified sound, and in the course of much tapping the tapped fingers became sore and it saved the physician this soreness. Skoda thought a moment about the material of which plessimeters were made, forgot his disgrace, resolved to experiment with ivory, wood, and metal to discover which was the most resonant. Also the thickness of the disk. Then he returned to the patient and the patient's reaction to a circle of ivory, wood, or metal being laid upon his skin and tapped. Could it alarm the patient? Could it frighten him so badly that it would retard his recovery or increase his illness? It was possible. No one could know what went on in a patient's mind. On the other hand, the patient had applied for relief of an illness. The illness itself was frightening to the patient, and his visit to the doctor or the hospital was another upsetting experience. And no matter what instrument a doctor used must produce terror. Terror was a normal expression of illness. One had then to ask oneself, were the stethoscope and the plessimeter justified? Whatever terror was

50

produced by these instruments, did the terror outweigh the benefits?

He had used the stethoscope and plessimeter on at least four hundred patients. He could now diagnose with not more than two dozen finger taps, no more than a minute of stethoscope listening. His diagnoses were almost invariably correct. By constant listening he could now distinguish between even the finest tones in a patient's breathing, between the differences in dry or fluid-packed tissues. He had entered an astounding new world. Then Klein had caught him. He saw again the fat little man with the pursy lips, the cold eyes, the wet nostrils. He heard Klein complain that he was annoying the patients with his tapping, his poking with a wooden tube. He heard himself review for Klein all he had discovered. He saw Klein look at him with hatred and disgust and contempt. He heard him warn that he must desist these unnatural experiments or leave the hospital. He saw the power in those eyes, the greed to exercise it, the knowledge of helplessness enjoyed. He had left Klein's office and gone straight to the wards, and he had tapped the plessimeter and listened with the stethoscope all afternoon. He had redoubled his tapping and his listening. He had made notes on almost five hundred cases when Klein caught him again. And now here he was in the carriage. He was dismissed from Vienna General, the greatest hospital in Europe. He was on his way to St. Ulrich's Lunatic Asylum.

But this method of diagnosis was tremendous. It was ludicrously successful, ludicrous because of its simplicity. The knowledge it revealed was fantastic. A lifetime of compiling such knowledge was not enough. Every moment of such a lifetime would have to be crowded with its study. In this world one would have to work with Kleins. There were many Kleins.

He worked at St. Ulrich's Lunatic Asylum four months. At the end of four months he obtained a job as a police doctor. He began to court those who could help him. He made himself liked by a minor official. This man Loberst, fourth assistant to the sanitary division of the city of Vienna in the poverty-stricken quarter of St. Ulrich, spoke to the third assistant, and the third assistant spoke to the second, and the second, after conferring with the first, obtained assurance for Skoda that if he left the lunatic asylum he would be appointed to examine whores, stitch stab wounds, set bones, and treat the sores of prisoners captured by the dozen policemen assigned to the district.

He was not long at the police station. He discovered politics. He would never again, in all his life, be unprotected. His weapon would be politics, more ruthless than truth, more efficient than ability, more flexible than money, more secure than knowledge. Politics was a small sin. What he knew, what he had discovered, was more important. And for a man who

51

knew what he wanted and had intelligence to direct him, politics was as simple as auscultation. Patiently, step by step, official by official, he manipulated, he planned, he plotted, he achieved. Less than six months after he was appointed to the police station, Joseph Skoda was back at Vienna General Hospital. His smile was as broad as ever. He was assigned to diseases of the chest. He tapped and listened to his heart's content. He met Klein and Klein greeted him coldly and warily. In politics one does not offend. Reprisals annoy one's backers. One accepts a situation and one preserves one's position. One gets along. Skoda was back at Vienna General. He was not back at Vienna General to avenge himself on Klein. His was secure. He broadened the field of his politics little by little. He was seeking now the post of professorship of internal medicine. Later he would seek to be head of Vienna General. He worked slowly. He worked day by day. Each day he gained a little. Each day he listened, he kept notes, he prepared a book on auscultation. His political gains grew. His book became fatter. His ear and his mind grew sharper.

In the year in which the carriage drove Joseph Skoda from the Vienna General Hospital to exile at St. Ulrich's Lunatic Asylum Karl Rokitansky was appointed at the age of thirty to be professor of pathological anatomy at the University of Vienna. He achieved this great distinction because of the concerted praise of his fellow doctors and his superiors. Upon sound advice from political sources which owed much of their power to the continued efficiency of the hospital and to the appointment of men whose work would be praise for their selection, Jacob Klein readily accepted Rokitansky as prosector of Vienna General Hospital. He discovered after he had voted that as prosector Rokitansky was to prepare subjects for anatomical dissection and that these subjects later would illustrate his lectures. There was no threat in Karl Rokitansky. The dead were his province. And Vienna General had plenty of dead.

In Moravia, eighteen-year-old Ferdinand Hebra prepares to come to Vienna to study medicine. In Buda, young Ludwig von Markussovsky receives private instruction, enters the final years before he begins at Vienna his formal medical education.

In England the first English railway has been built. Slavery had just been outlawed and 700,000 Negroes freed. Dr. John Hunter has announced that syphilis and gonorrhea are the same disease. Charles Darwin has set out on an expedition to South America. John Dalton has announced the atomic theory. R. Brown has discovered that cells have a nucleus. Richard Bright has discovered Bright's disease. Sir Astley Paston Cooper has performed an amputation at the hip joint.

In America, the telegraph has been invented, the first steamboat has crossed the Atlantic, the McCormick reaper has been invented, and the Colt revolver and the electromagnet. Usnea, a moss scraped from the skull of criminals hung in chains, is a popular physicians' remedy for nervous or wasting diseases. John Collins Warren has founded the Massachusetts General Hospital, George McClellan has founded Jefferson Medical College, Ephraim McDowell has removed the first ovarian tumor, working without anesthesia or antisepsis, a crowd waiting outside to hang him if the patient died and the patient singing hymns while he cut. Lenox Hodge has invented the pessary and J. L. Richmond has performed America's first Caesarian section.

The ovum, the mammalian ovum, has just been discovered by von Baer, but the basis of conception, the union of the spermatozoa with the ovum, will not be discovered for forty-one years, and not for sixty-nine years will the physiology of the menstrual cycle be described. There has never been an appendectomy, an operation on the gall bladder, an operation for the cure of inguinal hernia, a successful hysterectomy, a kidney removal, a prostatectomy, or an operation for a tumor of the brain.

Elsewhere in Europe, in 1834, Belgium has separated from Holland and declared itself a constitutional monarchy, Karl Marx is a schoolboy, Louis Philippe kings France after the Revolution of July, the fever of revolution spreads to Italy, smolders in Lombardy and Venice, in Hungary.

In Buda, Joseph Semmelweis, elder brother, has finished school, assists his father in the grocery. Karl is finishing agricultural school, is already apprenticed to a farmer. Philipp is studying to be a priest. August spends his summers as a carpenter's apprentice.

At Number One Burgauffahrt, on the evening of a pleasant Saturday in October, Joseph the father stands in the doorway. He bids farewell to sir teacher Hans Zimmerman. Sir Teacher Zimmerman waves back with difficulty; under both his arms are bottles of wine. When the teacher is out of sight, Joseph shuts the door, stands in the hallway a moment, thinking, then slowly climbs the stairs. Waiting where he had left him is Ignaz Philipp.

"I will study, Father! You will see! This time I will study!"

"You see how it is, boy."

"I know, Papa. I know, I know."

"Teacher after teacher."

"It is my fault. All my fault."

"What is it you want to do, boy?"

"Papa——"

"Do you want private instruction?"

"No, Papa. Papa I want——"

"Another school, maybe? Maybe that's it. They've given you a bad name. Such a thing is easy."

"Papa, listen——"

"I'll send you to a new school. A brand-new start——"

"Listen, Papa! You ask me what I want."

"What do you want, boy?"

"Papa, I want to quit school."

"You want to quit school?"

"Yes, Papa. Quit and be done. I'm no student, Papa. I hate lessons. I hate study. I want to stop—like Joseph has stopped. Like Karl will stop in another year. I want to help you in the shop, be a farmer, be a carpenter—anything."

"But you can't quit school, Ignaz. You're not ready! Look at me—I'm a grocer. Do you think I want to be a grocer? Do you think a grocer helps Hungary?"

"I'll help Hungary, Papa. I'll do anything. Only—no more school. I can't, Papa. I can't do it. It's not for me."

"Ignaz Philipp, listen to me. Boy, listen. This is important. I have just had a thought. How would you like—how would you like to go to Vienna?"

"To Vienna, Papa? To Vienna?"

"Now tell me, honestly!"

"Oh, Papa!"

"With fifty kroner—fifty kroner, mind—fifty kroner a month—just for spending money."

"Fifty kroner! Vienna!"

"You like to travel—you like adventure—— Oh, I know my boys, when you were just a little boy you even wanted to cross the bridge to Pesth . . ."

"Papa, Papa! What can I say?"

"Don't be hasty. Perhaps you won't like Vienna. There are many cafés there, singing and dancing, a big city, better than Paris, beautiful girls, many a strange sight . . . Eh, Ignaz Philipp?"

"Am I to go to Vienna? Is that your word? Am I really to go, then?"

"Will you study? Will you no longer talk of stopping school?"

"Now you will see, Papa! Now you will really see!"

"I am fifty-six years old, boy. All my boys are good boys. You are my hope. You will do what I would like to do. You will do it for me, Ignaz Philipp, and for your fatherland, for Hungary."

"Yes, Papa."

"In two more years—less, even—you will be through here at the university. You will go to Vienna. You, boy."

"To be a military auditor?"

"To be a lawyer."

"A lawyer!"

"First a lawyer. Perhaps there will be time to study at the same time to be a military auditor. You will study—in Vienna.

54

At Vienna University."

"I can't wait, Papa———"

"You will study law—you will study philosophy———"

"Anything, Papa———"

"And when the day comes—and it is coming, boy—you will be armed. You will be ready. You and I, boy—one person—we will strike for Hungary!"

"I am ready, Papa!"

"What is it you want to become?"

"Everything will be as you want it, Papa!"

They looked at each other.

"Go, boy. Study . . ."

Ignaz Philipp raced to Thérèse. He stammered the incredible news.

"And so—to Vienna, Mama!"

"I will tell you a thing. You must never mention it."

He shook his head quickly.

"Of all the boys, you alone, Ignaz Philipp, have not fought Papa."

"But I did, Mama! I just told him———"

"You don't know, my son. Joseph hates the grocery, he does badly, he is a great problem . . ."

"Joseph, Mama? Not Joseph, surely———!"

"Karl wanted to run away rather than study farming. Philipp cried because he is to be a priest. August hates the very sight of a hammer and saw."

Ignaz Philipp gaped.

"You alone, my boy, you alone have always made him happy. Did you know that? No. You didn't. But whatever Papa said you have always answered: 'Yes, Papa. As you say, Papa. Whatever pleases you, Papa.' You alone."

"If he would only punish me. Sometimes, when the teacher has been here, and then he just looks at me—and I think to myself, oh, please! Punish me! I have been so bad. I know how it hurts you. Punish me."

"He loves you, Ignaz Philipp. He would never punish you. He thinks his Hungary may be freed. Now he puts his longing in you, his hope in you, he will make you what he has never been, he would give you the fondest dream his life has ever given him . . ."

He flinched.

"I know. It frightens me, Mama. And it's easy for me to accept the career he decides. Because I don't really care what I do. To me one thing's as good as another. I don't seem to have any hungering for anything. No goal. No purpose."

She smiled gently into his troubled eyes. She took his hand and stroked it.

"It will come, Ignaz Philipp," she said serenely.

"I'm afraid it won't. I'm afraid that's the way I am."

"You're young. Your whole life's before you. I'll tell you something a woman knows. Every baby that's born comes into life with some qualities stronger. And the child grows. And one day he discovers all of a sudden that there's one thing he wants to do more than anything else in the world. Sometimes something happens and instantly he knows what he wants. Sometimes there's never any one thing you can say 'that made him decide,' that was the thing that decided him."

"I'm getting pretty old now, Mama. I'm sixteen. Karl knows what he wants, Philipp knows what he wants, all the rest know ———"

"Some know what they want to be when they're only four years old. Some are thirty and forty and fifty before they find out."

"Maybe for some people there just isn't anything."

"Oh yes. For everybody there's something. Fathers are proud of a baby. But all mothers hope. They look at the baby and wonder and hope."

"Don't hope too much, little Mama. You're like all mothers. You see me as better than I am. If you really knew———"

"You think a mother is doting? Foolish?"

"Blind, thank God?"

"No, darling. This thing they know. And maybe as a girl, and maybe after they live with a man and bear his children, they learn that somewhere in every man is his own notion of himself as he thinks he can be and dreams of being. It's always the picture of a great man. It gets strong and clear when he finds out what he wants to do. And then if the mother has made her faith in him be part of himself, and a good wife takes up where the mother leaves off . . ."

"And then———?"

"Why, then he could be born in a stable. That's what a woman knows. That's what she knows when she looks at her baby—all women, Mary or Magdalen. That's what I know when I look at you."

56

# SIX

IN Vienna, in the year 1836, three young men walked down Margareten Street into the entrance of an apartment house.

"Wait a minute!" One of them stopped.

"What's the matter?"

"We can't go plunging in like that!" The other two looked at him expectantly. "He might have a girl up there!"

"At this hour?"

"It's nearly noon!"

"Is there a bad hour for such a thing? No, wait! I'm serious! You know Semmy!"

"Maybe he's got two girls!"

"Maybe three! One for each of us! Come on!"

Up the stairs they pounded. At a doorway they stopped. The young man who was about to knock listened instead. He heard nothing. As he turned to the others he noticed a card tacked to the wood. He turned back to read it. The others bent to read with him. The card read: Ignac Fulop Semmelweis. They looked at one another in surprise. Then they turned and began to hammer on the door.

"Get up, wild man!"

"Hope of the Hungarians—arise!"

"Open, fellow collegian, open, dearest song leader, or we break the door down!"

The door opened. Instantly the three plunged into the room, one raced to peer under the bed, the second went straight to the closet, the third yanked aside the window drapes.

"Where are they?"

"Go away, imbeciles. Leave me in peace."

"Where are the women?"

"What women?"

"What women, he asks! You wouldn't know a woman if you saw one, would you? Look at him!"

"And what's the idea of the sign? Who in the sacred name of corpus juris is Ignac Fulop?"

"That's me, gentlemen. That's my name. In Hungarian."

"German isn't good enough for you?"

"That's right."

"All right, you Hungarian. What'll we call you tomorrow? Hunyadi? Arpad? What?"

"Yesterday he's Philipp—today he's Fulop. Let's call him Naci."

"Go away, fellows. I love you, but I haven't studied in a week. Today I have to study."

"Are you sure you haven't got a girl here?"

"Do you mean to say you didn't bring one? Do I have to be always the one who gets the girls?"

"What else are you good for?"

"To hell with girls! Look—we've brought something better than girls." Emil pushed a young man forward. "Look at this! This is Rudi! Meet Rudi. Rudi is going to be a real, genuine doctor. Do you know where we're going tomorrow morning? We're going to the Schwarzspanierstrasse—to the old munitions factory——"

"Rudi's taking us. And what do you think we're going to see?"

"We're going to see an actual anatomy demonstration!"

"Where they cut up bodies——"

"The real thing——"

"You're fooling!"

"Ask Rudi!"

Rudi nodded tolerantly.

"Oh yes. It's the real thing all right."

"Let me come too!"

"You'll faint dead away——"

"Hungarians can't stand the sight of blood——"

"It's all right with me," said Rudi. "But you'll have to behave yourself. No swooning or any other such nonsense——"

"You see what we do for you?"

"And tonight Emil here is giving a party. See that you're there."

"I've got to study. I've really got to study some time——"

He looked uncertainly at his books and papers strewn on a table. One of the young men promptly strode to the table and completely disarranged them.

"Oh well . . . I might as well . . . God! I hate law . . ."

"Who likes it?" They walked to the door. "You be there tonight, then!"

"I'll be there."

They clumped down the stairs, they burst into the street,

58

singing, they marched over the sidewalk toward the distant spires of the University of Vienna.

"He's a very amusing fellow, that Semmelweis."

"Straight from the country——"

"You should hear him sing in Hungarian when he's got a couple of quarts under his belt——"

"Remember the night he did that Hungarian dance?"

"We'll have fun with him tomorrow, Rudi!"

"I want to see his face when they start to cut up a body——"

"Is he a clown or what?"

"No, he's no clown. He doesn't even know he's funny. He's a Hungarian, that's all. A real peasant type. He's so simple he makes you laugh. We get a lot of fun out of him."

"Doesn't he know it?"

"Of course not. He thinks everybody is like him."

"I wouldn't want to make him mad. Not with that build."

"Don't worry. We've got him trained. You'll see him in action tonight."

Toward evening Ignaz Philipp put aside his books with a sigh of relief. Stimulated by the thought of the party, he had studied conscientiously all day. Now he rose, put on his student cap, shrugged into his coat, and left the room excitedly.

He went to a bakery.

"How much are these?"

"Twelve groschen the dozen."

"Have you got something more expensive?"

"Well, these little cakes here—but these cost a gulden——"

"I'll take them."

"The whole lot?"

"Wrap them up nice."

Carrying a huge box of cakes, he went to a tavern. He bought three bottles of wine.

Now, his arms filled, he walked to Emil's rooms. In the street an occasional man or woman turned to look at him. These Viennese, he thought tolerantly. Everything's strange to them but Vienna. They'll turn to stare at anything and they'll laugh at anything. Sometimes they even make you angry. But they're such madcap, laughing people at heart, how can you take offense with such children? Especially when they make you one of them and invite you to their parties. Let them laugh. Maybe in Hungary we'd laugh at them too.

He reached Emil's rooms. The district was for the wealthy. He walked over the thick carpets up the stairs, a little subdued by the elegance about him. From the second landing came a great sound of revelry. He smiled and quickened his pace. At the door he shifted the bundle and knocked. For a moment there was no answer. He raised his hand to knock louder. The door opened. An elegant young man his own age confronted

59

him with a smile of welcome. He saw the bundles. His smile disappeared.

"Take them to the service entrance," he said.

Ignaz Philipp glanced bewilderedly at the bundles.

"Do I look like a delivery boy? I'm invited here."

"I'm sure there's some mistake. Have you got the right address? Excuse me——" He started to close the door.

"Is this a joke?" Ignaz Philipp cried. He put his foot in the door. Emil appeared.

"Hello, Naci! What's the matter?"

"Am I supposed to be here or not?"

"Of course you are. Come on in. What have you got there?"

"I beg your pardon," said the elegant young man, "I naturally assumed you were a delivery boy——"

"Naci, this is Friedrich von Koenig—Freddie—this is Ignaz Philipp Semmelweis——"

"I bought some cakes and wine—I guess I do look like a delivery boy, at that."

"Give them to me. I'll take care of them," and Emil made his way through the crowded, noisy room. Ignaz Philipp grinned at the sight of the pretty girls, the sound of tinkling wineglasses, at his flushed and happy fellow students.

"Quite a party," he said, turning. But Friedrich von Koenig had disappeared. He stood, uncertainly. Emil rushed back.

"Come on, I want you to meet everybody."

They went from group to group. At each group the automatic smiles of welcome stiffened a little and the guests glanced inquiringly at Emil at the sight of Ignaz Philipp, the curious cadence of his German. The wine was poured more frequently. Ignaz Philipp found himself with a blond girl.

"And what do you do?" he asked her.

"I'm a dancer."

"Is that so? Now, what kind of dancing do you do?"

"Let's talk about you. Is it true you brought food and wine with you tonight?"

"Of course. How did you find out?"

"My dear boy, everybody knows it by this time." She looked at him with amusement. "Is that what they do in Hungary?"

"What's wrong with that? Bringing a little wine and cakes to a party?"

"You droll, wonderful man."

"In Hungary we have a poem about it, even—'Who brings but empty hands today'——"

"Wait, wait!" She rose. "A gentleman is going to recite a poem!" she cried. Heads turned toward them.

"Now, miss, I didn't say——"

"Please!" She took his hands, smiled at him, pulled him upright.

"A poem," she called out, "about bringing food to a party——"

Ignaz Philipp smiled good-naturedly.

"'Who brings but empty hands today——'" he began.

"In Hungarian! Please! In Hungarian!"

He shrugged. Raising his voice slightly, he recited the poem in Hungarian. There was a burst of laughter and applause. He saw Emil clapping vigorously. He took the blond girl's arm and led her over to him.

"So you recite poetry too!" Emil said.

"Isn't he wonderful?" the girl said happily.

"I wish there was a band. I'd like to dance with you. I've never danced with a real dancer."

Ignaz Philipp slipped his arm around her waist. She moved away.

"Don't dance with him," Emil warned. "That's the way he worms his way into a girl's confidence. He's the terror of the taverns."

"A dancer too?" asked the girl.

"Now you're making fun of me——"

"Don't be silly, Naci. Show her that Hungarian czarda."

"Not here."

"Go on, show her. How does it go—da-da-da-DUM-dum-dum——"

Ignaz Philipp grinned and put out his arms. The girl came closer. He put both hands on her waist.

"Watch, everybody!" cried Emil. "This is how they do it in Hungary!" He sang a few bars. Ignaz Philipp whirled the girl dizzily. She bumped into a chair. He stopped. He pulled out a handkerchief and mopped his face. The guests were smiling at him. He smiled back at them genially. He saw Friedrich von Koenig talking animatedly to a girl. He took the blond girl's arm and walked to him. Von Koenig looked up coldly.

"Well, are you having fun?" Ignaz Philipp demanded, smiling.

"I believe so."

The girl beside von Koenig raised a glass of wine to her lips.

"Freddie here took me for a delivery boy," Ignaz Philipp told the blond girl, delightedly.

"I could easily make that mistake again."

"No, you couldn't. Next time I'll come in the back way."

The girl on the couch choked suddenly. The wine spattered her dress. She rose hastily. She looked at her skirt in dismay.

"Don't worry—it's all right." Ignaz Philipp snatched out his handkerchief and rushed to her. He stooped. He lifted her skirt. He reached beneath and held the handkerchief against the stain.

"Get some salt, somebody!" he cried.

61

The girl looked at him, paralyzed. Heads began to turn. There was the sound of a giggle.

Von Koenig reached him, pushed him aside.

"Take your hand from under her dress, you clown!"

"What's the matter?"

Von Koenig took the girl's arm and led her back to the couch, his face white under the amused glances of the other guests. The blond girl watched happily.

"Go away, go away," von Koenig gestured irritably.

"I'm sorry—are you angry? Did I do something wrong?"

"I don't find you amusing. You're supposed to be amusing, you know."

"Oh, that's just because I happen to be from Hungary. To the Viennese all Hungarians are funny and to the Hungarians all Viennese are—well anyhow, different."

"Do you mean you're not an actor?"

"Me? You're joking. I'm a law student——"

"And those clothes you're wearing—they aren't a costume?"

Ignaz Philipp looked down at his best Hungarian suit.

"I apologize," said von Koenig. "I thought you were made up to play the part. That's why I thought you were a poor delivery boy."

Ignaz Philipp looked at von Koenig enviously.

"It's certainly not so fine as the suit you're wearing. That must have cost you all of fifteen gulden——"

"Feed quite a few starving Hungarians on that, couldn't I?"

Ignaz Philipp stared. He flushed. For the first time he saw the malevolence in von Koenig's eyes.

"I'll tell you something, Semmelweis. I'll tell you for your own good. I'm sure any number of Viennese find you foreigners amusing. But there's quite a few of us who don't. Kindly remember that. We don't like your manners and we don't like your quaint accent and we don't like your clothes. We don't like you. We think you ought to stay in Hungary, where you belong. And that's how all Vienna thinks except the few you're lucky enough to get a meal and an evening's entertainment from by showing how boorish you are." He continued to smile pleasantly.

"Are you trying to make me fight you? Is that what you want?"

"Good heavens, no. I'm just trying to stimulate you to be more amusing. That suit, now—couldn't you spill a little more soup on it? And that accent—why don't you practice—make it more singsong. Well, it's not for me to tell you. I'm sure you're very successful as it is." He turned to the girl beside him. "Come, dear. It's time to go home." He rose.

"I'll help you," said Ignaz Philipp. The blond girl put her hand on his arm. He shook her off and knocked von Koenig sprawling toward the door. The crash brought instant silence.

62

Emil rushed to him. The guests crowded around von Koenig, who picked himself up in silence and strode out quickly.

"What's the matter? What on earth are you doing, Naci?"

"Did you bring me here to entertain your guests like some damned tamed Hungarian bear?"

"Of course not."

"You sure you're not laughing at me? Because if you are I'll give you something to laugh about!"

"Naci! Calm down! What did he say?" He turned to the blond girl. "What happened?"

She shrugged. "Von Koenig got nasty. He accused my Hungarian of being a Hungarian." She turned to Ignaz Philipp and smiled. She put an experimental hand on his arm. She squeezed her fingers. "Muscles," she announced. "Come on, muscles. I'm going to pour you a drink. Then, if you like, you can take me home."

"I assure you, Naci," Emil said earnestly, "I had nothing to do with this—you mustn't blame me——"

Ignaz Philipp looked at him uncertainly. The blond girl pulled at his arm. They moved off. The party was beginning to break up. The girl poured him a drink. He drank it. She took his arm again. They left.

Next morning he was awakened early. The blond girl raised her head from the pillow.

"What's that?" she demanded sleepily.

"Shhh! I'll go see."

He opened the door a crack. On the landing stood Emil, his companion of the day before, and Rudi.

"Hurry up——"

"We'll come in and wait for you to get dressed."

"No, no. You stay out. I'll be dressed in five minutes."

He closed the door quickly. From the bed the blond girl stretched out her arms to him drowsily.

"Come on back to bed," she whispered.

"I can't. You go back to sleep, darling. This is something special."

"Ah, come on."

"I'll see you tonight."

He stuffed his shirt hurriedly into his trousers, wet his face, toweled it briskly, brushed at his hair, struggled into his jacket, and walked toward the door.

"Your shoes!"

He bent hurriedly, found his shoes, laced them quickly, seized his hat, and ran to the door. His hand on the knob, he halted, came back to the bed, kissed the girl, then rushed out.

In the street he walked beside them in silence.

"Our Naci is in a bad mood today," said Emil. "He wouldn't let us into his room and still he's in a bad mood. And look at the day! Look at this beautiful sunshine which you can feel

63

with your fingers! Look at the lovely people—look at this beautiful city!"

"I'll tell you something, once and for all. You can have your beautiful city. I'm not happy here and I never will be. And when I remember how delirious I was when my father promised me I could come to Vienna! My God! What a people! What insane, cruel people!"

"Go on with you, Naci. You like Vienna well enough at night!"

"Nothing the matter with the wine, eh, Naci?"

"Or the girls? How about the girls, Naci?"

"You're homesick, perhaps," said Rudi. "For a while I couldn't bear Vienna, either. The trouble with places like this is that they laugh all the time, and when they laugh you think it's because you're from out of town. But look about you, Naci. Look! Such places become old friends. Believe me. In time such things become old friends."

They had walked out of the Josephstadt now, the artists' and students' quarter, and Vienna was a city of palaces. Old Boom, clockbell in St. Stephen's Cathedral, spoke to the people briefly, knowing that time was of no consequence to them, and they looked up briefly, knowing that tone was important. On the glacis, townspeople strolled under the acacias, the lindens, the chestnut trees to the music of regimental bands, occasionally a couple would break into song. There was nothing better to do. There were endless shops, and endless smiles, and as they approached the Academy of Sciences and the university the Danube flashed briefly and down the Wollzeile the Vienna River, moving, always moving, and on the Prater the human stream moved as eternally.

"As a city it's wonderful," said Ignaz Philipp.

"Of course it's wonderful!"

"You booby, you're homesick, that's all."

"There are better places than Buda, you know!"

"Maybe so," said Ignaz Philipp. "But not in Austria."

"Only in Hungary, of course."

"Of course. Because in the people of Hungary there is nothing to distrust. These people, their whole lives, their whole careers are only making fun. When they are making fun of someone they are truly happy. They go about with a half-smile, waiting, waiting to stab you with their laughter. Do you look different? They laugh at you. Do you speak different? They laugh at you." He turned to Emil. "I'm not even sure about you!"

"Do you know how you talk, Naci? Do you realize?"

"You should set it to music, Naci. Singsong, up and down, cadence without meaning, like a—like a foreigner."

He glared at them. Abruptly his face cleared. He shook his head.

"It's insane," he said helplessly.

"It's just their way," said Rudi. "They laugh at each other too. You mustn't forget that."

"In Hungary it's different."

"Listen to our violin with one string. Ahh, we love you, Semi-Naci. Never mind the rest. And the girls love you. Tell me, can even Buda beat the girls of Vienna?"

"You've got me thirsty," said Ignaz Philipp. He stopped. "All this talk, talk, talk. Come on! Let's go get a couple of bottles and a couple of girls and see what it's like under the trees. What do you say? Let's make a picnic!"

The law students looked at each other, undecided.

"I've got to go," said Rudi. "I'm almost late as it is."

They looked at him, pondering.

"I'll show you girls," said Rudi. "And you'll need wine afterwards too. I promise you. They're a little dead, of course, not at all lively, you might say—on the other hand, is this something you get a chance to see every day? A real, honest-to-goodness dissection? The whole body laid bare, insides, everything?"

"I know a fellow once saw a dissection."

They looked at the park again.

"Come on," said Ignaz Philipp suddenly. "Are you afraid? Come on!" He linked their arms and dragged them onward. "Women! Living or dead, I love them all."

"Now, take it easy," said Rudi. "Don't disgrace me. No jokes, please. Be very quiet."

He looked at them anxiously, but they were confused now. He smiled, he clapped them on the back.

"You'll find it very interesting."

And with another encouraging smile he turned and led the way up the gray steps of an old munitions factory. They followed slowly, their hearts beating, determined smiles on their faces, terror, excitement, flight, dogged resolve, fascination, reluctance whirling in their breasts.

Their footsteps echoed in the stone corridors.

"The halls are empty," Rudi whispered anxiously. "We must be late." He walked faster.

The two law students were pale, Ignaz Philipp, vigorously fighting off the same dread, threatening his fears with the penalty of mockery, looked at them, their pallor heartened him; he forgot repugnance.

"Maybe," he whispered, "they'll give us a little souvenir. You know—a breast, perhaps. Or even a little piece of—ah—something else."

"Hush!" said Rudi. The law students became paler. He pushed open a small door. They held their breaths. He appraised them briefly. Then he turned and tiptoed through the doorway. They followed. He shut the door behind them. Instantly a nauseating odor of chlorine and putrefaction filled their throats. They were in an amphitheater.

Rudi made his way into a row of seats. Making themselves as small as possible, the others followed. On all sides the rows of seats rose steeply. They sat down. In front of each man was a flat surface for books, for writing. Gingerly Ignaz Philipp ventured a look to right and left. The amphitheater was almost full. No one was looking at him. Every man stared below. Hesitantly, fearfully, Ignaz Philipp looked also. A tiered gallery of seats formed a horseshoe. At the open end, far below, three steps led to the floor of the dissecting theater. At one side, on a high dais, sat a solitary chair, empty. And now he forced himself to look at what he had come to see. As he looked a voice ascended clearly.

"I have now exposed the abdominal cavity and I hold here the broad ligament, a fold of peritoneum extending laterally from the uterus"—he moved his hands to demonstrate—"to the pelvic wall." And the hands moved again.

Rudi leaned to him quickly.

"Do you know who that is?"

Ignaz Philipp peered at the group below. There were a dozen men, frock-coated, white-stocked, their hatbrims shading their faces. They surrounded an elongated oval, a wooden table. On the table lay the open body of a middle-aged female. One of the men was looking upward. In one hand he held a scalpel. With the other he tugged outward for their view from the opening in the woman the broad ligament of which he spoke. The speaker was somewhat tall, he was lean, his long face stared upward. He finished speaking and instantly he bent again over the opening.

"Naci!" Rudi jogged him excitedly. "That man—that's Berres! Professor Berres!" Ignaz Philipp looked at him, questioning. "Berres! Berres, himself!"

The amphitheater was quite still. The students were completely silent. They stared. They missed nothing. Few of them even interrupted themselves to take notes.

"—the round ligament," Berres' voice pierced upward.

Ignaz Philipp turned fearfully to look again.

Now the open body, now that which was happening in the theater smote him like beating wings. That shape was a woman, a creature, a mortal human. Panic, horror, clamped him. His soul shriveled. His mind screamed, fled. That which his eyes saw his brain strove to obliterate. Ignaz Philipp Semmelweis lay upon a wooden slab, dead; he lay below, he felt the wood, he felt the slab at his neck, he saw the men, frock-coated, his abdomen retched with the open wound they had made in him, he saw, he felt, he could not move. They were coming, they were coming again, the man, the man with the knife was bending over, the knife was descending.

66

He tore his gaze away. He looked about him. The two law students were looking at the floor between their feet. They would not look up. Rudi, entranced, stared below. The voice like a sword came upward again.

". . . the villous coat of the vagina is reflected over the *os uteri* into the membrane which lines the cavity of the uterus. *Pulpusum magus quam vaginae velamentum aliquoties reperi . . .*"

The voice was inexorable. It was detached. It was directed to no one. He shut his eyes. Rudi nudged him. Now shame smote him and he looked aside, licking his lips, to discover whether Rudi had seen him with his eyes shut. But Rudi was rapt. Ignaz Philipp looked at his two fellow law students. They were still watching the floor between their feet. He looked on at them, not daring to look elsewhere. And yet he knew he would have to look. Sooner or later, look he must. At the knowledge anger spurred him, anger kicked his disordered senses, and he held his sensibilities, brutally helping his anger rowel their panic, slash at their flight, marshal them into order again. He would not be bullied. He would not be terrorized. He would not be cornered. He froze his feelings. He took a breath. Measuredly, he expelled his panic. He set his teeth. He turned his head. He swallowed. He looked below.

For a time he saw nothing. Rigidly he gazed on. The black figures moved, the white figure was still, the scene was a daze, and he kept out its meaning and stared, and saw nothing, and would not look away.

Sometime, he did not know when, the scene below came to him clearly. The inexorable Berres, speaking without haste and without inflection, rose to him again and again, sounds without meaning, then there was silence. Without knowing the moment, Ignaz Philipp's shoulders which had been hunched hard and tight relaxed. Time passed. His sensibilities insensibly adapted, the fantastic disappeared, the horrible became commonplace, the unavoidable became bearable, he passed from resignation to pride, from pride, after a stumbling moment, to unwilling curiosity, and now, in that instant, he no longer saw the body. The dead human below had vanished. He focused harder. He looked only at a part. This was an organ, then, this was the uterus. Here life began, it looked strangely small, the shape was curious, here was the mystery, here the secret, and yet a baby could couch in it. But how?

"To the ovaries," the voice of Berres rose, "according to the idea of their structure entertained by different anatomists, various uses have been assigned. Their purposes have been differently explained. Some suppose them glandular and say they secrete a fluid similar to the male semen and which serves the same purpose. Others assert that they are ovaria in the literal sense, that they contain a number of vesicles, or ova, twenty-two in number and of different sizes, and that they contain a fluid like thin lymph. But all agree that the ovaria provide whatever the female supplies to the formation of the foetus."

He paused. The smell was horrible. The end of the scalpel, the wooden handle, still pointed to a barely seen, small, dark object connected to the uterus by an inverted triangle of tissue. Ignaz Philipp craned to see. He groaned inwardly; one of the assistants had stepped forward, obscured his view.

"It is perhaps not unfitting"—Berres laid down the scalpel, wiped his hands on a quickly offered towel—"to conclude to-day's lecture on a reflection which is in the province of physiology, and yet, nevertheless, I desire to speak of it in relation to that which we have just demonstrated."

He folded his arms across his chest. He glanced upward at the galleries.

"Whence comes this life? Here in our hands we have held its indwelling, the place wherein it is born. How does it come to pass? Is conception merely an assemblage of small particles already prepared?"

Ignaz Philipp recoiled. Didn't they know?

"Pythagoras supposed that from the brain and nerves of the male a moist vapor descended in the act of coition, from which similar parts of the embryo were formed. Hippocrates believed that equal parts of male and female semen mixed in the uterus. Galen thought the child was made of male semen and the female merely nourished it."

He paused. Ignaz Philipp waited, stunned.

"Harvey tells us that as iron, by friction with a magnet, becomes possessed of magnetic properties, so the uterus, by the friction of coition, acquires a plastic power of conceiving an embryo."

Friction. He pondered this.

"Leeuwenhoek, with the help of his microscopes, asserted that in semen of all male animals there were a number of animalculae in each of which were contained the perfect rudiments of a future animal of the same kind."

Aha!

"But the great Denman of England, pointing to procreation by two animals of different species, such as horses and mules, declares that this fact is a decisive and unanswerable refutation of Leeuwenhoek's doctrine of animalculae and that the moving parts Leeuwenhoek saw in semen were not animalculae but only parts fitted for organization."

Ignaz Philipp drew in word after word. His mind raced, his thoughts pounced, rejected, pounced anew. Only his ears and his brain were alive, the rest was Berres.

"Chemists presume that the male semen, being acid, and the female semen, alkaline, an effervescence arises when they

68

mix. Others imagine the male semen has the properties of milk, the female semen the properties of rennet, that the milk is thus coagulated, the foetus being formed from the curds and the waters of the ovum by those parts which resemble whey.

"And now, gentlemen"—he put his hands upon his hips—"some say that those things which are beyond the comprehension or which elude the observation of men of plain understandings are of the least importance in practice."

He swept them with his eyes.

"It is my earnest hope," he said quietly, "that no man here today shares this unhappy view."

He looked at them again.

"Whence comes this life? How—where—why—whence does it come?"

For a moment he looked down at the body of the woman, brooding. Then abruptly he turned, and, followed by the assistants, Professor Berres left the theater.

*My dear parents,*
[Ignaz Philipp began a new sheet], I have this day made a decision, which, based upon what I have seen or heard, and, as you know, all my life I have been indifferent to a career, and yet I hope, making this known to you . . .

He laid down the quill. He gazed past the student lamp into the darkness of his rooms. As usual, he could not think, the quill hampered him, it was impossible to write, writing was for the devil, it would not come, he could not make it. He looked back at the writing paper, he picked it up, he rolled it into a ball, it fell among a dozen others. He stared at his desk. After a time the face of his father rose before him and his mother. He held them fast. He put down a fresh sheet. He seized the quill.

*My dearest parents,*
I detest the study of the law. I could not be what you want me to be. Today I witnessed a dissection, I went laughing, fearful, disgusted, as a joke. I know now that I must be a doctor, that I cannot but be a doctor, and that I cannot help myself. I have found a life that has meaning for me. I give my whole soul to it. I beg your forgiveness. I plead with you to understand, and forgive. I have registered and will enroll tomorrow.

Your loving son, *Ignac Fulop Semmelweis.*

# SEVEN

IGNAZ Philipp Semmelweis began the study of medicine at the University of Vienna in the recorded year of man's effort, 1837. He brought to medicine the shape of his youth, given purpose, and this kneeled to the study of medicine. Humbly, he became a communicant. His books were Bibles. He absorbed them with anxiety and exultation. His days and his nights were without time, he ate the hours, unappeased, hungry, newborn.

The Academy of Medicine was temple and home. His rooms were a stopping place away from home. His spirit flamed in a chrism of consecration. His will was inexorable. The tissues of his mind stayed him, raging. The blithe years, the fitful, the capricious, the undisciplined, were terror now, and worthless. And he beat his head and read and reread and sat in lectures, numb with horror, understanding gone, praying the lesson to halt, to go back, to go more slowly.

To his fellow students his earnestness, his foreign clothes, his Buda-cadenced speech, the specter of defeat in his eyes, were compensation. They were angered by earnestness so naked. They solaced themselves for the defeats of the day by mocking him.

He presented a figure a little past middle height, stocky, compact, his shoulders sloping, his hands somewhat small, the fingers short, the palm broad. His face was oval, the lips smooth, a trifle full, partly concealed by a drooping mustache. His eyes were deep-set, black, wide-spaced, his forehead high, his hair thinning. His chin was cleft and rounded, his nose thin, the nostrils set well back. His coloring was full, his skin clear and fine.

There are some men on whose faces good and evil contend visibly as they react to good and evil in the world about them.

Of such men the world has little fear and even a smiling contempt, and this contempt is as much for the ingenuousness of the man as for any fear of injury from him. Ignaz Philipp Semmelweis wore such a face.

In his class was a tall, handsome, rich, well-bred Hungarian named Ludwig von Markussovsky, a young man his own age. To him Ignaz Philipp rushed when his books became impenetrable. And when lectures were blankness Ignaz Philipp walked humbly home beside Markussovsky, filling his notebook's blank pages, stopping in the streets to write against a lamppost, against his companion's patient back.

And when the traditional insolence of the Viennese toward all foreigners seemed a spear prodded only at himself, Ignaz Philipp listened hopefully to Markussovsky's reassurance.

He did not know how to suffer insults and derision. Injustice outraged him and mockery was flame to the quick tinder of his fury. He was accustomed to fight back, to debate with his fists the justice of the least considerable provocation. In Vienna derision and mockery buffeted him from all sides. He did not know where to fight back. For Hungarians, the Viennese had an especial contempt. His fellow students derided his clothes and his accent. In time his rage blunted and became bewilderment, and time then blunted even bewilderment. Now the intensity of his quest obliterated even open insult.

In his studies he had come now to the marvels of dissection.

Dissection of the human body, sanctioned by the state, was newly come to the world. Grave robbing had ended. This day Professor Kolletschka spoke lovingly of the new freedom and began the course in anatomy.

"I wish four gentlemen to bring the subject with which we will begin dissection."

He looked at the upflung hands.

"Mr. Schwartz . . . Mr. Tannen . . . Mr. Mueller . . . Mr. Semmelweis . . . you will be so good as to go to the basement. A caretaker will instruct you."

Ignaz Philipp thought as he trembled down the spiral wooden stairs, well, I have seen a body, I won't mind seeing it, but to touch it . . . will the skin be loose, will it turn in my grip . . . to see it is one thing. To touch it . . .

"I'll show you boys," said Mueller. "My father is a butcher."

"Don't bother showing me," said Tannen. "Show Semmelweis—Hungarians are born undertakers."

Schwartz tittered, his face white.

"Keep up your hearts, fellows, it's a corpse, it's true, but, after all, it might be a dead Hungarian!"

The staircase had ended abruptly. They were in a large, bare room. An old man sat at a battered desk. Perceiving them, he rose, shuffled toward a door. They followed. At the door he halted. He picked up a lantern. He lit it with the slow care of the aged. From a ring he chose a key. He opened the door. Ahead was blackness. He stood aside.

"All right, Mueller," said Tannen. "What are you waiting for?"

"Are you children?" Mueller cried shakily. He stepped into the blackness. Gingerly they followed him. The old man entered. He shut the door behind him. The lantern light, shrinking, touched a damp, cold room and a wooden table. On the table, beneath a sheet, lay a shape. Beyond the table, a shallow tank was a dark rectangle in the floor. From this arose an acrid, overpowering smell.

The old man swung his lantern toward the figure on the table. "Take him off. Put him on the floor." They looked at each other, trapped. There was no help for it. The old man tugged off the sheet. He held up the lantern. On the table lay the body of an old woman. She was nearly bald. Her feet were astonishingly naked, the crests of her hip bones stretched upward in her wrinkled skin, her hips were a bony cage too large for her thin body. Her breasts were flat, long, hanging a little over each side of her bony ribs. Ignaz Philipp was embarrassed. He looked away.

"Pick him up," the old man said. "Put him on the floor."

Ignaz Philipp shut his eyes. He put his hand to her wrist. The flesh was cold.

"All right," he said, looking at the ceiling, "come on, come on."

Mueller resolutely pushed forward and grasped her other wrist. Tannen and Schwartz clenched and unclenched a fist, set their teeth, grasped each an ankle.

"Pick him up," said the old man tiredly.

They lifted. The body was not stiff, not rigid. When Ignaz Philipp and Mueller lifted, the arms simply raised, the body did not move. They each put a hand beneath her shoulders. Now the four lifted her slowly, she was clear of the wooden table, they lowered the arc of her body gently to the floor. The old man stepped forward and replaced the sheet over her.

"This way," he said. He walked to the tank. Beside the tank were wooden poles. On the end of the poles was a blunt hook. He pointed to the tank. "Fish," he said.

"Go on, Tannen," said Mueller irritably.

"Come on, Semmelweis," said Tannen.

Ignaz Philipp picked up a pole. Tannen placed the tip of his pole gingerly a few inches below the surface.

"At the bottom," said the old man.

Ignaz Philipp pushed the pole through the dark fluid. The hook touched a rounded surface. It was hard, but it was too soft to be wood. The hook slid past, touched another. Suddenly it was entangled.

72

"Pull," said the old man.

Ignaz Philipp shut out thought. He pulled. The hook moved more freely. A body broke the surface of the fluid.

"Grab it," the old man said to Tannen. "Pull."

Tannen's hook found a leg. Ignaz Philipp perceived that his hook was about the neck. Together they pulled the corpse to the edge of the tank, up, over the edge, on to the floor where it lay dripping quietly.

"On the table," said the old man.

Rubbing their palms on their trouser legs, the four students lifted the wet body to the wooden table. Then on their trouser legs they dried their hands again. The old man dabbed a cloth at the body. From his pocket he drew a bottle of fluid with which he wiped the body again. He stooped, took the sheet from the dead woman, covered the body on the table. He picked up his lantern. He nodded his head at the body of the woman.

"Upstairs," he said. They grouped themselves about her, looked at her doubtfully. The old man started toward the door with the lantern. Behind him the room darkened. Promptly the four stooped, picked up the corpse, lugged her hurriedly after him. In the other room they paused while he locked the door. "Take him up," he said, without turning.

They stumbled to the staircase.

"I'll go ahead," said Mueller. "There isn't room for both of us."

"I'll follow behind," protested Tannen. "After all, Schwartz, I fished and you just stood there."

He dropped the leg he was carrying. Schwartz promptly dropped the other leg. "Just who do you think you are?" he demanded hoarsely.

"Well," said Mueller, and dropped the arm he was carrying and skipped safely up the stairway. The body tore from Ignaz Philipp's grasp. The old woman thumped drunkenly to the floor. They gaped. She made a very small heap. She lay naked, as a child might lay, helpless and beyond help. Ignaz Philipp stooped, gathered her against his chest, settled her a moment, turned, and began to climb the stairs.

At the entrance to the amphitheater Tannen grasped one of the dead woman's ankles. Mueller went swiftly to the head. Ignaz Philipp hugged her tighter. He no longer held a fearsome mystery. In his arms he held an old woman. He perceived with stunning force that she was simply dead. His mind spoke to him clearly: It is my revulsion against death and not Death which has made her abominable. It is a poor old woman, past pain. Death does not hold her. I do.

He pushed open the door of the amphitheater and walked quickly to the dissecting table, followed by the three. He placed her gently on the wooden slab. The others made sig-

73

nificant motions, touching her hands, moving her feet a trifle.

"To these gentlemen, for their labor in bringing this subject to the theater, will fall the privilege of first dissection," said Kolletschka. He placed four slips of paper in the dissecting table. "On each of these slips is written an extremity. They will dissect the extremity it is their fortune to select."

He looked at the downcast and indignant faces of Tannen, Schwartz, and Mueller. He turned to Ignaz Philipp, who was looking sidewise at the table, without expression.

"Since Mr. Semmelweis has elected to bring the lady to us singlehanded he shall have for his labor the first choice."

Ignaz Philipp stepped forward and picked up a slip of paper. He turned it over. He showed what was written upon it to Kolletschka.

"Mr. Semmelweis has picked the left arm. Mr. Semmelweis, you will begin by tracing the origin, the insertion and the innervation of the anconeus. Before you begin you will tell us, please, the origin——"

"Back of the external con—condyle of the humerus."

"The insertion——?"

"The olecranon and the shaft of the ulna."

"And the innervation——?"

"Musculospir*AL*."

"Musculospiral, Mr. Semmelweis."

He turned to the amphitheater.

"The function of the anconeus is to extend the forearm."

He turned back to Ignaz Philipp.

"You may begin, Mr. Semmelweis." He gestured to the instrument table. Ignaz Philipp felt the gaze of the amphitheater. He looked at the instruments. He inspected the sets of four. They appeared all alike. He made a small prayer that in the set he selected there would be no flaw which would direct attention to him. He picked up a wooden-handled knife and a wooden-handled hook. He walked to the dissection table. As he walked, as he felt the instruments in his hand, he became eager. He picked up the woman's left arm. Entirely fascinated, absorbed only in what he was about to do, he found the muscle.

Satisfied, Kolletschka had turned to Mueller.

"Select a piece of paper, please . . ."

Ignaz Philipp probed with his fingers that part of the dead woman's arm in which the muscle began. Now he felt for the point where it ended. Now, estimating with his eye the distance between those two points, he prepared to cut. He placed the scalpel on the skin. He drew it gently toward him. He looked for the incision he had made. Humiliated, shocked, confused, he stared incredulously at the old woman's soft white arm. On the skin was a small, scratched furrow. He was stupefied.

74

"Yes," said a low voice by his ear, "the tender skin of a human is tough, isn't it? It is incredibly tough. Pick up your scalpel, my boy. Stretch the skin lightly. As you cut, observe how deeply your knife penetrates. If you are going too deeply, diminish the pressure. If you are not going deeply enough, increase it. Try not to incise more than the skin. When you have incised the skin, study the fat layer, incise it. Study the membrane covering the superficial fascia. Incise it."

He walked on. Not a syllable had reached Tannen, preparing to incise the other arm. Tears rose in Ignaz Philipp's eyes. He held his head lowered a moment. The kindness was unexpected. He was totally unprepared for it. He swallowed fiercely. He addressed himself to the arm. Coldly, with exceeding care, he began to cut.

He walked to the chemistry class with Markussovsky.

"What was it like, Naci? Weren't you frightened?"

"I'll tell you, Marko—it wasn't so bad. But that skin—when it comes to your turn, remember what I tell you! It's tough!"

"What do you mean?"

"It's tough, Marko! You think: it's a woman's skin, a frail old lady, naturally it's bound to be tender; one cut and you're right through the table. Listen, Marko! Bear down, don't worry, it's really tough!"

"You looked fine. You didn't seem to be having any trouble."

"It was all right at first. Then I started to cut and I was paralyzed. That Kolletschka—he knew what was up—he just leaned over and whispered. Kolletschka—isn't that Hungarian, Marko? Do you suppose he's one of us?"

"I don't think so, Naci. No, I think he comes from Bohemia. He's really professor of medico-legal jurisprudence. Does a lot of dissecting, of course. Tell me, Naci, what did he say? And what was it like touching a dead body?"

"Well, it's quite a feeling, to begin with. There's a room downstairs with a tank in it. And you fish for them with poles with a hook on the end. And of course our Austrian and German friends—full of remarks—but when it came to anything serious—did you hear a bump up here?"

"Not a thing."

"I thought all Vienna heard it. They let her drop. The poor old soul. Right on the floor. Didn't want to handle her. Well, before that I didn't want to touch her any more than they did, she wasn't a her, you see, she was Death. But, after all, there she was on the floor, you'd have been so sorry for her, Marko, you'd have been like me, you'd have forgotten she was dead."

"Ugh! To pick her up like that! To hold her against you!

75

Naci! Even if she was living! What does it *feel* like—I mean to your hand——"

"They're cold, Marko. It won't bother you once you've felt it. It isn't fun, of course, but there's no terror after a while. It isn't pleasant, but——"

"Here come the Hungarians!"

Tannen, Schwartz, and Mueller spoke from a waiting clump of students.

"Here comes our brave boy!"

"Look at him, our little Hunky, look at the kind, stupid face, so good to old ladies——"

"Playing up to the professor, eh, Hunk?"

"Right outside the door," said Tannen, "he snatched her from us. We didn't want to make a scene——"

"And in he walks, our heroic peasant, carrying her single-handed——"

"If you think you made us appear badly you're very mistaken," Mueller said angrily.

"Why don't you go back to Hungary? Look at him. Look at his clothes. Do you know what you look like?"

"Where's your petticoats, Hunky? Isn't that the most important part of your national dress? I haven't flipped a Hungarian petticoat in ages."

"Why don't you leave us alone?" Markussovsky suggested.

"Oho! Now Hungarian nobility. Now it's protecting the poor peasant——!"

"We're not talking about you, Markussovsky."

"Why do you identify yourself with such boors?"

The initial bewilderment on Ignaz Philipp's face which had changed to stolid contempt now passed swiftly into anger. His face became swollen. An artery in his forehead pulsed. Markussovsky took his arm.

The door to the chemistry class opened. One by one they walked silently through the doorway.

"After class, Mueller!" Ignaz Philipp warned him. "You'd better be there. Wherever you are—I'll find you."

"I'm sorry, Marko."

Ignaz Philipp entered the classroom and with Markussovsky took a seat well in the rear. For a time he sat and stared at the lecturer, not seeing him or hearing him. Markussovsky covered a full page of chemistry notes.

"Naci," he called softly.

Ignaz Philipp hurriedly poised his pen over a sheet of foolscap.

". . . and although this course in elementary chemistry concerns itself for the most part with the uses of medicine, I find it expedient today to make a small excursion into the philosophical field of chemical conjecture . . ."

Ignaz Philipp looked imploringly at Markussovsky.

"Gases," hissed Markussovsky.

"As we know," the lecturer continued raptly, "azotic gas was discovered in 1772, by Dr. Rutherford, of Edinburgh. Azote in combination with oxygen gas, together with moisture and a very small proportion of carbonic acid, constitutes the atmosphere which surrounds the globe. Although it was discovered so short a time ago, it may well be that azote is one of the most important gases we know. It is an undecompounded combustible. It has never been applied to any medical or economical use. It is occasionally, although rarely, referred to as the nitrogen gas of Chaptal and the phlogisticated air of Priestley."

He looked about the classroom, and his manner became coy and waggish.

"I suppose this will someday be called the Age of Gas. Our discoveries in gases have been prodigious. The past fifty years have witnessed the discovery of azote, of fluorine, chlorine, carbonic-acid gas, and oxygen."

He paused. His eyes twinkled.

"There is another gas humanity's discovered, and which appears to be sweeping the continents. Its effects are very violent, and it is certainly the most destructive gas humanity has thus far discovered. I propose to call it Liberty Gas, since under this name it has already plunged France, Holland, Belgium, Italy, and North America into revolution."

The class tittered appreciatively. Ignaz Philipp laid down his pen. Markussovsky stared straight ahead.

"It is my sincere hope that none of my students ever displays the bad sense to inhale such fumes. The effects are usually deadly. Let us look for a moment at the effect this gas has had upon three doctors in France. Let us look first at Lavoisier, who tells us that oxygen and not phlogiston supports combustion. He was no politician, but once he helped add the French tax rolls. The inhabitants of France inhale the Gas of Liberty. Dr. Lavoisier is condemned to death by Dr. Marat and executed by Dr. Guillotin. One doctor condemned by another and executed by the invention of a third. Such melancholy happenings does the Gas of Liberty enforce upon this unhappy world."

Ignaz Philipp looked at his desk. It seemed to him that the professor must see his embarrassment. For a moment he wondered whether there might actually be men who preferred not to be free. He studied the lean Austrian on the platform. He was small. He might desire the strength and protection of some larger creature and readily trade his liberty for these things. And yet Napoleon was a small man. And so was Professor Berres. This lecturer has a weakness, Ignaz Philipp decided suddenly. Somewhere in him he has a weakness and knows it, and by being loyal to authority he protects himself

77

against the days of discovery. He smiled grimly at him. I know your secret, my man. You're my creature too. And then a wave of pity swept him for this earnest, weak man who was what he was and could not help himself.

The professor had made his joke. Now he returned to science. Now for a time Ignaz Philipp wrote eagerly.

". . . . water is one part hydrogen, eight parts oxygen . . .

". . . iodine may be obtained by digesting kelp in water . . . it destroys vegetable colors . . . phosphorus united with it burns with a great deal of heat but no light . . . it tastes hot and acrid . . . medicine has never found any purpose for iodine . . .

". . . charcoal has been recommended very highly for the cure of intermittent fever, for gangrene, and for ulcers . . .

". . . phosphorus was accidentally discovered by Brandt of Hamburg while attempting to extract from human urine a substance to convert silver into gold . . ."

Ignaz Philipp wrote with absorption and fascination. He thought pleasantly of poor Brandt back in 1669 doing tricks a child would be punished for in these times. But it was interesting, all the same. And he *had* got phosphorus.

"It is a great age we live in, an age of great discoveries. It is easy to see why many authorities feel that the last frontier has been explored and the unknown solved. We have discovered chromium and molybdenum, tungsten, columbium, selenium, and platinum. And platinum in solution with nitric and hydrochloric acid is an excellent remedy for syphilis. Our age has discovered palladium, yttrium, aluminum, sulphuric acid, chromic acid, lactic acid . . ."

Ignaz Philipp, entranced, wrote on and on. He was exultant with fact.

And he wrote of the new metals tungsten and selenium, of fifty-six acids, for many of which medical uses had been discovered, such as nitrous acid which the age had found of unequivocal advantage in the treatment of venereal disease. And he learned of tellurium and titanium, osmium, rhodium, and of iridium, whose medical properties were unknown. And he learned of uranium from which a peroxide of uranium had already been found which might someday have some medical use. And he learned of kinic acid, obtained from Peruvian bark, called by the French quinquina, whose medical properties were hardly explored . . .

Ignaz Philipp was surprised to find he had raised his hand.

"Yes, Mr. Semmelweis?" The professor was annoyed at the interruption.

"With respect, sir teacher—why do we learn these things if they are of no use to medicine?"

"How do you presume to know they are of no use to medicine?"

78

"Because you say so."

The professor reddened.

"This course is of chemistry. Presumably, medicine is a science. As practitioners of a science it behooves us to know all of a science that is known. At any time you feel your career will not be benefited by the ingestion of these facts you are at liberty to leave."

Ignaz Philipp shrugged. The lecturer glared at him. He resumed. But now his flight was spoiled. His oral argosy into this unparalleled era stopped. He returned to gases. He came to chlorine.

"As you entered this classroom I detected a peculiar odor which accompanied you. I deduced instantly you had just come from an anatomy lecture. The odor was chlorine gas, and chlorine is a most efficacious agent in destroying contagion and putrid exhalations of all kinds. It is in general use in the anatomical theaters of Europe and America and in the naval and military hospitals of Great Britain."

Ignaz Philipp and Markussovsky sniffed covertly of their clothing.

"In order to prepare this gas for the purpose of destroying contagion or miasmata of any kind it is only necessary to mix two parts of common salt and one part black oxide of manganese. Then pour over this mixture two parts of sulphuric acid. The fumes of chlorine immediately arise and are distributed in the infected atmosphere with the effect of destroying the miasmata."

Ignaz Philipp raised his hand.

"Mr. Semmelweis?" the professor acknowledged coldly.

"How does it work?"

"I have just explained to you, in terms that should be understandable to students eligible for this course——"

"With respect, sir. You have been most clear. I want only to know how chlorine gas attacks a miasma."

"A miasma is a noxious effluvium or emanation capable of bringing sickness and destroying life."

"Yes, sir. And how does the chlorine gas kill the miasma?"

"It makes a corpse, for instance, safe to handle."

"Yes, sir."

"Do you understand, now, Mr. Semmelweis?"

"How does it kill the miasma?"

"Mr. Semmelweis, you breathe, I suspect. And when you breathe, you breathe air. If you did not breathe air you would die. Now, how does air sustain life?"

"I don't know, sir."

"Ah! You don't know. But you know it does, don't you?"

"Yes, sir."

"In the same fashion, Mr. Semmelweis, chlorine kills a miasma . . . air supports life . . . chlorine kills a miasma . . .

it is, in short, the property of chlorine to kill a miasma. Are you happy, Mr. Semmelweis?"

"Will you pardon me, sir teacher?"

"Certainly, Mr. Semmelweis."

"I do not wish to be offensive."

"You are forgiven, Mr. Semmelweis."

"I have an unfortunate curiosity which plagues me . . ."

"A desirable quality in a student of medicine . . ."

"Therefore, air, as you say, supports life. But it always supports life. And chlorine does not always kill miasmas. Air's property is infallible; chlorine's property is not. I thought if there was some reason why chlorine did not always prevent the sicknesses and infections and plagues . . ."

The professor waited, heavily. But Ignaz Philipp had asked all his mind could offer.

"I see. That is very interesting. I may say that we have dealt with chlorine within the bounds this course offers. It seems obvious that an additional property of air is its infallible ability to support life and that an additional property of chlorine gas is its variability. Of both—the cause unknown. For the benefit of the class I may say that what we know of chlorine is of more than sufficient use for medicine's needs of today, tomorrow, and a thousand years from now. If there are no further questions, the class is dismissed. Tomorrow we will take up the thirty-six salts."

"You're a strange fellow sometimes," Markussovsky said as they walked down the hall to the class in botany.

"Because I asked questions? What's the matter, Marko?"

"No, it's all right, I guess."

"You were embarrassed, weren't you?"

"Weren't you?"

"What for? That's what we came here for—to learn, wasn't it?"

"I know—but—I should never have the courage, Naci. It—it just isn't done, you know."

"Ah, Marko, you have too much regard for formal classroom custom, you take these pip-squeaks of professors too seriously. They brought you up wrong."

"Ah, now, they're entitled to respect, Naci. You've got to admit that."

"They know more than I do, that's certain. But why shouldn't I ask questions?"

"Nobody else does, Naci. It makes you stand out. Every class the same. It looks—it looks bold, Naci. Almost impudent."

"Are you ashamed of me, Marko?"

"Wait! Wait! You know better! But you told me—'you know more about social customs and what's right and wrong

80

than I do, so advise me, Marko'—that's all I'm doing, Naci. I'm just trying to tell you."

They had ventured down a clinic corridor. There rose a sudden din of moaning shrieks. Around a corner came two men carrying a stretcher. On the stretcher the howling man writhed without pause. Ignaz Philipp and Markussovsky stood in the doorway as the stretcher bearers dragged the man on to a bed. One attendant left, smiling at the two students. On the bed the patient continued to scream and writhe.

The remaining bearer glanced at them briefly.

"Operation," he said importantly. Then to the other patients in the ward, most of whom had risen on their elbows, "Lie down, you others. There's nothing for you here."

The screaming man suddenly made an effort to throw himself from his bed, to leave his agony and escape to the floor. Hastily, the bearer yanked him back.

"What was the matter?" Ignaz Philipp licked a mouth suddenly dry, tried to sound offhand. The screams were rending him.

"Opened up his belly," said the bearer importantly. "Yes, sir, slashed him wide open, put their hands into his guts—you should see how they coil, like snakes, never stop—and cut out a big black tumor."

"Oh, he suffered . . ." breathed Markussovsky.

"Yes, he suffered, he must have suffered horribly, wide awake, feeling the knife, feeling the hands going into him," said Ignaz Philipp, as if the words could stanch the man's pain, comfort him with allies.

"*He* suffered!" the bearer echoed. "How about me? I had to hold him down. I stood there wrestling with this one for more than an hour, just holding him down while they cut."

"Why don't they give them something? Anything!"

"There's nothing you can give them. Not that helps much. They just have to endure it, that's all. And so do I. Hey!" The sobbing, screaming man, mastered by a sudden spasm, had tried again to throw himself from the bed. "I can't stay here all day." Holding the patient with one hand, he took a bottle from his coat pocket with his free hand. He uncorked it with his teeth. He motioned to a teaspoon. Ignaz Philipp picked up the spoon, the attendant filled it, dropped it into a glass of water.

"Thanks," he said. He stirred the contents of the glass. He held the glass to the man's lips. The man moaned, tried to swallow.

"Come on, Naci," said Markussovsky, white-faced. "We're going to be late."

"What's that?" Ignaz Philipp asked, looking at the glass.

"That? That's ether. Two teaspoons in a glass of water. Give

81

it after operations. Old, old remedy. Relieves the spasms. Tastes terrible."

"Naci!" Markussovsky called.

They walked down the corridor to botany class.

"Poor devil!" Ignaz Philipp said suddenly.

"Why do they have to suffer like that?"

"They should have got him drunk, at least. Do you suppose we'll ever get used to things like that?"

"I guess we have to, Naci."

"I guess the time will come when we won't even hear it. What is it they say? 'Pain is a normal expression of injury.' There's an odd refuge in a saying like that. It's true, of course. But it's strange how when you say it the panic leaves you."

"You become composed, almost."

"Detached."

"I wonder what will happen to him."

"Oh, he'll die, no doubt. No doubt at all, I think."

"They always do, don't they."

"From an abdominal operation? From opening a man up? My goodness, Marko! How many do you think survive a compound fracture?"

"Compound fracture——?"

"Where the bone breaks and breaks through the skin. Not more than one out of ten survives such a thing. Maybe not that many."

"Any broken bone?"

"Absolutely. Look! First of all they set the bone. Where the skin was torn, pus forms. Soon the part is black. It must come off. Off it comes. But—where they cut, more infection. And now the whole body dies."

"From a broken little finger?"

"From a broken little finger. From any bone. Break the skin —and you're dead."

"How do you know so much? Where did you learn that, Naci?"

"I listened around. I got to talking with some of the older students. You should hear them sometimes."

"You know something? You're going to make a good doctor, Naci."

"Study comes very hard to me. I wish I'd formed the habit when I was younger. I wish I could learn more. I wish I could learn everything. I can't learn enough."

"And before——?"

"I never had a thought in my head. Believe me, Marko! Not a thought. I'd have gone through law. Somehow I'd have become a lawyer. It would have meant nothing. Absolutely nothing."

"Until we became friends that's how I felt about medicine. Did you know that?"

"But now you feel differently, don't you, Marko? This searching! These mysteries. A man is sick, he doesn't know what ails him, you look at him, a message is written all over his face, a message plain, plain, plain to your instant glance. You take a powder, you add a liquid, you mix them, the man drinks—he's well! He looks at you. And his look licks your hand. Or it's a woman, maybe. Or a little child. Was there ever anything like it?"

"No," said Markussovsky slowly, "I guess there's nothing better. There's not much to life, when you come to think of it. It's trivial and soon ended. We don't even know if there's any real purpose. To be a doctor means a great deal to the sick. But it means more to him who knows what man is and cannot bear it."

"We know what a man is all right."

"We're beginning to learn."

"Sometimes I believe that every man walks with his identical and invisible counterpart. And this invisible man is his sickness, his head, his stomach, his legs, his trunk, all walk· ing beside him, waiting. The anatomy of this counterpart, that's the man I want to study."

"But that's simply medicine, Naci. That's exactly what we're studying. Anatomy is only physics and chemistry, function and reaction. A diagram. The other anatomy is medicine itself."

"Do you know something? I'm going to be very frank with you, Marko. These men, these teachers—they don't know much. They really don't. They know worlds more than I do. But they don't know much. They teach the same thing over and over. But if you ask them a question—then they are fin· ished."

"That's something I want to talk to you about, Naci. These men are paid to instruct us. What they instruct us has been legally specified. They are not bound to go beyond what the book says. Learn what they have to teach you, Naci. That's all."

"Do you mean I should stop asking questions?"

"I am going to be frank with you. Do you know sometimes it seems you are not really asking questions to learn an answer? Sometimes it seems you are just deliberately baiting them. Being fresh."

"Marko, I don't know much, Heaven is my judge, but I know this: there is an answer to everything. There is a man to ask the question. And somewhere there is a man to give the answer. How do I know he's not the man unless I ask the question?"

"You see, Naci, nobody else asks questions. You just take notes. That's all, Naci, that's the custom, that's the way it goes. That's protocol, my friend, they are teaching it to us even in that classroom custom. Protocol is perhaps the very foundation if not of medicine then of the practice of medicine. You see there aren't many laws governing doctors. We have to make our own. And the laws of protocol have been tested for many years. Naci, look! We're foreigners. We're already stamped, marked out. When we go against custom we're deliberately singling ourselves out for abuse."

"I'll go on asking questions, just the same. It's monstrous not to ask questions. I want to learn, I want to study, I want to swallow all knowledge, everything. Before I swallow I've got first to open my mouth."

"All right, Naci. You must do as you must do. But bear in mind what I've told you, friend. Try not to anger the instructors who don't like it."

"Give me a man like Kolletschka. There's an instructor for you."

"He doesn't know everything, Naci."

"Of course he doesn't. But he knows as much as the books know. And he keeps trying to find out more. Do you think he minds a few questions?"

They had reached the door to botany class. Botany was an important study for a student of medicine. From plants came many strange substances, a dozen or so having definite purpose in the cure of human ills. The distilled water of the cherry-laurel tree had been found to contain prussic acid which was a deadly poison but might perhaps be used as a narcotic. The gum from many a tree, and particularly the mimosa nilotica, was indispensable, and had even been found nutritious. Picrotoxin, obtained from the fruit of cocculus indicus, would neutralize acids. Serturner had made the poppy yield a substance sometimes called meconic acid, sometimes morphine, of which it was discovered that a half grain produced flushing of the face and an increase in muscular power, and morphine had begun to be used wherever it was desired to produce a flushing of the face and an increase in muscular power. There were untold possibilities in plants. There was caoutchouc, for instance, an elastic substance derived from South American trees which yielded a milky juice which hardened as it fell, and many resins and birdlime, and camphor and wax, and strychnine and emetin and nicotine. It was an age of which Hamann said that from a general knowledge of the possible it arrived at a thorough ignorance of the actual.

It was an age that taught Ignaz Philipp Semmelweis that one of the important constituents of bone is gelatin. That gelatin forms the whole of membranes and tendons and an important part of cartilage and ligament, and that albumen enters largely into the composition of bone. It was an age that had discovered uranium and which taught that muscle is nothing else than solid blood. Bile was explained as a substance which was separated from the blood as useless. Nothing was known of the manner in which secretion or assimilation took place. Positivism, a system which demanded proof of any postulate, had begun to replace metaphysical and teleological systems, which merely enounced a theory and relied on fantasy for its proof. Dalton had announced the atomic theory and Faraday and Volta and Ampère and Priestley and Davy had become bywords for electricity and its uses. The human brain, its purposes, and its anatomy were almost complete mysteries. Theses for a doctorate might be bought at a fixed price from groups of professional students. At Greigswald, a shoemaker, who had an itch to be called doctor, got his diploma from a dissertation on the curative properties of pitch. Many hundreds of thousands of pills were sold which would cure barrenness without even intercourse. Pitchblende was unearthed and Buffon discovered there is no essential difference between animals and plants. Organic chemistry was established, and spectrum analysis was discovered. Executioners sold human blood, which when fresh and frothy was esteemed as a cure for epilepsy, and it was sold on a fixed-fee basis in which the most costly blood was from a youth or a virgin and the cheapest was the blood of a hung Jew. There were three classes of doctors—physicians, surgeons, and country practitioners—and socially they rarely mingled.

This was the age in which Ignaz Philipp Semmelweis entered the temple of medicine. Each man makes his own temple, for the temple is in his thinking, and in the mind of Ignaz Philipp medicine was the very footstool of God.

He lived with Markussovsky that first year of medicine in Vienna, and he devoured the courses. His hunger for learning, his candor, his unabashed and naked desires for instruction were so angering to the Viennese that they came to detest the mere sight of him. Markussovsky they treated tolerantly and even with reserved friendship. He was a Hungarian, it was true, but he was not a boor, and he was not poor, and in Hungary he was actually the son of some sort of Hungarian noble. Moreover, he observed protocol, he had tact, he had even wisdom of a sort, not Viennese wisdom, to be sure, but a sort of urbanity all the same.

But Ignaz Philipp was candid, he was not adroit, he was fearless, he apparently had no shame and he had no manners. His clothes were plainly Hungarian, he fed badly and hugely, his success with tavern women was barbarous and notorious, when he was drunk he loved to be drunk and he said so openly and at the top of his voice. He was almost simple-minded, it seemed. In class he would stop a lecture any time he felt inclined, and then merely to ask some question on which no examination question could possibly be based. He did this knowing that it affronted the class and irritated the instructor.

If some casual barb against Hungary was said in his presence, as was perfectly natural in the Viennese manner, he had not the good sense to let it pass gracefully, or, like Markussovsky, to make some pleasant quip in return, which hurt nobody. He would, instead, instantly wage a furious and noisy battle from which one could not even escape by walking away with startled dignity. He would follow and scream at the back of one's head. He was a rebel, it was plain, and, for all anyone knew, a radical to boot. He had been heard to speak, or rumored to hear speak, of such a thing even as a free Hungary. It might easily be assumed that the secret police had their eye on him. There was dignity in medicine. And Ignaz Philipp Semmelweis had none of it, no nobility, no average social Viennese behavior, even.

The faculty showed their contempt for him openly. Only Kolletschka befriended him. But Kolletschka was not Austrian. Classrooms became difficult. Instructors refused to answer him or acknowledge his upraised hand. Goaded to reply, they directed at him venom, contempt, and open insult such as they thought might thenceforth discourage him from ever again presenting himself to their attention.

His classmates, who despised and hated him before the professors, were encouraged by the authorities.

Before the end of the first year a bewildered Ignaz Philipp decided to surrender, to leave Vienna and to escape to Buda to finish his medical training. He could not understand the hatred, he had done no harm, he intended no ill to anyone. All he wanted with all his soul was to be let alone, to study in peace, to get answers to his questions, to study all he pleased, to learn, unceasingly. He knew the penalty for being Hungarian. He knew he must endure what came his way. It was true, even in Hungary, he told himself reasonably, that a man from the country is looked upon by a man from the city with some disdain. One cannot change human nature. But the rest, the naked hatred he evoked, the sneers, the contempt, the insults, these were not for an honest man. It was like a sickness, and at last the only cure was to flee.

The year ended. He said good-by to Markussovsky. He returned to Buda and enrolled in the University of Pesth.

His father greeted him with love and understanding and disappointment and resignation. His mother defended him passionately. His brothers looked at him heavily and enviously, even the priest brother saying maliciously: "So we are going to be a doctor now. Tell me, Ignaz Philipp, what will we be next week?"

He settled down to life at home with a sigh, comforted and relieved. He was home. He was a Hungarian in Hungary. He found no contempt here and no insults, but only envy for a man who had the fortune to spend a year at Vienna.

86

The courses at the University of Pesth were a stunning disappointment. He endured his first year. Faithfully, Markussovsky kept him informed of the subjects and class work at Vienna. The comparison with the world Markussovsky described and the world in which he studied clamored at him daily.

He finished his first year at Pesth. He completed courses in anatomy, physiology, chemistry and botany, bandaging work and a very little obstetrics, materia medica, pathology, clinical medicine, clinical surgery, and slightly more obstetrics.

When his second year ended not even the urgent pleadings of his mother and the silent, reproachful face of his father could keep him at Pesth for another year. Markussovsky had progressed far beyond him. He wrote of great men and of studies which plunged Ignaz Philipp into fury and disappointment and frustration. He felt he had learned little. What he learned, he suspected. Equipment was poor, teaching was old-fashioned, courses were antiquated. For a man who had once studied at the great University of Vienna the University of Pesth was not even a good training school for veterinarians. He could not continue. He resolved what he must do. Come what would, he must do it. He must quit here. He must leave Hungary. He must leave his family, his home, the love ties, the ties of the cobblestones and the Christianstadt, the Danube and the currents of boyhood. He must return to Vienna. He returned to Vienna in 1840 to begin the remaining three years of his undergraduate study. He gave up his home and his country and his parents. He was a driven man, and he could not be denied.

# EIGHT

HE returned to Vienna. What he would receive at Vienna must outweigh bitterness and despite and insult. If there were to be penalties, he must bear them. What he sought was not in Budapest.

He lived by himself now. Markussovsky had taken fine rooms in the Alservorstadt with another student, Johann Chiari.

There were different faces when he re-enrolled.

He made a fresh start.

The first month was a nightmare of work. At Pesth they taught by description and by theory. In Vienna they used the clinical method. In this year he began practical work at the hospital and the clinics. His time was wholly consumed. He was enslaved. He was completely happy. In his lonely room he sometimes capered, danced, and sang with delight.

"There is something committed about this chap's strange avidity, his naked hunger," Kolletschka remarked one day during a pause in an instructor's meeting.

Professor Guntner, instructor in obstetrics, shrugged. "He has sufficient earnestness," he agreed dubiously. "I have not found him outstanding. I do not think he is much interested in obstetrics."

"Who is this?" asked Professor Hartman of Therapy.

"The Hungarian Semmelweis," said Professor von Scherer. "I don't know about you gentlemen, but in medicine and surgery he asks too many questions."

"Fortunately," said Ferdinand von Hebra, "we know the answers. In skin diseases, for example, we have the answers to everything except what causes skin diseases and what cures them. We are very lucky."

The group smiled uneasily and broke up. Hebra was difficult. His sarcasms were notorious. In the corridor Rokitansky drew Skoda aside.

"I think we shall have to do something about him," he said gravely.

"About whom? Hebra? You can't do anything about Hebra. Besides, he is right."

"No, no. I mean Semmelweis."

"He's Hungarian, isn't he?"

"I believe he is Hungarian."

"Well, what about him?"

"He's a tremendous student, Skoda. Amazing. Dogged and incessant."

"Brilliant?"

"I don't know."

"A memorizer?"

"He does more than memorize. What you tell him he thinks about, he rolls it in his mind, he makes side trips, he studies things not in the lesson, he examines from all sides. And then he asks questions."

"I don't know that I like questions so much. There aren't too many answers, you know. These divagations and being caught at a loss don't raise one particularly in the opinions of the know-it-alls one tries to instruct."

"What are you going to do when a student asks if disease isn't normal?"

"Tell him yes. Wait! Tell him no. Hold on, Rokitansky. What is it?"

"You see?"

"What were you discussing?"

"Disease."

"I would say—an unnatural disturbance in the body."

"We were contemplating a tumor. He said it seemed to him entirely natural for a tumor to grow, that it was the nature of tumors to grow, that a tumor grew according to natural law and was therefore not unnatural."

"He made this statement as a statement?"

"No, he asked it as a question."

"You know, there is something sympathetic there. For me, at any rate. I, too, find a question. Was the body made for disease? Or was disease made for the body?"

"Or were they made for each other?"

"I see what you mean, Rokitansky. That mind is working."

"You see?"

"He'll bear watching."

"I think—I think I'll take him in with me."

"To live, you mean?"

"He dresses so oddly. And he doesn't seem to notice his appearance, his coat is a little ragged, untended. I think he ought to be protected. A mind like that must, for the sake of

89

his career, realize that there are other things to medicine besides the study of medicine."

"Of that we can be very sure. By all means take him in hand, Rokitansky."

"You, too, keep an eye on him."

"Being Hungarian, he probably needs polish."

"I haven't been asked a question like that since I began teaching."

"Have you discovered an answer?"

"I don't know that I have. Can we say that disease is the relation of function and structure of the body to the function and structure of processes which determine the life span and qualify bodily activity and structure during that life span?"

"I don't know. But perhaps part of your definition smacks a little of the study of healthy tissue."

"A tumor is in perfect health, tissue in perfect health. There is nothing diseased about a tumor. Or, for that matter, there is nothing diseased about the process of sclerosis, or contagion, or anything else which occurs to or in the body. All seems to follow a perfectly rational, logical, and healthy plan."

"Life itself is a disease, Rokitansky. *Dis* means negative and *ease* means rest. The body is never at rest. Does human aim conflict with what the layman regards as disease? Is the body at war with health, with a normal process called disease? It is just as true to say that as it is to say that disease is at war with the body. Which, then, is the disease? The fact that man is discomfited by one process or the other is simply an error in creation. Man is merely present while these processes occur. We make our living helping him get along with the nature of things as comfortably as possible. And that, my dear Rokitansky, is why I am a bachelor. I could never forgive myself for perpetuating any such foredoomed nonsense."

"I think I shall ask him today."

"Do so."

"I think you are perfectly right in your concept, and I think I shall ask him today."

"My concept and I thank you. As for your friend, I shall do my best to give him a polish."

Joseph Skoda, leading clinician of the new Vienna school of medical thought, severe, wary politician, therapeutic nihilist, moved down the corridor, a short, stout figure, his walk as dogmatic as his speech, his spectacles glistening beneath a high forehead and a mane of black hair. His book was written, his position was secure, his clothes were queer, and he endured them for fear of offending his tailor.

In the clinic over which he presided he blinked at the class, singled out Ignaz Philipp, studied him, turned, and walked to the first bed.

"He has an intense face," he advised himself. "He has re-

90

bellion, that one. If he gets in trouble he may compromise his friends. Rokitansky may see trouble."

He turned to the class, grouped at the bedside of a young woman. Her pallor was startling. She peered through glazed eyes, indifferent to existence, On her chest he placed a small wooden disk. He tapped it with his forefinger.

"Do you hear that note? That is not resonant. It is dull. If the lung were hollow, the sound would be resonant. The lung is therefore, in the place where I put this disk, full." He moved the disk elsewhere on her chest. "The sound here is dull again. But there is a different timbre. The note is muffled. There is pus in this lung. We need hear no more. The patient has emphysema."

He moved on.

"What will you prescribe?" asked Ignaz Philipp respectfully.

Skoda did not even turn. He waved his hands indifferently. "It's all one," he said. "The diagnosis—that's the thing." He turned now. already at the next bedside. "The diagnosis—quickly."

Ignaz Philipp lingered behind and watched the pale one.

The patient breathed oddly. For a moment she seemed to be holding her breath, listening. Then, recollecting, remembering to breathe, she would breathe again.

"Come along, Mr. Semmelweis. You will see at the autopsy —I will be right."

And after class he drew Ignaz Philipp aside. "These patients—you must not lose your heart, Mr. Semmelweis. From Professor Rokitansky and Professor Hebra, too, I learn that much may be expected of you. Do not lose your heart to patients, Mr. Semmelweis. Let me tell you the patient is unimportant. It is the diagnosis, Mr. Semmelweis, that is the thing that is all-important. That is the thing that will make you a doctor."

"The professor is very kind," Ignaz Philipp said, dazed.

"Learn every sound your ear may perceive, Mr. Semmelweis, that is what I have to tell you. The chest and the heart of a human compose a symphony of sound. Learn the endless differences in pitch, in tone, in quality. They will make you wise. They are your Bible. Learn their slightest variation so that you have your diagnosis in an instant. Instant diagnosis, Mr. Semmelweis. Diagnosis confirmed by post-mortem. That will be your diploma, sir, a new diploma each time you are successful."

He held up his hand.

"Do not thank me. No gratitude, please. From time to time I will tell you more."

"I am grateful, sir professor."

"That is your problem. And also get a new coat."

91

Ignaz Philipp looked anxiously at his worn coat, the braid frayed at the lapels, a pocket torn.

"I will direct you to my personal tailor. Without fail, go to my tailor."

He wrote a brief note, pressed it on Ignaz Philipp, scanned him severely, and strode off.

As he walked to pathology class Ignaz Philipp was dazed but jubilant. Notice from the great Skoda was accolade. As he walked he looked upon the passing Viennese students with a melted regard that came very near to affection. "We shall get along together," he said to himself. "Give us time and we, too, shall get along. You shall see that I am not such a bad fellow, and I shall forgive you, and perhaps you are not so bad, either."

He pondered Skoda's advice. He conned it carefully. He did his best to remember each phrase, each intonation. "Do not lose your heart to patients, Mr. Semmelweis. I tell you that the patient is unimportant. It is the diagnosis that is important." Try as he would, seeking within himself to implement such doctrine, Ignaz Philipp could commit these sentences only as something Skoda had said. He committed them with respect. He could not make them his reasoning.

He watched Rokitansky dissect a cadaver. He made notes on the findings. Part of his mind brooded over Skoda's concept. He reviewed his own attitude. He was startled. As Rokitansky dissected he could project himself as a layman at a dissection and the next instant receive dissection as a medical student.

"This man," Rokitansky was saying, "during his life suffered much from a painful swelling in the abdomen, particularly in the upper right quadrant. He was a frequent victim of sweats. His work was often interrupted by fever."

He closed the man's hospital record, from which he had recited these facts.

"We have opened his abdominal cavity. What do we find? The stomach appears normal, though I should say there is a slight thickening in the outer coat. This, however, may have been normal for this particular individual. In any case it does not suggest that it was responsible for the illness which provoked the symptoms I have recited to you, and of which the man recently died. The greatest difference in the internal organs of the abdominal cavity of this subject appears to be in the liver. I have removed the liver, it is here beside his body. It appears far larger than the livers of yesterday's subjects, or of other subjects with which this class is familiar and has called normal. I will now open the liver and we shall see what we shall find. But before I do so I will tell you what I expect to find. I expect to find pus. I expect to find pus, because over a period of many years I have sought in many thousands of bodies for answers to questions which we cannot solve by taking notes or by inspecting the exterior. Death, itself a riddle, answers many riddles. I expect to find pus because, in the past, when the hospital has sent me cadavers to which were attached the symptoms of the disease which carried off this subject, I found that this type of abdominal swelling, fever, and sweat was always accompanied by pus."

He cut into a lobe of the liver. Instantly pus surged sluggishly from the cut tissue, spread over its surface, and began to drip onto the wooden table, spreading until it seeped under the side of the corpse.

Marveling, Ignaz Philipp willed to view this as a layman, and as a layman he was instantly disgusted. He suddenly smelled the putrefaction, the chlorine, even the raw alkaline odor of the pus itself. He found himself in the presence of death, of a corpse with a face and with members like his own. His impressions pointed to panic. Disgust and fear multiplied.

With an effort he directed himself to become a medical student again. The smell became commonplace, a normal expression of decay. The body receded in perspective. It was not the body which was being examined. It was the liver. The scene reduced itself to details. It was not the liver of a dead man. It was a liver. It was not liver, even, that he was considering. It was a problem. This problem wore the garments of liver and he was familiar with those garments. In addition, it contained pus.

"We have revealed the nature of a disease," Rokitansky was saying. "We have laid bare that which was in this man's life hidden from the eye of his physician. Henceforth, when as a doctor a patient comes to you complaining of abdominal swelling, of pain in the upper right quadrant, of sweating and fever, you will see more than an external picture. Your mental eye will see into him. You will see a liver"—he prodded the liver on the table with his scalpel—"a liver greatly swollen. It will contain a quantity of pus."

He surveyed the class a moment with great compassion.

"Do not be too exultant, my friends. Your next problem will be: What caused the pus to form there? And then: How shall I treat the patient so that the pus will go away and his liver return to normal? Remember this: We have uncovered the nature of the ailment which killed this man. We have not revealed the cause."

And that was the other thing that troubled him in his suddenly discovered metamorphosis, Ignaz Philipp reflected fiercely as he closed his notebook. When he looked at people in the streets nowadays he did not see them as people. He saw them as organisms. He saw them as products of function and he saw the function. He no longer saw his fellow humans as fellow members of the human race. He had become separate

93

from them. He saw his fellows clear-eyed, as they never saw themselves. He had become one of a group, all of whom shared the same secret, the same attitude, the same insight, the same knowledge, separate and apart from the mass of humanity. He had become part of a fellowship. It made him intolerably lonely. He thought of his brothers and his sister, and he struggled to regard them as loved ones and not as organisms, not as loved organisms. He thought desperately of his father and mother——

"You are sad today, Mr. Semmelweis."

He looked up. He saw, amazed, that the lecture room was almost empty, the last of the students was preparing to leave. Confused, he stumbled to his feet, swept up his books.

"Tell me, Mr. Semmelweis," said Rokitansky, "of what were you thinking just now?"

"I was thinking—with respect, sir professor—I was thinking——" Ignaz Philipp strove desperately to dismiss such disgraceful thoughts, to produce an answer. Rokitansky looked at him mildly, his eyes were kind, the lean face which was a façade for so much learning was unassuming, patient, genial, full of humility, aware, the mouth tender as a woman's.

"I was thinking that I have suddenly left the human race."

"Ah, so? Left the human race?"

"I am a medical student now. People are no longer people. They are organs and diseases and symptoms, chemicals. And their faces are messages which we, the initiate, can read, and I have knowledge that makes me one of a group, apart from them. My own family, even."

"It's strange, isn't it? As students we have all had that day. It is a troubling thing. Does it make you feel lonely?"

"Very lonely."

"It will pass. All your life a part of you will regard humans as tissue and as tissue problems. But the intensity of this, the emotions it arouses in you, these will pass."

"I fear very much, with respect, honored sir, that the more I study the worse this penalty will become. And I am only a student. Doctors must live in a world all by themselves."

"I will tell you a secret, Mr. Semmelweis. No layman ever feels that he will die. Deep within him he knows that someday, before it is too late, the secret of eternal life will be discovered. Others may die. But not he. And the doctor, Mr. Semmelweis, knows from the day he begins the study of medicine that someday he will die. He knows that nothing can save him. No layman ever really feels that he will become ill. He may fear it, but he does not actually believe it because he cannot imagine pain and make it real. All doctors know that illness is as inevitable as deterioration and they know this in terms of themselves. That is the difference, Mr. Semmelweis. To the

94

layman, the layman is immortal. To the doctor, he is very mortal indeed."

"I am doomed, then." Ignaz Philipp smiled a little.

"You are doomed, sir. You know the truth and the truth will not make you whole. And when you have completed your study, when you have committed a great host of facts so that they are a part of your thinking and are second nature to you, then people will become people again, and it will not be necessary for you to see everyone in terms of a subject. But you will always be a little apart. It is one of the unfortunate correlatives of knowledge. The things we know separate us from people who do not know these things. It does not make us superior, remember that, Mr. Semmelweis. It makes us separate. And one day, with a great rush, you will be overwhelmed by the incredible mass of things you do not know. You will be utterly humbled. That will be your link with your fellow mortals. On that day you will rejoin them."

Ignaz Philipp felt very tired. Partly, he suspected Rokitansky was offering comfort conjured to solve a problem. The words arranged themselves, they formed a pattern of thought. They offered a picture. But it was not a picture into which he could project himself. He was a little embarrassed.

"I thank you, sir professor," he said heartily. He hoped desperately that Rokitansky would not notice the insincerity in his mind. He was grateful for the time spent upon him, for the attention.

"You live alone, Mr. Semmelweis?"

"I do, sir."

"Good. The fact is I have for some time intended to supply myself with a sort of protégé——"

"A protégé, sir?" Ignaz Philipp echoed stupidly.

"Necessarily I prefer that he live with me. There would be no pay, unfortunately. There would, of course, be bed and board. I am told my cook is a great scientist. Would you consider, perhaps——?"

"Me, sir?"

"Of course you must have time."

"To live at your house?"

"Suppose you come to dinner with me tonight and test the cooking?"

Ignaz Philipp looked at Rokitansky a moment longer. He lowered his head. His eyes were full of tears and now they were overflowing. He stared numbly at the floor through the lenses of his tears. He saw his thick and cracked boots, the frayed ends of his trousers. At the back of his neck nerves tingled uncontrollably. He hunched his shoulders at the spasm.

Professor Karl Rokitansky, greatest pathologist in the world, looked at Ignaz Philipp compassionately a moment, then, inwardly deploring his own clumsiness, strode to the closet for his hat and coat. In the interval thus offered him Ignaz Philipp mastered himself.

"I want to tell you, sir—I want to thank you—I do not know how to tell you——"

"Have you no coat?" Rokitansky asked cheerfully. "Come along. You don't need one, anyway. For us old ones it's bitter cold."

In the carriage, Ignaz Philipp, lost for words, simply gazed at Rokitansky.

"We've got such a huge house," Rokitansky complained. "It was all right when we had our sons. Now they're gone into the world and have too-big houses of their own."

"Four sons you have, sir professor," Ignaz Philipp recited humbly. He wanted to show that he knew, that he was not too ignorant.

"Four sons," said Rokitansky complacently. His smile broadened. "Two physicians, two singers. One heals—the other howls. *Die Einen hei'en, die Anderen heulen.*"

Ignaz Philipp sniggered. He bit his lip. He looked at Rokitansky, who was grinning at him broadly, and now he laughed outright.

"You're going to be a great help to me," Rokitansky said. "Now we have laughed together, now we are friends." He looked at Ignaz Philipp anxiously. "We shall have to get you a coat. Probably you haven't had time."

"You must think me poverty-stricken, sir professor."

"Not at all, not at all——"

"I have a coat, home." He shivered. "Sometimes I forget."

"Of course——"

"I am not rich, but I have an allowance. Things are not too good in Hungary just now. My father has a grocery. But there is    rt of depression, we  re taxed so heavily, and the slightest sign of bad times, a failing harvest, a new tax——"

"Your unhappy country!"

"Still, I have enough allowance for a coat. I see I have been letting myself go, my trousers, my shoes . . . To tell the truth I hadn't noticed it. Dr. Skoda today offered to send me to his tailor——"

"To *his* tailor! My boy, Dr. Skoda is a great man and a great diagnostician. But he does not *buy* clothes. He *has* them, Somehow, miraculously, out of the void they appear, his tailor carries them to him and Dr. Skoda wears them. Where they come from no one knows."

"He does seem to dress a little—queerly," Ignaz Philipp said hesitantly.

"He will dress that way all his life. You know why?"

"I have heard the students say he is too kind-hearted to hurt his tailor's feelings by not wearing them," Ignaz Philipp said with no belief in his voice.

"And that, my boy, is exactly why he wears them." Rokitansky laughed uproariously. "And this is the same man who last year sued a clergyman for non-payment of a bill. Pleurisy, I think."

"How much he knows!" Ignaz Philipp said reverently.

"He is unequaled. There is no one like him." And then: "My boy, you are going to like this life. I can tell it. What do you think you will specialize in?"

"I hardly know, sir. Perhaps surgery?"

"Surgery is good. Surgery is fine. You have a lot of time to make up your mind. And I will be honest with you. I intend to proselyte. It is some time until you graduate. But when you do, I hope you will stay with us."

"Here in the university?"

"Here in the university. It is not too bad. We practice medicine here. Outside, medicine is a business. Never forget that. Business, business, business. A man has a good business or he has a bad business. It is openly—business!"

"Yes, sir. But when he gets up in the night to answer a call for help——"

"Business. He is unselfish as a plumber, a fireman, an innkeeper. It's part of his business——"

"But the long hours of study, the great part of his life he devotes to learning——"

"What tradesman doesn't do precisely this? Is there any class but a laborer which doesn't serve a long and arduous apprenticeship?"

"But he devotes himself, sir. He gives his life to relieve pain and suffering, to prolong life."

"That's because he wants to. And if he didn't do this, he wouldn't be in business. Remember that, my boy. Every man in this world does what he does because he wants to; even those who are dissatisfied with what they are doing make the most of it."

"Isn't that true, with all respect, sir professor, of life in the university? As a teacher?"

"True, my boy. Absolutely true. But no one can say we do it for the money that's in it. We get too little. We are the most selfish people in the world. We spend our lives doing exactly what we want to do—study and research. Our lives are pure science."

"And the motive?"

"For the human race, do you mean? Remember what I told you about the plumber and the fireman and the innkeeper, yes, and the policeman and the lawyer and, God help her, the midwife. Every member of the human race works for the human race."

He studied Ignaz Philipp's face.

"You are not convinced, I see."

97

"No, sir."

"You are thinking that we seek to relieve suffering and that this is so noble an endeavor that it cannot be compared with any other pursuit?"

"Yes, sir."

"It is very difficult to go around stuffed with nobility, but you will, as we all have, undoubtedly feel the awe with which the layman regards you as very pleasant, all the same. I, I do not feel noble. I do not feel consecrated even. I feel merely an unconquerable desire to know more and more and more. I wonder which I feel first—uplift at having solved a problem, or uplift at having helped the human race?"

"It is something to consider, sir."

"Did you go into medicine because you felt noble?"

"I went into medicine——" Ignaz Philipp was confused.

"There are many who do. I understand perfectly. I, myself, was so moved by pity for an injured horse I saw when I was a boy that I said to myself in that moment—I will one day be a doctor."

"Do you lose pity, sir?"

"No," said Rokitansky gravely, "I never have lost pity. But I have never cured anyone with it. And pity does not keep me a doctor. I am one with the human race with my pity, my boy. I have neither more nor less of it than they."

He looked at Ignaz Philipp, his eyes full of compassion and honesty. He thought to himself, I must tell you this, because you are a thinker, you have shown the capacity to think, this is how I feel, this is the honest tissue of my thought.

And Ignaz Philipp, looking back at him, saw the entirety of life in a university, where knowledge and service were maintained but were not for sale, where a man attaining greatness could be pure and honest as this gentle, incredibly learned man beside him. He remembered Skoda. There was politics too. Always the fabric of life was imperfect. Always the living were the sufferers.

Dinner that evening, for all Rokitansky's charm and kindness, was an embarrassed dream. Next day Ignaz Philipp moved his few belongings into the Rokitansky house.

It was a brief job, quickly done. He surveyed his new quarters with pride and delight. Rokitansky had provided him with a pleasant corner room that had been used by one of his sons. He was living now, he was actually living now, under the roof of this great man. He continued to assure himself of this with wonder. Mama would be proud. Mama would be so proud. If she could only see him, Mama would be so happy her eyes would shine.

Abruptly he left his room and dashed out into the shopping section of Vienna. He walked rapidly past window after window. He saw what he wanted, the moment he saw it he knew it instantly, in the window of a lace shop.

"That lace," he said to the shopgirl, "the piece in the window."

She looked at him doubtfully. She fished it out gingerly and spread it reverently on the counter.

"You think a woman might like this?" He fingered the edge of the foamy stuff diffidently.

"This?" She looked at him incredulously. "A woman would jump out the window for such a piece of lace!"

"It's not too—too—it's for my mother."

"Your mother would be mad for such a thing! Any woman would be! I thought it was for your sweetheart. For your mother?"

"Oh yes. No one else. It's not too fancy, is it?"

"Too fancy——!"

"Well, I'll take it then. I'll just take it."

"That will be twenty gulden."

"Twenty gulden!" He stared at her, then looked with new respect at the lace, fingering it uncertainly.

"That's Brussels needlepoint—applied on handmade net! That's treasure, that is. For a museum, maybe."

He fingered the coins in his pocket. He had thirty gulden remaining of his month's allowance and most of the month lay still ahead.

"We have lots of other lace, much cheaper. Here's a nice Venetian——"

"I'll take the other."

"The Brussels?"

He laughed aloud.

"Oh course," he said. "Naturally the best. You don't know my mother."

She wrapped it carefully, it made a small parcel, he put it cautiously into his pocket. Jingling the ten gulden that remained to him, he walked blithely to his new home. He sat at his desk and drew a sheet of notepaper toward him. He began laboriously to write.

*My dearest mother and father,*

I am feeling well and happy and hope you are the same. So much has happened to me that you would hardly believe it if you were here. I am living now in the home of Professor Karl Rokitansky. He has taken me in to live with him as a sort of protégé. It is a huge house and his sons are gone out into the world and of course he is a very great man at the university and wherever medicine is being taught they know of him well. He is a pathologist, an expert of disease, and he has done about thirty thousand dissections. He is a full professor. That means he is the head of the whole department of pathology at Vienna University. I can see Mama's eyes get bright as she reads this. It is really true, this Rokitansky has taken me up, and a few days ago Professor Skoda spoke to me kindly, he is another full professor, and also a Professor Hebra. I think it is because I have been studying so hard, but you needn't worry, Mama, I am taking good care of myself. So far I do not know what I want to do, what branch of medicine to practice. I think perhaps it will be surgery. I hope that will please you, Papa, because to tell the truth a surgeon probably could serve Hungary better than any other kind of doctor. It is a new field, besides, and I somehow like the challenge. I miss you both dreadfully, and all the others, too, but at a time like this, when I am so bursting with happiness, it is cruel to be so far away and not be able to hold hands and dance around the table. I kiss you both. I give you a great hug my mama, I love you with all my heart. I remember always everything you both told me. I am trying very hard. I wish you were here. Just for one little golden minute I would like to hold you, and you, Papa, to shake your hand. All my love,

Your *Ignaz Philipp*

P.S. This little bit of nonsense I enclose is from a store here. I thought Mama would like something from Vienna. The girl at the store said it was quite good. She thought it was for my sweetheart. And she was right.

He blotted the letter, folded it, slipped it with the lace into a heavy envelope, sealed the envelope with wax, and went out again to put it aboard the next stagecoach.

He went home heavy-hearted. For a wild moment he had been tempted to board the stagecoach himself. He thought of Thérèse's face when she saw the lace, and brightened a little. He went to his new room and began to study. Soon he was lost in his books.

The day following he met for the first time Professor Johann Klein.

# NINE

WHAT was it van Swieten whispered into the ear of Maria Theresa? What did he tell her, this great physician, summoned to cure the barrenness of the Empress of Austria and Hungary, what simple sentence did he whisper into her ear which made her start, redden, and which from that moment ended her barrenness?

Thereafter she bore thirteen children. He died, full of honors, never revealing what he had told the Empress. And as child followed child, a lying-in refuge for the luckless became one of her grateful ambitions.

Founded by Maria Theresa, the Lying-in Division was one of the three main divisions of the great Vienna General Hospital. According to her wish, "a secure place of refuge was to be provided for the many seduced females who are under the compulsion of shame and necessity, and for the preservation of the blameless, unborn offspring which they carry in their wombs, so that they may at least be brought to holy baptism. The strictest secrecy is to be observed in regard to the patients admitted and no patient is to be asked her name, much less for that of the father of the unborn child. No legal certificate is to be demanded of anyone, nor are husband or parents to have ground for action, if they have no other proof than that the person they have been seeking has been in this place of asylum."

Vienna had need of such a sanctuary. Marriage was almost denied the poor. It was forbidden for any citizen to marry who could not read or write. Times were perilous. Survival was more important than schooling. In this year, of 101,167 births, 44,773 were illegitimate.

The Lying-in Division of the Vienna General Hospital was divided into three divisions. The First Division, the Clinic for Physicians, was administered by Professor Klein. Johann

Klein was fifty-two years old now. His career was the preservation of his position. He did not depend on brilliance, for he knew brilliance only as an epithet, and he was wary of that which he did not understand. His tenure did not derive from a distinguished record, for he was not capable of distinction. At best he was an administrator. He thanked God for it. He had watched men attain distinguished records, and the higher they rose, the easier targets they presented their enemies. He had no sympathy for such men. They called attention to themselves. They were prey who presented themselves to the hunter.

Long ago he discovered that advancement was a perilous quest, an occupation. He believed in simple power, the power of combining with men like himself. He wanted only what he had. He was perpetually conscious of self-preservation. He moved slowly, carefully, watchfully. He weighed reports for the reaction they might produce in his superiors. The reports were not the histories of human beings but the stewardship of Johann Klein.. If he could have commanded destiny they would have remained exactly the same, year after year. He strove to juggle them accordingly.

He did not want attention. He did not want progress. He did not want deterioration. He wanted to go on being director of the First Division of the Lying-in Department of Vienna General Hospital. He had directed all his professional life to present to his superiors exactly the man they had appointed, to prove himself fanatically loyal to them or to anyone who should succeed them.

He regarded himself as a practical man, a man of the world, a sensible fellow, exacting, stern, and on occasion capable of being kind. There had been few rebels in his demesne. Sometimes he thought of Skoda, whom he had to banish to St. Ulrich's and mild enough he had acted even then.

Things turned out exactly right. Skoda, in fact, had been around to thank him soon after. He had learned his lesson, as any sensible young fellow should, and it hadn't taken him long to learn it. Now they both had their friends at court and Skoda was back at Vienna General and had even written a diverting treatise on the listening stick which had gotten him into trouble. The treatise was harmless, classifying the sounds of the chest by categories ranged according to musical pitch. It did a man no harm to write a harmless piece now and then. Lately, he had heard Skoda spoken of as the leading clinician of something called the new Vienna school and that he was about to be named first doctor of the hospital. Well, that's all right, Klein thought, he evidently hasn't learned everything, he doesn't know enough to keep his head down, sooner or later somebody will take it off.

He was polite to Skoda. On the other hand, it would not do to identify himself as a sympathizer. He had a position to guard. He was fifty-two years old. There appeared no reason why he should not maintain that position for a long time. In addition, he was a doctor.

The Second Division of the Lying-in Department was a clinic for midwives. It was administered by Professor Franz Xavier Bartsch, a careful, obedient, patient man, shy, kind, unobtrusive. His knowledge of medicine was neither profound nor shallow. Initiative might well have provided him a lucrative practice in the world outside the safety of the hospital.

The Third Division of the Lying-in Department was for patients able to pay for their treatment, and this division also was under the supervision of Professor Bartsch.

In this Third Division were the private rooms. Only the staff knew who entered these rooms. The pregnant patient brought with her any servants she wished, and usually her own cooking utensils and bedding and even her own furniture. To a great many highly placed ladies of the court, or Viennese society, the Third Division was a frequent sanctuary.

Patients unable to afford these Third Division private rooms could be accommodated in the Third Division in two six-bed wards or in a number of ten-bed wards and still keep their secret. No Third Division mother had to go through the public entrance of the Lying-in Hospital. For her there was a windowless corridor between two high buildings. Porters were on duty here twenty-four hours a day. The porter conducted the invariably veiled, masked, lavishly disguised applicant to the accommodation she whispered she could afford. Once in the sanctuary of the Third Division, the mother could remain until she chose to leave. When she left, she could take her baby with her. Or she could simply leave it behind. The Third Division had only two stipulations: payment in advance and the true name and address of the applicant; this she wrote privately. She then folded the paper, the physician sealed it before her, unread. The number of her ward bed or her private room was written on the outside. It was handed back to her. She locked it in a cabinet by her bedside. When she left the hospital, she took this slip of paper with her. If she died, the slip was opened, the address she had written was contacted, and her body returned to those who would claim it.

To the First or the Second Division went she who could not pay for her confinement. Here, also, was sanctuary. No visitors were allowed. Neither police nor relatives could discover her identity or presence, even with a court order. But though she was protected from the world, she was not barred from it. She could at any time receive the clergyman she desired or be attended by any private physician she chose and could pay for.

To be admitted to the First or the Second Division a widow or an unmarried woman must be a pauper with a certificate of poverty, or a soldier's wife, or a patient from some public institution. But only a pauper's certificate would admit a married woman.

If a woman gave birth to her baby on the way to the hospital she was admitted promptly and questioned later. Many an expectant mother had to travel so far to reach the hospital that her time overtook her and she had her baby in the public street, on the sidewalk, or lying in the gutter, on the way. These street-birth cases arrived carrying the baby wetly wrapped in an apron.

But there were well-to-do Viennese girls who had their babies thriftily at home and immediately afterward contrived to arrive at the hospital, with a certificate of poverty, passing as street births to obtain free aftercare.

If the umbilical cord still had a fresh look, if the baby had not been bathed yet, any woman who claimed to have had her baby in the street was admitted. Normally more than a hundred women a month had their babies in the open streets.

Women who were about to abort were admitted instantly.

Applicants to the First and Second Clinics were allowed to enter at the seventh month of pregnancy and in special cases even earlier. They, also, were allowed to wear veils or masks during their entire stay, if they wished, and the only work they were required to perform was to help keep their ward clean.

Once she had delivered her baby the First or Second Division woman was transferred to the nearby Foundling Home. Here she earned her board and keep by breast-feeding her own child at one breast and another child at the other. There was always a surplus of motherless children. Vienna's mother and child mortality was enormous. But the world was used to such deaths. There were years when in Paris the Hôtel Dieu lost more than half the women who gave birth there. There were four years when at the University of Jena not a mother left the hospital alive.

At the Foundling Home there would have been far too many motherless infants for the survivors to nurse. Fortunately, the infant mortality at the home offset this.

The Foundling Home was a two-story building. On each floor there were five large wards. In this home were placed all illegitimate children born at the hospital, all children left behind by the rich, and any legitimate child whose parents could not care for it because of sickness or poverty. The children were almost all breastfed. There were no laboratory tests for syphilis, tuberculosis, or any communicable disease. Any woman could nurse a child providing she had no obvious open lesion or any observable contagion. From 1784 to 1838 the records of the Foundling Home show that 183,955 babies were admitted, and of these 146,920 died. Eight out of every ten

104

infants never left the home alive. This balanced the deficit of mothers who died giving birth to them.

At the end of two months the mother was permitted to leave the Founding Home, her service as wet nurse having paid her confinement. She was given one dollar and twenty-five cents as a bonus. If she wished further employment as a wet nurse, a department in the Foundling Home easily placed her in a well-to-do home.

The child she left in the Foundling Home was sent to a country household. Peasants were eager for these children. When their own child reached eighteen years he was liable to army conscription. The foundling child could be sent as a substitute.

In the First Division at the nearby Lying-in Hospital there were wards for women who had already delivered their children, a huge ward for pregnant women waiting to be delivered, and a labor ward.

In each ward was an open privy, flush with the floor, covered with an iron grating to prevent women from throwing their babies into it, and not to be used by any woman until a week after she had delivered her baby. She was served during that interval with a wooden bedpan.

The First and Second Divisions contained 384 beds; in the Third, the pay division, there were fifty-seven.

In the rear of the Lying-in Division was a large military hospital unit. On either side of the Lying-in Division were the buildings reserved for contagious diseases. In the front of the division was a row of cesspools for an immense barracks near by, and this stink was the first breath drawn by the newborn infant, the last breath breathed by its usually dying mother. Beneath the Lying-in Hospital ran a large sewer, and in this place it had to run uphill with its contents. The side of the hospital was formerly a cemetery.

This day, as he reported with his class for instruction, Ignaz Philipp had no trouble remembering to wear his coat. The Viennese winter had come with ice and snow. The weather was bitter cold. He stood with his group in one of the First Division wards, waiting for the arrival of Professor Klein. The Réaumur thermometer outside registered fourteen degrees below freezing. There was a noise at the entrance. The class turned. Five shivering pregnant women had stumbled in from the street. Their dresses bellied in front of them, boardlike, ice-covered, frozen stiff with blood and fluid from the burst bags of water. One had her baby in her arms. The soaked apron with which she tented it was brittle with frozen blood and fluid. Within her, in her uterus, the placenta was still undelivered. With her free hand she held up her trussed skirt. Above her thighs, blue with cold, bloodstained, there

105

hung an icicle which issued from her vulva. It was the frozen, dangling end of the umbilical cord.

"Well, gentlemen!"

The class turned. Klein had arrived. He led them into the autopsy room.

On the wooden table at the head of which he took his place lay the body of a woman. From the cadaver the upper part of the trunk and the viscera had been removed. The uterus had been dissected out. In the cavity thus formed in the corpse had been put the waxen body of a dead, new-born child.

"Our problem today, gentlemen," said Klein, "will consist of two parts. First, we will take turns delivering according to various presentations."

One by one the class stepped forward. Ignaz Philipp was eleventh. As he prepared to insert his hand into the vagina of the dead woman his nostrils were suddenly overpowered by a greater stench than he could remember from any dead body he had handled. Involuntarily he paused and looked at Klein.

"Remember that smell well," Professor Klein said. "This woman died of puerperal fever." Then to Ignaz Philipp, "Go ahead, my boy, go ahead. Don't be gingerly. We have plenty of subjects."

Ignaz Philipp reached within the body. His hand found a foot.

"Grasp both feet, Mr. Semmelweis. One foot is not enough."

His fingers found the other tiny foot. He looked up at Klein. Klein nodded. Ignaz Philipp slowly drew the child through the pelvis, down into the vagina, feet first out of the vagina, out of the womans' body.

"It came quite easily," he said, surprised.

"Another baby!" Professor Klein called to an assistant. He turned to the class. "They wear out quickly," he explained. "Fortunately, we have more than we need."

Another child was placed in the woman's body. Its tiny limbs were arranged, its body placed so that its back was presented to the neck of the uterus.

"In all cases where the body of a child presents itself in any but the normal fashion, which is to say head first and with the back of the head uppermost, it is advisable to reach into the womb in the manner we are practicing, to seize the feet and then either to turn the child into the proper birth position or to seize the feet and draw the child forth in the fashion you have just observed. In the event of great narrowness in the pelvis, or of a presentation in which the face is presented uppermost, forceps are used. We will have an opportunity soon to witness this maneuver. In cases where the forceps fail there is an instrument which perforates the child's skull, thus permitting removal of the head and body in somewhat the same fashion as a cork is removed from the neck of a bottle. This, too, we will soon witness. Next student."

As the student advanced to the table the door of the autopsy room opened. Klein, who had been making last-minute arrangements to the body of the child as it lay in the dead woman, looked up indignantly.

"With respect, sir professor—five new women have come in. They are ready for your examination."

Klein turned to his assistant.

"You will take over the class. This man is to try his hand at a breech presentation."

It was a short walk, across the hall and into the next ward. He wiped his hands on the lapels of his coat.

An attendant drew back the bedcovers.

"Aha!" Klein smiled. He thrust his damp fingers into the warm body. "How do we feel? How goes it, Mother?"

Back in the autopsy room the door closed slowly.

The class in obstetrics crowded closer to the table.

"It is becoming too easy," the assistant protested suddenly. "This body is worn out."

Four students lifted the lifeless, hollowed body, dumped it into a wicker basket, covered the basket with a cloth. They lifted to the table another body, similarly prepared. The fourteenth student stepped forward.

"Fortunately for science, gentlemen, we do not lack for subjects." The assistant smiled reassuringly.

In the ward, Klein stepped from the bedside of the fifth newcomer. He straightened. He wiped his hands. He smiled genially.

"Be easy, Mother. We'll take care of you."

He walked into the hallway, crossed it, and reopened the door of the autopsy room. The class turned.

"Now then——" he said, and walked to the table.

107

# TEN

IN this era, this interval of men, synthesis began a clotting, an islanding, an agglutination. Discoveries and observations accumulated though the centuries were sifted and grouped. Patterns of chemistry, of physics, of treatment and of diagnosis became apparent. As the pattern was applied, progress was recorded. From this patient and sometimes quick and brilliant assembling of many facts and the fashioning from the many facts of a single fact this interval became a period of synthesis.

In England, Thomas Young stated the wave theory of light. John Dalton perfected the atomic theory. Richard Bright drew from a stock pile of medical facts compact weapons of comprehension for pancreatic diabetes, acute yellow atrophy of the liver, Jacksonian epilepsy, status lymphaticus, and that inflammation of the kidneys which is called Bright's disease. Penny postage began and five months later was taken up in America. Victoria was Queen. Ocean travel by steamship was established. Thomas Addison described pernicious anemia and used static electricity to treat spasmodic and convulsive diseases. Thomas Hodgkin shaped available facts on a disease which simultaneously enlarges the spleen and the lymphatic system and presented his findings so admirably that the disease became known as Hodgkin's disease. James Parkinson gave his name to *paralysis agitans*. Esdaile, Braid, and Elliotson used hypnotism successfully as an anaesthetic in surgical cases. These great names, Robert Graves, William Stokes, Abraham Colles, Francis Rynd, John Cheyne, John Corrigan, Sir Thomas Watson, Sir Charles Bell, Sir William Bowman, Syme and Fergusson, tidied the paths of medicine, collected facts, arranged them, synthesized.

In France at this time the great Dupuytren, Velpeau, Nelaton, Magendie, Bayle, Bretonneau, Corvisart, Pinel, Andral, Ricord, Alibert, Bichat flourished and their names were thunder and their work was lightning whose glare would light the paths of medicine forever.

In Germany, Schleiden and Schwann observed the cell, formulated the most important generalization in the science of the form and structure of organized beings, linked all living things with the statement: "There is one universal principle of development for the elementary parts of organisms, however different, and that principle is the formation of cells." The great Purkinjeshone, and Hyrtl, Henle, von Liebig, von Baer, Schönlein, Müller, Constatt, and Wunderlich. Doctor-Poet Johann Wolfgang von Goethe concluded that all parts of a plant except the stem are modified leaves, was unable to decide whether evolution was from foliage leaf to reproductive leaf, and was pained and amazed when Doctor-Poet Johann Schiller decided coldly, "This is not an observation, it is an idea."

In Vienna, Joseph Skoda, Karl Rokitansky, Ferdinand Hebra, von Oppolzer heaped fact upon fact, rose to greatness upon the eminence they assembled.

In Italy, Salvatore Tomassi, Francesco Selmi, who discovered and named ptomaines, Amici, Rolando, Panizza, Scarpa, Lombroso discovered and synthesized those things which made their names commonplaces in medical history.

In Russia, Nikolai Ivanovich Pirogoff introduced female nursing, established himself as the most important figure in the medical history of Russia.

The United States of America, of which there were then twenty-six states and seventeen million persons, was isolated from the great world of European science. Laboring in the wilderness, Ephraim McDowell, John Otto, James Jackson, North, Mitchell, Bigelow, Gerhard, Nathan Smith, Drake, Beaumont, Warren, William Morton, chronicled frontier prodigies.

In the world the average human lived less than thirty-three years. Twenty-five per cent died before the age of six years. Fifty per cent died before the age of sixteen years. One man in a hundred lived to be sixty-five.

Karl Marx prepared with Friedrich Engels to write the *Communist Manifesto,* and all the middle classes and all the lower classes of Europe, openly mutinous against feudalism, eagerly and loudly discussed revolt. Turner, Corot, Millais, Courbet, Delacroix led a new art movement. Chopin and Wagner and Liszt, Dumas and Victor Hugo, joined the spirit of revolt. Tennyson wrote doggedly of medieval legends.

It is 1840, and Ignaz Philipp Semmelweis has not decided whether he will be physician or surgeon or country doctor, they are ranked in that order and there are courses for each.

109

He continues to study both surgical and medical courses.
Many students have already quit classes to become country
doctors. In their first year these had attended an introductory
course on medical-surgery study, lectures on the theory of
surgery, general pathology and therapeutics, dietetics, prescrib-
ing and bandaging. In their second year they studied operative
surgery, the laws governing the practice of medicine, mid-
wivery and veterinary science. In several subjects, including
obstetrics, their attendance was not compulsory. In the third
year they attended clinics and reviewed the first two years of
study. Now the *landarzt*, the country doctor, graduated and
left Vienna for the remote countryside and the farmer, the
rancher, and the miner.

In 1841 Ignaz Philipp decided not to be a country doctor.
He tried to decide whether to be a surgeon. Until very recently
one of the duties of surgeons in Germany had been to shave
all army officers. Elsewhere in the world surgeons knew how
to shave, to cut hair, to spread plasters, to cut, and to bleed.
Less than seventy years before Vienna had established its first
surgical clinic. Now, surgery was emerging as a new science.
But a surgeon ranked below a physician.

It is 1842, and Ignaz Philipp continues to ponder a career
in surgery. Skoda and Hebra are uneasy.

"Can't you interest him in dermatology, Hebra?"

"He has no interest in skin work. My best pupils appear
to be those with some persistent minor skin disease."

"It is ridiculous. The very thought of such an excellent
young man becoming a surgeon is really unthinkable. He is
really becoming a fine thinker, Hebra. And Rokitansky is no
help."

"Karl thinks that what Semmelweis really wants is to *teach*
surgery."

"Karl hopes so!"

"I suppose none of us expects him to go out in the world
and practice. Do you?"

"Well, one naturally assumes—with the care we are taking
of him——"

"I don't know what particular care we're taking of him. Of
course it's always amusing to take an interest in a student
. . ."

"Still, if he *should* actually go out in the world, what is it
they say about my dermatology?"

"I know. 'It is the best practice. One's patients never die,
never get well, never get one out of bed at night.' Are you
being cynical, Ferdinand?"

"My dear Skoda. We have so many pupils. This is not the
first striking student. He will not be the last. It isn't what we
want. It's what he wants."

"Unfortunately we know better than he what's good for him."

In 1843 Rokitansky faced Kolletschka across ° dissecting table.

"What do you think, Jakob?"

"I think he will stay here with us."

"About the surgery?"

"I think he may teach surgery."

"Not practice it?"

"It is very delicate, you understand."

"I know, Jakob."

"I don't speak of it."

"Nor I."

"I believe, with you, his place is here, at the university."

"But he must make up his own mind."

"I say nothing direct."

"I would not dream of it."

"He is an underdog, you know. A Hungarian. He was treated badly his first year here. And all Hungarians grow up in an atmosphere of natural resentment. And surgeons are underdogs. One must consider that. He is a questioner, a challenger."

"I never speak ill of surgery, Jakob."

"Of course not. Nor I. But—perhaps——"

"You are thinking of Hebra and Skoda?"

"I think perhaps Professor Hebra, sometimes in his zeal to make a joke——"

"Yes. The mind of a student is a strange forming thing. The natural inclinations of mind and body mixed with the impressions of environment reaching to grasp that which is aptest for that individual, a reaching of which the individual is unaware. Have you ever noticed, Jakob, how many doctors die of their specialty? Is it the dumb mouth of the body, aware of the latent essence of its destruction, warning us to have ready a weapon to prevent its peril? No, I don't believe this surgery is his natural inclination, not his natural aptitude. I think he is espousing a cause."

"It is the one chink in his armor. He is not capable of universal detachment. His emotions——"

"In time, Jakob. In time they will pass. In time, and here in the university . . ."

"He dissects so beautifully."

"Yes, the best of all manual skills, that is the one he does best."

"And, of course, a surgeon——"

"Yes, Jakob. You are quite right. But little by little we are, I am sure, working him around. It takes patience. It takes caution. He has a fine mind. One must work very carefully."

111

"We might show him there is much actual practice right here at the university."

"That can be managed. Of course he does considerably more work in the clinics now than the ordinary student."

"He is good, Karl. He is all good. There is nothing bad in him."

"I know. We must keep him. We must look out for him. Well, the clinic. Well, let's see. Let's see what we'll see."

On the following day Ignaz Philipp dined with Markussovsky and Chiari. Markussovsky was planning to return to Budapest.

"Two years ago—a year ago even—I would have been worried, leaving you here alone," he said.

"Two years ago I would have returned to Buda with you," Ignaz Philipp said.

"We have gone a long way. A long, long way."

"Where have you gone?" Chiari asked pleasantly.

"Oh, it's not I who have gone anywhere. It's Ignaz Philipp here. He's the one. Living with the great Rokitansky—the intimate and favored darling of Skoda and Hebra and Kolletschka—it looks like you're bound for great things, Naci."

"What on earth do you say that for, Marko? My prospects are just the same as yours——"

"I wasn't hinting that you were teacher's pet. So don't take it that way. I was talking about your opportunities."

"What kind of opportunities do you think I have?"

"Now wait, Naci. One of us is being a little naïve. Let's put it this way. Willie Schmitt is a student at the university. He knows no one and no one knows him. Ignaz Semmelweis is a student at the university. He lives at the home of Professor Karl Rokitansky. He is befriended by Professor Skoda, Professor Hebra, and Professor Kolletschka. Which one has the brighter prospects?"

"All right, which one?"

"Are you serious?"

"Specifically, exactly what do you think any of these men can do for me? They could keep me from flunking. But I'm not in danger of flunking, thank God. On occasion, when they're not busy, I can have the extreme worth-while advantage of their conversation. I can learn something from listening. I hope I'm not giving the impression that I'm belittling them or tearing down fine and great men. I'm not being ungracious. I'm trying to answer your question. If I wanted money, they couldn't make me wealthy. If I wanted a fine practice, they couldn't send me patients. If I wanted fame, they couldn't make me famous. Exactly what do you think they could do?"

"Are you angry, Naci?"

"Not a bit. I'm just curious. And I'm uncomfortable. I don't like being viewed as a man of destiny——"

"All I can say is, I wish I were in your shoes," Chiari said enviously. "I'd show you destiny. I'd own the university in a week."

"No, you wouldn't. You'd be right where you are. They couldn't do any more for you than they can for me."

"You mean to say they couldn't have you made an assistant? That their recommendations wouldn't be any good if you wanted a job at the university?"

"Of course their recommendations would be good. If there was an opening. But they couldn't make a job. And they couldn't jump me over anybody's head. The university is run by rigid rules. There's unbreakable protocol and unbreakable precedence that governs us all. And you know that as well as I do."

"Have you tried for anything?"

"What would I try for? What do I want?"

"Really, Naci, you're a strange fellow——"

"I know you've been thinking that. You think I'm on the verge of a great career all on the basis of being taken up by a few officials. You think I'm an irreverent peasant because I don't know how lucky you think I ought to feel. Well, I am lucky that such men have taken notice of me. And I'm flattered too. But what else do you expect me to do about it? What is it you think I ought to plan on and hope for?"

"Don't be excited, Naci——"

"I'm perfectly calm, Marko. But you won't let me be one of you any more—you have a different attitude about me—I'll tell you the truth, you make me uncomfortable. You embarrass me."

"But you are strange about your intimacy with these men. You never talk about it."

"I swear to you there's nothing to talk about. They're busy men. I don't often see them. They have good will toward me and that warms me and gives me confidence. They've taken an interest in me. So I have to study all the harder. I don't flatter myself I'm the only student professors have ever taken an interest in or been kind to. There were students before me and there will be students after I'm graduated. And I'm not being wary. I'm just trying to make you understand the literal, living truth."

"But you *live* in Rokitansky's very house!"

"And I see him on an average of thirteen times a week. I see him at class an hour each day. And I see him at dinner an hour each night. I hear more from him at class than ever I do at dinner. He smiles, he nods, and he doesn't hear a thing I say. He's a sweet, pleasant, learned man, but he's working on a book. Most of the time I think he's forgotten I live there."

"I don't know." Markussovsky shook his head bewilderedly. "It's too much for me. You've upset one of my happiest delusions. I guess you're right, but—Naci!—when you think about it, isn't it even strange to you?"

"Yes. Everything's strange to me. But I don't want you to be."

"I won't. I'll never be."

"My life's completely changed ever since I decided to study medicine. I don't know what's happened. All I know is, here I am doing the one thing I'd rather do than anything else in the world. I'm not what I was, I never planned to be anything, I'm living a life I never dreamed of, thinking different thoughts, but I'm thinking the same way. No, nothing's the same. And it doesn't matter. The one thing that rises above everything else is medicine."

"Of course it does. For all of us. And as to the changes perhaps you've lost your roots. I wonder—— You live with Rokitansky. Are you at home there?"

"I don't seem at home anywhere."

"Are you unhappy, Naci?"

"Of course I'm not unhappy. Do you mean do I look back upon my childhood and yearn about how happy I was then? When I was home? I'll tell you something. My mother told me this once. When you think about how happy you were once upon a time the real happiness you have is right now, while you're thinking about it. Because in the days you were thinking about you weren't even aware you were happy. No, this is my life. I'm lucky, lucky, lucky to be living it. I'll go on studying in perfect bliss until they throw me out. And then I'll be a good doctor. I'll be really good. A small practice, a chance to experiment and study, a little security. That's all I ask of life. That, and a chance to help Hungary when the time comes."

"What are you going to do first, Naci? Are you going to stay on at the university?"

"I don't know."

"Are you going to specialize in surgery?"

"I don't know that, either. I just don't know, Marko. What are you going to do?"

"Marko doesn't have to practice for a living," said Chiari.

"No, that's true. I'm lucky, I suppose. My family has a certain amount of money."

"A certain amount!" echoed Chiari.

"There's one nice thing, Marko. For you, medicine needn't be a business. You'll never be one of the multitude who are doctors because they or their family respected medicine as a good business."

"There's nothing wrong with business, Naci. So long as it's honest."

114

"But I hate to see a merchant swaggering under our red gown, airing himself as some mystic figure with the powers of God, speaking strange words, the semi-divine recipient of some great secret. If a man is given greater dignity and greater privileges and special laws his concepts should at least be fit for the honors."

Markussovsky beamed at Chiari.

"You see? This is what it was like in the old days! Naci, I haven't heard you spout like this in two years. I thought, I'd begun to think, that Rokitansky had made you respectable."

"There's a lot in what Naci says, though," said Chiari, frowning. "I went with the eminent Dr. Brauner the other day to a rich patient. The moment we entered he set the servants to work, this one to fetch water, the other to bring wool, a third for milk. 'Make your presence felt!' he whispered to me. 'Set everybody running.' One of the family entered and instantly he pulled a grave and portentous face. Now that rigmarole isn't science and it isn't art. It's acting."

"It's business," said Ignaz Philipp.

"Call it whatever you like," said Markussovsky, "and say what you like, what we have studied and what we experience do set us apart. I don't approve of the mantle of mysticism any more than you do. But it isn't always the doctor's fault that folks view him with awe. Most people regard their persons as the visible evidence of divine handiwork. And it pleases them to regard that handiwork as a secret whose mystery is known only to God and the doctors."

"We're merchants. We have a specialized knowledge. It's for sale," said Ignaz Philipp. "We have a function to perform and well or ill we perform it. We're entitled to no more dignity, when you come to think of it, than the butcher, the plumber, the carpenter, or any other human who has specialized knowledge which he sells to his fellow humans."

"Not today," said Chiari. "The old days of hawking pills, the days when we served patients solely by naming their disease, those days are over. Medicine today is an art. I think someday it may actually become a science. I think we have a more important role than a carpenter."

"What really bothers me is the role we complacently preempt. The human body is *our* human body. Medicine is *our* medicine. It's like a carpenter looking with a proprietary air on all lumber and regarding carpentry as his property. To get away with this we draw on the ancient priestcraft. We dress mysteriously, we have our special costumes. We have our own language, our own magic gibberish. We have had laws passed to protect the omniscience to which we pretend. We protect one another like members of a priestly fraternity. We foster the belief that we are a mystery. The hold we have on people is their own fear, pain, terror, and ignorance. And we, too, are ignorant. We can say only that we know more than they know. We are pitifully ignorant."

"You'd better not let Rokitansky hear you say that."

"Marko, a man like Rokitansky doesn't have to be told how little he knows."

"It's true, you know," said Markussovsky tiredly. "We learn how to diagnose. We learn how to discover the nature of an ailment. We learn how to relieve some suffering. Not much. Well, I wanted to help people. But I can't see where therapeutic nihilism helps. I'll admit that's not my idea of a noble calling."

"A noble calling? I've heard a lot about the nobility of this calling. The unselfish sacrifice, the devotion to human suffering. We get up at nights when other people are sleeping, that makes us noble. We get up at nights like firemen or policemen or hotelkeepers! It's our business! We devote years to study because that's exactly what we want to do. And we get pleasure from it. We cause as much suffering as we relieve. We parade mystically with our imperfect knowledge, among the maimed and the doomed."

"Yes," said Markussovsky, "we're no nobler than our fellow animals. But then I never felt especially noble. All I want to do is practice medicine. And now it seems there really isn't much medicine to practice."

"I'm going to try to stay in the university," said Chiari. "I want to investigate. I'm convinced that if we turn up enough about the nature and cause of disease and its symptoms, we may give the next generation a chance at solving the cures."

"The university—that isn't for me, either," said Markussovsky.

"I don't know," said Ignaz Philipp. "I keep thinking that if I study long enough—— But I know this: Knowledge for the sake of knowledge isn't enough. I don't just want to accumulate knowledge. I want to use it."

"How?"

"I've been thinking about surgery," said Ignaz Philipp.

"Surely not surgery!"

"It's something positive at least, something you can grapple with."

"There you are again—treating diseases, not people. You can't save your patients, man! Not with surgery! Oh, you can get away with a little plastic work, a little tendon cutting, perhaps. But who recovers from anything else?"

"Did you hear about Cheselden cutting for stone? Fifty-four seconds! Cut through the perineum, grab the stone, in and out of the bladder in fifty-four seconds! And Dieffenbach—amputations in less than two minutes! And Langenbeck——"

"Yes, Naci, and von Graefe and Stromeyer and Simon.

116

Lightning operators. Is that what you want to be? A lightning operator? Why not study piano? You'll kill fewer patients."

"I don't know. I don't know what I want to do. All I know is I love medicine. I don't want to go out into the world quite yet. I want to learn more. I don't want to hurt people. I think I'll stay here at the university. I'll keep on studying. And when I've learned enough I'll go out and practice."

"Meanwhile we are at liberty to regard you as something less than nature's nobleman?"

"Meanwhile you are to regard me as a man who has studied six long years to discover what he doesn't know."

"Well, this much I know. You'll never stay in the university and teach, Naci."

"And why not?"

"Because everyone who teaches sooner or later writes a book. That's how you get ahead as a teacher. Skoda's written about the chest, and Kolletschka joined Skoda writing about pericarditis, and Lord knows Hebra's written enough, and your own Rokitansky goes at it morning, noon, and night. Can you imagine our Naci writing?"

"I would rather take poison."

"And he would too!" Markussovsky assured Chiari.

"To tell the truth every time I think about writing even my thesis I want to go home!"

"What's so bad about a little writing?" asked Chiari.

"Well, if you're like Naci, here . . ."

"In the first place, I hate Latin."

"He hates Latin and Latin hates him. And when it comes to German you may have noticed that he speaks it with a slight limp."

"Why not hire someone to write your thesis for you?"

"He can't do that, either. Our Naci is entirely too honest for anyone but his friends. What are you going to write about, Naci?"

"I'll find something."

"Ask Skoda," said Chiari.

"I think I will."

"And when you do, remember me to him."

"What for?"

"My boy," said Chiari pityingly, "you are wasted on yourself. Do you know that once in classroom, after class was over, Skoda spoke to me familiarly and I treasure the very memory? If I were in your shoes——"

"You must make the most of yourself, Naci. You really must, you know."

"Politics! Tell me, do you think Skoda owes his position to what he knows—or to politics? Of course there's such a thing as being lucky. I admit Kolletschka hasn't been too lucky. But who cares for that? He's doing what he wants to do. And as

117

for me—that's all I ask of life. That, and the subject for my thesis."

Next day he asked Skoda to suggest a subject for his thesis.

"My boy, a thesis discloses to the examiners how you think and the caliber of your thinking. It doesn't much matter what subject you select. I suggest you stick to diagnosis. I'll help you. Today. I want you to make rounds with me. From now on I think we'll find more clinical work for you."

In the first ward they entered Ignaz Philipp eyed a singularly beautiful child.

"Aha!" said Skoda, "you like that one, do you?"

They walked to the bedside.

"She's very lovely," said Ignaz Philipp.

"Then she shall be your patient. Take charge. What is your diagnosis, Doctor?"

Ignaz Philipp bent closer. The child was eighteen months old. Her blue eyes were sunk in her emaciated face. Her blond hair curled wetly away from the bluish-white forehead.

"Don't be in a hurry this once. Stay here. Study her carefully." Skoda turned to the ward attendant. "He will prescribe. This shall be his patient."

"She has the summer complaint," said the attendant. "She purges from the bowels constantly."

"Aha!" said Skoda. "It appears no doctor is needed on this case." He turned to the woman. "You are a diagnostician as well as a ward attendant?"

"With respect, sir doctor——"

"With a little more respect, if you please."

"I only meant to tell you——"

"Me? You need tell me nothing. This is the man you want to tell it to. Aha!" He turned to Ignaz Philipp. "What are you finding?"

Ignaz Philipp was bent over the bed.

"What is it, little maid?" he crooned. "What is it that troubles you? Would you like a doll? A nice doll like yourself?"

The child looked at him through blank, troubled eyes. She screwed up her mouth. She whimpered soundlessly. Ignaz Philipp glimpsed her gums. He turned back her upper lip.

"She has swollen gums," he said over his shoulder to Skoda.

"Yes. Do as you think best," said Skoda. "I leave you now." And he walked off, well pleased.

"Bring me a lancet," said Ignaz Philipp. The attendant sniffed and departed.

Ignaz Philipp sat on the edge of the bed. He held the child's bony wrist between his fingers. He felt the pulse. The pulse told him nothing. The skin was clammy. At the same time it was hot. "What is wrong with you, darling? What is wrong with you, little one?" he said to himself. Fever, diarrhea, emaciation, swollen gums, eyes bright and vacant. "What is wrong

118

with you, little one?" Some kind of fever, certainly. He drew
back the bedclothes. The stale odor of feces rushed to his nostrils. The child's legs were like a skeleton's, her ribs were a tiny
bony cage. He licked his dry lips. He had no assurance now.
Suddenly this was not a problem, but a living sick child. And
Skoda had entrusted her to him. And somewhere in what he
had studied was treatment for her. Fever, clammy skin, eyes
bright, and great emaciation. And diarrhea. Here and there
her skin was oddly spotted. Her abdomen was swollen, the
skin was tight. He thumped it as Skoda had taught him. It
gave back a drumming sound. He pressed his fingertips into
the frail flesh, watching the child's face, trying to elicit pain,
to discover a focus, a pain point from which to start working. The child moved restlessly. Her tiny, swollen abdomen
was tender. The attendant arrived with a lancet. Ignaz Philipp stood, wiped the knife on his sleeve, leaned over and drew
back the child's upper lip. He cut down to the teeth. Instantly
the child screamed, jerked its mouth wildly away. Blood
spurted onto the pillow. Stolidly, the attendant handed him a
towel. He pressed a bit of it against the gum, holding the
child's skull.

At the scream a woman came forward involuntarily from
a far corner of the room. She was standing by the bed, her
hands crossed and clasped to her chest as Ignaz Philipp
straightened and put down the knife. She peered around him
at the child.

"It's the mother," said the attendant. "Do you wish to prescribe?"

Her eyes summed him up, another student, another smart
chap, another know-nothing. And now the mother, too,
watched him, waiting.

"I will be back," Ignaz Philipp said coldly. "I will return
with her prescription in an hour. I will make it up myself."

"Doctor," said the mother. "Please, Doctor——"

"Yes, madam?" He tried his best to remember how Skoda
spoke.

"What is it? Little Lisl, will she die, Doctor?"

"She's perfectly all right, madam. I assure you."

And he walked quickly away from the ward. He tried to
think, as he walked, but he could not. His mind was confused,
his thoughts were meaningless and full of panic. He knew
nothing. He did not know what he was going to prescribe.
He did not know what ailed the child. He knew only that he
was full of gratitude at leaving the scene and that somewhere,
somewhere in the books to which he was straightway going,
was the answer. If it had been a class following Skoda, if he
had been a member of that class, if the question had been
asked—— Well, he checked himself, what would he have answered exactly? For that was the whole crux of the matter. "I

119

don't know," he answered himself. "But someone in the class would have had an answer. And I would have had an answer too." And Skoda would have been there. But this child, sick, not able to talk, to tell him anything, this poor, pitiful thing that was suddenly all his responsibility . . . this mother, begging him with her eyes . . . it might have been his own mother, his little sister, even . . .

There was nothing in Chelius, of course. Chelius, he reminded himself feverishly, Chelius was surgery. He leafed quickly through his books. Suddenly it loomed out at him from the printed page. Cholera morbus. He digested the symptoms rapidly. Cholera morbus all right. But those spots . . . no spots in cholera morbus . . . he heard Skoda: "Any physician knows that the really typical case of any disease is almost the exception rather than the rule . . ." There could be no question. It was cholera morbus. He fitted the symptoms to the symptoms in the book. Everything tallied. Quickly he wrote down the prescribed treatment. He returned to the ward. The mother was still standing at the child's bedside. Now he smiled at her confidently.

"You're not to worry," he said. "Where's the attendant?"

"She'll be right back."

"Fine . . . fine . . ."

He sat on the edge of the bed and took the child's wrist in his hands again. The pulse was much softer and seemed to have a double beat.

"Her tongue is so brown," the mother murmured anxiously.

"I know." He smiled up at her.

He touched her belly again. The child winced. He looked up. Her nose was bleeding slightly. Her tiny fingers curled and began to scratch weakly at her side. He bent to look closer. The spots again. Her skin was dotted with small, rosy, slightly raised spots. He pressed a spot. It disappeared. He removed his finger. The spot returned. He thought a moment. Then he smiled. The spots became laughably clear. He looked among the bedclothes, found a flea, showed it to the mother.

"Sometimes they bring them in," he said jovially, "and sometimes we have them here, all ready for them."

The child stiffened in a small spasm.

"Her bowel movements—all loose—like pea soup——"

"Now, don't worry." He rose and patted her shoulder. The attendant was approaching.

"Does she vomit much?" he asked the attendant easily.

"Oh, she vomited once or twice. She never eats anything. She coughs. And when we try to force food down—up it comes, naturally."

His mind moved happily among the assembled facts. Pain, spasm, purging, vomiting. It was cholera morbus all right.

"We'll put her on chicken broth," he ordered the attendant.

His voice was full of decision. "Large doses of chicken broth, no salt. No salt whatever. Give her"—he turned for a moment to look at the child—"give her up to a gallon. And simultaneously give her chicken broth by rectum."

He turned to the mother.

"And you," he said, "you go home and get some sleep. She's all right now."

"Oh, Doctor, God bless you, God bless you . . ."

"Oh, now that isn't necessary. You must pull yourself together . . ."

"Why don't you let her make the soup?" the attendant asked rebelliously.

"That's a fine idea," he said heartily. "Hurry, now! Rush home! Make a gallon of fine chicken broth. Bring it in the morning."

The woman rushed away.

"Make some for me!" he called after her.

He turned to the attendant. He was taut with pleasure. The face of the attendant did not reflect back to him his elation. She looked at him with barely concealed contempt. "Can she read my mind? Does she know how full of panic I was?" he asked himself, shocked. Then anger welled in him for her animosity.

"Well, woman?" he said coldly.

The attendant dropped her eyes. She compressed her lips. "There is another such patient," she said reluctantly.

Ignaz Philipp hesitated. In his triumph he was tempted. Skoda had not instructed him to attend any other patient by himself. Nevertheless the urge to repeat his triumph was unconquerable. He followed her toward the bedside of another child. The nearer he approached the higher rose his feeling of juvenile guilt. He was doing what he had not been told to do. There was no excuse of emergency. The child was Skoda's patient and he was well able to look after her. But here was an opportunity to practice medicine, to do the things he would be called upon to do when he graduated and had a practice of his own. Here, on this patient, he could practice as a doctor. He reached the bedside. He began his examination. The case was the same as the other child, the symptoms were identical except that this child had no spots.

"More typical than the other," he told the attendant. She looked at him impassively, then without being told went to fetch the knife. He cut down on the child's swollen gums.

"The same treatment," he said, rising. He felt oddly tired. The triumph was gone. He felt assured and confident and also humble. He thought to himself: "I have not really been a doctor. I have been an interpreter. I have been a man who knew where to look in a book and the book has told me what to do and I have told this attendant."

121

"The same treatment?" the woman asked. He thought he heard a searching tone in her question.

"Have you a better one?" he asked with cold politeness.

"So much good soup," the woman murmured.

"I beg your pardon?"

"As the sir doctor desires."

Now he walked from the ward, and as he walked the ward belonged to him. Every patient in it was his patient. He walked with surety, glancing right and left, diagnosing with a glance, at home in his own province, lord of all he surveyed. Here and there he stopped to speak with authority a soft word of encouragement. He was intoxicated with triumph and the power of knowledge.

Late that night, desiring again to drink of the same liquor, he came back to the ward.

He was astonished to find the child much weaker. Abruptly, triumph left him, he was chilled and sober in a wave of panic. What had happened? He directed his mind to review what he had read, what he had examined, what he had done. He had forgotten nothing. The child should have been relieved. At worst, it should have been no worse. He looked at the little girl again. Her breathing was much more difficult. Her body, which had been burning, was now somewhat less hot. Her eyes were glazed and without even infantile understanding. She had stopped tossing and lay in a stupor. She was no longer a case. She was a little girl, and he was an adult, and he must do something for her and he did not know what to do. The frightened face of the child's mother returned to his brain. He heard his own voice reassuring her heartily. He picked up the child's wrist again. The pulse was very soft, now, and definitely seemed to have a double beat. Across the bed, as he considered this, helpless, thunderstruck, the attendant put her hands on her hips.

"Doctor, don't you think this baby is going to die?"

Her voice was irritatingly loud.

"No, woman, I do not think so at all."

He listened critically to his own voice. It sounded self-assured. There was no break in it. No hint of panic. Dazed and confused, he bent forward, not to see anything, for his senses could no longer record intelligible sight, but to hide his panic by movement. He sat numbly thus, waiting, completely ignorant of what the child would do next and of what he should do if it reacted. As he sat, the child stopped breathing.

He looked at it. He waited for it to breathe again. "She has fainted," he thought. The possibility of death did not occur to him. There was no reason why the child should die. He was not treating a dying patient. Fainting was something that he could deal with. Gladly he pulled the child from the bed. He held it up, head down. Then he placed her on the bed again.

He had not brought her to. He seized her small shoulders. He began to shake her, at first gently, then with increasing violence. Still the child resisted him. Suddenly he leaned over her, and placing his mouth on hers began to breathe his breath into her with all his strength. Again and again he breathed great lungfuls into her tiny mouth. He stopped only when he was breathless. He watched her. She lay with upturned eyes. Her chest was still. Her body was bent a little, almost in an attitude of expectation, and this attitude was heightened by her upturned eyes and her small mouth, agape. He took her shoulders again and shook her. The attendant laid a hand on his shoulder.

"No use shaking that baby any more, sir doctor, because that baby is dead."

He stared at the child. For a moment he was completely numb. He had no thoughts at all. Then fear and guilt began to grip his bowels. Shame made him close his eyes. When he opened them he saw not his mistake but only a dead child, and "dead child, dead child," began to reverberate through his empty mind, and the child's remote face crushed his spirit beneath the infinite weight of parting and now grief winced in all his thoughts and he rose abruptly, full of horror and protest.

The attendant had gone. He looked about. The ward was quiet, sleeping. He went quickly to the other child he had examined. She was asleep, breathing uneasily. As he looked down at her it seemed to him she was weaker also. He pushed down her chin so that her mouth would open and he could look at her tongue. The child wakened.

"Now, now," he said soothingly.

But the child simply gazed at him, waiting. Her tongue was thickly coated. The edges of the tongue seemed browner than when he had last seen it. He looked about for the attendant, to order an enema. She had not returned to the ward. He went to a supply closet, found the enema apparatus, poured in a little water, brought it to the child's bedside.

"Now," he said, his face a cheery mask, "now we shall be better." The child watched him. He set the apparatus on the floor by the bedside. He approached the child. As he did so, he realized suddenly that he did not know what he was going to do next. "Give an enema. Yes, of course. But how?" He took up the child's wrist to give himself time to shape his thoughts. He remembered confusedly all the procession of students through the wards, himself among them, the enemas, the poultices, the blisters he had prescribed. He heard Skoda's voice asking: "And what shall we do for this patient?" He heard himself answering: "An enema containing such and such . . . A blister, composed of . . . A poultice, in which shall be mixed . . ." He saw the dutiful attendant making a

123

dutiful note. He licked his lips. How were those blisters applied? How were those poultices made up, how did one go about it, how were they put against the body, how held in place? How, how did one go about the simple business of administering an enema? What was the proper way of turning this tiny patient, of lifting her in bed? "Is this the brilliant pupil of Rokitansky, the pride of Kolletschka, the man Skoda entrusts with a human life?" he asked himself ironically. "My name is Semmelweis, and a few days ago I was called to demonstrate on a cadaver, before beginning pupils, an amputation Rokitansky himself called brilliant. Surely I can administer a simple enema. What an ignorant ward attendant can do, I can do."

He studied the patient. He considered. First of all, the water must run into the body. There must, therefore, be something on which to hang the water vessel. The tube then must be put into the anus, pushed past the sphincter muscle, pushed into the sigmoid flexure. But this is a retention enema. Therefore it must go farther up. How much farther? He visualized the child's descending colon. Much farther. Up, at least, to the transverse colon. He picked up the enema apparatus and looked for a nail on the wall. There was none. He put the apparatus down. He walked to the supply closet to look for a stand. The attendant entered.

"Give that child," he said, pointing to the bed he had just quitted, "a pint of chicken broth by enema." He tried to keep his tone level. He walked to the door. A sigh of relief welled in him. He was escaping. As he passed through the door, he slowed. With an effort he conquered his desire for flight. He turned defiantly and walked back to the bedside. He watched the attendant. He noted silently every move, each practiced gesture. When it was over, he walked again toward the ward door, not having uttered a word. As he passed the bed in which lay the body of the dead child, his first patient, he paused a moment, full of sadness, empty of panic, tired, almost detached. "The other one at least, that one shall not die. No, never." And as he walked from the ward he thought to himself with quiet bitterness: "At least now I know how to turn a patient, how to give an enema." And again, before he went to sleep, "I know so much. I know so horribly little. Diseases and corpses. Names and prognoses. But not enemas. And not people."

He fought a wild desire to rise and rush to the hospital, to sit at the living child's bedside. He lay still, commanding himself to know that such a flight would be self-indulgence. He pictured himself creeping from the house, racing through the streets to the hospital, forcing himself to enter quietly, taking up a vigil by the child's bedside. "And then what? If she changed color—if her breathing changed—her pulse—what then? What would I do?" Miserably, he tossed. His ignorance

124

was a living thing, detestable, full of agony. Guilt dried his lips. Horror and grief contended with guilt and ignorance to rule his panic. Suddenly in his confusion he saw the face of the dead child's mother, again he heard himself reassuring her cheerily. The vision jerked him upright. Instantly he was out of bed, flinging on his clothes.

He crept from the house like a criminal. As he rushed through the cold and empty streets to the hospital his mind whipped him ever to fresh speed, at times suggesting the sick child would be alive and well, completely cured when he arrived, and again picturing her dead, growing cold without breath, gone forever, like the first one. He reached the hospital. He made his way into the dark ward. From a corner a nodding attendant rose and goggled at him uncertainly. Abruptly he waved her back to her seat. The child was sleeping. He stared at her in the darkness, asking for a miracle, demanding his eyes to bore within and see the face of her ailment, the secret of her remedy. She had not changed. She breathed unevenly. Her mouth was partly open. A crust of thick saliva had formed in the oven of her fevered mouth and rimmed her lips. Occasionally one of her tiny hands made an unmeaning, spasmodic motion as if to clasp something. Cautiously he seated himself on the edge of her bed.

He knew, now, dully, almost with relief, that medicine was not for him. He was not a doctor. He was merely a student. What he had yet to learn could never be learned. Skoda, Rokitansky, Kolletschka, Hebra were an agonizing, an awesome distance removed. He could never know what they knew. The substance of their knowledge was beyond him. He pictured himself again, one of a tidy group of young gentlemen moving through the wards, clustered behind Skoda, standing beside a patient for ten or fifteen minutes, all examining the sick one minutely, detachedly, vying to be first with the right diagnosis, not to diagnose too quickly and be wrong, recalling a page of therapy and triumphantly suggesting the right remedy, moving on to the next bed, the next contest, the next triumph. And then out of the wards and back to the classroom. It had seemed so easy then. He had felt so bursting with assurance. Medicine was simple, really. One simply studied hard. One learned one's lessons. One applied them. And if one forgot, there was always the right book, on the right shelf, with the right answer.

But here was no problem, here in the bed on which he sat was no contest, no vying, no quick struggle to be first to remember. Here lay a human being, a sick child, the form of a small adult; here lay the passion of its mother and the quick love of its father. And it was disordered, it was sick, there was something wrong with it, something grievously wrong, and the cells of it cried out to him, Help me! Help me! and he could not answer. He could only pray. He could only sit and wait. He would wait. There was nothing else to do. And when it was over, when the child had recovered, he would leave, leave the hospital, leave Vienna, forever put behind him medicine, grateful that his ignorance could never harm another. He would not quit sorrowfully. He would embrace the outer world in a joyful tempest of relief for those he had not harmed. As to Skoda, he would make what amends he could. He had repaid his patronage and protection very badly. His vanity had tempted him and no desire to cure or to alleviate suffering. He had been momentarily intoxicated with a feeling of great powers and magic knowledge. Without Skoda's consent or knowledge he had taken charge of a patient. And he knew, doing this, that he was a student, not a doctor. He thought of the hour in which he would have to confront Skoda. His breathing came faster. His heart chilled. His stomach was a tumor full of pain and dread. No peace he had ever known seemed so sweet to him now as the thought that in a few hours he would be done with medicine forever.

The child stirred. From between its small, pale lips issued a slubbered sound, a ropy inspiration, a thick breathing, broken at the end with a little moan. He reached quickly for her wrist. The pulse was weaker, the double beat clearer. Each beat seemed now a definite double stroke. He looked at her, anguished, only able to watch. He confronted himself. Perhaps he had already waited too long. If there was a man who could help this child, that man was Skoda. From the beginning he had known that he would have to go to Skoda. It was no longer possible for him to bury this necessity. He would have to go to Skoda's house, to wake the great man up, to summon him out into the cold night, to bring him to see a ward patient, to save a patient who would have had an uneventful recovery if he had not interfered. But it was no longer himself that Skoda would be saving. Skoda must be brought to help a sick child. For himself, he was through. The child was now all that mattered. He looked away from the child's face. Through one of the high windows at the end of the ward the Vienna night was beginning to gray. He looked back at the child. She seemed to be sleeping more peacefully. She would be all right. There was still a vast reservoir of life left in her. For the first time he really prayed. It was done in a second, but it was quiet and empty of everything except gratitude and humility. He rose then and left the hospital to summon Skoda.

It was a long time before anyone answered Skoda's door. The sleepy servant at first refused to admit him. He ordered her to awaken Skoda. She goggled at him, dazed.

"You want a doctor. Dr. Skoda is a teacher. At the university, see? Go—get a doctor."

"I am a student of Dr. Skoda's. He will understand. Go

126

quickly. Tell him Semmelweis wants him to come to the hospital right away."

"But it is not time for sir doctor Skoda to go to the hospital. Sir doctor Skoda goes to the hospital only in the afternoons. You are making a mistake. You must find a regular doctor ——"

"Listen to me. You are not paying attention to what I am saying. There is a child sick. One of Dr. Skoda's patients is sick. He must come at once. Go! Rouse him."

"Listen to me, young sir. Dr. Skoda does not have sick patients. Dr. Skoda teaches. In any case, he does not rise until eight o'clock. No one has ever wakened Dr. Skoda——"

"Will you go up? Will you waken him at once?"

Ignaz Philipp looked about him. He saw the staircase. Mentally, he was preparing to push the servant aside, to rush upstairs, to go from room to room, if need be, looking for Skoda.

Skoda appeared at the top of the stairs. He was in his nightgown and he peered nearsightedly toward the candle held by the servant.

"What is it? What is it?"

"You must come to the hospital at once, Dr. Skoda. I'm afraid I have done something I should not have—a patient, a young child——"

"You, Semmelweis? What are you doing out at such an hour? What's the matter?"

"I need you, Dr. Skoda. At the hospital. That child you entrusted to me—I overstepped myself—I took still another one——"

"Your patient, is it? Don't worry about her. Is that what you've come here about?" He tried to see Ignaz Philipp more clearly. He had a sudden suspicion the young man was drunk.

"It's another patient, Dr. Skoda. Please! I have done something terrible—I——"

Ignaz Philipp slumped suddenly and put his hand over his eyes.

Skoda stared down at him, thunderstruck.

"Wait!" he called out after a moment. "I'll be right down."

He rushed back to his bedroom. What had the youngster done? Thoughts of a scandal at the hospital stabbed at him. He began to think of ways in which Ignaz Philipp might be protected and of ways in which he might protect himself.

When he clattered downstairs, still buttoning his clothing, Ignaz Philipp was gone.

"He went back to the hospital," the servant told him. "He said he couldn't wait."

Skoda rushed out into the night. This was bad, then. This was really bad. Young Semmelweis wasn't one to shout and rave. He was one of the quiet ones. And he knew far, far more than the usual student. If he had come to the house of the pro-

fessor, in the dead of night, to summon him to the hospital——
Skoda entered the hospital, ran down the corridor, entered the ward.

Ignaz Philipp was standing at the bedside of the dead child. Skoda stood beside him a moment. He saw the child was dead. He looked quickly about the sleeping ward. Everything was in order. Or were they all dead? He moved to look at another patient. The patient was breathing. So was the next and the next. He turned to Ignaz Philipp.

Ignaz Philipp looked away from the dead child.

"She died," he said, trying to keep his voice level.

"I see."

"I made a diagnosis, I verified it, I prescribed. I came back to sit beside her. And as I watched her, she died."

Skoda waited.

Ignaz Philipp walked to the bedside of the other child. Skoda followed, tense with waiting.

"And here is this other."

Skoda glanced at the sleeping child, saw what he saw, and turned back quickly to Ignaz Philipp.

"This one?"

"I took this one—you did not tell me to—I told the attendant I would prescribe for her——" He waited. Skoda said nothing.

"She seems to be sick of the same sickness."

Skoda leaned over the child for an unnecessary second glance.

"Yes," he straightened. "Yes," he said politely, "that seems to be very true."

"Before I do any more harm—before I disgrace you—disgrace the hospital—I had to get you—look, Dr. Skoda! It is such a little child, it's the child that matters, please, Dr. Skoda——"

"And this is all?"

"Help her, Dr. Skoda!"

"You have treated no one else?"

"Only this one."

Patients were beginning to stir, to sit up, to listen.

"Shall we walk into the corridor? Shall we consult there?"

He turned away and Ignaz Philipp walked with him.

"I will resign today," he said to Skoda in a low voice. "It is the blessing of God that I have killed no others."

"I see."

"I am an ingrate, and I do not beg you to forgive me. I ask only that you know from my heart how sorry I am. It is with complete relief that I leave medicine. I know now I was never meant to be a doctor."

They left the ward and entered the corridor. Skoda stopped. He put his hands in his overcoat pockets. Ignaz Philipp faced him, waiting for the remedy. Whatever came from Skoda's mouth would be the magic that would make the child's recovery certain. He waited, his mouth a little open. At last Skoda cleared his throat.

"Well, Semmelweis, that baby is going to die."

"Dr. Skoda! You don't tell me this baby is going to die?"

"I tell you that this baby cannot recover."

"But you will know what to give her——"

"She cannot live. She will die."

"But, Dr. Skoda—what will we do—what——"

"Semmelweis, this baby is going to die. She will expire before noon."

Ignaz Philipp hung his head. Guilt and sorrow crushed him utterly.

"I have done it," he said. "I have done it, I alone, I am the criminal, do with me what you will."

"I don't know that you have done anything, particularly. I don't know what all the fuss is about, really. She was going to die. I could have told you she was going to die—yesterday. I'm really surprised that you didn't see that yourself."

"She was going to die?"

"My dear Semmelweis, *all* of us are going to die, you know. This child was merely bound to die a little sooner. I wonder how you missed the signs? Tell me, my boy, what was your diagnosis?"

"I was confused, sir. If you had asked me then, I should not have been able to answer——"

"Children are almost always confusing. Even for me."

"After you left I went to my books. Soon the whole thing appeared to me quite plain. The child had cholera morbus."

"Not cholera infantum, eh?"

"No, sir. There did not appear to be prostration. Besides, she had been here more than five days. I believe death occurs in from three to five days, sir, after cholera infantum's onset?"

"That's quite right. It's evident that so far your reasoning was sound. I'm glad to see it."

Ignaz Philipp looked at Skoda uncertainly. The great man wasn't above an occasional joke. Perhaps this was one of his jokes.

"And you say the child will die, sir?" He waited, prepared to break into a hearty laugh.

"She will assuredly die. By, I think, eleven o'clock." Skoda was not joking. "Tell me how you arrived at your conclusion of cholera morbus?"

Ignaz Philipp frowned, painfully ticking off in his memory his research of many hours before.

"She had pain—abdominal pain—purging—she vomited—she had spasmodic contractions of her muscles—it is an acute catarrhal inflammation of the membranes of stomach and intestines——"

"I see. That is perfectly correct. Did you see mucus in her feces?"

"There was some mucus. The feces were quite green—pea green—like thick pea soup——"

"Like pea soup. Exactly. Always remember that. Like pea soup. And now the contractions——"

"She clenched and unclenched her little hand——"

"She clenched and unclenched her hand . . ."

"When spasms of pain gripped her, her muscles tensed——"

"I don't really think that's what the text means by spasmodic contractions. It must be much, much stronger than that —no, not produced by pain. Not so simple."

Ignaz Philipp waited humbly. The child's spasms might not have been the spasms Skoda had in mind. But they were certainly spasms. And the rest, all the rest definitely tallied.

"Now, as to the vomiting—a child vomits very easily, you understand. Vomiting is a symptom, certainly. But did she vomit persistently?"

"No, sir. She did not."

Ignaz Philipp had begun to shake. There was a roaring in his ears. He had killed two patients. He had missed a diagnosis. Please, God! he prayed, make it a complex disease, make it a disease I could not possibly have guessed . . . Ah, the poor children, the poor, poor babes . . .

"Now, as to those spots, Semmelweis—did you notice any spots?"

"Yes, sir!" he said, relieved. "They puzzled me at first. Then I remembered what you said about the really typical case being the exception and I cast about for an explanation."

"You found it?"

"I think so, sir." Skoda was playing with him. The child wouldn't die. It was going to be cholera morbus, after all. Now, if he would just utter the treatment—"I discovered fleas in the bed."

"I am not surprised," Skoda said dryly.

"No, sir. It is about time to try to get rid of fleas in our beds again."

"One must be very observant with spots, Semmelweis. Did you press these?"

"Yes, sir."

"Did they disappear on pressure?"

"Yes, sir."

Ignaz Philipp shut his mouth with a little click. Insect bites do not disappear on pressure. Rose-colored spots, disappearing when pressed, the child's nervousness, stupor, complete lack of appetite, its inability to contain urine or feces, the appearance of rapid wasting, the brown tongue, the cough——

"My God, Dr. Skoda!"

"Yes, my boy?"

"It was gastroenterocephalitis!"

"Exactly! Now we are getting somewhere! Have you seen Dr. Louis's fine work? I think we shall call it as he does— typhoid fever! That's what you were confronting, my boy. Now you have made the diagnosis you should have made in the first place. Typhoid fever, well advanced, in both cases exhibiting evidence of intestinal hemorrhage and perforation of the bowel. In short—they were doomed. Do you feel like a murderer now? No remedy is much good—for any illness. And these were beyond even our feeble bungling. What did you prescribe?"

"I took it from the book—a gallon of chicken broth—fed by mouth and by rectum——"

He stopped. There was the sound of footsteps in the corridor. He looked up. The blood drained from his heart. He paled. Tears started to his eyes. Down the hall, tiptoeing as rapidly as she dared, tenderly gripping a covered vessel of chicken broth, came the mother of the dead child.

Skoda glanced briefly at the woman, then at Ignaz Philipp. For the master of quick diagnosis the glance was more than sufficient. He understood instantly that the approaching woman was the mother of the dead or the dying child, that she was a poor woman, that she lived near the hospital, for the broth she carried was still steaming, that she was a laundress, for her hands were white and swollen, a sufferer from high-blood pressure, and a probable victim of kidney disease.

The woman had by now approached closely enough to recognize Ignaz Philipp. She came to him instantly, smiling. Another instant and the purport of his downcast head erased the smile from her face.

"What is it?" she cried. "What has happened?"

Skoda stared on at her silently. There was no doubt of hypertension. The kidney disorder would undoubtedly produce dropsy.

"Madam," said Ignaz Philipp, "I am sorry—I have to tell you——" He stopped. Skoda considered. It must then be the dead child, not the dying one, that was involved.

"Your child, madam, is dead. It expired, despite all the efforts of my colleague, sometime during the night. We have placed the cause of death as a disorder of the intestines called typhoid fever."

"She is dead?" the woman cried. "Dead? Little Lisl?" She seemed unable to grasp the fact of death. She turned to Ignaz Philipp. "But you told me, Doctor—you said she was well— you said——"

"I am sorry, madam—I am so very sorry——"

131

"Dead, madam," said Skoda. "You must bear up. It comes to all of us. It is a fact of life."

"But she was so little." The woman's face was ashen. She looked imploringly at Ignaz Philipp. Tears had begun to flow over her cold cheeks. She did not sob.

"Not too small to die," said Skoda. "Come, now, you will have others, perhaps you have already—think of them. Think of the others."

The woman turned a vacant face to Skoda.

"Madam," pleaded Ignaz Philipp, "there was nothing to do —I would give anything to bring her back to you—any-thing——"

"My Lisl!" the woman screamed suddenly.

"Be still, madam!" cried Skoda. Ignaz Philipp shut his eyes. He stood like a whipped schoolboy. His cheeks were wet.

"They warned me!" the woman shouted. "You are mur-derers, murderers, all of you! They warned me not to bring her to a hospital. What have you done to her? Where is my baby?"

"Madam!" said Skoda. He seized her shoulders. "If you do not conduct yourself quietly I shall have you removed from the hospital. There are other patients here."

The woman struggled in his grasp. "My baby!" she screamed again.

"It is no disgrace to be poor, but this place is provided for the sake of the poor. Such a child was your child. Neverthe-less she had every care that might be given to the rich. To those who can pay. You are fortunate, madam, that such a place as this is provided for people who have no means. If you have other children, it is quite possible we shall take care of them, too, in time. And of yourself and of your husband."

The woman eyed him, her face blank, the tears running from her face, falling upon her breast.

"My colleague conducted himself brilliantly. Your child was fortunate to receive his services. He did what he could in the face of the irredeemable. You owe him an apology. You will, in any case, contain yourself. You will not shout here. If you commit the least further outcry, I shall have you ejected."

He dropped his hands from her shoulders. The woman was quiet now. She looked uncomprehendingly at Skoda, then at Ignaz Philipp, then slowly back to Skoda.

"Your child is in there." Skoda pointed. He stood aside.

The woman did not move.

"In there," Skoda repeated, pointing again to the ward.

The woman surveyed them both again, her eyes begging the impossible. Then, a little hope still unconquerable in the corners of her eyes, she moved past them toward the ward where lay her dead child.

Skoda took Ignaz Philipp's arm. They walked on down the corridor.

"Hypertension," Skoda said briefly. "Unquestionably some kidney involvement. When she screamed—did you notice the chest sound? I think lower lobe involvement also."

"I felt very sorry for her," Ignaz Philipp said in a low voice. His shame for himself and for the scene he had just participated in was a fog of nausea in which he thought with difficulty.

"My dear Semmelweis"—Skoda halted—"I have been looking for an opportunity to speak to you on just this for some time. Your emotions are inappropriate. You must learn to detach them. They have no place in science. Pity, tears, sympathy have no known therapeutic value. As to your talk of quitting medicine, you can no more unlearn what you have learned than you can quit being a Hungarian because you dislike certain things about Hungary. You are what you are with the instruments you have been given. In time you will learn more. No matter what you are, you will never learn all there is to know, and your ignorance will always harm someone, be you grocery clerk, gravedigger, or engineer. Face that fact and leave your emotions behind you."

"I cannot bear to kill people. She looked at me yesterday with all her trust——"

"There you were as ignorant as she was. Hope is a dangerous emotion to play with. Give no one hope. Whether you are a doctor or not, all will someday die. There are no real remedies. All medicines are merely guesses. To do nothing is the best of all possible policies in internal medicine. Even to prevent death is merely to postpone the inevitable."

"I want to help people——"

"You help no one by running away. I will not even consider the possibility of your leaving. But if you left, do you think less people would die? Less would become sick? Less would need you? You talk nonsense, my boy. I, too, talked nonsense at your age. I have heard that you are accustomed to inveigh against medical protocol, against doctors standing together. Well, you have had a taste of it this morning. What do you think of it now? Do you think it would have done you or that woman or that dead child any good if I decided to be honest and throw a good student to the wolves as a scapegoat? And even so, being honest, could I honestly say it was you who caused the child's death? If you had diagnosed typhoid—what, then, would you have done about it?"

He clapped a hand on Ignaz Philipp's shoulder.

"It's been good for you," he said. "It's the best thing that could have happened. I tell you that frankly." His face broke into a smile. "Getting me up in the dead of night! Who but Semmelweis would have done such a thing? I thought you had

133

poisoned a whole ward! I was wondering how to word my resignation! Ah, now, another day has come, that baby is gone, there is a whole ward full waiting for us, we have to go on the same as ever. Come, now, we're up. By this time the mother has been sent away. We might as well call for the body, do the postmortem."

He took Ignaz Philipp's arm and walked down the corridor with him.

"Let's just look at those intestines. If we don't find Peyer's patches enlarged and necrotic—didn't you notice the child's spleen was enlarged?—I'll buy breakfast. What do you say?"

The body was brought. The postmortem was performed. Still full of sadness, Ignaz Philipp watched tensely. If the lymph follicles in the lower part of the child's small intestine were enlarged and sloughing dead tissue, then the child had died of typhoid fever and no remedy existed for her in the state of the disease in which he had taken her as patient.

"You see?" said Skoda suddenly.

Ignaz Philipp peered closely. His shoulders slumped. He sighed deeply.

"Typhoid beyond question," said Skoda. He put down his knife. He wiped his hands on a nearby towel.

"Come, now. We'll see what they have for breakfast. You lose, of course. But this time I'll let you off." He smiled at Ignaz Philipp and Ignaz Philipp winced, smiled shyly, sheepishly, still shaken.

They walked out of the autopsy room.

"Don't you think I have shown remarkable patience?"

"Yes, Dr. Skoda. I do."

"So do I. I like you, Semmelweis. We all like you. Now we will eat. Then you go off to bed. You're excused today. Go play with Markussovsky. Take care of yourself. And from now on—no more emotions."

Ignaz Philipp returned to his studies chastened and quiet.

"Do you know," he told Markussovsky, "I actually believed myself a person of learning. More than anything I am ashamed of how well I thought of myself."

"And have you found out yet what you will write your thesis about?"

"I am going to write about plants. You know, that's really all I know anything definite about. The life of plants. That, at least, harms no one."

"In Latin, remember—poor, poor Naci——"

*"De Vita Plantarum,"* said Chiari.

"The life of plants," echoed Ignaz Philipp. "That's what I'm going to write about."

"And tonight we're going out and celebrate. Chiari's got his appointment."

Ignaz Philipp looked at Chiari, surprised. Chiari beamed back at him.

"I'm to be an assistant instructor in obstetrics!"

"An assistant to the assistant assistant!" cried Markussovsky.

"Whatever!" Chiari assented. "Anyway, the appointment came down from the great Haller himself——"

"Chiari!" Ignaz Philipp cried, beaming. "You'll be my boss! You'll teach me now!"

"Don't be silly! You know more than I do!"

But Ignaz Philipp dropped to his knees on the floor and salaamed reverently at Chiari's feet. Markussovsky promptly kicked his behind. Chiari seized a nearby pitcher of water and poured it slowly over his head.

"Master!" spluttered Ignaz Philipp, and dived at his legs.

"It is the best thing that could have happened to him," Skoda told Rokitansky, Hebra, Haller, and Kolletschka. "Do you notice the change in him?"

"He doesn't seem so intense," said Kolletschka.

"Better for it to happen to him here, with us to protect him, than out in practice," Hebra said. "Now he'll settle down."

"It's very hard for the young to know that knowledge is the means and the end," said Rokitansky.

"He'll stay here now," predicted Haller.

"Of course he will," said Skoda. "At the best university in the world, safe, protected, following knowledge all his days —and what a job it's been just to give him all that!"

In the next three months Ignaz Philipp played joyously with Markussovsky and Chiari. He did not neglect his studies but he no longer studied with anxiety. A little time each day he worked on his thesis. A little time he crammed against the day of examination. He tried to avoid the clinics. At the bedside of patients he fought to ignore the patient, to think only of the illness and the remedy. He knew that the instant he relaxed, the instant he allowed the quick tendrils of his pity to reach for the patient, he would be lost, victim of emotions which had no place in medicine. He knew also that death was waiting to trick a man with pity, that pity was no weapon against the pitiless fact of mortality, that yearning could not cure. He did his best to teach himself this thing his masters had long ago learned and which they strove to pass on to him for his own good. In the evenings he rollicked, he drank heartily and cheerfully, the girls of Vienna had never seemed so fair or smiled so often. He sang, he danced, he wenched, he drank, and the rumors of his merriment reached the faculty and they, too, smiled, and remembered the time of their studenthood and wished they could dance and be privileged thus again. This was the Semmelweis they had been hoping for. This was the mixture, this was propriety, this would now be the balanced man of the university. He was a fine student, he had learned protocol, he reverenced knowledge, he could relax, he would be a fine teacher. Perhaps even a great one.

Skoda prepared to order him to attempt new researches and new attempts in auscultation, with particular regard to the stethoscope.

Rokitansky left off working on his monumental work on pathology to draw up a program of research into liver tissue with which he intended to entrust Ignaz Philipp.

Hebra considered attempting to divert him into skin-disease investigation and arranged quietly for him to take protocol at a private investigation he intended to conduct.

Kolletschka hovered hopefully in the background, instantly ready to help with any anatomical study that might occur to Ignaz Philipp, shyly hinting he would appreciate an assistant.

Professor Endlicher, overjoyed and amazed at Ignaz Philipp's sudden interest in botany, made him free of the botanical gardens, helped him with his thesis, guardedly imparted to him the curative powers of certain herbs he had just discovered. "I tell you," he said jubilantly to Skoda one day toward the end of the three months before graduation examinations, "this boy will one day be a botanist, a real botanist. He studies like I used to study. He soaks up knowledge like a sponge."

"Aha!" said Skoda later to Rokitansky. "When he told me that I said to myself, 'I thank you for your enthusiasm, my friend. I did not know this danger existed.' We'll take care of that! He'll be wasted on no botany, I promise you! Not after the pains we've taken. Botany! Sticks and leaves and dirty twigs!"

"What will you do? Do you want me to talk to him?"

"Do? What do you think I'm going to do?"

"Karl!" reproached Hebra. "Have you forgotten? Joseph's president of the board of examiners!"

There began the period of final examinations.

"Mr. Semmelweis," asked Professor Hildebrand, head of the department of internal medicine, "what is pain a symptom of?"

Ignaz Philipp observed him with dread.

"Of inflammation, of neuralgia, of swelling, of——"

"You have omitted one long pain!"

"Of sciatica."

Ignaz Philipp studied Professor Hildebrand's face. There was no expression there. The professor wrote a moment, then looked up.

"Mr. Semmelweis, what is hemorrhage a symptom of?"

Ignaz Philipp reflected a moment, gulped, and plunged. These were extraordinary questions. Suddenly he remembered that Professor Hildebrand did not like Skoda. His throat dried; he blinked in dismay. Professor Hildebrand listened, wrote, spoke, wrote again, all with never a change of expression.

"What is fever a symptom of?"

The two hours ended. Professor Rosas examined him in ophthalmology. Professor Wattman and Professor Haller examined him in surgery.

The day ended.

"I have failed," he told Markussovsky. "I know I have failed. There was not a smile on their faces. Not one."

"You worry too much. It was like that for all of us. It's only when they frown. That's when you have to worry."

"Remember," warned Chiari, "tomorrow comes chemistry. Remember Stauern. He's going to ask you what is gypsum. Remember what you must say."

"Calcium sulphate."

"No, Naci! Not calcium sulphate!"

"But gypsum is calcium sulphate!"

"That isn't what Stauern wants to hear. You want to flunk just say calcium sulphate. What Stauern wants to hear is calcium carbonate. And you *say* calcium carbonate!"

"But it isn't true! Anybody knows that gypsum——"

"Will your saying calcium carbonate *make* it calcium carbonate? Won't it be calcium sulphate just the same?" asked Markussovsky gently.

Ignaz Philipp subsided.

"Calcium carbonate." He shrugged helplessly.

"Calcium carbonate," he said next day.

"Good!" said Stauern.

He probed a foul-smelling bone fistula with a silver instrument. The silver emerged tarnished and black.

"What makes this silver black?"

"It is possible that it might be hydrogen sulfide——"

"It is possible you are ignorant of chemistry also! That is acetic acid. And it is acetic acid which dissolves the bone and it is acetic acid alone by which one recognizes osseous suppuration! Acetic acid! The principle of vinegar!"

And later that morning Professor Klein examined him in obstetrics.

"What occasions changes in the skin of pregnant women?"

"There is a certain tendency to darkening in certain areas —a—a deposition of pigment——" Ignaz Philipp glanced at Professor Klein hopefully.

"Good! What kind of pigment is it?"

Ignaz Philipp's mind clawed helplessly on the smooth cliffs of his memory.

"Well, well?"

"As far as I know there aren't any proofs, any investigations——"

137

"It's disgusting. Student after student! You're all alike. Evidently you, too, are a follower of this new positivism, eh? You must have your scientific proofs, eh? Your investigations? Let me remind you, Mr. Semmelweis, a doctor still relies upon observation."

Ignaz Philipp tried to think. He looked up, puzzled, mutinous.

"Oh yes," said Klein promptly, "you are going to repeat that there are no investigations, you are a man of science, I can see that. Let me tell you you are much too clever for anything so simple as observation of patients. Anyone can see that. But haven't you ever seen—haven't any of your fellow scientists ever told you—that carbon is deposited on the skins of pregnant women?"

Ignaz Philipp gasped.

"Yes, carbon! I can wipe it off with my hand! Thus the pigments are carbon!"

The second long day ended.

"I have failed," he told Markussovsky again. "If I didn't know it before, I know it now. What is this hostility? Why do they all behave so hostilely all of a sudden?"

"If you'd failed you'd have been told about it by now, I assure you. The word travels through stone walls. It has a special osmosis all its own. They're not really hostile. They all have some special theories, that's all. And they want to be sure you're a convert. Did you say calcium carbonate?"

"I said calcium carbonate."

"Then that's all there is to it, Naci. That's one thing you can rely on—if you said calcium carbonate—you've passed chemistry. Did he do his trick with a silver probe and diseased bone?"

"He did. And he claimed it was acetic acid——"

"Did you argue with him?"

"I did not."

"You're safe. What do you care what he thinks? Does it alter the truth? Give him the answer he wants—and pass the examination."

"Remember Galileo?" asked Chiari. "They made him recant and he recanted. But under his breath he said: 'The world revolves, all the same.' "

"Don't worry about it, Naci. You're almost through now. Tomorrow you give your thesis. Tomorrow, my boy, you can fight your silly head off. It's expected of you!"

Next day, in the examination room, he faced the commission which was to examine him on the thesis for his doctorate.

In the center of a small group of professors seated at a long table sat Skoda, president of the commission. He did not look up.

138

"The candidate, Ignaz Philipp Semmelweis, offers a thesis titled: *'De Vita Plantarum,'* " announced Professor Haller. There was a short silence. Skoda raised his head. He looked at Ignaz Philipp. There was no recognition in his eyes.

"You have written badly," he said coldly and levelly. "Your Latin is atrocious." He looked down at the thesis. It was true, the thesis was badly written. The Latin was almost childish. It wasn't possible, it seemed, that such a student could have fallen in love with botany on such short acquaintance. And yet one could take no chances. He must be broken of botany. There was no satisfaction in it. It was just a thing that had to be done. A fact. Skoda raised his head.

"Which plant liquid could replace quicksilver in therapy?"

Ignaz Philipp reeled, then rallied. There was nothing in botany which had been proven the equal or even substitute for quicksilver in the cure of any disease. The brutality of the attack dismayed him. Then forgetting Skoda and the amazing attack, he began to recite ailments which quicksilver had not benefited and for which quicksilver was specified, suggesting herbs to replace it. As he spoke his tone became more confident, more spirited. His reply ended. There was no sound from the commission, no change in their expressions.

"If there were no quicksilver, what would botany suggest in its place?"

Parrying endlessly, turning now to this questioner, now to another, attacking, defending, losing a little ground, gaining a little ground, Ignaz Philipp upheld his thesis. At the end of seventy minutes Skoda glanced noncommittally at his watch.

Ignaz Philipp ended. He stood waiting. Skoda looked at his watch again, shut it, rose.

He glanced for a moment at the faces of his fellows on the commission. They nodded almost imperceptibly.

"It is the sense of this commission," he said coldly, "that you have defended your thesis with care and thought worthy of finer studies." Now for the first time he smiled. "There is a poet in you, Mr. Semmelweis. I had not suspected it. I should like to presume that you someday write upon the importance of emotions in medicine. I have offered this theme to my students for a long time," he said, turning to the commission, "but so far none has done it. You"—he turned again to Ignaz Philipp, his eyes twinkling a little—"you would be the one to do it." He paused.

"I wish to become a healing doctor, sir professor," Ignaz Philipp said haltingly.

"You do not want to write, and I can safely assume that you do not want to practice botany, but medicine."

Ignaz Philipp bowed his head respectfully.

"All things have their limitation, Mr. Semmelweis. You

have had an opportunity to explore the limitations of botany. You may go."

On the bulletin board next day his thesis was graded Fair. His discussion was marked Bene. For the rest he had not failed a single subject. He had passed all. It was the second of March 1844. Until the fourth of March he and Markussovsky and Chiari did not draw a sober breath. The streets of Vienna resounded with their exultation. They awoke on the fifth of March in a tavern and through their aching heads laughed at one another's faces.

"Let us go home, at least, and change," said Markussovsky.

"You've got to be sober enough to graduate, Naci." Chiari grinned.

"Let's have a drink first, then go home."

"Let's go home first, then have a drink."

The letter was waiting on Markussovsky's mantel. It had been sent over by Rokitansky. Ignaz Philipp opened it, smiling at the familiar handwriting of his father.

"A little money?" asked Chiari, as Ignaz Philipp started to read.

"What's the matter! What's happened!" cried Markussovsky.

Ignaz Philipp held the letter and looked at them.

"My mother," he said harshly. "Oh, Marko! It's Mother! It's my mother!"

"Sick——?"

"Sick, Naci——?"

"She died . . . She's dead . . ." His face was an ache of bewilderment, like the face of a child beaten without cause. He sat down clumsily. They looked at one another. Suddenly he put his face in his hands and began to cry.

Later, much later, they helped him pack, they put him into a coach, they said what they could, they pressed their hands upon his. He frowned at them, bewildered. He could not keep the tears back. He did not know he was crying.

And so he went home.

A few days later his name was read out at graduation ceremonies. There was a brief flurry when it became evident he was not present. Then the name of the next candidate was called.

# ELEVEN

HE remembered nothing of the journey. His grief enclosed him. He was occasionally aware of jolting, of movement, on and on and on. The hundred-and-twenty-three-mile journey from Vienna to Buda took four days. The long hours droned miserably on. He was not conscious of the passage of time. He stared out at the landscape. He was unaware that it changed. He knew only that it moved. The movement lulled him. The fields were white. Snow sparkled in the sunlight. In the moonlight it lay clear and blue. He saw nothing. He thought only of his mother, gone from him forever, and he cried almost without ceasing. He thought of her face, of how it looked when he was a child. He thought of her smiling, he saw her frown, saw her good humor, her sadness, saw her face loom close to his before she blew out the candle, loom close, felt her kiss, saw her straighten, felt a small rebellion as she blew the candle, moved away. Terror exploded in him. He ripped the tissue of his thoughts and fled the fragments. She would kiss him no more. The terror died, drowned in misery, blurred in the swift anguish of his tears.

A passenger beside him moved nervously away, hunched toward the other side of the stagecoach. Ignaz Philipp was barely conscious that he was not alone. He was indifferent. He sat within the kernel of his grief. Somewhere, outside the shell, there was an inconsequent world.

The tears ran steadily down his cold cheeks. The stagecoach lurched, jolted on again. He remembered a day when they had romped together, she was like a young girl, that day, dancing in the garden, her skirts flying, her hair tumbling, and he chased her and she screamed, and suddenly, in mid chase, she whirled and stooped and caught him up and held him to her, panting. "I've caught you!" he cried, wriggling. "No, no!

141

I've caught *you!*" Through his tears he smiled again. Years later his older flesh creased into a smile, linked with that child and that mother again. And while he smiled the tears burst out sorely.

For that dancing girl, that lovely smell of mother, that intoxicating laughter, was dead now. She was gone. He could never hear the sound of her again, any sound of a thousand sounds of her living, her step, her scolding, her questions, her golden advice, her croon. In Vienna he could always stop in the midst of a day and in his memory hear her and see her. He could know that in just a few hours, a few days, he could be with her and the memory would be flesh and blood.

And now this was true no longer. This separation was not just for a little while. It was forever. She was dead. Ignaz Philipp knew what the dead looked like. He knew their silence, their odor, the touch of them, their passive remoteness, their separation from the living. That was how his mother was. He adored his mother. More than anything in the world he adored his mother. She was his conspirator, his playmate, the final authority on what was right or wrong, and always with love, with sober, patient, tender love, always for him, not what was right or wrong for the world but always for him, for him alone.

Sometimes it was as if she had no other children, no husband, even. But he knew that each of them, his father, his brothers and sisters, was given the same love. There was no refuge now. There was no longer any mother refuge. A chasm ripped through the thought of family. His mother was gone. He felt her hand on his shoulder. "Ignaz, do you know your father loves you best? You alone do not oppose him." He saw her grave eyes, he felt the love of her. It did not matter what she was saying. The steady tears spurted and fell.

After the funeral he sat in the grocery one day alone with his father. Joseph was changed. Ignaz Philipp remembered him as huge and towering, full of bulk, erupting shouts. His clothes now seemed too large for him. His skin seemed to fit him loosely. He had a grief remote. It was different from the grief of any of the children. He had lost something else in Thérèse, something the children could not know. He was a little strange now to all of them. His role had altered. Half of him had gone.

The store bell tinkled. The postman entered. He tiptoed in, his head was on one side, he hesitated a moment as if to speak a consolation, he shook his head, he tiptoed out.

"Bills," said Joseph quietly. "We get more bills than customers nowadays." He spoke without accent and without interest. "Here, Ignaz Philipp. Here are some letters for you."

Markussovsky, Chiari, Skoda, Rokitansky, Kolletschka, and

one from Haller. He opened them, read them quickly, passed them to Joseph.

"My friends, Father. They are sorry about Mama."

"From Vienna, eh? Your professors too?"

"Yes, Father."

"They think well of you, Ignaz Philipp. I'm glad to see that. I wish your mother knew."

"She knew, Father. I wrote. Writing is so hard for me. I could have written oftener. I tried to tell you both everything that was happening——"

"No one is complaining, boy. You're all right. You've done fine. Just fine. You're happy? You like what you're doing?"

"I've graduated, Father. I forgot to tell you."

"That's fine. I'm glad to hear it. Very commendable. You're a good boy, Ignaz Philipp."

"I didn't get my diploma."

"Ah, so? Well, that's how it goes. Don't worry about it, Ignaz Philipp. You're a good boy. You've always been a good boy."

"I can always get it. I have to go back to Vienna."

"Well, that's fine, then. Maybe they'll send it to you."

"No, I have to go back. I have to stand up and promise things. Officially. Not to hurt anybody, always to help people. Things like that."

"They ought to know you wouldn't hurt anybody. I remember once . . ." He sat silent. And he remembered Ignaz Philipp wincing in the market place while the barber shaved a man. ". . . I remember once . . ." And he remembered Thérèse's face as he told her this. "These bills!" he said. "Look at them. Every which way."

"Many bills, Father?" Ignaz Philipp saw his mother's strange, still face as she lay yellow-waxen in the coffin. "Many bills? Lots of them, eh? From everybody? Do you want me to help you? This is—— Do you want me to——"

"Just bills. They don't matter. Only bills. I wonder where Joseph is?"

"Yes. Now that you speak of it, I wonder . . ."

"Ah, this whole store . . ."

"Bad, Father? Bad, eh?"

"Throw it away! Out with it!"

"What can you do? What do you think?"

"From all your professors, now, Ignaz Philipp. That's good, you know. You'll have a fine practice . . . Soon, boy?"

"I don't know, Father. I hadn't thought about practice. I was going to stay there a while."

"Good, good. You know best. Don't worry. I can manage."

"Do you want me to start practicing, Father?"

"You do what you have to. You know best. Will you come back here?"

143

"I want to learn a little more, Father. You know—I don't want to hurt anybody—there's a lot to learn——"

"And then come back here. Back to Hungary, boy. Hungary needs you now as never before. It's true, boy."

"Lower your voice, Father."

"Everybody's a spy nowadays. They hear through walls. They run quick, the little mice, and tell the big mice. The big mice run to the palace and tell the rats. They're afraid now."

"All over Europe they say it's the same, Father."

"Revolution shakes the thrones, son. Everywhere but Hungary. Soon, soon, soon it's coming, it's coming here. Any hour, and day. They're frightened. They know. And we'll kill them all. Once and for all we'll be rid of them."

"Be careful, Father."

"It's been the same since the beginning. They crush us. They beat us. They enslave us. We revolt. Quickly they give in. We will get a constitution. We will be governed by Hungarians. We can speak our own language. Then the revolt is over. We lay down our arms. We wait. The promises are broken. The process begins again."

"This year Hungarian school children can learn their lessons in Hungarian, though——"

"A sop, my boy. A little sop. They're frightened. France is erupting again. Belgium and Holland have thrown off the yoke. The thrones are tottering, boy. All over Europe there is the music of clanking chains. The slaves are pulling at them. This time feudalism will die forever."

"And Kossuth is out of jail."

"It *is* good you weren't here when they jailed him. Wholesale arrests, men and women sentenced on suspicion, no trial whatever. The government opened any letters it wanted to. And Kossuth only tried to publish that we had been promised free speech, freedom of religion, our own constitution, our own language. And that we hadn't been granted these things the King agreed to. The schools are still full of spies. Everything relating to human freedom has been inked out of the schoolbooks. Yes, Kossuth is out of jail. At his trial they couldn't find a single witness against him. So they put him in jail for three years, anyway. And he's a member of the Diet now. We've won that much. It's coming, boy. There will be a revolution. It's coming any day."

"There's so much I didn't know. You don't hear in Vienna."

"No, you don't hear in Vienna. I can see that. I can understand that clearly."

"But even there, Father, they've had trouble. Lots of trouble. Even there they have begun to cry for freedom. It's dangerous to talk. But the talk goes on."

"They talk a lot in Vienna. They always have."

"But never before about revolt, Father."

144

"In the university?"

"Even in the university. Even in the medical school. The Conservatives support their conservative views on medical treatment by joining the Conservative political party. The Liberals wait their chance. The old ones cling to the past. Let anyone oppose them and he is a rebel, a political Liberal, his science, his proofs are political maneuverings by Liberals, and they rush clamoring to the Emperor. Yes, Father, even in medicine, you see. Even in medicine. Politics and medicine."

"The day is coming, boy. When it comes your place will be here."

"Yes, Father."

"Hungary, my boy. Your country. Hungary."

"You mustn't get too involved, Father. Speak softly. Be careful. Be prudent. Wait for the time."

"It doesn't matter, boy. Nowadays, it doesn't matter. Business is wretched, I might as well tell you. I don't know what's coming next."

"I don't think I'm going to be needing my allowance much longer—I think maybe I can give it up now——"

"That isn't necessary. That isn't necessary, boy. We've got enough to manage a little longer. But I've never seen times so bad. So much credit. So little money. So many poor. The country is bankrupt. We bleed our money into Austria, out of our veins into Austria, to keep the Austrian army strong enough to crush us. You see how things are . . ."

"I won't leave. It's clear my place is here. Helping."

"Oh, no, son. Your time isn't yet. Go back—what is it you have to get?—and when the time comes——"

"My diploma. I'll go back and get it and return to Hungary. I'm here now. I want to stay heré."

"You must go back, boy."

"It's my country, too, Father——"

"You must go back. There is nothing for you here. Prepare. Be ready."

"What you want, Father," Ignaz Philipp said at last. "That's what she always wanted."

Joseph fumbled tiredly among the bills. He put down his glasses, picked them up and put them on again. He bent and opened a drawer.

There was nothing more to be said.

"I will go back, Father."

"Yes," Joseph said absently.

The shop bell jangled. Joseph, his eldest brother, entered. Ignaz Philipp rose.

"Hello, Joseph," he said awkwardly.

"Hello, Ignaz Philipp." Joseph was noncommittal. "Father, I have only managed to collect a hundred kroner."

"Well, well, that's a hundred, at least . . ."

145

Joseph turned to Ignaz Philipp.

"People are poor these days," he said levelly. He inspected Ignaz Philipp briefly. He tried to think of something more to say "It's good weather. Fine."

"Yes," said Ignaz Philipp. He wanted wretchedly to be one of them. She was gone who made him so.

They had different lives now. They were alien people, not children, not brothers and sister, but adults, dreaming other dreams, apart even from one another. "I love you," he wanted to cry. "I love you all! I want you! I need you! Take my love! Be my family!" They moved about him decorously, curiously, their curiosity soon satisfied, they made conventional noises to one another and he responded. One day he shook his father's hand, bade him Godspeed, wandered into the street, stole quietly to the cemetery, wept there, died a little there. When night came he left the cemetery and took the stagecoach back to Vienna.

At high noon, on a bright April day, Professor Haller rose from his chair among the assembled faculty and stepped to the front of the dais. He carried with him a black cardboard box which he placed upon the lectern. He consulted a piece of paper. He looked up and surveyed the students before him. "Ignatius Philippus Semmelweis."

Ignaz Philipp rose. In the tail coat and the fine linen which Chiari, Markussovsky, and Rokitansky had loaned him he walked to the rostrum. He felt the eyes of the class assuring him he did not belong to any such raiment. Then triumph roared up in him, beating strong wings, his chest tightened, his breath came fast. The great moment had come.

"*Spondite,*" the Latin harangue began, "do you promise to live up to academic ideals, to work only for the benefit of your patients, not for money alone nor for the sake of anything else, and always to uphold your ideals?"

Haller stared at him. The trappings of ceremony vanished. The question was direct. He answered from the bottom of his soul.

"*Spondio!*" said Ignaz Philipp. "I promise."

The gold chain around Haller's neck glinted as he turned to the lectern. He picked up a black cardboard box and handed it to Ignaz Philipp. Within was his diploma. Ignaz Philipp bowed. Thereafter he went to the administrative offices of the university. He recorded his matriculation. He came to the last line of the form. "Is it your intention to live in Vienna?" Ignaz Philipp dipped his quill deeply into the inkhorn. He wrote in large letters: "No!"

"Not stay in Vienna?" Rokitansky asked gently that night. Skoda, Markussovsky, Chiari, Hebra, Kolletschka gathered about Rokitansky's festive table looked up quickly.

"It seems impossible, sir," Ignaz Philipp said apologetically.

146

There was a silence.

"Did you find some difficulty—home?" Skoda asked.

"It's not that I don't want to stay here———"

"There are no difficulties we could not solve," Skoda said slowly, significantly.

"I think I know what it is," Markussovsky said.

They turned to him.

"Things are not well in Hungary," he said diffidently. Ignaz Philipp watched him closely. "Naci here has just returned from the country of his birth. He feels perhaps his duty lies near his countryside . . ."

"Yes," said Ignaz Philipp. "Yes . . . That . . ."

"Part of your heart is buried there," said Chiari deferentially, "but———"

"It's no good saying 'but it's all one country,'" Skoda burst out. "Because it isn't. And we all know it isn't. You and I, Karl, we know that Bohemia is part of Germany. But we know where we were born. No, Semmelweis. It's no good saying that. But you can serve your country best—right here."

"Someday, when you go back, you will be armed to teach. The more a man knows the more he can teach. Do you know enough yet?"

Ignaz Philipp turned confusedly to Rokitansky.

"I know enough to heal—a little. At least I could be a landarzt."

"But you're no landarzt. You're no country doctor. You gain nothing by sacrificing yourself and dropping into such a life. And how would that serve your country better than lesser brains are already doing?"

"It's something else," said Skoda.

"It's my father," Ignaz Philipp burst out wretchedly.

What they had just told him he had told himself days before, over and over again. And yet each time the thought of his father, the face of brother Joseph accused him.

"Does your father ask you to return?" Skoda asked.

"No. He tells me to stay on until I am ready. But———"

"Is there any fight you can wage, say that you are back in Buda? Some campaign?" Markussovsky asked.

"There is none. I just feel———"

"I love your emotions." Skoda smiled. "You are feeling again. Pfooh with the facts! Pfoosh with the obvious! Let us feel!"

"I don't know what to do. I really don't know what to do," Ignaz Philipp confessed sadly. "Do you think———"

"Well," said Rokitansky gaily, "we'll talk of it tomorrow. We'll see how you're prepared, we'll figure something out. Tomorrow'll settle everything."

"What a poor household," murmured Skoda. "No dancing girls, no wine———"

"Hoh!" cried Rokitansky. "Where is that girl! Dance in here, girl! They're insulting us! Bring us some wine!"

"And be careful, Naci!" cried Chiari. "If you get any spilled on my shirt——"

"Or my coat——" said Markussovsky.

"Or my necktie——" said Rokitansky.

"He's got to be out of here by midnight," said Skoda. "He's got to put those pants back on the burgomeister that died in Ward Three this morning——"

"The pants," said Ignaz Philipp imperturbably, "the pants are my own."

"He's right," said Skoda. "Up or down—there isn't a girl in Vienna that wouldn't recognize those pants!"

The servant girl rushed in with wine.

"You see?" said Markussovsky. "The faculty knows everything. Even the girls of Vienna."

"To the pants!" said Chiari gravely. He raised his glass.

"To the pants—and the Hungarian inside them," cried Markussovsky.

They drank.

"Once again—to the girls outside them," shouted Kolletschka unexpectedly.

Ignaz Philipp looked about the table. His eyes misted. He thought of Thérèse. If she could have seen this. The faces smiled at him confidently, delightedly. These were his friends. They believed in him, they honored him. He lowered his eyes.

Next morning he sat with Rokitansky to decide his future.

"I have been so occupied with my writing. I have lost touch with so many things. I should have been advising you long before this. Tell me, it is surgery you want, isn't it?"

"Yes, sir. I want to be a surgeon."

"I am not going to pretend that I did not know this. We all knew it, Skoda, Hebra, Kolletschka—a student pins his interest to one thing one day and to something else the next. To tell the truth we had combined against you. We were pretty confident you would never continue with surgery. And if you did, we were sure we could persuade you to stay here and teach it."

"Teach surgery?"

"You'd have to study a little more, of course."

"But I don't want the academic life."

"You don't?"

"I don't mean to say anything—forgive me—but it seems so sterile—you learn so much and yet you never apply it——"

"Oh, we have our babies. We're not entirely sterile."

"Books, yes."

"Students too."

"But I want to practice—I want to help people—to make them well—to erase the pain from their faces——"

148

"Perhaps something one of us has said has put you off. You mustn't believe that Skoda means all he says, you know. He expresses himself strongly against medicines because so many of them have let him down. He hasn't been able to find any real scientific basis in them. He's not really a nihilist, my boy. It's his pupils who give him that name."

"I've heard him say——"

"I know. I've heard him too. But he's like the French, you see. Deep down he's a member of the expectant school. He thinks Nature is the best healer. And sometimes, most of the time, I'm inclined to agree with him. I don't practice. I can speak only from dissection. But often and often I've seen evidence of healing beyond our skill, healing by nature. I've seen the healed lesions of a tuberculosis of which the patient had never complained or been aware. And yet no medicine we have will cure tuberculosis. No, my boy. We don't throw up our hands. We devote ourselves to knowledge, to studies from which indisputable good may come. Skoda simply disdains remedies which have shown themselves over and over again mystic and hopeful and woefully fallacious. He contents himself with diagnosis. I am most interested in the anatomy of disease. We don''t throw up our hands."

"That is one reason I like surgery. It is concrete, at least, something provable . . ."

"You want to be a surgeon, then."

"I really believe so."

"You feel you are fitted for it?"

"It is you, sir, who can best tell me that. Myself—sometimes I am quite confident—sometimes not."

"You would make a good surgeon."

Ignaz Philipp flushed. His spirit leaped.

"Yes, you would make a good surgeon. Tell me, how many surgeons are there in Germany?"

Ignaz Philipp looked at him blankly. Surgeons? The world must be full of surgeons. Germany——?

"Take your time . . . name me a few outstanding men . . ."

"Well, there's Dieffenbach."

"Dieffenbach, of course."

"And von Graefe——"

"Yes——"

"And Strohmeyer——"

Rokitansky kept his serious eyes on Ignaz Philipp's flushed face. He nodded.

"And of course Langenbeck."

"Langenbeck."

"And Simon, and—and——"

"Precisely."

"There must be more. There must be dozens more."

"There are any number of barbers all over the world. But

149

we are speaking of surgeons . . . outstanding men . . . fine operators . . . the science for which Germany is noted . . ."

Ignaz Philipp waited.

"No, there aren't many surgeons, I'm afraid. And from your point of view this is fine. A small field, a young man aching to practice, full of science and honesty and skill. But there is a reason for so few surgeons. Actually there is barely enough work for those few we have. For surgery is the last resort. There it is, my boy. It is said, but you must face it. Surgery is the one cure more dangerous than any disease. Seven, eight, nine of every ten who undergo the knife never leave the hospital alive. You know this, don't you?"

"I had not thought of it quite as you put it——"

"No, a heart like yours thinks only that with what you have been taught and what you desire for humanity you can somehow reform all that. Am I not right?"

"I thought—with help—I could do better——"

"But we must admit that though you may someday be greater, you are not and will not for some years be as good as the men you have named."

"Yes, sir."

"And that these great men lose seven, eight, and nine out of every ten patients. Is that how you design to help the suffering? That is an insulting question. I withdraw it. I did not mean insult. The force of my reasoning carried me away. Will you pardon me?"

Ignaz Philipp put out his hands.

"I know. I wanted to be a surgeon too. There will be no surgery in our time. Shock, bleeding, and infection—these are the enemies of surgery. The planet holds no cure for them. Conquer them—and be a surgeon. Dare them and your patients die."

"There is another thing," Ignaz Philipp said in a low voice.

"It is money, isn't it," Rokitansky said confidently.

"My allowance comes less often now," Ignaz Philipp said humbly. "I have been home, I have seen why. Things are not well, you understand. Business . . . I should help . . ."

"But not in surgery. Another field, perhaps. There are many other fields. It isn't that surgery is well paid even. Think it over, my boy. I will help you. Think it over."

"Is there any field like obstetrics?" Chiari asked that night. "Everybody has to be born, at least."

"Every woman is a potential customer," said Markussovsky.

"Listen to us talk about customers," Ignaz Philipp said wearily.

"It's on your account, my friend!"

"You're the one who needs customers, Naci."

"Can't we say patients?"

150

"All right, patients. But what's the matter with obstetrics?"

"I don't know anything about obstetrics, for one thing."

"Oh, come now. You've learned something. You know as much as a midwife, at least. You passed your finals, didn't you?"

"I've never thought about obstetrics."

"Well, think about it, Naci. That's what we're telling you."

"But I'm not prepared."

'Well, and supposing you were prepared . . ."

The talk flowed on. Occasionally he noticed their faces, enthusiastic, animated. The past month pressed upon him wearily, the final examinations, the thesis, the death of his mother, his decision to set up as a surgeon, to leave Vienna, his talk with Rokitansky that day, the miscarriage of his unborn surgical career. Obstetrics, he thought, well and so obstetrics. And what do I know of obstetrics? I know nothing and care less. I know a little. I know what a student knows. Maybe I know more obstetrics than I think I know. Probably I know less . . . So, obstetrics . . . Still—it's a busy field . . . Skin work I do not like—definitely I do not like skin work—and as to remedies, what was it Rokitansky said about remedies? *The best course is to provide for the patient the most favorable conditions under which nature can heal . . .* That throws out most of medicine, all right, but it fits obstetrics, that's right! There's one field where a doctor can certainly provide the best conditions under which nature can heal . . . there, too, is Nature at her best . . .

"I beg your pardon?" he said aloud.

"No one said anything," Chiari said. "We've been sitting here waiting for you to say something."

"What did you say? What were you waiting for me to answer?"

Markussovsky threw up his hands.

"Chiari," he said, "I will toss a coin with you to see who will hit him over the head."

"We want to share the apartment," said Chiari. "We want you to move from Rokitansky's house and share these rooms. I'm going to move soon. I'm going to live in the hospital. We want you to live here while you take the course in midwifery."

"You know, babies . . ."

"First the man does something to the woman—and then they have a baby——"

"And they call for a doctor——"

"And the doctor gets rich——"

"All right, all right," said Ignaz Philipp. "I was thinking. It's very possible you're right. The more I think of it—— Yes, you're right. I'm going to have a try at obstetrics."

"Fine!"

"That's a very intelligent decision, Naci."

151

"You can enroll tomorrow. And just think! I'll be one of your teachers!"

"And you'll move in with us?"

Ignaz Philipp looked at Markussovsky without speaking.

"He's off again!" cried Chiari.

"Naci! Didn't we just ask you——"

"Marko," said Ignaz Philipp, "I've never been away."

They moved his few effects from Rokitansky's home. They went with him to the university and superintended his enrollment for the course in midwifery. Then they went rollicking out into Vienna. Ignaz Philipp left them early. He went to his new home. From a window in the apartment in the Alservorstadt he looked out over the glacis, the park, the wide parade ground, to the dim distance and the tall buildings beyond. He stood thus in the darkness a long time. The time for play was over.

Next morning he reported to Professor Klein.

"Your name?"

"Ignaz Philipp Semmelweis."

"Age?"

"Twenty-six years."

"Place of birth?"

"Ofen- -Buda . . ."

"Hungary! . . . Religion?"

"Catholic."

"I understand you know Professor Chiari?"

"Yes, sir."

"You will find him in the autopsy room, I believe. Your classes will begin immediately. You may now leave."

Chiari took him to the graduate students' quarters. He was allotted a bed.

"You'll see—you'll use it. I've gotten so I sleep more here than at the Alservorstadt. That's one reason I'm moving here for good. Anyway," said Chiari, "that's the first step. You're enrolled, you've got your bed, and you've now started your eight weeks' course."

"So far it's been easy."

"It's not too bad, Naci. You'll see. The first four weeks you'll be on day duty. The last four you work nights. The way we do, we work in pairs. There's forty-eight taking the course. We keep a journal covering each twenty-four hours and everything must be put down, medicine prescribed, observation, patient's complaints, and so forth. You and your partner will keep the journal three times for twenty-four hours each time, during the eight weeks' course."

"Pair me with a writer, Johann—I beg of you—a writer! How many patients are there?"

"In the whole Lying-in Hospital—four hundred and forty-one beds—usually full. In the Pay Division, which doesn't

152

concern us, fifty-seven. In the Second Division, where the midwives study under Bartsch, and which doesn't concern us either, one hundred and thirty. And here, my friend, in the First Division, two hundred and fifty-seven. And don't worry about the writing. I've paired you with Conrad Stiegler. That boy would rather write than deliver. Everything he sees, he makes a note. I had him as a student. Don't worry, I'm looking out for you, Naci."

"Two hundred and fifty-seven patients!"

"Come on, we'll walk through the wards on the way to class, you'll meet the other boys, I'll show you around. And, Naci! Before we start—one thing! Did you study under Klein? Remember! No jokes! Always with respect! Do exactly what he tells you and you'll get along with him fine. All right? Now come."

In the First Division there were eight wards. Six of these were for women in labor or women recently delivered. These six rooms were from fifty-four to seventy-two feet long and twenty-seven feet wide. The ceilings were sixteen feet high. There were thirty beds in each room. The beds were precisely equidistant from each other.

In a larger ward, a room one hundred and twenty-four feet long and twenty-seven feet wide, lay the pregnant women who had not begun labor and an occasional gynaecological case. There were sixty beds here.

In the labor ward, smallest of the ward rooms, were sixteen beds, fourteen for patients and two for the midwives on duty.

Each pair of wards was separated by a kitchen or by two small rooms.

"To get to the last ward in a row you have to go through all the other rooms."

"That's right, Naci. Shoes don't last long here."

"And the windows—so high——"

"Six feet above the floor. That's to prevent drafts. And, Naci! You'll notice the beds are exactly the same distance apart. Professor Klein is very strict about this."

"What is his thought?"

"He likes things just so. Order, Naci. That's the way he likes things. Don't, by accident, move any bed."

"What does he do, measure them?"

Chiari looked at Ignaz Philipp in surprise.

"Of course!"

Ignaz Philipp blinked, said nothing.

"Now I'll tell you about midwives."

"This is all new to me."

"Yes, you don't see that when you're a student. I know. Well, now, as to midwives. We've got ten of them. Ten certified midwives. One of these is chief midwife. She has to be present at every labor. And every morning she has to examine all the afterbirths to make sure they were all expelled intact. This chief midwife has an assistant. She's the housekeeper. She keeps the labor ward in order. The others take turn about, four on days, four on nights. Each midwife is assigned in rotation to a woman in labor or a woman just delivered. She has to remain with her patient until the labor is over. It's up to her to tie the umbilical cord, and she has to bathe and dress the baby and help the mother breast-feed the child for the first time. So much for midwives. They're an ignorant lot, poorly educated, peasants, mostly, but some of them, like the chief midwife, have had years of experience. I imagine she's delivered ten thousand babies in her time."

"And the others? Are they student midwives?"

"Those are just attendants, Naci. Just like in the other wards of the hospital. Just plain, dumb attendants. Each ward has three of them. The pregnant ones not in labor help them keep the wards clean. Now, it's time for Professor Klein! I've got to make rounds."

"But class——"

"Class comes right after rounds. Rounds twice a day. In the morning Klein makes them and myself and the provisional assistant. Four o'clock this afternoon comes the class. I've got to go, Naci! He can't bear tardiness. Find Stiegler . . ." Chiari rushed away.

Ignaz Philipp went in search of Stiegler, a mild, spectacled boy four years younger than himself, and Stiegler introduced him to those of his fellow students who were not on night duty and sleeping. Of the class of forty-eight there were twenty-one foreigners, graduates from other countries, eight from France, five from Italy, six from England, one from America, one from Russia.

At ten o'clock they went to the autopsy room. For the first day's class Professor Klein was present. Chiari and Gustav Breit, his assistant, moved decorously in the background.

"For some of you this room is familiar," Klein said. "You who came here briefly as undergraduates will find this course distinguished by the greater latitude appropriate to your diplomas."

He turned to the table, and Chiari and Breit whisked off the sheet which covered the female cadaver. The legs, the flesh, Ignaz Philipp noted automatically, appeared to have belonged to a woman in her early thirties. As in his undergraduate days, the upper part of the trunk and the viscera had been removed and the uterus dissected out. There remained the shell of a woman, neatly hulled.

"One of you gentlemen suggest an obstetrical operation," ordered Klein.

"Forceps delivery," a student called out promptly.

"Yes?" said Klein. "Another?" He waited.

154

The group shifted uncertainly.

"Decapitation——?" called out another.

"Perforation——?"

"Version——?"

Klein held up his hand.

"That is enough. Each of these will be done today. You may at any time ask that they be repeated."

He turned to the headless and chestless body. Instantly Breit went to a nearby table, drew off the sheet that covered it. From a row of small bodies he brought back a dead baby. He placed this in the body's abdominal cavity.

"Who asked for decapitation?" asked Klein.

There was a moment's silence, than a small murmur of laughter as the student stepped forward.

"We do not encourage levity," Klein said coldly. "There is nothing here provocative of laughter. During this course you will at all times conduct yourselves with the dignity your profession demands. I shall not warn you again."

He turned to the student who had come forward. On a small table near by he arranged a pair of nine-inch scissors, a blunt hook called a crotchet, a pair of forceps with claws, and a speculum.

"Decapitation is performed when the ordinary means of delivery have failed or cannot be employed and the child must be destroyed to save the mother. The first step is dilation. Dr. Breit——"

Breit placed himself by the side of the student. He indicated the speculum. The student picked it up, introduced it into the vagina of the cadaver, and paused. Breit whispered to him, and he picked up the scissors.

"For the rest of you gentlemen," Klein said, "we will practice abnormal presentations."

He led the way to another table, the sheet was removed, another female cadaver exposed, another baby placed in the cavity.

"The class will now turn its back."

Wonderingly, the class turned. Chiari quickly placed the child on its back in the cavity, the center of the skull slightly to the right of the cadaver's long axis. He then covered the trunk with the sheet.

"Still keeping your back turned, each of you gentlemen in turn will step backward to the table. Dr. Chiari will guide your hand to the vulva. You will then reach into the vagina. You will be permitted one minute to make your diagnosis. You will call aloud your idea of the position of the child."

One by one the class took its turn. Chiari noted down each diagnosis. When all had made an examination, Klein took the list from Chiari and quizzed each student on his findings. The sheet was then removed and the position of the child revealed.

155

Ignaz Philipp sighed. He relaxed. He had diagnosed correctly. The student studying decapitation had finished his work. The student who requested study in perforation advanced to the cadaver and was given a fresh baby. The remainder of the class practiced the diagnosis of presentation and position. The previous cadaver being no longer serviceable, a new one was uncovered.

At noon the class was dismissed for lunch. A half-hour later they returned and continued the activities of the morning. At four o'clock the group was assembled for rounds. They had used seven cadavers and twelve dead infants. The bodies of the women had been explored thoroughly and every student in the class had thrust his hands many times into each of the dead bodies.

There was at all times a plentiful supply of cadavers. Almost without exception the women had died of puerperal fever. As the class left the autopsy room, two new bodies were brought in. Breit stayed to prepare them for the next day. Those of the students who could find towels wiped their hands on the way out. The others wiped their hands on the lapels of their coats. They did this self-consciously, hoping that in a little while the garments would be sufficiently encrusted with blood, pus, and fluid to demonstrate the wearer's experience.

Klein, followed by Chiari, followed by the twenty-four students, began their long parade through the wards. There was time only for comments on the day's interesting cases. At each bed Klein paused briefly. Where necessary, he ordered medication. Where time permitted, the students were encouraged to examine the women.

"In the course of a day," Klein promised, "each student, after dissecting, will have an opportunity to examine from six to ten women, externally and by vagina."

Rags were provided, and for the protection of the examining student a pot of lard was offered his fingers for use as a lubricant.

Hours passed. The hands which had been plunged in death all day ceased at last their exploration of the warm and living. The day's rounds were over.

Ignaz Philipp and Chiari left the hospital and strolled home to the Alservorstadt.

"I'm putting you on as journalist tomorrow," said Chiari. "It's best that way, Naci. Might as well get it over. What did you think of it?"

"I learned things," Ignaz Philipp said. "Yes, I learned more today perhaps than all the obstetrics I studied as a student. There's so much, though, so much packed into a single day."

"Tomorrow you'll think today was a holiday. As journalists, you and Stiegler will keep all the records, as I told you——"

"Stiegler will keep the records, eh?"

"He'll never object, I can tell you that. But as journalist you won't have class tomorrow. You start duty right after morning rounds. You won't have time for regular meals. You'll have to eat on the run. After the clinic visits you and Stiegler will have to write out all the prescriptions you've put down in the book. Then you must distribute the prepared medicines. Next you apply leeches or vesicants and do whatever venesections are ordered. Next——"

"Johann! Wait! I'll never remember all this——"

"Naturally, Naci. When we get home I'll write it all down. You know how to bleed a patient, don't you? Never mind. The midwife will help you. And don't take any nonsense from midwives. They get above themselves very easily. Professor Klein is very firm about their being kept in their place. So! When you've finished with the treatments you admit the new pregnant arrivals, examine them to determine what stage of pregnancy they've reached, the presentation of the infant, and any small pelvises or big heads. If you find she's going into labor, you put her in the labor ward. If she's actually in labor when you admit her, just examine her and keep right on examining her until the bag of water bursts."

"They get a lot of examinations, don't they?"

"You may be certain of it. No women in the world get more attention, more scientific care. It's not at all uncommon when a woman's in labor and spends three days in the labor ward, say, because she's slow dilating, that she gets six clinic visits alone, and is examined each time by at least five students. That gives her thirty examinations—and that's not counting the many examinations she's given between clinic visits. Oh, there's no question about it. No money in the world could pay for the attention these poor women receive."

"Well then, suppose I admit a case in labor and the bag of water ruptures—what then?"

"Then she's assigned to a pair of day or night men and a midwife. They'll take over the labor. But if it looks normal, and everything seems likely to go all right, they'll turn the case back to you to deliver."

"Oh, my! And if after a little while it doesn't go so well——?"

"Then you have me called. I'll come right away. After a while, when you've picked up a little more, I'll stand by while you operate or do any of the things you do every day on the cadaver. There's just one thing you mustn't neglect: if you're allowed to conduct the labor, stay with the woman until she delivers the afterbirth. Don't leave until she does. That's all. When you're through you write down the age of the woman, how the labor went, the time of the labor stages, the condition, the weight and the sex of the baby."

157

"Do you think—would they start me so soon delivering as tomorrow?"

"Probably not. But don't worry, Naci, if they do. Just stand there and make the appropriate noises. They won't turn her over to you unless it's normal, and if it's normal, she'll do all the work herself. It's really nothing. You'll see. I don't have to tell you to pay no attention to the screams. Noise is a normal expression of pain and pain is a normal expression of labor. Anyway, they're not supposed to scream. They're supposed to save their breath for where it's needed. And one last thing——"

"Oh, Johann! No more——"

"No, this is nothing. It's a little custom, that's all. Whenever you serve as a journalist you're supposed to give the housekeeper and the attending midwives each a tip. That way you'll get more co-operation."

Markussovsky and Chiari dined together that evening. Ignaz Philipp stayed at home. He was very tired. He put his textbook on obstetrics by his bedside and the long list Chiari had written for him. He undressed, he got into bed, he began to read and memorize. His mind struggled through the crowded day's happenings. He discovered he had begun to have a mild dislike for obstetrics. He knew that he must continue, nevertheless. He saw plainly that he must soon support himself entirely. Obstetrics would be a prudent practice. Too, Hungary needed obstetricians. But if there were a revolution wounded men would need a doctor more than would birthing women. He determined to be doubly prepared. He resolved to cram surgery in whatever free time he could find.

The constant work among the cadavers was not pleasant. But it was a continuation of what he had been doing for almost six years. One never became entirely accustomed to the cold flesh, the constant odors, the chill fluids. But it was material that had to be dealt with, material from which one could always learn. He considered, impressed, the wealth of cadavers available. The course was really amazingly well provided with dissecting material. He had not realized that so many died in childbed. It was a relief to think of the examinations on living women. Warm and living flesh was infinitely more pleasant material. As he dropped off to sleep he smiled a little, remembering the curiosity with which he had gone on the first day's rounds. He could not remember the face of a single woman. The group had moved too fast. The women were faceless. He could remember only voices and vaginas.

"I've given him all he can handle," Chiari told Markussovsky. "So far everything has worked out as we wanted. I think the more work he has, the less time he will have to think. Right now that is best."

"Does he seem to like obstetrics?"

158

"I can't tell, really. He won't be able to know, either, until he's mastered enough to find out."

"It's good for Naci."

"I think so. I think it's good for anybody."

"But Naci most of all. We don't know what his qualities as an obstetrician will be. But as a human being he has the sympathies, the carefulness, the pity for people—his whole make-up—he might well have been born an obstetrician."

"You're probably right. But I think he'd make a better surgeon."

"Shall I tell you something, Johann? I think surgery would eventually break his heart. He's a fighter. And for even the bravest fighter there must be the reward of at least a few victories. No, Johann, surgery would break his heart. Surgery is not for fighters. Surgery is for men handy with their fingers. Surgery is for men with long memories and short purpose. Men who express themselves by dexterity, men careless of reward, to whom death is not failure. Men with a problem to solve in which life is only one factor. For Naci I think life will always be the issue. And I think that in time, as he met death after death, the fight would break his heart and he would end embittered and broken and a failure."

Chiari was silent. He was thinking of the death rate in the First Division. This week it had risen to 32 per cent. The autopsy room had twelve new cadavers each day. Every two hours another woman died. The miasma, the cosmic-telluric effects seemed to be unduly oppressive this season.

"We have our deaths too," he said mildly. "But it's not like surgery. He'll get used to them."

Ignaz Philipp was awakened by the sun. "That's what comes of going to bed early," he grumbled. He tried to sleep again. He tossed a moment, then gave up. He rose, he dressed quietly, he tiptoed out into Vienna. The morning drifted into the city, new washed. The sun minted the faraway spires of churches. The air was cool and moist upon the stone buildings and seemed to make a cushion of the very pavement. It was good to be alone in the city, it was good to feel the emptiness of the streets, it was luxurious to have the morning to oneself.

It was too early, still, to find an open coffeehouse. He stopped a moment and pondered. "Shall I walk about a while and make time pass?" Tentatively he walked a little, one block, then two. The novelty of the morning began to disappear. He stopped a moment on a street corner and from inside his coat he produced the list Chiari had made for him. He read it through for the twentieth time. Rested, his duties for the day almost committed to memory, the list no longer seemed so formidable. He strolled a little longer, considering the things he must do and how he must do them. He became conscious of hunger. He decided to breakfast at the hospital. He thought of the hospital eagerly. He looked at the nearest street sign. He was amazed. Somehow the hospital was just around the corner. In a few minutes he was at breakfast, eating among the night men just about to go off duty. He rose and went excitedly into the wards. He walked into one of the six large rooms in which pregnant women waited the onset of labor. This room was only partly filled. The women lay in their beds and watched him silently. He paused at the sight of the empty beds. From a nearby bed a woman said softly,

"The midwife has gone to breakfast, sir doctor."

Ignaz Philipp started a ·little. His hands tingled. Warmth flowed through his chest. The word "doctor" tingled in his brain. He turned to the woman with pleasure.

"Thank you," he said happily. "And how are you this morning? Are you well? Have you any pains yet? How did you sleep?"

"She snores," said a woman in another bed scornfully. "Can't you give her anything?"

"Ah, now! I guess it's not so bad."

"At least I don't have to be told to take a bath," the first woman told the ceiling, red-faced.

Ignaz Philipp looked away, embarrassed. Then he smiled. His professional demeanor vanished. The women ceased being cases and became human beings. They were no longer strangers with a history. They were women. He smiled conciliatingly at both of them. He glanced at the others. There was friendship in his glance and everyday sympathy. In the bed nearest him a watching woman who had been sprawled on the pillow pulled up the sheet to hide her bared shoulders.

"Well, well," he said awkwardly, trying to regain his official status, "no one appears to need a doctor here this morning. I must go and find some who do."

He smiled again, this time briskly. A woman four beds down had an incredible resemblance to his sister. He turned and walked toward the door. He stopped. He looked at the journal. A woman from Moldavia. Apparently it was her first pregnancy.

"Feeling all right?"

And before she could answer he nodded and walked again toward the door. In the corridor a bell clanged. The bell was stilled, as if a hand had been laid upon the clapper. Then it clanged again. A priest came into view. He walked with down-bent head. As he passed he shook the bell slowly once more. The ward was still. There was no sound but the bell. The women in the beds did not move. They kept their eyes strained on the doorway. The priest passed. The bell clanged again. Behind the priest two attendants carried a body. They passed. A second body was carried past. The bell clanged. This time it came fainter. The priest was far down the hall. It appeared

160

that the procession had ended. A rustling, a soft sigh rose from the women waiting their turn to go into labor. Then, instantly, the sigh was snuffed, there was rigid silence again. A third body went hurriedly past to join the other two.

"Three!" cried a woman behind him. There was a panic in her voice. "Only three this morning!"

"Only three!" another echoed shrilly. She sounded almost happy.

Around the doorway, into the ward, came a woman newly admitted. An attendant walked behind her. The woman was big with child. Her belly was a great round ball in front of her. Her shabby coat parted from the protuberance.

"In there," said the attendant. She pointed to a bed. The woman looked dazedly at the attendant. She saw Ignaz Philipp and stepped back a pace. She went to the doorway. She looked down the hall. From the distance came the fading clang of the bell. The woman stared.

"Come on, dear. Come on," said the attendant. She walked to the woman. She tugged at her coat sleeve. The woman came back into the ward. She took four unwilling steps. She halted. She looked around the ward. Her eyes were round, her mouth was open. Her breath whistled between her teeth. She blinked in mortal fear. She closed her mouth and swallowed.

"Now look here——!" the attendant said angrily.

The woman's dilated eyes focused upon Ignaz Philipp. She did not hear the attendant.

"It's all right, dear," one of the bedded women called out.

The woman did not hear. She was a trapped animal. Her hands were raised upon the top of her protruding belly like paws. The paws shook. Her breath panted loudly from her slack mouth. Drops of sweat rolled from her forehead down her cheeks. She stared at Ignaz Philipp. She got down on the floor. Clumsily, her huge belly rolling her as she moved, she crawled over the floor to Ignaz Philipp. The attendant did not move. The ward watched. The woman put her arms around Ignaz Philipp's legs. She clasped him behind his knees. Her breath came panting. He looked down into a broad face, dumb with fear. Her graying hair had loosened. Her eyes begged uncontrollably. Ignaz Philipp could not move.

"Please," the woman panted. "Please, boy—honored sir doctor—for the love of God, son—— Doctor—let me have my baby in the street!"

Still Ignaz Philipp could not move. He was unable to speak. In his ears there was a roaring noise. He saw Thérèse. Just so his mother's hair had been loosened. Just this gray. Just this woman's age when last he saw her. There was nothing about her that resembled Thérèse. There was only a woman, her hour come, begging as Thérèse might beg.

The attendant recalled herself.

"Here!" she shouted. "Here, now! None of that! Doctor—I'm sorry——"

"Only let me out," the woman prayed. "Oh, God—oh, sir doctor—boy, pity me——"

From a bed at the end of the ward a woman screamed suddenly. She screamed again and again. Another began to cry softly. There was a soft bumping sound. From their beds other women slipped to the floor, dragged their bellies big with child over the floor to his feet.

"In the street—please——"

"Only this once——"

"In the name of God, let us go——"

He looked at them. He shut his eyes. He could not deny them. Their pleading turned his tongue to water. He could not think. His heart cried out to let them go. His sick being cried to go with them.

"For my child, son——" the first woman screamed to him. The attendant reached her, slowly dragged her upright.

"For shame!" she cried. "Look at you! Back to your beds! What are you thinking of? What's got into you?"

"Only for a moment!" the woman prayed. "I will go right out—I will come right back—I swear it! Let me have my baby——"

"We will die, we are doomed!" another shouted.

"In the street!" shrieked the first woman.

"In the streets it's safe!" another cried.

"In the Second Division, at least—not in the First!"

"Not here! No one dies in the street. Only here. We won't bother you, honored sir doctor. We will bless you. We will have our baby—we will come right back in—you can do what you want with us——"

They cried all at once now. Another clasped his legs. Their faces were wet with their tears. They begged him and they pleaded. They cried upon Almighty God. The clamor filled the hall. Attendants ran in. White and still, Ignaz Philipp stood. An attendant peeled a woman's arms from his legs. The woman fell upon her face, groveling. Another seized at his shoes. Slowly the attendants dragged them away. The cries died. Now there was only desolate sobbing. Quite pale, still silent, Ignaz Philipp walked from the ward. He disappeared from their sight. As he walked unseeingly down the hall, he reeled a little. He spied the door to the autopsy room. Gratefully he let himself in. He closed the door and leaned upon it. Before him were the sheeted tables, and beneath the sheets were the mounds that were today's lesson. He took a deep breath of their dissolution and of the chloride of lime. He stood thus, staring a moment. Then, slowly, he began to cry. He cried for only a few moments. Abruptly he stopped. He dashed the

162

tears from his face. He gazed at the sheeted bodies. He tried to think. He began to chew his underlip.

It was thus that Chiari found him minutes later. Behind Chiari came Stiegler.

"One of the attendants said she saw you come in here," he said. "What in the world happened here this morning?"

Ignaz Philipp drew a slow, deep breath.

"Did they tell you?"

Chiari nodded.

"They're usually under better control. However—with a pregnant woman you can expect anything."

"Especially hysteria." Stiegler grinned.

"Especially hysteria," Chiari assented. He put his hand on Ignaz Philipp's shoulder. "Don't let it annoy you." A thought dismayed him. "Professor Klein's sure to hear of it." He shook his head angrily. "He hates scenes like that. It isn't orderly. Oh well, an assistant's life can't be always roses——"

"We'd better get started," Stiegler said. He pushed his spectacles higher on his nose and leaned to peer at Ignaz Philipp. "Sir assistant doctor Chiari says you won't mind if I do the writing——?"

"All right," said Ignaz Philipp levelly, "let's get started." He moved around Chiari. Stiegler clasped his record book proudly to his thin ribs.

"Call on me if you need anything." Chiari smiled assuringly.

Ignaz Philipp smiled with his mouth. He drew a deep breath, turned, and followed Stiegler out into the hall, into the depths of the first day's duty.

The long day ended. In all his life he had never been so occupied. He had never before made such demands upon his mind or body. He did not realize until he was on his way homeward that he had not eaten since breakfast. He understood why Chiari would soon move to the hospital. The short trip to the apartment seemed too much. Through the interminable hours he had done his best to think only in terms of medicine and study, to reject the patients as people and to regard them purely as cases. He had avoided looking directly into any woman's eyes. He had made himself oblivious to the sound of pain, to cries, to moans, to entreaties, and to weeping. He was aware of these sounds, but he forced himself to disregard them. As the day ended his struggle to disassociate himself became easier. "I suppose," he told Markussovsky, "that if one worked in a cannon factory someday one would get used to the noise and in time perhaps not even notice it." He was abjectly grateful that he need not be journalist again next day. He put his mind determinedly on his classes. He struggled to blot out the scene in the ward. He could not. It nibbled endlessly at the edges of his consciousness. He began to talk feverishly, talk almost constantly. The memory persisted. At last, hoping to exorcise it, he told Markussovsky. But the thing would not be exorcised so easily. He upbraided himself brutally. He sneered at himself that if he allowed such things to invade him he ought to resolve to forget the practice of medicine. Yet a part of him resisted the thought that one day he might actually become so hardened that such a scene would not affect him. Next morning, before classes began, he glanced covertly into the ward. The gray-haired woman was gone. The women who had joined her in the demonstration were gone also. He walked down the hall. He glanced in the labor ward. The women were there. They were in labor. It was difficult to distinguish their groans and their screams from the din of the women around them. He listened a moment, then he saw Chiari and went to join him in the autopsy room.

Chiari stood by one of the sheet-draped tables.

"Today you're really going to see something," he promised.

"Another childbirth death?"

"This one will be different, Naci——"

He broke off. The first students had begun to arrive. The room filled quickly. They looked to Chiari expectantly.

He turned to the table and removed the sheet. Before them lay a complete cadaver. It was the body of a woman in her late thirties. She was thin. Her abdomen was normal, her skin was unbroken, there were no visible evidences of any ailment or disease except that she appeared wasted. The class looked up from the woman to Chiari. Consumption, perhaps, Ignaz Philipp thought.

"This woman was admitted to the clinic in the usual manner. She was assigned to the First Division. The patient gave the following history: About a year ago she noticed a slight bleeding between menstrual periods. Her periods had always been irregular and when the bleeding became more frequent and more profuse she ascribed the leakage to untimely and protracted menstruation. She and her husband noted that she was becoming increasingly nervous. She began to be troubled by the frequency with which she rose in the night to urinate. Also, she became severely constipated. She felt no pain. She applied to the hospital because she appeared to be steadily losing weight and because lately her discharge of blood had become foul-smelling."

He looked up at the class.

"Are there any questions at this point?"

"Strongly suggestive of cancer——" said a student quickly.

"Cancer of the cervix and probably cancer of the uterus——" another said quickly.

A mumble of assent came from the class. Ignaz Philipp ruminated. It sounded like cancer. On the other hand, this woman was younger than those cancer of the cervix or uterus generally afflicted. He said nothing.

"Upon examination," Chiari began again, "we found the cervix uneven, soft in spots and hard in others. There were no other symptoms of clinical significance. A large mass could be felt on the right side of the cervix. Operation disclosed a large tumor some two and a half inches in diameter. The tumor was attached to healthy tissue by a short stem. The tumor was removed and when opened was seen to be composed of thready filaments and muscular tissues. Almost immediately after the operation the patient developed fever. She died forty-seven hours later."

He halted again and looked at the class.

"A polyp," said Ignaz Philipp. "A fibroid polyp."

"Right," said Chiari. "What looked like cancer and even could be construed as behaving somewhat like cancer was simply a fibroid polyp."

"But she died——" a student called out uncertainly.

"She died of a fever," said Chiari. "Look closely, gentlemen. Observe this woman closely." The class peered at the corpse, puzzled.

"She appeared to sustain the operation well. Under the knife she controlled her cries and screams quite well. She cooperated where she could. No more than two attendants were required to hold her down at any stage of the operation. She passed a restless night. She awoke early in the morning. She complained of pain in the region of her uterus, and of chilliness. She said the pain appeared to come in waves and paroxysms. There was no complete intermission. At times she seemed to be relieved by lying upon her face or by sitting up and leaning forward. At morning rounds Professor Klein found some fullness in the abdomen. Even very gentle pressure with the palm over the hypogastric region caused exquisite pain. Her pulse beat was one hundred and twenty strokes a minute. Her tongue was clean. She had been given two doses of a gentle laxative after the operation. These had not taken effect. Professor Klein ordered an immediate purging enema and prescribed a draught composed of one half ounce each of magnesium sulphate and manna.

"Before the draught could be compounded she began to vomit. When the draught was brought, she was ordered given a fourth part of it every fifteen minutes. The first dose was vomited. The other three were retained. At one o'clock in the afternoon her pulse was one hundred and thirty-two strokes a minute. Her abdomen had swelled markedly.

"Two hours later her abdomen appeared to have swelled a little farther. The pain in her belly was still marked but not so violent. A warm wet cloth was applied and appeared to

165

give her some relief. The purging draught now caused a plentiful bowel movement. She was ordered given ten drams of decoction of cinchona, eight grains of ammonium carbonate, two ounces of lemon juice, and thirty drops of spirits of lavender.

"At eight o'clock that evening the patient appeared to be in a dying state. She was vomiting weakly and frequently. She could retain no medicine. Her state being such as to preclude all hope, nothing further was attempted. Occasionally she was given cordials in small quantities. She died at half-past ten the same evening."

Chiari looked at the class expectantly.

For a moment they looked back at him. Then they looked down.

"Not even a guess?" asked Chiari.

There was no answer.

"Very well. I shall tell you what it was. Then we shall examine the cadaver to prove it." He folded his arms across his chest and surveyed the class a moment. "The woman died of puerperal fever."

The class started. Instantly a buzz began.

"She wasn't pregnant!" a student cried.

"She hadn't even recently delivered, had she?"

"No," said Chiari, "she had never had a child."

"But puerperal fever is a disease of pregnancy!"

"Puerperal fever," said Chiari, "is a disease."

"A disease of pregnancy!"

"It is a disease of pregnancy. But puerperal fever is due to epidemic influences. And sometimes these influences are so virulent that puerperal fever will attack even non-puerperal women—even women not in labor or recently delivered. It will attack even non-pregnant women."

The class waited.

"I see that there is nothing more to say," said Chiari. "I detect incredulity on a number of faces." Ignaz Philipp reddened and quickly looked down. Chiari turned to the cadaver. "The postmortem will have to finish the lecture."

The class grouped tightly about the table. In a half-hour the examination had revealed everything. The class sighed, looked up respectfully. Pathological changes in the parts which had been operated upon were unmistakably identical with those of puerperal fever.

"That was a fine case, Johann," Ignaz Philipp said when they sat at lunch together.

"It was a beauty, wasn't it? It's a good thing to remember, Naci. I think that kind of case was why Professor Klein singled me out to be his assistant. When I was taking my midwifery we had just such a case one day. Klein asked the cause of death. Everyone was stumped. I waited a moment and blurted out puerperal fever. He was surprised and very pleased."

"How did you come to make such a diagnosis? What made you say it?"

"Well, I thought to myself: 'This is the First Division. What do they die of here? What else but puerperal fever? Do any of them die of anything else? Very, very rarely.' So I just said puerperal fever."

"What luck! I bet no one could talk to you for weeks."

"It was a fine thing to happen, all right. A thing like that brings you to attention and doesn't do any harm, I can tell you. And, incidentally, Professor Klein has already noticed you. They told him about that hysterical outbreak in Ward Four yesterday and when he asked what you did while all this was going on they told him you conducted yourself with perfect dignity and coolness, that you never said a word. He was quite impressed. Professor Klein is a great believer in decorum, Naci. I told him you were very studious and industrious. He said he had heard that from others. So just watch yourself, my boy, and you'll be all right."

"Quiet, Johann? I couldn't move! I was transfixed! I hope to my God I never have to endure such a thing again. Those poor, poor creatures. God help them!"

"It doesn't happen often. They seem to have a fixed idea in their heads that when they come to the First Division they will never leave it alive. They fight like fiends to get into the Second Division with Bartsch and his midwives. And they are absolutely convinced that because many women have had their babies in the streets, on the way to the hospital, and have survived, that they, too, will be safe if they are allowed to deliver in the gutter."

"The poor devils. The poor, helpless things."

"Oh, I don't know as I agree with you there, Naci. It's true that enormous numbers of them do die. But then you can't combat an epidemic influence. What can you do with such a thing as puerperal fever? And as to being poor, it's true they're poor, they're supposed to bring a layette with them, you know, and one girl came yesterday bringing nothing else but a bit of rag for the umbilical cord—we insist they bring at least that— and she'd torn it off her dress at that. But God knows here they get the best medical treatment in the world in the best hospital in the world."

"What happened to her? Is she all right?"

"Who, Naci? Oh, the girl? I don't know. She delivered an hour or so after arrival. Seemed to have a little fever this morning. Shall we see? Would you like to see?"

They went into the ward where lay the women who had been recently delivered. They stopped at a bed. The occupant was a girl barely twenty.

"So beautiful," Ignaz Philipp murmured.

"She is, isn't she. That flaxen hair, those blue eyes, but look at that fever. Hello, miss," he said to the patient, "I'll bet you're from upper Austria."

The girl tried to smile. Her eyes were wide with anxiety. Chiari, smiling, felt her forehead. With his eyes he signaled Ignaz Philipp to feel also. The smooth skin was wet with sweat, burning hot. They took her pulse from opposite sides of the bed. Ignaz Philipp counted one hundred and twenty strokes a minute. He looked up. Chiari nodded.

"Pain in the belly?" Chiari asked.

The girl nodded.

"Pain where you had the baby?"

With an effort the girl separated her fever-dry lips.

"Yes," she whispered. "Like needles."

Chiari lifted the bedclothes. He sniffed delicately. He replaced the bedclothes.

"You'll be all right," he smiled. "Just do as you're told and you'll be fine."

They walked down the aisle between beds.

"Puerperal fever," Chiari said quietly.

Ignaz Philipp started. He walked to a nearby bed. In it lay the gray-haired woman who had clung to his knees.

"Hello," he called out, and forced his heavy lips to smile.

The woman stared obliviously at the ceiling. Her eyes were lackluster. Her lips were crusted and parted. Her breath came heavily.

"Another one," Chiari whispered in his ear. He turned away. Reluctantly, still looking at the woman, Ignaz Philipp turned at last and went with him.

From the corridor outside the clang of the bell approached. Then a hand over the clapper muted it. A step and then another clang of the bell. Again it was muted.

"We've got it bad this week," Chiari said. They left the ward. Down the hall walked an old priest. This time no attendant followed him. "He's on the way to give absolution. Wait a minute. I'd better tell him about the two we just left."

Chiari went to the priest, stopped him, spoke briefly. The priest went into the ward. Chiari and Ignaz Philipp walked on.

"There must be something, Johann!" Ignaz Philipp burst out suddenly.

"There's nothing can be done, Naci."

"There must be something! Somehow!"

"You're talking about puerperal fever, Naci——"

"I know. But there must be something——"

"They'll be dead within seventy-two hours."

They were dead within seventy-two hours.

They were on the tables, sheeted, ready for the class, four days later.

"Here they are," Chiari nudged him. "There're your friends."

Ignaz Philipp stared at the dissected bodies. He tried to reply. He was bewildered. He could think of nothing. There they were. They were dead. They had died of puerperal fever. So had the others, so had every sheeted body in this room.

"There's nothing can be done," he said slowly.

"It's a shame, Naci. But that's the way it is."

"Well . . . I'm going to read up on it . . ."

"You do, Naci. Get it out of your system."

"I'll read up on it."

"We've always had it, unfortunately. Long before you and I were born. As long as there have been humans. And we always will."

"You think I'm wasting time, don't you?"

"Naci, anybody who knows you knows better than to try to keep you from trying to investigate what you've set your heart on."

"I'm not doubting your word, Johann."

"It isn't *my* word, Naci. You know yourself——"

"I know. But I couldn't face those women if I wasn't at least studying, trying to stumble on something that maybe might help them——"

"Pity's a bad thing, Naci."

"I know it. You sound like Skoda. But I can't help it. I've got to try."

"He's off on puerperal fever," Chiari told Markussovsky that night.

"You're not going to get in trouble, Naci?" Markussovsky asked anxiously.

"Sure. I'm going to set fire to the hospital tomorrow morning."

But thereafter, when his day's classes were over, Ignaz Philipp went quietly to Rokitansky and Rokitansky happily provided him with cadavers, and Ignaz Philipp and Lautner, Rokitansky's new young assistant, and sometimes all three, worked into the night examining woman after woman, all dead, all dead of puerperal fever. And always he read. He devoured all that he could find to read. He came in time to know the cause and remedies almost by heart. The remedies were easy. There were very few of them. And all of them were worthless. The causes were more difficult. Authorities differed. In the end he committed the causes to memory too. There were twenty-eight of them.

June ended and July first he announced himself to Klein as an aspirant for the position of assistant. Chiari had received notice of appointment to the faculty. Klein looked at Ignaz Philipp's petition with satisfaction. The young man had proven himself studious and industrious and excellently quiet. He was pleased with him. He put the petition away. There was time, there was never any need for rashness. When the time came he would sign it. He would elevate Breit to be first assistant, now that Chiari was leaving. And Ignaz Philipp would fit in excellently under Breit.

For a few days Ignaz Philipp chafed impatiently.

"He does things slowly," Chiari said. "You cannot be impatient with Professor Klein. He takes his time. Be patient, Naci."

"How are his daughters?" Markussovsky asked suddenly.

"Never mind his daughters."

Ignaz Philipp looked at Markussovsky, astonished.

"What's up, Marko? What's he up to?"

"What are you up to, Johann? Are you getting anywhere? Or do the daughters take their time, like Papa?"

"Never mind—never mind——"

Ignaz Philipp whirled on Chiari.

"Why, Johann! When in the world——?"

"That's those nights he spends at the hospital, Naci. You know how it is with an assistant. They have to work so hard. If it isn't the hospital, it's the old man's daughters——"

"So that's why he never says Klein. That's why he's always saying Professor this, Professor that. Aha, Johann! What are you doing to the daughters?"

"Now, I'm not doing anything. I've just been around to the house now and then—I'm the assistant, after all——"

"Come on, Johann," said Marko. "Which one is it?"

"Are there enough for all of us?"

"You're being ridiculous! It's absolutely nothing, I assure you——"

"It's the oldest one, then," said Markussovsky. "In the first place because we've upset him, so it must be so. In the second place it has to be the oldest because——"

"Because Professor Klein loves order!" Ignaz Philipp cried triumphantly.

"Have your fun," Chiari said serenely.

Three weeks later he came home proudly engaged.

They celebrated the remainder of the week. July ended. Chiari moved from the comfortable apartment on the Alservorstadt. He took up permanent quarters at the hospital.

On August first Ignaz Philipp was duly promoted to the degree of Master of Midwifery. He became a provisional assistant in the First Division.

170

# TWELVE

FOR an instant, as he walked with Klein on his first day as provisional assistant, in that silent, purposeful march, both in step, faces grave, the eyes of the patients following respectfully. Ignaz Philipp felt pride full force. His exultance was brief. It was succeeded by embarrassment. He glanced to either side covertly. He had almost strutted. No one had noticed. He contemplated himself with disgust. Klein stopped at a bedside. Ignaz Philipp forgot everything and prepared to assist him. But Klein, ignoring the patient, had stooped and seized something on the floor. He showed Ignaz Philipp a curl of dust.

"You see?" he said triumphantly. "Dust!"

"How do you feel?" he asked the patient.

"I feel fine, sir doctor."

"Good." He walked into the aisle carrying the dust curl. "This place must be kept in order." He turned to the ward. "Is there anyone here who is having pains this morning?"

"No—none." The answer came promptly.

"Good. Now we find the attendant." He walked toward the end of the ward, Ignaz Philipp trailing. As he reached the last bed the attendant came hurrying in. He walked to her and held the dust curl before her eyes. The woman cringed.

"Last week, two beds out of line. A month ago, a dirty windowpane——"

"It was on the outside only. If I open the windows such a stench comes in from the sewers——" the woman said humbly.

"This day—dust!"

"I am sorry, sir doctor. If the director will forgive me——"

"I forgive you," Klein said coldly.

The woman looked at him swiftly, then hung her head.

171

"Now pack your belongings and be out of the hospital within the hour."

He walked from the ward. As they walked into the next ward he halted a moment and turned to Ignaz Philipp.

"Order, Dr. Semmelweis. What we must have—what we *shall* have—is order. Dr. Boer had a reputation for keeping this clinic clean. We uphold that reputation. God sends poverty, but not dirt. This is your first day as assistant. See to it that I never again find anything in any ward with which to reproach you."

He walked a little, in silence.

"I want to be able," he continued after a while, "to sit in my office and to know that at any hour of the day or night I may come where I will in the First Division and find every bed exactly the same distance apart, every floor precisely clean, every window entirely gleaming."

"I was noticing the sheets, sir director. On some of the beds they are changed as often as once a week. And yet——"

"On the expenses of this division as a whole and in the matter of laundry charges in particular my budget has been precisely established. I may say that in all my career here the yearly bills have hardly varied more than a few groschen. It is unfortunate that they vary even that much."

"With respect, sir director, because of the discharge, the natural staining, some of them, in fact, are very dirty——"

"They betray the normal consequences of hospital use. Their care conforms to the restrictions of their part in the budget. Naturally we do not expect that anyone should contemplate altering the budget in the slightest particular."

"I regret having mentioned the matter, sir director——"

"It is of no consequence. That is how one learns. I want you to feel free to come to me at any time between one o'clock in the afternoon and three-thirty to discuss any matter that puzzles you. In that way I shall feel you completely understand what it is I desire here. Punctuality, order, regularity, attention to the smallest detail—that is how one gets on, Dr. Semmelweis."

It was true, Ignaz Philipp reflected, that the First Division had a name for precision, for being well-kept, for being administered to near perfection.

"I shall try to be a credit to you, sir director," he said.

They passed into the labor room as the clang of the death bell entered the corridor they had quitted.

Late that afternoon, as he discussed the day and the journal with Breit, a midwife came to say that a patient in the labor room appeared ready to deliver. They went to the labor room. As they entered, an attendant was placing a screen around one of the beds. They went to this bed. The patient was a young woman.

172

"Well," said Ignaz Philipp, "getting ready to have your baby, are you?"

The girl smiled back pleasantly.

"I think so," she said. "It feels much that way." She was entirely calm.

"This is her third, Doctor," the midwife said.

"Well, let's just have a look."

"Put your legs up, dear," the midwife said. But the girl had already arched her knees and parted them.

Ignaz Philipp rolled up the cuff of his coat. The midwife handed him a pot of lard. He dipped his fingers in it.

"Now let's see," he said.

It was pleasant to examine warm and living flesh after the feel of so many lifeless tissues. He thrust his fingers softly and easily to the cervix. The girl was healthy. Her flesh was hot with the increase of blood to the pelvis, elastic, young, and great with life.

"How do you like it here in the hospital?" Breit was inquiring. "Are they treating you well?"

"Everyone is kind, sir doctor." The young woman smiled.

"Good. And your husband——?"

The smile faded from the girl's voice.

"I'm sorry——" she said. "I—the fact is——"

Ignaz Philipp's index and middle finger extended to measure how much the birth canal had dilated. There was room for both fingers and a little more. He withdrew his hand.

"I beg your pardon," Breit was saying earnestly. "Believe me, I have not the slightest wish to invade your privacy."

"It isn't that," the midwife interrupted. "She's married all right. She has a fine six-year-old girl, haven't you, dear?" The young woman nodded. "It's her husband," she explained. The young woman sighed.

"He's in jail," she said gravely. "He stabbed another man. They had a fight. They were drinking. Now he's in jail."

"That's a shame," said Breit. He looked expectantly at Ignaz Philipp.

"Two and a half fingers," said Ignaz Philipp.

"Everything else all right?"

"Perfect."

"Well, I'll leave you, then." He turned to the young woman. "You may have an hour or so to wait yet," he said. "Dr. Semmelweis here will take good care of you."

He nodded brightly and departed.

Ignaz Philipp sat in a chair by the bedside.

"That's a shame about your husband," he said.

"He's a good man."

"Well, you can't tell. Maybe they'll let him out."

"He's got a temper."

"Do you know what happened?"

173

"They were drinking, you see. The neighbors told me. My husband called the man a name. The man hit him. My husband took out his pocketknife. He stabbed the man here." She pointed to her right side beneath the ribs.

"The liver, eh? That's bad."

"It wasn't a long blade."

"I know. Even so . . ."

"Just a penknife."

"The man died?"

"I don't think so. I think he's somewhere in the hospital."

"I'll go to see him."

The young woman's face suddenly became anxious. Her features seemed to draw out, to lengthen. Her arms became rigid at her sides. Her hands clenched. She clamped her teeth together. Her lips bared. From her sieged vitals a groan spurted bitten splinters of agony. Ignaz Philipp looked quickly at his watch. It was ten minutes to five.

"How long ago did she have her last pain?" he asked the midwife.

"Twenty minutes ago."

He put his watch on the bedside table. He calculated. In twenty minutes or less she should have another pain. He timed the present seizure. The girl relaxed a moment, almost instantly stiffened again.

"Hah!" she cried. "Hah! Hah! Ow! . . . OW! OhGod! Oh God Almighty!"

She cried out again. Then, her teeth still clamped, her arms still rigid, she was silent. A fine beading of sweat misted her forehead. The spasm passed. Slowly the girl's jaws relaxed. Her teeth parted. She stayed thus a moment waiting, breathing heavily. Then her arms relaxed. Her hands opened. Her shoulders slumped. She turned her head on her pillow. She licked her lips. She smiled at Ignaz Philipp.

"A bad one?"

She nodded, still smiling with her mouth.

He took a towel and gently wiped her forehead.

"A hard one?"

"No, no. Not hard."

"Let me know when you feel the next one coming."

"Yes, sir doctor."

"Did you have any trouble with your other children?"

"Not a bit."

"Not even the first one, eh?"

"No. We had a little money then. My husband was working, we had a doctor, I had the baby at home."

"Well!"

"Yes. It was fine. The second one too. He died. He was only three weeks old. One day something happened, I think he swallowed something, he started to cough, he got red in the

174

face, in a few minutes, before we could lift a finger, he was dead."

"It happens. It happens. It's terrible, but it happens. Anyway—you've got a six-year-old girl——"

"She's so shy. We're great chums, sir doctor——"

"Yes. Good, and soon you'll have another chum."

"Am I going to be all right?"

"You're going to be fine. Tell me, does your husband want a girl or a boy this time?"

"He doesn't care."

"I never heard of a father who didn't care!"

"Not him! He says"—she paused shyly—"he says so long as it looks like me——"

"Good for him!"

"He's a good man."

"I'm sure of it."

"He's got a temper."

"Ah, well . . ."

"There's no work here. That's what's the matter. We're going to move. He would never have gotten drunk if things hadn't got so bad——"

"Maybe you'd like me to get a message to him. Would you like that?"

"My God! I wouldn't trouble the sir doctor!"

"No trouble at all."

"Please! I wouldn't dream——"

"Just tell me his address. I mean—where have they got him?"

"I think St. Ulrich's, but the doctor isn't to trouble——"

Ignaz Philipp turned to the midwife seated at the other side of the bed, placidly knitting.

"When the baby is born we can send a messenger, I suppose."

"Of course," said the midwife.

"Now, you see? So you're going to try a fresh start somewhere else." A warm wave of friendliness welled within Ignaz Philipp. The girl was honest, she bore her pains well, she was co-operative, intelligent, and serenely healthful. He was delighted at the lighting of her eyes when her man was mentioned.

"Yes," she said. "We're going to move. He's made up his mind. We're not going to stay in Austria, even. His father's got a farm—it's nice in the city—but when hard times come it's very terrible. But on the farm——" She broke off suddenly. "It's coming again, Doctor. The pain. It's coming——"

Quickly Ignaz Philipp rose. The midwife removed the bedclothing from the lower part of the young woman's body. Ignaz Philipp in almost a single motion dipped his fingers into the lard and then into the girl's body. He pressed his left palm

175

on the young woman's huge abdomen. Beneath that palm he felt the child gather itself. The abdominal muscles tensed. They became rigid. The contractions of the heavy uterus began slowly and powerfully. With his right hand he felt the birth canal slowly gape to the pressure behind. Three fingers slid into the canal easily. The neck of the uterus, a few hours ago a thick stump an inch long, projecting into the vagina, and in the center of which was an opening that would admit a thick knitting needle, was now stretched and expanded from a stump into a disk. The opening and the canal which would have admitted a thick knitting needle now would admit three fingers. But the head is bigger than the width of three fingers.

And the full bag above, the loaded uterus, now pressed and contracted, seeking to expel the child which filled it. The parts had not yet expanded enough. The birth canal must be wider. The uterus contracted again. The woman screamed. Ignaz Philipp's fingers felt the membrane which sealed the uterus surge, felt the waters within the membrane harden under pressure, felt the head of the child just beyond. The woman screamed again and again. Ignaz Philipp pressed with the palm on her abdomen. Suddenly his other hand, his wrist was wet with hot fluid. The membrane, the bag of water had burst. The uterus contracted once more.

"OhGod, pleaseGod, Ican'tStandit . . . Help me! Help me!"

"Pull on the sheet, dear, pull on the sheet."

"Don't scream," said Ignaz Philipp. "Save your breath to push."

The contractions stopped. The uterus suddenly relaxed. Ignaz Philipp withdrew his hands. He looked at his watch. It was five minutes after five. The pains had now begun to come at fifteen-minute intervals.

The young woman relaxed her grip upon the sheet. Her face was wet. Her hair was dampened now and hung lankly on the pillow. Ignaz Philipp mopped her face with the towel.

"Was it a hard pain?"

"No. Not yet. Soon, Doctor?"

"You're doing fine. You shouldn't have any trouble at all. I don't think it's going to be long now."

The midwife rose.

"Would you like me to get you some coffee, Doctor?"

"I'll go," said Ignaz Philipp. He turned to the young woman.

"Will you be good next time?" He smiled. "Will you remember? No more screaming—save your breath to push! Push hard! All right?"

"I'm sorry. I'll try."

"Sure you will."

He went to the journal on the way out. He searched for her bed number. He found it. She had actually given her name. He looked at it and drew a quick breath. Beatrice Czorny. The name was Hungarian. Her husband was a Hungarian! He studied the rest of the journal with sudden care. He left the ward, gulped half a cup of coffee. He set it down. He hurried back to the ward.

The young woman was as he had left her. The midwife sat by her side, placidly knitting.

"No pains?"

"No, Doctor." She smiled.

He looked at his watch. It was twenty minutes after five.

"What are you trying to do? Play games with us?"

"No, Doctor."

"I don't think that's a baby in there at all. I think it's just gas."

She studied his face.

"Was it like this with your other babies?"

"About the same."

"Did you have pains at shorter and shorter intervals and then at long ones?"

"No. They started much as these and then went on until——"

She gasped.

"Pain?"

She nodded.

"Remember! Use your breath to push! Don't scream!"

The pain smashed her. She held her breath. Her face swelled, grew red, grew red-purple. It smashed again. Her body arched. Her eyes protruded. It smashed again.

"Ai-eee!" she screamed suddenly. "No more! Ah, please! Doctor, Doctor!"

"You're screaming! You're not to scream! Push! Push hard!"

She rolled her eyes at him. She seized her lower lip between her teeth. She held her breath again. Her whole body seemed to swell. The pain smashed her. Her teeth ground down on her lips. Blood trickled from her mouth. She pushed. The pain smashed her. She pushed again. The pain smashed her.

"I can't!" Her breath guttered between her teeth. "I can't stand it! I can't! Oh God, OhGod,OhGodtakeit!"

"Stop screaming! Push! Now, listen to me!"

"Ai-eee . . . Oh God Almighty M-I-G-H-T—Y . . . EEEEEE!"

He put his face close to hers. He shouted into her open mouth.

"Will you stop that? Do you hear me? Stop it! STOP IT!"

Her eyes implored him. She clamped her teeth on her bleeding lip. Her face reddened, swelled, her eyes bulged. The pain smashed her. She strained. Her body bumped upward. She squeezed her eyes shut. Her red face was hardly human. The pain smashed her. She held on. The breath snorted out in a rush from her nostrils. The contractions slowed. The pain re-

177

ceded. Her face paled. Her knees hung limp. Her legs fell apart. Her body collapsed.

She breathed again. She sighed deeply. She sighed again.

"Hard one?"

She shook her head.

"Feel all right?"

She smiled weakly.

He looked at his watch. It was twenty-five after five.

"We're getting closer."

"Is everything all right?"

"Everything's fine. Only when I tell you not to scream—don't scream."

"I tried. Honestly, I tried."

"I know you did. You were fine. You were really fine."

"It's so hard. I thought I was going to—and then it burst out of me——"

"You save your breath. You need your breath to squeeze out. Help along."

She nodded. "I'll try."

"You're a brave, good girl. You're doing fine."

"Much longer?"

"Just a little longer now. You'll see."

"I think it's coming again."

"Get on your side. Quick!"

"On my side?"

"And bring up your knees."

The pain smashed her. She bit the sheet. It smashed again. She clawed at the mattress. Ignaz Philipp thrust in his fingers. The head was hard against his fingertips. The neck of the uterus was becoming a ring. It was very wide now. More than three fingers measured against the child's head. The pain smashed her. The uterus bulged. The head pushed against his fingertips. She screamed. This time the scream was deep in her throat. She made sounds now. She made only sounds. For this pain there were no words.

"Strain," cried Ignaz Philipp. "Harder. Listen! Move your bowels! Do you hear me? Move your bowels! Strain it out!"

The pain smashed her. The uterus bulged. The head pushed.

"Ahhh," she shouted deep in her chest, "ahhrgguh! . . . Hahhhh!"

"Come on, little girl. Come on, darling. This is a hard one, isn't it! This is what we want! What does your husband call you?"

She tried to smile at him. Her lips twitched. Her head jerked up and down on the wet pillow. A small gush of fecal matter spurted from her on to the bed.

"Boom-Boom——"

The pain smashed her.

"Ahhhh . . . Ahhhh, GOD! . . ."

178

"Well then, come on. Boom-Boom! Come on, girl! BOOM-BOOM!"

The head pushed again. The neck of the uterus widened grudgingly. His fingertips felt the large fontanelle. He withdrew his hand. He looked at the midwife. She arched her eyebrows to ask a question. He nodded slowly.

"Face up," he said quietly.

"I'll get the forceps."

He looked at the girl. He put his hand on her shoulder.

"You've done everything I've asked you to. You've been fine." He patted her gently.

Her face was wet and pale. She was smaller. She seemed, between pains, to shrink within her flesh. And the abdomen seemed more huge, the child thinly cased beneath the skin of her belly.

The pain smashed at her. She drew up her knees. From between her clenched teeth, her bared lips, came short, coughing grunts. He put in his hand again. Again he felt the greater fontanelle. His mind pictured the position of the child in the uterus. Normally, the child was born face down, facing the sacrum. This child's face was up, facing the girl's pubic arch.

The spasm passed. She turned her head. She tried to smile.

"Instruments?"

His heart yearned in a great surge of pity for the fear she now must feel.

"It's going to be all right, Boom-Boom. Be quiet, darling. Rest. Rest all you can. I promise you—it's going to be all right."

She smiled again and closed her eyes. He wiped the sweat from her face. The midwife arrived with the forceps. He wiped them carefully on his coat sleeve. He inserted his hand. He pushed his right forefinger between the tight neck of the uterus and the child's head, which was stuck there. His finger found the child's ear. With his left hand he slowly passed a blade of the forceps along his right hand, along his right forefinger, past the child's ear. Slowly, cautiously, he inserted the forceps deeper, easing the handle upward. He inserted the second blade. He locked the handles.

The young woman's body tightened. A deep rippling flowed in the muscles of her abdomen.

"It's coming," he said quickly to the midwife. "When she has her pain put your hand on her belly now, squeeze in, push down."

"I know, Doctor."

The rippling of muscle grew greater. The woman screamed softly. The pain was gathering.

"Don't scream! Boom-Boom! Listen to me! Help us!"

The pain smashed. The woman's head rolled weakly. Her teeth barely clamped upon her lip. It smashed again. Her face

179

swelled. It was dark red now. The tissues of it glistened with her sweat. Her hands pulled on the sheets. Her body arched. Sound ripped from her throat. The uterus fought to force out the child. Her skin ripped. Blood trickled jaggedly from the tear. Ignaz Philipp slowly raised the handles of the forceps. At the same time he pulled gently. The pain smashed again.

"You've got it," cried the midwife.

"Squeeze, darling," said Ignaz Philipp.

With a last, desperate exertion the young woman tensed and commanded her will to expel her entire body through her uterus. Again the pain smashed, and now she howled like a wild animal, and it smashed again, and again she howled. And there was a bloody froth on her lips.

Ignaz Philipp bent quickly to look. Bulging against the stretching vulva was a dark tumor. It was the top of the child's head.

"We're there, Boom-Boom. It's almost over now."

From the body of the young woman came a final feeble convulsion. Two hours ago she would have screamed in agony from it. Now it seemed but a cramp. She heaved upward. She lay silent. The head was born. Ignaz Phillip removed the forceps. He freed the shoulders. He pulled on them gently. Suddenly the body spurted into his hands. The child was born. He looked at it a moment.

"It's a girl, Boom-Boom. Your little daughter's got a play-mate."

She tried to smile but could not.

He scanned again the slippery, greasy, pale-bluish clay in his hands, the thick blue stem of the cord passing from its belly into the placenta still within the body of the mother.

"She's a fine baby," he announced happily. "She's perfect."

The midwife cut the cord. The child began a mewling cry. She tied a rag around the stump. In a little while another cramp came. With the cramp came the afterbirth. The midwife wrapped it carefully for later examination.

"It's over," said Ignaz Philipp. "That's all there is."

"I'm so tired, sir doctor."

"You're going to sleep too. You're going to get a good, long rest."

Usually three hours after delivery patients were required to walk back to the ward for women just delivered.

"Let her rest here tonight," Ignaz Philipp ordered.

Her eyes, exhausted, wet with pain, dimmed with gratitude. Her pale hand made a small groping motion on the coverlet. He put out his hand quickly. She pressed his fingers. She tried to raise his hand to her mouth. The effort was too great. Hastily he snatched his hand back, smoothed her pillow, held her shoulders.

180

"Sleep for me tonight, little one. There never was a better patient. Never! Sleep well . . ."

The midwife held up the baby. It had been placed on a pillow. To this pillow the baby was bound with a roller bandage, bound so tightly it could move only its head.

"Look, Mrs.! Look at your girl!"

"Isn't she beautiful?" cried Ignaz Philipp.

The woman stared and stared. And all the while her mouth smiled and all the while tears fell from the corners of her eyes.

"I'm going to have a message taken to your husband. What will I tell him? Would you like that?"

"Tell him—tell him the child looks exactly like Elizabeth——" she said shyly. She hung her head. "He thinks Elizabeth is the most beautiful girl in the world."

"Hah, hah!" cried Ignaz Philipp. "Next to Beatrice, eh? Next to our Boom-Boom!"

The midwife began to straighten the bedclothing.

"This time," Ignaz Philipp whispered to her, "put on some clean sheets."

She looked at him, doubtfully, startled. Then she smiled and nodded. Ignaz Philipp rolled down his cuffs. He wiped his hands on a towel.

"Good night, then, Boom-Boom," he said, and walked from the bedside, out of the ward. He tore a page of clean paper from the journal. He dipped a quill into the inkpot. On the paper he wrote clearly:

*Mr. Czorny*,
Your wife salutes you. You now have two daughters. A little baby girl was born to her this evening. Your wife instructs me to say the child looks exactly like Elizabeth. As her doctor I tell you the condition of both is excellent. As to yourself, be of good heart.

He signed his name. He folded the paper and on the outside he wrote: *"August Czorny, St. Ulrich's Prison."*

"There," he said. "That's the kind of writing I don't mind doing."

He walked out of the clinic and looked up and down the street. Across the street a youth was passing. He whistled to him. He gave the young man the note, fumbled in his pocket. He had only a few groschen and a silver six-kreutzer piece. Impulsively he gave the youth the silver piece, laughed happily at his amazement, watched him run down the street toward St. Ulrich's district. Now he thought of something else.

"Aha!" he said to himself. "The man with the liver."

He turned contentedly toward another part of the hospital. He walked with determination, full of triumph. The young woman and her husband had become his friends. As an attendant showed him to the man's bedside he decided what to say. The attendant left. He smiled down at the man, grimly. It was a swarthy fellow, one of ten thousand to be found hanging outside the doors of any tavern in the land.

"And how are you?" he asked, looking at the man fixedly.

"All right," the fellow said, surprised and cautious.

"I am Dr. Semmelweis. I just dropped by to see how you were."

"I got stabbed in the liver."

"I know. Are you in pain?"

"Oh no. They sewed me up."

"Yes. You look fine. You don't show any signs of internal bleeding."

"I feel all right."

"Probably you'll be out of here in a week."

The man stared at him curiously, warily.

"Well, I'm glad to see you're fine. I've just come from the bedside of Czorny's wife." The man started at the name. "She's just had a fine baby, a little girl. Aren't you glad?"

"Oh, sure," the man said carelessly, waiting.

"Yes, she went through a great deal. You know—it's pretty tough, not having your husband beside you at a time like that."

"It's not my fault."

"It's pretty tough to be in jail at a time like this."

"What did he have to stab me for?"

"You were both drunk."

"Sure. Only you don't go around stabbing a man. What kind of a trick is that, pulling a knife on a fellow? I've been in lots of fights. You never heard of me pulling a knife."

"And you never have, eh? I'm glad to hear it. I like to meet such an innocent fellow."

"I can't help it if he's in jail——" the man mumbled, confused.

"You're the one that has to bring charges against him. As I say—I just left his wife. They have a brand-new baby girl. And he's in jail. Well, I must be going. I'm—I'm very glad to hear your liver is all right," he said elaborately. "Yes indeed. You'll get the best of care, I promise you." He looked at the ceiling. "I'm glad to hear about your liver. Things like that can be quite serious." He looked at the man coldly. "I'll speak to the doctor on duty."

"It's not my fault," the man stammered. "Heaven knows it's not *I* who's to blame."

"Of course not. I just thought I'd tell you about the baby . . . really, it's such a lovely baby . . ."

"As to pressing charges—what kind of a man do you think I am?" He became suddenly virtuous. "I settle such affairs myself."

"That's fine." Ignaz Philipp beamed. The coldness left his

voice. "You know you're going to make that poor girl very happy."

"We were just quarreling and all of a sudden he pulls a knife on me . . ."

"You're a very understanding man. I'm going to see you get the finest of care. You ought to recover beautifully."

"Naturally a man doesn't press charges in such circumstances."

"Good-by, my friend," said Ignaz Philipp. "I'll tell her you're well."

"Will you speak to the doctor?"

"I'll speak to the doctor on the way out."

He left the bedside and walked from the ward, intoxicated with happiness. He had the best possible tidings for that fine young woman tomorrow morning. He stopped beside one of the journalists on duty.

"Good evening, Doctor," he said, and bowed.

"Good evening, Doctor," the man replied.

"I've been visiting one of your patients. I said I'd speak to you. Good evening again. Come over to maternity and speak to me sometime."

The doctor grinned. Ignaz Philipp walked out into the night. It was a fine night. He walked on the balls of his feet, springily. He was exhilarated, happy with the world. When he reached home there was no one to whom to tell his story. Markussovsky was out. Ignaz Philipp danced about a little, a senseless, joyous dance. Then he undressed, smiling. He slipped between the sheets. The bed had never seemed so soft. In a few moments he was fast asleep.

Markussovsky was sleeping heavily when Ignaz Philipp rose next morning. He dressed, he let himself out quietly. He walked briskly to the university. As he expected, Kolletschka was already in the dissection room.

"Good morning, sir," Ignaz Philipp looked about the room. "Where is Dr. Lautner?"

"I hope he is sleeping, Naci. How much sleep are you getting lately?"

Ignaz Philipp pointed to a nearby cadaver.

"Not so much as him."

"Still, you are young. When you're old as I am there will still be plenty of time for work."

"They keep dying, sir. They keep on dying."

"I don't think we will ever find the reason here."

"I know. We keep turning the same findings over and over. But the secret must be here. There is no other place to look for it."

"We've examined so many women dead of childbed fever, Naci."

"I can't help it, sir. There's no place else to look. And al-

183

ways—perhaps the next one will give up the secret. Perhaps we're overlooking something. Perhaps if we do enough post-mortems we will find it. And it will be something very simple. Something, perhaps, we have been looking at all the time."

"It doesn't do any harm to look, certainly. You're learning a lot of gynaecology, that's certain."

"That's right " He moved to a table and looked at the body. "The same sort of fluid in the thorax——"

Kolletschk₂ nodded sadly.

"A milky. putrid lymph in the lungs—pus around the ovaries—inflammation in the uterus—clots—some gangrene—the peritoneun₁ inflamed——"

"Always, always the same——"

"Blisters of pus and foul-smelling fluid under the skin——"

Ignaz Philipp swallowed.

"Well, there's nothing new here."

"No. Naci. Nor yesterday. Nor—— Do you know you've examined more than a hundred bodies now?"

"Not all of them are the same, sir. Some of them are slightly different——"

"Yes, that's true. But all of them——"

"All of them have at least one thing in common. They die. These are women, sir, healthy women. And they walk into the best hospital in the world. And they deliver healthy babies. And then they die. Why do they die? 1 don't know. How comes this disease? I don't know. But I see them every day. I look on, I observe, I watch them, powerless. But I have not yet reached the point where I can watch them indifferently. And so long as I continue to seek a cause and a remedy I'm not so ashamed at least to look them in the eye, one human being to another."

"Well, we'll keep on hunting, you and I, as long as you please. As for me, one never gets done learning anatomy. Who knows? Perhaps I will discover something too. You come here any time, Naci. I'll always be glad to help."

"You have, sir. You always have."

"Well, come on. Maybe you're right. Let's look at this one. She came in this morning."

He exposed the cadaver of a woman who had died of puerperal fever. Ignaz Philipp looked down at the body. It was a middle-aged woman. Her skin was pale and yellowish. Huge blebs, bubbles of pus and fluid swelled the skin on the left side of her chest Smaller bubbles, walnut-size, discolored her flanks. "Why did you die?' he said to himself. "What killed you? What is the mechanics of puerperal fever? How did you get it?"

Kolletschka came up with a handful of instruments. He watched Ignaz Philipp fondly.

184

"It's not easy to watch women die, sir," Ignaz Philipp said at last.

"It must be hard. Yes, it must be terrible. You must get used to it, though, Naci. Childbed fever has always been. It always will be."

"So healthy—and in a few days—dead."

Kolletschka sighed. He passed Ignaz Philipp a knife. From head to toe they began to ransack the woman, seeking the murderer. They worked in silence. They finished. They had found only murder.

"Curdled milk on the surface of the intestines—I wonder if that's really milk, sir?"

"Well . . . I'm afraid . . . that's what the textbooks say . . ."

"Milky, bloody fluid in the lower, middle, front region of the abdomen——"

"As always——"

As he left the anatomy room and walked hastily to duty in the First Division, Ignaz Philipp marveled, as always, at Kolletschka's patience, his quietness, his warmth, and his affection. He thought with awe of his good fortune in such a friend. "I'd like to do something for him, something wonderful." He snorted sadly. "What could a provisional assistant do for a man like Kolletschka? Buy him a book? He has the whole university library. He doesn't drink—he smokes, though! I'll look for a grand pipe. The best pipe in Vienna!" He winced. His allowance had not come again. He was far in debt to Markussovsky. In his pocket there were only a few silver pennies. Perhaps he could sell something. He spied the clinic and instantly he smiled, he forgot everything else, thinking of his young patient. He bounded up the steps. He restrained himself. He walked sedately into the first ward. He went swiftly from patient to patient. From the corridor he heard the clang of the death bell. He went to the journal. Seven women had died during the night. He shut the journal soberly. He sighed. Then he walked, smiling, to the bedside of Beatrice Czorny.

Her eyes were sparkling. He noted with surprise that she was very pretty. Her features so distorted and swollen last night had smoothed incredibly, she looked well, normal, rested.

"I feel fine," her eyes greeted him, doglike.

"You *are* fine," he said happily. "No pain, eh? Everything all right? You slept well?"

"I—I would like to ask you—I mean would the sir doctor permit——"

"Solid food! I'll bet that's what you want, solid food! Now, you be patient, Boom-Boom——"

"No, no. I beg your pardon, sir—with respect—I am so

185

grateful—would the doctor object—I want to give the child his name——"

Ignaz Philipp blinked. He was startled and pleased.

"My name? You want to name your baby after me?"

The young woman nodded eagerly. She watched him, her mouth a little open.

"Ah, no, Boom-Boom! You can't do that to a little girl! Do you know what my name is?"

She shook her head, anxious.

"My name is Ignaz, little one. What are you going to call her—Ignatia? No, no."

She thought a moment. "With respect—is the sir doctor married?"

"Me? Heavens no! I'm waiting for a girl like you, Boom-Boom!"

She smiled.

"Then there is someone dear to you——"

"No, no one, I asure you, no girl at all——" He halted suddenly. He stopped smiling.

"The sir doctor's mother?" the young woman asked softly.

"My mother's name was Thérèse," Ignaz Philipp said. He tried to keep any emotion from his voice.

"Then she shall be Thérèse!" The young woman laughed delightedly. "Is it all right, sir doctor? Do you permit it?"

"I thank you," Ignaz Philipp said awkwardly. "I thank you, young woman."

"It is for me to thank the kind sir doctor——"

He walked into the children's ward. The child, strapped to its pillow, slept peacefully. In its mouth was crammed the piece of cloth in which a spoonful of bread and milk had been wrapped. Ignaz Philipp removed the pap gently. The child slept on. He replaced it. He studied the small face. The midwife had molded the child's head, misshaped a trifle by the forceps. The infant looked quite healthy, normal, very well. She was beautiful, he decided. She was red, but she was beautiful.

"Little Thérèse," he said to himself. "Sleep. Sleep well, little Thérèse."

He swallowed. For an instant he pictured his mother standing beside the infant. An attendant walked to the crib softly. He turned away. He left the room. He prepared for morning rounds with Klein.

Rounds completed, he checked the journal. All patients had been attended to. Beatrice Czorny had been examined by himself, by the two night journalists, the two day journalists, Klein, and an interested student. During the balance of the day he assisted in classwork in the autopsy room. The day ended at last with four-o'clock rounds. The students wiped their hands and followed Klein, Breit, and Semmelweis through the

186

wards. Beatrice Czorny's temperature had risen a little. She was examined carefully. Neither the director nor Ignaz Philipp nor any of the four students who examined her discovered anything else of note to enter in her case in the journal.

At five o'clock Ignaz Philipp stopped again by her bedside. He reported that her husband had been overjoyed to hear about the baby and her good health. He related that her six-year-old daughter Elizabeth had been at the hospital during the afternoon and had brought a flower which the attendant would soon bring in. The young woman smiled happily. She told him she had spent the day planning life on the farm, planning all the new life. He described his visit to the patient her husband had stabbed. He said gravely, his eyes twinkling, he did not expect the man would press charges.

He examined her again briefly. The lochia cruenta, the sanguineous flow of the first few days after delivery, appeared to be scanty. Her eyes were somewhat bright. Her cheeks were flushed. Her temperature had risen. Her pulse was normal. Her bowels had moved.

"You're doing fine," he told her. "Rest is all you need."

The attendant arrived with the flower small Elizabeth had brought.

"There's no reason why Elizabeth shouldn't visit you," he said.

"But not this week end, Mother," the attendant said. "The folks you put her with are taking her out in the country."

"Monday, then," said Ignaz Philipp. "Good night, Boom-Boom."

As he walked home he thought of Kolletschka and the dissecting he would do with him the next morning. He wondered whether Markussovsky would ever practice. He decided that if he, himself, ever had so much money he would do years of research. He dreamed briefly of a vague but wonderful research institute for Hungary. He reviewed the day's patients. Mentally, he checked off those who had died. The wards were filled. More than 14 per cent of the patients were ill of puerperal fever. The percentage appeared to be dropping. Perhaps thirty women could be expected to go into labor in the next twenty-four hours. Five would die. He thought of a patient who had been in the labor room for three days. He wondered excitedly whether they would resort to Caesarian section. He recalled the Maternity Division's Caesarian record. In sixty years only five living women had been cut open for the delivery of child. All of them, of course, had died. But some of the children had lived. He thought of the infant Thérèse. He smiled happily. He thought of Beatrice Czorny. He frowned, remembering her slight fever. He reflected that perhaps she had been examined too much that first day. Tomorrow she would be better.

Next morning he dissected so long with Kolletschka that he

was almost late at the First Division. Klein looked at him sharply. Breit made morning rounds. Ignaz Philipp conducted class. At lunch he learned that the patient who had been three days in the labor room had died early that morning. There were four new cases of puerperal fever. He left lunch early. He went to the baby ward a moment to see the infant Thérèse.

"How are you, Thérèse?" he said shyly.

The child was well. It began to cry a little. The rag nipple had fallen from its mouth. He replaced it. He left the ward and went to its mother. Her eyes were much brighter. Her fever had risen. Her pulse was somewhat weak. He counted one hundred and twenty-two strokes a minute. He smiled at her reassuringly and went to the journal. Epsom salts had been prescribed for her. At eleven o'clock the preceding evening her after-pains which had been slight had become more frequent and severe. She had been hot and restless. She had complained of pain in her head and back. She had not slept well. Early in the morning she had complained of a fit of shivering. She had moved her bowels twice. She had retched but had not vomited.

Breit spoke from behind him.

"That's one patient we needn't worry about. She's got the constitution of an ox."

Breit read the journal, then straightened.

"I don't think there's much to worry about. She's been examined three times today. She's getting plenty of care. These little setbacks aren't uncommon."

"I've taken kind of a special interest in her."

"Oh yes. Her name's Czorny, isn't it. A countrywoman?"

"No, she's Austrian. Her husband's Hungarian, I believe."

"She's a good patient. She'll be all right." He looked at his watch. "Will you take classes this afternoon, please?"

At afternoon rounds the young woman's belly had begun to swell markedly. She felt slight pain when her lower abdomen was pressed. The lochia, the flow, had diminished considerably. The prescribed purge had produced five bowel movements, the last two watery. She said, smiling anxiously, that the pains had been much diminished by each bowel movement. More Epsom salts were prescribed and twenty drops of tincture of opium.

"I'll be all right," she told Ignaz Philipp after rounds.

"Of course you will." He laughed heartily.

"They won't let me nurse the baby."

"No, not yet."

"I nursed the others right away."

"Maybe tomorrow. Tonight you get a good rest."

He was not worried about her as he walked home, but he had begun to be concerned. "If she was a shade less healthy," he told Markussovsky, "we'd have trouble there. I'm sure of it."

"I know what you mean. No matter what the textbooks say, I always worry about the sickly kind. The healthy ones have their ups and downs. Occasionally they even seem to be coming down with puerperal fever. But they get better."

"I think you're right, Marko."

The journal showed next morning that she had slept fitfully. But from four o'clock until seven o'clock she had slept deeply. When she awakened at seven o'clock the pain in her abdomen had returned and was much stronger. Her bowels had moved well. The pains had now expanded from her lower abdomen as high as the pit of her stomach. It was difficult for her to move about in bed. She had headache and dizziness. At morning rounds more Epsom salts was ordered and it was directed that her abdomen should be gently rubbed with warm oil and covered with flannel wrung out in warm water.

Ignaz Philipp, who conducted classes again that day, stayed at her bedside after evening rounds until eight-thirty. He left much cheered. Her pains had begun to abate soon after taking the Epsom salts. Before he left the pains had become trifling and distant. Her abdomen was much less sore. Her pulse was stronger. It had slowed to one hundred and forty-two strokes a minute.

Next day, for the first time, his concern ended. She had a slight fever still. But she was alert and cheerful.

"You've got a really nice smile, young lady."

"I've got a lot to smile about. I feel fine. Can I nurse the baby today?" She held her breasts. "I ache."

"Ache, then. Wait one more day, little one."

She had passed a restful night. She said she was wonderfully refreshed by it.

"And the pains?"

"Very, very little. And not often."

He felt her abdomen. It was much smaller. It was only very slightly sore. She could turn in bed easily. Her pulse was full and soft. It had slowed to one hundred strokes a minute.

"Stick out your tongue."

Her tongue was somewhat brown, but not white-coated.

"Now I'm satisfied. Now I've got to leave you for patients who really need a doctor."

He pinched her cheek and walked away relieved.

At morning rounds Epsom salts was prescribed for her and continued warm flannels. The infant Thérèse throve. She was quite beautiful. There could be no question about it.

At two o'clock in the afternoon, while he was busied in another ward, an attendant hurried for a midwife. The midwife called Breit. After a brief examination Breit summoned Klein.

All the alarming symptoms had returned. The young woman

now groaned from great pain in her abdomen. She had begun to vomit. Her fever had risen markedly. Her pulse was one hundred and sixty strokes a minute. Her tongue was furred. Her abdomen had swollen. It had became so painful for her to move her bowels that she was unable to shift her body to a bedpan and her evacuations were now received on cloths. Ignaz Philipp came into the ward as Klein and Breit completed their examination.

"I think there can be no doubt about this," Klein shrugged.

"No, sir director."

"You notice also, Dr. Breit, the significant suppression of the lochia? Barely any discharge, thin-colored and I think foul-smelling." It was difficult in the ward to distinguish any one smell with clarity. Klein passed the napkin near his nose. "Definitely foul," he reported.

The girl stared at the ceiling.

"And how is our patient this afternoon?" asked Ignaz Philipp.

She did not answer.

"She seems to be a sick girl, Dr. Semmelweis," said Klein. Ignaz Phillipp's eyes widened. His brows raised. He still smiled.

The three walked from the young woman's bed.

"Puerperal fever," said Klein shortly.

Toward evening she began to demand quantities of water. Her pulse became much weaker. Her fever appeared to be higher. She tossed restlessly, moaning in pain at each movement. Her back, sides, and shoulders ached. She was distressed by paroxysms of labored breathing. Toward nine o'clock she had a desire for sleep. She dozed. Ignaz Philipp tiptoed from the bedside. He was still hopeful. Women had been known to recover from puerperal fever. There was no longer doubt. Beatrice Czorny had puerperal fever. He said little to Markussovsky. He was dazed.

He did not dissect with Kolletschka next morning. He rose even earlier than usual. He went directly to the First Division. The young woman was now much worse. She had complained during the night of a constant ringing in her ears.

"It sounds like somebody singing," she whispered. "Am I going to die? Is that it, Doctor? Can my husband come?"

"There's no need to talk like that, Boom-Boom. In the first place your husband can't come. You know the rules here. And anyway he's still in jail, poor fellow. And in the second place you know quite well you're not going to die."

Her lips were cracked with fever. She tried to lick them. Her tongue was dry.

"The pain is bad," she whispered.

He took her pulse. It was too rapid and too weak to count. She began in a little while to talk now of strange and random things. She whispered of a day the grocer had over-charged her. She scolded Elizabeth for ripping her only dress. Once she whispered that she saw a flock of pigeons.

"They dip so. They are so pretty. They wheel . . ."

Later it was evident that she could no longer control her urine.

"Boom-Boom! Do you understand me?"

"Hello, Doctor."

"Do you understand me?"

"Yes, sir doctor." She managed a slow, loving smile.

She closed her eyes. They fluttered open again. They were blank.

"My baby," she whispered. "See the carriage, darling . . ."

Her voice dwindled. He watched her helplessly. An hour passed.

Her breathing became hoarser. There was a rattling sound in it. He held her pulse. It beat faster. It became weaker. He could barely feel it. She sighed again. Her pulse stopped.

He sat there a long time, simply holding her wrist. He looked at her face. It had become quite peaceful. He rose and listened to her chest. There was no life left in her. He looked at her again. The fever flush was fading. Her face was young and beautiful. He left the bedside. His heart pounded. His throat ached. He forced himself to walk, to make rounds. He attended to his duties. He saw to other patients. He heard the clang of the death bell. The sound shattered his numbness. He stood still.

Suddenly he overflowed with horror. He went to the journal. He recoiled. It was no longer matter of course. Five more women dead during the night. Eleven more reported stricken. He stared at the ward, the women, the doomed. Young flesh and old flesh. Death after death. Shivering, he saw the women crawl to him, begging to have their babies in the gutter. The smell of the wards rushed upon him with all their odors of unchanged beds, blood- and pus-stained linen, the open sewers, the grated privies, and of women humbly rotting within their own flesh. On a sudden it was too much. He could stand no more. White and trembling, he stumbled to the office of Director Klein.

Klein looked up, surprised. "Has something happened? Shall I come?"

"We must do something! Something must be done!"

"Be calm, Dr. Semmelweis. What has gone wrong?"

"The fever, that cursed puerperal fever. Death after death. Every day more. They're dying, sir director, right under our very eyes!"

"I see. What was it you wanted me to do?"

"We've got to do something. It can't go on. It mustn't."

"I'm afraid you're wrong there, Doctor. I am sorry to see

191

you so upset." He sat down. "I shall like to ask you a few questions. To begin with—what are the causes of puerperal fever?"

Ignaz Philipp glared at Klein, breathing hard.

"All the causes?" he said with difficulty.

"If you please."

"With respect, sir director——!"

"If you please, Doctor."

"It is a milk fever——"

"Yes."

"Others say it is due to the suppression of the lochia."

Klein nodded.

"There is a theory that it is a putrid fever. There is also a theory that it is a gastric-bilious fever. It as an epidemic peritonitis. Another school holds it is erysipelas. Others say it is due to a miasma. There is a theory that it is due to the unstable condition of women. It is a krasis. It has been claimed that it comes from errors in diet, to chilling, and to emotional conditions——"

"That's enough. I see you are rather more familiar with your work than I expected. Lucas Boer taught that puerperal fever was milk fever. That is what I taught you. That, if you please, is how you will regard it. And the remedy?"

"There is no known remedy, sir director." Ignaz Philipp breathed rapidly. He gazed at Klein eagerly and expectantly.

"Exactly."

"And yet——"

"Henceforth, Dr. Semmelweis, you will regard puerperal fever as an ailment traceable to milk. You will regard it as an ailment for which no human mind has ever found a remedy. No remedy ever will be found. You will accustom yourself to the unhappy incidence and the consequent fatalities of this disease as one of the normal expressions of living and of giving birth, and you will behave toward it as a doctor is expected to react to the inevitable occurrences of life and of death."

"But, sir director——" Ignaz Philipp burst hotly. "Death after death, dying upon dying——"

"You have always the alternative of seeking a less distressing field, Doctor. Should you like to consider it?"

I will not stop, he said to himself then. I will never stop. From this moment on I will never stop.

"No, sir director," he said aloud.

"You are young, Doctor. I have informed you clearly that you might come to me with your problems between the hours of one and three-thirty." He looked at his watch. "It is now eleven-ten." He looked up expectantly.

"I am sorry, sir."

"Thus far you have been studious and quiet and efficient. I shall cancel out this morning's unusual performance against

192

your past record. You will go back to duty now. You will take this with you. As long as you remain here, you will remember it. I am going to quote to you what the Emperor of Austria said when he founded this division. 'Keep yourself to what is old, for that is good. If our ancestors have proven it to be good, why should we not do as they did? Mistrust new ideas. I have no need of learned men. I need faithful subjects. He who would serve me must do what I command. He who cannot do this or who comes full of new ideas may go his way. If he does not, I shall send him.' Do you understand, Dr. Semmelweis?"

"Yes, sir."

"You may go."

Thereafter Klein shook his head. He sighed and searched for a paper. He read it, he totaled it carefully. He went through the figures again. Death from puerperal fever in the past month was only 21 per cent. There had been worse months. There would be better. He put the paper away. At the end of the year the books would balance.

Shaking, protest blinding him with rage, Ignaz Philipp stumbled to the wards.

He was past feeling. He no longer felt anything. He drank the dregs and did not feel them. He went to the autopsy room and the class there. On each table lay a body. Many more were waiting. There were fair women and dark women. There were short women and tall women. And some were young. And some were old. And some were fat. And some were thin. Women of all creeds and of all kinds and of all shapes. And all were dead. The stacked corpses were always waiting. In a little while Beatrice Czorny would be thrown in with the rest. Then they would cut off her chest and scoop out her entrails. They would put a dead baby in the cavity. The students would practice. At the end of the day there would be no further use for Beatrice Czorny. There were no sick patients in this division. There were only the dead, the dying, and the living. As he lectured, another corpse was brought in. That night four more died of childbirth fever. They were dissected. The child, Thérèse, was used two days later, died of the illness that killed its mother.

Next morning he was at the anatomy room long before Kolletschka. He worked untiringly now, a man possessed, a man with one goal. When day was done he rushed back to the anatomy room. Patiently, calmly, raging, despairing, he dissected corpse after corpse, always the corpses of women dead of childbirth fever. Somewhere in these tissues lay the murder and the murderer. He sought without ceasing. He found nothing.

Some of the fury left him. He began to observe more closely. A part of his thinking became coldly detached. He began one day to gather statistics. Breit devoted more of his time to the students. He filled Ignaz Philipp's day with clinic duties.

"Give him enough ward work. Give him more than he can handle," Klein said. "He'll get used to puerperal fever."

At the end of three months Ignaz Philipp ceased to be a provisional assistant. But his status was still temporary. He now undertook all the work and responsibility of ordinary assistant. It became his duty to visit and examine every patient in the early morning. He was accompanied on these rounds by a throng of students and graduates, each of whom was privileged to examine the patients. In the afternoon he took the students around again and examined any patient who was in labor. He was also required to be ready day or night to perform all obstetrical operations or to help any midwife. He reported to Klein on the condition of patients twice daily. He gave clinical instruction in the wards. But each day he arose very early to work with Kolletschka, dissecting corpse after corpse, seeking the murderer. And in the evenings he now busied himself until midnight with a slowly gathering sum of statistics.

He made his first discovery. He discovered from his statistics that during six years three times as many women died in the First Division as in the adjoining Second Division. He looked up from his papers. A faint hope pulsed in him. His heart beat faster. He looked at his watch. It was after ten o'clock. He rose and went to the home of Bartsch.

Bartsch was preparing to go to bed.

"Won't tomorrow do, Doctor?" he said mildly.

"I have something of the greatest importance, I believe."

"I am sorry you found me thus. I had a hard day, you must excuse me——"

"It is of no consequence, it is I who should apologize for disturbing you at such an hour. Nevertheless——"

He laid his papers down on a table.

"I want you to look at these. I am going to leave them with you. You will want to study them."

"Mortality reports?"

"They cover the years 1841 to 1846. In our First Division there have been nineteen hundred and eighty-nine deaths. In your Second Division, Dr. Bartsch, there have been six hundred and ninety-one deaths."

"I know. It has always been like that. I don't know why. Professor Klein is in charge of both divisions. We do nothing in our division that you do not do in yours."

"Why do three times as many women die in the First Division as in the Second?"

"I have often wondered at it. Yes, I have often wondered."

Ignaz Philipp leaned eagerly to him.

"You have reached some conclusion? You have a theory?"

194

"No-o-o-o. I would not say a—a—conclusion. Some thoughts have from time to time occurred to me . . ."

"Will you tell me, please? Anything——"

"Well . . . really I haven't gone into it, you know . . ."

"Yes—but still?"

"Well, naturally there's the epidemic influence, the cosmic-telluric changes, the atmosphere, you might say—you're familiar with the way it spreads over districts and causes fever and particularly in women predisposed to it because they have just had a child . . ."

"Yes, Doctor." The weariness of the day left him. He was alert now. He gazed at Bartsch intently.

"Then I have also sometimes wondered—you know in your division you have students, all men. In the Second Division we train midwives, we have only women."

"That's true."

"Well, you know a man is by nature rougher than a woman. It has occurred to me that in making the examinations even their hands would be larger . . . and consequently . . ."

"I understand."

"Of course—and I beg of you not to mention this, for it might cause resentment—the First Division has acquired an evil reputation . . . women come there in fear and dread . . . they beg, they plead to be admitted to the Second Division . . . some of them seem to be convinced the First Division staff is responsible . . . I have seen them on their deathbeds in the First Division babbling brightly they were perfectly all right and needed no help solely to avoid medical treatment . . ."

"Every day," said Ignaz Philipp softly. "Every hour."

"So that I suppose fear plays its part . . . and surely, Doctor, perhaps modesty also . . ."

His voice trailed off. They were silent awhile.

"If other thoughts occur to me . . ."

"I shall be most grateful, sir." Ignaz Philipp rose, he smiled grimly, for the first time he had clues. "Shall I leave these papers?"

"Uh—no—I—ah—believe I am familiar with them——" He frowned a little. "Did you say only nineteen hundred and eighty-nine had died of puerperal fever in the First Division in six years?"

Ignaz Philipp looked quickly at the total. He looked up slowly.

"Yes . . . that is a little strange, isn't it! I'll check again."

He went back to the hospital, thoughtful. In the next week he checked his findings with Kolletschka, with Skoda, with Rokitansky.

"He appears to be obsessed with this single ailment," Skoda said later.

195

"I wasn't of much help to him," said Rokitansky. "My specialty is the appearance of the disease in tissue and not its causes or its cure. My mind doesn't work much these days. That Virchow has disabled me." He spoke this last sadly. He had recently issued a monumental work on pathology. Rudolf Virchow, a rising young physician-scientist, had promptly proven two of his important theories ludicrously false.

"Forget it, Karl. Your work will live long after Virchow is forgotten."

"He's right, you know . . ."

"That doesn't erase a whole work on pathological anatomy because two theories are wrong. Do another book. Forget him . . . What are we going to do about Semmelweis?"

"I wish I could help him. If he lets this run away with him he'll get in trouble. Klein doesn't like innovators."

"No," said Skoda reminiscently, "he doesn't, does he?"

At the end of two weeks Ignaz Philipp returned to Bartsch.

"I have examined the thoughts you advanced," he said deprecatively. "I'm afraid we will have to reject them."

"Today was a bad day, I understand."

"Eleven," said Ignaz Philipp briefly.

"New cases? Or dead?"

"The eleven? All dead. Seven new cases."

Bartsch shook his head sadly.

"And yet a few feet away we've been relatively lucky."

"First I examined the miasma theory. How, I asked myself, is it possible that the miasma struck down so many patients in the First Clinic, while under the same roof it spared the Second Clinic? For this I had only the absurd conclusion that the miasma, the so-called epidemic influence, is subject to miraculous fluctuation. This miasma hovering over us in the First Division declines in power the instant a patient crosses the threshold of the Second Clinic across the hall. At the same time, as another patient crosses the threshold into the First Clinic the miasma becomes deadly. The coincidence is absurd. Epidemic influences do not behave that way. When cholera breaks out, people sicken of it in the city as well as in the hospital. Yet when an epidemic of puerperal fever sweeps our clinic, hardly a case is reported in the city."

"I have heard it suggested that miasmas, epidemic influences, may hover over a single street, or a single house, or even a single person in a ward——"

"If that is true, why, then, does it hover consistently in the First Division and not the Second?"

"Yes . . . it's a strange coincidence, isn't it——"

"Too strange. One cannot accept it. For there is another thing. When an epidemic of puerperal fever gets too bad, we close the hospital. And that ends the epidemic. But when an

196

epidemic of cholera floods the city and we close the cholera wards, the epidemic goes right on."

"As I say, I have never given the matter much thought . . ."

"I am grateful to you for any theory, believe me. Now, as to the roughness of medical students and their larger hands, this also I have been compelled to reject. For what is the introduction of the index finger into the wide and long vagina of a pregnant woman as a cause of injury compared to the process of birth? If examination can produce fatal injury with only a slender finger, then the passage of a child through the same vagina must always be fatal."

"It's quite possible . . . you may be right . . ."

"Now as to modesty, as to injured modesty causing puerperal fever, I have been forced to reject this possibility also. Most of our patients certainly suffer from fear. But they do not suffer from modesty. First of all I cannot conceive how modesty could bring decomposed matter from without or produce decomposed matter within the individual herself. There is another thing. Many of our patients are frankly whores, loose and abandoned women. And all are poor and from the lower classes. Ladies of the highest class are, however, attended by men. Their patients do not die of puerperal fever in consequence of wounded modesty. Are we to attribute to our humble patients a tenderness of modesty such as the highest classes of the community do not claim? I cannot believe it."

"You are probably right. Yet these are not only my opinions . . . !"

"I know. I am aware that they are general. I have heard Professor Klein state them. Nevertheless, they are plainly illogical. As to fear, I cannot see how a psychic condition can occasion an anatomical change. Even accepting it, it must have taken some time before the First Division began to be feared. How about the patients who came before the First Division got its bad reputation? Why did they die? Fear does not explain the beginning of the mortality."

"It begins to look as though you had a lifetime of work ahead of you, Doctor. I am sorry I haven't helped you. I wish you luck."

Ignaz Philipp walked slowly back to the hospital.

Why did they die? Why did three times as many die in the First Division as in the Second? They were under the same roof. They were only a few feet apart. Their arrangements were exactly the same. They shared the same reception room. Why did they die? As he entered the wards he heard the distant clang of the death bell. He saw the women start in their beds. Some raised themselves, their eyes wide with horror. The priest was coming. Behind him followed death. The priest was coming to give absolution. Someone somewhere in the ward was going to die. What was it? Who was dying? Who was dying and did not know it? Was he coming this way?

Ignaz Philipp's heart tolled with the bell. He stopped. He watched the women. The bell knelled in his head. Another dead, or another dying. That bell, that priest, forever signaled one thing. He thought a moment. An idea tensed him. In his breast excitement grew. From the chapel of the Lying-in Hospital priests could walk to the dying in any ward in the Second Division without passing through any other ward. But to reach any ward in the First Division they must pass through all the rest. Ignaz Philipp walked purposefully into the corridor. He waited. A moment later the procession came into view. He walked directly to the priest. His breath came quickly.

"Father, I must speak to you."

The priest stopped.

"Yes, Doctor——"

"Is it a part of ritual that the bell must be rung?"

"It is customary."

"But must you? Must you absolutely ring it?"

"Why shouldn't the bell be rung, Doctor?"

"I will tell you why, Father. In this division we have a terrible mortality from childbed fever——"

"I know."

"We do not know the cause. It might be anything. It might be fear. And each time you walk down this corridor ringing the bell, each time you walk from ward to ward ringing it, the women start in horror, they leap up in bed, they imagine you have come for them. Each time you pass this happens. And, Father, you pass many times a day."

"I am only doing my duty, Doctor——"

"I know, Father. But I appeal to you in the name of humanity not to ring that bell. Come as you please—go as you please. Only this—I beg of you not to ring that bell."

The priest looked at the bell soberly.

"If you think it may help, Doctor——"

"I thank you, Father. From my heart——"

"I must hurry, Doctor." The priest, holding the bell by its clapper, rushed silently through the wards to the bedside of a dying woman.

"I am informed," said Klein next morning, "that you have persuaded the priests not to ring the death bell. May I know why you have taken this upon yourself?"

"With respect, sir director, it occurred to me that the patients dread the sound and that fear might be a cause of puerperal fever."

"I have heard that possibility. For that matter I have also heard overcrowding given as a cause. That seems to be a fa-

198

vorite finding of the committees appointed to look into causes when the epidemic becomes too severe."

"Overcrowding, sir?"

"Yes, if you like. And also because most of our patients are unmarried and depressed. Or because our patients get up too soon after labor. Or because the medical treatment is inferior. Or laundry, ventilation, chilling, diet. These are all hypotheses. And what is it we teach?"

"That the fever is caused by suppression of the secretion of milk."

"Precisely. I ask you again—concern yourself with your work. I do not require you to be curious. It is strange that I should have to remind you."

Klein forgot to inform the priest to resume ringing the death bell. The priest went about silently. Ignaz Philipp waited tensely. The end of the month came. He summed the deaths. They had risen slightly. The bell meant nothing.

He worked harder. In the evenings he read whatever work on obstetrics he could find. He consulted the greatest authorities. He explored overcrowding as a possible cause. And he found that the safe Second Clinic was more overcrowded than the deadly First. A week later he assembled all his research on the depression natural to unmarried mothers. The cause of greater mortality was not here. The same types of patients were in both the First and Second Clinics. There were as many unmarried mothers in one division as the other. He made a study of medical treatment. He found that it was the same in both clinics. The laundry was the same. The ventilation was the same. The same caterer supplied identical diets to both clinics. Patients rose after labor at the same interval in either clinic. The First Division continued to suffer three and four times as many deaths from childbed fever as the Second.

At the end of seven months he began a study of suppression of milk secretion. He discovered after three weeks of careful comparison that the incidence of this was the same in both clinics. He summed his records. In the course of the seven months there had been almost seven hundred cases of puerperal fever. That meant almost seven hundred deaths. He consulted his mortality records. He blinked. Something was wrong. There were a little more than two hundred deaths. But the disease was almost invariably fatal. Or was it? He rushed out to see Chiari.

"Virulence of puerperal fever abating?" Chiari laughed. "Oh, no, Naci. You're quite mistaken. What makes you think so?"

Ignaz Philipp showed Chiari his records. Chiari sobered.

"Does Professor Klein know you're keeping these records?"

"No, I haven't told him. He doesn't want me to investigate puerperal fever. But I think he knows that I've never stopped.

199

And I haven't. I can't. I must find out the reason for this murder. I don't want any trouble with him. I beg your pardon, Johann—for a moment I forgot he is your father-in-law now."

"He had a high opinion of you, Naci," Chiari said sadly. "It's too bad. It's a pity." He looked at the records. "You haven't told anyone else about the idea of the virulence abating?"

"I came straight to you."

"I'd forget these records if I were you," Chiari said. "Just forget you ever kept them. And, Naci—no one can do anything about puerperal fever. Why involve yourself? Do as you're told and you'll soon be on good terms with him again. I want to show you something—look here, this is the kind of research you ought to do!"

He took from his pocket a curiously shaped instrument.

"What's that, Johann?"

"It's something new I've invented. It's a decapitation hook!"

Ignaz Philipp frowned frequently on the way home.

"Marko," he said that evening, "why did Johann behave so queerly when I showed him these records?"

"Perhaps he feels Klein would resent it if he thought you were keeping records for your personal use."

"He would have said so. No, it was something else. Seven hundred cases of fever—two hundred deaths——"

"WHAT?" cried Markussovsky. "Who ever heard of such a thing—— Who ever——"

Suddenly it was clear.

"Wait, Marko! Wait!" He whistled, awed. "Do you know what that devil's doing? I see it now! Marko! He's sending his puerperal fevers to the General Hospital——"

"And there they're ascribing the cause of death to something else—probably some pal of his——"

"That's how he keeps the mortality tables down! It's that or he's deliberately diagnosing childbed fever as something else. That's why two years ago the table for this month showed 29.33 per cent mortality, and this month showed 3.22 per cent——"

"Remember? There was a committee investigation when they kept getting higher and higher?"

"Marko!"

"What are you going to do?"

"I'm going to keep it to myself. Now, I have a club. Now let him resent me all he wants. Now, I'll work unhampered . . ."

"You'd have to prove it, you know."

"And maybe I couldn't. But I could always raise the question. And Klein, my friend, Klein that behind-kisser who keeps his job only through the politics that got it for him, Klein doesn't like questions. Klein and Schiffner, the august director of the whole hospital, and Rosas, and the rest of the mandarins, no, Marko, they don't like questions."

"Where did you learn so much?"

"I've learned a lot. I know that von Tuerkheim, the liaison man between the court and the hospital, the man who keeps the Emperor informed of what's going on here, has no use for Klein and Schiffner and the rest. But the conservatives are strong at court. The battle never ends. Only a few years ago, when Skoda was up for Secundarius, Schiffner rebuked him publicly for making patients sicker by poking them with a stick, and another of them, Hildebrand, rejected his thesis on auscultation and percussion that the whole world's accepted now. They thought they'd settled Skoda. And when Hildebrand retired, the old guard appointed Lippe to take his place as head of the internal-medicine department. But Lippe died last year. And the old guard passed over Skoda again. They gave von Tuerkheim a list of candidates. And he threw out the whole list. He appealed to Nadherny, dean of Prague's medical faculty, to select the best of our men. And the result is—Skoda is now head of the department. And he is also Secundarius. Haller alone ranks higher. That's how it's ranged itself now, Marko. The old guard on one side, all reactionaries, all fumblers, all outdated—and on the other side the Skodas, the Rokitanskys, the Hebras, the Helms, the Oppolzers. And von Tuerkheim."

"Don't get caught between them."

"We know where our allegiance lies, you and I. For myself, when I think of medicine and politics mixing I get a feeling of nightmare."

"Then, Naci, why not slack off a little on this puerperal business? It can only embroil you. And look at you—how much weight have you lost? When do you eat? When do you sleep?"

"I could never stop, Marko. Never. Not now. Row after row of women, Marko, poor, friendless, and helpless, waiting to have their babies, waiting to die. Doomed from the day they enter. Day after day I see them. Night after night. I can't do otherwise, Marko. Their cries ring in my ears."

"Others don't seem to mind——"

"I know. I've discovered something. I've got a sickness."

"Tell me about it. Maybe I know something——"

"It's incurable. It's pity."

The months passed. Each day was like the last—endless work, endless research, endless failure, endless death. The year was almost ended and Klein had not yet made him official assistant. He reprimanded him almost daily now. And Ignaz had learned to listen with a smile. He looked directly into Klein's eyes and he smiled. Klein watched him coldly. He needed more excuse than a smile. He knew who Ignaz Philipp's friends were. He knew that Ignaz Philipp's reputation with the faculty was spotless, even among the reactionaries. Slowly and carefully, a hint here, a suggestion there, he began to undermine him. Klein waited.

In October, at Skoda's insistence, Ignaz Philipp took and passed a surgical examination. On November 30 he received the degree of Doctor of Surgery. Within two weeks Skoda's first assistant resigned to enter private practice. Ignaz Philipp thought until past midnight.

"It is not possible to withstand Klein," he told Skoda next morning. "Let me be your assistant. Klein cannot remain forever."

"I'll have to let you know," said Skoda. "There's Loebl, you know. He's the provisional. He's next in line."

At the end of the week the appointment of Loebl to Skoda's first assistant was officially announced.

"I'm sorry, boy. Hang on. Your turn will come."

The year ended. Month after frantic month Ignaz Philipp continued frantically to seek a clue to the cause of puerperal fever. In January he came upon a new theory. Authorities blamed male sperm for inoculating women with the fever. He began new research. At the end of January he had proven glumly that only by an incredible coincidence could three times as many men be poisonous to women in the First Clinic as in the Second. The deaths continued. Then they slowed. He grimaced as he watched them decline. Puerperal fever patients were being quietly transferred, undiagnosed, when the death rate in the First Division neared a figure that might disturb the Imperial Court. But there was a limit, he knew, to the number of cases the General Hospital could absorb. "There"— he smiled grimly—"there they have a death rate to consider also."

On the twenty-seventh of February, 1846, obeying almost overwhelming faculty pressure, Klein reluctantly appointed his first assistant. Now, if it was possible, he worked harder than before. There were still theories to explore. There was no lack of learned theories. There was no lack of authorities. One after the other his research rejected such verdicts as summer heat and winter cold, the immorality of the women, the pestilential nature of the timbers and mortar, of the very building which enclosed the maternity hospital. All these things to which childbed fever was learnedly ascribed were common to both divisions. But the First Division's death rate continued invariably higher, and day by day the women continued to sicken, to cry out, to implore him, and to die.

"I have examined every possible cause," he begged Skoda. "You must help me now, for I have exhausted the authorities."

202

"There are so many hypotheses. So many great men have made them with utter assurance. One of them, my boy, must be right."

"They are not right. Not one. I have tested them all. Not one is right. In addition to all I have reported on to you in the past months I have checked theories that it is caused by excess of blood—increase of fibrin—watery blood—damming up the circulation—the act of birth itself—diminished blood pressure—prolonged labor—insufficient contraction—even the authority who says learnedly that puerperal fever is some idiosyncrasy of the individual."

He paused, dejectedly.

"These things I *have* established: the longer the labor the greater chance of puerperal fever. A vast number of the babies born in our division die of what seems exactly like puerperal fever except that it does not attack their genitals. And those who give birth on the street before they reach the hospital, under arches, in gutters, on the sidewalks, they seem protected. What is it protects these street-birth women from puerperal fever in the First and Second Divisions alike?"

Skoda leaned forward. "Are you sure of that last fact?"

"Here are the records."

Skoda read them carefully. He looked up.

"You're right! My friend, we will demonstrate by statistics the smaller death rate among the street-birth cases compared with the First Clinic as a whole."

"What do you mean by demonstrate?"

"Wait. You will see."

Skoda next day moved for the appointment of a committee of professors to inquire into all deaths from puerperal fever, to prepare statistics on the comparative results in cases of street birth.

Klein instantly protested bitterly. Schiffner reassured him. He appointed a committee entirely friendly to the conservative group and he saw to it that the committee never met. He went quietly to the Minister of Education. The Minister of Education promised to help prevent any attempt at investigation.

Then he returned to Klein.

"But what's happening in the maternity division?" asked Schiffner. "What's this I hear that the First Division mortality is always higher than the Second?"

"There is absolutely no difference," said Klein. He looked at Schiffner steadily. "They are exactly the same. And where they are not there are good and sufficient reasons."

Ignaz Philipp next month sought Skoda again.

"I have found a new fact. In the Second Division patients sicken of puerperal fever in a scattered fashion—here a patient, there a patient. In the First Division they tend to come down with it in rows. Absolute rows."

"And what are you doing about it?"

"I will tell you. I am like a drowning man clutching at straws. I talked to Zipfel, Bartsch's assistant. He mentioned that they make a practice in the Second Division of delivering women on their sides. For the past month I've been delivering all First Division cases on their sides."

"And the results?"

"More patients die in the First Division than in the Second!"

"How are you getting on with Klein?"

"It's getting worse and worse."

In October of 1846 Klein moved suddenly and smoothly. He granted Breit a two-year extension of the appointment as first assistant which had expired months before.

Dazed, Ignaz Philipp was forced to relinquish his post. Once again he became merely provisional assistant. His contacts with patients were curtailed sharply. The blow was crushing. He faced now the prospects of waiting another two full years to become first assistant again. While the humiliation was still fresh Skoda, Rokitansky, Hebra, even Haller, maneuvered in vain to persuade Schiffner to countermand Klein.

"It is a scandalously arbitrary abuse of authority," cried Skoda.

"He is perfectly within his rights," Schiffner said indifferently.

They stared at him.

"Come, gentlemen! Even the young must learn to bear misfortune, surely! And I am not altogether unkind." They waited. "I gave him permission this morning to be absent in Hungary for a week——"

"Absent in Hungary?"

"To attend the funeral of his father . . ."

Ignaz Philipp returned from Hungary toward the end of October. His brothers and his sister had gone their separate ways. Now he was alone in the world. He was very silent. He began again to work in the morning with Kolletschka. Most of the rest of the day his time was his own. He read endlessly. He pondered quietly. He walked at night.

The death rate that October soared so high in the Maternity Hospital that it could no longer be ignored. A commission was appointed to investigate. The commission met in November. A week later it handed down its findings. It blamed the outbreak of puerperal on the presence of foreign students. There were then forty-two foreign students studying obstetrics at the university. Their number was cut to twenty.

At the end of November the death rate had dropped by

50 per cent. According to Klein's figures, from 10.77 per cent to 5.37 per cent.

At the end of December Klein's records showed the death rate to have fallen again. This time it was 3.21 per cent.

At the end of January, Klein produced figures showing the death rate had fallen to 1.92 per cent.

Ignaz Philipp tried once and then again to obtain access to the Maternity Division records. Klein laughed heartly. Even Breit smiled.

Ignaz Philipp returned to his reading. There was less than ever for him to do.

"I am going to England, Marko," he said at the end of January. "From all I can read they have less puerperal fever in their hospitals than any other place in the world. I am going to find out why. I am going to talk to their great doctors."

"But you don't know English, Naci. Do you?"

"No. But I have begun to study it."

He was partway through an English grammar when the news came in February that Breit had been offered and was going to accept a teaching position at the university in Tübingen.

"What are you going to do?" asked Skoda.

"I am still going to England."

"No, you are not going to England. You are going to be first assistant again."

"He will never allow it."

"He cannot help himself. There are rules that even he must obey. And one of these rules is that the provisional assistant becomes first assistant when the post becomes vacant."

Ignaz Philipp shook his head. He put his hand over his eyes.

"I am so tired, sir. Forgive me—looking ahead—I can see no hope for me here—I am tired . . . I am very tired . . ."

"You're going to have a rest."

Ignaz Philipp smiled wearily.

"I mean a trip. A good trip. A good rest. A new scene. A little play. How old are you now, boy?"

"I am twenty-nine, sir. But——"

"Twenty-nine means Venice. Have you ever been to Venice, boy? You are going to take my prescription. You are going to go to Venice and they will pump music into you and moonlight and laughter until you bulge so with it that there is nothing you can do but pump it back into those beautiful, lovely, black-haired signorinas. Do you hear me, boy? That's exactly what you're going to do."

Breit's appointment to Tübingen was to take effect April first. Skoda marched to von Tuerkheim. Von Tuerkheim went to Schniffner. Ignaz Philipp was given leave of absence until the end of March. Incredibly, a small sum of money accompanied the leave.

"We told them you had done a little extra," Skoda announced.

He put his hands on his hips. "Now—are you going to go?"

"I'm going to go."

"And are you going to come back?"

Ignaz Philipp looked at him levelly. "I'm coming back."

Skoda shrugged. "Naturally," he said.

Ignaz Philipp and Markussovsky packed their bags on the night of March first. On the second of March they were on their way to Italy.

In France, in England, in Scotland, in Ireland, in America, in Italy, in whatever country there were hospitals, women came to give birth to children. And puerperal fever in this year killed one out of ten, one out of twenty, one out of five, one out of three. And sometimes it killed them all.

# THIRTEEN

SPRING came late that year, winter lingered, at Graz travelers groaned about high snow in the Alpine passes. Ignaz Philipp and Markussovsky skirted the high Alps, the stagecoach rumbled southward toward Trieste. For a day they sat quietly. They ignored their fellow passengers. Always they gazed at the changing landscape, sometimes seeing it, sometimes staring blindly.

On the morning of the second day Ignaz Philipp said abruptly, "What I am looking for is in the First Division and nowhere else."

His tone was final. His mind was calm and assured. The last doubts had left him.

Thereafter the quaint countryside began to charm him. He smiled a little. The stagecoach stopped before crossing the Drava and he alighted quickly, pulling Markussovsky with him. He peered busily at the peasant huts, he pinched the cheek of a gaping toddler. The coachman called. They scrambled back into the coach. Ignaz Philipp sat in the lap of a middle-aged countrywoman. He rose hastily. The woman giggled. Two German merchants, stiff cold and formal, glared at him angrily. One had a cold. He spent most of the morning coughing in the faces of the passengers opposite him. Otherwise he was silent.

"Marko," Ignaz Philipp said in a little while, "have you got your gun loaded?"

"My gun?"

"Yes, but have you got it cocked?"

The Germans moved uneasily.

"Oh—my *little* gun!" Marko patted his pocket. "It's ready."

"Be careful. You know how easily it goes off. I'll never forget that poor fellow you shot in Buda——"

"But it wasn't my fault, Naci. I just patted it and it went off." He patted his pocket to demonstrate. The Germans moved as far as they could toward their side of the coach.

"Personally, I'm going to use a dagger. Bandits hate a dagger. It leaves marks on them and later they're easily identified."

The countrywoman gaped. One of the Germans cleared his throat.

"Excuse me—I am a merchant—were you speaking of bandits? Along this road?"

"I beg your pardon," said Ignaz Philipp, surprised. "I do not believe we have been introduced." He glared at the German.

"I am Friedrich Mansser. I am from Cologne. My friend is Adolph Gastheim. We are merchants."

Ignaz Philipp bowed.

"My name in Zuzel," he said severely. "Putzi Zuzel. My line is bedpans." He turned to the countrywoman. "Forgive the expression." They bowed to each other. "My friend is Willy Windel. He is a secondhand enema-can contractor." He turned to Markussovsky. "If you will pardon the expression." They bowed to each other. He turned then, and he and Markussovsky looked out of the window indifferently.

"You were mentioning bandits——" said Mansser diffidently.

"Bandits? Have you seen them already?" He and Markussovsky peered eagerly from the window.

The Germans swallowed. The countrywoman took out her knitting. She began to knit placidly.

"I sincerely express the hope we shall not meet any," said Mansser nervously.

"We don't care," Ignaz Philipp shrugged. "All they can steal from me is bedpans and all they can steal from my friend is a few secondhand enemas. If everybody will forgive the expression."

"It's the torture I'm thinking of," Markussovsky said.

"Yes, they're getting pretty clever. Last week they captured a Berliner. Do you know what they did? They made a little cut in the wall of his belly. Then they fished out a loop of his small intestine with a buttonhook. And then they pegged the loop to a tree and made him run around the trunk. Round and round and round."

"And what happened, in the name of God!"

"The police found him finally," said Markussovsky. "They unwound him. But he hasn't ticked very good since."

"We're almost certain to run into two or three bands this trip. I hope neither of you gentlemen deal in buttonhooks? They might remember——"

Mansser leaned forward.

"Diamonds!" he whispered.

208

"Diamonds!" echoed Ignaz Philipp, shocked.

"They're sure to find them," said Markussovsky.

"Will you listen to experience? There's just one thing to do. You must hide them."

"They're in a safe place," said Mansser. He wiped a little sweat from his forehead. His companion was very pale. He coughed and the spray flew in their faces.

"It's no good. There's only one safe place." He and Markussovsky shook their heads meaningly at each other. "We know."

"Please——" breathed Mansser.

Ignaz Philipp leaned forward. He whispered in Mansser's ear. The German straightened, red-faced, horrified.

"It's the only place," said Ignaz Philipp.

"Absolutely," said Markussovsky earnestly.

"One at a time," said Ignaz Philipp. "It won't hurt much. And they'll never think of looking there. They're Moslems, you see. It's against their religion."

"Don't bother to thank us," said Markussovsky modestly. "Courtesy of the road."

"What bandits?" asked the countrywoman suddenly.

Ignaz Philipp promptly fished out his ticket.

"Have you read your ticket? I thought not. Look here. Look close."

Printed in very small type in a corner of the ticket was the legend: "The management will not be responsible for accidents caused by natural catastrophes or highway bandits."

At the next stop where Ignaz Philipp and Markussovsky changed coaches the Germans alighted and ran hastily into the inn. They emerged barely in time to scramble aboard again. They ran awkwardly. They leaned against each other as they sat.

"I wonder when those tickets were printed," said Ignaz Philipp, watching the coach drive off.

"Sometime during the Caesars," said Markussovsky.

"You know something," said Ignaz Philipp meditatively, "putting those diamonds where they are ought to do the quiet one's cold a lot of good."

"They'll never cure his cold." Markussovsky grinned.

"No," said Ignaz Philipp. "But he won't dare cough."

From Treviso over the road the Romans built the stagecoach rumbled to Venice. In Treviso the red wine foamed but in Venice the Basilica of St. Peter pressed its age upon their mouths and they were silent. They sketched the tombstones of Capasantos and palaces and olive trees. They saw the ocean. They tasted the Adriatic upon their lips, salty, long before they saw its blue, and in the heart of Ignaz Philipp, a boy from Hungary who had seen only the Danube but had often sent his dreams down it, the ocean sent a great pain and humbleness and longing. And in Trieste the steam vessels lay idly, long lines of them, their hawsers languidly adip in the soft waters, like so many great ladies. Here the mountains crowded down to the sea; home they were green and trees browsed on them; here they were stripped, their ribs bared to the blown spume.

And wherever they went, enchanted, amazed, there were strange spicy smell, the odors of wild cookery and cargoes from far continents and the swagger of Levantine sailors and the crash of military bands, palaces and churches, bridges, and in the galleries pictures they had seen only in books, black gondolas, canals, flags, and the sound of chimes.

"Now you must fill yourself with beauty for the rest of your life," Markussovsky said quietly. He was suffused with deep peace. For the first time since they had known each other he saw Ignaz Philipp completely happy, and it was certain that he would be happy tomorrow. They had refuged in a strange place and they had escaped the world. For ten days there would be no problems, no death, no sickness, no hatreds, no agony. The long-silent death bell was replaced by the chimes.

And at nights there was festival.

The girl was blond, slim as a taper. Her eyes were somewhat deeper blue than the blue of the Adriatic. Her hair had been braided and was drawn over the top of her head where it resembled a crown. Vague and gleaming tendrils of it had escaped near her temples and moved with the air. She had a pointed chin, her cheekbones were round, her cheeks were golden and a little pink. Her slim body could only be guessed, but the thought was intoxicating. She had walked to the middle of the Marco Polo Bridge and she was looking absorbedly at a bolt of cashmere in a vendor's booth there. Ignaz Philipp was alone this evening. Markussovsky, tiring in the afternoon, had gone to their rooms and fallen asleep. Ignaz Philipp saw the girl and stood still. He gaped so long that passers-by jostled him and turned to look at him in amusement. He walked to a booth near by and from the corner of his eye he looked at her reverently. The girl appeared quite unconscious of his presence. After a time she put the cashmere down and picked up a bolt of Paisley. She peered at it closely. She held it to the light. She tested it with a long white finger. She put it down. She considered it a moment. Then she turned. She smiled full in Ignaz Philipp's face.

In a gondola that night they prowled the murky canals. The boatman sang. They kissed, and sprawled full length, they clung to each other, chest against chest, knee touching knee, toes pressed. They left the gondola without words, dazed, and their walking was not aimless.

He arrived in the rooms early in the morning. He woke Markussovsky. He babbled.

"But what was her name, at least?"

210

"Catharine . . . Catharine . . . I don't know . . . we just seemed to meet and . . . and . . . we looked at each other . . . and . . . the gondola . . ."

His voice trailed. He looked at Markussovsky, waiting to be helped.

"Don't worry, Naci. It's simple. Where does she live?"

Ignaz Philipp looked at him blankly.

"Where did you go?"

Ignaz Philipp shook his head.

"Where she lived."

He never saw the girl again. Because he kept looking for her wherever they were, he met Bianca. He met Bianca the very next evening.

Like Catharine, she spoke no German, only Italian. This time Markussovsky was with him. Bianca found Elena for Markussovsky, and for a while, in the time they floated over the canals, Ignaz Philipp took the gondolier's pole and made the gondolier sit at his feet, and then they tired of this and went ashore. And this time they found the girls' full names at least, and their addresses. But they never got a chance to return to them, for the next evening there was Madeleina and Josefina.

That was the night when they went to the bright and happy and noisy tavern and ate hugely and floated in a red sea of chianti and overheard at last above the din the bitter remarks from the next table that had been directed at them all the evening.

"But we are not Austrians!" Ignaz Philipp said, rising suddenly. He looked at the men earnestly.

"Just mind your business, foreigner. And leave our girls alone."

"Why do you come here? Haven't you got enough territory?"

"Can't we even have our little restaurants? Are you going to take them too?"

They spoke halting German. But the hatred in their faces was more eloquent.

"Listen! I am a Hungarian! My friend is a Hungarian! The yellow-and-black flag that flies above your country flies above ours also."

"Be careful!" shouted one; "they are spies and provocateurs; say nothing!"

But the first speaker was beyond caution.

"Go back," he hissed, "go back where you came from. Tell your Metternich that Italy is rising, tell him that Venice is not Austria and he cannot make it Austria, and we will be a republic again! We will be free! Run to your master, slave, and tell him!"

His companions pulled him away.

211

"He is very noisy," one apologized. "He has drunk too much wine——"

"We are making up a play, just a little play. He is rehearsing his part, that is all——"

"Just a little play, sirs, for a coming feast day——"

They passed from sight, out of the café.

The grip of Metternich on Poland was relaxing, Switzerland had revolted. Denmark defied him openly. Prussia was slowly deserting. German national feeling was rising. Divided Hungary was rapidly solidifying. A pope friendly to freedom was helping Italy rise. France regarded Metternich suspiciously. In England, Palmerston was definitely hostile.

The age of feudalism was drawing rapidly to an end. Europe's last despots gathered for a final stand. Nations clamored for consitutions, for free speech, for a free press, for freedom of religion.

They were subdued a while after the Italians from the next table had left, but more wine came, and afterward the evening passed pleasantly and then joyously and soon the dawn came and they walked uncertainly home, freshened with it, their eyes red with its rising. The days passed, the halcyon days, the golden days, vivid with great paintings, tumultuous with storied castles, with music, with wine, with unending curious things to explore and admire, with laughing girls and strange tongues and always the Adriatic. The last few days they lay in the warm sands of Lido, simply resting, musing at a blue sky, a galloping of dappled clouds, content to wait for sunset.

It was over at last.

On March 20 he and Markussovsky arrived in Vienna. They stepped from the stagecoach from warm golden spring into Austria's bitter winter. The next morning he reported for duty in the First Division. He was first assistant again.

"Well," said Klein, "this time I shall have perhaps your undivided attention."

"I have always tried to give you that, sir professor."

"Your comments are not necessary. Did you enjoy Venice? . . . fine . . . are you rested? . . . splendid . . . that will be all."

Ignaz Philipp walked to the door of the office.

"By the way, what was it Kolletschka was working on when you left?"

"He was experimenting with a stain he had developed for tissue mounted on microscopic slides—that and some work on lung tissue."

"I see. Perhaps that's what made him careless. One should devote all one's energies in that to which one is assigned. One hopes you profit from the lesson."

Cold, bitter cold clamped heavily on Ignaz Philipp's heart. He stared at Klein. His pulse pounded. He held his breath.

"What"—he licked his lips—"what's the matter with Kolletschka?"

"He's dead. Didn't anyone tell you? Died on the thirteenth of March. Cadaveric poisoning. Student pricked his finger while they were dissecting a corpse in class. We have a new provisional assistant. His name is Fleischer. See that he works. You may go."

He made his rounds mechanically. He led the students through the wards. He inspected the journal. Kolletschka was dead. He could think of nothing else. Jakob Kolletschka, aged forty-three, a true man, a friend, decent, gentle Kolletschka. He shut the journal. He walked from the First Division into the Second.

"What has happened, Bartsch? What happened to Kolletschka?"

"I'm sorry, Semmelweis. I knew it was going to be terrible for you . . ."

"Why didn't you write? Why didn't someone tell me?"

"Professor Skoda said no. Ah, man, you were enjoying yourself—what good would it have done?"

"Tell me, Bartsch. Tell me what happened?"

"It happened in class. He and a student were demonstrating visceral anatomy. The student was incising. He was clumsy and Kolletschka moved his hand to help him. The student nicked the end of his finger."

"And that's all?"

"It bled a little. It was a small nick, nothing much. Kolletschka went on with the lesson. You and I have had such nicks. But the next day he fell ill. He got worse. He was dead within the week. Cadaveric poisoning."

Bartsch looked down. Through the minds of both men rasped the refrain of agony in which men died of cadaveric poisoning.

"I thank you, Bartsch." Gentle Jakob. Gentle Jakob suffering.

"I'm sorry, Semmelweis. I know you were friends . . ."

"Thank you . . ." Jakob screaming, Jakob dead, Jakob dying.

He finished his duties that day in almost complete silence. He saw the faces of the sick and the agonized. But often the face of Jakob was on the pillow. And often the voice was Kolletschka's.

The next day he rose early and went to the dissecting rooms. He worked alone. Kolletschka was gone. That night with Rokitansky, Hebra, Skoda, he bowed in silence before Frau Kolletschka.

Scrupulously he resumed where he had left off almost a month before. He dissected. He reported at the clinic. He worked harder than before. Each case became his own case, to each woman he fought to give some solace. He looked at them, row after row, each mattress freighted with its weight of misery and fear, and his heart surrendered to them utterly.

They had no money. They were sick. There was no place else for them to go. And each knew she was in a place of deadly peril. Each knew the bed might be her deathbed. Their eyes begged reassurrance. They pleaded humbly to be healed, not to die, to have their babies and be released. They woke in fear and they bore in fear and they slept in fear. And that is how they died.

He set himself again to the hopeless task of saving them. He sat with them, he babied them, he fed them, he petted them, he worked with them as he had not dreamed a man could work. And he watched them die. A part of him died with them.

Nothing had changed. In the wards the beds were placed exactly equidistant. The same smells poisoned each breath. The patients were other patients than on his first day nearly two years ago. The faces were different. The bodies were the same. The poverty that brought them was the same poverty. The pregnancies had not changed. The killing went on. The screams and the prayers continued. The deaths had not changed. Nothing had changed.

The frenzied hours had come to nothing. All that he had worked for had come to nothing. He had worked in vain. The days of unending struggle, the nights of study, the weeks of research, the months of raging battle, the sum of his life and his prayers and his unquenchable determination was here in this clinic, this day. Here was the whole sum. And here was the sum of puerperal fever. He had altered nothing.

The killing went on.

There was agony and there was death, there was puerperal fever in the Second Division too. At Kiel, at Tübingen, at Jena, where there was no chance whatever, at Paris and Berlin and Milan and London, in Edinburgh, in far America, and wherever there were the sweet bodies of women, big with healthy child, the stink of death waited, the flood, the liquid corruption of epidemic waited to mingle with the clear waters of birth and the sound fluids of the living.

All this was in his records. His records had become a small book now. It was a book of death that showed the sums of death everywhere. There was no end to it. There was no end to his fight. There was no end to his failure.

The memory of Kolletschka rose gray in his mind at day's end, in the night hours. In the mornings, working alone in the dissecting room, the solitude was a fresh wound each day.

In the first ten days following his return to duty the death rate from puerperal fever which had subsided to an incredible 1.92 per cent rose abruptly to 3.60 per cent. He redoubled his dissecting. He rushed back to the wards and flogged himself to greater effort. The women screamed, they looked at him, imploring, he smiled a set smile, his eyes ached with pity, his hands detected the inevitable even as his voice tried to assure them. At the end of April the death rate had risen to 18.27 per cent. He set the figure in his records carefully.

He left the clinic early that evening. He met Bartsch on the steps outside the hospital. For a few blocks their way lay together.

"I can see by your face you've had no luck yet."

"I've had no luck. I've had nothing. Not even hope."

"Ah, well. It's not been a complete loss. All that dissection, all that work, you couldn't help sharpening your surgery and gynaecology."

"And what does it all come to? I know nothing. Against puerperal fever I am as effective as if I had never studied medicine at all."

"So are we all, friend, so are we all. So it has always been. You forget that, I think. Yes, it has always been. And it always will be. You have allowed this to obsess you. You must face the unfortunate reality. It is like death, one of the normal consequences of living. And like death—there is no remedy, no hope, no answer."

"I know. Perhaps it is really hopeless. Perhaps I have always known it. But always there were the women, begging, and always my heart bent down to them. And always there was this to make one hopeful, to tantalize endlessly: Why does the First Division have three times as many deaths and four and five and six and ten times as the Second Division? When everything is the same in both divisions—why?"

"Someday we will know. It will be a perfectly simple, perfectly natural explanation."

"But there will still be puerperal fever?"

"My friend, there will always be puerperal fever . . . women shall bear children in pain . . . And pain, pain reminds me! Have you heard about ether?"

"I've been so busy . . ."

"Well, it appears it's spreading like wildfire. A few whiffs, from all accounts, and the patient's dead to the world, feels nothing, you can cut him to ribbons—he comes to asking when you intend to begin!"

"Just plain ether? The stuff we give by mouth for headaches and muscular spasm?"

"The same ether. Some American stumbled on to it. Instead of putting fifteen drops in a glass of water and making the patient swallow it—which is all we've ever used it for—he found that by holding the ether under the patient's nose and letting him smell, the patient became completely unconscious."

"It's incredible. Are you sure? There must be some drawback."

"No, none. The Americans are all using it, the English have taken it up, the French are raving about it—and it was only discovered a few months ago. In London, the great Simpson is using it for women in labor—a whiff and their pains disappear!"

"Oh no!"

"Oh yes!"

"Why, we must get some! We must try it tomorrow! It means the end of those poor women's agony——"

"There *have* been a few deaths . . ."

"Aha!"

"And it's still new . . ."

"New! That ends it, then. I can hear myself: 'Professor Klein, I have here a new remedy! The greatest doctors in the world have tested it!' And I can hear him: 'New, you say? New, Dr. Semmelweis? And do they die of it? Well, that's the answer, Dr. Semmelweis. They die of quite enough things as it is. Does it end pain? Well, what's pain after all? Women don't die of pain . . .' No, Bartsch, new things are not for us."

"You're tired. You must ease up. Let things take their course, fall as they will."

"Yes, I'm tired. It's the truth. Good night, Bartsch."

He left Bartsch. He walked home. The streets were strange to him. It seemed to him that he had never actually seen them before. The world had become smaller. The city had become merely buildings. And himself had become a drab, sunken man, walking a hard pavement, his failure plain as the mark of Cain.

In the myriad millions walking upon the earth he walked in greater loneliness. He was not conscious of loneliness. He was conscious only of despair. He had not time to be lonely. He had not room for loneliness in his thoughts. He thought only of puerperal fever. The screams of women in agony rang in his ears. Time had not dulled those screams or blurred those imploring faces. Each scream was a new scream. Each death was a new death. They were whips driving him blindly into roads which ended miserably nowhere. But there was no relief. And there was no end. And there was no beginning. And there was no hope. And he could not stop.

And the years had passed. His mother and his father were dead. He had no home now. He had no wife, no child. He was too poor to marry. He was a Doctor of Medicine, a Master of Midwifery, a Master Surgeon. In nine years of unswerving devotion, of unsparing toil, of unvarying direction, he had attained the post of first assistant to a man who hated him, at a salary his father paid a grocer's clerk.

He was a dogged man. He was not articulate. He had no tact. He was not a great professor. He was not a great scientist. He had only pity.

This single unit in the cosmos, solitary, indomitable, drooping with failure, shut his eyes and beat at the unconquerable. He beat blindly and silently, without complaint and without respite. And failed. And beat again.

He walked home, a stooped, shabby man, indistinguishable from the myriad millions about him. He had come to this day.

He entered his rooms and Markussovsky was in a chair, waiting for him. Markussovsky leaped from his chair and grasped his shoulders, exultant and aflame.

"It's come, Naci! Old friend—it's come!"

In his clenched hand was a letter. He thrust it at Ignaz Philipp.

Ignaz Philipp looked at it, bewildered.

"From Hungary——?"

"The battle is about to begin. Kossuth is calling for volunteers. It's the revolution, Naci! At last, at last, it's the revolution!"

Ignaz Philipp opened the letter. The print leaped out at him.

"Fellow countrymen! Hungary's hour is at hand! We ask your blood, we ask your strength, we ask the blow that will free the Fatherland forever!"

Ignaz Philipp slumped into a chair. He put a trembling hand to his head.

"This is no riot, Naci, no student rising, no peasant revolt. This is the nation. This is the hour." He paused. He looked at Ignaz Philipp searchingly.

"You're coming, aren't you, Naci? Are you hesitating? Oh, man! Are you thinking of the hospital? You know what's there for you! The women—your search for a cause for fever? It's hopeless, Naci! You know it's hopeless, don't you?"

"Marko—wait, wait——"

"There's no waiting, old friend. Hungary needs us! Needs us *now!* The Hungary your father raised you to love beyond yourself, the Hungary you lived to fight for—Hungary's waiting. Is there a doubt, Naci? Is there a choice? Are you still hesitating? Do you give up so much?"

In the blood of Ignaz Philipp love of country began to heat. Old memory, old loyalty, old love, old hatred stirred. He clenched his teeth. His eyes warmed.

"I talk wildly. I know you. I know my friend. Forgive me. You have had nothing but shame here, nothing but injustice. My friend, what I have is yours—your future is mine. I am ashamed to speak of it. I have money. It is of no use to me. I do not want to practice. But you shall have an office, you shall have the finest office in Hungary—a laboratory—whatever your heart desires——"

"Marko——!"

"Don't reproach me. This was always in my mind. Now I

217

have a chance to say it. We shall live free men, in a free Hungary!"

They stared at each other, their eyes wide, their breathing rapid.

Hungary was rising.

"I leave in three days," Markussovsky said softly.

"In three days . . . fellow countryman . . ." he said.

The pent breath left Ignaz Philipp's taut body in a great spear of resolve.

They burned the letter. They talked endlessly into the night.

Morning dawned, this different morning, on an Austria unconscious of revolution.

Ignaz Philipp went to the clinic as usual. He tried to hide the fever that was growing in him. He saw the women and forgot the fever, he recollected himself and with his eyes bade them secret farewell. Wherever he walked, his footsteps said farewell.

At noon he went to see Skoda. There was nothing he could tell Skoda. Bohemia was not Hungary. But he could talk to him. Perhaps there was something he could say, some word, which would remain with Skoda, which might inflame that great man so that he would pick up the problem.

"I've seen the latest figures," Skoda said without preamble.

Ignaz Philipp shook his head.

"Yes, sir. They're rising . . ."

"Be careful, my boy. He may be using his peculiar bookkeeping to get rid of you. You go away—the figures go down. You come back—the death rate mounts. Keep your counsel. Don't be rash. Do your work. Be patient. Those who accept his figures—and his undiagnosed cases, and his cases diagnosed as peritonitis, typhus, and other things—they're all together, all in the same clique with him. Say nothing rash. Be careful. Wait."

"I am doing my best. But the problem is for you, sir. Excuse me, that I blurt it out, but your great mind, your resources, you will solve it, sir. I know it."

"Well, well . . . someday perhaps I will have a look at it . . . And now tell me! What is the latest? What have you found?"

"I will tell you. I will tell you an old story. Tomorrow it will be new. But there will be no change. You are at the hospital. You will admit a healthy woman. A sound, fine woman. This creature of God will come to you in the glory of health, groveling with fear. And you will tell her not to fear. You will use all your art. And she will have her child. And while you look at her, it will strike. There is, incredibly, a fever. There is vomiting. There is diarrhea. There is crunching pain. And now it is all over. In three days this healthy, praying woman is a burning, unrecognizable, insane corruption. And you will

218

watch, helpless. And now she is gone. And we open her up. And we find——"

"Lymphangitis, phlebitis, bilateral pleuritis, pericarditis, peritonitis, meningitis, metastases . . ."

"Yes, sir . . ."

"But you keep on trying."

"There's that one clue—that higher rate in the First Clinic. For me it's been a clue that leads nowhere . . . for you, sir, who knows?"

He looked at Skoda searchingly.

"Yes . . . well . . . you must do what you must do, boy. . . . Are you still working in the mornings? Dissecting?"

Ignaz Philipp nodded. He looked down.

"That poor Kolletschka . . . a great loss . . . to you, particularly . . ."

"I'll never forget him. Nor you, sir."

"And to go—that way. Well, we all have to go—some way. There's no remedy, you know. Still—cadaveric poisoning!"

"I don't know much about it."

"No. No one does."

"Only what happens."

"Only what happens . . ."

He left Skoda. With his eyes, with his thoughts, he said farewell to him. Tonight he would see Hebra and Rokitansky and perhaps Haller. Perhaps one of them might take over the search . . . There was not much hope. He clung to what hope there was.

He walked now to the graveyard where Kolletschka lay. It was in his mind to say good-by. Walking, he passed the morgue. He paused. He had never seen the death report. This, too, was Kolletschka, of his friend the last sentence.

He turned abruptly and went into the morgue. He entered the department of records.

He opened the file. He turned the pages. He came to the case of Jakob Kolletschka. In the kingdom of God there was the sound of blowing bugles.

He stared at the page, somberly. He began to read.

The body of Jakob Kolletschka had died of cadaveric poisoning.

He read on. The record was plain. It said:

In the upper extremity the lymphatic system was badly inflamed.

The veins were inflamed and swollen. The tissues of his lungs were inflamed. The heart was inflamed.

The inmost lining of his abdomen was inflamed, and the lining of his brain.

And wherever the murder traveled, in the abdomen, the lungs, the veins, the lymph system, the brain, the eye, there

219

was a milky fluid. There was the odor of putrefaction. There was the clear and stinking liquor of death.

The poison had leaped through him, from his fingertip to his left eye. There were swellings there.

The lymphatic system inflamed . . . The veins inflamed and swollen . . .

The record leaped out at him.

Lymphangitis . . . phlebitis . . . bilateral pleurisy . . . pericarditis . . . peritonitis . . . meningitis . . . and metastases . . .

He heard a roaring. He stared at the report.

He looked up. His breathing stopped. His ears rang with a clamor of Jericho. His eyes were blind with a great light.

He closed the book of records. He left the morgue. He began to walk. His mind read and reread the records. He saw the very texture of the paper. He saw the handwriting. He saw every word. And now carefully, delicately, his mind sifted the last case of puerperal fever he had dissected. He watched his knife cutting. He saw the tissues. He reported the findings. He compared them with the record he had just seen. Step by step, fact by fact, the cases tallied. There was one difference. Jakob Kolletschka had no uterus. In the woman the uterus and the cervix had been inflamed and the tubes and the ovaries. But the woman died and Kolletschka died. And the same thing had killed them both. His mind began slowly and carefully to select case after case, dead woman after dead woman. The dead were an endless procession. The cause of death was always the same. The symptoms were identical. The thing that killed Kolletschka killed the women.

And suddenly he remembered the dead babies, the heaped small ones, those who had died with symptoms like their dead mothers! The puzzling small ones, who could not have another small one like themselves in their uteri, the little boy infants who could never have a birth disease. And it, too, was clear now. They, too, had died of that which had killed Kolletschka.

Kolletschka had died following a wound.

But it was not the wound which had killed Kolletschka.

The wound was only a pinprick.

No man could die of such a tiny wound, a wound which shed perhaps four drops of blood.

What, then, killed Kolletschka? His mind went back to the dissection.

He pictured the scalpel. He saw it enter the flesh of the cadaver. It was shiny and clean. He saw the knife after the dissection had gone on a little time. It was foul-looking, corroded, stained, tarnished. Instantly he remembered his final examination in chemistry. He saw Stauern probe a foul-smelling bone fistula with a silver instrument. He saw the silver emerging, tarnished, black.

What makes this silver black?"
And he heard himself answering:
"It might be hydrogen sulfide——"
And Stauern:
"It is acetic acid . . ."
It wasn't acetic acid, of course. But if acetic acid had coated the dissection knife, Kolletschka would not have died of it. And hydrogen sulfide would never kill a man unless he choked with it. It wasn't hydrogen sulfide that had killed Jakob Kolletschka and it wasn't acetic acid.

No knife . . . No chemical . . . What remained?

He saw the knife. He saw the blade, black, coated with cadaveric material.

It was the cadaveric material. There was no other answer. The next thought was inexorable.

He saw himself dissecting women. They were dead of puerperal fever. He felt his fingers wet with the pus and the fluids of putrefaction. He saw those hands, partly wiped, entering the bodies of living women. The contagion passed from his fingers to the living tissues, to wounded tissues. He saw the women fever. He heard them scream. He saw them die.

He shook violently. He was remembering. Spurred by pity, he had plunged into dissection after dissection. He had dissected early in the mornings with Kolletschka. During the day he had dissected with the students. The more dissecting he did, the more infection he carried to the patients. And every student who dissected carried infection to the patients.

A new light blinded him. Now also the riddle of the clinics was solved. The First Clinic had a higher death rate than the Second Clinic because in the Second Clinic there were only midwives. And midwives did not do dissections.

Ignaz Philipp Semmelweis had discovered the cause of puerperal fever.

For a brief space that night, sitting with a stunned Markussovsky, the beloved fatherland begged in his heart and his soul. He heard the voice of his father. He heard the shriek of freedom. He heard the drums, and the exultant sounds of home. He heard the voice of Hungary. And in that clamor he heard high and clear, rising above all, the screams of women, the prayers of the dying. He heard their voices. He heard their agony. His mind and his hands held the answer now. He had solved the murder. The screams which had rung in his brain without ending for two long years rose higher, became invincible.

He could not leave. There was no other answer.

He turned his back on his country.

Now that, too, was gone.

"I must stay, here, Marko . . . I cannot help it . . ."

Markussovsky looked at him sadly. He drew a deep breath.

221

"And so we part, then . . ."

"I cannot . . . I cannot leave . . ."

"And if you fail?"

Ignaz Philipp looked at Markussovsky steadily.

"I have the cause of puerperal fever."

Markussovsky packed. That night he boarded the stage-coach for Buda and his fatherland.

# FOURTEEN

MARKUSSOVSKY was gone.

For a time Ignaz Philipp sat before the window and gazed at the distant parade ground. He thought of Buda. His boyhood rose in his mind in small and scattered scenes. There came to him again the feeling that he had grown up with, the feeling that the Austrians were guests in the house of Hungary who had inexplicably taken charge of the house and the hosts. The deeds done by the Austrians, the promises smilingly given and smilingly broken, the careful setting of noble against noble and landowner against peasant, the seizure of all the country's mails, the suppression of its newspapers, the imposition of another language on the children, the years of terror and casual pillage, the constant soldiery, rapine, and contempt burned hotly in his memory, and he began again to rage with bitterness and outrage.

He brooded now, sorely tempted, aching suddenly to return and fight. He thought of the hospital. Instantly the discovery washed over him, the fires of patriotism disappeared, a fever plucked at him to go to the wards, to apply his discovery, to begin immediately the end of the murder. His country was life. His countrymen were the living. He ached with impatience to begin. He knew that in a month after the discovery became known his work would be finished. For the first time in man's long history women would no longer die of puerperal fever. In all the world the women of the world would go to their childbeds in safety. The murder would stop. In a month the discovery could succor the planet. It was absurdly simple. The remedy called for no special equipment. The remedy meant only the slightest change in the routine.

To end puerperal fever one simply washed one's hands.

A basin must be placed in every ward.

A pitcher of warm water. A bar of soap. A supply of towels.

223

A gray horror swept him. He trembled, thinking of the women he had killed. No more must die. There was no time to lose. He seized his book of records. First, he said to himself, I must be honest. He dipped his quill into the inkpot. He began to write.

The variations in the mortality as they occurred in the divisions can be attributed to the special occupations of the various members of the staff. As an assistant I took special interest in pathological anatomy. I dissected endlessly to discover why these women were dying. The mortality soared. Consequently must I here make my confession that God only knows the number of women whom I have consigned prematurely to the grave. I have occupied myself with the cadaver to an extent reached by few obstetricians. However painful and depressing the recognition may be, there is no advantage in concealment; if the misfortune is not to remain permanent, the truth must be brought home to all concerned.

At the end of an hour he put aside his pen. He had written these few lines. Writing was unbearable. He was inarticulate. He could not express himself in writing. He labored endlessly over a single observation.

But it was not difficult to set down figures. He leafed through these grimly. He looked upon the record of 1842. It began in January with more than one woman out of five dying of puerperal fever. It ended in December with a mortality of one out of three. He leafed through 1843, which began with one in every five dying. He came upon April 1846, when one in six died. He speculated for a moment on the number of deaths attributed to phlebitis, meningitis, peritonitis, pericarditis, lymphangitis, typhus. All these were symptoms of the murder. They were all puerperal fever. The real total could never be estimated. The actual mortality including those patients hurriedly sent undiagnosed to the General Hospital must be double the written record.

He closed the book. It was done now. It was all over.

In a month puerperal fever would be a memory.

He was at the hospital before dawn. He smiled genially. He talked pleasantly to amazed attendants. He walked, exulting, from ward to ward. He walked, shuddering, past the autopsy room. Henceforth he would do no more dissecting.

He chafed to begin. He bit his lips to keep from crying out. He wanted to run through the wards, to rouse the patients, to cry to them all: "It's over, mothers! It's all over! There will be no more puerperal fever!" He mastered himself. The students arrived.

He tried to find words to begin. His eyes filled. They waited, wondering.

"There will be no more puerperal fever," he blurted suddenly. They looked at him in silence. He began again.

"I have found the secret of puerperal fever. Gentleman—it is all over. Professor Kolletschka—as you know, he died of cadaveric poisoning. The symptoms of which he died and the symptoms of women who die of puerperal fever are identical! There is no difference. I have seen the record. They are exactly the same."

They waited. He plunged on.

"It is we who are the killers. It is the cadaveric particles clinging to our hands which pass into the bodies of the women we examine."

They gaped, waiting.

"Gentlemen," he said, his voice breaking with strain and joy, "from this day on we will all wash our hands!"

The students slumped, disappointed. They began to look at one another significantly. They looked back at him coldly.

"Is it understood? From this time forth no student—no midwife—no one in this division ever again will examine any patient without first washing his hands as he enters the ward."

There was an embarrassed silence.

"May—may one know why, sir doctor?"

He controlled the swift flash of anger. He smiled. They were students, after all. "It's simple, boys. We must wash off those cadaveric particles. That is all. That is absolutely all. Now come. Now let us wash. With us begins the end of puerperal fever."

Some laughed. Some murmured angrily. Some shrugged. They went to the basins. Obediently they washed their hands. When they had finished he was waiting for them.

"Now let me see them."

This was incredible. There was something of a nightmare about this. Slowly, reluctantly, incredulously, they held out their hands. He examined them cheerfully and thoroughly.

"Now come. Let us begin."

He walked to the wards. They followed after him. Rounds began. The tour ended. The students prepared to go to class. One of them stopped.

"I beg your pardon, sir."

"Yes? You want to know more about the discovery, eh? Naturally! Fine! Come to me any time!"

The student stared at him.

"Will it be necessary to submit to that somewhat unusual performance every morning, sir doctor?" he asked, his lips tight.

"Of course. One must be very careful now. Every morning, gentlemen. And every afternoon. In short, every time you examine the patients. You see there's nothing to it. We simply —wash."

The students lingered. They looked at one another uneasily. Another spoke.

"With respect, sir doctor. Do you not consider this a somewhat humiliating performance?"

Ignaz Philipp stopped smiling. He frowned a moment, thinking. He decided he had not understood.

"Humiliating? To wash your hands?" He smiled. "I'm afraid —my thoughts were wandering—perhaps I didn't understand. You found something objectionable?"

"Some of us are undergraduates, sir doctor. Many of us are already doctors. Will you be pleased to consider——"

"We aren't schoolboys!" a student cried out.

"As you know, sir, the midwives line up every morning in the Second Division to have their fingernails inspected. We aren't midwives, sir, we are students and doctors. It is, to say the least, undignified——"

Ignaz Philipp looked at them open-mouthed.

"But—but I have only asked you to wash your hands——"

"Your hypothesis, sir, with all respect, is still unproven——"

"Are we required to make ourselves ridiculous for the sake of an incredible experiment?"

A vein in his left temple began to swell. It pulsed visibly.

"Enough!" he shouted. His voice rang through the wards. He glared at them, still incredulous. "It is I who am ashamed. I have spoken to you as equals. I speak to you now as your superior. This division is my direct responsibility. I am from this day on, knowing what I know, responsible for every death that occurs in it. I have made my position perfectly plain. I believe puerperal fever can be eliminated by washing the hands. I tell you this. I ask you merely to wash your hands. You will wash your hands. You will do exactly as I say. If you find my requirements unsuitable, you may pursue your studies elsewhere. You may transfer to Berlin, if you like, where one out of three die. Or to Kiel, where one of four die. Or to Jena, where *all* die. You may go where you like. But here—so long as you attend this clinic—until this thing is proven otherwise —you will wash your hands!"

In medicine the age of antisepsis had begun.

Klein came on the second day. As always, rounds began at Bed 1, in the labor room. Ignaz Philipp appeared in the doorway. Klein walked toward the bed. Ignaz Philipp walked quickly to bar his way. With a nod he tactfully indicated the basin. Klein looked.

"What's that for?"

"To wash your hands, sir director," Ignaz Philipp said in a low voice.

Klein drew back, His face reddened.

"Have you lost your senses? Is this some joke, Doctor?"

"I have made a discovery, sir director, which I believe will

226

end puerperal fever. I am positive I have discovered the cause. The remedy is simply washing the hands. It's really not much to ask, is it, sir director?"

Klein looked uncertainly at his hands.

"Why was I not informed? If there is to be any change in the routine of this division I am instantly to be informed. You are aware of that, Doctor?"

"You were not available, sir director. But I am happy to explain—to tell you all the circumstances——"

"If you have discoveries, Dr. Semmelweis, there is a certain, definite, well-known order for their presentation. One makes a report. One presents the report to one's director. One receives the director's permission to proceed."

"I put the report on your desk this morning, sir. I entered the procedure yesterday in the journal."

"But you began before you received permission. I am responsible for this division. I must remind you, you are only first assistant. If you execute unsanctioned ideas, and the patients die, it is I who am responsible. And is it possible, Dr. Semmelweis, that you have forgotten the code of ethics? Is it possible that you are now prepared to experiment on patients?"

Resolutely, his eyes dim with rage, his pulse pounding, Ignaz Philipp kept his voice even. Klein was no student. He was Klein. His dignity was offended. When he understood——

"The patients were hardly in peril, sir. The students and the midwives merely washed their hands."

"Morning rounds is not the time to begin some innovation based on a flight of your imagination. Order must be and will be preserved, Dr. Semmelweis. From now on——"

"Not imagination, sir director. Not imagination, but proof! If you have read the report I submitted, you will recall that I examined the death report of Dr. Kolletschka. I found that his tissues showed the same changes as the tissues of women dead of puerperal fever. That the dissecting knife carried into his body cadaveric particles which——"

"I am familiar with your report. It is not necessary to quote it to me. I am familiar with every comma in it. I pride myself, Dr. Semmelweis, on detail. I suggest you do likewise. I have read the full details of the coincidence. And now, if you please, stand out of my way——"

Ignaz Philipp reddened with rage. He barred Klein's way. His hands clenched.

"Will you accept the responsibility, then, of examining these women with unwashed hands? For I must tell you I intend to report this discovery."

"You have told me nothing of proven medical value."

"I am not fighting for myself now, Dr. Klein. I am fighting for these women. I have shown you plainly a means by which it is, to say the least, extremely probable that we can reduce the death rate in the First Division. I suggest to you, now, that such a reduction will be to your credit. I have found a means of ending puerperal fever. It is not expensive. It does not demand great change in routine. It cannot affect the patients adversely. It is simply washing the hands."

Klein had grown a little pale. He stared at Ignaz Philipp fixedly. Ignaz Philipp waited. Klein licked his thin lips.

"This is most irregular, Dr. Semmelweis. However——"

He walked to the basin.

"With respect, sir director—a most careful washing."

Klein stiffened. He hesitated a moment. Then he began to wash harder.

The death rate in the First Division began to drop.

Ignaz Philipp rushed to Skoda. Skoda listened patiently. At the end of two weeks he went to Skoda again. He found him with Rokitansky.

"Very interesting. One sees you're thinking, at least. But one week is not a discovery. It is merely a step in an experiment."

"But continue," said Rokitansky. "Continue by all means."

"As long as the soap holds out," said Skoda. "Come back in a week and let us see what we will see. Have you seen Hebra? He is looking for you."

"Yes, sir," said Ignaz Philipp. "But experiment or not—the logic follows—and the death rate is going down. No, I have not seen Dr. Hebra since last week. Is it important?"

"If he has missed you at the clinic he has probably gone home. Important? Yes, I should judge he considers it important. His wife is about to have a child."

"But that's wonderful!" beamed Ignaz Philipp.

"He wants you to deliver her."

"He wants me——?"

"I can understand your surprise. Yet somehow the opinion seems to have grown around here that you are a very competent obstetrician."

Ignaz Philipp was already at the door.

"Better hurry, boy. When he left she was having pains at three-minute intervals . . ."

On the twenty-fourth of May 1847 Ignaz Philipp delivered Mrs. Hebra of a healthy boy. Before the delivery, before every examination he had washed his hands for a quarter of an hour, soaping and rinsing, over and over. He delivered her at home. He had the sheets changed immediately after delivery. Mrs. Hebra recovered without incident.

To Hebra, to whom he had confided his discovery, he said only:

"Imagine how the same delivery might have gone one month earlier."

"It may still be coincidence, though."

"Yes. It may still be coincidence. But your wife is alive. And she is well."

At the end of May the death rate in the First Division had dropped from 18.26 per cent to 12.24 per cent.

He was beside himself with joy. But soon he frowned.

It was not enough.

Soap and water cleansed the hands. But wash as they would those students who dissected longest still wore on their hands the odor of the death room. The most conscientious students could kill the most patients.

What shall I use? he asked himself. What shall I use against these deadly particles?

Again his memory took him back to chemistry class. Again he heard the professor . . .

"I deduced instantly you had just come from an anatomy lecture. A peculiar odor accompanied you. The odor was chlorine gas—*and chlorine is a most effective agent in destroying contagion and putrid exhalations of all kinds . . .*"

*Liquor Chlorina . . .* ! He smiled grimly.

That day he ordered a quantity. He made a solution.

"Soap and water," he told the students at evening rounds, "is only partly effective. The odor of decay lingers. That is because the smallest particles are clinging to your hands in tiny crevices. From now on we will wash our hands in this solution."

There were angry murmurs. They turned sullen or exasperated faces upon him.

"Wash," he said. "Wash or leave the class."

They washed. He made the attendants wash in the strong-smelling solution. He made the midwives wash in it. They gritted their teeth. They daggered him with looks of hatred. They washed.

In this time Ignaz Philipp walked the earth in tumult. Night and day became the same to him. He seldom went to bed. Often he slept sitting up, in the labor ward. His vigil was almost unceasing. He watched any person who approached a patient. He looked at the journal twenty times a day. Elation kept his heart pounding. Every hour and every moment was filled with the thunder of discovery. He lived in the wards. With his eyes he embraced every patient, he protected them, his arms were around them. Klein was seldom in the wards now. He did not often attend classes. He busied himself with administration. Ignaz Philipp became the ruler of the First Division. He ruled with iron. He was absolute and unequivocal. He permitted no doubt. Resentment grew. He grew harsher.

"My manner is sometimes unfortunate," he conceded. "I do not mean to hurt your feelings. But these are human lives. Nobody will die of your hurt feelings. Thousands may die of your dirty hands. Wash, gentlemen! Wash!"

"But, sir, in science there is always room for the doubt—for the modification—for truth can be seen in many ways——"

"Here we do not permit doubt. Here there is nothing to discuss—until after you have washed your hands!"

June ended. The records were summed.

The death rate had dropped from 12.24 per cent to 2.38 per cent.

The wards were quieter now. The screaming had died down. The faces of the women did not implore so much. Here and there in their beds there was even a timid smile. Furtively, hope had begun.

He sat with Skoda, Hebra, and Rokitansky one night. From his pocket he drew the latest figures.

"We know all about you," waved Skoda. "We've heard about it."

"The death rate is dropping. It is dropping steadily."

"That's fine. Now prepare for the letdown. Prepare yourself now for the day when the figures soar again."

"I don't know, Joseph," said Hebra. "It's beginning to look as if he might be getting somewhere."

"Perhaps. Perhaps. All the same it's no harm preparing oneself for what we all have experienced. For the beautiful experiment gone wrong. For—for what usually happens . . . And now let's see those figures, my boy."

He and Hebra scanned Ignaz Philipp's records silently.

"Well," said Skoda at last, "it looks as if you might have something. Don't let your hopes rise too-high. Let's see what the end of July brings. Even the Second Division has been known to go epidemic in July."

Ignaz Philipp left. A little worry began to gnaw at the edges of his elation. Skoda's warnings rapped at him louder with each step. Halfway home he turned abruptly and returned to the maternity clinic. He looked over the sleeping wards. He peered into the delivery room. He spoke guardedly to the attendants, to the students on night duty. He looked at them all warily. He glanced at their hands. He saw that the basins were full. He went into the students' sleeping quarters and lay down. There were two deliveries that night. He assumed charge of both of them. The midwives looked at him with disgust. The students gave way and shrugged. He was oblivious to them. He attended the patients.

The days passed.

Toward the middle of June, Klein summoned him.

"I find that your experiments have become quite costly.

230

Your use of Liquor Chlorina is costing us at least fifty kreutzer per patient. You will discontinue using it immediately."

Ignaz Philipp wandered to the wards dazed. He called the head midwife. He placed her in charge. He went to Skoda. He asked for the use of his library. He scanned rapidly through chemistry textbooks. He found the works of the great Justus von Leibig. He read them for hours. He made a great pile of notes. He left Skoda. He went to a pharmacy. He bought chemicals.

When he returned to the Lying-in Division it was night. He went directly to the autopsy room. He mixed a solution. He removed the sheet from a cadaver. It had been prepared for demonstration of deliveries. He plunged his hands into the cavity. He rubbed them together. He poured over his hands the solution he had prepared. Then he smelled his fingers. The odor of putrefaction was still strong.

He made another solution. He repeated the experiment. He discarded the solution. He made another . . .

At about three o'clock in the morning he mixed a solution of water and chlorinated lime. He plunged his hands into the corpse. He used the solution. The odor had disappeared.

He set down the proportions of the solution. He estimated the cost. The total came to less than a kreutzer per patient. He smiled grimly.

The next morning Liquor Chlorina had been removed from beside the washbasins. In its stead was a large bottle of chlorinated lime solution. On Klein's desk lay a full report, together with costs.

The work went on.

July ended. The records were summed.

The death rate had sunk from 2.39 per cent to 1.20 per cent.

The news swept the hospital and the university.

Skoda, Hebra, and Rokitansky now began to spread Ignaz Philipp's doctrine. Haller attempted to compliment Klein.

"I hope, my dear Primarius," Klein said contemptuously, "that you are not of that number who regard this coincidence with the respect due a scientific fact. Rest assured, sir, welcome as your compliments are, your confidence in that young man is misplaced. His results are coincidence, sir. Pure coincidence."

"They appear to be facts, Doctor."

"Oh yes," said Klein. He smiled.

In August the death rate rose a little. It had been 1.20 per cent. Now it was 1.89 per cent.

Suddenly the death rate leaped to 5.25 per cent.

On a day in September Ignaz Philipp entered a ward in time to see four students pass by the basin, stop at a bed, prepare to thrust their unwashed hands into the body of a woman who had just delivered a child.

For an instant he could not move. He was stupefied.

A student pulled back the coverlet.

"Now, Mother, just spread your legs apart——"

The student bent over.

Ignaz Philipp rushed from the end of the ward.

"Gentlemen!" he shouted.

The students whirled.

"You stupid imbeciles! You clod-brained—you irresponsible —are you gone mad? Are you killers?"

They shrank, mortified, their faces burning, the patients listening.

"I don't like being talked to that way," one cried.

"Would you rather I took the sole of my shoe to you? Do you know what you're doing? Do you know what my orders are?"

"Look here, Doctor, with all respect, there are patients here——"

"No thanks to you!"

"Really, Doctor, these patients have gotten well before without any of this childish handwashing in your foul-smelling solutions——"

"You will leave the class. You will report to Professor Haller. You will not return to class. I will not have you."

The others fell silent instantly.

"I am not going to Professor Haller. I am going to another university. Some place where they behave with propriety and respect."

"You will leave instantly. Where you go is a matter of indifference to me. You will not now or ever return to this class. You are dismissed for insubordination and disobedience. That report will follow you wherever you go. And if you take my advice, you will leave medicine. You will cure more patients, resigned, than ever you will as a doctor. Now go."

The student left the ward in silence, passing red-faced between the rows of watching patients.

He paused in the doorway.

"You think that's the first time any of us have examined without washing our hands, do you?" he called mockingly. Then he disappeared down the corridor.

Ignaz Philipp turned slowly to the remaining students.

"Is this true?"

"Well, sir doctor, the fact is——"

"Is what he says true?"

They hung their heads.

"I have explained to you—I have told you why cleanliness is necessary—you have seen the results with your own eyes— and you *still* don't wash your hands? You deliberately flout me? You sneak? You evade for the joy of rebellion? You take these women's lives in your hands—for a whim?"

He spoke in a low voice. He could not believe it. His eyes were full of horror

"How long has this been going on? How often——"

"Not many times, sir doctor."

"Just once or twice——"

"Just to see what would happen——"

"Come," said Ignaz Philipp tiredly. "Come. I will show you what will happen."

He took them into the labor room. In a far bed, behind a screen, a woman was dying of puerperal fever. A great stench rose from about the bed. They stood by the bedside. She no longer saw them. Her eyes were glazed. Her breath left her chest painfully and returned in slow agony.

"Let us sit here, gentlemen. Let us sit here to the last. Let us watch her die."

And so they sat until the woman breathed her last.

He made the schedule of washing more rigid. The rules now ordered that anyone entering the labor ward must wash his hands in the solution of chlorinated lime. He assumed that cadaveric particles adhering to the hand were the sole source of infection and that this poison was destroyed after the chlorine washing. But he would risk nothing. In addition to the chlorine washing he also ruled that before proceeding to another patient, the examiner must wash his hands with soap and water.

Not all the students grumbled now. Most of them had become indifferent. But some had watched the death rate decline with awe. They had begun to look at Ignaz Philipp with respect. He was indifferent. He watched them all more closely than before. The death rate declined steadily.

The first week in October passed. A pregnant woman was admitted to the labor ward. She was placed in bed Number 1. In the morning Ignaz Philipp appeared with the students for rounds. They washed their hands with soap and water. They disinfected them with chloride-of-lime solution. They were inspected. They marched then to bed Number 1.

Ignaz Philipp smiled.

"Good morning, Mother!" He bent to examine her. His fingers signaled to his brain. He raised his eyebrows. He called for an instrument. He examined more closely. He straightened. He signaled to the students to begin their examinations. When they had done, he waited.

"I should judge that is cancer, sir. Cancer of the cervix."

"Adolf Kussmaul, isn't it?"

"Yes, sir."

"Thank you . . . Gentlemen?"

They chorused assent.

"You are quite correct. We have here a medullary sarcoma

233

of the cervix." Ignaz Philipp sniffed. "One observes it is foul-smelling. That is a normal expression of this disorder in this area."

They returned to the basins. They washed their hands with soap and water. They went to bed Number 2. They examined a normal case of labor. Her pains were coming at hourly intervals.

"You have a little time to wait, Mother . . ."

They washed their hands. They went to bed Number 3.

They continued from bed to bed until they had examined the last patient. They left the room. They went to the next.

In the labor ward they left there were twelve women. Within a week eleven of them were dead of puerperal fever.

The survivor was the woman with medullary cancer of the cervix. The rest had been healthy and normal.

In the night Ignaz Philipp walked the streets. In the days that followed he walked the wards with dread. In the nights he walked the streets again.

"It was bound to happen," Skoda said. "It was too good to be true." There was no satisfaction in his voice.

"The earlier decline in mortality—there was more than coincidence there," comforted Rokitansky.

"Check your procedure. Check again and again and again," Hebra begged.

Toward the end of October the woman with medullary cancer of the cervix was removed to the General Hospital.

The head midwife was a kindly woman.

"It is a mercy she is gone," she told Ignaz Philipp. She tried to make conversation, to draw him out of his gloom. "The ordinary smells in this place are bad. But this one——"

"I beg your pardon," said Ignaz Philipp. "I didn't hear——"

"It's nothing, sir. I was just remarking about the cancer smell. I'm glad it's gone."

"Oh," said Ignaz Philipp absently. "Yes, that's fine . . ."

The head midwife looked at him sympathetically. She walked away. Ignaz Philipp watched her, brooding.

What had she said? Something about smells. The cancer smell . . .

His mouth opened. The cancer smell!

His mind rocked. He swallowed, dazed.

That odor had come from putrefactive material.

He and the students had explored this woman and then marched from bed to bed. They had infected every woman they had examined.

Cadaveric poisoning was not the only cause for puerperal fever.

Puerperal fever could be transmitted from the living to the living.

Any putrid, infecting material carried by the examining finger could cause puerperal fever.

That evening he told the students what he had discovered. His face was white. He indicated the bottle of chloride-of-lime solution.

"Hereafter, in addition to soap and water, we will wash our hands with this solution not at the beginning of rounds, not as we enter each ward, but as the first step prior to the examination of every single patient. Before every patient. And after every patient. Is it understood?"

They nodded.

In October, in the First Division, there were these eleven deaths. There were two hundred and seventy-eight deliveries. The mortality was 3.95 per cent.

"Now," said Skoda, "I am willing to think that perhaps we have found something."

"Wait," said Ignaz Philipp. "You have seen nothing."

In the first week of November, in the First Division, there were no deaths from puerperal fever.

"There's no longer any use in waiting," said Skoda.

"What shall we do?" Rokitansky asked.

"You, Hebra, you and I shall see Klein. He is the one to announce it."

"Then tomorrow, my boy, be on your good behavior," said Rokitansky. "Put him in the best possible mood. Flatter him. Do anything."

"I will do my best," promised Ignaz Philipp.

In the morning, after rounds, he went to Klein's office.

"It is somewhat irregular to come here at this hour," he said humbly.

"The hours from one-thirty to four o'clock each day are at your convenience," said Klein. "You understand my feeling about order."

"I do understand, sir director. You will comprehend then the deep satisfaction that drew me here before the hour. I wish to report, sir, that thanks to your wise and able administration we may yet end this year with a mortality record lower than the Second Division."

Klein looked at him sharply. Ignaz Philipp's face was grave.

"It has been a privilege, sir director, to have worked with such a man as yourself."

"I find your admiration unexpected, Doctor. I would appreciate it even more if your hopes were based on science rather than emotion. The First Division's mortality rate has always been higher than the Second Division's. That is the order of things. It will, therefore, unquestionably always remain so."

"I had not thought about the order of things. You are probably quite right, sir director."

"Give a thought to the order of things, Doctor. Think of it oftener. It will help you."

"I shall, sir director."

"And in future——"

"From one-thirty until four o'clock, sir!"

"Thank you for your compliments. It is not necessary to be impulsive. You may go now."

"Thank you, sir director."

Ignaz Philipp bowed. He walked out humbly.

In the afternoon he watched from a ward as Skoda and Hebra walked toward Klein's office.

He did not see them leave.

In the evening he went quickly to Rokitansky's house. Skoda was there, and Hebra.

"We started with you," said Hebra to Ignaz Philipp. "We reviewed your work as a student, your postgraduate work, your long hours, the amount of work you did without complaint—we went over everything. We told him, God forgive us, how you respected him."

"The best we got from that," said Skoda, "was the response that you were a radical, a troublemaker, a man without order or tact or respect for duly-constituted authority."

"We proceeded to the discovery. We showed him that it had become general knowledge throughout the hospital and university that you had hit upon something that might well be a boon to humanity. We begged him to face the records, to acknowledge the falling death rate, to join in the plan to eliminate puerperal fever."

"It was then," said Skoda, "I offered him full credit for the discovery."

He paused.

"He was shocked," said Skoda. "He was shocked to his very core."

"He looked frightened," said Hebra.

"He considers the whole thing a wild concept, an irresponsible experiment which sooner or later will bring ridicule and contempt upon the whole Lying-in Division."

"He thought we were trying to trap him into being chief target for what he's sure will follow."

"Did you show him the figures?" demanded Ignaz Philipp.

"He said: 'Anything can be done with figures, gentlemen. We are all familiar enough with coincidence.' I asked him point-blank: 'Do you consider these figures a coincidence, Professor?' And he looked at me and blinked and said: 'Do you, sir professor, consider them anything else?"

In the second week of November a pregnant woman was admitted to the labor ward and assigned to bed Number 1. In the morning Ignaz Philipp appeared with the students for rounds. They washed their hands with soap and water. They next washed with chloride-of-lime solution. They were inspected. They marched then to bed Number 1.

Upon examination she was discovered to be suffering from a carious knee joint. An ulcer had pocketed the region with pus. The dirty dressing was replaced. They returned to the basins. They washed their hands and disinfected them with chloride-of-lime solution. They went to bed Number 2, and bed Number 3 followed, and so to the end of the ward.

The next day fevers rose in the labor ward. On the second day fevers rose higher. In nine days eleven of the women died.

Again there was no answer.

It appeared that every precaution had been taken.

Other women sickened.

At the end of November, this month which had begun with no mortalities reached 4.47 per cent. Out of two hundred and forty-six patients, eleven had died.

During the first week in December eight more died.

Now there was only one course.

The woman with the carious knee joint was placed in isolation. Everything that was used about her was kept from other patients. Attendants, midwives, and students were forbidden to touch her.

The deaths stopped.

No other women sickened. The mortality rate began to fall again.

"It must have been contact with something else or that the very air of the labor room was charged with the putrid matter," Ignaz Philipp decided.

"But isolation stopped it," said Rokitansky.

"Isolation stopped it."

"You know the answer, then," said Skoda.

"Henceforth," Ignaz Philipp told the students next day, "all such cases are to be kept in strict isolation." He entered the order in the journal.

The mortality rate dropped steadily. Day followed day and there were no deaths. December ended. The mortality rate for the First Division was 2.93 per cent. Eight had died out of two hundred and seventy-three.

"Well, Hebra?" said Skoda.

Hebra, editor of the *Vienna Medical Society Journal,* smiled.

"I had it written four days ago. And you?"

"I'm going to write to Prague. To Nadherny himself."

"And I," said Rokitansky, "shall put on my top hat and my ribbons and make a formal visit to Haller."

They turned to Ignaz Philipp.

"What are you going to do?"

He stood smiling at them, his eyes full of tears.

"I am going home and thank God for such friends. With

Klein—one doesn't expect much. With the students—well, even so not all of them are indifferent. But when the great men of the medical world—when Nadherny—when the others read the great *Vienna Medical Journal*—now, now I am happy. Now I know it is all over. In a month the murder will stop. My friends . . . my very dear friends . . ."

Before he went home he stopped at the clinic.

"There were some students here looking for you," said Zipfel, Bartsch's assistant. He had just been promoted to Privat-Dozent. "By the way, it appears you've made a great discovery. I've seen the year's records. My sincere congratulations, Doctor. It was a great work." He sighed. "I don't mind telling you—I almost made the discovery myself!"

"You did? How was that?"

"Oh, I had my thoughts, you know. All along I kept thinking to myself: There must be some answer, somewhere. Then one day I thought: Why not cadaveric infection? But I have to admit it. You were first. One can't admire you enough."

"Not cadaveric infection," said Ignaz Philipp gently. "*Any* putrid infecting material that may be carried by the examining finger . . . and isolation for all open, dirty cases . . ."

"Well, in any case, you're a lucky man. We're very proud of you, remember that."

Ignaz Philipp walked home. He remembered Zipfel's wise face, he heard him say again how he, Zipfel, had almost discovered the secret himself. He chuckled.

Outside his door waited a group of his students. They looked at him gravely.

"Come in, gentlemen, come in. What's the occasion?"

They filed in.

"Be seated."

But they remained standing.

He looked at them expectantly. They were all graduates. Kussmaul of Heidelberg, Stendrichs of Amsterdam, Routh of London, Arneth, who was replacing Zipfel; Wieger of Strasbourg, Schwarz of Kiel.

"We have come to say, sir——" said Kussmaul.

"With respect, sir doctor——" said Arneth.

"We want you to know we believe in you, sir," blurted Routh. "We have seen your doctrine work. We have seen what we have seen. Our term is ending. We are going to carry the news when we go home. And in the meantime we have divided Europe among us. We each of us will write to our professors at home. We each will write to the chief obstetrician in our cities. We have taken the liberty, sir—with your permission—the letters are already written . . ."

He bit hard. He swallowed. He dared not open his lips.

They looked at one another. Routh nodded. They stepped

forward in a smiling body and turned up their palms for inspection.

*Schwarz of Kiel. Kussmaul of Heidelberg. Routh of London. Stendrichs of Amsterdam. Arneth of Vienna. Wieger of Strasbourg.*

Skoda wrote that night to von Nadherny, head of the University of Prague.

In the *Vienna Medical Society Journal,* one of the most widely read medical periodicals in the world, Ferdinand Hebra, editor and head of Vienna University's Department of Skin Diseases, wrote for the world to see:

EXPERIENCE OF THE HIGHEST IMPORTANCE
CONCERNING THE ETIOLOGY
OF EPIDEMIC PUERPERAL FEVER
AT THE LYING-IN HOSPITAL

The Editor of this Journal feels it is his duty to communicate to the medical profession . . . the following observations made by Dr. Semmelweis, Assistant in the First Obstetric Clinic in the General Hospital of this city . . .

Dr. Semmelweis . . . for five years at the hospital . . . thoroughly instructed . . . for the last two years has devoted special attention to the subject of midwifery and has undertaken the task of inquiring into the causes . . . of the prevailing epidemic puerperal processes . . .

. . . observations aroused in him the thought that in lying-in hospitals . . . the patients might be inoculated by the accoucheur himself . . . and that puerperal fever was in most cases nothing else than cadaveric infection.

In order to test this opinion it was laid down as a rule in the First Obstetric Clinic that everyone, before making an examination of a pregnant woman, must first wash his hands in an aqueous solution of chloride of lime (Chloralis calcis unc. 1, Aqua fontana lib. duas). The result was surprisingly favorable . . . April and May . . . rule not yet in force . . . 100 cases of labor . . . 18 deaths . . . in the following months up to November 26 . . . 47 out of 1547 cases . . . 2.45 per cent.

From this circumstance the problem is perhaps solved, why in schools for midwives the proportion of the prevalent mortality is so favorable in comparison with . . . institutions for the training of medical students. An exception is the Maternité of Paris where, as is well known, postmortem examinations are conducted by the pupil-midwives.

Three distinct facts of experience may perhaps still further confirm the conviction . . . extend still further its scope. Dr. Semmelweis believes that he can prove that:

239

1. Owing to careless washing some student engaged in dissection caused the loss of several patients in the month of September.
2. In the month of October, owing to frequent examinations of a patient in labor who suffered from a foul-smelling medullary sarcoma of the uterus, when washing was not practiced.
3. Owing to a filthy discharge in an ulcer of the leg in one of the patients, several who were confined at the time were infected.

Thus, therefore, *the conveyance of a foul exudation from a living organism may be one cause which produces the puerperal process.*

In publishing these experiences we invite the directors of all lying-in institutions . . . to contribute the results of their investigations either to support or refute them.

In one of the world's most widely read medical journals in December 1847 this fact was brought out clearly: Puerperal fever is in most cases a cadaveric infection, but it is sometimes an infection by means of putrid exudation or discharge from a living organism.

The letters of the graduate students went into the cities of the world in early January. They were received in the British Isles where puerperal fever mortality records were the lowest in the world but where there was puerperal fever and even occasional epidemics of it, and where puerperal fever was for the most part regarded as a miasmatic contagion passed from patient to patient, or interpreted as scarlatina, erysipelas, or zymotic disease.

They were received in Norway, where the mortality was 15 per cent. Faye of Christiania received a letter.

They were received in Kiel, where the mortality was then 75 per cent, and in Berlin, where sometimes two out of three died, and Heidelberg and Italy and Strasbourg and Holland and St. Petersburg, in cities where sometimes four in a hundred died and sometimes forty.

They were received in Paris where the postmortems of women dead of puerperal fever were also performed by women. And there a casual observer could watch with the astonishment of Osiander the lively interest with which the young midwives took part in the cutting up of the bodies, how they with bare and bloody arms and with large knives in their hands amidst squabbling and laughter cut out the bony pelvis to make preparations for themselves.

In a small room in Vienna's Alservorstadt four men considered the millennium.

They sat in the shadow of a great university and in sight of the huge and sprawling Vienna General Hospital. The thoughts of these men were contained in one of the small buildings of this hospital, the small brick building that housed the Lying-in Division.

In this building puerperal fever had been conquered. The human race for the first time in the history of man could bear its young in safety. The dead of the ages, the known dead, filled the earth. And the wombs that might have borne the saviors and scientists, great priests, kings and dreamers of dreams, they lay there too.

And now this death that was born with every woman and walked her ways beside her would walk the earth no more. And now she walked whole.

"I am a little frightened," said Rokitansky at last. "I have been thinking of women. Of women everywhere. There is not a soul in the entire world this will not touch."

"It will come like an explosion, of course," said Hebra. "I can picture it—London—Paris—Africa—the remotest islands—'Have you heard? There's no more puerperal fever! It's gone! Gone forever!' "

"Imagine the universities," said Skoda. "Imagine the stupefaction as they read—as they check—as the first results come in——"

"To go into a ward," said Ignaz Philipp, "and not to hear screams—not to see death—not to see dying—to see gratitude in a woman's eyes and not terror, not mortal agony—to be able to do the duty of a doctor . . ."

"You'll be a great man now," said Hebra. "This university will be too small for you. You have done something more than save the living. These women will die and new women will be born and there will never be a woman born who may not owe her life to what you have discovered."

"They were dying," Ignaz Philipp mumbled, embarrassed. "They were screaming and dying. If you had seen them, if you had heard them—you'd have found a way. You couldn't have stood it, either. As long as I live I'll hear them."

"You'll hear a sweeter music henceforth," said Skoda.

"Yes," said Rokitansky, "you'll be St. Ignaz before long."

"See, here we sit in a room, and it spreads through the world. Even as we talk together, it's spreading," said Hebra. "It's out of Klein's hands. It's out of the university. It's out of Vienna. Presently it belongs to the world."

"I hope only that it spreads quickly," said Ignaz Philipp. "I want the first returns to be in this moment. I want to hear from the world. I want to know that it's started. I want to read the first letter."

A week passed. No reaction had come in yet from Hebra's article.

"It's too early," said Skoda.

"You're right!" said Rokitansky.

Ignaz Philipp nodded happily.

Next evening the first answer came from the world.

The letter was from Simpson of London.

He cited the low record of puerperal fever mortality in the British Isles. He said he was well aware of the lamentable conditions in the lying-in hospitals of the continent. He said that the properties of chloride of lime had been known in England for many years and that the contagious nature of puerperal fever was also English knowledge.

And that was all.

"He was in haste. He missed the whole point," said Ignaz Philipp, shaken.

"The great Simpson—is a great fool," said Hebra. "But that doesn't alter the miracle!"

"No," said Ignaz Philipp, "it doesn't alter the miracle . . . It doesn't keep the women of England from dying, either, with the remedy—the proof—now in their doctors' hands. Here," he said, white-faced. He handed Hebra the mortality report for the month of February.

In the First Clinic the death rate had dropped to 0.68 per cent.

# FIFTEEN

JANUARY passed. Each new day he woke with hope. He passed the day hoping. And when the post brought nothing, eagerly he willed the hours to pass until the new day. So the month passed. At the end he was impatient to be rid of it. Now he was nearer the day when the replies must inevitably begin. The day of the world's awakening. He frowned nowadays. He worried. Sometimes he could not understand the silence. But Hebra was increasingly confident.

"A whole month," Ignaz Philipp pondered helplessly, "and from the dozens of letters the students mailed—from your article, even—one letter! And that from Simpson."

"There is a thing coming which is going to end our troubles forever," Hebra said unexpectedly.

Ignaz Philipp looked up. Hebra hesitated, then leaned toward him cautiously.

"You know where our troubles come from. You know what blocks all progress in university and hospital. We are paralyzed with politics. The faculty is handcuffed with men who got their posts from a friend at court. They know little. They are shockingly limited. They are opposed to anything new. Medicine in Vienna can only be of their caliber so long as they rule the faculty."

"And the hospital. I know, Hebra. But remember—they are doctors—they are sworn to save human life, to prevent suffering—after all, there must be politicians in the human race, even doctor politicians—but even doctor politicians are doctors—and here is a truth—just a simple truth——"

"My friend, I am only a few years older than you, but I have spent those few years at the university. I have spent those years among jealous professors, anguished at any honor paid a fellow professor, seeking preferment, endlessly forming

243

cliques, separating, forming new cliques. The truth? My friend, the truth gets easily lost in such battlings. The truth has many sides and one seeks the side on which one's friends are represented. And one fights and dies there if need be."

Ignaz Philipp studied Hebra.

"You are trying to tell me something——"

"I suppose it must seem I've been rambling——"

"If what you say is directed at me it can only mean that I must leave Vienna and go into the world as a missionary, bringing this truth in my hands wherever women are dying."

"You won't have to do that. And you won't have to wait any longer. The time has come to take sides. Our politics are part of larger politics. And the reactionaries, the obstructionists of the university by their very presence have demarcated the liberals into reluctant groups. The groups have fused. Now they are a single, opposing group. Times are very bad. The wards are filled with indigent. The government is Metternich. Despotism has become intolerable. The students are becoming hard to restrain. And the reactionaries, deriving their position from the court, have become the party of the court. And the liberals have become the party of the people."

He looked at Ignaz Philipp questioningly. There was a little silence.

"Well, Hebra, you know where my sympathies lie, surely? You can have no doubt of me? I am a Hungarian. The people of Hungary have suffered from this monarchy more deeply and longer than the Viennese surely. My friend, if there's really fighting to be done——" His face flamed. He looked at Hebra warily.

"This time," Hebra said quietly, "there is no possible doubt of it."

"All my life I've heard about revolutions. When Markussovsky left I thought I'd be hearing of a Hungarian uprising within a week. It's come to nothing. One waits. One hopes. All my life it's been the same."

"This time it's inevitable."

"You'll see me in it then."

"I won't have to look far. You'll see me also."

"Hebra——!" This man speaking was the head of a department!

"We're going to win. And when we've won there'll be a new faculty. It will be based on merit. There will be no more politics to stand between humanity and a remedy for its suffering. We're going to sweep out the spies and lackeys, restore free speech and freedom of the press and freedom of teaching. And I'll tell you this: my Bohemia and your Hungary will be free too."

"What shall I do? Anything, Hebra. Give me something. Is Skoda part of this? Rokitansky?"

"Do your work until the time comes. Keep on with the doctrine. Never stop a moment. Skoda and Rokitansky are also democrats. But they will help best as ostensible neutrals." He wrinkled his nose. "It is repugnant to all of us. We are professors. We profess a truth which has no nationality. But now we have no choice. We have become a party in spite of ourselves. We are headed, incidentally, by Dr. Löhner. He is assisted by Professor Hye and Professor Endlicher."

"Professor Endlicher!"

"The same. Your gentle professor of botany."

"Löhner I can understand. But Endlicher——!"

"Did you expect him to side with the party of Klein and Rosas and Schiffner and Wattman?" Hebra asked gently.

Ignaz Philipp shook his head in happy wonderment.

"Endlicher!" he echoed.

"You can understand, then, how hard it's getting to hold the hot-headed students in check. And as to the poverty of the workers, I heard this morning that a woman in the poor quarter had been arrested for murder. She had killed one of her many children and served its flesh to the starving rest."

"Oh, now, Hebra——!"

"That's the charge. It's a matter of official record."

There was not long to wait.

On February 8 the people of France rose, overthrew the monarchy, and established the Second Republic. The news blazed through Europe. It was like a fuse. Outbreaks exploded throughout the Austrian Empire. On the third of March Kossuth addressed the Diet of Hungary and in the name of the people demanded a people's government. The news rushed to Vienna. The students of Vienna University begged for battle.

"This is the time!" cried Ignaz Philipp.

"Not yet," said Hebra. "First, we are sending Löhner to demand in the name of the university the removal of Metternich, freedom of speech, freedom of the press, and freedom of teaching."

Ignaz Philipp worked now in wards vibrant with crisis. He peered into the faces of the students, trying to guess who were liberals. He fretted over each one, for those who sided with the party of Klein might even extend the war to the patients, might deliberately neglect to wash their hands, might do anything. In the meantime he made sudden surprise visits to the clinic. His vigil was endless. Throughout the hospital and university tension became visible. What would the Emperor say?

On the twelfth of March Löhner and his deputation from the university returned with the Emperor's answer.

The Emperor, he said white-faced, had promised to consider the matter.

For a moment there was stunned silence. Then from the students there came a great shout of laughter.

245

"Now," said Hebra, "now it comes."

Outraged, the students took over the meeting. Their deliberations were short. Next day the Estates of Lower Austria were to meet. The students voted in a din in which their votes could hardly be heard to march in a procession from the university to the Landhaus.

"Come quickly," cried Hebra. He pulled hard at Ignaz Philipp.

"Where are we going?"

"Uniforms!" shouted Hebra. "Quickly, before they're sold out!"

They forced their way through the shouting students. Outside, Ignaz Philipp followed eagerly as Hebra rushed through the streets into the Josephsrader past the Lerchenfelder, into the Schottenfeld. He came to a small tailor shop. He burst through the door, Ignaz Philipp behind him. The proprietor looked up angrily. He saw Hebra. His frown vanished.

"Herr Professor!"

"I've come for the clothes!"

Without a word the proprietor walked to the front door, locked it, led the way to the rear of the shop. They decended into a cellar. In the glow of a candle Ignaz Philipp saw rows of tables, mounded, covered with sheets. The proprietor snatched off a sheet. The table was piled with the golden sashes of the revolution. On another table, under another sheet, were plumed hats.

Hebra picked up two sashes. He handed one to Ignaz Philipp.

"Roll it up. Hide it under your coat. Tomorrow—for the procession . . ." He found a hat. Ignaz Philipp found another. Hebra looked at the proprietor, a question in his eyes.

"Four gulden, sir professor," the man said proudly.

"Four gulden! More, surely!"

"That's what mine cost, sir professor."

Upstairs, the sound of pounding began. The first rush of students and professors had come for their uniforms.

Next day, dressed in the frogged coat of Hungary, the golden sash about his waist, Ignaz Philipp walked side by side with Hebra out of the great hall of the university into the Schotten Gasse and on to the Landhaus. His eyes were blazing. His heart pounded happily. He looked at Hebra, at the golden sash about his waist, the plumed hat on his head. Hebra looked back at him. They grinned. They walked in the center of a throng that filled the street from building to building. Wherever Ignaz Philipp looked he started with the fresh amazement of a familiar face. It was not only students. Here was Arneth, and Lautner, Rokitansky's assistant, here were dozens of other assistants. And here were full professors and Privat-Dozents and heads of departments, royalty of the faculty, men like

Hebra. There was little noise. The throng marched determinedly and grimly. And in the rear, joining the great procession, from every building flocked the townspeople. The crowd grew denser. Ignaz Philipp looked up. They were entering the Herren Gasse. They were under the archway which led into the courtyard of the Landhaus. In front of them was the building in which the Assembly was meeting.

The procession now halted. Ignaz Philipp looked about expectantly. On all sides men milled and waited. The marchers began to shift uncertainly. Students, thought Ignaz Philipp angrily, no leadership, no plan, just march. Now what? A few voices cried out, "Down with Metternich!" Then there was an awkward silence. It became crucial. The revolt was wavering.

Suddenly, in the hush, Ignaz Philipp heard a voice from the fringe of the crowd.

"Mein Herren!" the voice piped shrilly. "Gentlemen!"

"Give him room!" Hebra shouted unexpectedly from his side.

"Give him room!" shouted Ignaz Philipp instantly.

There was a commotion at the edge of the crowd. The students appeared to be wrestling with something. They hoisted. Someone shot up on their shoulders. It was a slight man. His plumed hat had fallen off. His sparse gray hair was blown in disordered wisps. He wore a thick beard.

"Who is it?" each man eagerly asked his neighbor.

"My God!" cried Hebra, staring.

"It's Fischoff!" shouted Ignaz Philipp.

Mild, unobtrusive Adolf Fischoff, professor of gynaecology, a man never known to have political opinion, a man who seldom spoke even at faculty meetings, began to utter publicly the first free word in Vienna.

For a moment Ignaz Philipp listened anxiously. If Fischoff fumbled, if he had cried out from a desire to speak and not with a message, if he fumbled now, this man unused to speech, or spoke uncertainly, there would be chaos. The sashes, the plumed hats, the procession would become ridiculous. The demonstration would be over. The revolt would be finished.

"Speak, man!" he shouted.

And from his side Hebra echoed, "Speak! Speak!"

"We will be heard!" shouted Fischoff. His thin voice carried through the throng. From the shoulders of the students he pointed to the Landhaus. "Our victory is in that building! Let us seize it. Does any man doubt why we are here today? We have risen, gentlemen! He who has no courage on such a day as this is fit only for the nursery!"

A great roar exploded.

Ignaz Philipp's throat was tight. He found himself gripping Hebra's arm. Tears smarted at his eyelids. His skin drew tight. His nerves exploded wave after wave of tingling shocks.

247

Freedom cried here. The freedom of country, of fellow man. Freedom for Austria. Freedom for Hungary. Freedom for thought. Freedom for the doctrine. The only passions of his life were caught up here, the two causes merged, became interdependent, became one.

The crowd strained to Fischoff now. And Fischoff clamored their dreams.

He cried out for freedom of the press. And they roared back at him.

He cried out for trial by jury. And they roared again.

Freedom of religion, freedom of teaching, freedom of learning, representation of the people, freedom to bear arms, cried gentle Fischoff.

But his voice was a fife and it shrilled what man could no longer live without, and the loose particles of them vibrated and merged and became steel.

And now he begged for Kossuth, too, and for the people of Bohemia and for Italy and for all the scattered nationalities of the sprawling Austrian empire.

*"Anschluss!"* he cried. "Union of us all! Respect for nationalities! A bond of constitutionalism! Only the free man can be faithful from his heart! And for the throne we are ready to devote the loyalty that derives from the splendid strength of freedom! I cannot live another day without my self-respect!"

He paused.

"Up! On! Into the Landhaus!" shouted a Dr. Goldmark.

Ignaz Philipp found himself shouting with the rest. The throng began to move on the Landhaus.

Inside the building the Estates had heard the rush of the massed people, heard Fischoff's voice. Some moved frantically to adjourn.

The doors burst open. Fischoff rushed in, the throng behind him. Ignaz Philipp stared at the frightened faces of the Representatives. From behind the crowd pressed inexorably. He and Hebra were wedged tight as their neighbors. He heard Fischoff call for silence. He helped cry silence to the crowd behind.

"We have come," said Fischoff without preamble, "to encourage you in your deliberations. We ask you to sanction our demands and to carry them to the Emperor."

Montecuccoli, president of the Estates, said hurriedly that the Estates were always in favor of progress.

"But we must have room and opportunity to deliberate."

He is too suave, thought Ignaz Philipp instantly. I don't like his polish. Be careful. He will manipulate us.

But Fischoff was assenting.

"I will stay here. A few of you remain with me. The rest—please—go back into the courtyard."

They looked about them uncertainly.

248

Part of the crowd began slowly to return to the courtyard. Ignaz Philipp and Hebra at last were able to move with the rest.

But outside the building, those who had been unable to crowd in and who filled the street were swept with a sudden fear of treachery. A great cry rose.

"Fischoff has been arrested!"

Instantly there was tumult. A window smashed. A door splintered. The roaring leaped to a solid thunder.

Quickly Fischoff ran to a balcony. There he showed himself with Montecuccoli. The din died at sight of him.

"Here is the president of the Estates," he cried.

"We will be represented," the throng shouted.

And Montecuccoli promised that a deputation from the crowd would go with the Estates to tell the Emperor the wishes of the people.

"Choose twelve men!" he shouted to them.

The crowd that remained in the Landhaus surged back into the courtyard. Ignaz Philipp and Hebra moved irresistibly with them, shouted the name of Goldmark and Lautner hopefully into the clamor.

The crowd picked up the names and shouted them up to the balcony. In the midst of the uproar a student shot up on the shoulders of the students. He waved a paper above his head. Ignaz Philipp's heart gave a great bound. The youth was dressed in the frogged coat of Hungary.

"It's a Hungarian!" he shouted at Hebra. "It's a countryman!"

The Hungarian youth was trying to speak.

"Louder!" clamored the crowd.

He tried again.

"What's he saying?" cried Hebra. "I can't hear——"

One word suddenly floated back to them.

"——Kossuth——"

"It's from Kossuth!" the crowd shouted, understanding suddenly, "it's Kossuth's speech!"

"Silence!"

"Gentlemen!" the youth began again. He heard his voice with despair. He looked down at the students. He spied a student wearing a Tyrolean hat. "Here!" he shouted to him, and shoved the speech at him. "Get up here. Tyrolean! Let them hear!"

Up in the air went the Tyrolean youth, up on willing shoulders, and his voice trained from boyhood to rebound among the Alps shouted the avalanche of Kossuth's speech.

While he read the speech the Estates in the Landhaus had gained time to make a decision. When the speech ended, one of the Estates came to Fischoff on the balcony and handed him the petition they had decided to present to the Emperor. Fischoff read it in amazement. He cried out to the crowd.

"They have agreed to ask for a report on the condition of the State Bank, and for a committee to consider reforms . . ."

He dropped the petition to the crowd, milling now in a storm of rage and scorn.

With his neighbors Ignaz Philipp reached vainly for the fluttering paper. A Moravian student seized it and shouting in triumph tore it into pieces.

"Into the Landhaus!" The cry rose again. Ignaz Philipp and Hebra fought their way back into the council chamber. The room was soon packed too full for movement.

"Is this the kind of petition we've asked you to take to the Emperor?" cried a student.

"Let's take the petition ourselves!" shouted Ignaz Philipp. "These are no people of ours!"

"These are Metternich's men!" Hebra shouted.

When the uproar died a little, Montecuccoli promised to present the original petition. The crowd parted as he and the Estates prepared to start for the castle. Suddenly their forward path was blocked as the crowd outside pressed in a moment. The next instant the pressure was gone, the President and the Estates were in the street, and Ignaz Philipp and Hebra and the crowd behind were catapulted into the street after them.

On one side of the throng there was wild activity. Ignaz Philipp stood tiptoe, craned to see better.

"Soldiers!" the cry arose. "Soldiers!" And they battled and shoved to reach the scene.

A regiment of soldiers had arrived. They had leveled their muskets. The crowd charged. An instant later, as he freed one arm and was about to free the other, Ignaz Philipp saw the regiment crumple and disappear. Now, as he pushed forward, he saw them again, milling a moment under the arches. The next instant he and the throng fighting irresistibly forward had pushed the soldiers the length of the Herren Gasse. They were in a clear space now, and stood uncertainly at bay.

A deputation from the crowd ran quickly to the mayor to call out the City Guard to protect the students. Refusing to listen to popular demand, the mayor ran to the Herren Strasse, rallied the soldiers, and retreated with them to better ground.

The unarmed students wavered.

But now from the suburbs, where the workmen lived, reinforcements streamed. Armed with poles and iron tools, they pelted into the center of town, tearing up stones for weapons as they ran.

The soldiers fired. The students surged back. In a moment Ignaz Philipp found himself overturning a wagon with Hebra and a dozen others. The barricade grew. From nearby houses furniture fell into the street, and as the soldiers reloaded, the barricade grew higher and stronger. The City Guard, summoned by the mayor, refused to fire and arms began to be passed out to the students. The soldiers gave way. From behind the barricades rose a great roar of triumph. It fell as if a knife had severed it.

Ignaz Philipp, his clothing torn, his hat askew, jumped on the barricade to see better. Hebra and a score more clambered beside him.

Cannon had been brought to the nearby Michaelerplatz. The Archduke Maximilian rode beside them. From that point the cannon commanded the Herren Gasse and every exit. Ignaz Philipp watched numbly.

"They've got us!" a workman cried suddenly.

"Let's die, then," shouted another.

The soldiers drew up behind the cannons. The master gunner and his men stood at attention. The street became very still.

"Fire!" cried the Archduke.

The master gunner, a Bohemian named Pollet, stepped forward.

He faced the Archduke. His voice came back clearly.

"I will not fire."

"What do you mean you will not fire!"

"Show me your orders. I obey the commander of the town."

"In the name of the Emperor," the Archduke shouted to the gunner's crew, "I command you! Fire!"

Pollet stepped in front of the cannon. He put his back squarely against a cannon's muzzle.

"These cannon are under my command. Until I receive an order from my commander and until necessity obliges it, let no one fire on friendly, unarmed citizens. Men! Only over my body shall you fire!"

Ignaz Philipp staring, open-mouthed, heart pounding, waited. Then with the rest he shouted a great roar.

The Archduke was riding away. Behind him followed the soldiers.

From another street, running with all their strength, their breaths sobbing in their chests, the castle deputation dashed back to the Herren Gasse. They had seen the Emperor.

Metternich had resigned. The revolt was over.

Now there was a tumult that shook the very buildings. Professors hugged students. Workmen hugged grave heads of departments. Ignaz Philipp and Hebra embraced as though they held victory itself. The street became a maelstrom of capering men, laughing, crying, and the next instant was half empty as students ran to shriek the news to the far ends of Vienna.

"Wait!" shouted Hebra. "Back to the university! Let's hold the university in case of treachery."

"My patients, Hebra," Ignaz Philipp cried suddenly, as they ran to the unversity.

"Tonight the head midwife is the best doctor in Vienna," Hebra shouted. "Tonight we guard the university."

That night the workers continued to riot in the suburbs. Metternich, who intended to retire to his suburban villa, found it burned to the ground and fled to England.

Next day, ignoring the Archduke, the Emperor announced freedom of the press. Minutes later he collapsed in a fit of epilepsy. Quickly the Archduke appointed Prince Windischgratz dictator of Vienna. He announced immediately that Vienna was in a state of siege. He instructed the soldiers to fire at will.

"But these are human beings," pleaded Fischoff.

Windischgratz eyed him.

"Human beings begin at barons," he said coldly.

The students refused to leave the university. At daybreak Ignaz Philipp stole quietly back to the clinic. He began his rounds. Klein found him thus, walking from bed to bed, dressed in the uniform of Hungary, his plumed hat in one hand, a forceps and a speculum in the other. He stared at him, stupefied. Ignaz Philipp turned. Klein drew back, trembling, and sped back to his office.

Ignaz Philipp finished rounds. It was the fourteenth of March. There had been fourteen days without a death. He returned to the university.

"They have torn down Windischgratz's proclamation," Hebra greeted him.

"He is going to have to kill every citizen of Vienna," Ignaz Philipp said grimly.

"They won't dare fire," cried a student. "Come on! We'll make them eat their bullets!"

The students needed no urging. They poured out of the university and into the Schotten Gasse again. This time they headed for the castle.

"There's going to be blood shed, Hebra," cried Ignaz Philipp.

"That's what doctors are for," Hebra replied, and they followed, running, after the rear of the procession.

"Hebra!" someone shouted. And again, "Professor Hebra!" They stopped and turned. A woman was running toward them. Hebra peered. Suddenly he clutched Ignaz Philipp's arm.

"It's Matthilde!" he cried. He turned to Ignaz Philipp. "For my wife!" he shouted incoherently.

He ran to the woman. Ignaz Philipp followed. As the woman saw him run toward her she turned and ran back in the direction from which she had come.

And suddenly Ignaz Philipp remembered.

"Is it time?" he shouted incredulously. "Is it time already?" He dashed ahead of Hebra and an instant later he passed the woman.

It was indeed time.

There was time to wash scrupulously, time to say a prayer. And then Ignaz Philipp proceeded to deliver Frau Hebra of another son.

"In full uniform!" Frau Hebra said proudly, as he made her comfortable.

Ignaz Philipp looked down at his frogged coat, his golden sash.

Hebra smiled proudly. "Leave me the sash, Ignaz Philipp. When he grows up I'll give it to him."

He took the sash and draped it over the head of the cradle. "Now we must go." He took Ignaz Philipp's arm.

"Where are you going?" cried Frau Hebra.

"We left the students marching on the castle. If we're lucky we may get there in time to save a few soldiers."

But the soldiers had not fired. And Windischgratz, shaken by the people's firmness, had appealed to Professor Hye to restrain the students. By evening the epileptic Emperor had recovered sufficiently to summon the Estates. Next morning he rode through Vienna in an open carriage. Cheers followed him. That evening, in an academic legion of professors and students, Ignaz Philipp and Hebra marched to the city gates to receive Kossuth and the delegation come from Buda to ask Hungary's freedom.

A responsible ministry was formed. The provinces waited excitedly. In Berlin, Virchow, hunted as a revolutionary, fled for his life. In Italy, in Venice, and Milan, the citizens rioted for freedom from Austria and the Emperor called on the Hungarians to help quell them. The establishment of constitutions began and the countries of the Austrian Empire, themselves a welter of nationalities, started to solve the distribution of freedom.

Ignaz Philipp bounded each day into a new world. He thrust his exuberance into the First Clinic. The wards vibrated with his exultation. An incredible thing was happening. He did not dare to speak of it. He and the head midwife looked at the journal, then at each other, and said nothing. Three weeks had passed. There had not been a death in the First Clinic.

The month's last week he slept at the clinic. At almost any hour of the night or the day he could be seen at any bedside. He examined everything, he checked, he examined again. The women, seeing him constantly about the wards, felt a vague terror.

"Why is the sir doctor here so much? What is he afraid of?"

"It's the childbed death, I think. There must be new deaths."

"I tried so hard not to come into the First Clinic. What is it they do to you here that—that——"

"Some say it's the doctors. Myself, I think it's the very bricks in this cursed place. When I knew I was fated here I touched nothing, you can be sure. Absolutely nothing."

"You should have been here the day he came in wearing his uniform. It was enough to frighten the fever into anyone."

They lay back, each of them wondering which of the others would never leave the hospital alive.

They had their babies. They rested. They left the hospital. Two hundred and seventy-six of them entered in mortal terror, bore their babies—and left.

In the entire month of March there was not a single death from puerperal fever in the First Clinic.

Ignaz Philipp continued to wear the Hungarian national costume, dark trousers with a strap for the instep, the frogged coat without lapels, the high collar banded at top and bottom, beneath the coat a white shirt, stiff white collar, a black bow tie. Nowadays he let the revolt go on and rarely left the wards.

"Do you think of nothing else?" Hebra asked him one day. "You must play a little, friend. You are becoming like a piano with one key."

"I am very tired, Hebra, and that is true. But we have not won yet, it seems to me. And until the doctrine is accepted I cannot afford a single puerperal death. An outbreak now would be very welcome to Klein. More than that, more than anything, you cannot imagine what a miracle it is to have a weapon. Not to be helpless any longer. To see suffering and to be able to relieve it."

"One thing—your troubles with Klein are over."

"Is he going to resign? What do you mean?"

"I mean that you will now have a chance to put your doctrine into effect officially. I mean that in a few days you will look back on all your struggles as a bad dream. Van Feuchtersleben, vice-director of medical-surgical studies, will ask tomorrow for a commission to be formed."

"Hebra! To investigate the First Clinic?"

"To investigate the relative merits of the entire faculty."

"Oh no. Never . . ."

"I told you. Remember? Now we begin to reap that glorious thirteenth of March."

The commission was appointed. The survey was made. The curriculum was ordered turned over to the faculty for full supervision. The university and the hospital reverberated with rumors that Klein was discharged, Rosas forced to resign, that a score of professors like them would be gone by the end of the

254

week. Ignaz Philipp made ready to take over the First Division.

The commission completed its findings. The report was published. Klein was safe. Surgery Professor Wattman and Director Schiffner were to be pensioned off. That was all.

Ignaz Philipp returned doggedly to his vigil. New riots occurred in the streets. The students and the workers had joined forces and had become a power no one could control. The foreign students had left Vienna. Because of the daily rioting patients were finding it perilous to reach the hospital from the provinces. In Hungary, the new free government ordered the Serb and Rumanian minorities of Hungary to speak only Hungarian.

But in April the mortality rate in the First Clinic was only 0.65 per cent.

And in April came the first letter of enthusiasm and gratitude.

It came to Dr. Schwarz, one of the students who had written to spread the doctrine. Proudly he sent it on to Ignaz Philipp. And Ignaz Philipp read it aloud to Hebra, Skoda, and Rokitansky.

It was from Michaelis of Kiel. It reported how the small Kiel lying-in hospital had been so plagued with puerperal fever that Michaelis had been forced to close it.

"When I received your letter I was again in the greatest distress. Our institution had been closed from the first of July to the first of November. The first three patients then admitted sickened, one of them died, and the other two were just saved . . . your communication gave me some encouragement for the first time . . . I at once introduced your method of chlorine disinfection into our institution . . . since the introduction of your method not a single case of labor has shown the slightest degree of fever with the exception of one in February . . . I therefore thank you for your communication with all my heart; you have perhaps saved our institution from destruction . . . I beg of you to greet Dr. Semmelweis on my behalf and to offer him my thanks . . . when I think of the deaths I, myself, must have caused . . ."

"You see?" said Skoda. "That is only the first. Now the replies will start coming from all over the world."

"You must save that letter," said Rokitansky. "You must frame it and keep it always."

"I am going to write to him tonight," said Ignaz Philipp.

"Tell him to write his experiences to other lying-in hospitals," said Hebra. "Tell him to send me a report for the *Vienna Medical Journal*."

Ignaz Philipp began his letter shortly after ten o'clock that evening. He finished at three o'clock in the morning. First he thanked Michaelis awkwardly for writing a reply. Then he described in detail the methods of chlorine washing he had

255

tried. He devoted a page to the statistics of the First Division. He told his hopes, he begged that Michaelis write to every obstetrician he knew. He wrote Hebra's request that a copy of the Kiel results be sent the *Vienna Medical Journal.* He reiterated his gratitude and prayed for Michaelis' fortune.

He sealed the envelope. He closed his eyes a moment and thanked God.

Michaelis never received the letter. Brooding over the deaths, heavy with a sense of personal guilt, he left Kiel one afternoon, alighted at Hamburg, and as the train started threw himself under the wheels.

Dr. Litzmann who replaced him promptly announced that the tragedy was a great loss to medicine and could have been avoided if Michaelis had not allowed the Kiel lying-in hospital to become overcrowded. He added that in Kiel it was customary for puerperal fever to start in the open country and the towns and to spread to the hospital.

In Vienna the mortality rate in the First Clinic for the month of May was 0.99.

The women by now had become accustomed to the sight of Ignaz Philipp steadily patrolling the wards in the national costume of Hungary.

"I have heard that the First Clinic is not having so many deaths these days," a newcomer said uncertainly.

"There is something funny going on, you can be sure of that," the patient in the next bed said. "I think myself that just as many are dying. I have seen that doctor come in the wards late at night——"

"He comes in all hours——"

"What I think perhaps is that he steals the dead out when no one is looking."

The newcomer shivered. The ward in which she lay was fetid with the peculiar odor of parturition, sweet, animal, heavy, and this diffused into the odors from the open grating at the end of the ward which served as privy, and from the smell of putrefaction from the leaky sewers which served the whole great hospital and ran beneath the lying-in clinics.

"I don't want to die," she said plaintively; "do you think I will die?"

"Do you think any of us want to die? Perhaps it's your turn, perhaps not. Don't worry about it. Worry when you go into labor. That's when the stink steals into your flesh."

"None of us know. Don't listen to anyone. And leave the doctor alone, you with the big mouth. He's a good, kind man. He smiles at you, at least."

"And now that he's here everybody washes."

"Aha! Everybody washes! Listen to her! Do you know what a student told me yesterday? Yes, and I've heard it from midwives and attendants, too, for that matter. They wash their hands because we're dirty. That's what your good doctor advises them."

"Just because we're poor and have to come here——"

"I didn't know he said that——"

"He said that, and more——"

"So we're dirty, are we——"

Ignaz Philipp entered the ward on his way to the labor room. He walked from bed to bed.

"Good morning, Mother . . ."

"Good morning, sir doctor."

"Feeling well, I see?"

"Thank you, sir doctor."

And to the next and the next, his trained eye missing nothing, seeing no fever, no glazed eyes, hearing no screams, passing thankfully from this ward into the next and the next and then to the labor room.

It was a cavern of low moans this morning. Three women were in labor simultaneously. The journalists were busy. The midwives bustled among them. Ignaz Philipp watched them wash. He patrolled from bed to bed until the deliveries were completed.

He saw little of Klein in these months, for which he was profoundly grateful. But he made sure that the beds were at all times equidistant. He held the attendants rigidly responsible for keeping the floors clean, the windows polished.

He saw Skoda and Rokitansky only rarely. The council on curriculum had become a battleground for reform and reactionary groups. The fortunes of their adherents and assistants rose or declined as the heads of the university fought for control.

With Hebra he heard sad news from free Hungary. The Slavs, Croats, and Rumanians, outraged at Kossuth's determination to denationalize them, struck back. Hungrary fell into civil war. In October the Austrian Government sent Viennese regiments to intervene. The students protested. Rioting in Vienna began promptly. The Emperor fled. Windischgratz laid siege to Vienna. Free Vienna surrendered.

On November first Windischgratz entered the dazed city. Immediately the reactionary Schwartzenberg ministry was appointed. Its first order was to wipe out all traces of the revolution.

Now silence settled ominously over the university. The liberals went their troubled ways. The old order had terribly returned.

Klein appeared in the First Clinic again. He began to take special interest in the patients. Ignaz Philipp listened, amazed, one morning as Klein made a small joke. Klein took over a few classes also. He had aged markedly. He seemed, a bewildered Ignaz Philipp speculated, to be trying to ingratiate himself with patients and students and midwives for some reason.

His hopes rose again. A letter arrived from Tilanus of Amsterdam. It was an entirely friendly letter. He said he was not prepared to give up the principles by which he had conducted a lying-in hospital for twenty years. He declared that he firmly believed in the contagiousness of the miasma which attended puerperal fever and that spring and winter were the most miasmatic periods. "We often had the experience of the spread of an epidemic in the hospital by the admission of a patient already infected, and the conveyance of a contagion to other women owing to the atmosphere in which they were thus placed."

He agreed with Ignaz Philipp on the importance of cadaveric poisoning as a cause for puerperal fever. He quite agreed that the mischief might be made less by chlorine disinfection. But he could not believe that the evil would be ended solely by washing. He closed his letter wishing Ignaz Philipp every success.

"A good letter," said Hebra. "We have here a liberal and a broadminded man."

"It's curious. He half agrees with my doctrine—I will send him a copy of our records. Thank God for his sympathy, anyway. Perhaps when he sees the proof——"

"That's two good letters and one bad one."

"That, Hebra, and the year's record."

"Is it going to be low? Low as you hope?'"

"Low as I can keep it, Hebra. I keep my fingers crossed. I hope this year to make a record that can't be ignored. Perhaps that will do it. We have tried letters. We have tried publication. A year and a half has passed and we have had a rough letter from England waving the British flag in our impudent faces, a letter praising us from a man who killed himself because the doctrine was true and who was promptly succeeded by a man who kills patients instead, and a letter from a friendly Dutchman who is only half convinced."

"Our golden chance came with the revolution——"

"Yes, Hebra, and with the revolution it ended. No revolution will ever unseat Klein, depend upon it. I don't understand what's been happening. I can't begin to comprehend it. I haven't Skoda's admirable and agile mind, or Rokitansky's serenity, or your quick tongue and fine brain. But I still must believe that this apathy is a nightmare of coincidence, only a nightmare. And I have the records of the First Clinic for last year, dropping, always dropping, and for this year——"

"March and August and not a death——"

"March and August and not a single death. Twice in one year. And when the year is over—when the figures are added —when the world sees them——"

"My friend, I am going to write another article."

"You cannot, Hebra. Please, I beg of you! You are known to have been a member of the Academic Legion—you can only get in trouble. You are the head of a department. Don't, Hebra. Don't. Let the record speak for itself. It will be enough."

Hebra's second article appeared in the *Vienna Medical Journal* in December. It repeated the first article. It concluded:

This highly important discovery, which is worthy of a place beside that of Jenner's smallpox vaccination, has not only received complete confirmation in our lying-in hospital, but assenting voices have been raised in distant foreign lands expressing belief in the correctness of the theory of Semmelweis. Among the letters received are those from Michaelis of Kiel and Tilanus of Amsterdam, from which especially we select corroborative testimony. Still, in order to obtain for this discovery its full influence, we would, in the most friendly manner, request all the directors of lying-in hospitals to set investigations on foot and to send the results obtained to the editor of this *Journal* whether they support or refute the theory.

They were reading the article, Skoda, Hebra, and Rokitansky, when Ignaz Philipp burst in upon them, pale and shaken. He carried a piece of paper. He set it down before them. On it were written the total puerperal fever mortalities for the year 1848. The First Division had shown a mortality of 1.27 per cent. The Second Division had shown a mortality of 1.33 per cent. For the first time in the history of the Vienna General Hospital the First Clinic was lower than the Second.

"Now the problem is ended," Rokitansky cried. "Now, my boy, you have only to sit and wait."

"No," said Skoda, "this is surely not a time to wait. Not with this record."

"Now," said Rokitansky, "is the time to wait. I have always felt that patience was your best weapon. Patience defends the truth. No other method in medicine can succeed. You have your discovery, Semmelweis. Perfect it, continue with it, be patient. In time, a little here, a little there, the world will have it. And listen to me! You cannot fight the world."

"I am not trying to fight the world, sir. I am trying to fight death."

"He's right, Karl," said Hebra.

"Of course he's right," said Skoda.

"You will see," Rokitansky said. "The women you save today will die tomorrow. But the world you fight this morning will kill you this afternoon."

"This record," said Skoda, "will be our weapon. We couldn't have a better one. It is almost unbelievable. Now we have

259

something that must force their hand. Now we will see what our reactionary friends will do."

"What's the first step?" cried Hebra.

"A commission!" said Skoda firmly.

They groaned.

"Really, Skoda——"

"Another commission——?"

"But this one will be different! No more laymen. This will be a commission of doctors. And the question will be unequivocal. We'll stand or fall by it. They can't ignore it. And when the findings are published the doctrine will become official." He hit his forehead with his open palm. "I should have thought of it before."

They stared at him, waiting.

"It's very easy," he said triumphantly. "I will simply propose to the faculty tomorrow that a commission be appointed to test the discovery. It the commission finds the doctrine good, it is to be made official practice for this hospital. If they find it bad, it is to be discontinued immediately."

"You've got it, Joseph," said Rokitansky.

"Of course I've got it."

"They've got to face it. And they can't wiggle out," said Hebra.

"We really haven't waited long," said Ignaz Philipp, troubled. "There's been no chance for tests yet. You are men of position . . . shouldn't we wait? . . . Should you really be offering yourselves as targets?"

"Sometimes, my boy," said Skoda, "science and humanity need a little help."

Next day he presented his request for a commission before the assembled faculty. The majority of the professors concurred at once.

Rosas objected.

"By even referring to the high mortality of previous years in the First Division, Professor Skoda is deliberately holding Professor Klein up to insult—and at the same time criticizing the judgment of the faculty which appointed Klein and which has kept him in office."

"The petition asks," said Skoda, "that a commission of doctors be appointed to examine a discovery which has apparently stopped an epidemic of puerperal fever and which has since diminished mortality."

"I warn you," said Rosas, "that such an investigation will hamper the freedom of action of professors and dozents. Lectures on special pathology and therapy will have to be discontinued. The petition is using the pretext of a discovery to cast aspersions on one of the oldest and most trusted members of the faculty. This investigation can only bring disharmony and upset the established order of things and disrupt the unwritten law of co-operation among doctors."

The faculty voted. The petition went to the court.

Jubilantly the four men danced about Rokitansky's home, shook one another's hands, clapped one another on the shoulder. Happily, smiling, Ignaz Philipp walked the wards, joking with the midwives, smiling the fear from the faces of the long lines of women.

At the court of Ferdinand I, Klein and Rosas moved swiftly and frantically. They moved from courtier to churchmen, they summoned their friends, the wheels of their organization began to move.

On February 18 the court issued its answer. It was read by Baron von Sommaruga, Minister of Education.

"Regarding this continuous feud between the College of Medicine and the First Clinic, it is unfortunate that in the name of science and scientific discovery the morale of women in labor should be thus undermined and abused.

"Any investigation by the faculty should only be devoted to something appropriate and useful.

"The commission, the inquiry, are not asked for in good faith.

"Any investigation may be undertaken only by Professor Klein himself.

"The Minister feels that the subject is sufficiently important to warrant investigation. However, since this is a time when there is no epidemic, this is hardly the time to try to find out the causes of childbirth fever.

"The validity of the supposed discovery can never be proven by any comparison between the favorable conditions of the present and the unfavorable circumstances of the past."

Ignaz Philipp received the news dully. Now, he was completely bewildered.

"But I've asked for nothing," he said. "Only the truth established—is it good—or is it not good? If it's good—let's start saving lives with it."

"Apparently," said Rokitansky, "it's not so simple. And yet —I can't believe the answer myself . . ."

"Patience," said Hebra. "Wait for the letters . . . wait till the *Journal* is read abroad . . ."

But Klein and Rosas had had a narrow escape. It must not happen again. The organization went quickly to work.

In a few days the pulpits of Vienna resounded to a mass attack on Joseph Skoda, his life and his teachings. Doctors met to denounce him. The attack was city-wide, swift and thorough and brutal.

"Materialism!" shouted the clergy.

"Rank, utter materialism," echoed the doctors.

At the university the faculty listened, amazed.

261

"I will resign, if you like," Skoda told Haller.

"You will do nothing of the kind. I am sorry, Doctor, for the hurt this must have caused you——"

"Oh no." Skoda smiled. "They haven't hurt me, Dr. Haller. My work is talking, not listening. If I stopped to listen I'd never have time to talk. Me they have not hurt. Never. But we actually must do something about the new doctrine. And it comes from our own university, Doctor, this discovery . . ."

"It's ridiculous," said Haller. "Really, it's possible to become quite irritated with Dr. Klein. Yes . . . I see we must do something . . ."

The four met at Rokitansky's house that night.

"I don't know what's he's up to," Skoda reported happily, "but when Haller, when the Primarius himself begins to move for us——"

Ignaz Philipp shook his head unhappily.

"But it's so simple," he said. "I can't understand all this moving of heaven and earth—all they have to do——"

"Don't worry about it, boy. It's all taken care of now."

"Any letters, Hebra?" asked Rokitansky.

"Not yet. It's still early."

"That's right!" Ignaz Philipp smiled. "Klein one can understand—politics I begin to see is inevitable—but out in the world—away from such a situation—where all that's involved is a doctor and a suffering patient——"

"And remember," said Rokitansky, "there are others here who feel as we do. We're not alone."

A few days later they sat in the university auditorium. Primarius Haller confronted the faculty. He presented his annual report on the Vienna Hospital. He came at last to the Lying-in Division. He paused. He put down his papers.

"I should like now to speak of a discovery by Ignaz Philipp Semmelweis, a member of this university, assistant to Professor Klein. This discovery, described so ably by Ferdinand Hebra in the current *Journal* of the Vienna Medical Society, is one for which the human race may well be proud and profoundly grateful."

Ignaz Philipp sat stunned. He listened open-mouthed. Suddenly the blood rushed hotly to his face, his spine dug into the wooden seat, he wished himself buried from sight.

Skoda smiled serenely. Rokitansky listened gravely. Hebra rammed his elbow into Ignaz Philipp's ribs.

"The importance of this discovery for lying-in hospitals and for hospitals generally speaking, especially for the surgical wards, is so immeasurable that it appears worthy of the attention of all men of science, and it certainly deserves due recognition from the high authorities of the state."

In front of them and a little to the left Klein and Rosas sat, their faces stony.

"I herewith formally propose that Ignaz Philipp Semmelweis be invited to address the Vienna Medical Society."

More could not be said.

With a burning face Ignaz Philipp rose and accepted the invitation. Then, his ears roaring, embarrassed to the depths of his being, he made his way awkwardly through the congratulations and the friendly smiles, an assistant knighted by the head of the hospital.

He fled.

In a few minutes he was back in the sanctuary of the First Clinic, back among the women and the midwives and the students and the things he knew and loved and understood.

Now Haller had spoken. Now the world would listen.

Now the future of the doctrine was assured. Now was the hour of truth.

Ignaz Philipp's term as assistant expired on March twentieth. As was customary, he requested a two-year extension. On the advice of Rokitansky he added that he hoped to strengthen the evidence of his opinions about puerperal fever by the success of another two years' treatment.

The extension was refused. His job had vanished.

In a few days he would be dismissed from the First Clinic. Dazedly he gathered his belongings. He said good-by to the head midwife, to Bartsch and Arneth and to a few students. He stood for a time looking soberly into the autopsy room. It was almost empty. He went into the babies' room. He watched them awhile. In the bed nearest him an infant began to cry. The rag pacifier had fallen from its mouth. He replaced it. The child stopped crying. He left the babies' room. He started to go through the wards for the last time. There were no screams now. No death bell. He moved absently. He entered the first ward. The chlorine solution, the washbasins, had disappeared. A midwife saw him. She grinned.

"No more washings, sir doctor!"

They were safe, though. So far, they were safe. They lay in their beds, big-bellied, and they no longer crawled to him across the floor. These few were safe. For a little time they were safe. Until tomorrow.

He passed the first bed, and the second.

From behind him one of the women blew a loud noise of derision. He walked on. A small hysteria of laughter crashed about him.

"Good-by, Hungarian——"

"Go back to Hungary, Doctor—that's where they need you——"

In a bed ahead a woman sat up.

"We hear we're too dirty for you to touch, sir doctor——"

"Too dirty for your fine Hungarian hands——" She spit after him as he went by.

263

He walked through the ward. After the first he heard the patients only dimly. He looked at them gravely. His face was calm and without expression. In the doorway between the wards Klein appeared. He looked at Ignaz Philipp coldly. He walked with him through the remainder of the wards. They walked in silence. In the same silence they parted. As he opened the outer door his successor, Carl Braun, came to him. In his hands he held a bottle of chlorine solution.

"I believe this belongs to you, Doctor," he said.

Ignaz Philipp took the bottle, bowed, looked about him for the last time, and left the clinic.

He heard the door close behind him.

It was a clear March day.

He was on the sidewalk. He began to walk toward the park. He walked a long time. It was night, finally, and he went home.

# SIXTEEN

HE SAT in his room in the darkness. He wanted no lights. The dark was a mantle for his spirit and his sick heart. The blows his memory beat at him were muffled by it. From this cave of darkness he stared into the night at the Alservorstadt. His blood had leaped and kicked with rage. Now it pulsed coldly with dull hate. His mouth twitched. In the darkness he fingered the raw and secret wounds of rejection and shame.

He heard footsteps. He cringed as they approached his door. He heard Hebra call, heard him knock, shrank as he turned the knob. He heard his footsteps recede and die away. He sat in silence. He sat thus for a long time. He rose at last in the darkness and groped toward the bed, he undressed, he thrust his body beneath the blankets. He lay without movement. He loosed his thoughts again.

. . . it is terribly necessary that I do not feel sorry for myself . . . I must think clearly . . . first . . . let us face what has happened. Let us look it full in the face. To lose a job as an assistant is a disgrace. I am disgraced. There are those who know the circumstances. There are many to whom I must have failed in some way, failed as an assistant. I can't help that. The plain fact is I have no job . . . I must keep on . . . there will be no money coming in . . .

The salary, the thousand gulden a year, would stop now. Of his patrimony remained eighteen hundred gulden. He must move to smaller and less expensive rooms. It made no difference. These rooms were too large, too empty without Markussovsky.

. . . this is no defeat . . . it was time I stopped being an assistant. As Privat-Dozent I will give the doctrine authority. I will lecture each day. Each lecture will be a new indoctrination. I don't much like getting paid by the students. But it's

265

the system. It's the way it's done. And I can practice, I can have patients while I teach . . . They'll go all over the world, those boys . . . and wherever they go they'll spread the doctrine . . . that's one way . . . that's one sure way. . . .

He thought of tomorrow. He would enter no wards tomorrow. He would open no journal. He would see no patients. He would see no women safely delivered, safely up, safely out of the hospital.

And abruptly he stiffened in shame, remembering the women. They were safe and they were whole and he had saved them. And for this they had spit at him. He shook his head in wonderment. It was too much to understand. He must try to understand a little piece at a time. He began again. He saw the scene. He heard their mocking. The women . . . the very women . . . perhaps they wanted to die, after all. Perhaps a touch of fever would help them, a flick of agony, a flash of grinding pain. Maybe that was what they wanted. Klein's way . . . that's what they deserved . . . Klein.

And the anger left him. He remembered. He saw Klein whispering to a patient. He saw attendants, students, toadies of Klein, whispering, silent when he appeared. It was Klein, of course. The poor women . . . what could they do . . . what could they know . . . sick and desperate . . . ignorant . . . unstable . . . the poor devils . . . how could you blame a poor, sick woman . . . He smiled a little. Even Mama wasn't always reasonable . . .

The poor devils . . .

He was back at the clinic. And outside the clinic, stretching far down the streets of Vienna, was a long line of women, a year's patients, six thousand women. They were the poor and the hopeless, he saw their faces, and some were hungry and some were shamed, and some were beaten, and the line moved slowly into the hospital. They were six thousand women and each woman was alone. Their bellies big, their hour come, they marched in, and as the doors closed upon them the screams began, the air burned with their fever, wailed with the first mewling of their babies, the air was alive with begging eyes. And the line would not stop. They were stacked now, the first to come, row upon row of them, their bodies were still warm, and behind the eyelids the trapped eyes gazed on, imploring, fearing, helpless, and the dead.

And in his hands and brain was life. He had life for them all, for every woman, for every line marching into every hospital in the world. They must not die so. They must not. He had the gift of life. There was no time to lose.

He saw them, he saw himself, he saw all humanity, frail and doomed.

Frail. And doomed.

He fell asleep seeing the sickness in every human face, no

face without its sickness, and death the quick and slow and waiting doom.

He rose, saying to himself, in an agony of pity, frail and doomed. He dressed hurriedly. He rushed through the streets, and all the faces turned their message, the same message, clear and inexorable. Children, middle-aged, old people, their faces eddied by, their paths, their fate, the same. Every human.

He found Skoda.

"I must have a job," he said. "I must start immediately. Anywhere. In any capacity. Will you help me?"

Skoda nodded.

"It's already been arranged. We're going to get you appointed Privat-Dozent."

"Is there no chance of working with patients? I thought perhaps if you knew someone at Prague, or Berlin, or——"

"First of all, we do not want you to go elsewhere. We want you to stay here. Secondly, if there are any openings at these places they are invariably filled with their own men. I need hardly tell you that to be appointed Privat-Dozent is a promotion. You may engage in private practice. And as Privat-Dozent you may indoctrinate your students to your heart's content."

"That's true, isn't it——" Ignaz Philipp waited hopefully.

"It's one thing to spread a theory by keeping records for a long time and then addressing a small audience on the subject. It's quite another thing to send students all over the world, each man a nucleus of new instruction wherever he goes."

"You're right, sir. You're absolutely right. There were a handful came to me last year, voluntarily, each man promising to write someone back home—but as Privat-Dozent——"

"Instead of a handful you'll have hundreds. And when a mere assistant says something, that's one thing. When a Privat-Dozent says it, that's something else."

Ignaz Philipp's heart beat rapidly. His thoughts swirled with the fumes of exaltation.

"How long—that is—when do you think such a position——" He had a fierce desire to leap into the air, to kick his heels like a schoolboy. He tried to speak diffidently.

"Can you wait a month?"

Ignaz Philipp grinned. He bit his lip.

"Oh yes."

"The new list of appointments will be out in a month."

Now Skoda smiled too. Ignaz Philipp gripped his hand hard.

"Now go away and let me work. Somehow whenever I see you the air is full of emotion. Go somewhere and keep busy for a month. Why don't you brush up on dissection? You're going to have a lot of demonstration along with your lectures —Mr. Privat-Dozent."

Ignaz Philipp walked proudly through the university streets. He was completely happy. He found Rokitansky.

"It occurred to me you might be in today," said Rokitansky. "I presume you are looking for some ladies. Well, here they are, waiting for you. Henceforth, I'll save all the puerperal cases. Dissect away to your heart's content."

There were days when the month passed rapidly. There were days when he was sure the month would never end. At night he studied his records, prepared lectures, imagined himself delivering the doctrine step by step. He would be tactful. There would be no shouting, absolutely no shouting. He would speak smoothly, subtly, quietly. But there was haste too. He would show them the urgency, the great haste with which they must set the doctrine in effect. He pictured himself speaking this suddenly enormous thing:

"You have seen, gentlemen, how in two years suffering dwindled, deaths ceased. That was only here in Vienna, in a single clinic of the Lying-in Hospital. Now picture to yourselves the whole world, your comrades everywhere, you pick up the mortality reports, you scan the past year, like a clap of thunder the deaths have stopped everywhere. When you have heard the din of endless torture, as I have, you will know how loud will be the thunder of that silence . . ."

It would not do to be too dramatic. He must find words to speak quietly. But they must see, all the same. Perhaps the records would speak loudest of all. He rose early every morning. He dissected until evening. It was like the old days, the days with Kolletschka, the days when every hour was crammed with search and question and dexterity and joy.

He opened a note from Hebra one afternoon toward the middle of April. "Come to dinner tonight."

He had visited with no one for weeks. He thought of the evening with pleasure. He put the note in his pocket and returned to the cadaver he was dissecting. As he picked up his scalpel he thought of the Hebra children. He hesitated. Abruptly he made up his mind. He laid down the scalpel. He went to the sink and washed his hands. He scrubbed thoroughly, but as he thought of the children he scrubbed faster.

A half-hour later he knocked on the door of Hebra's house.

"But you were coming tonight!" Frau Hebra cried. "Ferdinand sent me a note—for dinner, he said——"

"This is a professional visit." Ignaz Philipp grinned. "I have come to see my babies." He walked past her into the house.

"Everything is a mess—it's a shame you should see the house this way——"

"Yes, yes, everything's a mess. Anyone can see that. The floors are blinding me, the glass is like diamonds—why do I waste my time talking to you? Where are the children?"

From the next room a small figure came at an unsteady run, grabbed Ignaz Philipp's leg and clung there.

"HaHA! Young Ferdinand!" Ignaz Philipp grabbed the boy and flung him up at arm's length.

"Look at him. He's a mess. Put him down and I'll clean him up——"

"You leave him alone. He belongs to me, don't you, Ferdinand? You're my boy, aren't you, Ferdy? Say Uncle Naci, boy. Say Uncle Naci!"

He rolled the child back and forth in his hands. The youngster bleated with delight.

"He doesn't talk, Naci. Is he all right? I mean, not talking yet?"

"Ahhh! What do you know about talking! Talking's for women. All you think of is talking." He slung the child under one arm. "Come on. Where's the other one?"

He followed Frau Hebra upstairs.

"He says da-da, and mum-mum, and I think he says wassy. But shouldn't he be talking by this time?"

"Woman, supposing he could talk? What would he talk about? Are you lonesome? If you want a companion, if you want someone to talk to, I know a nice young Hungarian doctor who'll be glad to entertain you when your husband's away." He rolled the child out from under his arm and set him upon his shoulders, where the youngster instantly began to pound his head.

"All the same——"

"All the same, have a girl next time. She'll talk your ear off."

"And I can't break him from wetting himself——"

"Have a girl. But remember, once he's housebroken he's housebroken for life! But you can never trust a woman. Now if I were to frighten you, right now——"

From down the hall came the sound of a baby crying.

"Wait till I get you married. I'm going to find a girl who can smack you. You say worse things every time I see you."

He grinned delightedly.

"HO!" he shouted up to the boy.

They entered the nursery. Ignaz Philipp went straight to the cradle. Over the head of it still hung the golden sash. He picked up one end of it, pleased.

"You still keep it, eh?" He sighed. "What days, what wonderful days."

"The only thing wonderful about them was that I always knew where to find Ferdinand. I'd listen for shooting and shouting and I'd know there was Ferdinand. Fine days for a wife."

He had stopped fingering the golden sash. He was looking at her oddly.

"What's the matter, Naci? What's happened!"

He pursed his lips. His eyes widened. He blinked.

"Either I'm bleeding to death——"

"Naci!"

"Or the ceiling's leaking——"

She put her hand to her mouth, dismayed.

"Or——" He looked up at Ferdinand, sitting imperturbably on his shoulders. "Hey!" he cried out, and swung the youngster down. "What are you doing, eh? What are you doing to your uncle Naci?"

She rushed to the child.

"Ferdinand! What have you done! Didn't I tell you to ask Mama? Didn't I? Sitting right there without a word—— Oh, Naci! Oh, I'm so dreadfully sorry! You bad, bad Ferdinand, you, bad, bad——"

Ignaz Philipp had taken off his coat. He looked at it.

"It's not blood," he said ruefully. "It's Ferdinand."

She snatched the coat from him, her face crimson.

"Here," he said. "Take the vest too. Don't scold him, Frau. I think we got the shirt in time. It's only water. Don't worry about it."

"You see what I mean?" she cried in despair. "You have to watch him like a hawk." She knelt and began to tug off the child's rompers. "Wet! Wet clear through." The baby in the cradle, who had fallen silent at the sound of their voices, now began to cry again. Ignaz Philipp grabbed Ferdinand and held him under his arm. He walked to the cradle and scooped up the crying child.

"Wait until I put some fresh pants on him——"

"Ah! Leave him alone. I like him better this way."

"But he's all bare! His bottom's bare!"

"That's the way I like 'em. Go on now. Dry my coat. A fine reception a doctor gets in this house. No wonder his father stays away."

He lay down on the floor.

"Naci! You're going to get filthy——"

"Go, woman! Go!"

She raised her eyes to heaven, shook her head, and left the room.

Ignaz Philipp piled the children on his belly.

"Now," he said. "Now, you two boys. Now here's Uncle Ignaz." He lay luxuriously a moment. "Boom-ditty-boom!" he shouted suddenly, arched his body, bumped the floor. The little boy screamed happily. The baby dribbled.

He shook his forefinger at the two mites on his belly.

"Don't wet me," he warned. "If you wet me I'm going to wet you back!"

Up went the belly again and down he bounced and down the children bounced with him.

270

"Boom!" he shouted, and rubbed his face in the baby's neck, "Boom-ditty-boom . . ."

An hour later Hebra found the three of them sleeping on the floor in a corner of the nursery. The boy slept with his head pillowed against Ignaz Philipp's side. The baby lay in the crook of his arm.

"You need children of your own," Frau Hebra said at dinner.

"I think I've heard you mention that once before."

"I'll say it again too. Why don't you get married, Naci?"

"Hebra! Will you beat her, please? She's matchmaking again."

"Ferdinand!" said Frau Hebra.

"I'm sorry. I was woolgathering."

"He just can't seem to leave the classroom behind him when he comes home."

"Did you have a hard day, Hebra?"

"No-o-o-o . . . nothing out of the ordinary . . . don't mind me. What was she doing to you?"

"She's trying to get me married again."

"You should see how he is with the children. He's hungry for children. Why don't you have your own?"

"I will. Maybe I'll get married first."

"It's time you got married. You don't need to be a millionaire, you know."

"No"—Ignaz Philipp grinned at them—"all you need is a job. A good job. And maybe—from all I hear—just on the chance, mind you—the job I'm looking for is coming right to me."

"Naci!"

"Hasn't he told you?"

"The fact is——" said Hebra.

"All he ever tells me is the bad news. What is it? What kind of job are you being offered, Naci?"

"Hebra, I'm ashamed of you. It's a Privat-Dozent, Frau."

"A Privat-Dozent! Really?"

"That's what's being arranged. I tell you when I think of it I could burst. It could hardly be better."

"But when?"

"It's due now, eh, Hebra? Any day, Frau. Maybe to-morrow."

"Oh, Ferdinand! Isn't it wonderful?"

"What do you know about Privat-Dozent!"

"Why, now he can get married!"

Ignaz Philipp looked at Hebra curiously. He seemed to be smiling only with his mouth. He looked tired.

"I suppose you've already got some woman picked out for him?"

"Oh, I know dozens of women. You'll see."

271

"You know something? I don't need a woman. I've got all the women in the world. They're my girls. Every one of them."

"You can't fool me. Still, you'd like to get married."

"I would. Do you know—for the first time in my life—perhaps being here this evening, playing with the children—I'd like to have a home of my own. Up to this moment I'd never even thought about it. I'd like to be like my father and raise a large family and have a fine wife like—well, a fine wife."

"And now you'll be able to."

"Yes, and more . . . much, much more . . ."

He turned to Hebra.

"What do you say, old friend? Will you talk to me when I'm a Privat-Dozent?"

"What's the matter, Ferdinand? You sit there like a lump."

"I'm sorry." Hebra smiled. The smile vanished. "Naci—I've got bad news for you."

"What news could be bad news? What's troubling you? Frau, get your man a glass of wine. Get up on the table and dance for him."

Hebra looked at the table. He felt a little sick.

"Ferdinand!"

"It's the Privat-Dozent. The list was posted after lunch."

"Yes——"

"You're not on the list. They didn't give it to you."

He was not able to remember clearly the rest of the evening. It passed somehow. As he walked homeward Frau Hebra's voice came to him dimly, staccato with indignation. He saw Hebra's embarrassed sorrow. For a few moments he had been Privat-Dozent. He had held the prize and planned from it. His mind reeled with the bitter disappointment of loss. His life had been built around the appointment in a lightning reconstruction. It was gone. It was snatched away. He shook his head dazedly, viciously, to clear it.

"What now?" he asked himself. "What next? What now? How shall I plan? What shall I think about?"

He was passing the hospital. Dim light showed in the windows of the First and Second Clinics. He halted. He imagined the attendants dozing, the journalists on night duty walking from ward to ward. He saw the women, some asleep, some moaning softly, their heads twisted on their necks as women lay in labor. He yearned to go in. On a sudden impulse he opened the door and defiantly walked through the empty anteroom into the Second Clinic.

Arneth looked up. He gaped. He rose at once and came to him.

"Dr. Semmelweis! How are you? Is there something I can do?"

"I was just passing by——"

"It's good to see you. Will you sit down?"

272

"No, thanks, I'm just going to stay a minute——"

"Doctor—I'm sorry about the appointment—I want you to know how I feel about it—there's quite a few of us——"

"It didn't take long for the news to spread, did it? I only heard of it myself an hour ago."

"If you want the latest gossip, go to the university. If you want the news before it happens, go to the hospital. Undoubtedly something much better is waiting for you. Believe me, I have never a doubt of it. Now that you're here, would you like to see your old hunting grounds?"

"Yes. Yes, I very much would. Yes. To tell the truth, when I saw the lights burning I—well, here I am."

"Come on, then. It'll be a pleasure. But don't expect too much."

They left the Second Division and walked across the hall into the First.

Ignaz Philipp restrained a gasp. The familiar rows of beds loomed whitely in the darkness. But the smell was now overpowering. Arneth glanced at him quickly, nodded sympathetically.

"Wait," he whispered.

They left the ward and advanced into the next. On their beds the women tossed feverishly, one cried out, a midwife hurried to her, the stink of death was frightening. It was all the air to breathe.

In the labor room two women were gripping the sheets in the first torment of labor. There was the deep, throaty sound as of cats moaning. Here the smell was unbearable. The moaning exploded in three short shrieks, then became low moaning again, as before. Four beds were quiet. There was no movement. They watched intently. There was no breathing.

"My God! My dear good God!" whispered Ignaz Philipp.

They walked back to the Second Clinic.

"What's happened, Arneth? What in the name of the dear Jesus has happened?"

Arneth nodded.

"It's happened. Now you've seen it."

"But how? A year ago I had things fixed—there wasn't a single death—not a single case——"

"Yes. I've heard about it. You had it down to zero per cent, didn't you? Well, it's risen a little, Doctor. It's now 34 per cent."

"Thirty-four per cent! One out of three! What are they doing?"

"Well, first Braun stopped the washing altogether. The women began to come down with fever. In a week eleven died. The babies died as fast as the women. Braun considered. He set out the basins again. I came in and watched them. The students washed as they pleased. Some washed. Some didn't.

273

Those that washed promptly soiled their hands all over again by picking up dirty instruments. They really don't know any better. They seem to think that there's some magic connected with it, if you wash why that's enough, you don't have to be clean. You just have to wash. Well, of course the death rate continued to rise. And two weeks later Braun angrily ordered the washing stopped altogether. I heard him talk to Klein. 'You see?' he cried. 'The damned washings have nothing to do with it. If anything, washing just makes matters worse. And Klein looked at him. 'Naturally,' he said. 'What did you expect? I'm really a little surprised at you!' "

Ignaz Philipp stared at Arneth, white and sick.

"But they're killing them in there. They're deliberately killing them!"

"No," said Arneth softly, "it's the cosmic-telluric influence, Dr. Semmelweis. That's what's killing them." He smiled bitterly. "I'm sorry you had to see it . . ."

"But they can't," cried Ignaz Philipp, "they can't just continue—it must stop—someone must tell them——"

"They can. And it will continue. And it won't stop. And no one can tell them."

"But you, at least——"

"A mere provisional, Doctor."

The night bell rang. A sleepy porter shuffled out to admit a moaning woman. She halted on the threshold. She gave a last look at the street. Then she stepped inside and the door closed behind her. She clasped her hands. She looked at the porter.

"The First?"

He nodded apathetically.

"Yes, lady."

She looked at him a moment longer. A shuddering breath shook her.

"Oh, my God!" she whispered. Then her shoulders sagged. Her breath sighed out in surrender. Her chin dropped to her chest. Dully, she slouched away behind the porter.

"It doesn't matter," he told Skoda next day. "It happened and it's over with. Can you get me on next month's list? Will you try again, please?"

"Of course I'm going to try again. And of course it matters. It matters most vehemently."

"I wish you could have seen what I saw last night."

"I hear the rate's risen pretty high again."

"By God, I can talk to the students! I can do that! I must! I must get started!"

"I'm going to talk to Haller this afternoon. This time there'll be no tricks. And no failure. Did you hear anything about your application?"

"Not a word."

"Not even to answer you! All I can say is—be patient!" He said it grimly, with promise.

Ignaz Philipp walked home rapidly. His spirit was sore and he had begun to get a little angry. The veneer of protocol he had acquired during his years of study was at best thin. It was difficult for him now to survey the situation in which the women found themselves with medical detachment. He had always looked at facts bluntly. He had learned to shape them in his mouth so that he usually voiced them diplomatically. Now he rebelled. The plain truth was that men were men whether they were doctors or ditch diggers.

And a doctor could be ethical and criminal. To kill patients could become, if one allowed oneself to think that way, not the same as killing human beings. And yet those dead women and the women who would die tomorrow would not be any more dead if a murderer and not a man of honor had killed them. Klein and doctors like him were murderers. And they would continue to murder.

Medicine protected him.

And there was no law that could make him answer for his crimes.

He was beyond the law. He was a doctor.

Two pieces of mail awaited him. One letter was from Wieger, from France. It contained a medical journal and a letter.

*Dear Dr. Semmelweis,*

You will remember me as one of your graduate students. Perhaps you will also remember that day when with Kussmaul, Routh, and others, I pledged myself to write home the news of your discovery. Soon after despatching letters to Strasbourg and Paris, I left Vienna. On my return home, chafing because of the lack of response to my communications, I took the liberty of submitting a full account to the *Union Medicale.* I submit the publication. I have no words to comment. Here, as elsewhere in France, the mortality rate continues appalling. One week last month we reached 41 per cent. That is all I have to tell you. That and my undying assurance that your doctrine is still my doctrine and that my belief in it will never waver. *Philip Wieger*

His spirit leaped joyfully. The letter was an entire surprise. He thought of Wieger with pride. He had a feeling of bond, of kinship with the young man. It came to him that Wieger was a disciple. The impact of this word suffused him with pleasure and embarrassment. He remembered the *Union Medicale,* and reached for this distinguished medical journal eagerly. His fingers trembled a little as he studied the front cover. He had hoped to see the discovery in a foreign language, but it was a

275

hope without confidence. Now here was a French medical journal. Now the simple truth had reached the physicians of France. Now the women of France could be saved too. Somewhere in this journal was the first publication on the cause and cure of puerperal fever in a foreign language. He leafed through the journal. The article eluded him. He began again. He leafed through more slowly. He read each imposing opening page. He frowned perplexedly. Wieger must have made a mistake. He must have sent the wrong journal. He reached the last pages of the medical journal. His eyes picked up a familiar phrase. He halted instantly.

"On the prophylactic means used against puerperal fever in the great Vienna Hospital . . ."

There was Wieger's article. There it was in its short entirety.

*It had been printed under the title: "Doubtful Anecdotes."*

This was the answer from France. He closed the journal quietly and pushed it away. Disappointment and sadness weighed him, frustration was lead in his heart. He had failed again. He sat crushed, unwilling to think. His hopes had been very high.

The remaining letter was from England. He held it in his hands, unopened. He looked at the envelope and nodded his head slowly. He tried to accustom himself to the fresh blow it must contain. At last he felt ready. He opened it. A letter and a few pages torn from a periodical sifted out. He opened the letter. It was from Routh, an English graduate student. He would not be tricked another time. This time he was prepared. Glumly, grimly, he began to read.

*Dear Dr. Semmelweis,*
Although my letters to London, sent while I was a student of yours, produced no response, I beg leave to submit the enclosed which I believe will be of interest to you.
Faithfully, *F. H. C. Routh*

The printed pages had been cut from the *Medico-Chirurgical Transactions,* official journal of the British Medico-Chirurgical Society.

Unwillingly he began to read. The article was titled: "On the Causes of the Endemic Puerperal Fever of Vienna." Followed a full account of the discovery, as described by Dr. Routh in a speech before the Society. There was no laughter here, no derision, no Gallic pleasantries. Dr. Routh was the first Englishman to proclaim the Semmelweis doctrine in England.

The article ended. The comments of Dr. Routh's hearers followed.

Dr. Murphy, Professor of Midwifery at University College Hospital, mentioned a case he knew of an eager German stu-

276

dent who seldom missed a post-mortem. Puerperal fever seemed to attend him. Wherever he went new cases occurred. He stopped attending post-mortems. The fever subsided promptly.

Dr. Copland, who many years before had approached the problem on the basis that puerperal fever was caused by a miasma of contagion and advocated cleanliness, rose to say that the facts stated in Dr. Routh's paper were so convincing that he could scarcely doubt their accuracy.

Mr. Moore said that the number of post-mortems performed at Vienna was remarkable. He cited the low number of post-mortems performed in England. He felt that in any country where a great number of post-mortems were performed the Semmelweis doctrine might well deserve consideration.

But here was no contemptuous dismissal. Here, for the first time, was a flicker of serious consideration. From England. From Simpson's country. Ignaz Philipp reread the article unbelievingly. He read it again. Slowly he digested this morsel of hope. Slowly his sadness began to drop away. One did not need many such letters. A few more such reactions in England and this small candle of truth could start a blaze that might light the earth. A letter here—a meeting there—a sober consideration—a faithful trial—slowly or rapidly, in a month or a year, the discovery would become the world's. It must come through disciples, then. It must come about through students. Through the young men. He paused. He smiled a little. It came to him that he was not many years older than Routh. He passed his hand self-consciously over his head. His hair was very thin now. In a few years he would be quite bald. He fingered his face. There were deep lines between his brows. He had lost weight. His face was becoming lined.

But in his heart and in the deep tissues of his body he was invigorated. He was no longer tired. He began to plan. He began to think of the future with resolution. He no longer despaired. He chided himself irritably. An hour ago he had been disappointed and crushed. He had read an adverse reaction. But that was only one letter. He had not received an appointment as Privat-Dozent. He had waited only a month. And it had seemed the end of living. But a new month was coming. A month was only four weeks. The students would carry his message. The students would practice the doctrine. The important thing was the students. And as Privat-Dozent he would lecture, he would indoctrinate, he would prove, he would instill them with all he knew, and all he hoped, and all that must be done. A new month was waiting. A new list would be posted at month's end.

Next day he moved to smaller rooms. In the evening he went to Skoda.

"How do the chances look? Did you see Haller?"

277

And he showed him the letter from Routh. Skoda read it carefully. He read the article. He rose.

"Come. Let us go see Rokitansky. He'll want to see this."

"I'll tell you what we must do," said Rokitansky. "Now it has started. Now we must move with great caution."

Skoda and Rokitansky looked at Ignaz Philipp. He flushed.

"You want me to keep my mouth shut, isn't that it?"

"There's no use saying anything at this point. It is easy to say the wrong thing——"

"Or to say the right thing—wrong."

"Precisely. Now we must move with caution. We must take no chances. We must say nothing."

"You don't think, sir, that we should give Routh's letter to Hebra to publish in the Vienna journal?"

"I don't think it's necessary," said Rokitansky.

"It might even stir up resentment," said Skoda. "We must do nothing that will keep you from getting appointed Privat-Dozent at the end of this month."

Ignaz Philipp looked at them eagerly. He waited. He could not restrain a smile. He was full of joy.

"You've never done any experiments with animals," Skoda said thoughtfully.

"That's a fine idea," Rokitansky said instantly.

"I'll be glad to. I have no equipment—no place to work——"

"You will spend the month experimenting. You can use my laboratory. And I'll even lend you my assistant, Lautner—you know Dr. Lautner?"

"I know him well. He's a fine young man——"

"Keep a careful record," said Skoda. "Work hard—speak to no one—keep to yourself—these experiments may well be a factor which could even set the seal on your appointment."

He found Lautner in the dissecting room.

"I have just come from Dr. Rokitansky," he said, smiling anxiously. "I have always admired your work, Dr. Lautner, and now he tells me that if you are willing we shall work together."

Lautner smiled, surprised.

"It will be a pleasure, Dr. Semmelweis. What are we to work at?"

"He said we might use his laboratory. He suggested a series of animal experiments. It's—it's about puerperal fever."

"I see." Lautner's tone was guarded.

"Yes . . . Perhaps you would allow me to explain my theory . . ."

"Of course, Doctor. Please do."

"It begins a long time back. When I was provisional assistant in the First Clinic . . ."

"Yes, Doctor."

278

"I had begun to notice that the death rate in the First Clinic was invariably much higher than the mortality in the Second . . ."

Step by step he reviewed the discovery. Lautner laid down his scalpel. He sat upon an autopsy table and listened.

"You will want to see records . . . I have kept many notes . . ."

He spoke with pleasure. He detailed all he had learned with absorption. He reviewed the dramatic drop in death as if it had occurred yesterday. When at last he finished, it was with reluctance. He had been living in a world of facts. Now he came back to a world that was not fact. He looked at Lautner. He waited.

"That is most interesting, Doctor." The young man's tone was still guarded. But now there was a degree of warmth in it. He was prepared to co-operate. He looked forward to performing the experiments. I have succeeded, Ignaz Philipp exulted. Think what I could do in a lecture room. Think of that coming day. He wants only to be shown.

"Have you any thoughts on how we should begin?" Ignaz Philipp asked politely. Lautner shifted at the compliment. Ignaz Philipp said quickly: "You see, I am on my good behavior. They tell me I am too blunt, want tact, have no manners. It is true. I have never learned to say in a cautious paragraph what can be said boldly in a sentence. I have heard that I am only a Hungarian peasant from whom not too much can be expected. Forgive me in advance if I ever seem offensive. Believe me, it is not in my heart."

"I believe you," Lautner said, confused. He had heard gossip about Ignaz Philipp's manner.

Ignaz Philipp smiled.

"Well, let's see what we'll see," he said happily.

"Shall we use rabbits?"

"By all means rabbits. The noblest birth experiment in Nature. Let us go and buy some multiplying rabbits. And tonight, if you please, we shall dine together. And tomorrow—if it suits you—we shall begin."

The experiments began. Lautner watched politely, holding a rabbit which had delivered young fifteen minutes before. Ignaz Philipp dipped a brush moistened with exudate from inflammation of the lining of a human uterus into the rabbit's vagina and uterine cavity.

"If the theory is correct," said Ignaz Philipp gravely, "this exudate should produce in the rabbit the same inflammation as it produced in the human it killed."

Lautner nodded. He was interested. But he expected nothing. They waited. Days passed. Suddenly the rabbit died. Together they opened it. The rabbit's uterus was inflamed, coated with the same sort of exudate which they had introduced into it. Throughout the body there were other zones of inflammation. More exudate. Lautner considered this soberly. Ignaz Philipp wrote down the experiment.

"Rabbits have greater resistance," Lautner said suddenly. "On the next one let us make repeated infections."

"You're sure, Doctor, you don't feel a miasma hovering over us?" Ignaz Philipp was smiling broadly.

Lautner flushed.

"It's been taught, Dr. Semmelweis, for many hundreds of years, now . . ."

"I know . . . I know . . . Well, we shall see . . ."

"And this time let us not infect so soon after delivery."

"Agreed."

The second rabbit was infected twelve hours after delivery. This time the brush was introduced several days in succession. Two days later the animal manifested pain when the brush was introduced. Its uterus contracted and expressed a yellowish exudate. Lautner looked up, startled. Ignaz Philipp smiled at him grimly. I am going to make a convert here, he vowed. I am going to make another convert. The animal died eleven days later. In the uterus there was the same inflammation, the same exudate. And in the lungs. And elsewhere in the body.

Lautner worked now with great gravity.

"Do you begin to see, Doctor?" Asked Ignaz Philipp gently.

"Certainly on the basis of these two rabbits—one might say——"

"Two rabbits, Doctor. And nearly six thousand human beings. These are my proofs. But come. Let us start another . . ."

The third rabbit died in six days. The uterus was inflamed and coated with exudate. This time, instead of the lungs, the infection had attacked the liver and the large intestine, and the exudate was in these places also.

The month had nearly ended. He worked a little nervously now. He slept badly. Lautner watched him sympathetically.

"I'll tell you what it is," he said abruptly one day. "I am waiting for an appointment. An appointment to Privat-Dozent."

"Oh, I'm sure you'll get it, sir."

"Yes, this time I really dare hope.'"

He laughed uncertainly.

"But it's making me nervous, you understand——"

"Of course I understand. But don't worry, Doctor . . . really . . ."

Four days before the list of appointments was posted Haller sent for him. He dressed with great care. His coat was threadbare, he noticed, startled. He wiped it with a wet cloth. He brushed it anxiously. He shined his shoes. Nothing must be left to chance. Nothing must happen now.

His heart beating, success animating only his eyes, he presented himself gravely to Haller, Primarius of the university. "I have sent for you," Haller began slowly, "to explain two things."

He is going to tell me about dignity and decorum. I must let him know with all the sincerity I possess that I am going to conduct my lectures with perfect professional——

"I feel strongly that it is my duty to give you this news since it involves both of us and in a great sense I am responsible."

Students, now . . . thousands of students . . . students like Wieger, students like Kussmaul, students like Routh . . . students from the entire world . . . disciples at long last, disciples for the doctrine . . .

"It is with the keenest regret I have to tell you again that your name will not be on the list of appointments to Privat-Dozent."

Ignaz Philipp's face continued to smile a little in anticipation. In his brain his thoughts toppled, his hopes crashed. His body became numb. His mouth opened. He could feel nothing.

"It is useless to tell you that your friends Dr. Skoda and Dr. Rokitansky and Dr. Hebra and others on the faculty are shocked and saddened by this news which they have already had from me. I rely upon your patience to persevere, to wait for next month's list."

He waited, his square, kindly face turned sorrowfully to Ignaz Philipp.

"Yes, sir," Ignaz Philipp said at last. His voice was a stranger's. It came from the depths of him, tortured, hoarse, a disembodied croak.

"It is no secret to you that the faculty is divided. There is great opposition to progress. Unhappily these opponents present a solid front. In the liberal group are men of many opinions. Unwittingly, with sad consequences for you, it was my unhappy fate to offend some of our own group. There are other dissensions in this liberal group. Professor Hyrtl, I tell you this in confidence, does not always see eye to eye with Professor Skoda. He is opposed to Dr. Skoda's theory of therapeutic nihilism. He feels also that Dr. Brucke is sometimes inclined to theorize too much . . ."

Ignaz Philipp listened dully. In his swirling cosmos he was grateful for the sound of Haller's voice. Another month . . . another month . . .

"Professor Dlauhy and Professor Heller, liberals both, have always been a little at odds over questions of method . . . it was I who precipitated these differences into the unhappy division which produced this unhappy result . . . I delivered my yearly report . . . you will remember I praised the results of your experiments . . . Surgeons Schuh and Dumreicher listened as I cited uses of prophylaxis in surgical cases . . . you know the rivalry between medicine and surgery . . . I am a

281

physician. They are surgeons . . . I learned too late that they resented my advice."

He fell silent. Ignaz Philipp waited miserably. There was no one to blame, of course. These men were all on the Liberal side.

"I understand, Dr. Haller," he said huskily.

Haller nodded slowly.

"Yes . . . you are suffering . . . believe me, I am suffering too . . ."

"And the women are suffering . . ."

"And the women are suffering . . . I can only assure you, Dr. Semmelweis . . . I can only give you my personal assurance . . . that next month . . . next month . . ."

In his room that night Ignaz Philipp tossed his brushed coat on his bed. He sat down and examined the book of his personal records. His money was dribbling slowly away. Now from his patrimony there remained not enough to buy instruments to begin private practice. With care, with profound care, the sum that remained might be made to last a little longer. He rose. He went to the bed. He picked up his coat. He brushed it. He hung it carefully in the closet. He examined his shoes. The soles appeared still stout. He undressed. He washed his socks and his underclothing. His shirts must be pressed and laundered. The ruffles were fraying. He took needle and thread. He was also a surgeon and a surgeon at least could sew. He finished. He set the shirt aside. In the bureau were two more suits of underwear. He took one out. He looked at the bureau somberly. There was no need for a bureau. He resolved to sell it. Every penny was important now. He had three suits of underwear, five pairs of socks, a dozen handkerchiefs, three shirts. They would fit easily in his carpetbags. He was too numbed to consider it longer. He turned out the light. He got quietly into bed. He lay there, thinking.

Early in the morning, just after dawn, he rose and reread the fine letter from Routh. He pored again over the article that accompanied it. He refolded the letter and the cut pages reverently. He put them back in their envelope. He sat awhile, trying to remember Routh as a student. He recalled Wieger. He shook his head sickly, remembering the heading: "Doubtful Anecdotes." Poor Wieger, he thought, alone in Strasbourg, trying to spread the doctrine alone. Standing up manfully, ignoring the laughter, a young man facing his elders with courage. It was his student. It was his disciple. Wieger must not, he would not fight alone.

Painfully he set about writing a letter of hope and praise to Routh. An hour later he had covered only two sheets. He finished the letter, sealed it, set about writing a letter of hope and praise and confidence to young Wieger.

Later he went to the dissecting room. Rokitansky looked at him sorrowfully, then hung his head.

"I saw Dr. Haller," said Ignaz Philipp. His heart filled with pity suddenly for these fine men, these great men of the university, who had failed like probationers.

"Sir Professor," he said gently, and managed a smile, "I want you to know—it's all right—I understand—these things happen—I'm grateful—believe me . . ."

Rokitansky looked at him tiredly.

"I'm best at the dissecting table," he said wryly. "It seems I don't know much about anything else."

"You shall tell me that next month, sir. Next month when I am Privat-Dozent and we look back at all this and wonder. And laugh."

He nodded his head knowingly. He smiled again. He left the dissecting room to find Skoda and later Hebra.

"Do you think I have lost confidence? Believe me, I am full of confidence. These things are nothing. What you do for me is everything. Beside the discovery even I am nothing. Wait until next month, my friends. Then we shall begin. Then we shall see."

And in the afternoon he resumed his experiments with Lautner. His face was beginning to ache now from constant smiling.

"I am so sorry, Doctor. So very sorry."

"It seems we go up today—we go down tomorrow—the day after, who knows?" He smiled ruefully. But his spirit was sick.

"Ah, well, today we begin again. Let us see now. How do you feel about the discovery? How do you begin to feel? Tell me frankly."

"I am beginning to think—I am wondering if I am not helping on the threshold of something—something very significant."

"But you are still thinking about the theory of miasma a little?"

"To tell you the truth I am not entirely convinced that miasma cannot be one of the causes."

"Well, we will try to rule out miasma. No one knows what miasma is. No one knows what puerperal fever is. To explain the inexplicable in terms of the unknowable is not exactly good science, eh? Today we will show you that miasma is not hovering over these rabbits. It is so easy to make up names like miasma and cosmic-telluric influences to explain something we know nothing about. To me they are just rubbish."

"Frankly, I'm beginning to wonder."

"That's good enough. A wonder is healthy. But there are other trashy theories. There's also wounded modesty, and fear, and ventilation, and being located on the banks of a river—oh, there's dozens of them. I'm not even going to attack these

283

idiocies. But I had a letter from a Dr. Routh, a former student, who read a paper on the discovery in England. And unfortunately he stressed one point only. He stressed the very thing you and I have been working on. Cadaveric poisoning. Today we're going to do two things—we're going to destroy the theory of miasma for you—and also the chance that you might feel that only cadaveric poison can produce these findings."

He looked at Lautner fondly.

"This time we will use the blood of a man who died of marasmus, of tissue starvation. There is no pus here. This is a clean death. We will begin an hour after birth."

The brush containing the blood mixed with a little water was introduced repeatedly. The rabbit was placed in a cage with a rabbit whose vagina had been painted with pus. The first rabbit remained completely healthy. The second rabbit died. Now Lautner became excited.

"They were both in the same cage——" Ignaz Philipp emphasized.

"And if the theory of miasma is correct, the miasma that killed one should have killed the other!" Lautner said excitedly.

"Unless this was a particularly nimble miasma that for reasons of its own kept hopping about, eluding one rabbit and hovering determinedly over the other."

Lautner looked at him a moment. There was nothing he could say. After a moment he simply smiled.

"Now as to cadaveric poison——" said Ignaz Philipp beaming.

They infected rabbits with the exudates from a man dead of typhus. But the rabbits died with the symptoms of puerperal fever. Always the same symptoms. Inflammation and pus in the infected uterus, inflammation and pus elsewhere throughout the body. They tried again, this time with the exudate of a man dead of cholera. The rabbit died of the symptoms of puerperal fever.

"Lest it be the brush which causes injury we will use a small syringe——"

But there was never any change.

"The introduction of any infected material into an injured surface which has access to the blood stream causes puerperal fever."

Lautner shook his head in a jerk of assent.

"Do you believe this?"

"I do, sir."

"It is all clear?"

"Yes, sir."

"Will you help me? Do you see now that when we wash the infected brush with soap and water, wash it well, and then follow this by rinsing it thoroughly in chlorine solution, we will remove the infection and may touch the rabbit with the brush safely?"

"I will help you with all my heart." Lautner spoke thickly. Sincerity choked him.

"Tomorrow we will take another rabbit. We will wash the brush as I have said."

News of the experiments spread through the university. Lautner begged permission to tell his friends what was happening.

"That is what I want," Ignaz Philipp said exultantly. "Tell the whole world. Nothing could please me so much." He sobered. "But remember this. Let it sink in. Here we watch dying rabbits. In the wards human beings are dying. Think of that, Lautner. Think of the living women you know."

From the university reverberations of the experiments reached the Vienna Hospital, reached the First Clinic.

In the laboratory Ignaz Philipp read a note from Chiari. "I shall wait no longer. I want to congratulate you now. We shall be Privat-Dozents together. Your reputation—your good name is made."

"He is right, you know," said Lautner.

"Perhaps he is. Perhaps he is," said Ignaz Philipp cheerfully. "It does seem—well, it's good to hear from him." He laughed aloud. "We're going fine, eh, Lautner? Just the same, for his sake, I think I'll burn this note. He's Klein's son-in-law, you know."

"I don't think there's anything Klein can do to discredit you this time. I don't see why he'd want to."

"Chiari—we used to room together. It seems so long, so long a time ago. Chiari and Markussovsky—you wouldn't know him—and myself. He's a good man, Johann Chiari. He's got his own problems . . . Klein? Well, I'll tell you, Lautner. There will always be doctors like Klein. I don't think the Kleins of this world are in the majority. But while other doctors are healing people, the Kleins are making a secure position for themselves. They don't use medicine to do this. They use the protection of medicine and the politics of medicine. And because of the way medical liberals split up among themselves it's the Kleins who really run the universities and the hospitals."

"I wonder if it wouldn't be better if the state were to run the hospitals, the Crown, the government?"

"Isn't that what's happening? Klein owes his power to politics, not medicine. He is a courtier. And that power comes from the court. The final decisions come from the court. The government therefore runs the university and the hospital."

"Do you think there can ever be anything else?"

"As long as politics and not the wisdom of medicine governs us, I don't think so. I used to think that if the revolution was

285

successful—if we became a republic—everything would be solved. But there would surely be men devoted to governing and not to healing. Wieger, a French student of mine, once told me a curious thing. There was a rich man in his country almost a hundred years ago who had an idea—'A plan of a hospital association in which by means of a very modest sum each member will be assured in case of sickness of any kind of assistance which he may desire.' He died poor in 1773, still trying to persuade the government to sponsor it, or people to subscribe to it. I can't help but feel that a man's poverty is the responsibility of the state. And his body is medicine's responsibility to God."

He laughed a little.

"I haven't gone on like this since I was a student. Back in the days with Chiari and Markussovsky. That's the way we used to talk all night sometimes."

"I wish I'd been with you."

"You'd have heard quite a lot of nonsense, I promise you. But it makes you feel good all the same"—he stretched his arms—"to talk a little now and then."

"You talk very well. You'll make a fine lecturer."

The month was almost up.

Ignaz Philipp grinned happily.

"You've brought me luck. Yes, you've brought me real luck. I'll tell you ... . Tomorrow we'll start some surgical experiments. We'll try the prophylaxis in surgery."

"Let's begin tonight," said Lautner. "Let's go have supper, sir, and come back."

"Ha! We're beginning to make a good team."

Lautner's face shone.

They left the laboratory. The door shut behind them. They walked down the steps. They stood on the sidewalk a moment. Two policemen stepped out of the shadows.

"Dr. Lautner?"

"I am Dr. Lautner."

"You are under arrest."

They took his arms. He drew back.

"Is this a joke? Who are you looking for?"

Ignaz Philipp recovered. He pushed a policeman aside.

"Let go his arms. What do you think you're doing? Do you realize what kind of a mistake you're making?" He glared at them indignantly.

"You're Dr. Semmelweis, aren't you? Stand back, Doctor. Here is the one who's made the mistake. Come along, Dr. Lautner . . . the charge is sedition and inciting to rebellion."

Lautner marched off between them, silent, stunned. Once he looked back over his shoulder at Ignaz Philipp, his mouth open, pale, bewildered.

Ignaz Philipp stood irresolute.

"Don't worry, Lautner," he shouted suddenly. "It's a mistake—I'll clear this up in a moment——"

He rushed off to find Rokitansky. With Rokitansky he rushed to Haller. It was incredible. But it was not possible to get Lautner out of jail. The warrant had been countersigned by the Minister of Education. In the dignified university the news exploded with horrified speed. It was recalled that Lautner had been a member of the Academic Legion.

"I was a member too," said Hebra. "And so was Dr. Semmelweis. And so was half the university and the hospital."

The Minister of Education said nothing. On the second day Lautner was released. He emerged from the jail in company with a group of thieves who had served their time, a handful of prostitutes, and a score of vagrants. It was announced officially that the charges had been withdrawn for lack of evidence.

Ignaz Philipp and Rokitansky were waiting for him. They said nothing. There was nothing to say. They walked with him toward his lodgings.

"The whole university is outraged," Rokitansky said finally.

"They wouldn't even let me in to see you," grated Ignaz Philipp.

"It doesn't matter. I promise you. It doesn't matter. It's all done."

"The charges were completely false," Rokitansky pleaded anxiously. "Think of that, Lautner—everyone knows that——"

"It's my fault." Ignaz Philipp nodded dully. "You were working with me. Things were going too well. If you hadn't been working with me . . ."

Lautner stopped. His face was very pale.

"It's not your fault, Doctor. We all know where this attack came from. It's easily seen that this was aimed at discrediting you. But it happened. That's the horror of it. It really happened. I must go. I must go at once. When an outrage like this can be created by men of medicine you are none of you safe. I cannot leave quickly enough."

"You have such a promising career," Rokitansky said in a low, shamed voice. "Your career is just beginning—I have great things planned for you . . ."

"Do you think I could ever walk about the university without shame? It is true I am disgraced. But I know also it is a disgrace even to be here."

They could not dissuade him. They went with him to his rooms. They sat miserably while he packed.

He was gone next day. He went to Egypt. In a little while they heard he had been made court physician there. In a little while he sickened there and died of a fever of the country.

"There is still hope," said Skoda. "He was vindicated, after all. And you have still the proof of the experiments to show."

287

Ignaz Philipp nodded sadly. But in his heart he could not doubt that this time at last his application would be granted. He prepared his opening lecture.

He waited. The month ended. This time no list whatever was posted.

The days passed. Spring was warm that year in Vienna. Calm returned to him. In the spring, in the park, seeing the green births, watching the Danube, listening to children, it was impossible to continue to despair. He began to hope again. He dined with Hebra. He romped with the children. He smiled fondly at the golden sash. The world was new. Again Vienna had just been minted.

He went with Skoda and Rokitansky one night to the brick courtyard of a tree-shaded inn on the banks of the Danube. They listened quietly to Beethoven. They waved their steins to Offenbach. They heard the Danube splashing beneath the violins dreaming Liszt. They stamped their feet with the whirl of dancers bobbing to Straus.

"Suppose one day a crazy man approached you and said to you," said Skoda, "suppose he said to you: 'Ignaz Philipp Semmelweis, you good-for-nothing dismissed assistant, you are going to be elected a member of the Royal Academy of Physicians!' "

He thrust his leonine face closer to Ignaz Philipp's face. He stared at Ignaz Philipp fiercely.

"I'd find out what kind of beer he was drinking and buy a barrelful," said Ignaz Philipp, the corners of his mouth twitching.

"You know the new list of appointments will be out soon?"

"I know I'd better be getting a job soon or find a wealthy widow who likes Hungarians."

He sobered suddenly. He peered closer at Skoda. There was no smile on Skoda's face.

"I haven't been altogether idle, boy. Tell me—do you think being a member of the Royal Society will help you get the Privat-Dozent?"

Ignaz Philipp's pulse began to jump.

"Look at him," cried Skoda. "Rokitansky! Look at that vein in his temple!"

"You're joking, sir. You're surely joking——"

"I never joke, my boy. What do you say to that vein, Karl?"

"If I were a doctor I'd send him to a good doctor."

"Please! You can't mean it, sir——"

The orchestra had swept into Meyerbeer. His mind whirled with it. To be elected to membership in the Royal Society! He thought of Thérèse, he thought of his father Joseph—even if it was a joke—if they could hear—and then suddenly his excitement gave way to panic. He was a simple young Hungarian again, come to the great city of Vienna . . .

288

"I've got a better treatment," Skoda was saying. "Are you listening to me, boy? You will take the prescription on the night of June sixth."

"In our company——"

"In the Hall of the Royal Society!"

"I beg of you——"

"In the Hall of the Royal Society!"

Ignaz Philipp bit his lip. Tears filled his eyes. It was true then.

"It's true?" he faltered.

"What do you think we're celebrating about!" Skoda exploded.

The remainder of the evening leaped and capered groggily in his memory. The headache he bore next day was a sweet and happy proof that the evening had not been a dream. He had no ambition for place. It had never occurred to him that such an immense honor could be conferred on him. Sometimes he hoped briefly and vaguely that one day he might become a Professor of Midwifery. He dreamed no higher. He would have been content to remain an assistant, even an assistant under Klein. He cared nothing for dress, nothing for money. Since his discovery he had forgotten even to speculate on a professorship for his old age. He did not think of himself as a man of destiny. He did not think of himself at all. He had become a directed call, his motivation, his life, his personality, fused by pity followed the grail of his mind and his courage.

Now, his eyes downcast, his hopes surging, he walked with Rokitansky and Skoda on the night of June sixth to the Hall of the Royal Society. He heard his name called. He heard a confusion of voices. The votes were counted. His eyes still resolutely down, he walked with Skoda and Rokitansky out of the hall again. He had been elected a member of the Royal Society of Physicians.

"Doctor of Medicine," cried Hebra jubilantly. "Master of Midwifery. Master Surgeon. Member of the Royal Society!"

"I think it will be a little difficult now to ignore any application you may make for Privat-Dozent."

"Yes, my friend," Skoda nodded contentedly, "this honor is going to be just a little hard to ignore."

He was still far in the clouds of enchantment a week later. The list of appointments was to be posted in another fortnight. Hebra found him in a chemistry laboratory. He was making solutions of chlorine.

"What do you think?" he cried joyously. "I believe I've found a new solution strength! What do you know about stink chemistry, Hebra? Come help me."

"You're getting ready, eh?"

"I'm going to make up enough to give every student a small bottle. What do you think of that?"

Hebra looked down.

"What's the matter? What's happened?"

"What are you doing these days, friend?" Hebra asked diffidently.

Ignaz Philipp thought a moment. He waved quickly to the laboratory.

"Today, I've been here," he cried. "Why, Hebra? Yesterday, yesterday I dissected a little, the day before—— What's happened? What's the matter?"

"And your practice—are you practicing?"

"Hebra! What practice?"

"I thought perhaps you had picked up a patient or so, just to amuse yourself, just to——"

"Man, where would I practice!"

"That's right. No calls, of course, to—a patient's home . . ."

Ignaz Philipp began to laugh.

"Hebra, you look like an owl! What's the matter with you? Are you trying to tell me that Frau Hebra is again making a baby?"

"No," said Hebra.

"What then?" Ignaz Philipp smiled appreciatively.

"There's a rumor suddenly going around that you're supporting yourself performing abortions."

They stared at each other.

"A rumor that . . ." said Ignaz Philipp slowly. The vein in his temple began to beat thickly.

"I never doubted you," said Hebra.

"A rumor . . ." Ignaz Philipp repeated hoarsely.

Hebra's lips drew to a thin line.

"Is there a better way to offset the effect of election to the Royal Society?" he asked harshly.

Ignaz Philipp gazed at him, stupefied.

Next day he learned from Arneth that there were stories that his operating technique was responsible for the First Clinic's death rate. The rumors spread, grew monstrous, leaped misshapen over the walls of the university into the town.

He heard each new tale with horror. Skoda laughed at him.

"They're desperate now. They did this to me also. Remember? I'm still here, you see."

"Something should be done, all the same," said Rokitansky.

"I've already done it," said Skoda. "Come on, boy! Smile!"

And reluctantly, and later relaxed and reassured, Ignaz Philipp smiled and hoped again.

The night before the appointment list was to be posted Haller gave a dinner at his home. The faculty attended. At Haller's right side sat Ignaz Philipp. From down the table Skoda winked.

"Has anyone here heard any rumors lately?" he called out

in a loud voice. There was a moment of confusion. Heads turned to look at Ignaz Philipp. Then Haller clapped Ignaz Philipp's shoulder and began to laugh. In another moment the laughter was general. The rumors died there.

But the harm had been done. The list was posted next day. Ignaz Philipp's name was not on it.

They held another council that evening.

"I'm beginning to think you're some bird of ill omen," Hebra said vexedly.

"I'm sure of that," said Ignaz Philipp. "Or a criminal. I feel quite a lot like a criminal. It's what I'm trying to do, undoubtedly." He did not smile. He looked about him coldly.

"I'm joking, friend."

"Yes. Of course you're joking. Forgive me for not laughing." Hebra reddened.

"No need to be angry," Skoda said softly. "We're all in this. It hurts us all. It appears as if it's just going to take time, that's all. It won't be done in a day. We must now relax. We must move slowly, without emotion, planning each step, waiting, watching. That's how this is turning out."

"I know. We sit here and manipulate and contrive and spin webs, a dainty word here, a thrust there—and what are we doing it for? Is this a dream? Am I imagining all this? Why are we abashed? This thing is true, isn't it? It's no disgrace, it's no shame, it's something to shout, something to pound on a table, something to push in their faces! Why do we sit here? What good does it do? What are we waiting for?"

"You can't go rushing in like a mad bull, you know. That's what you'd like to do, one can see that. You'll never get anywhere that way. You can't force people to swallow something you've made them too resentful to swallow. I don't care how good it is. And I don't care how true. You're going to have to learn patience, my boy."

"I've been patient——"

"So far."

"I've buttered my tongue and greased my knees and smiled and made pious noises."

"So have we all."

"But if I shouted so the mountains fell I couldn't make the noise of one woman screaming. That's a noise you don't seem to hear. I don't know why."

"We hear it all right," said Hebra.

"We hear it, my boy. I told you long ago pity was an emotion. And if you let emotions drive you then you can't plan, you can't think, you can only tear your hair and shout. There'll be plenty of time to shout when you get on the lecture platform. Right now we have to think, all of us. We have to think how to get you there."

291

"All right. I'm sorry. Hebra—forgive me. Skoda—I ask your pardon. Isn't there something else I can do?"

They sat silent, considering.

"The plain fact is"—Hebra shook his head—"you're trapped."

"Suppose I went to England for a while. I was thinking of that before."

"As an assistant?" asked Skoda.

"Yes, as an assistant. Until the appointment comes."

"First of all, you'd find no change. Even the pay is the same. You'd get a hundred pounds a year, just as you got here."

"I don't mean the pay!"

"Man, the English appoint Englishmen. Just as we appoint our own. In every hospital and every university in the world the rivalry is intense for position. The jobs go to the natives. There's no chance for an outsider."

"Will you loan me a little of your patience?"

"I'll tell you something. You think as a citizen but you're a doctor. And that's something else. You're part of an old, old organization. You're going to have to start thinking as a member of that organization. You're going to have to accept it as it is."

"You can't face life with both attitudes," said Hebra. "You've always been a rebel, friend."

"You've both been rebels. You—Hebra—I've fought beside you on the barricades. And you, Skoda, you were such a rebel that Klein exiled you to St. Ulrich's asylum. You saw a truth, both of you, and you couldn't stand it. You exploded. What are you trying to tell me? I'm no different from either of you."

"We've rebelled, yes," said Skoda. "But within limits. There's much I could still rebel about. But it wouldn't be logical for me. Or for Hebra. Or for you. Not the kind of rebellion you mean. Not a continual war. I'm a doctor. Take it all in all, I've done well under the medical system. I've accepted it. I've learned to take the unbearable along with the triumphs. I like the system. I enjoy its benefits. And I must accept its penalties."

"And this is one of them," said Hebra quietly.

"Yes," said Skoda, "you know well what I think of this situation. I agree that it's intolerable. But let's look at it calmly. Let's face it. Let's take time. Let's work it out. In this medical cosmos it takes twenty years to get a new idea into a textbook and twenty years to get it out after it's outmoded. That's the system we're living under. Let's plan accordingly. Nothing else will do."

"I agree with you. My intellect agrees with you. But my whole being shouts to me that women are dying."

"And you want to save them tomorrow morning—or, better —yesterday morning."

292

"Yes, that's what I want to do."

"All right. I understand you perfectly. Now understand me. Stay away from the clinic. Don't listen to them. Don't think about them. They're going to go right on dying. There isn't a thing you can do about it until you're in a position to stop it. Now will you face it? Will you face that fact?"

Unaccountably, as Skoda said this, Ignaz Philipp thought of Beatrice Czorny, of the girl whose husband called her Boom-Boom, of the baby she had named Thérèse, of Thérèse herself, and of love and of home. But in that same instant he knew it was useless to protest further. He forced himself to subside, to wear the appearance of acceptance, to listen calmly, as if Skoda had finally conquered. He knew he was an alien, in that moment, unassimilable, an alien in his own society.

"Yes," he said dully. "Well, we must do what we must do . . ."

"Of course," said Skoda. "And we will win too. These things are not defeats. They are merely checks. You must see the whole pattern. Now we will bring up reinforcements. Now we attack again."

"Is there something else to do?" Ignaz Philipp looked up, incredulous.

"Something else? Why, of course there's something else. Get me the records of the First Clinic."

"From Klein?" Hebra asked dubiously.

"Certainly from Klein. Don't shout at him and don't be ugly. Simply go and ask him quietly for access to the records."

Ignaz Philipp compressed his lips. He sighed wearily.

"I'll need all the records you can get. I need them for a speech. I'm going to address the Imperial Academy of Sciences."

"On puerperal fever?"

"On the cause and the cure of puerperal fever. As discovered by Ignaz Philipp Semmelweis."

"Oh, friend . . . !"

"Don't 'Oh, friend' me. And stop looking like a woman in labor. Get me those records."

Ignaz Philipp sighed luxuriously and happily. He rose.

"Are you satisfied?"

"Completely."

"Do you see hope again?"

"You should have been on the barricades, sir. You would have maneuvered Metternich into joining the revolution."

"Go on, go on. Get me the records . . ."

Ignaz Philipp rehearsed his approach and his speech all the way to the First Clinic. At the door of the clinic he paused. He remembered Klein's pattern of hours. Scrupulously, anxious not to irritate him, he withdrew to wait until one o'clock. He walked in the park. He rehearsed himself again. He weighed each sentence. He tested it for Klein's reaction. He tried to make each word harmless.

He walked back to the clinic. He began to tremble a little with anxiety and apprehension. He scolded himself angrily. His mind kept veering to the importance of the official records. He wanted to think only of approaching Klein. But Skoda must have the records if he was to speak. And upon his speech depended the Privat-Dozent. Skoda was going to champion him openly. He began to breathe rapidly.

"Stop it!" he cried to himself. "Stop it, you fool!"

He drew a deep breath. "Good afternoon, sir director," he said to himself silently, "you are in good health, I see. I am very glad . . ." He walked up the clinic steps. He opened the door and walked into the clinic.

The smell of death rushed to him. He looked up once. Braun was not in the wards. Gratefully, he looked down, he looked neither to right nor left, he walked rapidly through the wards to Klein's office.

Klein looked up. He sat back in his chair.

"And to what do I owe this signal honor, Doctor?"

"Good afternoon, sir director. You are looking well, I see. I am glad."

"I am glad to hear it, Doctor."

"I did not want to trouble you. I know how busy you are. Operating a lying-in hospital can leave you little time for visitors. You see how it is, though. How well I have learned what you taught me. Here I am—at the hour you liked."

He paused. He smiled ingratiatingly. Klein said nothing. He gazed at Ignaz Philipp calmly.

"The fact is, sir director, I've come to you for help."

"I'm always glad to help my old students where I can."

"I knew you would say that, sir. I remembered your many kindnesses . . ."

"Well, perhaps so . . . perhaps so . . . I'm glad you feel that way . . . You're leaving Vienna, perhaps? You'd like a letter?"

"No, not exactly leaving Vienna. It's something else. I'm collecting a little material . . . a paper, perhaps . . ."

"I see. That's very intelligent."

"Yes, sir. I'd like access to the First Clinic records."

Klein's expression did not change. He smiled pleasantly. He nodded his head a little.

"You'd like to see our records . . ."

"I'll come at night, of course, I won't be in anybody's way. The sir director is extremely kind."

"That's quite all right."

"I beg humbly to thank you. With all my heart."

"There's no need of that, Doctor. You can't see the records."

Ignaz Philipp gaped. He swallowed. He reddened.

"I—I—mean the official records——"

"Of course."

"And you won't let me see them?"

"Not under any circumstances whatsoever."

"But the records, sir director—hospital records——!"

"Was that all, Doctor?" He continued to smile gently.

"Listen, sir director. I ask you in the name of science——"

"I am a very busy man, as you have observed. We are all busy here. Very, very busy. Perhaps someday, when we are not busy . . . but then we are always so busy . . . so very busy . . ."

"I see." Ignaz Philipp smiled mechanically, choking down his rage, fighting the blinding tempest of anger that flashed and rocketed in him. He kept rigidly still for a moment. He knew that if he moved or spoke he would have to leap across the desk and pound at Klein until the brains oozed from his cracked skull. The moment passed. He breathed deeply. He shuddered.

"Good day, Doctor," said Klein, and turned back to the papers on his desk.

Ignaz Philipp walked quickly from the clinic. In the street Chiari stopped him.

"Where are you rushing to, Naci? Are you trying to snub me?" He looked closer at Ignaz Philipp's face and stopped smiling. He looked quickly at the clinic. He took Ignaz Philipp's arm and walked beside him down the street.

"It's no good, Johann," Ignaz Philipp said thickly. "I tell you it's no good."

Chiari said nothing. They walked in silence. After a time the rage burned out. Ashes remained. He turned to Chiari and managed a wry smile.

"What in the world happened, Naci?"

Ignaz Philipp shook his head.

"I wanted to consult the records. I went in humbly. I virtually licked his hands." He spat. "All I wanted was access to the official records of the First Clinic." He shrugged helplessly. "Another hope gone."

"Let's go up to your place. Why do you go near him, Naci?"

"Skoda is going to address the Imperial Academy on my discovery. He wanted the records. You're going the wrong way, Johann. It's down this way. I've moved."

They walked a little in silence.

"I wish I could tell you what to do, Naci. I put up with it as long as I could to keep peace in the family. A month ago we had it out. I haven't seen him since. That's where we stand. So Skoda's going to speak on puerperal fever. You're getting plenty of attention, Naci."

"I don't want attention. All I want is to be Privat-Dozent. Like yourself."

They had reached Ignaz Philipp's rooms. Chiari looked about him.

"Need the money, eh?"

"I need it, yes. But it isn't the money," he said, as they climbed the stairs. He paused on the landing. "It's a funny thing, Johann. This discovery is an obstetrical matter. And the only people who help me are a skin specialist, chest specialist, and a pathologist."

There was a letter under the door.

"It's from Hungary," cried Ignaz Philipp. "Come in, Johann. Sit anywhere——"

Chiari looked about the small room, at the bed, the table, the two chairs. He sat on the bed. Ignaz Philipp went quickly to the table and opened the letter.

"From Marko!"

Chiari jumped and came to him.

"What does he say?"

Ignaz Philipp read swiftly. He passed the letter to Chiari.

*My dear Naci,*

We parted queerly but I have never felt the fact of parting or the reason for our parting was any fray upon the bonds that keep us friends. In this world men follow many beliefs but beliefs change; and friendship is not a belief. Beliefs change, friend. I believed that Hungary would someday be free. When her hour came I went happily to help deliver her. Tonight I am sick at heart for what has been born here. Our freedom has meant only the freedom to enslave others. Our first national act was to march on Italy, at Austria's request, to put down the Italians' revolt for freedom. Since then we have attempted to make Hungarian the language of the Slovaks, Ruthenians, and Croats within our borders. We have denied them representation and imprisoned them when they protested. We have denied national rights to our Serbs and Dalmatians. We are a divided country. As if this were not enough, our generals desire a constitutional monarchy; Kossuth and the others want a republic. They are preparing to fight to the death over it. And while they fight the Serbs, the Slovaks, the Ruthenians, the Rumanians, the Croats, the Dalmatians, the men of North Hungary also gird to fight for their right to freedom. Perhaps we have not learned yet that you do not rule with freedom but share it and are ruled by it. I think our days are numbered. Great bloodshed is inevitable. And when we are prostrate, waiting, Austria will march on us again. And then—farewell to free Hungary. Only our dreams are free, friend. Only the Hungary we hold in our hearts. Perhaps that will be enough. Is it well with you, Naci? I have heard no more of your discovery. Did you find a flaw in it? I miss you sorely. Give my regards to Chiari and our friends. Even a brief note will be welcome.

Your friend, *Marko*

"I think he is tired," Ignaz Philipp said uneasily. "The situation he speaks of can only be temporary. A sort of adjustment in a newly free country—things settle down—justice rises——"

Chiari shook his head.

"I don't know, Naci. You must have heard these things too——"

"It is so easy to hear rumors in Vienna. No, Johann. We are free now. It won't be easy to enslave us again. We have waited centuries for this. Setbacks are inevitable. But to be Austrian again—no, no, Johann. That, at least, can never happen."

"Well, we must write Marko. It is good to hear from him. Tell me, Naci—I am your friend—do you need money?"

"No, no. I need help. Not money. I need to get that appointment."

He looked at Chiari reflectively. There was no need asking him if he had read Hebra's articles on the discovery, heard of Haller's praise for it. He must have done so. The evidence of the discovery was convincing. If Chiari had not lectured on it to his students, it must have been because Klein was his father-in-law. And if he had lectured on it, he would have mentioned it.

"Perhaps," he said tentatively, "now that you are free to think and speak as you please you will go to hear Skoda speak?"

"I will be there, Naci. But what will he do about records?"

Ignaz Philipp smiled. Suddenly he had remembered something.

"He will have records, Johann."

"Naci, I beg of you! Don't do anything rash!"

Ignaz Philipp went to his bags. He pulled forth a thick sheaf of papers.

"I'm not going to steal them. And we won't need Klein. I've got records of my own. Let Klein challenge them. They're duplicates of all he has."

Now the days passed swiftly. Ignaz Philipp worked long hours over his precious records. He put them in order. He indexed them. He assembled statistics to prove each existing theory of puerperal fever wrong. And when he had done, he went with them to Skoda. Together they reassembled them to implement Skoda's speech. He passed the birth clinic daily. He heard the cries. He smelled the dead. And each day he

297

looked at the windows and vowed grimly: Women, you shall have a voice.

He wrote to Markussovsky. He waited vainly for an answer. On the sixth of October that part of him which was patriot reeled and was shattered and fell dumb before grief. Dismembered by civil war, Hungary had fallen to an invasion from Russia. And Russia, championing monarchy, had promptly handed her back to the mercies of Austria. Freedom was over. Hungary was enslaved once more.

He could not weep. The disaster was too great. It ripped beyond his time, it scattered the dreams of his father and his father before him. For days he walked about Vienna numbly. His grief was a darkness that shrouded even his hopes for the discovery.

But the time for Skoda's speech before the Academy of Sciences was very near. And within him was that which was of an eternity beyond country. And from the fabric and the flame of this he fashioned new hope and he buried his dead yesterdays and hope drew him from his knees and he pressed on.

In the Imperial Academy of Sciences Skoda delivered a full testimony to the discovery of the cause of puerperal fever and the methods by which all mothers everywhere could be protected. In addition to the records Ignaz Philipp had supplied him he had also obtained records of the Lying-in Hospital at Prague and he cited these also, to show that conditions implored science for relief.

Ignaz Philipp tingled with victory. The future was a joyous sound of trumpets. There was no debate. The Academy promptly voted to include Skoda's address in its official transactions. A member rose and formally demanded that a special report be prepared.

"I wish to present to you the man who has made this discovery and whose records have made my talk possible, Dr. Semmelweis. Will you rise, please?"

In a nightmare of embarrassment Ignaz Philipp rose, bowed awkwardly to the applauding members, sat quickly down.

"I propose him now for membership in this Academy."

He was elected almost instantly.

"—A final motion. I propose that Dr. Semmelweis and Dr. Brucke, Professor of Physiology, be voted the sum of one hundred florins with which to carry on further experiments on puerperal fever in the interests of the Academy."

The transactions of the Academy echoed throughout Vienna, past Vienna into Germany and Prague. Reports were mailed to Paris and London and Milan and St. Petersburg.

"Now there is nothing that will ever hide the truth again," he said reverently and happily. "Now the way is finally clear. In a month the doctrine will be everywhere."

Skoda nodded.

"If you like you can go listen to your women again." He smiled. "I don't think you will hear them much longer."

"And what further do we do?"

"Isn't that enough? God save me from men with a discovery! We'll sit a little and wait for the reactions."

In Prague the Lying-in Hospital was in charge of Antonius Jungmann. He was an old man who had given full authority to his assistant, Wilhelm Scanzoni. And in Prague, when the explosion of Skoda's speech echoed, Scanzoni blazed with anger. In an official paper he had described in 1846 how he had discovered that puerperal fever was caused by blood changes brought about by cosmic-telluric influences.

Scanzoni's reply to Skoda and the simple truths of the Semmelweis discovery came swiftly.

"There is nothing new in this so-called discovery, for it has long been known, even in Vienna, that puerperal fever is more frequent in lying-in hospitals."

They read the reply with amazement.

"What does he mean by that?" Ignaz Philipp shook his head, dazed.

"I don't know." Skoda shrugged. He read on.

"Although no one ever requested us to do so, or even officially suggested that we do so, when rumors of the chlorine washing success reached us we gave the method a fair trial here in Prague. It was our unhappy experience that chlorine washing raises the mortality instead of lowering it."

"It's impossible!" cried Ignaz Philipp.

"You can imagine how he carried out the washing." Hebra laughed.

"And now," said Skoda, "we come to the rub."

"It is apparent that Dr. Skoda, by holding up the Lying-in Hospital at Prague to criticism and scorn in citing our records before the Imperial Academy of Sciences has placed upon us an obligation we dare not ignore. I herewith demand the appointment of a committee which will thoroughly investigate the conduct of the Lying-in Hospital and which will once and for all establish management or mismanagement."

"Now what do you think they will do?" Skoda challenged.

"I don't know," said Ignaz Philipp, bewildered. "Their mortality is even higher than Vienna's."

"My boy, they will use medicine's sovereign cure, a plaster of medical politics. Watch and see."

In Prague the requested commission was promptly appointed. Deftly Professor Jungmann prevented it from meeting on the grounds that the investigation must wait for an epidemic to make observations.

And in Vienna, a month later, Zipfel published a report

in which he fully supported Scanzoni's cosmic-telluric theories. In Prague, Scanzoni was appointed Privat-Dozent.

At the Lying-in Hospital Bernard Seyfert succeeded him. He published instantly a treatise on puerperal fever which echoed all Scanzoni had written, and added two points of his own. The first point was that puerperal fever began in the countryside and from the countryside spread to the lying-in hospital. The second point was a remedy he had discovered.

"It is my practice to keep all my puerperal-fever cases among my healthy cases. In this way my puerperal cases gain courage. If I moved them, as has been advocated, the stricken women would surely suffer injury to their morale."

"I don't believe this," said Ignaz Philipp flatly. "I read, but I cannot possibly believe my eyes. If this is an indication of how an easily proven means to end puerperal fever will be received throughout Europe——"

"It's only Prague." Hebra laughed. He turned to Skoda and Rokitansky. "What have you got to say of Bohemia, gentlemen?"

"We were only born there," said Rokitansky. "And if Scanzoni and Seyfert are a national disease I assure you it's not contagious."

"You can get your best appraisal by glancing over the statistics with which Seyfert proves his arguments," said Skoda. "I recommend those bookkeeping methods to all lying-in hospitals, everywhere."

Guilelessly, Seyfert had added his statistical proofs. In the month of January he showed that Prague's Lying-in Hospital had suffered a morbidity of 30 per cent. Of these eight recovered. And ten died. And twelve were transferred to the general wards. The mortality for the month, he concluded carefully, was therefore obviously only 10 per cent.

The replies checked Ignaz Philipp only so long as it took him to recover from bewilderment.

"The records are perfectly clear," he said confidently. "They have only to see how the deaths declined here in Vienna and try the same easy method themselves. Europe is not Prague."

Carefully, laboriously, editing endlessly, he composed a long and patient letter to Scanzoni, mailed a second to Seyfert.

And now, lest the world have any misapprehensions on how Vienna felt about the new doctrine, Carl Braun, Ignaz Philipp's successor at the First Clinic, published an official report.

"There are thirty causes for puerperal fever," he wrote, and listed the whole thirty.

"The first cause is pregnancy itself."

Among the remaining causes he included wounded modesty, cosmic-telluric influences, fear, bad ventilation, suppression of milk, suppression of the lochia, the change in seasons, the climate, cold weather, constipation, location on the banks of a river, and a feeling of guilt.

"In England," he concluded, "there is generally a low mortality rate. It is also a fact that in England only married women are admitted to lying-in hospitals. In Vienna, as is well known, the majority of patients are unfortunate women, unmarried. It is obvious that if one is to seek for a remedy, a most powerful remedy, indeed, is marriage.

"As to the so-called discovery of chlorine washing it has been tried here and proven a failure."

Undermined at home and mocked from nearby Prague, the discovery appeared doomed before it could honestly be tried. Ignaz Philipp bowed to depression too heavy to be moved. Weariness gnawed his resources. He viewed his hopes, lackluster, through gloom whose profundity darkened his days.

"You must write!" Skoda scolded. "This is no time to mope. Nothing has been defeated. Courage, man! Sit down and write the whole etiology and the prophylaxis."

"Hebra has written it. He had written it twice. Haller has spoken of it officially. You have lectured on it. The students have written on it. What more is there to explain? There is nothing I can add. It's this simple: If you want to stop women from dying of puerperal fever, wash your hands."

"You've stopped experimenting with Dr. Brucke, he tells me . . ."

"There is something unreal, sir, in performing all over again the identical experiments I did with Dr. Lautner. It is a waste of time and money. The experiments simply prove the same thing."

"I am trying to make you understand that experiments are impressive. That's the main thing."

"But it's solemn nonsense——"

"I'm going to warn you, then, and I want to warn you very seriously—Braun, Scanzoni, and Seyfert must be answered! If you believe in your own doctrine—if you want it to succeed—if you intend to relieve suffering mothers—you must answer them."

"How?"

"Your hope is the Vienna Medical Society. They invited you to address them. There is your answer."

It was true. Remembering, his hopes rose immediately. He wrote the Society, formally asking for an opportunity to speak. The Society promptly set a date. And now, again undaunted, he began feverishly to prepare material for an address.

He stood before the Society on the fifteenth of May. He spoke without notes.

Simply and briefly he explained the manner in which he had discovered the cause of childbed fever.

Patiently he explained the methods he had used to prevent it.

He related the records of his results, the spectacular drop in the death rate, the two golden months which were free of any puerperal fever whatsoever.

"Cadaveric poisoning is only one infection which can be conveyed to pregnant women. There was a month in which I believed it the sole factor. Then infectious material from a carious knee joint killed eleven women—shortly before we transmitted infection from a medullary cancer of the cervix and killed eleven more."

The members of the Society listened intently. In the rear of the gathering sat Klein, his arms folded, his face expressionless.

"The English lean heavily, and the Americans universally, on the theory of contagion. They believe it can even be carried in the clothing of a physician and that, standing by the bedside only, the contagion will escape into the air and become an atmosphere of contagion.

"But childbed fever is not a contagious disease, for a contagious disease is understood as one which produces the *contagium,* by which it is spread. And such a contagium produces in turn only the identical disease in another individual. Smallpox is a contagious disease, because smallpox produces the contagium by which smallpox is again engendered in another individual and no other disease. Scarlet fever cannot be produced from a case of smallpox; on the contrary, one can never produce another disease from smallpox. And the same is true of scarlet fever and of any other disease caused by contagion.

"But such is not the case with childbed fever. This disease can be produced in a perfectly healthy woman in labor or recently delivered by diseases which are not childbed fever. I have described to you how it can be caused by discharges from a cancer and by the exudates from a carious knee joint. It can be caused by the pus from typhus. It can be caused, in short, by any decomposed organic matter from any disease.

"Childbed fever is therefore as little a contagious disease as it is a specific disease in itself. It develops from an animal organic material which has become ·putrid. This material may come from a diseased living organism or a corpse. It is taken into the blood mass of a woman in labor or a woman recovering from labor. It will not pass through unbroken skin. It demands injury for access. And once in the body it produces a blood dissolution which promptly presents the well-known exudations and metastases."

He paused. He had been looking straight ahead, as he spoke, over the heads of the members. Now he looked at their faces. They were staring up at him, intent and absorbed. His spirits soared.

"Since childbed fever is caused by putrid particles it is necessary to observe rigid precautions so that they may not be introduced into women. These precautions comprise rigid cleanliness. The method is not complex. It is not expensive. It does not require profound alteration in routine. It cannot possibly affect the health of the patient adversely. The hands must be washed thoroughly with soap and water, and then washed with chlorine solution. And nothing must come in contact with the patient which is not rigidly clean."

He sat down. For a moment there was silence. He looked toward the rear of the hall. Klein still sat expressionless, his arms folded across his chest. But now a doctor rose.

"I make this motion, that Dr. Semmelweis be asked to elaborate on his theory at the next meeting."

More? he thought to himself. All right, I will tell them more. I will tell them the same thing all over again if necessary. Now at least I have gotten a hearing.

The motion was passed.

Hebra carried him off to dine at his house.

"Now," he said jubilantly, "you must work out an elaboration."

"You know, it troubles me, I don't see how to elaborate, really. What more is there to say?"

"Oh, there's always a lot of loose ends, little things. Bring up the matter of prophylaxis in surgery, for instance. You showed how surgical cases can transmit childbed fever, you've shown how rigid prophylaxis prevents surgical sepsis, elaborate on that. And next time hit back at Scanzoni, Seyfert, and Braun. You said nothing about why their attempts with chlorine washing didn't work."

"Answer Zipfel too?"

"Answer everybody. Every fool in Europe, if necessary."

"Stop talking so much and eat," said Frau Hebra.

They ate heartily. Now they laughed a little. Victory seemed very near.

Seyfert countered quickly with another article.

"The worse the weather, the more childbed fever. Epidemics come in winter and disappear in summer. And to say that putrid material can be washed from the hands by soap and water is an exaggeration, to say the least. For chlorine as a disinfectant simply does not exist."

Zipfel followed with a second article.

"Patients I examine before I go to the autopsy room are the first to die. But those I examine after I come from dissecting very seldom die. Therefore, washing the hands is valueless. It has also been my experience that just as many women who had their babies in the street die as those who come to the hospital to have them."

Zipfel was promptly promoted to Privat-Dozent.

Once again Ignaz Philipp sank into despair. Once again he rallied.

On the eighteenth of June he addressed the Medical Society for the second time.

"Dr. Zipfel was once kind enough to loan me his records. They indicate in his own writing that street births rarely are followed by childbirth fever. This fact is well known in every lying-in hospital in the world. His records, which are available to any member of the Society, show in his own handwriting that when he and the assistants dissected in the Second Clinic the mortality rose. When they stopped dissecting, the mortality dropped."

He looked directly at Zipfel.

"He has forgotten. Or he has grossly misrepresented the facts."

Zipfel looked quickly down. Klein sat in the rear, his arms folded, his face impassive.

"Now as to chloride of lime as a disinfectant—it is ludicrous to pit Seyfert as an authority against Gustav von Liebig on such a question. I quote Europe's, perhaps the world's greatest chemist, I quote Liebig who has written: 'That which has been discovered by Dr. Semmelweis cannot be doubted by any un-prejudiced man. The only cause of puerperal fever is decomposed material. Chloride of lime undoubtedly possesses disinfectant properties.' I repeat, gentlemen, despite Seyfert and on the authority of Liebig—chloride of lime undoubtedly possesses antiseptic properties.

"I did not discover the disinfectant properties of chloride of lime. I only brought them into use."

He waited. A doctor rose.

"How then, Doctor, do you explain that at Prague and at Vienna chlorine washing has not been successful?"

"If childbed fever is caused by the conveyance of decomposed material to a wounded surface, and I have proven this and will undertake at any time to prove it again and as often as is needed, then that which will remove decomposed material will prevent childbed fever. Soap and water will partly remove such material. Soap and water followed by chlorine washing removes it entirely.

"Unfortunately, there is no magic in this. It is not some witches' rite. It is not a mere motion. The washing cannot be perfunctory. It must be rigidly thorough. One cannot wash one's hands carefully and then pick up a contaminated instrument. One cannot bring contaminated material of any kind in contact with the genitals of a woman in labor or one who has not healed from the wounds of labor. And since it is decomposed material which causes childbed fever it is obvious that neither at Prague, nor at Vienna, since I was first assistant, has decontamination been complete."

Another doctor rose.

"It is a fact, Doctor, demonstrable from your own records,

304

that childbed fever appears more prevalent in the winter than in the summer months."

"If prophylaxis is not observed that is true. And it is also true, gentlemen, that the winter months are indeed the dangerous months. The records will show that during the winter months we have the most students and that therefore the most dissecting is done at the time. Here, then, is the only influence of the weather. In winter it is more pleasant indoors, even in an autopsy room. In summer there are better things on a student's horizon than staying indoors in an autopsy room when the park, the street, the Danube beckons."

He waited. There were no further questions. He bowed stiffly and sat down. Inwardly he grinned. His heart was triumphant. A small discussion began to murmur among the members of the Society. A doctor rose.

"I move," he said, "that Dr. Semmelweis be invited to address us again, to elaborate further."

He looked at Skoda vacantly when the meeting was over. "I don't know," he said tonelessly. "I don't really know—is this a joke?—is all this just a monstrous joke——?"

"This next time will turn the trick. You can't seem to see it, my boy. But you've won. You've really won."

Rokitansky encouraged him quietly. Arneth came to him with praise. Since Zipfel had been promoted out of the hospital washing had begun at the Second Clinic under Arneth and the mortality had dropped. His eyes lighted at that. Hebra prodded him with hope. Skoda dinned encouragement.

He flung himself into his notes again with new zeal. He read feverishly, he made notes, he collated all experiments.

On the fifteenth of June he addressed the Society for the third time.

He began this time at the very beginning. He related the discovery again. Step by step he proceeded through the application of the preventive. Fact by fact, he refuted all objections. He spoke patiently and simply. He left nothing unsaid.

And at the end his patience ebbed a little.

"I have now shown, on three occasions before this body, that puerperal fever is caused by decomposed material conveyed to a wound. I have shown that it is a pyemia, a pus in the blood. I have shown that a man can infect a woman with this pyemia and that a man can infect another man with it—for so Kolletschka died. I have shown that it can arise after surgery as well as after childbirth and in the nonpregnant as well as the pregnant. I have shown that it can be prevented. I have shown how it can be prevented. I have proven all that I have said with facts, with records, with laboratory experiments and with human beings. I have talked a great deal."

There was a small eddy of laughter at one side of the hall.

305

The blood rushed to his face. The vein in his temple began to pulse.

"But while we talk and talk, gentlemen, women are dying. And doctors are killing them. There is no lying-in hospital where women are not dying of childbed fever. And their children with them. And we talk, gentlemen. We talk and talk and talk. And it is not necessary to talk. I am not asking anything world-shaking. I am asking you only to wash. In the name of pity—stop the murder of mothers, gentlemen. Wash your hands. Wash everything that contacts a patient. Stop this murder. For God's sake—*wash your hands!*"

He stopped. He was trembling. He unclenched his cramped hands. He glared at the assembly. There was silence. He sat down.

Dr. Kilian arose. He was Professor of Obstetrics at Vienna University. He had just published a textbook on obstetrics. The chair respectfully recognized Dr. Kilian. There was an expectant silence.

"This is the first time I have heard about this doctrine," he said mildly. "I have never heard about it before—therefore I am unable to discuss it."

Ignaz Philipp blinked. Here and there in the assemblage rose a few gasps.

"But it has been my experience," Dr. Kilian continued gravely, "that if one puts plenty of lard on one's fingers as a lubricant, one will find that one has achieved complete protection for the examiner—as well as for the women." He paused a moment to think further. "I confess," he concluded, "I confess I do not see how, if one has lard on one's fingers, one can either transmit cadaveric poisoning—or incur it."

He sat down. Ignaz Philipp lowered his head. He stared at the floor between his feet. It was hopeless. There was a shuffling. Someone else had risen.

"I am happy to report that the heavy mortality which a few months ago raged through the Foundling Hospital has now abated——"

Ignaz Philipp looked up in astonishment. The speaker was Dr. Bednar, chief physician of the Foundling Hospital. Bednar caught Ignaz Philipp's eye. He smiled. He continued.

"Cases of sepsis of the blood of the newborn are now quite rare. For this we have to thank the discovery of Dr. Semmelweis, lately assistant in the First Obstetric Clinic. His discovery has conferred untold benefits. He was able to investigate and explain to any reasonable man's satisfaction the cause and means of prevention of childbed fever which formerly ruled in such murderous fashion in the Lying-in Hospital. All medicine," he said loudly and firmly, "owes Dr. Semmelweis a deep debt of gratitude. So do all babies. And all women." He sat down.

306

The blood thundered in Ignaz Philipp's ears. It was the beginning. It was beginning at last, at long, long last. . . . The chair recognized Dr. Zipfel. He cleared his throat. Ignaz Philipp waited. It was going to be very difficult for Zipfel to reply to all this. A brief throb of sympathy for the trapped man swept him. Zipfel raised his eyes.

"I fail to understand in what manner Dr. Semmelweis presumes to allow himself to be credited for this discovery. I am prepared at any time to show that it was I and not Dr. Semmelweis who discovered the cause and cure of childbed fever. And that is to me that any credit for this discovery is due."

Ignaz Philipp turned slowly to stare at Zipfel. He half-rose. Before he could gain the floor Dr. Helm, temporary director of the General Hospital, was addressing the meeting.

"It is impossible for me to contain my indignation at any attempt to rob Dr. Semmelweis of priority as discoverer of the causes and cure of childbed fever. It is idle for anyone here to attempt this. Dr. Zipfel's claim is incredible in view of his previous attacks on the very discovery for which he now claims full credit.

"The cause of childbed fever is exactly as defined by Dr. Semmelweis. The results of the prevention he advocates are so plain that I feel ridiculous standing here championing them. Dr. Semmelweis presents records. They are not contested. I ask you to consider those records. How do you explain the mortality of the past three years? Coincidence? Accident? It is fantastic that there is even any discussion. It is the plain duty of every physician to practice what Dr. Semmelweis preaches and to pray in gratitude for his discovery."

On his right Hebra squeezed Ignaz Philipp's hand hard. Kiwisch of Würzburg rose quickly. Dr. Kiwisch was one of the chief obstetric authorities in all Germany.

"Unfortunately, gentlemen, the theory of cadaveric poisoning is not at all new. It is an old, old theory. It was proven long ago. I have had a high mortality in my clinic for many years. In one year it reached as high as 26 per cent. But I can assure you—the epidemics always declined when good weather set in."

Ignaz Philipp's face darkened.

"But I've just answered that," he whispered to Hebra fiercely. Hebra pointed. A doctor had risen.

"I wish to read a report from Dr. Scanzoni: 'Childbed fever, I state emphatically, is caused by chilling, by wounded modesty, by mental excitement, by fear, and by miasmatic cosmictelluric influences. There is no other cause. There is no cure.' "

Ignaz Philipp stiffened. He gazed blankly now, straight ahead. Through the hall murmuring began to be louder.

Dr. Lumpe rose, once an assistant to Klein, now Privat-Dozent.

"I can speak with familiarity of the First Clinic," he said confidently. "With all respects to my colleagues, the cause for childbed fever in the First Clinic when I served there, as now, is due to the patient being admitted four days before delivery. This makes for bad ventilation. It is also a fact that childbed fever is just as common in private practice as in a lying-in hospital." He smiled broadly. "As to the theory of Dr. Semmelweis, it has only one fault. It is far, far too simple. It is so simple that, like Columbus' egg, it is worthless." He sat down, smiling happily.

Ignaz Philipp shot to his feet.

"It is very peculiar in view of what Dr. Lumpe has just said that the Second Clinic is always more overcrowded than the First—because patients avoid the First and desire mightily to get into the Second. Since the Second Clinic is more crowded than the First the ventilation in the Second must be worse than the First—this bad air which Dr. Lumpe speaks about. But in the First Clinic more patients died. The rest of Dr. Lumpe's comments—like Columbus' egg—are simply not founded on fact."

There was a little silence. The chair recognized Heinrich Bamberger, Professor of Internal Medicine at Würzburg.

"I wish, first of all, to make it clear that my position is exactly that of my colleague, Dr. Kiwisch. In addition I wish to state what has apparently been overlooked. Gentlemen, the symptoms of puerperal fever invariably arise first. When the symptoms have established themselves, there then arises the blood poisoning of puerperal fever. The general symptoms precede the local processes."

At the sound of the next voice Ignaz Philipp, who had buried his head in his hands, whirled.

The speaker was Chiari.

"What the learned doctor is trying to tell us," he said abruptly, "is that a patient first has the pain and swelling and deformity of a broken arm and then breaks his arm. It is a very interesting hypothesis."

A few rows back of Chiari, Klein listened, white-faced.

Lumpe rose.

"I will not believe to all eternity that the examining finger, impregnated with cadaveric poison, is in any way the conveyor of infection."

"Puerperal fever is caused by bad ventilation and by a miasma—a change in the weather is definitely the deciding factor."

From the assemblage came cries.

"Sit down!"

"Chiari was talking!"

"Why should Chiari continue? He wasn't saying anything!"

"Silence! . . . Quiet, please . . ."

But before Chiari could resume, a Dr. Hayne rose. He was a visiting Englishman.

"I have listened to the proceedings with some interest," he said indignantly. "I don't believe there is any reasonable question of priority in this matter. In 1830 I published a report on the effect of miasma on calves."

A little bitter laughter rose and mingled with the scattered angry voices.

From the chair Rokitansky asked:

"Does Dr. Chiari wish to continue?"

"I wish to say that in every particular I have found Dr. Semmelweis' conclusions correct. I have examined all the records, I have repeated his experiments, and I have watched the mortality fall as his remedy was applied. There can no longer be any reasonable doubt in the mind of any physician open to the pleading of reason. Up to this time I have for various reasons refrained from public advocacy of what my mind told me was true. As Privat-Dozent in the University of Vienna, my lectures will in future admit the truth of the Semmelweis doctrine and urge its application upon every student who listens to me."

A small uproar was beginning in the assembly room.

Abruptly, in the rear of the room, a chair overturned.

"He lies!" a voice shouted.

"You're a fool!" shouted another.

The august assemblage rose, necks craning. The next instant the two speakers had thrown themselves upon each other, fists flying. An instant later other doctors joined in the melee. The assemblage milled and shouted.

On the dais, Rokitansky pounded for order. Below him Ignaz Philipp sat. His hands were clasped in his lap. He stared at the floor.

"Call the police!" someone shouted above the din.

Abruptly the fighting stopped, the clamor began to subside. Abashed, the membership sat down again.

"Gentlemen," said Rokitansky, "these are the facts brought out in this discussion."

He summarized the proceedings. He paused, then, and looked mildly over the Society.

"The discovery of chlorine washing is of unquestionable value," he said abruptly.

He looked down at Ignaz Philipp.

He raised his eyes and gazed serenely over the meeting.

"I stand," he said, "in honor of the discoverer."

Chiari rose promptly. Then Helm, Arneth, Skoda, Hebra, and Haller.

The meeting was over.

"Tonight," said Skoda grimly, "the celebration is coming out of your pocket."

And when they sat about a table in the Prater, "Now, my boy, now apply again for Privat-Dozent. Now let us see them stop you."

Hebra jumped up. He raised his stein.

"To the next Privat-Dozent——"

The others rose quickly. Ignaz Philipp grinned bashfully. They drank, they clapped his shoulders, they sat down.

"It was a long fight——"

"A long, long fight——"

"But you see—we won!"

"Now you can spread your doctrine, my friend——"

"And save women until there's enough to go round for all of us——"

It seemed now that in Vienna the professors and the doctors spoke of little else. Ignaz Philipp listened happily.

"But there were many—there still are many—who haven't accepted the discovery," he said cautiously.

"Yes," exulted Hebra, "but the students, my friend. Have you forgotten the missionaries to be? The students you'll lecture?"

In September his hopes really soared.

A letter arrived from Simpson of London. Simpson had had time to consider the doctrine. He admitted the error of his earlier letter. He declared his acceptance of the doctrine.

And at the end of September Professor Kilian resigned. The post of Professor of Midwifery was now invitingly open.

"Is there a chance?" Ignaz Philipp breathed hopefully. "Do you think there's a chance—would they consider——"

"I can think of no one better qualified," said Haller firmly.

A few days later the Minister of Education hurriedly signed his assent to Ignaz Philipp's application for Privat-Dozent.

The appointments were posted.

Now there was no containing Ignaz Philipp's joy. He walked happily past the Lying-in Clinic. Once he even blew a kiss at the closed windows.

The Minister of Education's appointments went to the printer. The official catalogue of classes and instructors for the coming year was being prepared.

The printer picked up Ignaz Philipp's appointment. Where the Minister of Education had written ". . . is appointed Privat-Dozent with demonstration on the cadaver and the phantom . . ." a line had been drawn. The words: ". . . on the cadaver," the all-important words, had been penned out.

They had not been stricken by the Minister of Education.

The forgery could have been committed only by the Professor of Obstetrics or the head of the Lying-in Division.

Professor Kilian had left the university. The head of the Lying-in Division was Johann Klein.

The catalogue was officially published.

Ignaz Philipp studied it, stunned. By the forgery he had now been relegated to a post beneath provisional assistant, in which he had started five years before. His hands had been bound.

He looked at it again. There was no possible doubt. The words stared back at him blackly. There was no conceivable way in which the cause and cure of childbed fever could be demonstrated on a leather dummy.

He walked home. His thought were a nightmare. The years of his life spun past him. On the stairs he reeled. He clutched the banister. He breathed thickly. He entered his bare room. He sat on the bed, thinking. He sat a long time. It grew dark. He made up his mind. He rose. He walked to the window. He looked in the direction of the university and the hospital. He turned. He walked abruptly to his bags. He packed them roughly. An hour later he was in a stagecoach, bound for Hungary.

# SEVENTEEN

THE streets of Buda, which knew nothing of sadness and were impervious to failure, opened their stony arms to receive him, closed upon him protectively, kissed his soles with their cobblestones, and welcomed him home.

He hurried through the familiar avenues and each was a thudding song. He went directly to the house of Markussovsky. He knocked, he stood in the street, his two bags in his hands, and waited. Two men sauntered down the street. He turned with surprise. They had stopped on either side of him.

"Having trouble, friend?" The man spoke Hungarian.

"My friend lives here," Ignaz Philipp said, smiling at the sweet music of the language.

"Been traveling?" asked the second.

"Just come from Vienna," Ignaz Philipp said. He knocked again.

"Let's have a look at what's in those bags," the first said quietly.

Ignaz Philipp turned quickly.

"I beg your pardon?" He snatched the bag in his right hand from the man's fingers. "Hey! I'm a countryman! Would you rob a countryman?"

"Make no trouble, friend," the second man said. Citizens walked past, their heads averted, pretending to notice nothing. The second man drew from his pocket a sheet of paper weighted with ribbon and red wax. "State Investigator," was inscribed upon it.

"What on earth do you want with me? Do you think I'm a thief? I'm a doctor. My name is Semmelweis——"

"We don't know what you are. Now, open those bags."

The door opened. Markussovsky emerged. He gaped at the sight of Ignaz Philipp.

"Naci!"

"Hello, Marko . . . I'm back, you see—will you tell these men——"

"Yes, gentlemen?" said Markussovsky.

"I was just standing here at your door, waiting, and they came up—that one has a paper—State Investigator——"

Markussovsky's smile dwindled. He looked at the men with sudden comprehension.

"There's no point standing in the street," he said smoothly. "Come in, gentlemen."

They went past him into the hallway. There they turned and waited.

"Your friend is evidently new here," the first man said to Markussovsky.

"I was born here, right here in Buda," Ignaz Philipp said. "What's the matter? Have I done something?"

"That's our job to find out," the second said impersonally.

"I assure you gentlemen," said Markussovsky, "this man is well known to me. He is a doctor. Perhaps you have heard of him. His name is Semmelweis. I will vouch for him, personally."

"If you want to look at my bags," said Ignaz Philipp, "look here—" He began to unbuckle the bags. They were both quickly open.

"Of course we don't want to make trouble. Perhaps there's really no need of taking him to the city hall for questioning——" the first man debated.

Markussovsky's hand went unobtrusively into his pocket, and emerged again, closed.

"You've been very kind, gentlemen," he said. "Perhaps you'll drink to my friend's homecoming . . ." He took the first man's hand and shook it. The man nodded. He transferred his hand to his pocket. He jerked his head toward the door.

"Come, Posip," he said. "It's evident we've made a mistake." They walked back into the street. Markussovsky shut the door behind him. He shook his head as if to clear it. Then he opened his arms wide.

"Naci!"

They hugged each other. They stood apart, smiling, inspecting each other.

"You've just got in? Have you come back to stay? Tell me! What's happened?"

Hours later, when all had been said, Ignaz Philipp turned to Markussovsky.

"What's happened here? Who were those men?"

"Did you get my letter?"

"Of course——"

"Well, you know what happened afterward. And after

313

that—well, this morning was just a mere sample. Body and soul we belong to Austria again. And now the country is overrun with spies. They make their living denouncing people, there's a fixed sum for each denunciation—or you can buy them off as I did this morning."

"But I hadn't done anything——"

"That doesn't make the least difference. All they have to do is denounce you. Then you go to jail. Maybe you get out. Maybe you just lay there, forgotten."

"They spoke Hungarian, Marko!"

Markussovsky lowered his head.

"I know," he said. "That's the way it is now, Naci. That's just a detail. No public meetings are permitted without official permission. It is forbidden to gather in the streets in groups of more than two people and then for not more than a few moments. Even the meetings of the Hungarian Academy of Sciences have been prohibited. When doctors ask to meet they are allowed to do so only if a police official is present taking down every word that's uttered. The city has been proclaimed in a state of siege. The Medical School has almost expired. Medical writing and teaching have almost ceased. Von Balassa, the Professor of Surgery, went to jail for asking a student to speak Hungarian. He was only released a week ago."

"And you——"

"I make old bones. I do nothing. There is nothing to do. In the war I felt of some help for a while. I was a military surgeon. I set a few bones, plugged a few holes—now you're here maybe I can live again. What are you going to do, Naci? What's your first plan?"

"I want to see Buda. I want to see my family——"

"Your family's gone, Naci. Your brothers are scattered to the winds. When the revolution came they changed their name to Czemereny, Semmelweis in Hungarian, they're in hiding now, wanted men. They don't dare come back. I looked up your sister. Her husband was killed in the first week's fighting. She was living in the country . . . I think she's moved . . ."

But the house was there. He stood in the cobbled street before the house in which he was born and it faced him serenely. The store was boarded up, many of the windows were broken, the doors were locked and sealed. But it was home. He touched the stones with his palms, secret and alone with old memories, and with that contact he touched boyhood and Father and clung an instant to the rustling skirts of Mother. And he walked lingeringly away from it and came back again and it faced him serenely still, and he left it comforted at last and walked to the Christianstadt. He walked

314

with Marko through the hills of Buda. He stared across the Danube at the plains of Pesth.

And before the day was done a brook of youth had begun to return to its dry bed in him and resolve dipped its wheel to the stream and moved, and he stirred, and his head lifted.

"You see what it is," said Markussovsky. "It was never any Vienna, friend. And now——"

Ignaz Philipp smiled grimly. "Well, I can't just lie down and die . . ."

"No, you can't do that." They looked at each other, Markussovsky who had given himself to give his fellows freedom and Ignaz Philipp who had no other thought than to give them life.

"You'll be well received here, I can tell you that."

"I've got to find a room and I've got to find work."

"How are you fixed, Naci? How's your money?"

"I haven't got much. I'm just about broke."

He grinned. Markussovsky looked at him a moment, then grinned back.

"Naci, you've put new life into me. I swear the world looks entirely different. Now at least I've got a mission. I'm going to get you started."

He sat late that night in Markussovsky's home, writing three letters. One was for Skoda, one for Hebra, one for Rokitansky.

"What did you say?"

"I thanked them. I thanked them with all my heart. They're my friends. They can't help but understand. There's nothing really to understand. And there's something else, Marko. They were fighting for the truth and a clear remedy. The truth didn't leave Vienna with me. Neither did the remedy."

Next day with Markussovsky he crossed the bridge over the Danube into Pesth. They went to the university. It was housed in an old building, two stories high, a former palace of the Jesuits. The interior had been rebuilt for classrooms by removing the walls between the cells of the monks. They entered through the baroque doorway. As they walked in the smell of cabbage filled their nostrils and frying lard from the caretaker's rooms in the cellar. On their right, in a narrow classroom, a professor read a lecture on topographic anatomy. In the rear was a dissecting room and a small chemistry laboratory. They ascended to the second floor. On one side was Professor Balassa's surgical department, with thirteen beds. An attendant brushed by them bringing water from a fountain in the courtyard. They stopped him.

"Where is Professor Birly?" asked Markussovsky.

"He's downstairs," the attendant said shortly, and walked off.

They found Birly.

"We have heard of you here in Pesth, Dr. Semmelweis."

Birly was an old man, short, thin, he stared up at Ignaz Philipp with watchful, birdlike eyes, Professor of Obstetrics at Pesth University.

"You'll be glad to know he's come to live here," said Markussovsky. "Perhaps to teach . . ."

"You'll be welcome," said Birly. "I make you welcome, sir. Have you made application?"

"No," said Markussovsky. "I told him he'd best come here to see you first."

"Splendid, splendid." He looked at Ignaz Philipp gratefully. "There's plenty to do, I assure you. And not many of us to do it any more. Still—we're managing . . . we're managing," he said proudly. "Would you like me to show you around?"

They entered the dissecting room. A shabby young man stood at a dissecting table, surrounded by students. He looked up.

"Dr. Bognor, allow me to present Dr. Semmelweis——"

Bognor's face lighted.

"Oh yes. We've heard of you, Doctor . . ."

Ignaz Philipp's wrists tingled with pleasure. He looked at the body on the table.

"A typical case of severe gangrene," Bognor said, "as you see——"

"Dr. Bognor assists Dr. Balassa in surgical instruction," said Birly.

Bognor dropped his scalpel and went to a pail of water in a corner of the room. He rinsed his hands.

"I expect we don't have all the advantages here you enjoyed in Vienna." He smiled.

"I don't mean to interrupt you, Doctor," Ignaz Philipp protested.

"No, no," said Bognor. "It is time to make rounds, anyway."

As they left the room he returned to the table, straightened the cadaver, covered it with a sheet.

"I hope to see you later, Doctor," he called.

They passed from room to room.

"There's no reason," said Birly as they mounted the stairs, "why the faculty shouldn't accept you instantly, Doctor. I will be glad to share instruction with you. Now, let me show you what will probably be your rooms."

They entered the Obstetric Clinic. There were five cubicles. They totaled a space three paces wide and eight paces long. In this area of two hundred and forty square feet were twenty-six beds. One of these rooms was barely large enough for a bed. Ignaz Philipp looked from its single window down to the courtyard. On one side was the well from which water was drawn for the building. On the other gaped an open pit

316

in which the slop pails were emptied and in which all the hospital's fluids, pus, blood, and sloughed or dissected tissue, were thrown. Near this were the rotting dustbins. Next to the dustbins stood the privies. Beyond the courtyard was a cemetery.

They walked into the next room. Ten beds were crowded here. In the first bed a woman lay dead.

"Puerperal fever," said Birly briefly. "She should have been taken out last night."

In the next bed a woman writhed in agony.

"More puerperal." Birly shook his head irritably.

Four other women lay dying. Four lay silent.

"These others are suffering from other diseases," Birly waved at them. He pointed: "Typhus . . . Cancer . . . Smallpox . . . And she's something we haven't diagnosed yet . . ." He frowned. "I really must speak to Bognor . . ."

They walked into the tiny delivery room. In one of the three beds a woman lay in labor. A man bent over her. At the sound of their entrance he straightened and turned. It was Dr. Bognor. He wiped his hands upon his lapels.

"We meet again." He smiled. "Well, what do you think of our place, Doctor?"

"Fine . . . fine . . ." said Ignaz Philipp. He licked his lips. He smiled mechanically. Involuntarily he looked at Bognor's hands. Hurriedly he looked away again. Bognor and his hands had come directly from a gangrenous cadaver and he had just finished examining a woman in labor.

"Doctor," Birly said petulantly, "I see another woman has died of puerperal fever. I have strict orders regarding purging. Why was she not purged?"

"Excuse me, Dr. Birly. I myself made up the dose."

"It could not have been strong enough. If her bowels had moved she would not have had puerperal fever."

"I am sorry, Dr. Birly."

"We must be more careful."

"Her bowels really moved, though. You may look for yourself, sir. That pail by her bedside still contains her last movement."

"Then they must move and move again! Please, Doctor!"

"Yes, Dr. Birly."

The sternness left Birly's face. He sighed and smiled.

"You young men . . . you young ones . . . poor Dr. Bognor has his hands full. He is also our coroner . . ."

They left the university. They walked down the street. When they had turned a corner, Markussovsky turned to Ignaz Philipp, his mouth working.

"Well?"

"My God, Marko!"

"You see?"

"But it's unbelievable!"

"Are you glad you came home?"

"But, Marko——!"

"You can't believe it, can you? Well, here's your chance."

"Did you hear Birly?"

"I did. My friend, he believes his notion heart and soul. Every year he opens the obstetric course with a ringing philippic. It's always the same. The cause of childbed fever is constipation. Give purges—stop childbed fever. 'Bowel Birly' the students call him. But he's not bad, Naci. You'll get along with him. Come on, now, and enter your application."

That night a dozen doctors gathered in Markussovsky's home to meet Ignaz Philipp. He warmed to their welcome, before the admiration in their eyes. To them he was a man from the fabulous Vienna, from the great Vienna General Hospital itself. A man from whom things had been heard. He swam in a happy sea of talk.

"I have heard your theories with much interest," one doctor said toward the end. "And when I heard them I said to myself, 'Ah! Wait until he comes to Pesth! Because here, Doctor, we do hardly any dissecting at all. And yet our women die of childbed fever. I think in one bad time the record went as high as 60 per cent. How do you explain that, Doctor?"

Ignaz Philipp stared at him. It was apparent that the full doctrine had not really penetrated here at all.

"It is not only cadaver poisoning," he said, remembering to be patient. "It is any decomposed material . . ."

They heard him out. They nodded brightly. It was evident that they still did not understand.

"It will be interesting to see the results of any experiments you may do here," one said friendlily. There was no conviction in his voice. But there was no enmity.

A letter from Pesth appeared in the *Vienna Medical Journal.*

"Dr. Semmelweis, well known to you as a Dozent of the University of Vienna, is to lecture with Professor Birly at the University of Pesth, on practical obstetrics. For which purpose he has been granted also two rooms in the St. Rochus Hospital."

Vienna shrugged and turned the page.

"I want never to hear his name mentioned again," said Skoda. "For me, henceforth, it is as if he never lived."

"It is a pity," said Rokitansky sadly. "It is a very great pity . . . he was too brusque . . . always too brusque . . . impatient . . ."

Hebra, whose children he had delivered, said nothing.

In the Imperial Academy of Sciences Professor Brucke rose and moistened his lips.

He drew from his pocket a thin sheaf of bills.

"Dr. Semmelweis has left in order to make his home in Pesth. I herewith return you the grant of one hundred florins." He sat down. There was no comment.

In Pesth, Ignaz Philipp sat with Professor Birly and smiled determinedly.

"You want the surgical department divorced from the obstetrical department. Well, that's all right, I think. Bognor's got enough to do without obstetrics. Anyway, at the University Clinic we don't admit any obstetrical cases during August and September. And St. Rochus only accepts obstetrical cases in those months. In August and September we close the other university clinics for a thorough cleaning. The rest of the year St. Rochus, our city hospital, accepts only gynaecological cases and an occasional labor with complications . . . Yes . . . all right . . . henceforth you'll handle all the obstetrics alone . . ."

"How many would you say—in the course of a year——?"

"Oh, anywhere from one hundred to two hundred cases."

Less in a year than in a single month at Vienna, Ignaz Philipp thought, dismayed. He smiled on.

"Now as to this washing business——"

"Yes, sir."

"It's part of this theory of yours, isn't it?"

"I'll be glad to explain—I'll be very happy——"

"No need. No need, I assure you. I've heard every word of it. You're going to find it difficult, I warn you, to prove any cadaveric poisoning here. Our students don't dissect, you know." He looked at Ignaz Philipp with a little restrained triumph.

"But you see, sir, as I told some doctors the other night——"

"Never mind, Dr. Semmelweis, never mind. You shall have your way. Wash to your heart's content." He looked at Ignaz Philipp kindly. "Listen to an old man, my boy. I've got a theory and you'll never find one sounder. Puerperal fever is caused by improper functioning of the bowels. All you need is a good laxative, a sound purge. You listen, friend—give them laxatives! I'm an old, experienced hand at obstetrics. I've been at it forty years. Believe me—I know what a good laxative does. It saves lives."

"I promise you—I shall always keep their bowels open!"

"Good! Then we shall have no trouble, you and I. And you may carry on your experiments as long as you like!"

Markussovsky was waiting for him that evening.

"I have someone home who wants to see you."

Ignaz Philipp did not recognize him. The man was tall, thin, his black eyes sparkling beneath a high forehead. He was almost bald. He looked at Ignaz Philipp, grinning.

"You don't remember me, eh?" He bent deliberately, and

319

watching Ignaz Philipp he began to rub his knee. Ignaz Philipp watched him, bewildered.

"Not remember Poldi?" Markussovsky said reproachfully.

Ignaz Philipp clapped his hands to his face.

"Poldi! Not Poldi Hirschler——!"

"*Dr.* Hirschler!" said Markussovsky. "He teaches internal medicine."

They went out into Buda, they ate, they drank hugely, they talked past midnight.

"Everybody's watching you, you know," Poldi said. "I hope this doctrine of yours works."

"It will work," Ignaz Philipp said grimly.

Poldi looked at him hopefully.

"We've got to drum up some practice for him," said Markussovsky.

"Send me some patients, Poldi!"

"You know I will. I've only got fourteen myself. You'll have to introduce him around, Marko. But you, Naci, you ought to get enough patients from the hospital in a little while."

"Well, in the meantime, the job pays nothing. I don't get any salary——"

"And Birly's got the best and the most pay patients, naturally, and those he can't handle he distributes to the men who are already here," said Markussovsky.

"It's going to be hard," said Ignaz Philipp. "I wish you'd tell me what to do."

Markussovsky folded his arms.

"You really want to know?"

"I'll do anything you say."

"Well, the first thing you do is get a new suit of clothes."

Ignaz Philipp looked dubiously at his shabby, stained coat.

"You've been a university drone, my friend. It's all over you. Henceforth you're going out in the world. You're going to get patients. You're going to build up a practice. You're going to get a few social graces. You're going to learn the things that every doctor has to do if he wants to be successful——"

"Listen to him, Naci——" Poldi admonished.

"But I'm no—no drawing-room monkey—I'd just feel foolish doing the things that come naturally to you fellows."

"You're going to learn to dance——"

"You can imagine me dancing!"

"And you're going to ride horseback——"

"The only horse I've ever seen was under a policeman."

"And you're going to sip tea——"

"Oh, God! From a cup——"

"And you're going to be seen! Everywhere!"

Ignaz Philipp shook his head. He began to laugh.

"All you need is one baroness," Poldi said earnestly.

Ignaz Philipp stopped laughing and still smiling shook his head.

"No," he said, "it's a beautiful picture"—he began to laugh again—"but——"

"But you haven't got money? We'll loan you the money."

"I wasn't thinking of money. I was thinking of how I'd look —dressed up and dancing."

"Better get used to it. Naci, there's nothing else for it."

"The school year is just beginning——"

"It'll take you only a few hours a day. You'll see. You'll have long, dragging days on your hands."

The first days did not drag. Tactfully, as kindly as he could, he separated surgery from obstetrics. He had all the lying-in rooms cleaned. There was no running water but he lined one wall in each room with pails of water. He set out basins and a supply of soap. He made up a quantity of chlorine solution.

There began then the delicate matter of instructing attendants. Their good will was vital. The slightest defiant deviation might mean the beginning on an endemic. He was a new Ignaz Philipp. He spoke gently, politely, patiently; often he bit the inside of his lips, often he walked from a room to hide rage. Always he tried to appear imperturbable. This was not Vienna. This was his own Hungary. He remembered the backward Pesth he had once quit in disgust to return to Vienna. Pesth was worse now. Medicine had stagnated. The revolution had completed the ruin. He sighed often. It was difficult to see a future here. But small as it must be, the demonstration of the doctrine was going to be exact and incontrovertible.

The first classes began.

At the University Clinic there was no classroom for obstetrical lectures. He lectured in any room which was not in use. For bedside demonstrations there were twenty-six patients. His class contained twenty-seven medical students and ninety-three midwives. Time seldom permitted all of the one hundred and twenty students to examine each of the twenty-six patients in any one day.

At the clinic the largest of the three rooms barely offered regulation space for six beds. Here ten beds had been crowded. When he entered this room for bedside demonstrations the students trooping after him quickly filled all space and overflowed into the bed-filled smaller rooms on either side and into the corridors beyond. Those with him craned to see. Those in the other rooms and in the corridors stood hopefully on tiptoe or stood on chairs. It was necessary for him to shout so that the farthest student might hear. His voice was often drowned by the screams of the patient. He cried out each step of the examination and a description of what they could not see. He conducted demonstrations on the phantom in corridors, on window sills, in doorways, on the stairs, in the laundry room. But no one was permitted to examine a patient who had not first washed with soap and water and followed this with chlorine solution. All utensils or instruments which might contact a patient were similarly cleaned. And, imperceptibly at first, but soon rapidly, just as in Vienna, the death rate from childbed fever began to drop.

He rose at six o'clock each morning. By eleven o'clock his work at the university and at nearby St. Rochus was finished for the day. From that hour he was free to attend his private practice and to earn the means with which to support himself. He had no practice. The severest economies might extend the funds remaining from his patrimony to support him eight more months.

"You've got to face it, Naci. It's going to take time to get patients. How much time depends entirely on yourself," Markussovsky said at the end of the third week.

"A few patients are bound to start coming in," Ignaz Philipp said hopefully.

"But there are only two ways of getting a solid practice. People will come to you because of your reputation or because they meet you socially. When your doctrine is shown to be successful here, your reputation will be made. But that will take time. It will take many months. In the meantime——"

"I've got to live," Ignaz Philipp said ruefully.

"Why don't you gamble? Instead of trying to stretch it out, why not spend a little money, buy some clothes, get out among people, have some fun at the same time——"

"How much clothes would I need?" Ignaz Philipp demanded abruptly.

The rest of the day they spent with a tailor. Next afternoon they bought linens, hats, shoes.

"I'm going to gamble too," Markussovsky cried. "You'll pay me back when the experiment's a success." And he led Ignaz Philipp back to the tailor and ordered a riding habit.

"But I don't know how to ride," Ignaz Philipp protested happily.

"Ah, but you will."

"I've got no horse."

"We'll rent you one."

"I feel absurd—this whole thing seems like a silly dream."

"But you're happy, I can see that."

"I'm happy as a child. I'll tell you the truth, Marko, I'm enjoying every instant. I've never had so many things."

"My friend, life is just beginning."

Markussovsky's enthusiasm occupied all his days. The creation of Ignaz Philipp as a successful doctor with a large and fashionable practice gave him purpose. Ignaz Philipp submitted docilely. He was as engrossed as Markussovsky.

"But I am sure," he told Balassa at one of the evening gatherings at a café, "that any day someone from my old neighborhood is going to confront me and shout: 'Hey! Here's Ignaz Philipp Semmelweis—the grocer's boy! What are you dressed up like that for?'"

"And I'm equally sure," cried Poldi, "that they'll never recognize you."

"Not all of us, you know," said Balassa, "were so lucky as to have a father in the grocery business."

The small group of doctors who met and talked and roistered mildly had begun to look forward to their meetings. They called themselves "The Roast Beef Club," though not openly, for all clubs were forbidden, and often they talked as much medicine as nonsense. And in this group Ignaz Philipp and Markussovsky were the nucleus. And Ignaz Philipp, whose existence had been spent among a half-dozen men in Vienna, relaxed and was nourished and discovered great pleasure to be among his fellows.

He wore new clothes now, stylish and opulent. He plunged into the new life with all the zest and health and good spirits he naturally possessed. He learned the new dance steps. He took riding lessons. And in the evenings Markussovsky did his best to push him into what remained of the social life of Budapest.

"You need a girl," Markussovsky said critically.

"I am ready to fall in love with anybody."

"But it mustn't be just one girl——"

"I'm ready for dozens——"

"Because then it might be bad for business."

Thereafter he escorted a different girl each week.

"You look warm, Naci," Markussovsky teased him one night at a ball. "Is that Julia Eszterhazy heating you up?"

"She's wonderful," Ignaz Philipp beamed. "They're all wonderful. But I haven't got your languid social physique. When I dance, I dance with all my peasant heart. You know I've really learned to love dancing, but it's very hard on the shirts."

They went into a cloakroom. Ignaz Philipp found a package.

"Stand at the door and keep guard for me, will you?"

Markussovsky stood, his back to the doorway, watching. Ignaz Philipp unwrapped the package. Carefully he took out a fresh shirt. He removed his coat. He struggled out of the damp and rumpled shirt he wore, wrapped it, and put on the fresh shirt.

"Naci, you're a madman. How many is that tonight?"

"That's my third. That's the last shirt I brought with me."

They returned to the ballroom.

"How fresh you always manage to look!" the auburn-haired

Julia Eszterhazy exclaimed. "It's so close in here. Really, Doctor, I envy you."

"He has a secret method," Markussovsky said gravely. "If you were a patient of his I'm sure he'd have to tell you."

"Oh, would you, doctor?"

"What would I do with a patient like you?" Ignaz Philipp whispered. "So young, so healthy, so beautiful——"

The waltz began. He extended his arms. They whirled off.

"And last week I am sure you said the same thing to Maria von Zemplen . . . and the week before to Augustine Weidel . . ."

"Never! No, never!"

"And next week you'll have entirely forgotten me—and you'll be saying it to someone else——"

"It's a wonder to me, looking at you, holding you so close, that I am really able to talk at all."

He tightened his arm about her. His eyes half-closed.

"I might just come to see you . . . sometimes I have the oddest pain——"

"In your heart?"

"No . . . it's further down . . . and last week I had the most peculiar feeling . . . Dr. Semmelweis! You're not even listening!"

"Yes, I am! You've got a pain——"

"I *had* a pain!"

"Aha! You should never have pain. You're too lovely. Give your pain to me."

"Shall I come to see you?"

"Some afternoon I will come to see you. Shall I wait until the pain comes again?"

"Next Wednesday," she said, "at three o'clock——"

Ignaz Philipp pressed her closer. The music shifted to a czardas.

The days were full now. One night he went to the theater for the first time and sat stunned, amazed and delighted. Thereafter he went regularly. He listened enraptured to the French singer, Anna La Grange; he saw the great Rachel. In the afternoons he went hunting in the countryside or riding in the parks. Sometimes Markussovsky rode beside him, mounted on the same horse he had ridden in the revolution. Sometimes he rode with other doctors. There was little to do for doctors in Budapest these days. After a time they began to call their group the Academy of Horseback Riding Doctors. "It's better than doing nothing." Surgeon Lumnitzer shrugged. "I've got all those expensive instruments I bought years ago in Paris—and nothing to cut but corns. And my own, at that."

But in the mornings he worked without smiling among the twenty-six patients who filled the tiny rooms allotted him. He enforced rigid discipline. He attended each confinement.

He watched the students warily. The attendants had learned to expect him at any hour of the day or night. There had been one death in January. But February and March were passing without even a single case of fever.

In the middle of March, riding with Markussovsky, he fell from his horse. Markussovsky picked him up. Ignaz Philipp's right arm dangled. He had broken the humerus.

He attended his lectures with his arm in a sling.

He had begun to care for a few patients. Among the first of these was Julia Eszterhazy.

"Do you really want to know the truth?" he asked her one day.

"Of course I do. Unless it's something obnoxious."

"Well, the truth is there's nothing wrong with you, my dear."

"But my headaches——"

He rose, and selecting a bottle began to pour a little into a smaller bottle.

"What's that?"

"That's a physic. You don't need it—but here you are."

"You perfectly dreadful man!"

"No, I'm not. Not really. I'm not dreadful and you're not sick. There's no use pretending, and you're a charming patient, but I've decided I just can't take your money."

Julia Eszterhazy left indignantly.

"Now, what are you up to?" Markussovsky asked him later.

"I saw Julia Esterhazy and she says——"

"I know, I know. I told her she wasn't sick. She's not, Marko."

"She never was. She's probably the four healthiest girls in Hungary. But she's also the four richest——"

Ignaz Philipp wrinkled his face, smiling.

"I can't do it, Marko! I just can't."

"But you've *been* doing it!"

"I know. But I—I can . . ."

"And last week Mrs. von Fleigel——"

"Really, Marko! All she had to do is exercise a little and stop eating so much——"

"Do you tell a woman like that: 'Now, madame, you go home and drink a lot of camomile tea. You're only bored. Having nothing to do, you think of illness?' "

"What would you tell her?"

"I'd tell her anything. What does it matter? She'll simply go to someone else, who'll be glad to take her money. If she's bored, let her pay for medical entertainment. Of course you can take her money!"

"But she's not really sick——"

"Until you get a practice of exclusively sick people you're

going to have to do what any other doctor does—take them as they come and be glad they're coming!"

"I suppose you're right——"

"Of course I'm right. What do you suppose you're cutting such a fine figure for? And you've begun to make a little money, haven't you?"

"That's true."

"Well, stop losing patients and save your honesty for the clinic. That way you'll make a success of both."

He came home one morning to find a woman waiting for him.

He looked at her without recognition. She put out both her hands.

"Ignaz Philipp! It's Julia——"

He swept his sister into his arms. They clung to each other. They cried a little. Now he held her at arm's length.

"But little Julia! You've changed—you've——"

The woman before him had a lined face, her hair was graying, she was thin, her eyes were anxious and beaten.

"Little Julia . . . !"

"I heard you were back——"

"But why didn't you let me know? I've looked for you everywhere."

"Oh no, Ignaz Philipp. You see my husband—during the revolution, well, he became a soldier, of course—they watch me closely still——"

"But where do you live, Julia? What do you do?"

"I live in the country. I live very quietly. I have a little money——"

"Where is August? And Philipp? And Ignaz? And Karl? And——"

"They're all scattered, Ignaz Philipp. I don't know where. We changed our name to Czemereny——"

"I know."

"And they're gone. They're in hiding, wherever they are." She plucked at her dress nervously.

"It isn't good for you to be seen with me. I shouldn't have come. How does it go with you, Ignaz Philipp?"

"Not come? My own sister? You come whenever you want. I'm your brother. You must come to see me or I must go to see you."

"You look—prosperous. Things go well?"

"It's all sham, Julia. Just clothes. Not many patients."

"You've hurt your arm!"

"It's almost healed. Next week I'll take off the sling. I broke it. Horseback riding."

"You? Horseback riding?"

"All sham, Julia. All just sham. It seems a doctor has to get out. He has to be seen—attract people—dance——"

326

They talked a long time. He looked at her lovingly.

"You must stay. We will have dinner together."

"Oh no, no. I must go now. I have stayed too long. When I go back they will ask me where I've been. I'll tell them I came to the doctor." She smiled faintly, but almost instantly she rose, looked about her warily, and walked to the door. "I have to go back now. I really must. I'll come again, Ignaz Philipp."

"But stay at least for dinner——"

She shook her head, smiled at him, and was gone.

With April came warmer weather. The clinic, the St. Rochus rooms, now operated almost as in the best days at the First Clinic in Vienna. On May 20 he was made honorary chief of the St. Rochus obstetrical department. His practice had begun to grow. Now, instead of horseback riding, he learned to swim. He joined a bathing club and floundered happily about a private pool fed by the Danube. In June there were gay little picnics on the little islands in the river.

Toward the end of June he received a letter from Arneth.

I left Vienna shortly after your departure. I went abroad on my wander-year. I have been to France and I have been to England. And wherever I went I tried to lecture on your doctrine. Now I have returned home for a while and I am soon to start out again. It does not go easily, dear doctor. In England, though they have no knowledge of the cause of childbed fever, they are nevertheless very clean in their practice and consequently, with the exception of an occasional epidemic, their mortality figures are quite low. But in France——! I cannot tell you how many women die of childbed fever in France, for no one really knows. It is worse than Vienna. Of that I am sure.

I went to see the great Dubois, but he put me off impatiently. "We have our own method for dealing with the cadaver problem!" he told me. It appears that some doctor in Provence came to him recently and proved to him, gravely, that there was some basis in cadaveric poisoning. This Provence doctor had two patients, and one of them sickened and died and he dissected her that same afternoon and attended his other patient that night. You can imagine! At any rate, Dubois politely asked me to come back the next day to watch a lecture and demonstration.

I presented myself at his office next morning. At first I was sure I had entered the wrong office. Such a clamor! There were four women, all yelling at the top of their lungs, and Dubois was yelling louder than the rest. "Six francs!" the women shouted. "I tell you, you shall have four!" Dubois thundered. I looked at the women more closely. They were painted, their clothes were poor but garish, it was obvious they were prostitutes. Oh, ho! I thought to myself! This Dubois is arranging an evening for himself! Four, no less! He must be insatiable! He saw me then, and approaching me, red-faced from his exertions, begged me to wait for him in the amphitheater. I withdrew. Through the door I could hear the tumult break out afresh. "Five, then!" Dubois shouted. "Five francs, and that's all!" The noise dwindled.

I went into the amphitheater, grinning. I found an empty seat and sat down. A few moments later in walked Dubois. And behind him came the four prostitutes. Oh no! I thought. Not here! And then to my amazement Dubois pointed brusquely to the table. One of the prostitutes calmly boosted herself to it, lay down, and hoisted up her skirt and petticoats!

And now one by one, under Dubois' direction, the students came down and began to examine her. The lecture proceeded. When the first prostitute got tired of being explored, she got up and a second succeeded her.

And that, my good doctor, is a fair sample of Dubois and French obstetrics and gynaecology. As you see, he has solved the problem of cadaveric poisoning. Instead of dead ones, he uses live ones. They were very lively.

Later, I asked him about chlorine washing. He shook his head instantly. He said that in the first place it won't destroy cadaveric particles and in the second place he's almost convinced it will eat up healthy tissue. And in the third place he isn't using cadavers. He admitted there was still childbed fever, but he said there wasn't any remedy for miasma or cosmic-telluric influences.

There you have it. I am going to rest awhile. Then I shall return to the fray. I am going to return to France first. Then I shall go on to England. Of this you may be sure: I will never rest until I have seen your discovery accepted. If not here— at least abroad.

Faithfully, dear teacher, *Von Arneth*

When he read the letter, Markussovsky laughed.

"What are you looking so thoughtful about?" he demanded.

"I don't know, Marko—sometimes this new life makes me guilty——"

"You must learn this. You're just one man. You can't fight the whole medical profession singlehanded."

"I wake up nights, my heart pounding. I've dreamed that I've found a cure and they won't accept it. I'm wet with sweat. I shudder from my nightmare. I rub my eyes. I'm awake— and it's true."

"What are you going to do about it? Don't you see what it's brought you so far?"

"My God—must I die for it? Is my life a price?"

"Naci, I'm going to say something familiar. Something you

328

beg of other people. I'm going to give you a piece of advice. Wash your hands."

Ignaz Philipp winced. He shook his head.

"You've got the clinic, Naci. You're putting your doctrine into effect there. No one's preventing you, are they?"

"That's true."

"And I hear, not only from you but from others, that the mortality has almost ceased——"

"One death so far this year——"

"Well, you see then! You're practicing your doctrine—and you're making a little money to boot! All you need now is one big member of the nobility, one important patient——"

"It's fine, Marko. Believe me, I'm grateful. It's fine as far as it goes. But——"

"But what?"

"This is something for the whole human race! Don't you see that? For every woman! For England and France and wherever a woman's in labor and dying! And here I'm practicing in a worn-out hospital, in a university that should have been condemned at least by the revolutionary cannon—on exactly twenty-six patients! That's all the rooms will hold. Perhaps two hundred cases in a whole year. What can I prove? Tell me, what?"

"If it's true for twenty-six patients it's true for all patients——"

"And meanwhile all I can save—out of the thousands that are dying needlessly—are two hundred patients a year. I should be out, Marko. I should be going around the world, doing what little Arneth is doing——"

"Naci, my friend, the human race——"

"Spare me, Marko. I can't think of them that way. To me the human race is a woman, dying."

"Does Birly interfere with you?"

"Never. He's kept his promise. He lets me do as I like. He won't let me explain what I'm doing, though. He won't hear a word. All he wants to know is that I'm giving the women plenty of physics. Then he's happy."

"Be patient, Naci. I know what you want. Be patient . . . just a little longer . . ."

But Ignaz Philipp, restive now, began to write secretly to other hospitals, other universities, asking hopefully for a job.

In July, at a swimming party, he slipped on the edge of a pool and fell, fracturing the lower bones of his right arm. He was able to deliver his lectures and to supervise the clinic. But he could accept few new patients and was again forced to refer part of his painfully gained practice to other doctors.

He began to brood a little. There was no encouragement to his applications for a job elsewhere. He was still unable to feel settled in Budapest. A sense of living in exile from Vienna began to oppress him.

In August, Balassa asked him to consult on the Countess Gradinish.

Markussovsky hugged him jubilantly. Poldi pounded his back.

"You've done it! You've finally done it!"

"The Countess Gradinish herself!"

"Now you'll have all Budapest at your doors, Naci! You've got the choicest plum of all Hungary. Good old Balassa!"

"But be careful, Naci," cried Poldi. "Handle her with delicacy!"

"Let me warn you," Markussovsky begged. "She's a very paragon of nobility! She's the absolute ruler and arbiter of Budapest aristocracy! She's a terror! The word dignity was invented for her. She's remote as an iceberg."

"Be careful, Naci! Be very careful!"

"Wait, wait!" Ignaz Philipp pushed him away, bewildered. "I'm not going to marry her! I'm just going to consult with Balassa———"

"That's all you need, my friend. The news will be all over Budapest the minute you enter the castle!"

He dressed carefully. He met Balassa. They drove to the castle. A porter opened the iron gates. They marched decorously to the door. A footman admitted them. A second footman took their hats. A third footman waited at the huge, curving marble stairway. They marched slowly up the steps behind him. They walked down a thickly carpeted corridor. They came to a heavy door. The footman knocked gently. The door opened instantly. A maid bowed them in. In a huge bed, heavily overhung with dark red velvet, propped high on four snowy pillows, lay the Countess Gradinish. They came to the bedside. Balassa bowed. Ignaz Philipp instantly followed his example. They straightened. They stood, waiting.

"Good morning, gentlemen," the Countess Gradinish said heavily.

"Good morning, Grafin," they chorused, hushed.

She motioned with her hand. The maid bowed and left the room. Balassa placed his bag upon a table. He opened it. Ignaz Philipp looked at the countess. She was a woman in her sixties. Her face was thin, yellowish, claylike. Her white hair was scanty and from it came a faint and costly fragrance. Her eyes were gray, dull, the white somewhat muddy. Her lips were pale and a trifle bluish. Her hands, rigidly still on the silk counterpane, were mottled faintly. The bones and the tendons made straight lines, the skin appeared to have been drawn over these like a loose glove.

"The Grafin is in pain?" Ignaz Philipp asked gravely.

330

For answer she made an impatient small movement with the lifted fingers of one hand.

Ignaz Philipp walked to Balassa.

"I am going to examine her," Balassa murmured. "Then you examine her also."

Ignaz Philipp walked back to the bedside. He bowed. "With the Grafin's permission——?"

She bit her lip. A small flush of red invaded her cheeks. She lowered her eyes. She nodded her head.

Ignaz Philipp gently drew down the coverlet, the blankets, the sheet.

"If the Grafin will raise her legs—bend her knees——"

Balassa came to the bedside carrying a towel and a speculum and a pot of lard, rose-scented. They washed their hands. Ignaz Philipp took the towel and the pot of lard. The countess stared resolutely at the ceiling. Her face was white now. Balassa dipped his fingers in the lard. He smeared a little on the speculum. He bent over the bed. For a moment she held her knees stiffly together, then grudgingly she unlocked them. Balassa made his examination. He straightened. He nodded to Ignaz Philipp, took the pot of lard, wiped his hands on the towel. Ignaz Philipp anointed his fingers. He bent over the bed. The countess was flesh, now, simply tissue. His fingers questioned these tissues. They reached the cervix. They pressed. The countess winced. The fingers noted this, pressed on, felt on, explored, sent their messages, withdrew.

Ignaz Philipp straightened. He looked sidelong at Balassa. Balassa nodded almost imperceptibly. He drew the bedcoverings over the countess. Ignaz Philipp finished wiping his hands. They withdrew to one end of the huge room.

"What do you make of it, Doctor?"

"There is unquestionably growth there," said Ignaz Philipp.

"Exactly. Of a spongy quality—typical, I should say——"

"There's her age too. And yet I thought I felt definite shape——"

"Would you say so? It seemed to me irregular. No, I'm quite positive . . ."

"Probably you're right. Yes . . . I'm sure you are . . ."

"Shall we say, then, medullary cancer of the cervix?"

Ignaz Philipp nodded slowly.

They walked back to the bedside. The countess turned her head. She looked at them levelly.

"Well, gentlemen?"

"It is difficult to tell you——" Balassa began.

"Come, come." She addressed them as servants.

Balassa bowed.

"My confrere and I have decided—it is our unhappy duty to inform you—the countess is suffering from cancer of the neck of the womb."

331

Her expression did not change. Her face became a little paler.

"There is no possible doubt?"

"There is no possible doubt."

"And the remedy?"

"There is no remedy, Your Highness."

She gazed at them, as if waiting. They looked back at her. After a time she drew an audible breath. She nodded her head at them shortly. She turned her face on the pillow, then, and resumed staring at the ceiling. They bowed. Balassa took his bag. They walked quietly from the room.

Outside the door the maid and the footman were waiting. The maid returned to the room. The footman ushered them downstairs. There, the second footman handed them their hats. The first footman opened the door, closed it behind them. They marched down the walk, entered the waiting carriage, and drove away.

"There's no doubt about it in my mind," Balassa said firmly.

"No, I suppose not," Ignaz Philipp said slowly.

"You seemed to have a doubt back there?"

"It was just that I thought I felt definite form——" He smiled and expelled a breath. "It's good to get out of there."

"The old girl's pretty stuffy, all right. She's a stickler for form and dignity. Her pride is famous. She took it well, though."

"Yes . . ." Ignaz Philipp smiled.

"What are you smiling at?"

"I was just thinking—with all that blue blood—every inch of her a countess—I was wondering if—yes, it must be! Since it's hers even her cancer is noble also."

"I'm sure she thinks of it that way."

"The poor girl . . . if she had to have cancer, at least it was a noble one . . . it gives her courage . . ."

"And it gives me courage also. A noble cancer—a noble fee."

The fee was huge. But there was more than the fee. That afternoon Ignaz Philipp had difficulty entering his own rooms. They were crowded by expensively dressed women and a few men. They had all come eagerly to be attended by the same doctor who had had the honor to be summoned by the Countess Gradinish. One by one Ignaz Philipp examined them dazedly. A few were actually sick. He dealt with the rest briefly.

"Your health is consonant with your age, madame. I assure you this draught will make you no better——"

And to an elegant and elderly man:

"There comes a time, sir, when such pleasures fade for the best of us. This medicine I am giving you contains jalap and alcohol. It cannot harm you and it cannot help you. What you need are new sexual organs."

And to a young woman:

"Your trouble seems to be with your bowels. If you don't move, dear lady, neither will your bowels. Get out and exercise. Eat less. Drink more water."

But now they were not indignant.

"Such a wonderful doctor . . . so vigorous . . . no wonder the Countess Gradinish favored him . . . so original . . . I feel refreshed, positively refreshed . . . just seeing him . . ."

And one was a young woman, barely twenty.

He listened to her chest, he tapped as Skoda had taught him, he listened again. When she had dressed he took her hands.

"Is it true?" she wavered.

"Yes, my dear, it is true."

She blinked at him. She bit her lip.

"I know . . . I've been told . . . I just hoped . . ."

"Perhaps a dry climate——" he urged softly.

"I've just come back from Egypt . . . well . . . have I long?"

"My dear, will you do something for me?"

She nodded hopefully.

"Have pleasure. Live quietly. Live well. Draw one breath at a time . . ."

Markussovsky and Poldi were jubilant.

"You must move to larger quarters soon. You should start looking around right now."

"I'll just wait and see how many are there tomorrow."

"All right, my skeptical friend. You'll see. Tomorrow there will be even more."

And there were. And on the third day it became evident that Markussovsky was right.

"My simple apartment is bigger than the whole university birth clinic. And now I actually have to look for a bigger apartment. And all because a countess has sickness."

"What's her outlook?"

"Bad, Marko. Very bad. Cancer of the cervix. Medullary."

"Ah, well! this is a world in which each man is nourished by another's cancer. Poor old countess. You know, I'm surprised."

"That she has cancer?"

"No . . . That she permitted an examination . . ."

"Ah, but she's a sick old girl, all the same . . . she'll be suffering soon . . ."

"Wasn't she suffering?"

Ignaz Philipp frowned.

"No . . . no, she wasn't . . . pain on pressure, of course

. . . but it's a rotten life lying there, waiting—under death sentence——"

"Well, I'm sorry. But I can't help being tickled for you, all the same. You're a made man. Look at you! You who used to go around looking like a home for moths and soup stains. I wish Chiari could see you now!"

That night, as he undressed, he tried to stop thinking about the countess. There was something about her case that fretted him. He did not know what it was. He reviewed his examination. He tried to determine why he felt even slightly uncertain. He tested each fact again. He shrugged, finally, and went to bed.

He awakened around midnight. He sat up in the darkness. He was thinking of the Countess Gradinish. It was almost as if he had not been asleep. His mind raced rapidly and clearly over the symptoms his fingers had explored. It was not the symptoms that had awakened him. It was a word, the name Chiari. And as he thought of Chiari he went instantly back in his memory to his student days, to the day he palpated an old scrubwoman in the Vienna clinic. He remembered the slightly rounded form his fingers felt near the old scrubwoman's cervix. Instantly he heard Chiari's voice.

"Uterine polyp . . ."

And he saw himself nodding, a little vexed that Chiari had spoken before he had been able to get the same words out. And now his memory, his digital memory, felt others, felt dozens.

And again he remembered what his fingers had felt within the Countess Gradinish . . .

A shock of dismay smote him.

"That poor woman!" he cried aloud. He jumped from his bed. He pushed his feet into slippers. He snatched an overcoat. He struggled into it as he ran through the doorway. He grasped his bag. An instant later he was in the street, running. He found a carriage.

"The Countess Gradinish," he shouted. And the startled driver inspected him a moment, then shrugged and drove off.

At the castle gates Ignaz Philipp leaped from the carriage.

"Wait for me!" he ordered, and began to jangle the small bell. There was no answer. He was just about to open his mouth for a shout when the gatekeeper stumbled into view. He peered through the darkness.

"Dr. Semmelweis!" Ignaz Philipp cried. "Let me in at once!"

The gates opened. He raced up the walk. He knocked on the door. He waited. He knocked again. There was no answer. He began to pound. Suddenly the door opened. A half-clothed footman held up a light. He gaped at Ignaz Philipp.

But Ignaz Philipp had pushed past him, and his slippers clattering on the marble steps, his nightgown trailing beneath his open overcoat, he bounded up the stairs. At the top of the stairs he turned and without hesitation rushed to the countess's bedroom door. He burst into the room. The countess was reading. She looked up, amazed.

"Your pardon, Highness——"

He stripped back the covers.

"How dare you——"

"A moment, please!"

He lifted her legs. He thrust them apart. The next instant he had worked his fingers in and was examining her. She stared at him, paralyzed, speechless. Suddenly she winced. He smiled happily. He withdrew his fingers. He turned toward her his happy grinning face. He bowed low.

"I congratulate Your Highness! It is not cancer! It is a simple tumor near the cervix!"

She stared at him coldly. He looked down. He was suddenly aware of his nightgown and slippers. He looked up, embarrassed.

"Forgive me! It came to me as I was fast asleep. I knew the torment and worry you must be suffering. Before I knew it, I was on my way here."

"You may leave, now, Doctor . . ."

"Yes. All the same you will sleep better . . ."

He turned. In the doorway were the startled servants. He walked quickly past them. He wondered, vexedly, how much they had seen. Downstairs, he buttoned his overcoat. The still-dazed footman opened the door. The carriage was waiting. He rode home. He threw off his coat jubilantly. He kicked off his slippers. He got back into bed. He sighed happily, thinking of the reprieve he had brought the old countess. His mind relaxed. Shortly he was soundly asleep.

At the clinic next morning the students greeted him with expectant smiles.

"Good morning, good morning," he called out. "Everyone smiling? Everyone so cheerful this morning? We shall have a good day."

The students looked at him, delighted. At the rear of the lecture room there was a small burst of happy laughter.

Markussovsky was waiting for him at eleven o'clock when he left the university. Ignaz Philipp looked at his friend's face, startled.

"What's happened to you?" he demanded. "Are you in trouble, Marko?"

"Oh, Naci, Naci! What in the world have you done!"

"Done? Who? I? I've done nothing! What's the matter?"

The news had raced through Budapest society. The Countess Gradinish's doctor had run through Budapest in his nightshirt, he had burst into the castle in the middle of the night, he had pelted headlong into the bedroom of the most dignified woman in Hungary, yanked off her covers, and plunged his hand into her.

"Well, it's more or less true, of course, but——"

"But there goes your practice."

"See here, Marko! That woman was suffering. I can't help her pride. What's cancer beside pride? Any time anyone wants to wake me in the middle of the night and tell me he's made a mistake—I haven't got cancer——"

"Couldn't you have waited until morning?"

"Suppose it was you, Marko. You know what cancer is. Why, people have killed themselves when they found out! If you had been diagnosed as cancer—would you have wanted me to wait until morning?"

Markussóvsky shook his head dolefully. Then, slowly, he began to smile.

"I'd have given anything to have seen it, though!" He grinned. "Imagine! The Countess Gradinish!"

"Now that I think of it, I guess she'd rather have the cancer," Ignaz Philipp said tiredly.

There was only a trickle of patients that afternoon. The great chance had gone. He sat in his office, pondering this. He thought a long while. And at last he sighed in relief. He said a small prayer of thanksgiving. He was free again. He need no longer ride in the park. He could swim, hike, hunt when he pleased. The things he had found good in the life he had worn like a strange coat he could return to, at will. The rest he was done with. He had not fitted the pattern of a successful doctor. He had tried honestly, and even with pleasure, to become something he was not. And now it was over. He could be himself again. A little had been added to him. The rest he gladly surrendered. He had wasted time. The dying had no time. He winced. There was no doubt where his life lay. There was no doubt of the road. The direction was clear. He heard the call again, strong, clear, and inexorable. He lifted his head. He returned to it with all his heart.

# EIGHTEEN

HE summed his life shrewdly now. He saw himself clearly. He perceived the entire scope of his work at the university. His world contained twenty-six patients. He could teach twenty-seven medical students for whom obstetrics was not a required course, and ninety-three midwives, mostly peasant girls who understood perhaps half he told them.

He read Arneth's letter again. Childbed fever raged throughout the world. He had a sure and certain miracle of life for women and babies of the present and future. It was not just for Pesth. It was not for twenty-six women, not for a mere hundred women a year. It was for tens of thousands, for women speaking every language and in their hour the one language, the cry of the helpless, the cry upon God of a woman in pain.

In a medical journal that month was a notice of a medical vacancy. The post of Professor of Obstetrics was open at the University of Prague. Within the week he had obtained a leave of absence and set out for Prague. He left the stagecoach in Vienna. There was barely time to reach the Prague train. He flung himself panting into the railway coach.

"Welcome!" a voice cried coolly.

He looked up. In front of him sat Chiari and Arneth.

They laughed delightedly. They wrung each other's hands. At last they grew quieter.

"You're going to Prague—to apply for the professorship?" asked Chiari.

"Johann, you should see Pesth! Prague seems like Heaven!"

"We're going too."

"No!"

"Yes . . . here we are . . . three chafing men out to better ourselves!"

337

"I wonder which of us they'll take?"

Chiari shrugged helplessly.

"Who has the prettiest eyebrows?"

"What is it like in Pesth, sir?"

"I don't like to talk about it even. Everything is stagnant. At the best it was always far behind Vienna. And since the revolution it is incredible."

"But in Pesth, at least, you're free to demonstrate the doctrine."

"Yes, I can demonstrate to my heart's content—within the limitations of the foul old buildings, the tiny rooms, the antique equipment. I can demonstrate to my heart's content— among twenty-six beds——"

"Only twenty-six beds, Naci? Truly?"

"Twenty-six beds! No more. That means from one hundred to two hundred patients a year. There was never a month at Vienna when I didn't care for more than two hundred. More in a single month in Vienna than I can care for a whole year in Pesth . . . and everything so backward, so backward . . . not over two dozen instruments in the whole clinic, surgery included . . . no running water in any room . . . the whole obstetrical clinic is five rooms and the whole five rooms would fit in one living room fifteen by sixteen feet . . . no lecture room . . . no hope of anything better . . ."

"Naci, Naci . . . it must cost you a lot to say this. I remember what a patriot you are . . ."

He smiled.

"I'm ashamed, but do you know I separate Buda and Pesth when I say all this? It's true. I was born in Buda. It's all one city, of course. Separated by the river . . . you see how it is. One loves wholly. One grows older. One divides and divides until the 'wholly' one loved becomes a little particle."

"Would you return to Vienna?"

"A year ago I would have laughed at that, and the hate that rose in me with my laughter would have dissolved my very teeth. But there is only one Vienna."

"Vienna's not changed, Naci. Things are just the same. Carl Braun out-Herods Klein. He's all that Klein is, but he's sharper-tongued. Your name is never mentioned at the clinic without contempt."

"And how about the childbed death rate?"

"That's the same too."

"It's a pity that his sharp tongue can't remedy it. It's obvious that he'll never descend to anything like cleanliness."

"It's not only Klein and Braun and Rosas and Scanzoni and Lumpe and Kiwisch and all the rest," said Arneth. "It's France too."

"That was a wonderful letter you sent me. I enjoyed every

338

word of it. It gave me courage one day when I was forgetting . . ."

"There was something I didn't write you. In January I addressed the French Academy of Medicine and gave them a full
story of the discovery. Orfila was chairman. They rejected the
whole thing, emphatically."

"Oh well . . . they'll always have French whores to play
with . . . and plenty of corpses, damn the swine . . ."

His face reddened. The artery in his temple began to pulse.
They looked at him in alarm.

"I lectured at Edinburgh, also," Arneth said hastily. "They
listened with deep attention there. I think in England there is a
real chance——"

"Forgive me. They are wearing me thin-skinned. It's no
good being angry. I learned that long ago. What chance would
you say I had if I went to England? Or France?"

"There is no chance, none whatever," said Arneth. "They
have their own men. There is so little chance even in Vienna
that here you see me forlornly applying to Prague—with my
betters."

"Well, we can't stop, that's all. I beg of you—don't stop. To
stop is to turn your back on murder. Knowing it is being committed. Knowing you have the means to prevent it."

"I gave a lecture on something that seemed to me rather
odd," said Chiari. "I had a case of pyemia in a woman recovering from labor—without any inflammation of the womb."

"It doesn't amaze me."

"But without inflammation of the womb?"

"Of course. Johann, I don't think you—— Well, maybe
you've forgotten. The whole essence of the discovery of the
cause is this: that any decomposed material conveyed to an
injured surface—any injured surface—can produce pyemia.
What we call childbed fever. Kolletschka, who had no womb,
died of a wound in his finger. Men can die of it and women
can die of it. Women in childbirth are particularly vulnerable
since the womb is so injured and so open during childbirth."

"It was the first such case I'd ever seen."

"Don't you remember that polyp long ago? That woman
from whom a growth of the uterus was removed, and who died
with all the symptoms of childbed fever? And who wasn't even
pregnant?"

"Really, Naci," groaned Chiari, "someone should write all
this. You—you should really write the whole thing."

"But it's been written. You know it's been written. It's been
written over and over. Hebra wrote two articles on it which
went all over the world. Arneth here and a dozen of my students were obliging enough to write their professors back
home, and some even followed this with articles in their own
medical journals when they returned from Vienna. Skoda has

spoken of it before august medical bodies and the minutes have been made a written official record. I spoke on it, described the whole thing from start to finish, before the Vienna Medical Society and the full report was written—written and printed in full. Have you forgotten? There's nothing to add. It's all been written."

Chiari shook his head dolefully.

"Do you know," said Arneth slowly, "it's true of your discovery as it has been of every discovery in the whole history of medicine. When we take our medical oath we undertake to lengthen life and ease suffering. We are all united in seeking new means. And every time a man has come forward with a demonstrable truth, a remedy for good, the profession seems to have done its best to crush the discoverer and hide the discovery. No quackery—no criminality—nothing seems to make us so furious as a discovery."

"It's the oldest disease of humanity," said Chiari. "It's not only medicine, my friend. So long as there are trees there will be crosses."

"It's an odd reward. I never, never want to be a discoverer. Even Harvey——"

"When Harvey discovered the circulation of the blood," said Chiari, "he ended one of man's deepest ignorances. But even before Harvey discovered it, the blood circulated just the same. And if he had never discovered it, circulation would have functioned serenely. It was a great discovery, it shed a tremendous light—but it ended no suffering. It saved no life. If he had never made the discovery no one would have been the worse for it."

"Well, well," said Ignaz Philipp, "perhaps it is as Skoda said —perhaps it takes a little time. All the same, I wish you no bad luck, friends—but I hope I get this job at Prague . . ."

They were rejected, all three, on the grounds that they did not speak Bohemian.

"I don't really blame them," Chiari said, on the way back. "They have their own men to think of."

"But they speak German, and they understand German!" cried Arneth.

"No, he's right," said Ignaz Philipp. "You can understand it. Myself, I always lecture in Hungarian." He grimaced. "Perhaps that's another disease of humanity. In the body the cells produce each their own kind, with their own language of function. They keep to this jealously. Perhaps in many ways we're an expression of our cells. Perhaps there is an anatomy of nations. A physiology of the body politic."

"This from you, Naci?"

"Trains should never have been invented. They make a person longwinded."

"Are you going to stop over in Vienna?"

He brooded over this. He had been trying not to think of it.

"You should, you know. You should at least stop long enough to see Skoda and Rokitansky and Hebra and perhaps Haller."

"They have not even written me."

"You never were much of a letter writer yourself, Naci."

"But I wrote them . . . It hurt a little not to be answered . . ."

"I don't imagine—you're a fair man, Naci—I don't imagine it sat too well, the way you left."

"What would you have done, Johann?"

"For half what you went through? I? I would have thrown up my hands before I even started!"

"I'll go. I have to return to Pesth. But I'll stop for at least the day. I'd like to see them. I'd really like to."

Rokitansky greeted him sadly.

"I've always liked you, boy. You're much like my own sons. You were treated very badly. But I wish—I wish you'd stayed."

"I miss you. I miss you all, sir. But there's this, too, only a man left Vienna, not the truth."

"Ah, the truth. Who knows what's true for any of us? The highest and the purest aim of man is study. All else is of little worth. The only man a man can help—is himself. Nevertheless, we are all what we are. I know you feel you must persevere. I beg of you—walk quietly. Be patient. Let the truth lead you. Do not try to lead the truth."

Ignaz Philipp left him. His heart was heavy. He reverenced Rokitansky. He was humble before the greatness of his knowledge. And he berated himself angrily because he saw unerringly that in Rokitansky's mind the truth was of itself enough. He felt a little ashamed that he was able only to think of and to be moved by the coarse and earthly plane of people.

He sought out Skoda. And Skoda greeted him coldly.

"You've made your bed, my boy. You're an adult. You know what you're doing. I won't pretend I wasn't hurt when you ran off and left us, who were your friends, with the whole tempest to battle."

"With respect, sir, what were you fighting for?"

"The same thing you were."

"And has that disappeared? Did it go with my going? If I died, would it die with me?"

"I'm a chest specialist, my friend. Not an obstetrician."

"Yes, sir. And have you become a chest specialist first and a doctor second? Are your duties to the whole human race? Or just to their chests?"

"My duties don't include running away and leaving my friends in the lurch, I can tell you that. You're not the only one who's had to suffer for what he believed in, you know. I've

341

had a little experience with Klein myself. When the stethoscope was new, for instance."

"But you outmaneuvered him in the end. You have that kind of cleverness. You were exiled to an insane asylum for a while, then to a police surgeon's job. But it didn't last long. You know well how to fight, how to be politic, to be smooth and artful. Those things aren't given all of us. We suffer who haven't them."

"I'm sorry for you. You let your emotions run away with you. The very pity which makes you strive so, which appears to be your mainspring, will always prevent you from thinking clearly. You will always be impetuous. You deserve better, boy. Do you know what they are calling you now in Vienna? They call you the Pesth Fool. *Der Pesther Narr.* Virchow started it."

"They do so? That hurts. I won't say it doesn't hurt. But do they wash their hands?"

"Of course not!"

Ignaz Philipp rose in fury. His hand crashed down on Skoda's desk.

"Well, they could call me adulterer, parricide, and thief— they can spit on me and curse the mother who bore me—and if they wash their hands I will smile at them. I will humbly thank them. I will get down on my knees and praise the breath that calls me fool. Only let the murdering dogs wash their hands!"

"Your face is very red, my friend. That pulse in your temple is pounding again. You must take care."

Thus Ignaz Philipp remembered him. He saw that face through a red fog and then the red receded, he mastered himself, he shook a little, he was calm again. They spoke a little further. He left soon after. But it was thus that Ignaz Philipp remembered him resolutely as he walked to Hebra's house, and afterward, all the days of his life.

He heard Skoda's voice again from long ago, a voice in a classroom: "A quick diagnosis—confirmed by the autopsy. That is the highest good in medicine." And: "The remedy? My friend, there are no real remedies." He was swept by a flush of gratitude that a man with such views could ever have championed him.

Frau Hebra and the children were in the country.

"I don't believe you stopped to see me at all," Hebra cried at Ignaz Philipp's disappointed face. "A man who loves children so much ought to have children of his own. Why don't you get married, Naci?"

"You don't get married on nothing, Hebra. But I'd like a home all the same."

"You've already given up too much. Settle down. Build a practice. Make a family."

342

"Tell me, Hebra. Tell me honestly. Is there any chance for me here in Vienna? Any chance at all?"

Hebra avoided his eyes.

"What's that matter with Hungary, friend? You should make a great success in Budapest!"

"So that's the answer, then."

"I'm going to hurt you, Naci. I'm going to tell you the truth. Do you know what they're calling you here?"

"The Fool. The Pesth Fool . . ."

Hebra put his hand on Ignaz Philipp's shoulder. His heart ached with sympathy.

"If I could do something . . . If I could only do something . . ."

Ignaz Philipp sighed. He smiled.

"You can do something. You can kiss the babies. Give my love to Frau Hebra. And see me to the stagecoach."

"What are you going to do? Why don't you stay over-night——"

"I'm going to do the only thing that's left for me to do. I'm going back to Pesth. And if Pesth is the only pulpit I can have I'm going to make it the biggest pulpit in the world. I'm going to save women. Maybe I can only save twenty-six bedfuls. Maybe I can only indoctrinate a dozen students. But nothing's going to stop me. As long as I live I'll do with what I must. And I'll never stop."

"God help you!"

"I never mattered. From the moment I read Kolletschka's death report—believe me, friend—I never mattered."

"Well, take care. And, Naci, if you ever need me——"

The stagecoach rolled off into the night.

When he returned to Pesth he set himself to his lectures and to the supervision of the clinic as to his life's work. He made that tiny unit the whole scope of his being.

"If it's small," he said to himself grimly, "so much the better. It gives me greater time for more attention."

And he guarded now the smallest detail.

In November his first year ended at Pesth. He went to Birly. He laid a sheet of paper before him.

"I have the honor, sir," he said jubilantly, "to present a year's report."

"Good, good! Let me see!"

"The year before I came there appears to have been a mortality of 13 per cent——"

"Yes, yes. We had the usual epidemic then. Yes . . . 13 per cent . . . and now?"

Ignaz Philipp, wordlessly, pointed to the sheet of paper. There had been two hundred and seventeen patients. There had been one death. The mortality for the year was 0.46 per cent.

"Hurrah!" crowed Birly. "You see, my boy? I said it all along. I congratulate you. Physics, that's the thing! I've always said it! Give them purges! Keep their bowels open and you'll have no childbed fever! But this is amazing! This is indeed a great triumph!"

"With respect, sir—that single death—that was the case Dr. Bognor examined just after dissecting the gangrene death—when I first came——"

"You see? Over and over I've warned Bognor to give purges! One might as well yell out the window! Why," he cried indignantly, "if he'd physicked that woman we might have had a *perfect* year!"

"But you see, sir, we've instituted thorough washing now. We wash away those cadaveric particles, that infectious material which——"

"Bother your theories, Doctor!" Birly said, smiling happily. "You know and I know that it's physicking that's done it. And I'm proud of you. A good doctor is a doctor that carries out orders!"

Throughout Budapest the amazing news spread rapidly. It spread beyond the university, beyond the clinic, even among the poorest citizens.

And now his practice which had dwindled to only ten patients began to swell, to grow soundly, to promise help.

In that month Rosshirt of Erlangen published a textbook on obstetrics in which he stated that puerperal fever was caused by the stretching of the uterus which inflamed the peritoneum.

"How can any man's mind conceive that the normal expansion of the uterus during pregnancy could inflame the body's inner lining!" Markussovsky marveled.

"It's the blandness, the serenity of it that makes me rage," groaned Ignaz Philipp. "And in a textbook, mind! Perhaps he tears this page out and soaks it in water and makes the women drink it as a remedy."

"Be calm, Naci. Don't let an ass's braying upset you."

"But he's infecting women—he's letting them die—and a mind like that is head of a famous department—and writes textbooks——"

He calmed. He returned to his work. But there arrived in Budapest also that month a new textbook, written by Kiwisch. And Kiwisch had not changed. He pronounced that childbed fever was a disease peculiar to lying-in women. He said it was caused by a miasma and a shock to the nervous system.

"But what are you so furious about? He's said all this before."

"I know! But read this!"

Ignaz Philipp pointed with a shaking finger.

Kiwisch had written that Drs. Semmelweis and Skoda had now spoken more fully and more definitely than formerly on

344

the origin of childbed fever being connected with cadaveric poisoning.

"Neither Skoda nor myself has written a word or uttered a formal syllable on the subject for two years! That's just a plain lie and very calmly delivered!"

"But, Naci! You mustn't work yourself up so! You're the one that's suffering—not he."

"Me? It's the *women* who are suffering, Marko! Look here——"

The type stared out boldly.

". . . I still continue to make post-mortem examinations and go direct without special precautions to perform obstetric operations, and I could not find room in any single case for the suspicion that I had thereby caused an outbreak of puerperal fever . . .

". . . still in those institutions where there is a possibility of infecting a lying-in woman by decomposed animal material (cadaveric poison, wound secretions, decomposed puerperal effluvia) their influence must be avoided as far as possible, and it is necessary for this purpose to employ the measures in use in England and introduced by Dr. Semmelweis, chlorine disinfection and fumigation . . ."

Markussovsky read and blinked.

"You see? He's actually adopted the prophylaxis and he's actually arguing against it on theoretical grounds. And he's read every article on the subject and heard everything I had to say about it and he's still deliberately misrepresenting that only cadaveric poisoning can infect women."

"But is he actually adopting the prophylaxis? I think he's just being cautious, giving it lip service. Because see what he says—he continues to make post-mortem examinations and go direct to women in labor—without washing——"

"Another textbook! Every time this happens I've had another failure. The truth is set back again. Another thousand, another ten thousand women have been doomed."

In December, Kiwisch died. He was succeeded as Professor of Obstetrics at the University of Würzburg by Johann Chiari.

"I'm glad. I'm glad with all my heart. Now we have Würzburg! Now you will watch the mortality drop!"

"Don't be too sure of Johann, Naci. He won't fight too hard."

"I'm as sure of Johann Chiari as I am of my two hands!"

In Würzburg, Chiari did what he could, met opposition, and where he could he compromised. Würzburg greeted his first attempts indignantly. The "Pesther Narr" had become the subject of derision in the obstetric clinics of Vienna and the discovery was held up to ridicule in every lying-in hospital of Germany and Austria.

In December, Arneth wrote that he had addressed the

French Academy of Medicine again, and awaited their answer. No answer was ever made.

But in Pesth the deaths had stopped.

In the twenty-six beds of the university clinic and in the two months of each year when the surgical department at St. Rochus gave the use of two rooms for obstetrical cases, the women of Buda and Pesth came to have their babies and knew, as they planned to come, that they would emerge alive, and they crossed the thresholds and smiled.

Ignaz Philipp worked grimly on. There were evenings when he walked the streets of Buda alone, fevered for more scope, for more patients, desperate to spread the truth in a world thunderclap. And when his legs were tired at last and his mind had calmed he made peace with things as they were. And he planned long dreams and nourished the small flame he had lit and guarded it jealousy and each month was a new hope that tomorrow, surely, tomorrow, at the very latest, the world would wake with a start and the truth would be everywhere. All his hopes were in Budapest now. From this small clinic, if he kept proving and saving, month after month, the news must one day be the world's.

Perhaps tomorrow.

In the next year Busch of Berlin declared for the world that all measures to prevent epidemics of puerperal fever had failed and that the only effective means of stopping an epidemic was to close the lying-in institution.

"The fool! The contemptible, murdering fool! Here are the measures—here is the proof—how long, how long will it go on——"

"Naci, you must stop raging. You will do yourself harm. Please, please, Naci——!"

"Why shouldn't I rage? Why don't the heavens open?"

"Look at your face." Marko led him to a mirror. "Look—how you tremble! Look at the vein in your temple!"

Ignaz Philipp passed a hand over his eyes. He drew a deep breath. He sighed. He tried to smile.

"I'd hoped that this year, finally——"

"Come on. We'll go out. We'll dance."

"I don't want to dance."

"We'll go to the theater, then. Please, Naci! I need a good show."

But that year there was only one death in the university clinic's obstetrical department. One single childbed fever death.

And the next year Scanzoni published a new edition of his book on obstetrics. In this he again ascribed childbed fever to a miasma. There was one bit of new material. Scanzoni now boasted that he had been among the first to oppose the Semmelweis doctrine.

And while Ignaz Philipp was plunged in misery and æ-

346

spair from which not even Markussovsky could rouse him, a book arrived from Arneth. It contained the record of his journeys on behalf of the doctrine. It paid high tribute to the cleanliness of Edinburgh and London.

And Ignaz Philipp rose with new hope. He worked harder. He watched more closely.

"You guard those patients as if they were your kin!" Birly said indignantly.

"Sir doctor, they are!" Ignaz Philipp said grimly. Then he smiled. "They get the best purges in Budapest!" he assured Birly.

"That's right," Birly cackled happily. "Keep purging them. And believe me—I don't forget you. I talk about you everywhere. Before you came we used to have to close the Lying-in Clinic regularly—just to stop the deaths. And now——"

"Seven hundred and four births—four deaths!"

"Four years—and four deaths! Keep at it, Doctor. Purge them all. Then we won't have any deaths."

He was balder now. He no longer dressed so carefully. He had bought no new clothing. He had become a little corpulent.

"You must exercise more, Naci," Marko scolded. "You must get out a little. Just sitting at the Roast Beef Club night after night isn't helping. You need a doctor. Better still—a wife——"

"A wife," mused Ignaz Philipp.

"Yes. A wife. You'll never find one in the clinic, you know——"

"I'll tell you what I'll do, Marko. I'll look for one for you! You look for a wife for me—I'll look for one for you!"

"Doesn't anybody occur to you? Anybody at all?"

"To tell you the truth I'm waiting for one that looks like you."

Markussovsky rubbed his hand over Ignaz Philipp's nearly bald head.

"Is this why you're letting that mustache of yours droop so low?"

"That's a Hungarian mustache, my friend. It wouldn't hurt you to grow one."

"Well, suppose you bring that Hungarian mustache with you and see how much *gulyas* you can push through it."

They went to a little restaurant near the river. They ate gulyas, they swabbed about their plates with torn chunks of bread, they gulped the red wine, they sipped the Tokay.

They went down to the docks and a boatman poled them slowly down the waterfront. On the one side the lamps of Buda twinkled, above were the stars, and on the left the bright glow of Pesth's cafés, and now a czardas and now a polka and now a waltz came to them faintly. They lay back and rested.

"In a month it'll be too cold for this . . ."

"Another month . . . another month . . ."

"We'll go to theaters, then . . ."

"How it flows by . . . softly as the Danube . . . Julia Eszterhazy came to me yesterday . . ."

"She's huge . . . and she was such a pretty girl too . . ."

"She's due. I think she'll have it any day now . . ."

"And Poldi Hirschler ought to be a papa soon. . . ."

"Little Poldi . . ."

He sighed.

"I wonder who there'll be for me?" Markussovsky sat up.

"Oh, you're an aristocrat—you'll marry another."

"I never did believe in that, you know."

"Well, you can always have me."

"You know something, Naci? Pesth has been good for you. You've learned to relax a little lately."

"It's true. I fight my mornings through. And then there's nothing to fight. It's a long day, Marko. And now I've got patients too."

"You've got a good practice, Naci."

"I have one luxury. I take only the sick."

"You could be a rich man, my friend."

"I've got enough. I'm making as much as my father used to make. Enough for eight children . . ."

"You'd better start raising them."

The months passed. In 1854 Mends of Vienna blamed childbed fever on bad ventilation, crowding, and miasma. Almost simultaneously Hamernik of Prague said loudly that even cadaveric poisoning could not cause childbed fever because there were epidemics in England and Russia where little or no dissecting was done.

In the seven years since the discovery of the cause and the simple prevention of childbed fever had been clearly announced at least seventy thousand and perhaps a third of a million women had died of childbed fever. As to the babies, there was no counting.

And in Pesth, Ignaz Philipp heard these things, and counted, and now his shoulders had begun to sag a little. He watched the clinic still, but it was automatic now. He had begun to gray. The year ended. The new year began as the year before it. January ended.

He had finished a demonstration one day early in February and was on his way to the street when Professor Lenhosset called his name. He turned in the doorway.

"Will you hurry, please, Doctor? It's Professor Birly——"

The old man lay on the floor of the chemistry laboratory. His eyes were closed. His breathing was stertorous. His face was pale purple. His collar had been loosened. Beneath it his neck appeared small and stringy, Ignaz Philipp ran to him.

He got down on one knee. He took the old and bony wrist between his fingers. The pulse was imperceptible. Ignaz Philipp bent quickly and put his ear against Birly's chest. The heart beat uncertainly, querulously. It skipped, it faltered to a strange music, low pitched, rough, churning, blubbering. He began to count. The music stopped. Beneath his ear there was no sound whatever. He pressed his ear harder. The bony chest was silent. He looked up. Birly was dead.

Ignaz Philipp looked at him a moment longer. Then he put his hands on his thighs and stood up. The room had begun to fill with doctors. Their faces were startled. They peered at Birly, then at Ignaz Philipp, who still stood silent.

"Well, Doctor?" Balassa asked politely.

"He's dead."

They pursed their lips. One or two mechanically shook their heads. The rest nodded. A few edged apologetically out to spread the news.

"Will you call the wagon?" Lenhosset called after them.

Ignaz Philipp bent and straightened Birly's open coat.

"Mitral, Doctor?" someone asked.

"Mitral," said Ignaz Philipp briefly. The others nodded knowingly.

The wagon clattered into the courtyard. The voice of the driver came to the dusty laboratory.

"Whoa!" he growled. "Stand still."

The driver and his helper entered the room. The doctors made way for them. The driver halted at the sight of Birly. He tipped his cap respectfully. Gingerly he bent, nodded his helper to Birly's feet. They lifted him easily.

"His hat!" someone said.

An assistant ran out hurriedly. Ignaz Philipp followed the driver and his helper as they lugged Birly out of the laboratory. As they reached the back entrance the assistant hurried up. Birly's hat in his hand. He put it on the old man's chest. It fell off as they labored down the steps. Ignaz Philipp picked it up quickly. He brushed it off as he followed them to the wagon. They let down the tailpiece. They shoved the body gently over the rough wood floor. They turned to Ignaz Philipp.

"You know his home? Where he lives?"

The driver nodded. He turned away.

"Someone ought to go along," said Ignaz Philipp. "To prepare the widow——"

From the doorway Lenhosset spoke.

"There's no one there. He lives alone. Only the housekeeper."

The driver looked again at Ignaz Philipp, then turned and with his helper mounted the wagon seat. Ignaz Philipp looked at the hat he still held. He brushed it quickly again. He leaned into the wagon and put it carefully on Birly's chest. The wagon moved off.

He entered the clinic building again. A few doctors still loitered there, Lenhosset, his own assistant Fourmic, Balassa's assistant, Grigorin.

"Well," said Fourmic, "he lived a long time."

"Active right up to the last," said Lenhosset. "That's the way I want to go."

Ignaz Philipp went home. He was shocked and confused. Birly was gone. Birly had been a voice and a presence, clothed, patterned, meaningless. Death nudged Ignaz sharply into a surge of fellowship. A pattering of sadness and pity and a little fear fell upon his heart. He shook his head. In that instant, and for the others as that instant came to them, Birly was more alive dead, than for years he had been living.

Late that same afternoon a strange patient came to him. She was a middle-aged woman in some pain.

Ignaz Philipp took her name, looked at her questioningly. "Were you referred to me——?"

"I'm a patient of Dr. Birly's. I understand he's dead."

"This morning——" Ignaz Philipp stared at her.

The woman clicked her tongue.

"A great sorrow. He was a fine man. He always took such good care of me——"

She pointed to her left leg. She pulled up her skirt. The flesh was bandaged above the knee.

"It's started to hurt worse than ever——"

Automatically he began to unroll the bandage. His thoughts were whirling. Death was death. Still . . . when a doctor died . . . Birly was barely dead . . . and here was his patient . . . is there no loyalty among them, he thought bitterly . . . her doctor . . . her savior . . . and he was barely cold . . . and instantly, without compunction, she had hurried to another . . .

"Oh!" the woman cried out. She grimaced in pain. He removed the bandage. A partly healed ulcer confronted him.

"A vein broke down, Dr. Birly said . . . you know, I feel very lucky you could take me. They say you're so busy . . ."

Were they all like this? Was this the whole human race? And when he died, before he was cold, would they do this to him too? His heart winced from a great blow of loneliness. The love in him wrung its hands in defeat.

"Were you his patient long? Did you know him well?"

She smiled sadly, reminiscently.

"He delivered me. I've been his patient since I was a little girl."

"He was a fine doctor," Ignaz Philipp said bluntly.

"He was a fine man." Her eyes filled with tears. "He was a great, great doctor. Yes . . . since I was a little girl . . ."

She blinked at her leg. "Is it healing at all, Dr. Semmelweis? Do you think it will ever get well?"

He continued to dress it.

"Does it pain?"

"It pains constantly. I have to sleep just so. Not to roll on it. And it prickles."

"Are you afraid you'll lose your leg?"

The color left her face. Her eyes widened. Her mouth opened. She licked dry lips.

"Yes," she whispered.

"You won't."

She nodded anxiously.

"It'll be all right."

She rose, still gazing at him, studying his face alertly.

"Come back in three days."

"Yes, sir." She swallowed. "Oh, thank you, Dr. Semmelweis. I'm so grateful . . . I feel better already . . . ah—how much——?"

"There will be no charge."

"But, Doctor——"

He waved his hand brusquely.

It had been on his tongue tip to tell her to take the money and buy flowers for Birly. He stopped himself with a great effort. Unwillingly he realized that she was not indifferent, not even cruel, only living, the puppet of process, a collection of cells, a vessel of pains and fears, pains and fears indomitable. Tugged here, yanked there, eyes wide, seeking a succorer.

When you had pain, you went to a doctor. When he died, you went to another.

"Well, and why not?" demanded Markussovsky. "What do you expect them to do?"

"It's disillusioning, all the same. She looked at me with the same gratitude and adoration she must have given Birly yesterday. And the fault's with me. Now, all of a sudden, I understand, I'd gotten to believe that I was the dispenser of ease, the wellspring of cure, the fount of help, the source of remedy— even the remedy itself. I'm just a middleman," he said wonderingly. "I'm a medical travel agency. I've studied the roads and I tell them which one to take. I'm not the road. I'm a guide."

"It seems to me we talked about this a long time ago," Markussovsky said dryly. "In those days, as I remember, you were very loud in protest against doctors feeling themselves the essence of quinine, the power of opium——"

"It's a terrible thing to say, but Birly's death is good for me. Do you know I've just been drifting along lately—maybe even getting calloused——"

"It's good for you in more ways than one," Markussovsky said softly. He smiled grimly.

"What, Marko? What do you mean?"

"We'd better start to work—and quickly. The post of Professor of Obstetrics is now open."

He stared at Markussovsky. He drew a deep breath. Wild hope blazed suddenly in his eyes.

"Oh, Marko!"

They turned. Poldi Hirschler had come in.

"I just saw your man Fourmic talking earnestly with Tormay, the district medical officer," he cried excitedly. "They were on their way to Director Tandler's office."

Ignaz Philipp stiffened, then smiled.

"Don't worry about Fourmic. He's a good boy."

Markussovsky looked at him unsmiling.

"Good enough to be Professor of Obstetrics?"

"Oh, Marko! Calm down. He's only been my assistant for a month——"

"Stranger things have happened," Markussovsky said ominously.

"You have to watch yourself, Naci," Poldi said anxiously.

"But who else *could* they appoint? I'm honorary chief of the obstetrical department at St. Rochus—I was more than Birly's assistant——"

Protesting, he went with them to see Balassa. Still protesting he called upon Lenhosset, Tormay, and finally Tandler.

"He seems to think it's just going to fall into his lap," Markussovsky said.

"Why do you suppose young Fourmic went to see Tandler?" Balassa asked gravely. "To put in a good word for you?"

"Why not?" Ignaz Philipp asked, flushing.

"Are you really so naïve still?" demanded Markussovsky.

"I'm still honorary chief at St. Rochus——"

"That's fine. But the administration naturally wants to be in Vienna's good graces——"

"They only recommend, you know——"

"The actual appointment comes from Vienna——"

"And just how do you think you stand at Vienna?"

But the times had changed. In Vienna the Minister of Education searched the records vainly. Ignaz Philipp had done nothing for seven years to merit censure. He was known to the Austrian authorities as a patriot, but no longer as a political Hungarian citizen. The prevailing policy had shifted to conciliation. There was some danger of arousing Hungarian sentiment. And, finally, reluctantly, definitely, he had no rival in Pesth worthy of serious consideration.

The Minister of Education pondered.

In Budapest, Markussovsky and Balassa hurriedly and carefully penned the last words to a short article, sent it posthaste to the *Vienna Medical Journal*. When Hebra read it, he smiled happily and rushed it quickly to the printer. It was published a week later.

The passing of Professor Birly is noted with deep regret. The late Professor of Midwifery was an honorable man whose sudden death has caused the deepest sympathy and regret in the widest social circles. He was a man of learning, and possessed all the endowments required in a teacher, and yet it would not be going too far if we expressed the opinion that long before his death he had ceased to be a professor of midwifery according to the present-day requirements of medical science, teaching the manifold methods of diagnosis and the new ideas with regard to pathology so urgently demanded in every good school of medicine. It is no indiscretion to mention that both professional and public opinion supports the appointment of Dr. Semmelweis to the vacant professorship . . . Dr. Semmelweis, when assistant in the Lying-in Hospital of Vienna, acquired, owing to his lectures and his courses of practical and operative obstetrics, a reputation extending far beyond the boundaries of the monarchy; and he has attained already a great position in medical practice in our city . . . If the recently revived scheme of erecting a new lying-in hospital is carried out, and proper facilities for teaching are afforded in it, then will be opened up to our energetic obstetric specialist a wide field of activity and a new era in obstetric science will commence in our fatherland.

Ignaz Philipp read this, thunderstruck. Markussovsky smiled at him smugly.
"But this is wonderful!"
"Of course."
"Marko! It's you! Why didn't you tell me?"
"I'm afraid of your conscience, my friend."
"It's wonderful! I—I—can't—I'm speechless! . . . And a new building? . . . Wàit! 'If the recently revived scheme'— who revived the scheme?"
"I did," said Markussovsky calmly. "Right now. With my little quill and inkpot." They grinned at each other. "And you can thank Balassa too."
In July the Minister of Education handed down his decision.
Ignaz Philipp Semmelweis was appointed Professor of Theoretical and Practical Midwifery at the University of Pesth. He had become a full professor.
The celebration lasted until nearly dawn. Everyone was his well-wisher now, no face was absent, and they trooped from Markussovsky's house to the café they called the Roast Beef Club, and from the club to Balassa's house, and then to Ignaz Philipp's lodgings, and soon the carriages whirled them hilari-

ously back to Markussovsky's. Fourmic clapped him on the shoulder and bawled congratulations at him as if he had never, never connived frantically to get the post. Tandler smiled on him benignly like a man who had never sought an excuse to avoid the recommendation. Lenhosset applauded as if his loyalty had never wavered. Tormay spread his hands and demanded what other choice could possibly have been made. And Poldi Hirschler cried openly, for pleasure, and Balassa nodded and smiled, and Markussovsky was everywhere, triumphant.

It was still dark when Ignaz Philipp found his hat and slipped unsteadily away. The night air was cold and sweet. He lifted his chin to it. He opened his mouth and it cooled his throat. His thoughts rose and fell, reeling. He wondered how much was wine and how much exultation. He shrugged, uncaring. He made his way unsteadily over the bridge. By the time he reached the Buda side he had sobered a little. He mounted into the Christianstadt. Now the streets were silent. He turned a corner. He was standing in the Burgauffahrt. He stood there in the darkness. He had come home. He put his hands to the stone of the house where he was born. He opened his soul to the things it had contained. In that contact there rushed into him all that had loved him best and been kindest to him and was simplest. It filled him. He could hold no more. He turned. He put his back against the stone. He nestled to it. He looked far into the dark reaches of the streets. He lifted his head and looked at the sky. His eyes filled. The tears welled slowly to his cheeks.

"Hello, Mutterchen," he said huskily.

The sky was paling. Such as he was, bearing his prize, he had come home. Lonely and longing he stood. He breathed softly. He stood faithfully. Now a small wind flickered. The light was stronger. The dawn had come. Over the plains of Pesth the sun was rising. The street became a street again. The home had become an old stone house.

He straightened. He stood away from the wall. He looked about him covertly. He turned, he looked at the house once more, he sighed a great breath, he made his way back through the Christianstadt, over the bridge into his rooms in Pesth.

When he awoke it was past noon. He sat up startled and guilty. Then he remembered. With a dazzling, intoxicating flash of delight his memory leaped within him. He was another man now. He was a new and added human. He explored the feeling. Not a Provisional—not an Assistant—not an Interim—not a Privat-Dozent—but a Full Professor!

He sprang from bed. He dressed rapidly and carefully. He went directly and purposefully to the university.

The days passed. Markussovsky seldom saw him. The long and idle evenings were over. He rose at five o'clock each morning. Saturdays and Sundays he worked all day and far into each week-end night. He scanned his realm fiercely. The means of teaching at the university and the hospital had rotted, derelict, in the neglect of years. In the whole six-hundred-bed hospital there were only three doctors and two surgeons. Patiently, eagerly, detail by detail, he began to rearrange the obstetric course. He had almost nothing to work with. Never had the beds seemed so few, the space so cramped. More and more patients were imploring admittance.

"Hereafter," he told Fourmic one day, "we can admit only patients who are actually in labor."

"Do you think so, Doctor? Very well."

"And we will hurry them out on the ninth day. Even earlier."

Fourmic smiled diplomatically.

"What are you doing with that bedpan!" Ignaz Philipp cried abruptly.

An attendant halted and turned sullenly. She stood silent. Ignaz Philipp strode to her.

"Give me that!" He snatched the wooden vessel from her hand. He sniffed at it. He thrust it back at her. "Go clean it!"

"I've just cleaned it, sir professor!"

"Go clean it! Do as I tell you! When I tell you clean—I mean clean——"

"You can't get rid of the smell!"

"I can get rid of the smell as easily as I can get rid of you! Go! Dip it in chlorine solution!"

The woman walked off, muttering angrily.

"They seem to get worse and worse, don't they?" Fourmic said mildly.

"They'll be clean! They'll follow orders! And remember, Doctor, I'm holding you strictly responsible——"

Fourmic bowed.

Ignaz Philipp walked to the window. In six years there had been nine hundred and thirty-three births. And only eight deaths.

He looked down into the courtyard. It was a hot summer day. The open plain that was Pesth baked under the heat. He raised the window a crack. Instantly the smell from the open sewer, the dustbins dotted with rotting flesh, the privies, rushed into the stifling sickroom.

He put his hand to the wall. He snatched it way. It was blistering. In the walls were the three chimneys of the laboratory beneath. The air was stifling with the heated stench of sickness. The century-old walls were moldering. The floor was buckled wood, gray with age; the cracks gaped, partly filed with the caked refuse of the centuries.

"I beg your pardon, sir professor——"

Fourmic had come to him.

355

"The students are ready. The patient is in labor——"
He followed Fourmic out of the tiny room, made his way through the students thronged in the corridor, pushed into the delivery room. It was hardly larger than a small kitchen. It had been a monk's cell. He made his way between the three beds crowded into it. Behind him pushed the students. The room was soon jammed. Eighteen had made a place for themselves against the walls and between the beds. The remainder of the one hundred and twenty crowded and jostled and craned from the corridor and the tiny rooms on either side. In the other two beds two women were moaning in labor.

"They've got an hour or so to go yet," Fourmic said. He pointed to the third bed. "She's been having trouble."

Ignaz Philipp edged his way to the woman. Now he smiled. "Having trouble, Mother?"

The woman nodded dumbly. The bed was wet with her sweat. Her hair hung dankly. Suddenly she shrieked.

"It hurts, sure it hurts. Don't let anybody tell you it doesn't hurt. But it's going to be all right, Mother. You just wait. It's going to be all right."

The woman moaned. He rolled up his sleeves. He turned to the students.

"I am now going to make an examination. This case should have delivered two hours ago."

From the next bed a woman screamed.

"What did he say? I didn't hear . . . What? . . . What?" In the corridor the students pressed closer, hands cupped behind their ears.

The heat was a solid mass. The sun burned remorselessly through the single window. Ignaz Philipp dashed a rivulet of sweat from his eyes.

"It's ninety-eight in the shade," Fourmic said deferentially. He brushed his sleeve across his face. The perspiring students pressed closer. In the bed the woman writhed in torment.

"Observe first!" Ignaz Philipp shouted. "I wash my hands!"

". . . what . . . what's he saying? . . ." came from the corridor irritably.

In the bed farthest a woman howled as pain crumpled her.

"With soap!" bellowed Ignaz Philipp. "Most thoroughly!" Fourmic handed him a towel. The water in the bucket was warm. He bent tenderly to the woman. "In a moment, Mother. In a little moment."

"Now the——" The second woman screamed again. "Now the chlorine——!"

They stood tiptoe to see. He rinsed carefully. Time was thick heat. From the students crushed in the small cubicle sweat dripped steadily. Ignaz Philipp shook the drops from his face. He bent to examine the woman. He looked up at Fourmic.

"Now he's examining her!" Fourmic bawled promptly. Behind him, in the bed touching the back of his legs, a woman began to moan, exploded in a roar of pain. In the bed before him, a few inches from his knees, the woman stiffened in sudden agony.

"Ohhhhhhh-AH! Aurrrrr-UH!" she howled.

Ignaz Philipp turned his head to Fourmic.

"Feet!" he said.

"The presentation is feet first!" Fourmic shouted.

" . . . I can't hear a thing . . . what? . . . what did he say . . ."

"He's going to have to do a version!" Fourmic shrieked.

From the bed behind the woman began to howl again. In the room the heat crushed closer. Ignaz Philipp swayed a little. It was becoming difficult to breathe. He tried again. He turned the child. His hand still in the woman at the lip of the womb, he gestured with the other to Fourmic.

"Now he's using forceps!" Fourmic screamed. "I'm handing him the left blade!"

"Oh, God!" the woman implored. "Oh, God—AHH!—I-I-I-I—HAUGH—*I CAN'T STAND IT!*"

"A little, Mother, a little, little more," Ignaz Philipp gasped. He slid the forceps along his fingers. He placed it over the head. He put out his hand for the second blade. Sweat drenched his eyes. The light faded. He groped blindly. He could no longer breathe. He rose, reeling. He waved helplessly to Fourmic. Half fainting, he fought and pushed his way through the packed and stifled mass that jammed the corridor. He staggered to the stairs. He sat down. From behind Fourmic's voice shouted:

"I'm putting in the second blade——"

The voice came to him half-drowned in a wild wail of labor. The nearest students were trying to clamber on one another's shoulders.

" . . . did you hear what he said . . . what? . . . I can't hear a thing . . . he's using forceps, I think . . ."

Ignaz Philipp sat a moment longer, breathing heavily. His strength returned. He rose slowly. He walked down the stairs. He made his way into the street. The air cut at him in a hot blast. He clambered into a carriage. In a little while he was home. He lay there, gasping.

"It isn't only the building, the lack of water, the stink, the open privies, the sewers, the lack of even elementary things," he groaned to Markussovsky and Hirschler that night. "It's the attendants, God help me! I've got the whole Lying-in Hospital staff to fight——"

"They've never been trained to cleanliness." Hirschler shook his head.

"Balassa tells me that Fourmic indicated to Lenhosset that you seemed to treat them roughly——"

"Unfriendliness, resentment, even disloyalty——"

"What you need is a new building!' '

"Right now I'll be content with fresh linen. Just, please God! enough clean sheets!"

"Walk carefully. Don't antagonize Tandler!"

"I'll bear anything. But before the year is over they're going to be clean. They're going to know what clean means. And as to the students—what am I going to do? How are they going to learn? They can't see a fraction of what's going on—they hear even less—and on top of that two thirds of all births take place at night—when they're not there——"

But the work, somehow, went on. His time passed now in a steady fever of labor. He got little sleep. He was perpetually watchful. There were nights when he slept in a classroom. He gave Fourmic an assistant. He begged, he implored, he threatened, he cajoled the sulky attendants. He hovered tenderly over the mothers. He watched them leave shakily with their babies. He fought the days, he clambered over the days to the weeks, he battled the weeks, and day by day and week by week and month by month a sort of order crept into the tiny bedraggled cosmos that had become all his life.

The year ended. He had managed to race not two hundred, but five hundred and fourteen patients through the wards. Two had died.

The year's record in the aged and foul clinic and hospital of Pesth was 0.39 per cent.

He sat down. He heaved a great breath. He drew a sheet of paper toward him and began to write. He wrote a full report. He sent the article to the *Vienna Medical Journal*. He waited, tired but happy. It had been worth it.

The article appeared. Beneath the article was an editorial note.

We thought that this theory of chlorine disinfection had died out long ago: the experience and the statistical evidence of most of the lying-in institutions protest against the opinions expressed in this article; it would be well that our readers should not allow themselves to be misled by this theory at the present time.

Hebra was no longer editor.

He read. The blood choked his face with rage. He paced his rooms, caged, delirious with anger.

Death in Vienna's wide, clean wards that year ripped the life, screaming from six hundred and ten women.

In Paris the Maternité was closed when of thirty-two women admitted to labor thirty-one died in the space of nine days.

In a month the great Virchow, oracle of middle Europe, published his full and eagerly awaited findings on childbed fever. It was caused, he announced, by insufficient contraction of the uterus, overcrowding, and miasma. "Nervous excitement," he advised, "and milk-making will prevent it."

An important new textbook, written by Spaeth, Braun, and Chiari, appeared. And in this book Braun serenely set down the thirty causes of childbed fever, beginning with the first cause, pregnancy itself, and running through fear, shame, chilling, miasma, modesty, lack of milk, to a new item, cadaveric poisoning, which he shrugged and ranked twenty-eighth.

"What is Johann doing in such a book? Why didn't he come out for what he knows to be true?" Ignaz Philipp looked at Markussovsky, pale and shaking.

"Be calm, Naci. Be calm . . . we'll write . . . we'll find out . . ."

"Even Johann . . . even Chiari . . ."

"Calm, Naci . . . calm . . . we'll write . . ."

But Chiari was dead of cholera even as they talked.

And Klein died. Ignaz Philipp waited, hardly daring to hope. If ever there was a time—an opportunity——

But Carl Braun was appointed to take his place.

The world seemed larger, now that Klein was gone. A weight, a threat, a watching evil lifted from Ignaz Philipp's mind. His heart lightened. He turned to Markussovsky.

"We need a medical journal. We need a paper in which we can tell the world what we are doing. If not for the sake of the women, the very pride of Hungary itself demands it. Start a medical journal, Marko."

They raised some of the money at the Roast Beef Club. They planned a series of lectures. They revived the Pesth Medical Society. They rallied a renaissance. And Wagner, Kovacs, Bokay, Lumnitzer, Hirschler, Andreas, Sabestyan, Balassa, joined them eagerly.

In December, Primarius Moleschott wrote from the famous University of Zurich, offering Ignaz Philipp the post of First Doctor and Full Professor of the Zurich Obstetrical Hospital.

Fiercely and proudly Ignaz Philipp turned it down. He plunged into his work with greater vigor, greater vitality. Next year, he vowed sternly, next year would be perfect. He began to prepare a formal request for a new hospital. His face was showing lines now. He had begun to stoop a little. He was thirty-eight years old.

In February he stepped from a building in which he had just seen a patient. He reached the sidewalk. He turned sharply. He collided with a passerby. The breath was driven from him. He stooped quickly. He had knocked down a young girl. He seized her hands. He pulled her upright. Her eyes were violet. She was just of his height. Her lashes curled thickly, her brows were like a swallow's wing. She set her hat on her dark curls. She gazed back at him and her face crinkled, she laughed, her full red lips parted over white teeth. Her slim figure heaved breathlessly. She tucked a handkerchief into her lacy bodice.

"Well?" she said. His mouth opened. He heard himself stammer. He looked into the eyes of Maria Weidenhofer and his head whirled and in a moment he was walking her home. It seemed he was walking beside her.

He felt her hand on his arm.

He looked at this girl. His heart gave a mighty surge.

# NINETEEN

HE WALKED beside her so greatly conscious of such precious personage that it seemed to him the world aware stood dazed on either side to see them pass. He looked about him covertly, sure of universal scrutiny. She looked at him quizzically. At once he tried to make a sentence. "But you're beautiful—how beautiful you are! I am your slave, I love you!" rushed to his tongue, and desperately he held it back. He glanced at her, fearful that she had heard his heart. He looked quickly away. He must say something. Something quickly, oh, God. Something matchless that would make her turn to him with awe, knowing her true man, and say with her eyes you have won and I will never let you go. And suddenly a brilliant inspiration came to him, new minted, clever, gay, worldly, original, sophisticated, knowing, invincible. He turned to her, his heart pounding, his lips stiff.

"How does it happen I've never seen you around Pesth?"

And Maria trembled with awe and delight. He looked so strong, he was so poised, an older man, and who would have dreamed of such a thing to say? She smiled at him boldly.

"I've been here," she assured him.

And now he smiled helplessly. Now when this look burst upon her, Maria stared and in her heart an old wisdom stirred and asked a question and held a quiet light to certainty. And that which flowed between them held them fast, and her hand on his arm trembled a little.

And so they walked and gazed at each other, and there were no words at all. And sometimes they turned to smile upon each other and were instantly drunken and looked away. And once he thought to speak, and in the same instant she spoke, and they looked at each other confused.

"It is such a day——"

361

"How cool the air is——"

Like two golden balls the sentences rolled dazzling and collided.

"You were going to say——"

"No, no! *You!*"

They laughed in delight.

"You know I don't even know your name. I've knocked you down and I don't even know your name."

"I'm Maria Weidenhofer." The words were strange to her.

"Maria Weidenhofer!"

"It's not a very pretty name——"

"Not pretty——?" He was staggered.

"Well, if you think so——"

"Think so!"

"I like men's names better."

"Oh no! Never!"

"Some men's names are very nice——"

"A man's name?"

"Yes."

"I can't think of a single name——"

"Men with a mustache have nice names . . ."

"Is that so! Do you know that never occurred to me. I never even thought of it." He looked at her, awed at this profundity.

For a moment she was about to tease him. But her heart was a candle guttering in pity, melted with his confusion.

"I don't know *your* name," she said gently.

"Me? Oh my! Oh, forgive me!"

"That's all right. I do the same thing——" She looked at him expectantly. He opened his mouth.

"My name is——" She smiled. His mouth closed instantly. "My name is——" It returned to him. "—Ignaz Philipp Semmelweis!" he said in a rush.

"Ignaz Philipp Semmelweis," she mused happily.

"My friends call me Naci," he said apologetically.

"What a fine name! What do you do?"

"I? What do I do? Oh! I'm a doctor!"

"A doctor!" She looked at him with respect. His heart danced.

"Yes," he said, "I'm a doctor. And you, what do you do?"

"I don't do anything."

"Nothing at all?"

"My father is a silk merchant. Have you heard of him? Weidenhofer and Company?"

"I must have heard of it. It sounds very familiar——"

"No, it doesn't. You're just trying to be kind."

"I thought I heard of it from somewhere."

"You're a doctor. Why should a doctor know about silk? But he's a big merchant, all the same."

362

He licked his lips.

"I'd like to meet him."

"Would you really?"

"Oh, very much. And your mother too."

"I want you to."

"Perhaps today, then. Now? Right now?"

"All right," she said, "let's go now."

And they looked about them and discovered where they were and turned and marched toward her home.

Frau Weidenhofer looked at Ignaz Philipp, surprised. She turned to her daughter.

"This is Dr. Semmelweis, Mother." Frau Weidenhofer looked from one to the other. The air was charged. Their faces were open letters. Instantly she was alert.

"Come in, Doctor, come in." And to Maria she said, as much to reassure herself, "Your father will be home shortly."

They seated themselves. Frau Weidenhofer looked at them expectantly.

"I bumped into your daughter——" he began, smiling.

"He knocked me down!" Maria said gleefully.

Frau Weidenhofer smiled uncertainly. She looked about the stiff and meticulously ordered furniture for reassurance.

"On Neuen Welt Street," said Ignaz Philipp explicitly.

"He is a doctor," Maria explained.

"So you told me." They looked at her expectantly. "It—it was good of you to bring Maria home," she said, besieged. "Dr.——"

"Semmelweis," said Maria promptly. She laughed. "He bumped into me——"

They looked at each other. They said everything. Their look ended.

"He bumped into you——" Frau Weidenhofer said mechanically.

"And I would like your permission to—to——"

Frau Weidenhofer clasped her hands tightly above her breasts in a world gone suddenly mad.

"Oh, where is your father!" she cried, rising hastily. She smiled desperately. "Dear, dear, dear!" She ran to the window. "He is always late nowadays. He must be coming! He must be coming now! Any minute!"

"Mother——"

"You know how your father is. Always late. I can't imagine——"

"With your permission——" began Ignaz Philipp.

There were footsteps in the hall. Frau Weidenhofer flew to the sound, met her husband in the doorway. Ignaz Philipp and Maria rose.

"This is Dr. Semmelweis," began Frau Weidenhofer.

"How do you do——"

"My name is Semmelweis. I am a doctor. I have met your daughter Maria. I have come here—I would like your permission to marry her——"

Weidenhofer drew a deep breath. He peered closer at Ignaz Philipp. Then his eyes twinkled.

"Well, Maria?"

"Well, the fact is—well, I'll tell you, Father—well—well, yes . . ."

Ignaz Philipp looked at her, stunned.

"But, Karl——!" cried Frau Weidenhofer.

"Look at them!" He spread his hands, laughing. "What can you say?"

"But we don't even know this man——"

"He bumped into me——" said Maria.

"Maria, will you please stop saying that!" She turned to her husband, at bay. "They bumped into each other on the street, and he brought her home, and now he wants to marry her."

"Neuen Welt Street," Ignaz Philipp said carefully.

"You see?" She looked despairingly at her husband.

"Well"—Weidenhofer laughed, it seemed he could not stop laughing a constant bubbling laughter—"he's honest, isn't he?"

"Karl!"

"All right, all right, Anna. But what's the use? You can see at a glance—— All right, then. Now, young man . . ."

"Yes, sir."

"Let's have dinner. And then let's begin at the beginning."

"I had just come from a patient——" Ignaz Philipp began eagerly.

"Later, later. First—dinner!"

Weidenhofer ate heartily. Ignaz Philipp and Maria lifted their forks, lifted food, put their forks down, lifted them again. Frau Weidenhofer sat dazed. The meal ended. The table was cleared.

"Now, let's sit right here and see what we have."

"Father——" began Maria.

"Later, later. First I want to be the head of the house. Dr. Semmelweis?"

"Things happen quickly," Ignaz Philipp began, groping.

"Yes, they have a way of doing that."

"I—I don't know where to begin——"

"Tell us about yourself!"

"Well, I was born in Buda—and I went to medical school in Vienna——"

"You mean—you're *the* Dr. Semmelweis?" he asked slowly.

Frau Weidenhofer looked at her husband quickly, then at Ignaz Philipp. Maria instantly smiled with pleasure.

"Well . . . I suppose so . . ."

"Well! Well!"

"I'm full Professor of Obstetrics at Pesth University——"

"I know." Weidenhofer nodded.

"I have a fair practice . . ."

"You should!"

"I am a bachelor—my friends are probably unknown to you—Professor von Balassa, Ludwig von Markussovsky, Poldi Hirschler—August Hirschler, that is—Professor Lenhosset——"

"There's enough vons in the list, at all events!"

"My father was a grocer. I was born in the Burgauffahrt. In Buda."

Maria sat rigidly. If she had spoken she would have cried. Wave after wave of tingling shocks raced under her skin.

"My father was a silk merchant," Weidenhofer said gravely. "And my grandfather was a farmer."

"But Karl—Dr. Semmelweis!—they've just met—they can't have known each other more than an hour—let's take time—let's be calm, all of us—let's——"

"They're not going to get married tonight, Anna." He turned to Ignaz Philipp. "Not tonight," he warned solemnly.

"I'm abrupt . . . I just blurt out . . . it's my cursed nature . . . I know better . . ."

"My boy, it's been my experience, and I daresay as a doctor it's been yours, too, that things don't happen on a schedule in this world, even if we do look at our watch to see if it's time to be hungry. She's a good girl, she's just eighteen, and she's our only child. And of course this is a shock."

"It's incredible!" moaned Frau Weidenhofer.

"Have you anything against the doctor, Anna?"

"I'd like to know him better. Is that asking too much?"

"She'd like to know you better. Maybe, in time, she'll want to marry you herself . . ."

"Karl——!"

"She's right," said Ignaz Philipp. "I wish I had a mother and father to take you to. But they're dead."

Frau Weidenhofer caught her breath.

"I'm sure Dr. Semmelweis understands, Karl——"

"And I'm sure he does too. Let's leave it at that. There's no use making myself ridiculous playing the heavy father. We love our daughter as we do ourselves. But I'm a man of business. And, I hope, sensible. It's obvious what has happened. It's obvious that you're honest, that you come to me, man to man, that you're no fly-by-night, that you're in fact a man of considerable standing. We'll give it a year. We'll leave it at that. We'll see what happens."

Ignaz Philipp beamed at him dazedly.

"Agreed?"

"Agreed!" croaked Ignaz Philipp.

"Papa!" cried Maria, and instantly burst into tears.

Ignaz Philipp, staring at Weidenhofer hypnotized, thrust

out his hand. Weidenhofer seized it. Frau Weidenhofer put her arm about Maria, and, still dazed, began to cry also.

"All right, all right," shouted Weidenhofer, "this is not a funeral, this is not a funeral. I'm a plain, sensible man of business who knows a fact when he sees one. Let's have a little wine!"

Sometime, much later that night, Ignaz Philipp knocked on Markussovsky's door. Markussovsky rose and let him in.

"I'm going to get married."

"Oh, my God!"

"I'm going to get married."

"Sit down, for God's sake. I'll call a doctor."

"I'm going to get married."

"Naci!"

"It's true . . ."

Next day he called for Maria with Markussovsky. They went to dinner.

"You're making me lonesome," Markussovsky said finally. They turned to him, surprised.

"I sit here carrying on an animated conversation with myself and you two sit there looking at each other."

"We've got years to make up for," Ignaz Philipp said exultantly.

"He's a bachelor, you know," Markussovsky warned. "Set in his ways. And," he said carelessly, "the very devil with the women."

Maria smiled. "I should be surprised if he wasn't," she said gravely.

"That's a fine thing to say," Ignaz Philipp said indignantly.

Maria smiled at Markussovsky friendlily.

"You're a bit jealous, you see. I can't blame you for that. You've been bosom friends so long. And now you think I'm going to separate you. And also . . . you're not the least bit sure that I'll be right for him . . . or that he isn't making some mad mistake."

"Oh, my," cried Markussovsky, confused. "Oh, what kind of a woman have you got here!"

Ignaz Philipp grinned at Markussovsky's red face. Maria put her hand across the table and took Markussovsky's hand.

"If he likes you—I like you. And to tell the truth, I like you too. All on my own."

Markussovsky bowed his head.

"I'm beaten. I haven't a word——"

"You came here all prepared, didn't you——"

"I had a knife in every pocket," he confessed.

"It's wonderful, isn't it?" She sighed and sat back happily.

"I'll say one thing for you. You're well mated. Tell me, what makes you so infernally honest?"

"I was brought up that way."

"A pair of blurters if ever I saw one."

The evening passed. They brought her home.

"I'll wait for you in the carriage," Markussovsky said.

They stood alone on the steps.

"Tomorrow?" he asked softly.

"Of course tomorrow."

"We'll go boating?"

"Boating would be wonderful . . ."

"Oh, darling! The river's freezing——"

"Of course. It's February——"

"We'll do something——"

"Anything."

He looked at her awkwardly. She stared back.

"Do you know," she said suddenly, "you've never even kissed me!"

He took her in his arms. The perfume from her furs was sweet and sharp in his nostrils. His face rested reverently a moment against her cold face. He felt her lips against his cheek. He turned his face slowly. Her lips were suddenly against his. He pressed them softly. He pressed harder. The world was a flame, floating, she pressed her body to him help-lessly, the cosmos became a roaring void. His arms tightened around her. Their heads bent to one side. He pressed her lips hungrily, blindly, harder. She tore her head away. He kissed her neck.

"Naci," she whispered shakily.

He straightened. He dropped his arms. She put them back.

"Oh, God," he whispered.

"I know . . . darling . . . tomorrow?"

"Tomorrow," he said hoarsely.

She looked at him. She took his face in her hands. She lifted her chin, her eyes half-closed.

"Tomorrow," she whispered. She made a kiss with her lips. He reached for her. Softly she held him off. "Tomorrow . . ."

She turned to the door then and swiftly let herself in.

He stood, staring at the blank door.

After a long time he turned and walked down the steps, back to the carriage.

The days passed, an impatient blur of time, the minutes ached, the hours yearned, the weeks groaned, and always there was laughter, and wild longing, and quick delight and amaze-ment over little things and large things and each other.

And when it was May they could bear waiting no longer.

"Why is it we're waiting?" Ignaz Philipp asked one night.

Across the table Weidenhofer wiped his mouth carefully and leaned his elbows on the table.

"Go on," he said, "last month was good, but this month you are ready with something even better, eh?"

367

"Father——!"

"We really mean it, sir."

"In March it was because you thought you could get leave only in March. In April it was because you both had found a perfect house that couldn't possibly be had after April. Now it's May. All right, let's hear about May."

"I'll tell you what—in another week—in just one more week, mind—she'll be too old for me!"

"Do you doubt any longer, Father? It's cruel to wait—just for nothing——"

He looked at his daughter critically.

"She is getting a little gray," he admitted. "Beginning to stoop a little." He nodded. "Eighteen years is a lot to carry around . . . especially at eighteen . . ." He turned to Frau Weidenhofer. "Well, Anna?"

Frau Weidenhofer's mouth opened to protest. She closed it. She looked at their pleading faces. She smiled wearily. She shrugged.

"June—June at least," she begged.

They were married in June.

There would be no honeymoon. They had planned to go to France and then to England. They had pored over maps, besieged friends who had traveled, planned the trip detail by detail. But a week before the wedding two women in the clinic sickened suddenly. And as he looked at them, shocked and incredulous, he knew they had sickened of childbed fever.

"I can't leave," he decided miserably. "I can't—we can't go. I'd have to leave them. I haven't been strict lately. I've been happy. Almost I'd forgotten. And if I go—if I turn my back on them—two cases already! More in a week than we've had in a year . . . I don't dare, Maria . . . I just don't dare . . ."

"But don't be unhappy about it! What difference does it make? We can always go on a honeymoon . . ."

He worked desperately over the two cases. He gave them fluids, he purged them, he did the few things medicine knew. And slowly, and agonizingly, and luckily, they recovered. They were convalescent. He left their bedside to go to the church.

"Let me at least get married in peace!" he said coldly to Fourmic.

"I've told you, Doctor, I don't honestly see how it could have happened. We've washed, we've all washed——"

"All I had to do was let up a little——"

"We did exactly as if you were here!" Fourmic protested.

"Childbed fever is caused by decomposed particles. That's all. I ask you to remember that. It comes from no other cause."

"I'm as sorry about this as you are, Doctor——"

"I'm going to the church now. I'm going to get married. I want to leave here in peace. I won't want to worry that the moment I'm out of the door some filthy attendant or some stupid student is going to poke a dirty bedpan or a dirty instrument or a pair of dirty hands into one of these few patients. We've had a very narrow escape."

"You can leave in perfect confidence, Doctor."

"I'm holding you strictly responsible."

"Rely on me. Good luck, Doctor—congratulations——"

"Thanks. Thanks, Fourmic. Now, remember——"

And he walked from the university, jumped into a carriage, and arrived home in time to change clothes under the supervision of an exasperated Markussovsky, to lose the ring, to find it again, and finally to arrive at the church.

He had not been in a church for a long time. He had never before suspected it of comfort. When he was a child he and his brothers had gone to church automatically, it was one of the cardinal points of a compass of living, a thing one did to please Mother, like hanging up one's clothes, helping Father in the store, taking a Saturday bath, going to school. As a medical student he went as often as was needful to maintain that status of citizenship and that respect for one's childhood fears and obligations for which a harried young man could grudgingly spare the time. As a doctor he had little time for any other form of worship than the solace and redemption from pain of those who presumably served God more regularly.

Now as he entered the church in which he was to be married he was charmed by a feeling of quiet and the luxury of serenity. This was a repose that seemed immovable. An infinity of supplications had been breathed here, pain, crucial distress of mind, desperate begging for the least and the greatest things human minds could ask. The dim church remained untouched, its high dome rose serenely, its walls rose in a placid communion of stone, detached, remote, cool, and hushed in the everlasting silence of stone. And he, who had spent his life among the entreating, to whom desperate prayers or the shattered screaming of the last appeal, to whom endless supplication, burning words, imploring eyes, folded hands were a daily fixture, familiar as beds, bandages, blood, and the dry smell of chemicals, discovered intermission here, a sense of suspension and freedom and ease, a place of prayers in which he was not called upon.

They had come a little early, despite Markussovsky's fears. He knelt for a space, not praying but content. He heard a small bustle at the church door. He prayed quickly, in a remembered and dutiful form of words. Then he thought a moment, asked the good will and blessing of Heaven on Maria, was about to rise, remembered the two women convalescent from childbed fever, prayed for them and for an end to childbed fever, opened his eyes, rose, dusted his knees, and forgot everything in the sight of his advancing bride.

The wedding meal was eaten at no small waterfront café, no thriving middle-class inn of the inner city, but at a restaurant on the Andrassy Avenue itself. All the Roast Beef Club sat about the table, Markussovsky, Poldi, Hirschler and his wife, Father and Mother Weidenhofer, and for the occasion even Julia, his sister, had been prevailed upon to come and now sat quietly, occasionally ceasing to brood and venturing a timid and uncertain smile. At the head of the table sat Ignaz Philipp and next to him was Maria. Their heads ached with the noise, their attention was endlessly divided by the shouting friends and by the power of love which drew their attention to each other. Ignaz Philipp responded to the toasting, gazed gratefully at his friends, was awed by their good will. Maria looked at him with adoration. She took his hand beneath the table and pressed it thankfully.

Lenhosset thought of a toast.

"To the new lying-in hospital," he rose and cried excitedly. "And to the man who will be its director!"

Ignaz Philipp struggled to his feet and drank quickly.

"You're not supposed to drink to yourself," Markussovsky shouted. "Sit down and save your strength for tonight."

"I'm drinking to the new hospital," Ignaz Philipp answered imperturbably. "Even though I know we'll never get it."

"You'd better get it soon," Balassa said. "I hear you had two cases of fever in a single week. Not even you can hold back the tide singlehanded."

"It's not the hospital!" Ignaz Philipp's face began to flush. "It's the stupid imbeciles who work there!"

"You'd better muzzle Fourmic, old man. That's not the way he's telling it."

Ignaz Philipp jumped up.

"I'll muzzle Fourmic! I'll get rid of him and every sulky dirt-lover along with him! I've had enough! I've had absolutely enough! These deaths were deliberate murder—by deliberate murderers—on helpless patients—by contemptible, cowardly swine!"

He was shouting now. They looked at him, silent and amazed. Maria pulled at his sleeve, tugged and tugged. Markussovsky rose quickly and went to him. Weidenhofer frowned, perplexed. Frau Weidenhofer put her hands to her breast. The rage passed quickly. He shook his head hard. He managed a smile. Trembling and pale, he sat down. Awkwardly the guests began to talk again; soon the wineglasses lifted and the uproar recommenced.

"Naci, Naci, you mustn't let anything upset you, do you think you're a firecracker?" Maria scolded him, smiling. He heaved a deep sigh and smiled at her and soon he was part of the uproar. Music began. Markussovsky claimed Maria. They whirled about the dance floor.

"Poor Naci—he's had too much to drink." Maria smiled.

"I wish you were right," said Markussovsky.

"Why, Marko! Of course he's had too much to drink!"

"You're a woman with a problem, my girl. You've got a rival. There's another woman in your life before you even start. Her name is childbed fever."

"I don't know what you're talking about."

"Didn't he ever tell you about childbed fever?"

"The first day he took me out. And once a day ever since. I love him when he tells about it. He gets so earnest and intense."

"I know——"

"What's the matter, Marko? It's the man's whole life!"

"He's been through a lot——"

"He's told me."

"I wonder if even he could tell you. Days of it, weeks of it, months of it, years of it. It's been never-ending. He's rubbed raw. I'm worried, Maria. He explodes so easily nowadays. A man can only stand so much strain. Even a man of his enormous vitality can have a nervous breakdown."

"Marko!"

"Oh, Maria, forgive me. I'm sorry. This is no time to talk of such things——"

"Of course I forgive you. I've noticed how you changed the subject whenever childbed fever came up. To tell the truth I was sometimes a little irritated with you——"

"You see how it is. And we love him. He's the finest man I've ever known and it's not worth it, Maria. It's all for the sake of women who never heard of him or who forget him the minute they leave the hospital——"

"I don't think he cares whether they're grateful. I think he just can't bear to see them suffer. I think he suffers worse than they do."

"Calm him down, Maria. Make him peaceful. I thank God for you, for the happiness you are, for what you can mean to his life. And, Maria——"

A waiter was hurrying toward them, threading his way between the dancers. He looked at Markussovsky. He nodded meaningly. Markussovsky immediately took her arm and led her, surprised, back to the table.

"Come on," he ordered Ignaz Philipp. Ignaz Philipp stood quickly and wonderingly walked with them to the door. They walked out of the restaurant. They stood expectantly on the sidewalk. Ignaz Philipp and Maria looked inquiringly at Markussovsky He gazed back at them in mock exasperation. He pointed to a horse and carriage standing at the curb. They looked at the horse and carriage, then, uncomprehending, back at Markussovsky.

"It's yours, stupid, it's yours!" he shouted at last.

"Ours!" They ran to the carriage.

"It's my wedding present. Something every doctor needs!" Maria flung herself upon him, squealing with delight. Ignaz Philipp stared at him, blinking back the tears.

"Now you won't have to run around Pesth in your nightgown!" Markussovsky roared.

They trooped excitedly inside again. Hours later they rose at last. They made their way to the door and the waiting carriage in a torrent of shouted admonitions and cheers.

"Henceforth you can bump into her all you want!" Weidenhofer yelled.

"Karl!"

"Give me a granddaughter, at least, to make up for my daughter you're taking from me——"

They got into the carriage, rice and shoes raining about them, they drove off toward the apartment that was the Weidenhofers' wedding present.

He had never imagined such content. The days were short now, they passed in complete happiness. And the weeks grew richer, each day was a fresh and smiling marvel. Each day they drew closer, they slipped into each other's thoughts and hopes and happiness.

Maria could not bear to be alone all day.

"Go visit your parents, darling. Go see Frau Balassa—Frau Hirschler."

"I don't want to see anybody else. I want to be with you."

"But, Maria—my darling—I have to make rounds—I have to see my patients——"

"I'll go with you!"

"But how, my angel—how will you go with me——"

"I'll carry your bags into all the houses!"

"No, no, darling! It wouldn't be proper, it wouldn't be ethical!"

"Then let me ride with you in the carriage."

"Maria, darling——"

"Oh, please, Naci! Just let me sit beside you and ride from house to house with you while you make calls."

"Well——"

"Oh, Naci! Oh, thank you, thank you!"

He rose at six o'clock, at seven o'clock he was at the university, beginning the day's lectures, inspecting the wards, demonstrating. At ten o'clock he came home. She was waiting for him with breakfast. They ate happily together. Then, while he packed his bag or made up medicines, Maria rushed to tidy the dishes, hung up her apron, presented herself, inspected him, brushed him carefully, and together they walked out of the house into the waiting carriage.

He clucked at the horse. The carriage moved off. She squealed happily and squeezed his arm.

"We're together! The doctor and the doctor's wife! Isn't it wonderful, Naci?"

"It's perfect," he said. "But I feel guilty. It's all right now, but what will you do when I'm with the patient and you have to sit out here all alone, nothing to do? And just sit there and wait. And wait. And wait."

"I'll tell my rosary."

"Your rosary!"

"Every woman's got a very special kind of rosary. I'll sit there and I'll think of the day we met and what you said and the night you first kissed me. And how you look, and whether your shirts are lasting, and if I hadn't better feed you less starches. And what our baby will be like and whether I want it to have your nose or mine and what color eyes they will be. And when we have to visit Mama, and whether you like me in blue with my hair some other way. And——"

She broke off and nodded at him sagely.

"*You're* the one that's going to be bored. Not me!"

"All right, darling. But sometimes you're going to have to wait a long time."

"I'll make up stories about what you're doing inside. 'My husband's in there,' I'll say. 'He's doing a very critical operation—that man's florins are inflamed—he's performing a removal of the groschen——' "

He roared happily.

"I'll remove every groschen in sight!"

"And you have to tell me everything. Everything, Naci! I'm bursting with curiosity. Now I'm a doctor's wife. Isn't this wonderful, making rounds together? What's the first case?"

"Oh, Maria, you won't be interested in such things. Honestly, sweetheart, there's nothing sensational. Just the same old things. This is a young girl. She's got syphilis."

"Ooh, Naci! A bad girl!"

"Sure! And the cavemen were punished with cold until they discovered fire."

The carriage stopped. She slumped blissfully in the seat, dreaming long, contented thoughts. In a little while there was the sound of a door closing, and he jumped into the carriage beside her and they drove off again.

And the next patient was a man with malaria, a meek little man with a hypochondriacal wife, and he would never get well because she kept taking his pills.

And they chattered and chuckled about this, and the carriage drove spanking and when they turned a corner he sud-

373

denly swooped and kissed the palm of her hand and she kept her hand secretly closed over this and when the carriage stopped and he went to the next patient she opened her palm slowly and looked at it hungrily, triumphantly, all the time he was gone.

He was shaking his head when he got back into the carriage.

"Can't save that one," he said soberly.

"Oh, Naci! Does he know it?"

"Maria, nobody ever knows it. They're always astonished, always taken by surprise. It's the one thing we're all sure of and the one thing most people can't adjust themselves to. Other people will die. Not them."

"But it's no fun to think about."

He shook his head resignedly.

"All right, puss, we won't think about it."

"And don't sound so lordly!"

He grinned. He pinched her thigh.

"Others, Naci—never us."

He nodded promptly. "Others, Maria—never us."

"And now you've got to eat. This is outrageous. I won't let you do this. You should have had lunch a half-hour ago. Is this what you do to yourself every day? I'm ashamed of you!"

"One last call, sweetheart. I've got to see this poor man. A cart ran over him and crushed his bladder . . ."

And so they spent the days together, the long, happy, quiet, beautiful days. And each day she rode with him while he made his rounds, and waited in the carriage, and sometimes she brought a bit of sewing to pass the time and sometimes she tried conscientiously to digest a ponderous medical book, and mostly she sat quite still, her hands folded in her lap, and looked off into the distance and dreamed golden, humming dreams.

She would be there when he came out of each house, and he would try not to run to the carriage, and he would sit beside her, feeling her warm body next to his, and each time she spoke he was startled, hearing the music of her voice for the first time. She was a tumult of delight in his bursting heart and the hours prickled with moments when his need for her was so humble and swelled so huge that he was numbed and his chest hurt from containing it.

He said nothing in such moments. But she would look at him suddenly, poignantly aware.

"I adore you, Naci . . ."

"I love you, little Maria . . ."

"I'm as tall as you are!"

"You're my little girl . . . Maria . . . maybe we'll have one of our own soon?"

374

"How can you tell when a woman's pregnant, Naci?"

"Well, her periods stop, of course, that's the first sign, and in a couple of months the cervix gets quite soft and rather bluish . . ." He turned to her excitedly. "Why? Maria—tell me! Do you think you're pregnant?"

"Ah, I wish I was. No, no. I was just curious—what you see, Naci, you look at so many women—there . . . you see one after the other . . . you—you must get sick of it. Tell me, Naci, how can you like—well, how can you like——"

Her voice trailed helplessly. He looked at her and chuckled.

"Well, I'll tell you, darling. I put on another pair of glasses . . ."

She grinned back at him, her cheeks scarlet.

"So you've been worrying, eh?"

"I just thought—I couldn't help wondering—after all, I'm a woman——"

"You're my darling!" he said, and his eyes burned suddenly. She snuggled against him, comprehending, and he clucked to the horse and they whirled swiftly toward home. Behind the carriage they left a trail of physics and pills and bandages and sorrow and relief and pain and happiness. And tomorrow would be another day, and then another, and each day they would set out again together.

Now, in these early months of 1857, the clinic seemed almost to manage itself. There were no more deaths from peurperal fever. The attendants kept grudgingly clean. Fourmic appeared to cease his eternal fawning and political maneuvering. The women came to fill the tiny rooms, had their babies, and, while another waited at the bedside, arose and went into the world again, carrying their babies. The students presented the same problem, but Ignaz Philipp had become almost resigned to it now, and tried always to meet it with the good nature he brought with him each day from his home.

He stood before his class, somewhat taller than many of his countrymen, well-set-up, a little corpulent, florid, and healthy, his head growing always more bald, his eyes deep-set and kindly. He looked out over the group of twenty-seven medical students and ninety-three young women to whom it was his duty to communicate all that man had learned about the delivery of babies and the care of mothers.

"Well—are we all prepared to learn today? I shouldn't wonder that you were more prepared to learn that I am able to teach you."

The men looked at him moodily. Midwifery was not a compulsory subject of examination for a doctor's diploma. It was a useful thing to know, and one made money from it now and then, after one graduated.

The women, the young girls, smiled worriedly, straining to catch each word. Most of them were peasants, most of them were illiterate, they had come to learn what they could learn, as quickly as they could learn it, and then to return to the countryside and take up the occupation of delivering babies for a living.

"Yesterday we discussed the unfavorable position of the head," he began softly. "Today we will progress to face cases." He waited a moment. The class settled down. He was lecturing today in the surgical lecture room, temporarily vacant.

"Of laborious birth, face cases are the most difficult and troublesome. Because of its length, inequality, and roughness, the face must occasion greater pain. And from the solidity of the bones it must yield to the propelling force of labor throes with more difficulty than the smooth, movable bones of the cranium. Success in delivering such cases rests heavily on preserving the strength of the mother."

"Too fast, too fast," some of the women protested.

The medical students turned and looked at them contemptuously.

"The variety of the face cases," Ignaz Philipp proceeded slowly, with a reassuring smile toward the women, "are known by the direction of the chin. For the face may present with the chin to the pubes . . . the sacrum . . . to either side . . ."

"What is 'sacrum'?" one of the women cried out.

"And 'pubes'?" cried another.

The medical students slumped indignantly.

Patiently, Ignaz Philipp stopped the lecture. He explained what sacrum meant and pubes. He picked up the thread again.

"The rule in all these positions is to allow the labor to go on till the face is protruded as low as possible. It is often as difficult and hazardous to push back the child and to bring down the crown or vertex as to turn the child and deliver it by the feet."

"What's vertex—what's the vertex, sir?"

"Now you know what vertex is! Remember? We've used the word vertex a dozen, four dozen times. Here"—he slapped his head sharply—"here is the vertex."

"Perhaps the sir professor should explain the word feet to her!" a student cried indignantly.

"That's enough. That's enough now. Be gentlemanly! These girls have to understand too."

The lecture went on.

". . . because the occiput cannot properly be cleared of the perineum before the chin has descended as low as the inferior edge of the symphysis of the ossa pubis . . ."

"Please—please!" the women cried despairingly.

"Oh, my God!" the students groaned.

Ignaz Philipp reddened a little. He drew a deep breath. He turned to translate for the women. He mastered himself to speak patiently.

". . . because the hind head"—he thumped the back of his

head—"can't be worked clear of that muscular area at the bottom——"

"What bottom?" a girl's voice called helplessly. "Bottom of what?"

Ignaz Philipp's face swelled. The artery in his temple began to distend, to pulse. He tried to restrain himself. Suddenly his hand slapped down on the desk.

"What are we talking about?" he yelled. The women jumped. The students shut their eyes and slumped in their seats resignedly.

"You said the bottom of something," the girl faltered.

"And what are we talking about?" he exploded. "Do you think babies are born through the rectum? The bottom of her vulva, that's what! You know what a vulva is, you stupid blockhead? Shall I draw you a picture of the difference between a man and a woman? Don't you even know that?"

The girl burst into tears. Almost instantly women on either side began to weep also. The students tore at their hair, they groaned, they put their heads down on their folded arms. Other women began to cry.

Ignaz Philipp's temper passed. He looked at them, he listened remorsefully.

"Now, now," he called out. "Don't cry, don't cry . . . you mustn't be hurt by a little noise . . . it's all right . . ."

The girls stopped crying and subsided to a few fearful sniffles. They lifted woebegone, imploring faces.

"I don't blame you a bit. Not a bit. That's how it is with our Hungarian girls. Good girls. Virtuous. How should they know what they've got down there?"

The women laughed, they could not help themselves, in an instant they were sunny again, the tears drying on their faces.

The lecture went on.

"We come now to excrescences of the *os uteri*——" The women lifted their heads. "I'll explain this to you in a minute," he said hastily.

He lectured in Hungarian. But there were not enough technical words in the language. Sometimes he had to speak German to explain what he meant. When he had finished, when the students understood, they sat writhing with impatience while he went back to Hungarian—and translated from the medical words to the simple, everyday expressions an unschooled woman from a farm would understand.

The lecture ended at last. He shook his head wearily. Each day it seemed to become more difficult to cram into the few hours enough instruction to complete a course. He walked, sighing, to the wards where he would demonstrate the state of pregnancy, labor, and delivery for the handful of the hundred and twenty who would be able to hear him, the half-dozen who would get an actual glimpse of what was going on.

In a moment wrangling would start as the whole hundred and twenty, whispering fiercely, fought to examine each of the twenty-six patients, who waited their onslaught with daily dread.

He passed among the beds, and as he came the faces of the women glowed, they raised on their elbows to see him, they smiled, they called to him cheerily. Even the women in labor forced themselves up in bed to smile at him. And for each he had a quick chuckle, a joke, a pat on the backside, a pretended peep of delight at a pendulous breast, a quick murmur of sympathy for a woman in torment. They waited for him, they followed him with their eyes, adoringly.

But for the attendants his arrival brought apprehension, for his eyes were everywhere, he could see dirt where one had just cleaned, he seemed to smell it out. And when he found it his rage could be heard in the street. He conducted no feuds, he was rigidly strict, but he was fair, he tolerated no abuses, he demanded only the rigid cleanliness whose interruption for a careless moment he knew would bring an epidemic.

This day, as he entered the largest of the tiny rooms, Fourmic hurried toward him, pale.

"A new case," he whined. "We can't explain it——"

He turned and went into the tiny ward, Ignaz Philipp close behind him. He reached a bedside. He put his hand instantly on the woman's forehead. The skin was burning. He whirled on Fourmic.

"Sir professor—I beg of you—listen to me——"

"Do you remember what I told you?" Ignaz Philipp advanced on him. Fourmic retreated.

"I took care of this case myself!" Fourmic cried rapidly. "I tell you I washed—I washed and washed again—I saw to her utensils—nothing has touched this woman——" He was badly frightened but he was obviously sincere.

Ignaz Philipp turned from Fourmic. He would deal with him later.

"Move her," he ordered. "Move her instantly."

The head midwife hurried in.

"We can't explain this, sir professor—I assure you—we have done everything——"

"Never mind. Never mind now. Move this woman."

"We have no room, sir——"

"Move her into the corridor. Put a bed in the hall. Hurry!"

A bed in the corridor was hastily made up. The woman was lifted to it.

And there, three days later, she died.

But on the second day another woman sickened, and then another, and when the woman in the corridor died, four women were mortally ill.

Now Ignaz Philipp barely left the hospital. Balassa and

378

Hirschler cared for his private patients. The carriage rides with Maria were over. He arrived home late each night, his shoulders stooped, grief tearing his heart, bewilderment, fear wild within him. His life's work hung in the balance, once again. He stood on the steps a moment before entering. He drew a deep breath. He curved his lips into a smile. He straightened his shoulders. He drew a deep breath. Then he banged open the door, calling cheerily.

"Maria! Come kiss your husband."

And Maria would fly from the window where she had been waiting for him and watching him, and pretend she had been surprised in the kitchen. She would run to him, smiling in amazement.

"You home, Naci? I didn't hear you come in. You're late, aren't you?"

"Little trouble at the hospital." He shrugged, smiling. "Nothing serious . . ."

In the night she would awaken and put her arm fiercely across his sleeping body and bite her lip softly and stare wide-eyed, praying.

The deaths continued. In one short month he bowed to more deaths than he had seen in any year in nine years.

He drove himself mercilessly. He drove his staff relentlessly. He walked the wards, haggard, his eyes reddened, stumbling for lack of sleep. He examined everything. He redoubled the chlorine washing. He stopped the students' examinations. He stopped Fourmic's examinations, and young Bathory, his assistant. No midwife, no attendant was allowed to touch a patient. He made all examinations himself.

The deaths continued.

One morning, faltering desperately down the corridor, the screams of two dying women piercing his ears, he happened to glance into the largest room. A nurse was helping a new arrival into bed. The covers were thrown back. He gaped incredulously.

On the bottom sheet of the bed the patient was preparing to enter was a large, dark stain. For a moment he stared, paralyzed. Then he stumbled into the room. His face was deathly pale. He looked wordlessly at the bed. He looked at the nurse.

"New arrival, sir." She smiled. Then to the woman: "Get in dear, get in, you'll catch your death of cold——"

"Stop!" He found his voice. "Stop!" he shouted hoarsely.

They looked at him, amazed.

He pointed a quivering finger at the soiled sheet.

"Do you know what that is?"

"It's lochia, sir," the bewildered nurse said. "Discharge. From the last patient——"

He stared at her. She could hardly think coherently.

"You mean—you were going to let her lie down—on that?"

"Yes, sir. Is anything wrong——?"

He seized her suddenly by the back of the neck and forced her head down to the sheet.

"Smell it!" he roared. "Smell it, you blind dog! There's your murder—you murderer—that's what you've been doing—you've killed them! You've killed them all!"

He gave her a great shove and she sprawled across the bed and whirled, her hands raised defensively.

The head midwife ran in.

"There's your murderer!" He pointed at the supine attendant. "She's been putting healthy patients in these filthy, fouled, stained, stinking sheets—she doesn't even change them——"

He advanced on the attendant, his hands curled. The head midwife seized his arm.

"She shouldn't have done it!" she cried rapidly. "But remember yourself, Doctor——"

"What am I going to do?" the attendant whimpered. "I can't help it if there's not enough sheets to go around—I can't put them on the bare mattress——"

Ignaz Philipp turned to the midwife.

"It's true." She nodded. "It's very true."

He ran to the linen closet. Perhaps a dozen sheets lay on the shelves.

"If I use those," wailed the nurse, "then we have none until next week—and the bed I was putting her in is the cleanest we've got!"

Ignaz Philipp looked at them each in turn. The breath was spurting through his nostrils in sharp gasps. Suddenly he ran past them to the bed. He seized the sheet. He gave a mighty yank. The sheet left the bed. He made a ball of it. Without a word, clutching it tightly, he ran out of the ward, out of the university, into the office of Administrator Tandler.

Tandler looked up as Ignaz Philipp rushed in, breathing heavily.

"Ah, Professor! I've been meaning to call you in. Sit down. I hear we're having quite an epidemic—your theories don't seem to be working——"

"Theories!" Ignaz Philipp exploded. He shook the ball of sheet. "There's your epidemic!" He advanced on the desk. Tandler rose and retreated. "There's your stinking epidemic!" He pushed the foul sheet under Tandler's nose. "Smell it! That's death! Smell it well! It stinks, doesn't it! Sixteen dead for want of enough clean sheets!"

"Really, Doctor——"

"Sixteen dead—would you like to come and hear the last of them die?—sixteen dead, because the great Pesth hospital hasn't enough clean sheets for the mothers of Hungary—so a yearly financial report will look nice—sixteen dead——" He followed Tandler around the office shaking the sheet in his face.

"I'll take it up at my earliest opportunity—the Honorable Minister for Culture and Education controls expenditures—I merely recommend them—be calm, Doctor, this is highly unnecessary——"

"You'll take it up, will you? I'll give you something to take up."

He threw the sheet on the floor at Tandler's feet. He walked rapidly out of the room. He ran downstairs to his carriage. He drove directly to a store.

"One hundred sheets!" he called out as he entered. "Hurry!"

"One hundred sheets——?"

"And one hundred pillowcases!"

"Now?"

"Now!"

Three clerks hastily ran to the shelves, to the rear rooms, they ran to the carriage, heavily laden. They ran back for more.

"And who shall I charge these to?"

"Charge them to me! Dr. Semmelweis! Send the bill to this address."

And he jumped into the carriage then and drove at a gallop back to the hospital.

"A clean sheet for every bed!" he thundered.

"Yes, Dr. Semmelweis——"

"Not only when a patient leaves! The moment a sheet is soiled—remove it!"

The death stopped instantly. No more women sickened.

But the year was ruined. The record was a target, now, no longer a shield. Doctors began to speak guardedly about the inevitability of childbed fever. The Semmelweis doctrine was a fine thing, no doubt, but—well, one had only to look at the record. It's true Dr. Semmelweis blamed it on sheets, it's true the epidemic seemed to be over. But then who really knew what caused childbed fever, when all was said and done? The epidemics came—and when they were ready to go—they went.

Ignaz Philipp groaned helplessly. He lost weight rapidly. Maria would wake in the night to see him striding up and down the room, his fist noiselessly hitting his open palm. A fortnight after the epidemic halted an article appeared in a medical journal, written by Anselm Martin, of Munich, citing a Munich epidemic, and stating learnedly that the cause of childbed fever was unknown.

And in the next mail was a copy of the *Dublin Quarterly Journal*. And in this Dr. Murphy, Professor of Midwifery at University College, gave a full report of the Semmelweis doctrine and did his best to explain its tremendous value.

In another week or two news of the Pesth outbreak would

begin to spread inexorably through Europe, nullifying the Murphy article, canceling all he had suffered for, dooming more women irrevocably.

There was one thing to do. He drove home from the clinic, absorbed, coming nearer to the brink. He entered the house. For once he did not call out for Maria. She came to him swiftly.

"Is anything wrong, darling? Are you all right, dearest?" She inspected him anxiously. He smiled tenderly.

"Nothing's wrong." His face relaxed.

"Good, my sweetest. Good, my angel. Hurry and change! We're going to Mama's tonight."

He shook his head.

"No, darling. Not tonight. I've got something I must begin— have we got paper?—pens?"

She stared at him in astonishment. "Are you going to write?"

"I'm going to become a writer . . ."

He walked to his study. She looked after him, her mouth open.

He sat down at his desk. He found a sheet of paper. He trimmed a quill. He dipped it into the inkpot.

He began to write another sermon, from another mount. He began to write the life and death of human women. He wrote the title boldly,

THE ETIOLOGY, THE CONCEPT,
AND THE PROPHYLAXIS OF CHILDBED FEVER
And below it,
*By Ignaz Philipp Semmelweis. . . .*

# TWENTY

BEFORE him stretched a sea of notes and data. He plunged happily. He had preserved his laborious notes meticulously. The records of the years were heaped in his desk. There were deaths here, and the reasons for deaths. There was prevention and the reason for prevention. There were thousands of cases and thousands of days and proof after inexorable proof. He began to assemble the annihilating logic of statistics.

And each night, to document his facts, to present a universal picture, he wrote long letters to the heads of lying-in hospitals throughout the world, asking for their experiences with childbed fever.

Elsewhere, in England, France, Germany, Austria, Bohemia, Switzerland, Denmark, Sweden, Russia, Italy, wherever there were lying-in hospitals, perhaps as few as ten thousand women died of childbed fever each year. And perhaps as many died as thirty-five thousand. And perhaps five times that. Each year of those eleven years.

In his professional career he had applied his discovery to the delivery of eight thousand, five hundred and thirty-seven women. And in those eleven years one hundred and eighty-four women had died of childbed fever. His mortality record, since his discovery, was 0.02 per cent.

Without cquipment, without gleaming tile, in tiny rooms suffocating with the exhalations of open sewers and of privies, with inadequate bed linen, indifferently washed, without rubber gloves or sterilizers, antibiotics, wonder drugs, with ignorant and unfriendly and disloyal helpers, before even a knowledge that germs existed as the cause for infection, he had achieved a mortality rate from childbed fever lower than the world has ever known.

He set to work now, once again, to persuade doctors by these official records to adopt the simple principles by which women bearing children and the unborn doomed to die might still be saved.

He spent long hours on a single page. He puzzled endlessly over each sentence. He wrote and rewrote. He was not articulate with a pen, it was a strange and dismaying instrument he did not like and had not learned to use persuasively. But the statistics, the figures, they were articulate. He dipped his pen. He consulted the records. He checked and checked again. He wrote slowly, laboriously on.

Maria sat near by. She sewed. She watched him with pity and compassion, yearning to relieve him, to take his labor to herself. In the mornings he went briskly to the clinic. His work at the university finished, they made rounds together. Usually he made a last trip to the clinic; a careful, final inspection for the day.

For the rest, they were content with each other. When she could detach him from a part of his routine they went on long walks together. Sometimes in the evenings Poldi Hirschler and his wife or Markussovsky would visit them.

The knowledge that Ignaz Philipp had begun to write spurred Markussovsky. In late January he announced excitedly that he was ready to send to the printer the first copy of the *Orvosi Hetilap,* the first medical journal Pesth had seen since the *Orvosi Tar* was suspended during the revolution.

"I know you're busy on your great work—but if you could possibly find the time—if we could have an article by you——"

"Of course, Marko." And he stopped work on the *Etiology* to write a synopsis of the doctrine and the effect of its application in the Pesth Clinic.

And it was in February that Maria faced him, troubled, across the dinner table.

"I wonder if I'm sick, Naci?"

He put down his fork carefully. His heart gave a great bound of fear. He forced emotion from his face.

"A big healthy girl like you! Why do you say that?"

"I think something's wrong."

"Do you have any pain, darling?" He rose and walked slowly to her side. He put his hand against her forehead. He felt no fever.

"I feel all right." She hesitated. "But—nothing happened to me this month!"

"Nothing happened to you . . ." He savored the words slowly. Fear fled. His eyes widened, in his ears was suddenly the sound of beating wings. "Nothing happened to you, darling?"

And at the look on his face her own eyes widened, comprehending.

"Naci—do you think?—tell me, Naci——"

"Wait, now! Wait! It's too early to think——"

"Oh, Naci! A baby! Oh, my. Oh, my——"

"Now, don't let's get our hopes up——"

"A baby!"

She jumped from her chair. She smoothed her dress over her belly and looked at it searchingly.

"Not yet, foolish angel! There won't be anything there for months——"

"It's there, though! I can feel it!"

"No, you can't feel it. Not yet."

"I know it's there! I know it!"

But he was wiser than Maria, and knew well that one month was no real test, and prayed it might be true, and did his best to cushion her against the chance that it wasn't, and she laughed at him happily and began to sew in earnest.

And March passed, and she grinned at him triumphantly. And April. And now there was no longer any doubt.

"A baby——!"

"Our own baby——!"

"We're going to have a child, darling!"

He charged about his ways remade, strength surged in him, during lectures he paused and smiled, to the bewilderment of the students, in the wards he gazed fondly at his mothers, drawn to them by a new bond of understanding, sharing their hopes more vividly, caring for them with new compassion and gentleness and fierce protection. And Maria's lovely face wore a soft smile almost constantly now, and her features seemed to blur a little and her eyes became placid. When they walked, when they went to the homes of their friends, they began to touch each other surreptitiously, reassuringly, they looked at each other yearningly, endless glances full of meaning and love.

In the nights they lay awake, thinking long thoughts, speculating, planning, their minds caressing each new thought in a lovely anguish of intolerable joy.

"It will be a boy," Maria would whisper suddenly.

"Maybe a girl . . ."

"If it is a girl we will drown it, as the mothers do in China."

"You will not drown my daughter."

"I will put her head in a bucket."

"Maria!"

"I want to give you a boy."

"You're not the only one that's giving. I did something too."

"You! What you did!"

"You couldn't have a baby without me, just the same."

"Don't you want a boy?"

"Of course I want a boy. But most of all I want a baby."

"Our own child, Naci . . . our very own . . ."

And he tensed and reached his arms to her in an unbearable access of longing and delight.

In May her slim, boyish belly had begun to round a little. She stared at it, stupefied with triumph and pride.

"Cover yourself! Look at you—lying there admiring yourself!"

"Look at it, Naci!"

"You're going to catch cold——" He came to the bed.

"See how big I am!"

He looked down at her, trembling with pride, tingling with the sight of her loveliness. He bent quickly and kissed her belly.

"Look! Don't kiss me—look!"

"That wasn't for you. That was for the baby."

"When will I get bigger, Naci?"

He pulled the bedclothes over her.

"A peanut like you will probably never get any bigger!" He struggled to keep his voice from shaking.

"Really, Naci——!"

"My darling, you're going to get big. You're going to stick out in front like—like your backside had slipped around in front—then you're going to start complaining, 'Oh, Naci! I'm getting too big——' "

"Never!"

" 'Oh, Naci, Naci! Make me smaller!' "

"I want to be the biggest pregnant woman in Budapest. Bigger."

"Maybe you ought to have a maid, Maria. What do you think?"

"What for?"

"I don't want you lifting things—heavy things—and I don't want you stretching, reaching——"

"I want no maids in my house for my husband to look at. Get that right out of your head. I'm a perfectly healthy girl. Go on to your foul clinic and leave me alone with my baby. Such things to say for those pretty, tiny ears to hear!"

He bent to kiss her. Their lips met. Suddenly she wrenched her head away. "Naci!" Her eyes were wide.

"What happened? What's the matter?"

She stared at him. "It—it moved!"

He looked at her, his mouth open, his mind racing.

"Are you sure?"

"It moved, Naci! It moved! It moved!"

He sat down on the bed, weakly, and began to stroke her arm.

"It's alive now——"

"Yes, darling. Now it's alive . . ."

As May neared its end she began to plan for an anniversary party.

"It's too much work," he worried. "We'll go out—we'll go to the same restaurant where we had our wedding supper——"

"No, Naci, I want it to be in our own home. I'm a woman and I want to show off a little. I want people to come and I want to have the feeling that I'm showing them all we've got." Her eyes danced.

"I wonder what Papa and Mama will give us?"

"Oh! Papa and Mama——?" He smiled back, inwardly appalled. He had forgotten about an anniversary present. "Well —I suppose—well, good-by, darling—I have an appointment —a patient—I forgot——"

And he rushed to Markussovsky.

"What will I get her? Tell me, Marko!"

"What does she need?"

"I don't know."

"Has she ever mentioned anything?"

"I—I don't know."

"Oh, my God! What a brain! Full professor—director of a lying-in hospital—great discoverer—come on, come on! We'll go to the stores . . ."

On the way to the stores Markussovsky had an inspiration. He hurried Ignaz Philipp to Weidenhofer.

"What has she always wanted? Something you've heard her say?"

"Ever since she was a little girl," Weidenhofer said promptly, "she has been begging for a pair of diamond earrings."

"Wonderful!" Ignaz Philipp beamed as they walked along again. "Now everything's easy!"

"Easy! Do you know how much diamonds cost?"

"More than Maria?"

"More than you made in a year as assistant!"

"That's fine! I've got that much."

He gave them to her just before the Hirschlers arrived, as she was giving her hair a final pat, as she was reaching for her jewel box to put on the plain gold earrings she cherished.

"I wouldn't put those on," he said, trembling with excitement, his voice uneven.

"Why not, darling?" She turned, surprised.

"Gold," he said, his lips stiff. "Bad for pregnant women."

"Really? I didn't know——" She looked at the gold earrings, surprised that they had suddenly become dangerous.

"Try these," he said diffidently, and brought the package awkwardly from behind his back.

"What is it? What have you got?" She tore the wrapping from the tiny box. She opened it. She sat down. The diamonds winked at her merrily. She began to cry. "Oh, Naci, Naci . . ."

"Now, don't cry. Don't excite yourself. Remember the baby!"

387

But she was already fastening them in her ears. She stared at the mirror, dazed.

"Diamonds—real diamonds!" she whispered.

"You look beautiful!"

"The size of cannon balls!"

"For my darling . . ."

Her hands flew to her mouth.

"But they cost a fortune! Oh, Naci! You shouldn't——"

"Give them to me. I'll take them back." He put out his hand. She seized his wrists. She looked earnestly at him.

"For the baby——?"

"For you, my angel. For you alone!"

He pulled her upright. There was a knock at the door. The Hirschlers had arrived. In a little while the small apartment was filled. There were the Hirschlers and Balassa, Markussovsky, the Weidenhofers, Lenhosset, and young Bathory. They ate the dinner Maria had cooked, exclaiming with pleasure at each new dish, and Ignaz Philipp at the head of the table beamed proudly.

"My wife!" he cried out repeatedly. "What do you think of her?" He put his arm around her waist. "Come! Tell me!"

And Maria pinched him, and he beamed on, intolerably happy.

Later, he took Markussovsky into his study to show him the small pile of papers that was to be the *Etiology*. Markussovsky nodded soberly. He turned to his friend. He put his hand on his shoulder.

"You're lucky, Naci. I used to worry about you—worry about you a lot. But now you'll be all right."

He worked fiercely now, proudly. The book began slowly to grow. He read, he devoured periodicals from all over the world.

Cocaine had been discovered, and aniline dyes, and spectrum analysis. Darwin had published *The Origin of Species*. The Atlantic cable had been laid. A new railroad had been finished connecting Budapest with Vienna. The Bessemer steel process was four years old. Ether and chloroform had come into general use. Florence Nightingale had begun the profession of nursing.

The replies to his letters began to arrive.

The first reply was from Levy, of Copenhagen, to whom the doctrine had been explained long ago by Michaelis.

We don't permit students to dissect any longer while they are taking their six months' course in midwifery. No precautions are taken except ordinary cleanliness; it is a very unusual thing for the staff to employ chlorine disinfection. At any rate many people appear to be predisposed to infection and puerperal fever assumes many forms. Your indifference and inefficiency in applying methods of investigation are, to say the least, regrettable . . .

Ignaz Philipp put aside the *Etiology*. Patiently he wrote a long letter to Levy, regretting that Levy still viewed childbed fever in the same way as he had regarded its cause and prevention eleven years ago, explaining doggedly the complete doctrine, sympathizing with the epidemics that still swept Denmark's lying-in hospitals, citing the almost unbelievable records of Pesth.

From Litzmann, who had replaced Michaelis long ago at Kiel, came the next letter.

We have instructed our students to take greater care in cleanliness . . . but the chief cause of the better results lies with our care taken to prevent overcrowding . . . This foresight Michaelis did not exercise. Further, it is evident that childbed fever begins in the country and the town and not in the hospital, to which it still unfortunately spreads . . .

Ignaz Philipp laid down the letter.
"What's the matter, dear?"
"Oh, it's nothing. Nothing at all. Just an . . . unusual . . . letter . . ."
"Your face is red. You look strange. I wish you'd stop reading those letters."
"I can't stop."
"Well, be calm, then."
"I'll try . . ."
A reply came from Steiner, at Gratz.
"You look happy——"
"An old pupil, darling——"
"What does he say?"
He began to read.

"Infection of all sorts occurs at the Gratz Lying-in Hospital . . . the dissecting room is the only place where the students can meet and pass the time when waiting for their midwifery cases, and they often devote their time to dissecting or studying and manipulating preparations. When they are summoned to the Lying-in Hospital, which is just across the street, they do not make any pretense at disinfection; some of them do not even wash their hands . . . The patients might as well be delivered in the dissecting room . . ."

He lowered the letter. They stared at each other.
"It's unbelievable, Naci. I don't believe it!"
He read on.

389

"As it is, the students cross the street with hands wet and bloody from the dissecting; they dry their hands in the air and stick them a few times in their pockets and at once proceed to make examinations . . . It is no longer a riddle to me why after a clinical meeting the medical officer of Gratz exclaimed: 'The lying-in hospitals are really nothing but murder institutions!' "

Virchow, who was then viciously attacking Darwin, did not deign to reply to him. Scanzoni, Braun, most of the great names of Germany and Austria continued serenely to teach and to practice the theory of miasma and the thirty causes of childbed fever, beginning with the first cause, pregnancy.

The Paris Academy of Medicine conferred learnedly.

Depaul suggested that the only prevention of childbed fever was the construction of smaller hospitals. Beau rose and stated that childbed fever was a local inflammation, the treatment being large doses of quinine. Hervez de Chegoin followed. He said that childbed fever arose in the uterus. Trousseau tried to make himself heard with the statement that childbed fever seemed also to attack men. But the great Dubois intervened at once. He began to speak of the bilious appearance of the disease. Cruveilhier said it might possibly arise from a wound origin. But Danyau rose stoutly.

"For me childbed fever is a malady of miasmatic origin! The allegations concerning the transmission of the disease by the medical attendant, as mentioned by Semmelweis of Vienna, lately referred to as the Pesth Fool [laughter], are not convincing—and appear to have found few supporters in Germany."

Cazeaux pronounced it a mysterious influence, cause unknown. Bouillaud said earnestly that it was a special condition of pregnancy. Dubois summed for them all.

"It is nothing but an epidemic and they bring it to the hospital, these women pregnant or in labor, already infected. The remedy is to close the lying-in institutions."

The report of the meeting of the French Academy reached Budapest.

In the living room Maria sat happily with her father and mother.

Ignaz Philipp appeared suddenly in the doorway of his study.

"There must be a God!" he shouted hoarsely. "There must be a God who sees these things!"

His face was purple. His features were swollen with rage. In one fist he clenched the copy of the Paris meeting.

"Almighty God!" he yelled, and began to tear the papers into great shreds.

Maria rushed to him. She threw her arms around him.

"Naci! Naci, darling——"

He stared at her. Suddenly he began to cry. The Weidenhofers looked at each other. Abruptly Ignaz Philipp shook his head fiercely. He stopped crying. He tried to smile.

"From Paris, Naci? From France?"

He nodded brokenly.

"I'm sorry," he said, shamed. "I'm very sorry."

"Everyone knows the French are dirty," Frau Weidenhofer said indignantly.

"They might at least copy the English," said Weidenhofer.

Ignaz Philipp looked up. His face began to redden. The pulse in his temple beat faster.

"In England," he cried, "they sometimes bury them two in a coffin to conceal the horror!"

"It's all right, Naci," begged Maria. "Be calm, darling. Finish the book. Once and for all they'll have to see . . ."

They looked at each other. His face relaxed. He tried to smile. She pressed his hand. The evening passed. They talked determinedly of other things.

Next day Weidenhofer came to Maria while Ignaz Philipp made his rounds.

"I don't like the way his eyes looked last night."

"He had cause to be angry, Father. Believe me. For eleven years now he's proven over and over again the reason women die of childbed fever—he's begged them to listen—he's shown them how easy it is not to have it—and after eleven years—this!"

"He gets too excited. I don't like it."

"You don't have to like it."

"Maria!"

"He's my husband! When he wants to get mad he can get mad! He's the finest man in the whole world! He can do what he pleases and I don't need anyone coming here to criticize him! Do you understand, Father? You or Mother or anyone!"

Ignaz Philipp put aside the *Etiology* and began long and patient replies to the letters. Endlessly he went over the old ground, endlessly explaining, endlessly citing the results. After a month he resumed writing the book. He wrote determinedly, slowly, fact upon fact. This time the murder would end. The book would end it.

But each afternoon Maria made him stop work for a space. And sometimes they simply walked the streets of Pesth, or roamed about Buda. And sometimes they sat with their arms about each other's waists, on a boat floating slowly down the Danube. And sometimes they headed the carriage for a long drive into the countryside and a quiet picnic. Maria was quite large now. She regarded herself with satisfaction.

"It's going to be a big baby. A great big boy."

"Our baby, Maria. Can you believe it? Our very own."

"But a boy."

"I don't care, Maria. I just want a baby. Our baby."

"I can't wait, Naci . . ."

"I can't either . . ."

In late July the head midwife came upon Fourmic and the head attendant examining a woman in labor.

"But your hands!" she protested. They turned. "Aren't you going to wash your hands? You, Niesler, you know better! I won't have it!" The head attendant reddened sheepishly.

"We've had a fine year so far——" the head midwife began stubbornly.

Fourmic laughed contemptuously.

"Really, my dear head midwife. Are you still committed to the eccentricities of our good director?"

The head attendant laughed appreciatively.

Suddenly the deaths began.

Ignaz Philipp rushed about the wards frantically. He pitted everything he knew against this new invasion. He became gray with fatigue. His face was lined with worry. He stole from his bed at nights to sit up with dying women, to try to pull them back to life by the very force of his despairing will. And the next day another died, and then another, and, one dreadful day, two. At the end of three weeks he was reeling and haggard. He had checked the washing, the utensils, there was plenty of linen. The death toll reached eighteen. In the wards were two cases of gangrene of the genitals. He could not isolate them. There was no room. He put two attendants to watch them, one of these the head attendant. He gave them the strictest order to touch no other patients. And one day he came into the wards unexpectedly, in time to see the head attendant examining a woman in labor.

He rushed to the bedside. Bathory came up in time to intercept him as he sprang at the woman.

"Get out of here!" he screamed. "If you're not out of this hospital in five minutes I'll have you arrested." He struggled with Bathory, trying to reach her with his hands. The woman fled.

Shakily, Ignaz Philipp tried to compose himself. He drew back the covers to examine the frightened patient. He recoiled.

"That stain! Was that stain there when you got into this bed, Mother?"

The patient nodded, speechless. A young attendant came up timidly.

"She didn't change the linen very much, sir director——"

Fourmic came in.

"What's the trouble?" he asked easily.

Ignaz Philipp looked at him steadily, his face white. He pointed to the bed.

"That is your responsibility, Dr. Fourmic——"

"Oh, now surely, Doctor——" Fourmic began deprecatively.

"Head Attendant Niesler has been discharged. I caught her examining this patient against my repeated and vehement orders—issued in your presence——"

"And a good thing you did, sir director! I've always thought she was careless!"

Ignaz Philipp stared at Fourmic fixedly.

"I hope you're not displeased with me, sir director——"

Ignaz Philipp turned and left the ward. He left the university. He walked the streets, numb and defeated. He walked a long time. Finally he turned toward home.

From the window Maria watched him, saw his slumped shoulders, his dragging walk, his bent head. She watched him as he climbed the steps, saw him compose his face, straighten his shoulders, draw a breath, force himself to smile. She heard his knock. She made herself wait a moment. Then she walked quickly to the door, smiling.

"Home so soon? Have you come to see the doctor? Who shall I say it is?"

"Just an old man. Just an old, old man looking for a young wife . . ." He smiled at her fixedly.

She took his arm and drew him inside.

At the university, Fourmic meditated, where Ignaz Philipp had left him. He made up his mind. He waited until Ignaz Philipp was out of the building. Then he went swiftly to the office of Administrator Tandler.

When Ignaz Philipp arrived at the university next morning a letter from Tandler was on his desk.

Reports have been made confidentially which have to do with manifold inefficiencies and imperfections in the obstetrical clinic of the Imperial and Royal University, that, for example, through the negligence of the head midwife not only are the bedclothes of the women seldom changed, but even the bloodstained bedclothes of dead women are spread under newly admitted women, and, as a result, the mortality has reached such a high point that, on one day, even ten women died.

This fact must be even more shocking in view of the appeal last year for more bed linen which was granted so fully that the high cost of providing it did not escape the notice of the Honorable Ministry for Culture and Education . . .

Shock after shock, blow after blow. Ignaz Philipp picked up his pen wearily.

. . . There were never more than two deaths in one day . . . the disaster is due entirely to chance and offers fresh

393

and tragic proof of the correctness of my views on the origin of childbed fever . . . it was the head attendant and not the head midwife who was responsible, and this guilty person has been discharged . . .

He finished the letter. A phrase from Tandler's official rebuke returned to his mind. ". . . Reports have been confidentially made . . ."

He picked up his pen again. He wrote a second note to Tandler.

I should be obliged to you if you will find some post for Dr. Fourmic, whose energies and understanding entitled him to better leadership than I am able to give him. He is an excellent worker and has a busy mind. As of this date I shall respectfully expect his transfer elsewhere.

Fourmic left. Bathory was appointed assistant. The wards became quiet again. The book called. He resumed his work upon it. It would be necessary now to overcome this new mischance. The book must do it. He worked harder.

Maria suffered under the heat. He watched her anxiously. He brought flowers, he fanned her, nights she would awaken and find him standing over her, watching, smiling. Toward the end of August the heat abated. The crisp weather of September brought relief. At the clinic, Bathory labored without respite. Each day the wards were cleaner. Each day Ignaz Philipp seemed to have a little less to do. And when he smiled, seeing these things, Bathory tingled with worship and threw himself into the work harder than before.

September was passing. Maria, in the last few months, seldom rode with him on his rounds. Now she stopped accompanying him. Her belly had become huge.

"He moves all the time, Naci. Is he coming soon?"

"He'd better. You'll burst."

She patted his face lovingly.

"He's going to be a comfort to his father, after all the trouble he's had . . . he'll make it up to you, darling . . ."

"Do you feel all right, Maria?"

"I feel fine. I feel pregnant—but I feel fine. He'll have blue eyes, Naci——"

"Violet, like his mama——"

"Blue, Naci. I want them blue——"

"And I can play with him——Oh, God, how long I've waited for a child of my own——"

"But you must be gentle with him—you mustn't beat him when he's bad——"

"Beat him! Beat my baby?"

"What will he be, Naci? Will he be a doctor, like you?"

394

"I'll tell you something, Maria. He'll be exactly what he wants to be!"

"Suppose he wants to be a street cleaner!"

"Then he'll be a street cleaner. I'm not going to ruin a good street cleaner to make a poor doctor."

"He'll be the finest doctor in the world. Next to his papa."

He drew her on his lap.

"I'm going to bounce him on my knee—Boom-ditty-boom-ditty-boom-boom-boom——"

"Don't shake me, Naci! Stop! He's kicking! He knows what you're doing——"

He threw his arms around her.

"I love you, Maria . . ."

"I adore you, Naci . . ."

They sat awhile in silence.

"He'll make up to you, Naci," she murmured drowsily. "He'll make up to you for everything . . ."

September ended.

Now the days began to pass one by one. They waited warily. She moved slowly, sluggishly. He hovered over her. He became more frantic each hour he was away from her. He brought home a maid to watch her, to run to the hospital after him.

"Soon, Naci?"

"Any day now, little Maria."

"I hope so. I hope it's soon."

"Any day now . . ."

"Hurry, baby . . . hurry, little son . . ."

On October fourteenth he turned over the clinic to Bathory. He asked Balassa to call on those of his patients who were seriously ill. He hurried home. As he stepped from the carriage the maid burst from the door, dressed to run to the hospital.

"Hurry, doctor," she cried, halting at the sight of him. He raced up the steps. She ran after him. From the bedroom came the sound of an animal in pain. Maria was in labor.

He rushed to the bedroom.

And now for his own wife and best beloved of all the world began that hour, that endless process of time and slow destiny from whose inexorable agony no woman could be spared. He wiped the sweat from her wet face. He sat silent. His heart bled, his brain staggered, his knuckles were white, and he was her husband. And she cried out and he listened, staring, alert, and he was her doctor. And between the pains they smiled at each other, white-faced. Toward evening he began to move about her swiftly. He washed his hands for the seventh time, he rinsed them again in chlorine solution. He bent over her. His hand entered her body. He began the timeless exhortation of the hour come.

"Don't yell, Maria . . ."
And she screamed.
". . . Save your breath, my darling . . ."
And her face purpled with the effort.
"Strain, my darling, my angel, harder, harder."
And she strained.
". . . Harder . . . harder . . ."
She collapsed, breathing heavily, spent. Almost immediately she leaped with new agony. A trickle of blood began to flow from her torn flesh.
"Hard, now! Harder! Squeeze! . . ."
"I can't . . . I can't . . . I . . ."
"Harder! Squeeze! Push! Strain!"
His hands closed on her huge abdomen. His fingers gripped, contracted, wrung her belly.
*"Now!"*
The head pushed out. It rested there, in the world, waiting. He turned its shoulder. He drew it forth. There was a faint cry. The child was born.
On the bed Maria was quiet. He cut the cord. He handed the child quickly to the maid. He went to the bedside. She opened her eyes. She stared at him mutely, questioning.
"A son, Maria! A boy! A fine, wonderful boy! An angel of God!"
"A boy," she said weakly. "A boy," she whispered again. She closed her eyes. A tear crept from beneath her eyelids. He bent and kissed it, kissed her on the mouth, ran to the foot of the bed.
In an hour all had been done. The child lay in a cradle beside the bed. Maria, sponged and clean, dozed weakly. An hour later she heard the child cry and awakened.
"A boy?"
"A boy, darling. Really and truly a boy."
"He cries loud . . ."
"He's a warrior!"
"Our boy . . . our son, Naci . . ."
His hand closed over hers. He could not speak.
At eleven o'clock there was a knock at the door. The maid admitted Bathory. Ignaz Philipp drew him to the door of the bedroom. He gestured to the dim figure of the sleeping Maria, the tiny cradle. Then he drew Bathory away.
"A boy!" he whispered. He grinned hugely, his eyes wet.
Bathory shook his hand happily. Then his face sobered.
"What's wrong?" asked Ignaz Philipp.
"It's a breech, sir. A bad breech . . ."
In the carriage Bathory turned to him apologetically.
"She's getting weaker. She wanted the priest. I think it's hopeless . . . but you said always to call you . . ."
"You've done right, my boy. Absolutely right."

396

He leaped from the carriage. They entered the clinic. By a bedside in the delivery room a priest read quietly from his breviary to the moaning figure in the bed.

Ignaz Philipp looked at the woman an instant, then ran quickly to wash. He hurried back to the bedside. He bent over the woman.

It was a frank breech, the thighs flexed, the legs extended on the child's anterior surface. His hands moved deftly, the courage and the knowledge of the years flowed into him, he was skill now, all skill and resolution. Bathory looked on, amazed. The child's heels appeared. He turned the body slightly. Now the hips were free. He moved again. An instant later the child was free to the shoulders, then the neck. And finally the head came safely forth.

He stood back. He went to the buckets and began to wash. A half-hour had passed. Bathory came to his side, dazed.

"I don't believe it!"

"Don't chide yourself. I had a little luck too."

The priest was shutting his breviary.

"Maybe he had something to do with it." Ignaz Philipp nodded. He dried his hands. The priest was starting toward the door.

"A moment, sir!" he called.

The priest turned. Ignaz Philipp grinned at him.

"I've got a job for you."

"Yes, Doctor?"

"A baptism!"

The priest smiled.

"Tonight? Bring it to me tomorrow."

Ignaz Philipp strode to him and took his arm.

"Tonight!" he said. "For my baby we waste no time!"

The maid admitted them.

"He's been crying pretty loud," she said doubtfully.

"Of course he's been crying loud! We've got a fighter there!"

They entered the bedroom. Maria awoke. She blinked at the sight of the priest.

"What will we call him, angel? What will we call your little warrior?"

She shook her head.

"Naci! At this hour of the night!" She smiled happily. "Call him—what else but Ignaz?"

He stooped. He held the baby in his arms. He drew the cover from its head. The priest began the service of baptism. The holy drops sprinkled on the tiny forehead. The child screwed up its small mouth. He gave a hard, loud cry. Ignaz Philipp looked at him, surprised.

He turned his head and winked proudly at Maria.

The service ended. The priest left. He sat down in a chair by

Maria's bedside. She began to breathe quietly. He closed his eyes for a moment. When he awoke it was morning.

"You could sleep under a waterfall!" said Maria reproachfully. "Listen to him! Listen to that son of yours!"

The child lay in her arms. They looked at him tenderly.

"Our son! Our boy! Our very own!"

The child which had been quiet a moment now began to mewl an odd, hard cry.

"Isn't he loud? Isn't he wonderful?"

Something stirred in Ignaz Philipp's thoughts, something, he could not remember what, tugged at his memory uneasily. Suddenly he bent. He put his hand on the child's head. The child cried loudly.

"Is something the matter, Naci? Is anything wrong?"

"No, no. Everything's all right."

"Our boy . . . our own little Naci-boy . . ."

After noon the child's crying became louder. An hour later it cried again, less vigorously. It died at eight o'clock that evening.

The dead baby lay in its cradle beside the bed. Ignaz Philipp lay beside Maria. He tried to take her in his arms. She turned her wet face. He began to sob. Their tears ran together on the pillow.

Somehow the next day passed. And then the next. Small Ignaz was buried. A part of them was buried with him. After many days they could bear to talk about him.

"We'll have another, darling . . . I'll give you another . . ."

He had been daydreaming. He started and went to her side.

"I don't care, Maria. I've got you."

"We've got each other."

"You're my baby. You're enough for me."

"Forever, Naci . . . forever and ever . . ."

Markussovsky tried to draw him back to the book.

"Give me a piece of what you've done—just a piece of it. I want to publish it in the journal."

"Later, Marko . . . later . . . I don't want to think of it now . . ."

"You've always told me, Naci—it's the women, the other mothers—it's for them——"

"All right . . . come . . . take what you want . . ."

And Maria thanked Markussovsky quietly.

"He'll see it in print," Markussovsky whispered, "he'll get enthused again. It'll take his mind off—off——"

"Yes," said Maria. "Yes, Marko. You're a good friend."

The excerpt from the *Etiology* appeared in the journal. Ignaz Philipp roused a little. He returned to his work. In December a letter from the university presented him with the sum he had spent from his own pocket for bed linen more than a year before.

The year ended. They began to smile timidly. There was laughter in the house again. And in April Maria was with child, with a new child.

Now they kept close, now he hovered over her, silently, watching her every move. In the evenings she sat with him in his study and while he wrote feverishly on the book she did her best to unravel the disorder of his accounts; in the days they walked hand in hand, his eyes ever alert, watching her.

On November twentieth Maria bore a daughter. And they called her Mariska. And she was their delight. And a month passed, and the child bloomed rosily, and he raced home betimes to play with her toes. And the second month passed and the child gurgled at them, sputtered happily while they hugged each other and romped with her. And in the third month she was more beautiful than ever. And in this month Mariska sickened suddenly and died.

Now they clung to each other fiercely. Now they saw no one. His face had become deeply lined. He was almost entirely bald. He stooped heavily. He walked slowly. He rarely smiled. She clung to him. Sorrow had quieted her. She was no longer blithe. She was grave now, and she spent the long days at the window, waiting for his return. They spoke little. They had no need of words and no use for them. They no longer wept. There were no more tears.

He worked silently on.

In April he composed a letter to the government, asking for a new lying-in hospital. His pen moved slowly over the paper.

. . . the clinic is situated on the second floor, and indeed in the furthermost part of the building, so that the poor women in labor must not only travel considerable distances from the city but are compelled to drag themselves up two flights of stairs and down a long corridor . . . so that births on the stairs are not a rarity . . .

What have I done, he asked himself, what have I done to deserve all this . . . when will it stop . . . what have I done . . .

The old and rotting walls . . . the impossibly small rooms . . . no running water . . .

His pen wrote tiredly on.

Markussovsky, who had been appointed a Court Minister, took the letter, presented it in person.

"He must be cheered," he told Bathory. "We must uplift him. I am going to get him a new hospital if they kill me for it. Somehow we must make him keep trying."

"Courage—pity—mind . . . these three . . . no man can have more . . . no man but he can have so much . . ." Bathory said simply.

Ignaz Philipp wrote on. He watched with pathetic attention and wistfulness the progress of his doctrine in Europe. He was occasionally cheered by some solitary valiant who rose in some odd corner to support the discovery. But the deepest disappointment was his general, unfailing portion.

In July he roused. The government had granted his request for improvement of the clinic. The Lying-in Hospital was to be moved to the outskirts of the city. He began to write more swiftly. Maria smiled. She held him in her arms at night. She hugged him. She whispered love into his ear. And he reached for her, sad and content.

In August came the day when the *Etiology* was finished.

With Markussovsky and Maria he walked, to the printer's, dazedly carrying the huge pile of manuscript.

That night they returned to the olden days, they feasted in the Andrassy, they jumped into the carriage and whirled to the Roast Beef Club, they heard music, they danced, they laughed, and drank again.

The *Etiology* was published in August.

The great work was done. He sent it out into the world.

He smiled now. He waited confidently.

In a little while he laughed aloud. In November Maria had conceived again . . .

# TWENTY-ONE

NOW the year came bright with refreshed promise. The days were jubilant with waiting. The nights were soft and triumphant with love.

And he walked the earth like a man freed of a great and final duty, of an obligation to belief and art and life itself. All that he was, all the years of his life went out in that book. He had framed the fabric of his life and the imprint of his soul in those humble words, and they went forth with a prayer not for honors, and not for money, but simply to give life.

There could be no quibbling now, no misunderstanding, no complaint of ignorance. Within those pages, honestly documented, clear, patient, logical, and shining with the ardor of perfect truth, was an end to the ancient doom of motherhood, the death that waited all women from the day they were born.

It was complete.

It had been said. It had been proven. The way was shown. He waited. He walked his ways serene, a man whose broken life had been made whole by a faith beyond hope.

And from the world of medicine which received the *Etiology*, from universities, hospitals, and clinics, from the eminent and the renowned and the revered leaders of medical opinion, the answers were prepared swiftly.

"What will you do now that they have the book, now that childbed fever is over?" Maria demanded. "Poor Naci! You're going to have to live peacefully."

"We'll take a trip. We'll go to England, finally, and France. And maybe Russia. We'll go on our honeymoon."

"First I'll have the baby."

"Then the honeymoon."

"No, I've changed my mind. I want to be the first woman in our family to have a baby on her honeymoon."

From Prague, where the mortality reached 26 per cent, the first answer came from Breisky.

"No one but Semmelweis has observed any advantage from this prophylaxis, this strange washing. Childbed fever is caused by the unknown."

"It's just Breisky," Markussovsky implored swiftly. "You're not going to take that to heart? It happens to be the first answer . . . it's unfortunate . . . but surely, Naci . . ."

"He's only got to try, that's what I don't understand. For fifteen years now that's all I've been begging. It's simple, just try it, it can't hurt the patients, and here's the proven record that it stops the dying. And now I've made a book of it——"

"Come on, Naci, come, my angel. We'll go for a walk, the three of us——"

"We'll have a good dinner——"

"And we'll dance—smile, Naci! Come on, darling, smile for me!"

And within the week came letters from Dommes of Hanover, Pernice of Greifswald, Pippingskjold of Helsingfors. And they had read the book with surprise and great interest. And they had hope and would try.

Bathory smiled happily watching him stride about the wards that week. And the women smiled to hear his jokes again, and he lectured his class—which had grown now to eighty-three medical students and one hundred and ninety-nine midwives— with renewed patience, and at night he ran happily up the steps and he was reborn.

And while his heart sang, his spirit leaped, came a humble letter from Kugelmann. From Kugelmann of Hanover, a young man, a student of Michaelis.

401

Permit me to express . . . the holy joy with which I read your work . . . to a colleague I felt compelled to declare: This man is another Jenner . . .

It has been vouchsafed to very few to confer great and permanent benefits upon mankind, and with few exceptions the world has crucified and burned its benefactors . . .

I hope you will not grow weary in the honorable fight which still remains before you . . .

Ignaz Philipp lowered the letter.

"My God," he said when he could speak, "my dear God . ."

And Maria, her eyes streaming, tugged at his arm.

"Open the package, Naci."

With the letter had come a parcel. Beneath the wrapping was a book. He opened it. A sheet of paper fell out. On it was written:

"I humbly beg of you to accept my gratitude in my most prized possession."

He opened the book. It was a first edition of Jenner's original work, autographed by Jenner himself.

The *Etiology* had gone out into the world.

And there the little space of hope abruptly ended.

In the next weeks the venomous spears, the unending blows of the mighty sank in his heart, beat him without mercy and without pause.

The great Virchow, the man to whom all the world of medicine looked with reverence, rose at the German Society for the Advancement of Natural and Medical Sciences and said coldly that childbed fever was caused by erysipelas and inflammation of the lymph glands. And such men as Billroth and Weber acquiesced.

Ignaz Philipp sat down instantly, desperately, to reply. And even while his first slow sentences were shaping, Hecker of Munich protested indignantly,

"The strictest cleanliness is of little use in preventing such colossal outbreaks of childbed fever as we experience here. The doctrine of Semmelweis is one-sided, narrow, and erroneous."

"You've stirred them up," Markussovsky told him anxiously. "You see, Naci? You've got them aroused."

"Yes," said Ignaz Philipp wearily, "yes. Oh yes . . . yes . . . Well . . . I must answer, that's all . . . I must answer . . . the book . . . apparently, the book . . ."

"You leave the book to me. I'll take care of the book. We're not through yet. We haven't even begun . . . Come on, Naci . . . we've been through this before . . ."

402

"What do you want of me? Tell me, Marko! What do you want of my life?"

"I'm all for you, Naci. Be calm, old friend . . . be calm . . ."

"I'm sick of it, I tell you! I'm sick of these pompous asses—I'm sick of murderers who kill more than they cure—I'm sick of their airs, their low voices, their deep bows—I'm sick of their games—this is no game, this is life and death—I'm sick of liars—I'm sick of thieves—I'm sick of the whole filthy pack!"

He paused, ashen, trembling, and spit on the floor. Rage welled blinding again. He spit once more.

Without a word Maria left the room, came back with a rag, got down on her knees, and silently began to wipe the carpet.

"I've got to go now, Naci," Markussovsky said awkwardly.

"What are you going to do?"

"I'm going to put a piece in the *Orvosi Hetilap*. I'll give them something to open their eyes."

"Yes, that's right. That's good. That's the thing. Go on, Marko, you go ahead. That's right. That's the way to do."

Markussovsky looked at him, confused.

"We'll go to dinner tonight."

"Yes. That's right, Marko. That's fine."

Markussovsky left. Ignaz Philipp bent, took the rug gently from Maria's hand, raised her to her feet.

"It's all right, you know, Naci. I wasn't doing it to reproach you." He looked at her and nodded, not hearing. "Marko will write a good piece, he'll show them! Isn't it wonderful of him?"

He stared at her without answering.

"Naci!"

He sighed. He sat down tiredly.

"Yes, it's wonderful. That's what it comes to. Now it's wonderful. That'll make up for everything. Yes. Now we'll have a fiery little piece in a paper no one sees, written in Hungarian. And I can look at it, if I'm fool enough. I can fill my eyes with it. I can stare at it and make myself forget the world, forget the dying and the tortured. And I can see only that wonderful piece, which says everything I want, and be content. Yes . . . But nobody else will see it, Maria. Nobody where it matters. We are great men, Maria. See how we dedicate our whole lives to the relief of the sick and suffering. That is how we want you to think of us. Will you remember that, Maria, next time you pay our bill?"

She began to cry softly.

"No, don't cry, Maria. I've done my best. No, really. There is nothing more to say."

He nodded dully when the *Orvosi Hetilap* appeared, and a few days later he nodded again at an article by Fleischer, written in Hungarian. Bathory excitedly brought him *Froriep's Notizen.*

"What's this? What's this, my boy?"

He read the ringing defense of the doctrine. He gave the small journal indifferently back.

"That, that's fine! Isn't that fine, sir?"

"Yes, yes . . . that's fine . . ." He walked off. Bathory stared after him.

Now Maria set herself to cheer him. She took him, unprotesting, on long walks. She ignored his silence. She chattered brightly, determinedly, on. She called in Markussovsky, they drew him out of the house, to the theater, to Poldi Hirschler's. Slowly his sadness became gentler. One night they went to the Weidenhofers'.

"I don't really want to go, Maria."

"I know, but if I let you alone you wouldn't want to see anybody."

"That's right."

"But it's only right—you know that, sweetheart——"

"Yes."

They went to the Weidenhofers'.

"What's so glum?" cried Weidenhofer. "You look as if you'd lost a dozen patients!"

"Now, Father——"

"I've lost ten million." Ignaz Philipp stared at him steadily. "I've lost a hundred million. I've lost women who this moment are opening their mouths in the first birth pang. I've lost tomorrow's—all over the world a line of women are going into birth clinics—going to their deaths—I've lost them all."

"Oh, now surely not that bad——"

"I've lost the babies—how many great men—what suffering they might have lived to relieve—how they might have changed the world—God only knows. I've lost them all. I've lost the womb that waited to bear more. I've lost them all. And tomorrow I'll lose them again. And the next day. And the next and the next."

"But really, Naci, they're not your patients——"

"I am a doctor. Let me tell you something, Herr Weidenhofer. I know what it means to be a doctor. In my heart is the truth. All sickness is my sickness. All death that can be prevented is my labor—and if I know what will cure them, all women who are dying, are my women . . ."

"We'll talk of something else," Maria said.

"No, no. Your father does not seem to understand. Look, Herr Weidenhofer, I will explain it to you——"

"It's all right. I understand."

"And I tell you that you don't understand. You understand nothing."

404

"Naci! Why are you angry with Papa? Papa hasn't done anything to you."

"You're tired, Naci," Weidenhofer said tolerantly. "You're letting this thing run away with you."

"Do you think so?"

"Surely. A few weeks' rest—a few days in the country——"

"I've just told you that women are dying. What do you recommend? Come, you be the doctor. What do you suggest, shall I rest a little? And maybe they'll stop dying?"

Weidenhofer shrugged.

"If you're going to talk that way—I was only trying to help. You've spent your life trying to prove something. You've proven it. You've written a fine book about it. You've sent it to those who can put your theory into practice and stop a great evil. And they read it. And they'll have none of it. Well, what's there to do, then? What's any sensible man to do?"

"Just quit trying."

"That's right. You can't fight the human race. You've got your own life to live—and my daughter has a right to happiness, I'd like to add——"

"Weidenhofer, now I know what you are."

"Now, just a minute——"

"Now I see you through and through——"

"If it comes to that I've had my doubts about you for a long time, young man."

"Father, please—Naci——"

"No, no. He doesn't insult me in my own house!"

"How about the baby!" Frau Weidenhofer suddenly cried fiercely.

"What kind of man doesn't even send to tell the grandparents a baby's come! Tell me! I'd like to know! Tell me, since we're on the subject of knowing all about each other, what kind of man calls in a priest suddenly, at midnight, to rob the friends and the grandparents of the pleasure of a baptism——"

"Who knows," interrupted Frau Weidenhofer, "but the child might have been saved even——"

Maria stepped in front of Ignaz Philipp.

"Are you mad?" she shouted at her parents. "Do you dare?"

"The baby could not have been saved," Ignaz Philipp said levelly. "My son was doomed."

Maria turned, startled.

"He had hydrocephalus," Ignaz Philipp said quietly. "He had water, fluid, where it did not belong, in his small head."

They were silent.

"You can't blame that on Maria," Frau Weidenhofer said uneasily, at last. "She's always been healthy——"

"You'd like to blame it on me. I know. But I've always been healthy too."

"You might have told us. Look at her. You didn't even tell your own wife."

"I've known it all along!" Maria lied fiercely.

"I'm sorry I came here tonight," said Ignaz Philipp. "I don't think I'll trouble you again."

"As you please," said Weidenhofer stiffly.

"I didn't know you preferred to see post mortems on little babies. Next time there's another dissection I'll be sure to let you know. There's quite a bit to it. You'll revel in the details—you're a fine, sensible man—I won't try to protect you——"

Weidenhofer paled. Frau Weidenhofer began to cry. Maria took Ignaz Philipp's arm and drew him from the house. They were silent on the way home. At the door of their house he turned to her and laid his hand on her arm.

"Forgive me, Maria. They're your mother and father . . ."

"I wish it hadn't happened. But you're more important. We'll all forget. You'll see. It'll be forgotten."

And later, as they lay in bed, she stroked his arm.

"Was it my fault, Naci?"

"No, darling, no, angel, no, my life. Oh no, no, no, no . . ."

"Truly, Naci? Not to spare me?"

"Maria—if the water had been outside the brain tissues—it might have been tuberculosis. In one of us. But it wasn't. It was deep down, in the ventricles, in the brain itself . . ."

"What causes it, Naci?"

He thought a moment.

"Outside the window is a tree, a fine straight tree. Nature makes billions of babies, billions of trees. Once in a long time one comes forth imperfect. It's luck, Maria, just plain bad luck . . ."

She sighed and blinked into the darkness.

"And for Mariska—God only knows. Illness strikes a child in a quick breath, they can't talk, they can't tell you where the pain is, in a moment they're gone . . . that's how it happens sometimes . . ."

She ran her hands slowly over her belly.

"Naci—this time——" she quavered.

He grasped her quickly. He drew her into his arms so fiercely that she gasped.

"This time it will be all right!"

"Our bad luck's over, Naci . . ."

"It's gone, my angel. It's all, all gone . . ."

He woke briskly next morning. It was as if the outbreak at the Weidenhofers' had cleared the air. And the next day, reading a periodical, he saw that a former student, Siebold, had deserted him and walked fashionably into the glittering ranks of medicine's aristocracy. He was depressed only briefly. And then this defection seemed to add to the small surge of force that had animated him from the family conflict.

He returned to his mission. He applied himself with decision to answer his latest critics. The book must be defended. It must be defended if need be, to his last breath. It must not be put aside. It must not die. If by some stroke of the pen he could arouse interest in it again, if by his replies he could find new champions, new disciples——

He began to write the *Ofener Briefen,* the open letters. He wrote to Spaeth. He wrote to Scanzoni. He wrote to Carp. He wrote, breathing hard, to Siebold of Göttingen.

As he ended the letter to Siebold—"what has happened, dear Siebold, for you saw the doctrine work—what has happened to make you doubt the evidence of your senses?"—a tremendous thought exploded in his brain.

If you truly seek the truth—if you sincerely desire, as I desire, to end this horror—I propose this in the name of humanity: Arrange a meeting of German obstetricians. Let it be held in any city in Germany. Let it be held, if possible, in August or September. Let us debate the entire question. Let us decide it, once and for all.

Now he resumed his work with fresh ardor. He lectured Bathory endlessly. He prowled the wards. He neglected his practice. Sometimes he would pause beside a woman and twitch off her bedclothing to peer at the sheets. Or he might stroll into a closet and suddenly dart to a bedpan, snatch it to his nose, smell it. The attendants redoubled their efforts. They dreaded his appearance. And when he was absent Bathory had formed the habit of appearing at odd hours and gazing alertly everywhere as Ignaz Philipp did.

That summer in Budapest the thermometer was too hot to touch. The temperature rose to nearly a hundred degrees. In the house Maria fanned herself listlessly. Once again she was huge.

"My back hurts," she complained. And Ignaz Philipp rubbed it tenderly.

"You're like a woman, Naci . . . you know just where to rub . . . your hands are so tender . . ."

"It's little enough I can do."

"Would you like to have this baby? Would you like to have it for me?"

"Is something wrong, love? Is something troubling my angel?"

She nodded, her eyes never leaving his face.

"I dread it, Naci . . . I'm afraid . . ."

"Not afraid—not really afraid——"

"With the others we waited for our child. Our child, Naci. Now we're waiting for a baby."

He stroked her in silence.

407

On the tenth of August Maria bore a baby girl. They watched it, their hearts pounding. They ran to its slightest cry. It was a beautiful baby, healthy, strong——

"She cries so little, Naci! I'm terrified——"

"It's because she's healthy—nothing hurts her——"

"Perhaps—perhaps she's—— Oh, Naci! could she be mute?"

They gazed at each other in terror.

"Now, now, now!" he said loudly. "There's nothing to be afraid of, angel! Look at her! HaHA!"

The little girl was baptized in the Innerstadtischer parish church, decorously baptized to the satisfaction of the Weidenhofers in the presence of all their friends. She was given the name Margit. She received the drops of water on her forehead with a squeal of delight, she crowed and waved her arms vigorously, she gurgled. Maria and Ignaz Philipp watched her, wet-eyed. And afterward she throve. She grew larger. She was completely happy, completely healthy, and daily a little more beautiful. They watched her tenderly. They adored her. But she was like a visitor. Anxiety never left their hearts.

Eighteen hundred and sixty-one was roaming toward its end. The anxious months of fall and winter were come. On the record of the clinic this year depended the fortunes of all women present and future. The clinic was and must be a testament to the book. Now his labors and Bathory's attacked even the stairs, the bed slats, the windowpanes, the very doorknobs. The attendants ended each day exhausted. A vast smell of chlorine filled the entire building.

A miracle was happening. As the days passed the miracle grew.

He and Bathory looked at each other. They did not dare to speak of it. They hardly dared breathe. The attendants watched them and slaved harder. Maria prayed. She took the baby to church and made a novena. Markussovsky watched excitedly. He ran to Balassa. No one mentioned the miracle in Ignaz Philipp's presence. No one dared. But among themselves they spoke of nothing else.

"In such a building!" Markussovsky smashed his fist despairingly into his palm. "In such a place!"

For the clinic was located in the Landstrasser now, in the ancient Kunerwald house, on the second floor, above a surgery. Once again there was no running water. And now there was not even a fountain. Waiting attendants rushed to the street when the Danube water sellers appeared, dipped their pails in the wooden barrels, lugged them upstairs.

There were no rooms for isolating contagious or infected cases. There were not enough beds. Patients were often on straw, on the floor. The year ended.

And in this place, and under these circumstances, he ended the year with not a single death of childbed fever.

With a mortality record—not for one month, not for two—
but for an entire year—of 0.00 per cent.

He stared at the world, his shoulders back, his head high,
triumphant.

Budapest rang with the miracle.

And even as they celebrated, the Ministry in Vienna was
demanding an investigation. The appointment of a new commission.

For in Vienna at the First Clinic, under Braun 43 per cent
were dying. And at the Second Clinic, under Zipfel, one out
of every three never left the hospital alive.

"Can they ask any more? Can any human want other
proof?" Markussovsky cried exultantly.

"You've done it!" crowed Balassa. "They can't ignore this
now!"

And Ignaz Philipp and Bathory hugged each other and
danced a jig about the ward, and Ignaz Philipp kissed the head
midwife and the patients laughed and cried, and groaned and
laughed again. Now in Buda the attendants grinned proudly,
and stood in a line to shake his hand.

And Markussovsky rushed to the *Orvosi Hetilap* and sent
a feverish article telling Budapest's joy and Vienna's sorrow
out into the world, to England, to France, to Russia, wherever
women were dying.

And at the house Ignaz Philipp and Maria, holding little
Margit between them, danced a polka and kissed each other,
and kissed Margit, and thanked God and waited the great day.

There was no great day. The miracle at Pesth was ignored.

The doctrine was condemned more violently than ever
before.

In Vienna, Zipfel said the women had died of a miasma for
which the only sensible cure was to close the hospital.

On behalf of Braun the *Vienna Medical Journal* referred
severely to "the sad illusions entertained by Semmelweis regarding the infallibility of his prevention."

In England, Denham of Dublin dismissed the proof and the
doctrine contemptuously. "It is a waste of time to comment
on this. Women in childbirth die of a poison taken in days
before labor."

It was all wasted, it was all in vain, it was as if nothing had
happened.

And there were some, receiving these fresh and incredible
proofs, who were indifferent merely, and laughed tolerantly.
And in their clinics women died to the music of their deft
laughter. And there were some who shrugged and did not even
laugh. And in their clinics the women died also. Woman after
woman, death after death, the heaped dead choked the
morgues, were buried two to a coffin, lay stacked in rotting

heaps, cold, barren, yanked away to make room for the freshly silent, for the oncoming others.

But in Pesth, in the facilities of a stable, without running water, lying upon straw, they did not die.

And there was a reason. And it was a simple reason.

And it had been told again and again.

And Ignaz Philipp in his mind's eye looked out over Europe, looked out over the world, and his mouth opened, and there was nothing more that he could say.

For a few days he went about silent, trying to think of something. And then one night his thoughts rebelled. They stopped. They had come to a blank wall. Behind them the mighty and unconquerable force of his message pushed inexorably. His head hurt suddenly. He staggered. He climbed the steps to his house. He paused. He studied himself. He entered the house.

"Marko's here!" Maria called. She looked at him closely. "Are you all right? You look pale. I'm going to take Margit to Mother's. Marko wants you to go to the Roast Beef Club."

"All right," said Ignaz Philipp vacantly.

"It'll do you good."

"Bad and good. Good and bad."

Markussovsky came into the hall and took his arm.

"Don't bother to take your coat off. We'll go right now."

"I see. All right. Yes . . . I'll be sure . . ."

They left.

This night Balassa was at the restaurant and Bokeis and Wagner and Hirschler and Lenhosset. Later, young Bathory came in.

Ignaz Philipp drank his soup.

"I'd like some more, please."

"More soup?"

"More soup."

He began the second bowl silently.

"It's a curious thing," said Balassa. "I understand a Dr. Broca has discovered the speech center in the brain. What do you think, Bokeis?"

"I haven't seen the paper."

"I'll lend it to you."

"What do you care about the brain, Balassa?" asked Wagner.

"Oh, I know. I'm just a surgeon. But ever since Helmholtz measured the velocity of nerve current ten years ago the whole area's given me a kind of secret fascination."

Ignaz Philipp ate with complete concentration.

"I can't keep up with things any longer," confessed Lenhosset. "There's too much new for me. Max Schultze defining protoplasm and cell, von Mitteldorph operating for gastric fistula——"

"And I found something for you, Semmelweis," Balassa interrupted. "It was in one of the French journals. Lemaire had a piece discovering the antiseptic properties of carbolic acid——"

Ignaz Philipp ate stolidly on.

"More meat," he said quietly.

Markussovsky slipped from his chair to Balassa's side.

"Please," he whispered urgently. "Say nothing about puerperal fever! I beg of you. Nothing to excite him."

Ignaz Philipp looked up.

"But I was only mentioning carbolic acid——" Balassa said, surprised.

"What is he saying to you?" Ignaz Philipp demanded heavily.

"Now, Naci," said Markussovsky, "it was nothing for you, my curious friend. Nothing at all——"

Ignaz Philipp put down his fork.

"He was trying to keep you from talking about childbed fever, wasn't he!"

"Believe me, Naci," said Balassa earnestly, "it was nothing, absolutely nothing——"

"I won't have it, do you hear me?" He got up, knocking over his chair. "It must not be silenced! Are you betraying me, Marko?" he shouted. "You too? Now you?"

Markussovsky walked to him quickly. He put his arm about Ignaz Philipp's shoulders. Ignaz Philipp threw off the arm indignantly. He faced Markussovsky, his fists clenched, breathing heavily.

At the table his fellow doctors watched, paralyzed with astonishment. Balassa regained his wits.

"Lemaire," he said loudly; "we were talking about Lemaire. He's discovered antiseptic value in carbolic acid."

Ignaz Philipp turned his head. He looked warily at Balassa. He looked back at Markussovsky. His rage passed. He sat down. He began to eat again.

In the days that followed Markussovsky slowly and artfully began to draw Ignaz Philipp's attention to gynaecology.

"You used to be such a skillful operator, Naci. Remember?"

"That's all past. That's gone. All gone."

"It's such a pity to throw all you know about it out the window."

"Yes, it's true, Marko. I learned a lot."

"All those dissections—day after day——"

"That's true, that's true . . ." His fingers flexed.

"How many hundreds, thousands perhaps——"

"Oh, a lot, Marko. Unquestionably . . ."

"And how badly we need a good gynaecologist . . ."

"Well, I'll see . . . I'll see . . ."

"And for the students too . . ."

411

He revived his interest in gynaecology. When his work at the clinic was finished, he went to St. Rochus. There, in the rooms set aside for him for obstetrics, he plunged into gynaecological work.

"It's play," he told Maria. "Just play, darling."

"It's good play," she told him stoutly. "They're lucky they have a man like you."

A new idea came to him mildly. He began to operate, using the same prophylactic technique he had advocated years before, the prophylaxis that worked so well against childbed fever. Perhaps, he thought, revolving this new idea slowly in his mind, perhaps if I demonstrate what absolute cleanliness will accomplish in surgery—perhaps then it may be accepted for women in labor—it's not much chance, of course —but perhaps if it works out well——

He lifted his head. In the street people were staring at him. He looked away, confused. He walked rapidly home. He had been talking to himself aloud.

His skill at gynaecology began to be talked of through the university. Years of dissection had given him amazing skill. For a time he concentrated on removing tumors of the cervix. He operated with the strictest cleanliness. At St. Rochus the air became suffused with the smell of chlorine solution. And in these days, when a human with a bone broken through the skin was almost certainly doomed to death from infection, when the knife still meant almost inevitable death, he operated without loss of any life whatever.

In his lecture he had come to speak invariably about the doctrine of childbed fever. Whatever the subject, his speech soon dwelled on this. He became increasingly severe. At examinations he would shout in fury when a student appeared not to have grasped his teachings. He commenced to fail students ruthlessly.

And Maria, when these things reached her ears, worried and pleaded with him.

"They'll do you a harm, beloved. You mustn't be too harsh with them. Who knows what they'll do?"

"I've heard about their threats. Well, I'll tell you what they'll do. They'll do nothing."

"My darling, I'm worried. I can't help it. I love you and I'm worried."

He lifted her chin.

"Child, you don't understand. If a law student doesn't learn something it can only cost a client money. But if a medical student doesn't learn something—it can cost the patient his life!"

"Gah!" cried little Margit. "Gah-GAH!"

"She means Daddy!" Ignaz Philipp announced proudly. He stooped to her. He lifted her high in the air and danced off with her. The child screamed in delight. He lay down on the floor. He sat her astride him.

"Bounce, beautiful! Bounce on Daddy's big fat belly!"

"I don't know which of you is the bigger child!" Maria moaned.

Ignaz Philipp thrust out his arm, seized Maria's leg, pulled her so that she toppled upon them.

"Naci! My dress—you'll hurt the baby——" And instantly she fell to tickling him until he roared and rolled to safety behind a chair.

He wrote the results of his operations eagerly, describing the technique of prophylaxis. And Markussovsky rushed them into print in the *Orvosi Hetilap,* article after article, burnished with humility, faltering with hope.

In May he interrupted the articles long enough to launch a new attack for the doctrine, reopening the open letters, writing fresh material to refute Braun and the eternally malignant Scanzoni. They were long letters. Toward the end he sent them out unfinished, writing on them: "Continuation and conclusion to follow." Secretly he sought out all the world's medical journals. He read the rebuttals, the attacks, the scorn. They brought him to desperation. But they drew him. He could not stop reading them. Their glibness paralyzed him. He felt powerless, unable to answer.

He clung to Maria. Her belly was huge again. From their bodies was coming another child. They waited fearfully. He summoned Bathory. On November 22 Maria bore him a son. He was baptized Bela. He was a robust boy, with Maria's violet eyes, her long body, her dark hair.

"He's all mine," crowed Maria.

"But he's got something of mine you could never give him!"

"You're a pig, Naci. Baby, your father's a plain pig."

Now he clung to her. He had become silent. He spent long hours in his study. When she looked in at him covertly, he was at his desk, staring at the book, not moving. And in the night she might awaken to find him gone from bed, to hear him pacing in his study. And one night, hearing voices, she rose and tiptoed to the study, and he was sitting at his desk, his chin in his hands, talking quietly to dead Ignaz and dead Mariska.

He spent less time at gynaecology. He returned to the clinic. He became remote, abstracted, empty of plan. His hope was not dead. But it had become helpless. It throbbed dully. It gave him no rest. He felt alternately impotent and restless to begin something, he knew not what.

In January, Markussovsky went to London. He returned in March glowing with news of a new operation, removal of the ovary. He spoke with awe of the operations of Charles Clay of Manchester, Baker Brown and Spencer Wells of London, and Thomas Keith of Edinburgh.

"Tell me what they did, Marko. Tell me exactly."

"I thought that would fetch you! Now listen carefully."

And Markussovsky described to him, step by step, all he had witnessed.

"It's a great thing, isn't it, Naci? But it's a long way off."

"I don't think it need be such a long way off."

"It's all right for the great hospitals of London, Naci. It won't be done here for another ten years."

In June Ignaz Philipp performed the first ovariotomy in the history of Hungary. The news spread from St. Rochus to every physician in the nation.

And at St. Rochus a small group of doctors and assistants conferred anxiously.

"He's an obstetrician, after all, not a surgeon."

"He's got his surgical degree, though."

"That still doesn't make him a surgeon. He's got his own field. Now he seems to be taking over ours."

"I say let a man stick to his specialty and let us stick to ours."

"Let's not have any fights—no trouble—no excitement——"

"He's pretty well entrenched, you know—"

"Well, I'll tell you what we'll do . . . if we're all together in this it ought to be simple . . . He was appointed by the state, after all . . . and this happens to be a city hospital . . ."

In July Ignaz Philipp was removed from the staff of the St. Rochus Hospital.

A brief notice in the official minutes of the Ministry announced that his position on the staff was incompatible with his university position.

He was notified at the clinic. For a time he said nothing, he remained motionless, staring impassively out the window. After many minutes he rose deliberately, put on his hat, and walked from the university. He walked into Pesth. He bought flowers. He walked home, his arms filled with blooms. Maria was watching for him at the window. She ran to the door.

"Naci—Naci, my darling——"

"It's not too late. It's never too late to bring flowers."

"My poor absent-minded baby. You remembered, darling. Are you thinking of our anniversary? Don't you remember you brought me flowers weeks ago?"

"But it's been a long time. One mustn't let such long times pass."

"Where in the world is there such a lucky woman as I am! Who has such a husband! Do you know I adore you? Do you know that, Naci?"

"I have only you," he said slowly.

She put the flowers down and took him in her arms. He moved his head on her breast.

414

"I'll tell you something. I think I'll give up my gynaecological work at St. Rochus."

"But you were expecting great things from it, Naci. You were hoping that——"

"It's better that I stop. The clinic is enough. Will you understand?"

"Naci, I'm glad of it. I know what's in your heart. I know you can't help yourself. But I've watched you get more and more tired. Your health is more important, darling. I watched you from the window today and as you walked your left leg seemed to drag a little."

"I'm tired. I'm very tired."

"Are you all right, though, Naci? Are you feeling well otherwise?"

"Do I seem ill, Maria? Do I seem ill to you?"

"No, never! I just worry—you know—you're my baby——"

"Are you sure, Maria?"

"Sure, sure . . ."

He left to make his rounds. He had been gone only a few minutes when Markussovsky arrived. He told her what had happened. Maria bowed her head. She began to cry.

"He told me he was going to give it up."

"Poor, poor Naci . . ."

"He wanted to protect me—not to let me know—to feel bad—he brought me flowers . . ."

"We must take extra care of him, Maria."

"Are you trying to tell me something, Marko? Is anything wrong?"

"Nothing, Maria. But he's tired——"

"Are you keeping something from me?"

"Maria, look at me! I'm your friend too! Wouldn't I tell you?"

"He's been overwrought. Blow after blow. All his life. There just doesn't seem to be any letup. Is he never to have happiness, Marko? Like other men? Will it never end?"

"You've given him happiness he never dreamed of, Maria. You're his happiness."

"Now we must shield him."

"That's right. Now we must keep all friction away, give him a chance for peace in spite of himself."

Ignaz Philipp was troubled. He looked at himself in the mirror closely. He had noticed a slight pain in his head at intervals. Occasionally, thinking deeply, he suddenly realized he had been speaking aloud.

"I am getting old," he told himself uneasily. "I am forty-five. And already old. I must be careful."

For a month he devoted himself only to the clinic and his patients. He rested. Sometimes he came home early and took naps. He became peaceful. Criticism in medical journals

415

which a few months before he would have received with rage, with baffled fury, ceased to move him. He read them apathetically. He frolicked with the children. He entertained a few friends. He went out peacefully with Maria. His life became placid.

In the *Vienna Medical Journal* came an article charged with the bubbling wine of hope. The Austrian Government, debating a new lying-in hospital for Prague, had invited certain eminent medical men to answer questions on puerperal fever. Among these were Rokitansky, Skoda, Oppolzer, Virchow, Hecker, and Lange of Heidelberg.

The government asked this question:

"According to the present position of science regarding the contagious origin and extension of childbed fever, is the theory established for certain, is it probable or is it possible?"

And to this question Virchow answered: "Childhood fever is the effect of a predisposition."

And Hecker said: "It is caused by a miasma."

And Lange replied: "It is caused by an infection from decomposed material."

And Rokitansky, Skoda, and Oppolzer said unequivocably: "The doctrine of Semmelweis is established beyond any question."

Ignaz Philipp stirred. He crept from his lethargy. It was not too late to hope. He began to nourish his hope again. He read the article over and over.

And while he read, while he smoothed the paper, while he debated within himself a new letter, perhaps, or a new article, a weighty envelope arrived from St. Petersburg.

The letter was from Professor Hugenberger. He enclosed a report of the proceedings of the Medical Society of St. Petersburg.

The *Etiology* had been discussed at five consecutive sessions. Arneth, now a Professor of Obstetrics in Russia, had taken a leading part in the discussion.

Only two members had been steadfast in their miasmatic faith. They were overridden. One of the results of the discussion was a resolution to issue rules for the guidance of midwives in which henceforth it was to be the duty of every Russian midwife to apply the Semmelweis prophylaxis in her practice. For Russia, the doctrine might now become official.

"You will see from this," wrote Hugenberger, "how many followers you have in the Far North, and how strongly the younger men support you. By that alone much is gained, for it is in their hands that the future lies."

Ignaz Philipp resumed writing again. He composed several articles for the *Orvosi Hetilap* covering the Russian discus-

416

sion. He was exuberant. His tone was milder. He smiled now. He looked to the future with confidence.

The reaction he waited for in the medical journals of Europe came very quickly. He read them all. Once again he viewed them with staggered disbelief. The same objections he had disposed of over and over again were thrown up exultantly, as if they had been fresh inspirations. He waited a week. He became calmer. The disappointment was a dull pain which no longer sickened him. He addressed himself to the labor of answering them. Once again he began at the beginning. Patiently and laboriously he covered the old, old statistics. Midway in his first open letter he paused. He laid down his pen. He walked from the study.

When she saw the weary, worn expression on his face Maria ran to him. He put her gently aside. He went into the bedroom. He sat in a chair, looking out of the window. And there he sat silent and would not answer.

Maria put on her hat and went quickly to Markussovsky. When they returned to the house he was sitting as she had left him. His expression had not changed. They spoke to him. He continued to stare out the window. After a long time he turned and gazed at them dully. Maria was sobbing quietly.

"As a friend," Markussovsky said softly, "as a privilege— will you let me write the letters for you . . ."

He drew a deep breath. He nodded. He got up, walked to the desk, took a thick sheaf of papers, pressed them into Markussovsky's hands.

"You write," he said tonelessly. "Tell them . . . the sun is sometimes . . . when one considers . . . Marko . . ."

"I'll do it. I'll take care of everything——"

Ignaz Philipp put his hand confusedly to his head.

"A certain pain," he said. "My thoughts seem . . ." He shuffled to the desk. He drew out a copy of the *Etiology*. He gave it to Markussovsky.

"I've got a copy——"

"It's all here . . . you'll find everything in order . . . just now it seems . . ." His voice trailed vaguely.

Next day he rallied, he wrote feverishly on ovariotomy, he busied himself again with the clinic. He began to eat hugely. He helped himself more often to wine. He grew careless of his appearance.

And Maria watched, and pondered, and loved him, and waited for peace.

One day, returning from the university, Ignaz Philipp found himself walking on the bridge across the Danube. He looked about him, startled. Then his knees shook. Trembling, he made his way to the railing. What am I doing, what has happened to me, where have I been? He put his hand to his head which had begun to throb. Fear flooded him. Is it pos-

417

sible—is my head—can I be—— He shook with horror. He stood at the railing. He drew deep breaths. He scolded himself angrily. He frowned. He made his way slowly back to the house. He looked narrowly at passers-by. He sighed in relief. They did not appear to notice him.

Now he became more gentle even than before. He played endlessly with Margit and Bela, he walked with them, he was forever bringing home new toys.

And Maria held him tight, and he clung to her, and he smiled now, he was always smiling.

"They're our children finally," he said one day.

"They've always been our children, angel."

"I know. But now they're really ours. Now we can keep them."

Her eyes filled with tears.

"Have you felt that, too, Naci? I thought it was only myself."

"No, we didn't dare enjoy them . . . it's true . . . after the others . . ."

"But now they're ours."

"Yes . . . now they're really ours . . ."

"And life is good, Naci . . ."

"Yes, now life . . . life is smoothing . . ."

The pattern of the days linked quietly together, became calm, they looked at each other, their eyes luminous with secret, with a new joy, with deeper love. Maria was pregnant.

They sat together through the long evenings of spring content to hold each other's hands, to sit silent, to dream.

And in July Maria went to her bed, laughing. She bore a daughter.

And this was the miracle. From the beginning the babe seemed to him Thérèse.

They christened her Antonia.

And he loved Margit, he adored small Bela, but Antonia was his delight.

He hung over the cradle, studying her features endlessly. There could be no doubt of it. The face of his mother looked back at him. Each night he hurried home, rushed past Maria to the nursery, bent to study her again. He never wearied of this. He was content to sit there, forgetting everything, absorbed in the baby's placid face.

"I must give her something to be proud of," he said excitedly one day.

"If her father isn't good enough for her, I'll throw her out," Maria said instantly.

"No, no, no . . . you don't understand . . ." And he started to write a book on obstetrics. He went out to the Roast Beef Club. He harangued Markussovsky over and over. He solicited opinions. He wrote furiously. In a month he began another book, a manual of gynaecology. He wrote more feverishly than before.

He came home from the clinic one day ashen and trembling. Bathory helped him from the carriage, helped him into the house. Maria flew to him.

"Don't be excited, Frau Semmelweis. The doctor has been working too hard. He'll be all right."

He took gently from Ignaz Philipp's clenched hand a sheaf of papers. They were the latest news from medical Europe and England.

Spaeth in Vienna had written authoritatively that washing was not harmful but that it was bad ventilation which caused childbed fever.

In the French medical journal Dubois had written: "To call attention to this subject of prophylaxis is to exhibit sheer inanity. One hardly comprehends why the medical profession in Germany has taken the trouble to refute it."

Braun had suggested that to prevent childbed fever one should warm the bedpans.

Virchow had written: "We should perhaps recognize the merit of Semmelweis in restraining the ravages of puerperal fever in his clinic, but the infection is not such a special kind —cadaveric poisoning—as Semmelweis alleges."

And in the *London Lancet,* by the great Robert Barnes, was an article which was to hamper the introduction and application of the doctrine in England for at least a quarter of a century after.

"Pregnancy," opined Robert Barnes, "often produces a profound alteration of the blood. I believe with Mauriceau that pregnancy is a disease of nine months."

Maria stared at the wrinkled papers.

"He happened to get hold of them," Bathory said apologetically. "I don't know how . . ."

They led him into the bedroom. They undressed him, silent all the while, and put him to bed. He lay there, staring at the ceiling. Bathory poured a glass of water. He found Ignaz Philipp's bag. He opened it and selected a pill.

"Here, sir, with respect, Doctor—take this——"

He held the pill to Ignaz Philipp's lips. Ignaz Philipp swallowed the pill and afterward, docilely, the water. He lay back. He tried to smile at Maria. She fell to her knees and put her arms about his head, holding it to her breast. Bathory left them thus. After a while Ignaz Philipp breathed evenly. He slept.

He returned to the clinic next day. He gave up writing. He no longer responded to Markussovsky's eager and constant offerings of good news. He worked at the clinic, he attended his patients, he came home. He played quietly with the children. He studied small Antonia. He clung to Maria. Sometimes he would wander up and down the living room, muttering, denouncing his antagonists.

"You must stop it, Naci. You are only wearing yourself out."

"Excuse me. Excuse me, Maria." He would stop, startled. "I did not realize . . ."

"And tonight we are going to the Hirschlers'. They are naming the new baby for you!"

"For me, Maria? Really for me? Oh, Maria—oh, let's hurry—isn't it wonderful?—a boy, Maria?"

"Of course it's a boy! I've bought a new hat and—Naci! What is it? What's the matter?"

His head was bowed. He sighed in complete dejection.

"Aren't you going to get ready, darling? What's happened?"

"I can't go. Never, never, never . . . no . . ."

And later, "Forgive me, Maria, don't leave me, darling, forgive me . . ."

"You're all I have . . . all I live for, Naci . . ."

She stroked his body gently. She soothed him. After a time he slept.

His lectures became a great burden. As always, they were interrupted endlessly. Nowadays, when he was interrupted, his eyes would fill with tears. He would be unable to continue. He would leave the room. On other days he would forget to bring his notes. What is the matter with me, he would rage silently, I forget everything, I remember nothing. Please God, what is happening?

His walk became unsteady. He continued to eat to excess. One morning in June, sitting on the edge of his bed, he suddenly conceived a means of spreading the doctrine everywhere. It was a hazy idea. He rose and walked about the room, trying excitedly to recollect it. He thought deeply. The first step was to collect all available material. He walked into the living room.

"Naci!" cried Maria. He turned to her, smiling.

"In front of the children!" she cried again. She stared at him.

He looked down at himself, stupefied. He was naked.

That day, walking home from the clinic, it became suddenly clear to him that his doctrine belonged to all humanity. He stopped. An elderly man was approaching him.

"I beg your pardon," Ignaz Philipp said courteously. "It occurs to me that you may be unfamiliar with my doctrine of prophylaxis in childbed fever——"

The man stared at him horrified, moved off quickly. But Ignaz Philipp had forgotten him. A young man and a young woman were approaching arm in arm. These were the people, these, these young ones, they were the ones who must know——

"You are about to be married, yes? I want to warn you of a certain danger—when you have your child the doctor must wash—see to it—rigidly clean—I must warn you——"

He walked off. They looked after him, amazed.

That night he went straight to Antonia. He sat by her bedside. He gazed down at her, muttering strange words.

And Maria, watching from the doorway, drew back into the living room and put her hand to her mouth. An insight, dreadful and inexorable, stabbed at her brain.

Next night he sat quietly at his desk, working. She was a little reassured. She watched him uneasily.

In July he sat at a faculty meeting. The members discussed the university problems. They came finally to the question of a new provisional obstetrical assistant.

"Dr. Semmelweis," the chairman called, "we will now be obliged to you for your views on this subject."

He rose. He remembered Vienna. He remembered the day when he first became provisional. He remembered the heavy toll of death in the First Clinic, the low mortality of the Second. He remembered the midwives, his respect for them for the women they did not kill. The honest women . . . honest women, all . . . what could be more fitting at this time than the vow of their calling? His eyes dimmed with tears.

"Dr. Semmelweis?" said the chairman.

He drew from his pocket a folded sheet of paper. He opened it. He began to read aloud:

"I swear by the Almighty and all-knowing God that I shall never mistreat patients entrusted to my care——"

It was the oath of the midwives. He read it to the end. He sat down. He put his head on his arms. His shoulders heaved. His tears fell silently.

Bokeis, Wagner, and Balassa brought him home. They gave him sedatives. They bled him. They removed all sharp instruments, all knives, anything pointed.

He recovered slowly.

"Something—something is the matter with my head," he said perplexedly.

"You're my child. You're my good, sick child," whispered Maria.

He slept.

Later that night Markussovsky came, and Bokeis and Wagner and Balassa.

He heard them enter. His brain was clear. He was ashamed. He shut his eyes. They saw him thus, when they came to the doorway, and nodded, and tiptoed away.

421

In the living room they talked to Maria in low voices.

"Our only chance, our only hope of saving him is Vienna," Markussovsky said sadly. "There is no other hope, Maria."

"But they can cure him—he can certainly be cured——" she begged.

"If you will permit him to be taken away——"

"It need not be for long——"

"But he must go to Riedel, at the asylum, in Vienna——"

"Otherwise——"

Maria began to sob brokenly.

Ignaz Philipp wondered incuriously why she was crying. He raised himself on one elbow. He was going to go to her. Suddenly it came to him clearly what it was they were talking about. His pulse pounded with fear. He fell back to the pillow. He was insane. They were going to put him away. He was going to an asylum. His palms were wet with cold sweat. His mind raced. There was time. But there was still time. His fears left him. He smiled to himself cunningly.

Next day he rose early. He lifted Antonia from her bed. He walked up and down the room with her for hours. Before noon he slipped away from the house. He went to a printer. He wrote busily. He commanded his intellect. He handed what he had written to the printer.

"Tomorrow!" he commanded.

"But I cannot—it is impossible to print them so soon——"

He drew out fifty florins. He handed them to the printer.

"Tomorrow!"

The printer nodded. He walked rapidly to his forms.

That night Maria sat him in a chair and pressed cold compresses to his head. A wild hope beat in her that somehow this would pass, something would happen, perhaps the compresses . . .

Margit and Bela came and stood by his chair. He put his hands on their shoulders, drew them to him.

"Papa's very tired," he said.

"Papa's tired," they echoed gravely.

Maria led him to his bed. She sat beside him. She held him in her arms. He fell to kissing her, to stroking her hair, he touched her, he clung to her as if he could never have enough.

Next morning early he crept from the house. He went directly to the printer. The man tiredly handed him a huge pile of circulars. They were printed in bold letters. They said:

Young men and women! You are in mortal danger! The peril of childbed fever menaces your life! Beware of doctors, for they will kill you! Remember! When you enter labor unless everything that touches you is washed with soap and water and then chlorine solution, you will die and your child with you!

422

I can no longer appeal to the doctors! I appeal to you! Protect yourself! Your friend, Ignaz Philipp Semmelweis.

He put the bundle under his arm. He went out into the streets of Pesth. He ran to every young man, every young woman. He pressed his handbills on them. He would not be denied.

They were gone. He had given the last handbill away. He smiled. There was one last thing. There was now the greatest, the best thing of them all. He walked rapidly toward the Landstrasser. He began to run. He ran faster. He reached the clinic. He burst into the dissection room. The startled students gave way. He ran to the table. On the wooden slab lay the body of a woman. He seized a knife. He slashed the belly. He slashed again. From the cold and gaping wound the stinking fluids of putrefaction welled thickly. He slashed again. He stood back. He raised his left hand. He cut his fingers. Then he plunged the hand into the corrupt and rotting darkness of the woman's belly. His fingers reveled there. The open wound sought among her pus-blistered tissues.

He drew forth his hand.

He sighed. He was free. He walked quietly from the room.

At the house Maria and Markussovsky were waiting for him.

"Where have you been? What happened to your hand?"

"I've been out for a walk. A little walk. A little walk in the country. I'm tired now. My head——"

"Of course you're tired, darling. We're going away for a rest——"

"To Grafenberg——" said Markussovsky.

"To Grafenberg?" he asked mildly.

"For the cold baths," said Markussovsky. "They'll do you good, Naci. I'd like to go myself . . ."

"They'll make my darling well, all well, my precious darling . . ."

"Tomorrow," said Markussovsky.

"Yes, yes. Fine. We'll go to Grafenberg—my head——"
He turned suddenly to Maria. "You'll bring Antonia!" he cried loudly. "Antonia must go too . . ."

"Antonia shall go, beloved . . ."

He grinned at them.

"My friends . . . my two best friends . . . I love you . . ." His eyes filled with tears.

"I'm tired . . . I'm so tired . . . I'm so very tired . . ."

Now the garden was empty. In a little while it would be dawn. It was very dark. He was alone. He bowed his head. He was very tired. He walked unsteadily to the table. He sat down. He put his head upon his arms. He fell asleep. They left next day for Vienna.

From the moving railway coach, standing beside Bathory and Maria, who held Antonia, he waved farewell to Markussovsky, Balassa, Wagner, and Bokeis.

Buda faded. He strained for a last glimpse of the Burgauffahrt.

After a time they led him gently back into the coach.

# TWENTY-TWO

FOR a while he was content to sit at the window yearning toward the rocks, the earth, the trees of his native land. He gazed at them hungrily. The train sped smoothly on. A sense of departure, of infinite loss, dismayed him as each new scene was set before him and then was whirled away. Tears came to his eyes. He turned to Maria. He held out his arms for Antonia. The child had fallen asleep, her small mouth at her mother's breast. He took her gently in his arms. Softly he began to hum an old, old song, "A Cloud Comes Down."

"Why are we going to Vienna?" he demanded suddenly. He looked about him anxiously. "If we are going to Grafenberg, why are we going to Vienna?"

Bathory bit his lip. He looked helplessly at Maria.

"We are going to Grafenberg, darling. But we are going by way of Vienna. Is that all right?"

Her cheeks reddened with shame. It was incredible to her that he would believe such a thing. At any moment now he would become his normal self and laugh at her.

"It's all right," he conceded slowly. "You're with me now. But tomorrow you return and bring the other children to me at Grafenberg."

"I will, my darling. Tomorrow."

His eyes grew fond and soft with love.

"Do you know I love you, Maria? Do you know how much?"

"Yes, my angel . . . yes . . . Maria knows . . ."

"Do you remember I promised you a trip? You see? Naci keeps his promises."

"I remember . . ."

Bathory walked to the rear platform.

"A trip for Maria, I said . . . a fine trip . . . and here we are."

She tried not to cry.

"It's always as if I first met you," he said wonderingly. "Is it that way with you? The day I first saw you. And my heart——"

She put out her hand.

"Please, Naci, my darling——" She put her face in her hands. She sobbed brokenly. I shall stop the train, she told herself abruptly. I will take him away. I will keep him with me always. It is I and I alone who will make him well. She heard Markussovsky decide upon Reidel. She became confused. Her decision faltered. Perhaps they knew best. Perhaps in this way she would have her man again, her darling, her child, quickly. And forever.

"Bathory!" Ignaz Philipp said suddenly. He rose. He put the sleeping Antonia tenderly on the seat.

"Stay with me, Naci——!"

He looked at her, his eyes quite clear.

"I must find Bathory . . ."

He went to the rear platform.

He stood beside the younger man in silence, watching the rails, watching the countryside spin away beneath their feet.

"It goes, my friend. Thus it goes." Bathory started. Ignaz Philipp had spoken in a normal tone.

He put his hand on Bathory's shoulder. He looked at him affectionately.

"You think they will make me well, son? For I must go on. And while I am gone, my dear friend, I beg you by God do not let this murdering continue. Hold up in your heart the feeling what it means to heal a sick person. Save the mothers, save the unborn little children."

Bathory bowed his head.

"What they have done to you," he said brokenly. "What they have done to you . . ."

"Never be afraid or ashamed to possess pity. It is the love of God, made mortal . . ."

"I swear it. Believe me . . . I swear it . . ."

Ignaz Philipp folded his arms.

"God is my witness . . ." His voice trailed. He spoke to himself. Sooner or later the time must come. No man might conjecture. Perhaps tomorrow, like a thunderclap, men will rub their eyes and birth will be sweet. The pleading faces of the suffering lifted to him. It is all right, mothers, now you are safe. He smiled. He advanced serenely to the bedside.

"Put on your coat, sir doctor," Bathory said quietly.

Ignaz Philipp looked at him mildly. He perceived with surprise that he had taken off his coat. He put his arms back into the sleeves. He looked about him. He saw vaguely that he was on a train. He bade himself remember that he must ask Maria about this. He turned to Bathory and smiled brightly.

"I'm very hungry," he said expectantly.

He sat quietly, smiling often, nodding contentedly, for the remainder of the journey.

At the Vienna station Hebra was waiting with a carriage.

He saw Ignaz Philipp and paled. It was difficult for him not to weep at the sight of this ravaged face, these hollowed eyes, these stooped shoulders, this shambling walk.

Ignaz Philipp shuffled to him at once. He took Hebra's hand.

"Well, Hebra, so you're here, are you? Now I'm your patient. Will you heal me?" he laughed delightedly.

Hebra helped him into the carriage.

"Heal, heal, heal, heal, heal," he chuckled. The carriage drove off.

"Do you still remember Vienna, Doctor?" Hebra begged. "Do you see that house? Do you remember this street?"

"Aha!" He pointed triumphantly.

"Yes, that's the beer garden . . ."

The carriage stopped. Ignaz Philipp looked about him, troubled.

"Yes, you remember. This is my house."

In the doorway Frau Hebra stood awaiting them.

Ignaz Philipp jumped shakily from the carriage and ran to her.

"Frau Hebra! Little Johanna!" He held her hand lovingly. "Do you remember when the little boy was born that spring? And the guns cracking? And I could tell Ferdinand it was a boy?"

"Come in, come in!" And she turned quickly to hide the tears.

They sat about the round table in the dining room. Frau Hebra's trembling hands poured coffee. Maria held Ignaz Philipp's arm. He turned to her lovingly. He patted her cheek.

"What happened to your hand, friend?" Hebra asked.

He put his hand out at once.

"Look here, Ferdinand, how it hurts. Such a little thing. I had to operate this morning, a Czech girl called Czorny, nothing difficult, I must have cut my finger."

The hand had already begun to swell. The lips of the cut gaped and like clenched teeth the white bone grinned through.

Hebra pushed back his chair and got up.

"Do you know what we'll do? I'll tell you what! We'll treat that at the clinic. Come on, Naci! Let's go have a look at the new clinic!"

Ignaz Philipp stood docilely. He looked at Hebra levelly. Then he turned his head slowly and looked down at Maria. He smiled.

"You won't come with me . . . I don't think so . . ."

Maria began to tremble. Frau Hebra came to her swiftly. She put her arms about Maria's shoulders. She held her in the chair.

"No, no, dear. You remain here with the little child."

"Good-by," said Ignaz Philipp gently. "Good-by, my darling."

He bent, then, and kissed Antonia on the forehead.

"Naci! My beloved!"

Ignaz Philipp turned brightly to Hebra.

"Come! Let's go see the new clinic."

In the carriage he sat between Bathory and Hebra. Now there was no life in his eyes. He answered only yes and no. His voice was a dull monotone. The carriage turned down the Alservorstadt. He lowered his eyes. They reached the asylum.

Dr. Reidel was waiting.

He drew Ignaz Philipp into the doorway.

"We will do our best to satisfy the professor. The room will soon be in order. Meantime, let us walk in the garden."

He nodded to Hebra and Bathory. He shut the door.

The two men waited a moment, gazing at the shut door. Then reluctantly they turned and got into the carriage.

"There is a great man," said Bathory. "There is the greatest man we will ever know. There—in that asylum. And we are not worth it. We are none of us worth it."

"No," said Hebra, "it is probable that we are wholly maimed, blind, imbecilically cruel, ungrateful, that the thoughts by which we live make our very presence here on earth fantastic. And yet—I think we will always have men like him."

"We don't deserve it."

"No . . . But what we are composed of is shining and indomitable. It is not shoddy, and it is wholly pure. It is the cell which is eternal, beyond good and evil, the mortal and immortal symbol of the Almighty. And because of this the covenant will continue and the world and our petty thoughts which people it will continue to receive redeemers."

"And now this sweet and gentle and bewildered and raving man bears the burden of what we are not. Now he stumbles. Now he carries the cross," cried Bathory bitterly. He gritted his teeth. "But to the end of time Medicine will bear this guilt and the human race will share the burden and the disgrace."

"And the cell," said Hebra gently, "will function on, hampered by one less human ignorance, bearing us with it to a goal we cannot plan."

The sun was westering. The men sat silent. The carriage drove on.

In the garden, in the courtyard above which the asylum

427

rose on all sides, Ignaz Philipp walked with Dr. Reidel a space, smiling at the flowers.

He stopped. He looked up at the buildings.

"Why are all the windows covered with bars?" he said suddenly.

"For protection," said Reidel. "We don't want anyone to get in."

Ignaz Philipp nodded sagely.

A white-coated attendant came up.

"Where is Dr. Hebra?" Ignaz Philipp demanded.

"He had to leave—he took Dr. Bathory—they went to see a patient."

"I see . . ."

"Your room is ready now, Doctor."

He shambled obediently after them. His body was quite weak. He felt ill. His mouth was parched. His sight blurred. His bones had begun to ache.

He entered the room.

"Here I am," he whispered, "a sick fellow. But Ferdinand is going to get me well again. He's the only one in whom I have confidence."

He lay down on the bed. He closed his eyes. Reidel and the attendant left noiselessly. The door closed behind them. A lock clicked. He sighed. He tried to sleep. The wound in his finger, red, inflamed, scalding, thumped and pounded remorselessly. His upper extremity was paining. His brain ached. In his belly he felt a searing knife.

He opened his eyes. The room was dark. He had been asleep. He leaped from the bed. He stumbled to the door. He twisted the handle vainly. He began to pound the wooden panel. He shouted.

Suddenly the door opened. An attendant blocked the doorway.

"What is it, Doctor?"

"It's dark! It's late, man! I must go to my patients!"

"Tomorrow, Doctor——" The attendant held him off.

"Tomorrow? Are you crazy? They need me! They need me now!"

The attendant struggled with him.

"They're sleeping, Doctor——"

Ignaz Philipp beat at him wildly. His face was distorted.

"Let me go, you fool! Only I know what my duty is! My patients are waiting! I must heal them!"

The attendant stepped back a pace. His arm swung out. He slapped Ignaz Philipp a stinging blow across the face. He waited. And again he slapped him, this time across the eyes.

"Back to your room——!"

His arm swung again. Ignaz Philipp threw back his head. From his throat shrieked a wild scream of rage. He flailed at

428

the attendant. He became raving tissue, terrible in its delirium, cruel and tragic and unconnected from reason. Mind faded, sank, disappeared. The attendant fell beneath him. As Ignaz Philipp rose he was borne down again beneath other guards. He rose again and was drowned beneath a fresh wave. Shrieking, bellowing, battling with superhuman strength, he was carried down the corridor by six attendants. They rushed him down a flight of steps. They came to the dark-chamber. They kicked open the door. They gave him a final buffeting and flung him in. They slammed the door. They turned the key. They left him there, howling, begging to get out.

In the morning Maria came smiling.

"No, no, Frau Semmelweis," Reidel said. "Not today. He's not well today——"

"My God! Let me see him!"

"Tomorrow . . . perhaps tomorrow . . ." He closed the door.

She left. She returned each morning, frantic, choking with hope. She left in despair.

In the dark-chamber Ignaz Philipp lay sometimes on the bed, sometimes on the floor. He groped once a day to a pan of food and a wooden cup filled with water, pushed into the blackness through a quickly closed trap. His rage was spent. He moved weakly. The flesh hung in small tatters from the wound in his fingers. His brain throbbed with pain. He breathed with difficulty. His loins, his groin, his abdomen pounded with pain.

"You had best leave him here," Hebra told her one day. He had come to the asylum with her. He had left her outside. He had conferred outside the dark-chamber door with Reidel. He looked at her meaningly now, his face pale.

Maria searched his face.

"No!" she cried suddenly. "Never!"

"You had best."

And when they turned her away next day she took Antonia and went to the train to go to Pesth, to gather Margit and Bela, to return and bring them with her. She had made up her mind. There was no indecision now. I am coming back. I will take him away. I will keep him with me always. My darling . . . my beloved . . . my good, sick child . . . Her head ached intolerably suddenly. She felt dizzy and weak. In Pesth it was necessary to help her from the train. She was carried home and put to bed.

On the thirteenth of August, in a small consulting room in the asylum, Hebra and Reidel faced each other across a table. On the table lay Ignaz Philipp. He breathed painfully. His eyes were closed. The tissues of his lungs were inflamed. The inmost lining of his abdomen, the lining of his brain throbbed sluggishly. In the room there was the odor of putrefaction.

His left arm was hugely swollen, the skin was blue-black. From the grotesque arm dangled a decaying hand, the joints of the fingers laid bare, the cartilage rotted, the bones flecked with shreds of rotting tissue.

In the distance the noon bells of St. Stephen's pealed, quivered over the golden city, trickled softly into the room. Far down the corridor a priest came slowly, and as he walked the bell he carried tolled an older story of a longer time.

Ignaz Philipp opened his eyes.

Hebra bent down.

"Are you there, old friend?"

From the glazing eyes the mists cleared for a moment. The lips trembled. The whisper was barely audible.

*"I will never stop . . ."*

The light of his eyes flicked. His pulse was a thread.

*"No . . . never . . ."*

The light died. His mouth opened. He was gone.

# EPILOGUE

*When I with my present convictions look back upon the Past, I can only dispel the sadness which falls upon me by gazing into that happy Future when within the lying-in hospitals, and also outside of them, throughout the whole world, childbed fever will be no more . . .*

*But if it is not vouchsafed me to look upon that happy time with my own eyes, from which misfortune may God preserve me, the conviction that such a time must inevitably sooner or later arrive will cheer my dying hour.*

IGNAZ PHILIPP SEMMELWEIS

The body of Ignaz Philipp Semmelweis was removed to the autopsy room of the General Hospital. There, where he had dissected as a student and where Kolletschka received his death, he was dissected by Meynert and Scheuthauer, Rokitansky's assistants.

He died of that which he had devoted his life to eradicate, and of that common disease of humanity, significant to the profession which for a brief time he graced.

His body after dissection was removed to the morgue.

From the morgue it was transported to Schmelz Cemetery, an obscure place of burial which has in its turn long since died also.

His passing was chronicled among the minor notes in two paragraphs in three Vienna newspapers.

At St. Rochus he was succeeded by Drs. Walla and Diescher, who had opposed his doctrine. The mortality rate at once began to rise and in a short time outstripped the nightmare days of Vienna.

His doctrine was ignored and misrepresented for years after his death.

By 1890, as the older men died and young men replaced them, the doctrine began to spread, to become universal.

In 1891 a Hungary suddenly conscious of her greatest son took his body to Budapest for burial over the strenuous protests of Austria and Germany, where it now was claimed that the Pesth Fool was a German.

In 1906 a statue was unveiled in his honor in the city of his birth.

In the world today puerperal fever has by no means disappeared.

The children and the mothers his doctrine saved, the great men and women who live because he died, are as countless and unimaginable as the waves of the oceans.

His sister Julia married Peter von Roth, who became a congressman. She died at the age of ninety.

His brother Philipp died under the name of Czemereny, a canon, aged ninety years.

Antonia, his darling, was married in 1882 to the Royal Chef at Pressburg Castle and bore two sons and two daughters.

His beloved Maria lived past the turn of the century with her daughter Margit.

His son Bela, who worshiped his father with a silent and utter intensity, grieved for years after his death, and, despairing that his father's teachings ever would be accepted, killed himself at the age of twenty-five.

*It is the doctrine of Semmelweis which lies at the foundation of all our practical work of today. Through all the details of prevention and treatment, the temporary fashions and the changes of nomenclature, the principles of Semmelweis have remained our steadfast guide. The great revolution of modern times in Obstetrics as well as in Surgery is the result of the one idea that, complete and clear, first arose in the mind of Semmelweis, and was embodied in the practice of which he was the pioneer. . . .*

SIR WILLIAM JOPPA SINCLAIR

*Professor of Gynaecology and Obstetrics*
*University of Manchester*

*Without Semmelweis my achievements would be nothing. To this great son of Hungary Surgery owes most.*

JOSEPH, LORD LISTER

*Professor of Surgery*
*Kings College, London*

The beginning was with God.
And the end, also.